L' Amore

'The Luminara Series'

Book 2

By
SJ Molloy

Published by SJ Molloy
ISBN Ebook – 978-0-9899879-2-9
ISBN Print version – 978-0-9899879-3-6 (Paperback)
Editor – Maxann Dobson - The Polished Pen - www.polished-pen.com
Developmental editor – James Ramsey - The Polished Pen - www.polished-pen.com
Cover Art, design and graphics – Design Divaz – www.designdivaz.com
Interior design – Lucinda Campbell - www.design.lkcampbell.com
Interior design, paperback – Kassi Cooper

L'Amore Playlist

Chantal Kreviazuk – Feels Like Home

Lonestar – Amazed

Carrie Underwood – Before He Cheats

LeAnn Rimes – I Need You

Bryan Adams – When You Really Love a Woman

Kings of Leon – I Want You

Andrea Bocelli – Vivo Per Lei'

Emeli Sande and Labrinth – Beneath Your Beautiful

Leona Lewis – I Got You

Mama Cass – Dream a Little Dream of Me

Eva Cassidy – Somewhere Over the Rainbow

Andrea Bocelli – Because We Believe

Snow Patrols – Chasing Cars

The Lumineers – Ho Hey

Mumford and Sons – The Cave

John Legend – Ordinary People

The Goo Goo Dolls – Iris

Kristina Train – Dark Black

Pink – Just Give Me a Reason

Lady Antebellum – Singing Me Home

Kid Rock & Sheryl Crow – Pictures

Rihanna – We Found Love

Shania Twain – You've Got a Way With Me

Kristina Train – I'm Wandering

Norah Jones – Come Away With Me

Norah Jones – Turn Me On

Testimonials

SJ Molloy, first time British Author from Scotland, has found her way into the hearts of the US and all over the world. I found this book really refreshing in that the back story of the heroine was thought provoking and there was enough detail to get the idea without it being gratuitous. The book in my opinion was very well written. The book definitely had a 50 Shades feel to it, and the sex scenes were very erotic. Well done, SJ Molloy, you will be reaching for the next book in the series like I did!

~ Books and Beyond Fifty Shades

"SJ Molloy writes her stories the way that we talk about books—with Heart and Passion. Reading her characters' intense chemistry makes a person yearn to reach out and possess that themselves. This author has left a huge imprint on me, and I cannot wait to see what she deals out next."

~ The SubClub Books

Contents

Prologue i
Chapter 1:Home 1
Chapter 2: The Tour 22
Chapter 3: Old Flame - New Fire 47
Chapter 4: Insecurities.. 58
Chapter 5: Intrusions 68
Chapter 6: Reconciliations 87
Chapter 7: Senses 99
Chapter 8: Episodes... 112
Chapter 9: Revelations 126
Chapter 10: Workout.. 134
Chapter 11: Famiglia.. 146
Chapter 12: I'm sorry 163
Chapter 13: Dream a Little Dream.............................. 166
Chapter 14: I'm all his.. 175
Chapter 15: Dark Black.. 191
Chapter 16: Compromises.. 201
Chapter 17: Gifts of the day 208
Chapter 18: Trust Me 222
Chapter 19: Uprising Michael Parks........................... 238
Chapter 20: Runner 242
Chapter 21: Guilty as Sin 253
Chapter 22: The colour Blue 267
Chapter 23: Men in Black 281
Chapter 24: Devil's Advocate...................................... 293
Chapter 25: Pamper Night.. 304
Chapter 26: Truth!.. 316
Chapter 27: Picture Book 335
Chapter 28: The Highlands 349
Chapter 29: Mother's Intuition.................................... 359
Chapter 30: Church 379
Chapter 31: Angel 398
Chapter 32: Ghosts... 412
Chapter 33: Queens and Kings..................................... 422
Epilogue: Michael Parks" Inferno Burning.................. 438
Glossary of Characters 443
Acknowledgements.. 448
About The Author: Bio 454
Share and review 456
Author Links 457
Coming soon by SJ Molloy.. 458

"Those who deny freedom to others deserve it not for themselves." –
Abraham Lincoln (1809-1865)

The best laid schemes o' Mice an' Men,
Gang aft agley,
An' lea'e us nought but grief an' pain,
For promis'd joy!
(The best laid schemes of Mice and Men
oft go awry,
And leave us nothing but grief and pain,
For promised joy!) – Robert Burns (1759-1796)

The strength of a family, like the strength of an army, is in its loyalty
to each other – Mario Puzo (1920-1999)

Lust is a gift. It's the desire for souls so beautiful.
Love is a gift. It's the lust for souls deep within.
Light is a gift. It's the love for both souls illuminating. ~ *SJ Molloy*

Dedicated to

Granny and Grandpa R
&
Granny and Grandad B

Thank you for never hushing me when I had so many words to share and for encouraging me to tell my stories and paint my pictures. I hope I make you all proud, I love you and I miss you.
xxxx

Prologue

The cosy sunroom at Lexi and Cameron's grandparents' highland cottage is the perfect room to relax, drink tea, and admire the beautiful scenery of the Cairngorms National Park. This traditionally Scottish dressed room is situated off the kitchen. An extension to the picturesque white washed building, purposely facing south to gain maximum sunlight exposure.

This is the room that Alexander and Elizabeth Robertson have utilised as their go-to family room for breathing space, consolations, and reflections. Over the years the inviting sunroom has been subject to many deep and meaningful family discussions, some private and some more open.

These discussions very seldom encroach into the open living room area of the house, for that is a room for undisturbed trouble-free thoughts. The discussions which take place in the sanctuary of the sunroom typically stay within the confines of these glass walls. Today is no different.

Casey Huddersfield, the therapist, has of course been privy to many of these discussions over the years. Some light and casual, but many of her chats have indeed been deep. Today she is having another private session with Lexi and Lucca together because she hoped that being here at Lexi's grandparents' property would help Lexi be more relaxed and responsive.

Unfortunately, today is another dark, depressing day. The sky is grey with ominous clouds overhead, and the downpour of torrential rain has been relentless in the last twenty-four hours leaving the heavens open to an almighty rainstorm.

Even with the murky, gloomy colours and wild weather of today, the views across the national park are still breathtaking. The Scottish Highlands always appear magical and enchanting, even on an eerie foreboding day like today, Casey thought, and therefore she admires the captivating view while waiting on Lexi and Lucca to join her.

Casey has spent the best part of the morning with Grace Robertson, Lexi's mum, and these particular chats with Grace always last a relatively long time. It has been a while since they last spoke, and they have a lot to cover and catch up on.

Casey's lucky that she doesn't need to watch the clock today, so it allows them both a comfortable pace to talk without rushing. Here, Casey can allow as much time as desired, thus demonstrating once again she's a diligent and a considerate therapist.

She welcomes Grace warmly and gives her time.

Grace is understandably tired after her long session. After thanking Casey, she expresses that she wants to take a nap before dinner but will wake Lexi up from her sleep to ask her to come downstairs.

Casey feels an overwhelming compassion to pour her heart and soul into helping this family. At first Casey was apprehensive about taking Lexi on as a patient because she had worked so closely with Grace—her friend—over the years and thought from a professional perspective that there should be some boundaries and she shouldn't get involved with counselling Lexi as well. Casey thought it would be awkward initially and too hard to give both Grace and Lexi an equal amount of undivided support and attention. But when Lexi was referred to her all those years ago by a previous counsellor, it only took reading through her case file before she decided to make Lexi her priority, and she has never faltered with being patient and supportive to both Grace and Lexi.

The girl deserves it every bit as much as her mother.

For Casey, this is the quintessence of her career, being able to comfort and support this family. Admittedly, it's difficult at times. She has to be extremely impartial and keep her integrity, and she can only hope her efforts are making a difference.

This case is the very reason why she chose to become a therapist. After all, the family is dear to her and they had endured the worst, most unimaginable tragedies. She owes it to them.

She hates to use the common word *psychologist*, as it's off-putting to some of her other patients. She wants to counsel and not to dissect, therefore Casey believes in equivalence, and her warm, empathetic approach helps her gain the trust of her patients. Casey maintains her title as a therapist. And she's a great one at that.

After informally greeting Lexi and Lucca in a warm embrace, Casey takes her seat. Lexi remains silent, pouring some tea for each of them with a shaky hand, and then sits back in her wicker chair worrying her fingers in front of her mouth in a nervous dance. Lexi thinks about the deep, private conversation she and Lucca had with Grace just a few nights ago on this very wicker sofa.

They discovered their fate.

Casey can't help but notice that the beautiful girl, who normally looks so radiant, appears to be pale, tired, and very sick.

Worn down ... again.

Shattered and broken.

It tugs on Casey's heart to witness her fragile like this. Truly, it makes her feel desperate to help in any small way she can. She wants her to get better and would love positive results for her. For them both. Lexi has always been relatively closed, and today she seems exceptionally tense and guarded. *Afraid.*

It reassures Casey that Lexi has such an attentive, caring, and protective fiancé as Lucca. When Lucca called and explained their circumstances, it shocked Casey at first but it was a very pleasant surprise. Ultimately, it's clear that Lucca is the perfect partner for Lexi, and there's no one she'd rather see her with. He's everything she needs. Casey knows Lexi will be well looked after and will indeed receive the love she deserves from Lucca.

Although she's delighted for them, it still feels somewhat surreal to Casey that Lucca and Lexi are now romantically together because they were both individual patients of hers. Fate definitely intervened here. It pleases her very much because Lucca has a lot of love to give and Lexi requires it in abundance.

Breaking the ice, Casey congratulates them on their recent engagement and then enlightens them both about her husband Terrance, a dear friend of Lucca's. Terrance caught up with Lucca early this morning and is now out in the fields, clay pigeon shooting with the dogs. Lexi will get the chance to talk with him afterwards at dinner.

Lucca entwines his fingers with Lexi's and lifts their connected hands up to his mouth. He tenderly kisses the back of her trembling, delicate hand and kisses the impressive blue diamond of her engagement ring, then sets their hands back down to rest on her lap, giving her reassurance. But he never lets go of her; they remain connected.

Unified and bonded.

"Lexi, are you still writing in your journals? I have to say that was a huge step for you and I'm very proud of you. I have you to thank for that, Lucca. I'm so happy you were able to help with that."

"Well ... I was before ..." Lexi speaks in barely a whisper and drops her head, a habit she often demonstrates when she's nervous.

Lucca immediately places his fingers under her chin and lifts her head to meet his loving eyes. They briefly exchange silent words using only their engaged eyes: crystal blue with brushed chocolate.

A simple yet powerful understanding between them. Lexi smiles and relaxes.

He has her.

"Did you think it helped you, writing in your journal?" Casey politely asks, breaking Lexi and Lucca's moment to move forward with her questions.

"Eh ... I believe it did, yes." She's much clearer in her answer this time. Casey trusts Lucca calmed her nerves and has given her the encouragement she needs with the warmth of his eyes. Despite looking very ill, Lexi seems to blossom under Lucca's loving influence and his touch. She flourishes.

"When you say did? Aren't you writing your feelings down now?"

"No ... yes ... um no ... I keep picking up the journal intending to write, but since last week, since the ..." Casey notices Lexi's becoming uncomfortable talking about the recent turn of events so she interrupts.

"I think you should continue to write, especially now at this time with everything that's going on." Casey sips her tea and smiles, admiring Elizabeth's trademark design ... a purple thistle on the side of the china cup.

"I know I should, but when we left Tuscany I was filling pages with happy words ... happy feelings and nice memories, and I thought that I'd carry that on. You know ... like my new chapter, my new start. But when I start to write now, all I feel is pain, grief, and darkness. That's where I was before Lucca, and I don't want to go back. It makes me want to tear the pages and get rid of the words. The dark words."

Lexi reaches for something to fidget with. The tassel on the tartan shawl is weaved and flicked absently through Lexi's fingers. Both Lucca and Casey realise that Lexi is restless because she frantically teases and rolls the strand of soft wool between her middle finger and thumb.

Breakthrough.

"What you're telling me is that you're still compartmentalising and filing your thoughts. By putting them to the back of your mind and ignoring them, you're only creating a much bigger issue for yourself for when you do finally address these worries. Acceptance is a gradual process. Denial isn't healthy, Lexi. It's good to break down these worries as they come to you and progressively manage them. Small steps." Casey places her cup down on the thistle designed coaster, tilts her head, and removes her red spectacles as if she's looking at Lexi through her own eyes. The warmth and sincerity of Casey's tone mimic the soft and kind sensitivity in her eyes.

Lexi remains silent. She's contemplating Casey's words. Lucca brushes his thumb over her hand and the ring on her fourth finger but looks over towards Casey, giving her an appreciative knowing nod of his head.

"I guess I feel like I am going back that way and I can't, not now. I don't want to. I want to look forward to life and not be dragged backwards." Lexi meets the warmth of Lucca's eyes once more. He has the unconditional look of love, and it's all it takes to fill her eyes with emotional tears. She gazes at him helplessly as if she's apologising.

Another awful habit. If she isn't saying it, she's expressing it. Something that's been instilled in her from an early age. During her abused years she was constantly forced to apologise.

It tears Lucca apart to see her upset and distressed. He wishes he could just take away her pain, fears, and anxiety and erase her bad memories completely. Sadly, he can't, but he can smother her in love.

His love.

The love.

L'amore.

He wants to give her the best life imaginable. Privileged and filled with hope and promises, he intends for her to never have to want for anything. It's his aspiration to help her with her angst in order to achieve clarity, and he needs her strong, especially now. He feels she needs this session, even if it hurts her, because it's better for her in the long run. It takes all of his willpower not to cancel the session seeing how sad his beautiful girl is.

She is so close. He believes in her.

They need to persevere, if only for today.

Casey reaches in her pocket for a handkerchief and wipes the glass of her spectacles before placing them back on her face. "That's understandable, but I would say that sometimes in order to move forward, we need to go back and start again. Address those old fears and emotions before you can embrace new ones, better ones. If you can't identify and accept the old haunts, then how will you paint your image of happiness, a new beginning, and for that matter accept them?" Casey raises her brow inquisitively.

Lexi is confused and wrinkles her nose, glancing towards Casey with a puzzled look on her face. Lexi wonders why she is talking in riddles today. Normally, Casey is to the point. Perhaps it's the informality of today's session. Casey chuckles and relieves Lexi of her uncertainties.

"Okay, so imagine your journal is a mood board, or if you like, a painting. It's merely a tool, a piece of art to help you visualise and express what's in your mind at that given moment. If you feel dark, your painting would be black. One day, when you feel bright, you'll go back and read over dated words which depict ... describe your darkest times. By that time, you will wonder what it ever felt like to experience that particular feeling because you'll be too busy in your present, painting your new brighter visions, that the old will seem like a very distant memory. You rewrite or repaint. Just because the words are down on paper doesn't mean that you need to reflect and relive those feelings the moment you re-read them. And you won't, you will be making new ones."

"I suppose." Lexi is still unsure. She has no intention of writing down some of her worries, especially after the drama and turmoil of the last week. Bright future or not, surely it would hurt her to even look back over the words because it would reinforce those memories. And after witnessing the pain and hurt both Cameron and Lucca had after reading some of Lexi's first journal, Lexi knows that if it's too upsetting for others to read, then it will crush her to look back over the words. It would almost be like reliving it again.

"Are you worried about others reading it? What they will think? Because I want you to remember that the journal is for you and not for them. It's to help *you* accept and move on, and *you* need to stop worrying about what other people think. This is about *you* gaining clarity." Casey's tone remains soft and gentle but she emphasises the word *you*, pointing out that this is very much about Lexi. That thought alone makes Lexi feel even more vulnerable. She accidently pulls at the tassel on the shawl with her jitters, tearing it off, then looks down at the wool strand in her hand.

Lifting her head, she notices Casey steals a quick glimpse at Lucca then back towards Lexi. That's when Lexi realises the extent of her questions; Casey must know that Lucca had a negative reaction to reading her journal. Why else would Lucca share this information with Casey? It occurs to her that if Lucca shared the information with Casey, then he must be seeking his own solace and acceptance through therapy again, but he hasn't mentioned anything to Lexi about needing advice or help. Lucca has always been focused on helping Lexi and making her his priority.

It doesn't particularly worry Lexi that Lucca has mentioned this to Casey, because if he needs his own counsel and Casey can help him understand more than she can with her words, then so be it. Although Lexi did agree to share her honesty, and surely that meant allowing Lucca to read the things she wasn't able to say. The thought makes her feel nauseous because now she's thinking of Lucca and how she doesn't want to inflict anymore upset onto him.

"You know Lucca and Cameron read my journal?" Lexi asks, already knowing the answer.

"I know that Lucca has; we have spoken about it. I love that you are learning to communicate with Lucca, and that is very important, but I also think right now, you need to keep up your journaling for your own benefit. Lucca is always going to be here for you and I'm sure that when you want to talk, he will listen. If you want him to read your words, then that's something as a couple you need to agree on, but don't get hung up on what others think. Right now it's what you think that's important." Casey lifts her cup for another sip of tea, while Lexi's cup has been left neglected.

As usual, Casey makes a fair point. Lucca has agreed to help Lexi anyway he can and to give her time. He has always shown compassion and understanding even when he finds things hard to digest himself. His hand tightening over Lexi's confirms he agrees with Casey.

Lexi finally lifts her tea and takes a sip. "I ... don't know how to. I mean ... before, I was writing purposely to explain things to Lucca which was hard, but it seems even more challenging now. After the revelations this week, it would be nothing but dark and it's too hard. It's too hard to read back over."

Lexi shakily holds the cup in both hands then turns to watch the remnants of rain drops making their way down the window. Understanding now why it was difficult for Lucca to read her journal, why his heart felt crushed and he was sickened. He was distraught and the thought of rereading her words makes her feel this very sentiment. *Distraught.* She sits the cup back down and feels Lucca's warm hand on the small of her back when she reclines against the cushion.

"Let's say on my blank canvas is shading, but every time I feel new, special emotions or a glimmer of hope, I can sketch over it, adding to it until eventually I've erased the page of darkness to eventually build something colourful. The shade is the foundation and needs to be there, but now seems inconsequential because I only notice the colour. It's more obvious." Casey scribbles in the air with her hand as if she is sketching her picture.

"You're saying I need to accept it and move on, aren't you?" Lexi slumps back, the heat of Lucca's hand providing her with a reassuring gesture that he has her, that he is here for her.

"Yes, that's exactly what I'm saying. I don't expect you to ever feel the same emotions that you feel today or yesterday, but if you write how you feel now and what you want to feel, then chances are if you believe you can feel these desired emotions, then you will. Trust yourself to believe you can, and you will."

"It sounds as if you're suggesting I'm to reprogram my entire thoughts." Lexi knows from years of therapy and experience that as much as she tries to remain positive and focused, she will always be a worrier: paranoid, nervous, and sceptical.

"Your mind is very powerful, yes, but you'll be drawn more to what you want as opposed to what you had. Here's another example: if you had written in your journal two years ago that you were lonely and you wanted to meet a man like Lucca, you'd look back on that page and think, 'I can't remember feeling lonely' and it will make you all the more grateful you don't feel lonely now. You would accept the old in order to accept the new. Negativity attracts more negativity, which is why you counterbalance; having something positive to focus on means you're closer to receiving it."

"That sounds idealistic. I'm not sure I'm at a stage to write about how I feel. Sure, I know how I want to feel, but there are words I simply can't write." Lexi edges closer to Lucca so her thigh touches his. The closer the contact with him, the stronger she feels. She can't get close enough. Their bodies connecting envelopes her in the warm love she has grown to depend on.

"It's not that you can't write them; it's because you won't. You are still filing and cataloguing your thoughts, compartmentalising. Put it down on paper then underneath, write the opposite—how you want to feel. You're one step closer to feeling it and trusting you will receive it. In my experience people already have it, they just need to realise it's already there. For some, that's the bigger picture. Seeing the words."

Lucca uses this opportunity to support Casey. "I like the sound of that, Casey. It sounds similar to the law of attraction and very positive." Lucca's tone is upbeat and brimming with spirit. He knows his sweet girl is processing everything, but she's hostile. Maybe if he reinforces the positivity behind Casey's suggestions, his girl will believe him ... It's a good idea.

Lexi looks at her fiancé and smiles. A warm sincere appreciative smile. He always knows how to say the right things at the right moments.

"Think of it as the ask-get approach." He winks and Lexi blushes a shade of bright pink. That approach certainly proves beneficial in other areas of their life. Maybe it will work here as well.

"I'm sorry. You think I'm being negative, don't you?" Lexi's voice is so soft, sweet, and gentle that it melts Lucca's heart. He wants to pull his sad girl over onto his lap and wrap her in the tightest embrace he can, next to his heart, and never let her go. He'd let her ask and he'd give her anything she wanted.

"No, baby, I think you are scared. You have been extremely positive given the circumstances, and you are strong. I admire your courage and strength. It may be something to think about though, if it helps you. Casey is right. You should be focusing on the words however way it makes sense to you. If that means writing the counterbalance of your negative with positive words in order for you to move forward, I think you should do it."

Casey sits back, watches, and listens to the discussions between the two of them and doesn't interrupt. She has merely planted the seed, and in order to grow together as a couple, Lucca and Lexi need to learn how to nurture these ideas. *Together.*

"If you think it is easier, do you want to say the words to me first before you write them down, and then write your happy words under them, will that help?" Lucca is a very intelligent man, insightful and ever so considerate. This happens to be the opposite advice he gave her while in Tuscany, but he's prepared to try anything that will help her.

Lexi sighs. She looks weak, lifeless, and utterly spent. All these extra ideas today are mentally draining for her. Lucca will take her back to bed after the session, to talk with her more privately and to hold her, always to hold her in his caring arms.

He knows this is tiring for her, but she needs a fresh perspective to get her through their next chapter. The last thing he wants is for her to be depressed and closed off. It's not good for her.

More tears trickle down Lexi's cheeks. Casey passes her a tissue to wipe her eyes but then sits backwards again, opening up the space between them to allow Lucca to work his magic.

Lexi swallows down a lump in her throat. "I ... I don't think I can say it again. I know I told you what you needed to know and you struggled hearing it. I don't want to upset you anymore, and it might be too raw for me to talk about it just now," she sobs.

He pulls her in close to his chest and nuzzles against her soft, glossy brown hair. She buries her head into the crook of his neck, and he allows her to cry while he caresses her with gentle, caring strokes of his hands.

Casey is about to excuse herself to give them some privacy when Lexi sits upright and wipes her tear streaked face. Lucca kisses her lips chastely then kisses her temple before wiping a tear with the pad of his thumb. "It is okay, Lexi, you are doing great," he soothes.

"No, I want to do better. I want to try and be positive. I mean ... for us. I'll try and write the words down and then write something optimistic next to it, if you think it will help, and when the time comes, we can talk about it again. That's if you want to." Lexi gradually loses the frigid tension in her body while fully addressing Lucca, turning to gaze up at him and gently squeezing his hand.

"There is my girl." Lucca beams the most loving, sweet smile, his eyes glistening as he shows her that sexy dimple that she loves. She blushes again and modestly returns the smile. He's so goddamn proud of her and could not love her more even if he tried.

"So what do I do? Write down Take Life – Give Life? It's a bit ironic."

Lucca strokes her delicate, slim arm while Casey adoringly watches the two of them in their tender moments. She sits forward and changes her body language, willing to answer Lexi's questions.

"If you want to. You write down whatever words make sense to you. How you visualise your happy future, what you want to experience and feel, opposed to what you have undergone. Yes?"

"I'm worried that anytime I read it, no matter when in the future it is, I'll always feel that dreadful guilt, that horrible shallow feeling. The one that reminds me I'm a mur ... I'm a mur-de-rer," she stutters.

Finally, she says it. She says it out loud and it feels good to get it out.

Lexi is worried that these feelings will never leave her. That she will always be taunted by the reality that she has taken someone's life. His life.

"Baby, listen to me. What you have done, it was an act of bravery. You must stop feeling guilty because you are a hero, nothing else. And you *have* given life. Please accept that it is a blessing, a gift, the strength you found. You are an inspiration, strong and beautiful, kind and loving. You did a remarkable thing and what you had to do. It was smart and intuitive and he is gone thanks to you. We are all indebted to you because I would not have you in my arms everyday if you had not." Lucca moves an unruly tousled wave of hair from her face to behind her ear and brushes her cheek with the pad of his thumb.

Lucca tries to convince her. She gives a pitiful shake of her head but grips his hand in a gesture of appreciation, thanking him for his confidence and reassurance.

"If you feel compelled to read over those words at any point, you will have the optimistic words beside it bringing you back to your present. That feeling may never go away, Alexis, but it will fade in time and become distant. Inconsequential. You need to move forward and embrace your next chapter and stop agonising over things out of your control." Casey sips her tea and breaks off some shortbread to nibble on. "How about I drop by after my holiday and see how you feel in a week's time, and you can let me know how your writing has gone. Things should get brighter through time and with positivity. Right now, I'd like to talk about those dreams you've been having."

I'm trying to escape. I'm running through the Australian bush.
He's chasing me ... he's shouting at me ... my bare feet are hurting and bleeding.
It's dark ... it's hot.
I'm scared.
I can't get away.
I need to get away.

Lexi knows Casey has her best intentions at heart, but in a week's time she doesn't know where she'll be. She hopes she'll be protected and safe. This unsettles her and adds to her anxiety, because all she ever wanted was to feel secure. Right now she just feels vulnerable and in limbo.

Then, after another glance into Lucca's mesmerising eyes, he has her.

Safe.

Protected.

Secure.

She smiles and nods her head, agreeing with Casey. Lexi realises then that the reality is, it doesn't matter where she'll be next week because Lucca will always be with her. And where there is Lucca, there is lust, love, and light.

And where there is light, there will be no darkness.

Chapter 1: Home

Lexi – three weeks earlier

Stretching, I turn around, weaving my arms around my fiancé's brawny chest, and gaze into the sparkle of his bright, azure-blue eyes.

Lucca's eyes.

Taking in his handsome, glorious body and his sexy smile, I melt into him.

"Morning, beautiful," Lucca whispers before placing soft kisses on my lips and moving a soft, unruly brown wave from my face.

"Hmmm, what time is it?" I ask, smiling as I gaze at my exceptionally large and exceptionally heavy blue diamond ring resting on his chest. Lucca rubs his thumb over the generous stone.

"We need to get up and organise the packing of your things to take over to our house, but maybe after I do this ..." Seductively, he kisses and bites my neck. I fling my head back, giggling in response. "Then maybe I will do this ..." He runs his hands over my breasts, cupping them and causing them to swell, and my nipples to harden like the diamond on my finger.

I love morning sex.

I love him.

Moaning with pleasure, I purr, "Hmmm, I like this game."

"Then maybe I will do this ..." he teases in his sexy, husky bedroom voice. He trails his fingers over my navel and straight to my pelvis, then underneath the seam of my lace thong. I part my legs while I wiggle and pulse sensitively for his touch, then jerk up quickly when Doris starts barking from outside the bedroom door, startling me into reality.

Damn!

The game was just heating up.

I have missed her so much while being away in Tuscany. I feel guilty that I didn't give her a lot of attention last night when I arrived home from the airport, but I was exhausted and just needed to sleep, despite her trying to suffocate me with affection. I missed Cameron last night too and never got the chance to see him as he was working a late shift. Hazel and Dominic waited up for us to arrive from the airport, and I was delighted to see them but it was too late to stay up and gossip about our travels.

Pouty lip. That will work. I'm pining for Doris.

Lucca stops his seductive teasing and looks at me. "Baby, is this dog going to be a problem? I want you desperately, but she is wrecking my mojo here, and I am not sharing you. I think she needs some obedience training," he drawls as he continues to ravage my neck. Pausing, he glances up at me through his black feathery lashes.

God, he is beautiful, charming, and all mine.

I look at him with my big brown eyes and exaggerate my pout as I trace my fingers over his lips.

"No way. She is not getting in the bed, Lexi. We are not starting this."

"Lucca, just five minutes for a cuddle. She used to get in here with me, so it's not fair to shut her out now. I promise I'm all yours, and when you take me to your house later, I will be all yours over and over again while we have fun in your bed. And a promise is a promise."

Lucca sighs reluctantly, losing his grip on me so I can get up. "God, you are fucking adorable. And it is not my house; it is our house now. Okay, let her in, but she will be getting kept in the opposite side of our house, Lexi, and nowhere near the bloody bedroom."

I smile and lean over, kissing him appreciatively. As I jump out the bed, he smacks my ass and shakes his head. I open the bedroom door.

Tornado …

She jumps on me, throwing me back on the mattress with her long, grey, velvety legs and wrapping them around my neck as she nearly smooches me to death. I can't stop giggling. Lucca is horrified.

"Lexi, fuck. Are you okay?" he panics.

"Yes, she's just playing. Where's my little ray of sunshine? I've missed my little cupcake so much. Have you been a good girly?" She wags her tail frantically, burying into my neck as she whimpers and whines in response to my baby talk. I squeeze her so tightly I could crush her, but she doesn't mind at all.

"Fucking hell, this is not happening. I have seen it all now," Lucca grumbles. Doris turns around and pounds on top of him. She licks him as she whines and whacks me with her wagging tail. "Lexi, can you get your dinosaur to jump down?" Lucca moans, trying to push her off him.

I giggle. "She likes you. Just pet her like last night and she'll leave you alone," I reassure him. He rubs her head, and she purrs with delight, then rests her chin on his muscular chest and stares up at him with her human-like amber eyes, sussing him out. I love that she has warmed to him.

"I do not fucking believe this. That dog is spoiled rotten, but I do think she likes me, so that is a start." He cocks his head to the side, eyeing her up and grinning crookedly.

"You two need to get along, and I think you do actually like her," I say playfully.

"She should be a working dog, Lexi. Not a lap dog." He moves, but Doris pins him down to the bed. Gripping him with her huge paws, she nuzzles her head under his arm.

"Admit it, you love her," I tease. Smiling, I watch Doris show Lucca lots of friendly attention.

"Not nearly as much as I love you. Right, you have had your five minutes. I want you back now." He frowns and curls his lip mischievously, showing his dimple.

"Done deal," I mumble as I drag Doris off Lucca's lap by the collar and out into the hall. "Hazel, can you take her out please?" I yell downstairs.

Lucca is ready to give me a lecture on my dog, but before he does, I seductively sit on top of him, straddling his groin. I slide myself down so my breasts press against his chest.

"It starts with five minutes. Then that bloody thing will want in bed with us all the time, and that is not happening. You are all mine, baby," he says, pressing his erection between my legs rubbing my throbbing ache for him.

"I'm all yours now," I reply, twirling a soft wave of my hair and lifting it up to brush seductively against my lips.

Burning me with his bedroom eyes, he rewards me with his sexy dimple smile. He rolls me over, placing his dark, bulky arms at either side of my body and holding me. I lift my hands and grasp his defined biceps then wrap my legs around his waist and link my feet at the bottom of his back, rocking my hips up to meet him. His breathing becomes heavier and needier, and his dark shaggy hair flops around his face as he gazes straight into my eyes.

Turned on.

No end.

He kisses me, groaning into my mouth as his wet tongue tangles dirtily with mine. It sends a surge straight to my wanting, damp sex. My butterflies have woken up and are fluttering their wings in response. My sensitive nerves and tissues are pulsing for him, and my arousal is drenching my tiny thong with excitement.

Rubbing my fingers along his indented contours and protruding veins of his upper arms stirs so much greedy anticipation.

I let go of his upper body and wrap my arms around his defined, smooth back, pulling him in closer towards me. Inhaling his sexy scent drugs me, makes me lose control. I trail my fingers over his firm ass and grip it.

"Fuck. I need you so fucking bad," he groans as he slides his hands down my side and over my hips, hooking his thumb under the thin strap of my lace thong. Grabbing the thin material, he moves his hips back, giving space between us so he can rip them off me.

"I will buy you new ones," he pants through gritted teeth before I protest.

He's going to be buying me a lot of new lingerie at the rate he tears through them, but I love his primal approach; his animalistic prowess has me caged inside his unforgiving, dominant possessiveness, and I can't seem to get enough.

He trails his hand up the contours of my hips and outlines my breast, flicking his thumb over my diamond-hard nipple.

Heaven.

Dropping his head, he kisses, licks, and teases my erect nipples in turn. He moans, his hot breath warming the wet flesh of my breasts.

"Fuck, you taste so good."

Groaning, I grab Lucca's hard, violent cock, tightening my grip on his thick length. Stroking and teasing his rock-hard tight skin, I tug back and forth towards my clitoris allowing his swollen head to touch me in just the right spot. I hold his heavy sack, massaging his testicles and rubbing his pre-ejaculation against my clitoris.

He bites down on my breast with the sensation of my touch. "Jesus, that is fucking good ... I feel it, baby. Tell me what you want. I want you to feel," he demands. "I want to please you. Do you want my fingers ... my tongue ... my cock? Tell me what you want to ease that ache."

All of it.

"I want your tongue, your fingers, and your ... cock." I can't believe I just said that word out loud! But in the heat of the moment and with all the sexual experiences Lucca is threatening me with, I'm beginning to lose some of my inhibitions.

Before I finish my sentence, his head is between my legs, and his tongue is dancing around my wet, fleshy folds, stimulating my sweet spot while his fingers slide inside my swollen core with one finger pressed at my back entrance.

Sweet contact.

Sweet sensation.

Sweet Jesus.

"Jesus, Lucca, it's so good, don't stop," I breathlessly moan as I tighten my grip on his hair as he continues with his oral masterwork, and I buck under the glorious torture. Closing my eyes and biting my lip, I dig my nails into his scalp.

"Baby, open your eyes. I want to see you." Sexy, smouldering eyes drown me, and it's the sexiest vision.

Holy shit!

After a pause, he drops down, picking up speed with his tongue and pressing deeper into my front wall with his fingers. It's driving me crazy. I thrust up to meet his tongue and sheath his fingers farther in my core.

"Baby, you are close. Fuck my tongue and come for me," he demands as his thumb presses my sweet spot and his tongue slides into my hot narrow avenue.

Italian sex god.

Expert.

Climbing to a soaring smash, I cry and scream, kicking out my twitching feet behind his back, throwing my head to the side and rocking my hips to his sweeping tongue penetration as I ride out the electric waves of my orgasm.

"Shhh, Doc. We are not alone," he chuckles.

My cheeks are flushed, and my heart is pounding. I feel a little dizzy, clinging onto the last current sparking my nerves.

He's right—we're back in my own house in Scotland, the home I share with my brother Cameron and my best friend Hazel, and I know they are both here.

I'm mortified.

Oh dear Lord. I hope they didn't hear me.

"I can't wait to get you alone in your house," I say as I grab his hair and pull him up my sweaty body to my lips. His thick lips are swollen, wet with my juices, and wanting to claim my mouth.

Devour.

"It is not my house, it is our house. You will be screaming at the top of your lungs when I fuck you senseless there."

Oh my God.

"I need you inside me," I blurt out in desperation. This is still new. I never thought I could be so confident or make demands like this, but I know it turns Lucca on.

"Fuck, you are so hot right now. I need to take you hard if you will let me," he growls.

"Do it. I want you, all of you, any way I can." I push my chest up to his and rock my hips towards his mighty cock so that my wet folds strum against his raging rock.

I love that he still has some sort of boundaries. He knows when to ask and when to take. He has read my journal, the old one and the beginning of the new journal and has pretty much figured out my personality. My moods, my insecurities, and as of recent … my desires.

One day, I'll speak them instead of writing them in my journal.

"I am going to fuck you senseless," he blazes then flips me over in a quick move. Spreading my knees, he holds me on all fours, wrapping his hand around my stomach and snaking his fingers to my pelvis as he pulls me towards his hips.

"Lexi, hold on and bite your lip. Remember we are not alone. This will be hard," he assures. I rock towards him, and he slams inside me.

"Oh my God, I ... I need this." Don't stop," I moan as he pushes, rams, and buries into me. I feel as if he could pound me to the very core.

I grab the headboard with both hands and drop my head between my arms, clenching my teeth and closing my eyes. Then I push myself back to meet his intense intrusion.

"Fuck, you are too fucking good. I feel so goddamn good in you." Lucca drives into me, his fingers rubbing my wet, throbbing clitoris as he builds me up until I'm almost at my cusp of ecstasy.

It's a race to orgasm, and he's grunting deeply, coaxing me to finish. He thrusts again, but with more conviction as he pushes me further up the bed, causing the sheets to burn my knees, flicking his fingers quickly over my clit. I bury my face in a pillow to muffle my cries as I reach an intense pinnacle.

Euphoric.

Torturous.

Blissful.

Eruption.

"Jesus, fuck," he grits roughly. Then with one final thrust, he fills me with his hot sperm. My legs are shaking, my knees are red from the friction, and my hands ache from clenching the bed.

I surf out the waves of pleasure, dragging out the cavernous penetration until Lucca releases his fingers. He releases his cock and flips me around again then slumps down on me.

He rubs between my legs, smearing his sperm over my folds then up to my navel and settles it on my breasts. Nuzzling into my neck, he kisses me repeatedly and nibbles my ear.

"That was fucking amazing. You okay?" he gasps into my ear.

"Uh huh. I'm great. You blow my mind. I love you," I drawl breathlessly as I allow my heart rate to descend slowly.

Lucca leans on his side and lifts me around to face him, pulling me into his contracting chest. The cloudy cream smothered on my skin makes me stick to him like glue. He moves some wavy, soft, just fucked curls from around my face and rubs the pad of his thumb across my lips. "You have no idea how much I love you, what you do to me, how you make me feel. And fuck, Lexi, it just keeps getting better." His blue eyes sparkle at me with sincerity, love, and gratification.

I kiss him softly and sigh, completely content in my post-coital glow. "I really can't be bothered with packing today, but I suppose I will need to get on with it. Besides, we have another matter we need to attend to."

"Yes, plenty more sex, any which way." He rubs his fingers down my back and cups my ass.

I giggle. "Yes, plenty of that, but we need to check in with Cameron and Mr. Carlin and call my grandparents and my mum."

"Okay. Well, I will help you pack up, then yes, we do need to make the calls." He looks at me, his eyes serious. "Lexi, I want to do this right. I want to ask your grandfather's permission. It is the right thing to do, but I would rather he met me first, so we should pay them a visit very soon. I cannot very well take his *Apple* without asking for permission to bite, and I understand that this may be a shock for them because we have not known each other long."

Lucca is right; it's the respectful thing to do. I know they will love him, and I do miss my grandpa. I'm quiet as I contemplate my thoughts, becoming slightly antsy in his arms. I feel sad that our romantic holiday is officially over, and I have to face the crazy screwed-up reality of my life again. This reality is ultimately making me restless, and I worry about what my mum will think.

"Dolcezza, what is wrong? What are you thinking?" He lifts my chin and looks straight into my eyes.

"I'm just thinking that my grandparents and my mum will love you. They'll be delighted to know I'm happy, and how much progress I've made since meeting you. I'm just a little worried about seeing my mum and how I'll manage. It always seems such a struggle, and I don't want to go back to that dark place I was in before meeting you, and if she's in her own dark place, it upsets me. I hate to see her like that because I love her so much. Sometimes she is better than others." I bite the inside of my cheek nervously.

"Hey, I am going to help you. I love you, and I will not let you back into that dark place, I promise you." He tightens his grip on me and kisses my temple.

Promise.

A promise is a promise.

"Lucca, I don't always cope great when I'm around them, and I'm worried you won't like it. I just ask that you be patient with me."

I drop my head slowly and sigh, but he lifts my chin up. "What have I told you about doing that? Keep your chin up so I can see your beautiful eyes. I understand now how difficult it is for you. I love you, and nothing you say or do will change that. Please relax and stop worrying. I have got you."

"Thank you, Lucca," I say, tracing my fingers over his jaw, his dimple, and then his lips.

"I need to clean up before I shower. Can you get me a towel from the bathroom?"

"Sure." He kisses me, then jumps up, giving me a great view of his sexy ass. He throws on his jeans and turns around to wink at me with a cheeky, dimpled smile before walking out the door to the bathroom down the hall. I admire my ring again while he's away, feeling the nicest rush of warmth rippling through me.

True perfection.

True happiness.

True bliss.

He's taking his time. I can hear him talking to someone before he returns, shaking his head as he grins, and I'm not sure if it's in a good way or not. He hands me a towel, and I dry myself off between my legs.

"Who were you talking to?" I ask.

He leans over to kiss my lips, then my breasts. "Never mind, but you do have visitors downstairs."

Oh my God—I hope no one heard us having sex.

Fuck!

File S for silence. Silence me next time I'm mid-orgasm. As much as Lucca has been good therapy for me, and worked wonders in helping me with my issues, I'm still filing. I'm so used to it that I don't think it will ever go away.

"What do you mean never mind? Who was it?" I challenge him, raising my voice in panic.

"Fuck, Lexi. You are getting me horned up again with that fiery shit."

"Stop trying to distract me." I stand firm and assertive with my hands on my naked hips. "Bloody pest!"

"Okay, calm down. I was speaking to *Anna*," he says, frowning guiltily.

"Why is Anna here so early? Oh, I'm going to bloody kill him."

Rage.

Riled.

Realisation.

My brother has not kept his word and is, in fact, cheating on Rachel with Lucca's younger sister. Fretting, I open my drawers to pull out some sleep shorts and a vest top and throw it on quickly.

"Lexi, do not go barging in there. He can do what he likes. They are both adults. You need to let it be, Doc," he says with amusement in his voice. This just confirms that he does condone this and it doesn't bother him, which makes me even angrier.

"It's not funny, Lucca. Cameron should not be cheating on Rachel like this. I love your sister, I do, but it's not appropriate. My brother is a jackass, an absolute friggin' halfwit."

I storm out of the room leaving Lucca sighing in exasperation and running his hands through his hair. I head down the hall and bang on Cameron's door. "You've got two minutes to get downstairs. Both of you! Anna, I know you're in there," I shout.

Anna opens the door and squeals before hugging me tightly.

She has just-fucked hair but is dressed in smart work clothes and smells of expensive perfume. Cameron is sprawled across the bed, naked like a rock star with the duvet covering his modesty and nothing else.

"Hi, Sis. Good holiday?" he asks casually.

"Don't you 'hi, Sis' me. What are you two playing at? Cameron, you have a girlfriend. This is not fair to Rachel, and it's not fair to Anna."

"Lexi, relax. I am fine with it. I am not going to be moving in. It is just a fling, and Cameron has spoken frankly, so I know where I stand. I am just having a bit of fun." Anna tries to reassure me with a confident explanation.

"And Rachel? What about her?" I glare at Cameron and then Anna with the most distasteful scowl.

"We have a very open relationship. I don't expect you to understand it, but we see other people. Period," Cameron adds, mussing his hair with his fingers.

Disgusting. I'm going to kill him. "What is wrong with you? Why would you do that? It's—"

"It's not wrong, it's normal for Rach and me. We have an understanding. I don't need to explain, Lex. For fuck's sake, just because you don't—" Cameron shrugs and scuffs his bare feet across the carpet.

"Sleep around?" I retort, hand on my hip.

"Yes." He sighs, holding the nape of his neck.

Lucca is standing behind me. "Orianna, why have you not left for work yet? You told me you were going. I am going to fire your ass, and then you will need to find some other boss who lets you gallivant at your leisure all over the fucking place."

"Calm down. I am going in today, but I was just visiting Cam, and I wanted to congratulate you both." She squeals and claps her hands. It's not lost on me that she's changing the whole direction of this confrontation I'm trying to have with Cameron.

Hazel comes running up the stairs in her pyjamas to see what the commotion is. She grabs my waist and hugs me senseless. "Are we all friends up here?" she asks warily, looking around at everyone trying to suss out what the problem is.

I give Cameron my best "we will talk about this later" look. He mutters something under his breath and shakes his head.

"Congratulations again, you two! I am so, so happy for you both." Hazel hugs me tightly, before releasing me to wrap her arms around Lucca. I giggle as he shuffles restlessly.

Hazel grabs my hand. "I know I said this last night, but bloody hell, that is not a ring, it's a blooming boulder. It's beautiful, Roo. I love it!"

Anna's eyes light up. "At least you picked a decent diamond, Brother Dearest. You do have impeccable taste. Lexi, it is amazing, very beautiful. I am so happy you will be my sister-in-law!" she says enthusiastically.

Cameron jumps up out of bed naked, and I blush and look away. He has never covered up around the house, but I'm embarrassed as Lucca and Anna are here. Hazel doesn't flinch; she's seen it before, but Anna smirks and lifts her eyebrow as he turns around to pull on jeans and a T-shirt.

He walks up to the doorway where we have tightly grouped together in the narrow landing area. "Congratulations, baby girl, I'm so, so happy for you. I love you. You know that, right? Even when you're scolding me. I'm glad you have Lucca. He's going to take great care of you, and I'm glad to see you home. I missed you."

He hugs me and I snuggle into his neck, forgiving him briefly for his infidelity because I did miss him too, and his embrace reminds me of the heart-to-heart we had in Tuscany when he came over for a few days, causing my heart to skip a beat. I know we are going to have to talk about it again at some point in proper depth. I respect him massively for sharing his own ghosts with me and thinking about it does draw my attention away from his infidelity, which seems inconsequential for now because he reminds me how much I love him regardless of his flaws.

He shakes Lucca's hand. "Congrats, mate. Take good care of her. She means the world to me."

"I will, you do not need to worry. She will be well looked after. Lexi *is* my world." Lucca wraps his hands around my waist, closely pressing himself against my back as he rests his chin against the side of my head.

"Is this a private party up here?" Samantha asks, standing behind Hazel.

I scream and let go of Lucca, forcing myself against her and wrapping my arms around her neck.

She squeezes me tightly. "I'm so glad to have you back but also delighted with your news. Good God, you've been busy, my darlin'. Let me see this ring."

I nervously lift my hand up, and her eyes nearly jump out her head. "Oh my God. Girls, get up here, you need to see this!" she yells down the stairs, grabbing my hand to admire my rock. "Your ring is gorgeous, honey. Now are you going to introduce me to your handsome man?" She smirks as she drinks Lucca in.

"Lucca, this is Samantha. Sam, Lucca." He has her charmed in no time. He does the double-cheek kissing, and I can tell she's hot and bothered, but she is trying to keep her composure and act professional, more business-like instead of one of my best friends.

She blushes and I think she's trying hard to make a good first impression on Lucca.

Shit, I wish he'd put a shirt on to cover his sexy body.

Carrie, Jessica, and Lucy all come pounding up the stairs, but stop and gaze at Lucca when they reach the top step. Their mouths drop like bloody goldfish. Lucca laughs, and I see Jessica elbow Lucy in the ribs.

I can barely breathe. There is just not enough room on this compact landing, but I'm deliriously happy to see the girls.

"Girls, this is Lucca. Lucca, these are my girls. Carrie, Jessica, and Lucy," I proudly say as I look at the girls with the biggest smile on my face.

He kisses them all on both cheeks, causing them to melt under his sexy ways. "It is a pleasure to meet your beautiful girls. Ladies, I am charmed."

So are they, evidently.

He gives them a sexy dimple smile, and my eyes silently tell him to quit that because that look should be reserved only for me. He chuckles.

"I told you she had an Italian god," Hazel blurts.

Anna giggles as Lucca bows his head, letting his dark wavy side fringe sweep over his eyes. I do believe he's a little embarrassed at being under the microscope of all my friends.

"Ladies, it is a pleasure to meet you all, and I would like to thank you for taking good care of my girl and being such good friends to her. I am going to throw something on. I will be back in a bit," Lucca says.

"Don't bother, Lucca. We rather like your body, so feel free to kick about like that, boss," Hazel replies impishly. Lucca shakes his head and smiles before kissing me and walking back towards my room.

I smack her arm. "Cut it out, Skip," I chide, and the girls all laugh, jibbing at Hazel as well.

It's nice to be back with them. I introduce Anna, and they are all polite and welcome her openly, although I can sense from some of the disapproving looks exchanged between them that they are wondering what the hell is going on. I assume Hazel hasn't told them about Cameron and Anna. I then hug Jess, Carrie, and Lucy in turn, but I can tell by Lucy's body language that she is shocked by Cameron and Anna's fling. I give her an extra cuddle to reassure her and whisper in her ear that I will explain later.

"I can't get over that ring. It's monstrous, bloody hell," Carrie says. I smile and let out a little happy sigh, raising my shoulders contently.

"You look amazing, Lex. You have a fantastic tan, and you look so happy. It's lovely to see," Jessica says, rubbing her hand down my arm.

"Thank you, Jess. You wouldn't believe the time I've had with Lucca, and how special I felt. Well ... how special I feel, actually."

Cameron shuffles past us and squeezes through to the top of the stairs. Lucy looks up at him and blushes, then looks across to Anna who is dressed to kill in a navy tailored pencil dress and high heels. She's bothered that Anna is leaving Cameron's bedroom; I can tell.

Hmmm.

"Cameron, put the kettle on," I say. He looks back at Anna, cocking his head and winking with a devilish, sexy grin, then looks at me sheepishly and nods his head.

"Lexi, I am just going to help Cam in the kitchen and make some calls. Have you called Mamma and Papa yet to say you arrived home safely?" Anna asks.

"Yes, we called them last night from Marco's car on the way home from the airport." Marco da Vinci is Lucca's oldest friend and his right-hand man. He is Lucca's driver, all-round organiser, and business advisor. She kisses me again and squeezes my upper arms. "I cannot believe how excited I am. Seriously, I am thrilled for you both."

I smile. "Thank you, Anna. It means a lot. I'm very lucky that Lucca has such a wonderful family."

"You are so sweet. You will have me crying in a minute. Right, girls, who wants tea?"

"I do," they say in unison.

She wiggles past us and struts down the stairs, leaving an impression.

"She seems really lovely. I can see how you and Anna got on so well, Hazel. She's very outgoing," Jess says.

"We all really hit it off. She's fun, fun, fun, and that girl has her family wrapped around her little finger," Hazel replies.

"Two peas in a pod then?" Samantha says sarcastically.

Hazel rolls her eyes. "Oh lighten up, Sam. Some of us know how to relax and have fun, you know, you should try it," Hazel retorts.

Lucy is very quiet. That file will need to be revisited. Friend in need of care—my care.

"Girls, I'm going to grab a quick shower, then I'll come down and give you the holiday-dolliday debrief." Normally we would have sleepovers and a DBB: *drunk, bed, and bitch* in bed, catching up on gossip, but I guess it will need to be over a cup of tea this morning.

I walk back into the bedroom to find Lucca sprawled on my bed with his hands behind his head, grinning up at me. "Your friends are really nice, and they seemed pleased to see you." He smiles. "I thought I would give you a minute alone with them."

"Thanks. They are, and I'm delighted to see them. It feels like forever since I last saw them, even though it has only been five weeks. It's the longest I have ever gone without seeing any of them. I'm going to have a shower now. I'm desperate to catch up and tell them about Tuscany." I sort through some clothes sitting at the top of my suitcase and feel my heart twinge with happiness that all the girls are here.

"I am coming in the shower with you," he says as he jumps off the bed.

"It's not big enough for us both, and not when we have a house full, Romeo." I shake my head and index finger, smiling at him playfully. My shower is the standard square cubicle, fit for one, not what Lucca is used to with his opulent bathrooms at the villas and his farmhouse.

"We will fit, but we will need to wait until tonight before I fuck you again. Then I can make you scream good and proper." He cocks his head, his shaggy hair sweeping across his forehead. He smiles showing me his brilliant white teeth and dimples. The heat in his eyes sears through me. My full system goes into overdrive when I hear him say the word "scream." It does crazy things to my insides and dampens my sex almost instantly. Typically, I'd be petrified with his choice of words, but hearing them from his lips is erotic.

He makes me scream with pleasure.

With pain.

Pleasure and pain.

I love it.

"You fucking destroy me when you scream. I know you are thinking about it now, I can tell," he says as he runs his tongue down my neck. Damn, he's good. And apparently psychic. I might need to do some vocal exercises to prepare my throat for said screaming.

He pulls my hand and leads me down the hall towards the bathroom. This will need to be a cold shower—freezing, in fact. We fit in the shower cubicle, but it's a tight squeeze, so I stay pressed against his chest, placing soft, wet kisses on his shoulders as he cups my ass. There is something exceptionally lovely and intimate about the heat of our bodies so close and just holding each other. Special.

After drying, Lucca puts clean jeans and a white V-neck on that are on the top of his case and I put a white silk vest and black and white textured miniskirt on from the new collection Lucca bought me in Tuscany. This isn't what I would normally wear here at home, but it seems like such a waste not to wear them. I do have a lovely tan, and I'm more relaxed about my appearance since meeting Lucca.

As I throw my hair up in a shaggy bun, Lucca moves a stray wave over my cheek and behind my ear.

"You are beautiful. I love when you wear your hair up like this. It is such a turn on watching you unravel it, letting your hair tumble down your back." He kisses my lips and runs his hand up under my skirt, cupping my ass.

"You're not so bad yourself, but you're being a core tease," I reply, returning his kisses. I'm so hot for him right now, but we have visitors, and I need to catch up with the girls.

Taking his hand, we walk downstairs to a hyperactive Doris doing her excitable dance in the hallway. The girls have locked her out of the lounge. Sam!

Doris follows me into the kitchen, nudging her head on my legs, looking for some attention, so I lean over to hug her again, stroking her and rubbing her ears. Lucca leans against the counter, shaking his head bemused as he peels a tangerine he has lifted from the fruit bowl. The sight of him leaning casually against the counter peeling a tangerine is doing nothing for keeping my sexy need under control.

Oh my goodness, maybe I'm one of those obsessed sex addicts.

I have sex on the brain.

Around the clock sex.

Sex, sex, sex.

Needing to distract myself from these thoughts, I open the back door to let Doris out, inhaling some fresh air, then take Lucca's hand and enter the lounge. My eyes light up, and I put my hand over my mouth. There are engagement and congratulation banners and balloons everywhere!

Lucca tightens his grasp on my other hand.

"Wow, what a lovely surprise. Thank you, everyone. This looks amazing, and it's very thoughtful." Tears prick at my eyes.

Lucca wraps his arms around my waist, and drops his chin on my shoulder as he looks around the lounge. "Yes, thank you, girls. It looks great."

I love how he always manages to stay so endearing and down to earth. Even though he has such a privileged life, he's grateful over some latex balloons and foil banners.

Jessica jumps up and walks over to grab my hand. "I'm so happy for you. It's been a long time coming. You deserve this happiness, darlin'. I love you, Lex, we all do."

"You're going to make me cry, Jess," I choke. Lucca kisses the side of my head then takes a seat next to Cameron.

"Lex, don't cry. You'll set us all off," Carrie says as she stands and comes over to hug me.

I break down sobbing at their kindness. Sam, Hazel, and Lucy jump to their feet and hug me in a tight circle as the tears trickle down my cheeks. "I'm so sorry, I'm just a little emotional. I've missed you all, but I've never felt this happy," I blubber.

Lucca appears worried with my emotional distress, his forehead pinched.

"Don't worry, mate. This is what they do. They get all smoochy and fucked up with that crying shit. Wait until you witness them on the wine. It's like a fucking car crash," Cameron says to Lucca.

Hazel scowls at him, but Anna giggles at his remark.

Lucy gives me an extra squeeze. "Don't be sorry. You deserve to be emotional; it's a special time. We're just so glad you're happy. You worried the hell out of us when you had to have surgery. When Hazel called we were so sick with worry and ready to jump on a plane to come and be with you."

Carrie runs her hand over my wrist. She's a nurse and assesses the small scar, saying it's very neat and tidy. It's still playing up, not enough to wear the sling all the time, but I'm taking strong painkillers and not letting Lucca know that it continues to give me grief. I'm trying to forget all about that awful night, and he feels guilty enough about it, so I don't want him feeling any worse than he does. I watch Lucca bow his head. I can tell he's uncomfortable as he listens to them talk about it.

"Come and sit down and give us your holiday chat," Samantha says. I take her hand and sit on the sofa, wiping my tears.

"Hazel, will you make more tea, please? Where is Dominic, by the way? At work?" I ask.

"Yes, early meeting, but he'll be home for dinner. I've been cooking up some of those dishes Maurizio taught me, and Dominic thinks he has died and gone to heaven. It's great he's moved in here with me because now we can save money for the wedding."

I'm glad Dominic has moved in here with her too, but it will be strange not living with Hazel. We've been together every day since we started at the University of Glasgow, and I'm going to miss her and her outrageous personality. And even her messiness to a certain degree because that's what defines her.

"Lexi, I love your outfit, you look amazing," Samantha says.

"Thank you. Wait until you check out all the new clothes I have. They're unreal."

"That's good. Do you by chance have a cream pencil dress in this new collection, because your mutt ruined mine," she gripes.

Busted. "Yes, sorry about that. I'll buy you a new one." I frown and nervously bite the inside of my cheek.

"No, you won't, but I might raid your wardrobe when I need to borrow something." Sam shakes her head and smiles.

"Okay, deal."

Lucca smiles at me. "You okay now, Doc?"

"Yes, just got emotional seeing the girls and all of this." I move my hand around the lounge towards the decorations, and he smiles, nodding his head with understanding.

"Cameron, mind taking me to pick up my car? I will need to bring over some boxes to pack up Lexi's stuff." Lucca turns around to address Cameron, stretches, and yawns then checks the time on his watch.

"Sure, mate. Let me grab my keys."

"Anna, are you not supposed to be somewhere?" Lucca asks her impatiently. She jumps up when Cameron and Lucca stand and hugs Lucca tightly. He kisses her forehead and holds her close. "I love you, Orianna, and I am grateful for your support, but I need to ask you to get back to work. You have a lot to do for the Edinburgh Club di Energia launch."

"Fear not, Lukie boy. I am going to the office just now. I just want to spend time with you two, is that so bad?" She giggles.

"Do not push it."

She hugs me, squashing me with enthusiasm, then says her goodbyes and follows Cameron out into the hall.

Lucy is sitting next to Samantha—very quiet, indeed.

Hmmm.

Noted and filed. *Again.*

Lucca wraps his arms around my waist, and as he kisses me softly on the lips. I blush. He runs his hand repeatedly over my wrist, closing his eyes and pressing his forehead against mine, breathing heavily. He's still hurting deeply about the accident, and pondering on it because Carrie brought it up.

"You sure you are okay?" he whispers.

"Yes, I'm fine. I'll see you when you get back."

He lifts my wrist up and kisses it sweetly. Samantha notices. Shit! Interrogation is on her agenda; I can see it in her eyes.

"Ladies, it has been a pleasure. Thank you again for making this special for Lexi. I hope to see you all very soon. Please, come over to our place anytime." He double-cheek kisses them all in turn, because he expects them to be gone when he returns.

Hazel returns with mugs and a pot of tea. Placing the tray down, she smacks his ass as he walks away. "Catch you, boss," she chirps.

Lucca shakes his head as he walks out, but the sexy dimple smile is definitely there. I can sense it.

We pour fresh tea, and I tuck my legs at my side to snuggle on the couch as I hug my "Little Miss Nervous" mug trying to get warm. My body temperature has become acclimated to the Tuscan sun, and I'm shivering being back home.

The girls have taken my engagement ring and are passing it around, asking all about how my romance happened. They know the basics because Hazel has already told them, so I fill in the gaps.

Although they are delighted for me, they are surprised I allowed Lucca into my heart and fell for him so quickly.

"He is absolutely flaming hot, Lex. Hot-hot-hot! A definite keeper," Sam says. I smile, sliding the ring on my finger.

"How cute is it that he is so close with his baby sister? Far too sexy," Jessica adds.

"Right, dish the dirt. Is the sex as hot as hell?" Sam asks.

Oh my God!

"They are at it like bloody rabbits," Hazel blurts out. They all start giggling.

"Swiftly moving on," I say, blushing, trying to distract them as I feel the heat from my burning cheeks.

"So what's the deal with the wrist?" Sam challenges, picking up my hand running her finger over the scar then she tsks and shakes her head.

I bite the inside of my lip and hold the back of my other hand against my mouth as I move my fingers up and down. "Nothing to tell. We'd been drinking, and I fell and fractured it."

Narrowing her eyes she protests. "Bullshit. You're lying, I can tell. We love you, and love that you're happy, but I think you're hiding something." Sam's not letting this go, and although I'm annoyed and don't want to divulge anything, I'm also glad they're concerned about my welfare.

"I told you, it was an accident. Lucca was holding me, and I was wriggling. He was drunk and tripped over a sun lounger cushion and dropped me."

Yelling.

Running.

Collapsing.

"Oh, is that why he was looking guilty and continually rubbing your wrist?" Her facial tension relaxes and she seems to accept that by softening the glossiness in her eyes. The others nod and smile sympathetically in understanding.

"Yes, he feels awful about it. Now let me tell you about all the sightseeing we did!" Steering away from what could have been an awkward conversation, I tell the girls about the farmhouse, Lucca's grandparents' villa, and about his parents' villa. I tell them about Florence and the exquisite hotel we stayed in, and they love to hear about The Luminara Candle Parade, the opera and the fairy-tale garden on the night he proposed.

Then I tell them about the white silk journal he has given me, and all the romantic writing he has scrolled inside of it.

Lucy sighs. "Oh my God, he can't be real. He sounds too perfect and such a romantic."

Breakthrough! Lucy has finally found her voice this morning.

Twirling a curl of my hair, I smile so much that my cheeks are sore but drop my face when I see Lucy is glum, maybe over the Cameron-Anna escapade. I would love her to find some happiness, some love, and to have a little male attention and romance of her own.

"He does sound exceptionally romantic," Jess adds.

I can't help my sigh. "He is. He's very loving and attentive. He is romantic and an amazing chef, and considerate, and generous, and caring."

And a sex God.

An hour later, Cameron and Lucca return just as the girls are leaving.

"Are you planning on having an engagement party?" Jess directs to both Lucca and me.

"It's not really my thing, I don't want any fuss," I mumble, unsure of Lucca's intentions.

"We need to talk about it, but whatever Lexi wants is fine by me. It might be nice to have something small to commemorate it, Doc. What do you think?" Lucca asks, searching my face for approval.

I shrug. "Maybe we can have a small intimate meal or something," I say impulsively on the spot. Lucca's appeased. His eyes are all twinkly, clear blue and loving. Very loving.

"We'll look forward to it," Carrie says.

I kiss them all, hugging them goodbye. Lucca begins carrying the boxes upstairs as Cameron slouches on the sofa, hanging one leg over the side with an arm stretched across the back of the sofa.

"What's your plan for today?" I ask Cameron.

"I might go back to bed, and I have a song to finish that I've been working on, then I'm playing seven asides with the lads later."

"Lucca, can you come with me? There is someone I want you to meet." I throw my studded, suede sandals on and shout for Doris. Lucca holds my hand, and I pick up the gift bag before taking him next door to meet Mr. Carlin. I let myself in and smile when I see him sitting in his chair in the lounge.

"Oh, not that bloody dog again. I thought I'd get some peace now that you're back," Mr. Carlin grumbles. Doris has flown upstairs with his slipper, whipping her tail on the banister, and I can't help but giggle. She'll be off to find something she can chew no doubt.

Mr. Carlin stands up when he sees Lucca. He shuffles about, mumbling and straightening his tie, then puts his thumb under his suspenders and straightens his spine.

"Mr. Carlin, I'd like you to meet Lucca Caruso, my fiancé." I smile.

"Well, son, get in here so I can meet you properly and evaluate you," Mr. Carlin says.

18

Lucca looks stunned by his abrupt manner, but he walks over and shakes Mr. Carlin's hand. "I have heard wonderful things about you, Mr. Carlin. It is an honour to finally meet you."

Mr. Carlin eyes him up first then fixes his glare straight into Lucca's eyes, quietly studying them for a few moments. "You have kind eyes, son. You're doing well so far," he says diplomatically.

"Thank you, I think," Lucca says, shrugging his shoulder.

I walk over and give Mr. Carlin a huge hug. Usually, I rub his arm with my hand in gesture, or I pat him on the back, so he's surprised by the affection I'm showing him.

"So you've decided to take a leaf out of Hazel's book and spread your wings. I'm glad. It's about bloody time, lassie. It isn't healthy keeping all those insecurities in," he mentions.

"Why is that blooming heating on at maximum? I'm cold, but even I feel sweltered in here. Honestly, you're going to fall into a coma with that heating up so high. No wonder you sleep as much." I moan and then storm into the kitchen in a stupor to turn it down.

"Lexi, you're only back two minutes, lassie, and you've started that bossy nonsense. I need the heat. Don't have as much body fat anymore to keep me warm, and you'll put me in a coma before anything else, young lady."

"Lucca, sit down and talk to Mr. Carlin," I say, ignoring his comment. "I'm just going to check his fridge and the mail." I check the fridge and notice he has prepared meals in the frozen compartment. "Where did you get the meals from?" I ask.

"Hazel made them up. That girl is not as bad as I thought. She's not as good a cook as you are, Lexi, but she definitely learned a few things over there." He pings his suspenders, insinuating he's put on a few pounds in weight.

Another massive thank you that I owe her. I know her meals will be healthy ones because she's a nutritionist, and I could bet my life it's all the Swiss chocolates he's eating that's putting added weight on him.

"So, how are you getting on with the home help Lucca arranged for you?" I ask.

"Which one?" he replies.

"What do you mean which one?" I chide while Lucca quietly chuckles.

"Well, the first one, Fiona, she never bloody talked. I'm bored enough, so I was not having that. Then the second, Terry, kept moving my whiskey to the top cupboard and treated me like a geriatric. Now I have Julie. She's nice, very bonnie girl and tells me her grandfather goes to chess club in the village, but she can't cook worth a monkey." He cleans his spectacles with a handkerchief.

I glance at Lucca and roll my eyes. "Told you he was insufferable."

"Lexi, I have ears and can still hear." He harrumphs and rolls his eyes then taps the side of his ears reminding me they are in good working order.

I shake my head. "I wanted to let you know that I'm moving into Lucca's house, but I'll still be over to check on you every day."

"Aye, I know. Cameron told me. As long as you know what you're doing, lassie. I know you wouldn't make an irrational decision off the cuff unless you felt safe and content. You must be something special, son, to gain her trust so quickly. Just don't abuse it." He glares at Lucca with a beady eye.

"Lucca wants to ask Grandpa properly if he can ... you know ... marry me ..." I trail off.

"There, it's back, the hesitation and uncertainty. Lexi, you need to face these fears and stop worrying. You're provoking anxiety with these thoughts. You were happy until you mentioned up North," he glowers. Mr. Carlin knows my family and knows how challenging it can be for me, especially when Mum is sick.

"Lexi, look at me. It will be fine. You will be fine. A promise is a promise, right?" Lucca says compassionately with a steady tone. When I look into his eyes, I can't help but smile and reach for his hand.

"There is my girl." His tone is soft and loving as he rubs his fingers over my diamond ring.

Mr. Carlin starts coughing, breaking our moment. "Well, if I hadn't witnessed it, I wouldn't believe it. Looks as if you have found your light, lassie, right there in your fiancé. You're going to be just fine. Can I retire now?"

I giggle. He can be so warm and loving when he's not grumpy or moaning. "No way. You told me you need to keep your brain active, so I'm keeping you on your toes. I'll lift something out of the freezer for your dinner, and if you're lucky, you might get some of Lucca's home cooked meals sent over. He's very good at cooking, better than I am."

I hand him the gift bag, and his sagged, wrinkled eyelids rise. "There is a bottle of Macallan Fine Oak 18, and a new flask that I had engraved. I also got you some chocolate truffles, a new belt, and a shirt."

"You're a sweet wee lassie, and Eleanor would be so proud of you. Thank you, sweetheart. Perhaps I'll wear it to this chess club in the village," he adds, looking in the gift bag. He shakes his head when he sees Doris tearing into the daily newspaper. "Oh, I give up. I hope you're taking her with you," he complains as I pick up the shredded paper and tell Doris off for being naughty.

Leaving Lucca to chat with Mr. Carlin, I lift his meal out the freezer and make him tea. After saying our goodbyes, we head home and spend hours packing my things, only stopping to grab a quick sandwich at lunchtime. I slump back on the bed, absolutely exhausted after such a busy weekend and travelling last night.

"Are you ready to go? I will make us some dinner," Lucca suggests.

Yawning and stretching, I nod. "I can't get up. I'm so tired."

Lucca leans over and kisses my lips, then trails his fingers up the inside of my sun-kissed legs and under my miniskirt to cup my sex, giving me a tease of what will come tonight.

Giggling, I say, "Okay, point made, Mr. Caruso. I'm getting up, but I will expect lots of TLC."

"Oh, you will get more than that. Trust me."

Chapter 2: The Tour

Grabbing my mail and keys from the kitchen, I stop in slow motion and feel a nervous, rippling rush cascading down my body, making me a little weak and tingly.

I never thought I'd leave here, and especially not with a man. I thought Hazel, Cameron, and I would live together indefinitely. In my own little world I hoped we would, even though deep down I anticipated that Hazel would move on when she marries Dominic. Yet here I am, taking flight and fleeing the nest.

My stomach knots and I feel a little queasy with apprehension. I actually can't quite comprehend that this is, in fact, real and happening. It wasn't long ago that I was an independent woman with rules, boundaries, trust issues, and a whole lot of mental files, and now the direction of my life has changed completely. In theory talking about living with Lucca was so much easier when we were in holiday bliss, but now it's actually happening, I find it a little overwhelming.

That's what love is doing to me, confusing me with an array of new uncontrollable feelings I can barely contain.

My new love.

Our love.

The love.

Consumes.

Encases.

Covets.

My needy body and mind.

Love refills my gasping lungs to allow me to breathe. Love lifts my wings to allow me to soar and fly higher towards the light. Love nourishes, protects, and cherishes my inner vulnerability. Love is teaching me to be resilient.

Love is Lucca.

I know I'm making the right decision loving and trusting Lucca, but it doesn't avert me from my nostalgic notions. Opening the back door, I sit on the back step and look at the small green lawn with the little gnomes dotted about that Eleanor and Mr. Carlin helped me with after a day trip to the Clydeside Garden Centre.

Every time I'm in this garden, I think of Eleanor and part of me feels as if she is present and it makes me wonder if I will still have the spiritual feeling of having Eleanor close to me after I leave here. This very step is where I broke down emotionally after one of my sessions with Casey, and Eleanor showed me comfort. It was the first time I allowed myself to cry as an adult after holding my tears back for so many years. Eleanor encouraged me to let it all out and helped me feel, and for that I will always be indebted to her. I can picture her standing right there in the empty spot next to me with her lemon blouse and apron on.

Doris bangs through the door, distracting me from my musing, and nearly knocks me off the step as she barges into me. Instinctively, she lays her head on my lap, as if she senses I'm upset, and I use my thumb to rub her grey velvety fur while she whirrs away with contentment, closing her eyes and humming relaxing under my touch.

"There you are. Why are you sitting out here?" Hazel asks.

My bottom lip quivers as I look at her with worried eyes. She sits down next to me, and I place my hand on her knee—she understands me.

"Look, you're only five minutes down the road. We'll see each other whenever we want, and nothing will change. Not really. I'm so proud of you, Lexi, and you have my blessing. If I thought this move wasn't good for you, I would tell you, but I think it will be the making of you. Truly," she assures me.

"I'm scared."

Hazel reaches for me, pulling me into her side, comforting me by stroking my hair. "Well, of course you're scared. You wouldn't be human if you weren't. Lucca is your first relationship, and lucky for you it's full with nothing but love and conviction, so you just need to embrace it and go with the flow. It's understandable you have doubts, but, Lex, you are in a very fortunate position. You get to start all over."

Does this mean if I start over, I'm disregarding what I have here? What I've worked hard at achieving since moving away from Mum and my grandparents? I have independence and a simple, orderly life. Does it mean I'll be disrespecting Eleanor's memory by moving on?

I look up at her and move my head in a small side-to-side shake as I bite my inside lip and grasp the hem of my skirt.

Hazel presses her lips together, swallowing back a lump in her throat, her eyes pooling with moisture. "Oh, Lexi, don't. Please, don't … it will all work out fine. You will be five minutes away, and Lucca will take good care of you. If he doesn't, then Dominic and Cameron will have his balls." Her voice is breaking, and she's trying not to cry herself by supporting and convincing me.

I wrap my arms around her neck, burying my head in her blonde locks. I miss her already. I miss our DBBs in bed, our coffee nights and wine nights, our barbecues and morning runs, coming home from work and watching chick flicks. I even miss her moaning about what's healthy to eat and what's not, and I'm not even away yet.

Cameron walks out of the kitchen with three shot glasses in his palm, joining us on the step. "Slippery nipples. Bottoms up, girls."

"Lang May Yer Lum Reek Rum," the three of us chant in unison, clinking shot tumblers before we slam back the Bailey's with Sambuca. Feeling the warm, strong, creamy liquor burn my throat, I set my shot glass down on the ground, putting my hands over my face and crunching forward into my knees. Nostalgia is making me terribly emotional.

Cameron stretches his arm around my shoulder. "It could be worse. You could be moving to Tuscany. At least you're here, and I promise nothing will change. We'll see you all the time."

My feet feel ice cold on the stone ground, even though it's late June and supposed to be summer. I shiver as I hop side to side on the cold stone slabs.

Hazel comforts me, hugging me fondly as Doris does her affectionate animated dance, pawing at my knee. Lucca and Dominic join us, and he stands behind me and places a hand on my shoulder. He senses I'm fretting; he just knows.

"Doc, if you want to stay here another night we can move you out tomorrow. It is no hassle. However long you need."

Turning, I look up at him with sad eyes. "No, it's okay. I want to go to yours tonight. I'm just processing, that's all."

Lucca is trying hard, and I feel guilty for being miserable. I lift my feet up and stretch my legs across Cameron's knees, and then Cameron wraps his arms around me. I tilt my head leaning it on Cameron's shoulder, wondering if we will still comfort each other like this now I have Lucca to care for me.

Hazel jumps up. "Well, I'd like to celebrate. For one, I can leave as much mess as I like without being hounded, and for two, no more dog shit on the back lawn, and for three, lots of bathroom solo time. Oh, and when Cameron's at work, Dom and I can make as much noise as we like in the bedroom."

Dominic laughs at her forward confession. "And that is my future wife," he says with cheeky sarcasm, stretching his hands towards her. Dominic is good for Hazel; he will only pull her in if it's totally necessary but gives her a lot of free rein, which is more than I can do sometimes.

"Lucky you," Cameron mutters under his breath.

"Hey, I heard that, Cammy, and need I remind you that I've been turning a blind eye so far with the whole Anna situation, you are the lucky one," she blurts.

After some friendly banter and reminiscing about our garden barbecue days, Cameron lifts my legs off his knees and stands up then takes my hand to yank me upright. "Come on. We should get moving." Before I lock the back door I have a final glance at the gnomes Eleanor and Mr. Carlin helped me pick out.

Leaving the front door open, the boys head out front. Cameron puts Doris and her bed in the back of his jeep, and a few more boxes on the back seat. After saying goodbye to Hazel and Dominic, I lift my bag and walk outside slowly. My mouth drops when I see Lucca standing in front of his car. Another Aston Martin by the look of it, but it's a completely different model in a shiny black gloss. Rolling my eyes, but not surprised at all, I press the key fob for my little Ford Focus but realise I shouldn't drive yet with my fractured wrist. The rotational movements could be problematic still.

Damn.

I give Hazel my car keys.

"Nice wheels, Lucca," Dominic says.

Lucca nods his head smoothly and then opens the door for me to get in. I notice his registration plate is CAR US04. I remember him telling me that his dad Antonio bought Marissa CAR US01 as a wedding present. Antonio has number 02, Lucca's brother, Savio, has 03, his other brother, Armando, has 05, and Anna has 06.

I wave to Hazel and Dominic before getting in.

"You okay, Doc? I am worried about you," Lucca asks.

"Yes, I'm fine. It just feels as if a chapter is closing on me if that makes sense. I'm not all that good with change. It might take me some time to adapt." I lower my voice with embarrassment, but I promised him honesty.

"It is a big thing. A lot has happened for us in the last few weeks. You are doing so well and have made great progress; you should be very proud of yourself. Try to embrace it and live for today. I promise to be patient, and I will give you as much space as you need. Although I am looking forward to spending all my time with you. I want to make you really happy. You are my life now, so I will love you endlessly. Make you feel alive, just like I promised." He places his hand on my neck pulling me towards him and circles my nose with his before kissing it then my lips.

I know he will.

Leaving me breathless, he pulls away to look at me with that very promise in his eyes. Love. The promise of love.

"You're right, I'm just being idiotic. Please don't think I don't want this, because I do. I want to live with you very much. It's just such a big step for me."

"Please do not call yourself idiotic. You are anything but," he firmly says.

We drive up the tasteful, vintage, tree lined street of historic red sandstone houses. Cameron has pulled over to allow Lucca in front. Arriving at the private gate, he punches in a code opening the gates to allow us access. I roll my eyes. Of course I knew his property sat at the end of the street, and I've heard it's spectacular, but being this close and now entering through the private gates feels somewhat surreal and intimidating.

"What model is your car?" I ask, changing the subject.

"It is an Aston Martin V-12 Vanquish, do you like it?" I remember he also drove an Aston Martin in Tuscany; he obviously favours them.

"Yes, it's great. Very flash. When I'm cleared for driving again which I think will be soon actually, I'll need to get my car back. I need it for work."

"I think I will get you a new one."

"You're not buying me a car. My car is just fine, thank you. I love my little fokey. It does me just fine," I say assertively, straightening in my seat, shocked he would even suggest that I need a new car.

He laughs. "You would be safer driving a golf buggy than that toy car. I intend to get you two cars. Something suitable for Doris, and something sleek just for you."

Hmmm. *We'll see about that!*

My mouth drops in awe as we approach the gigantic house. Oh my goodness. It looks like a castle—a fortress—and absolutely stunning. I had no idea that this is all behind those gates. Lucca told me that it's a category B listed building dating back to 1802 and that he has spent years carefully restoring and renovating it. I knew his house would be impressive, but I'm astonished as I didn't expect this.

The house is made of traditional red sandstone and stretches over three levels with a separate coach house at the side of the building. There is a large, landscaped circle with a beautiful fountain in front of his home and several parking bays.

The cobbled driveway leading to the house is bordered by gravel at both sides with lush green trees and a large, vivid green lawn on either side. The trees and hedges start along the wall at the front gate's edge and continue around the perimeter of the property. Ivy climbs along the tall red sandstone walls and towering trees make it very private indeed.

"Wow, you live in a mansion," I say, looking out the window in awe.

"We live in a mansion," he corrects.

"Who lives in the coach house?" I ask, a little awed by the scale of everything.

"My housekeeper and gardener, Rose and Peter Smith. They are very loyal and good people. There is a granny flat out the back as well for any family or friends who stay over, and an extension onto the back of the main house. Anna's known to show up from time to time to take advantage of my pool, so feel free to warn her off if she pesters you."

Lucca effortlessly swivels the car around the circular fountain centrepiece and swiftly brakes in front of the main entrance. My stomach twinges with nerves and anticipation as Cameron pulls up behind him. Lucca gets out, opens the car door for me, and takes my hand. He presses a code on a panel near the front door allowing the main entrance gates to close behind us.

Cameron opens the jeep trunk, and Doris catapults out the back and bolts off exploring. I giggle watching her but nearly jump out of my skin when I hear a smash. She's gone and knocked over a huge stone plant urn near the front door.

"Lucca, I'm so sorry. I think she's a little excited."

Laughing, Lucca adds, "It is only a pot, so do not fret, but we are going to have to get her to obedience classes." I release his hand to go and pick up the shattered stone. "What are you doing? Leave it. Peter will get it."

He drags me back to his side while Cameron shakes his head in amusement. "Told you, mate, the mutt is a fucking liability. That dog is going to wreck this place." Lucca nods his head and rolls his eyes in agreement with Cameron.

A tall, sandy-haired man wearing a cable knit red sweater and brown cord trousers walks out of the house. Walking over to Lucca, he shakes his hand, then holds both his hands for a moment before patting his shoulders. "Well, young man, you going to introduce me to your beautiful new lady?"

Blushing, I stay close to Lucca's side.

"Peter, I would like you to meet my beautiful fiancée, Lexi Robertson. She is the lady of the house now. If I am not here, please make sure she has anything she needs."

What's with the lady?

"Yes, Lucca, absolutely. It's a pleasure to meet you finally, Miss Robertson. I hope you will be very comfortable. If there is anything at all, please just ask me or my wife Rose." He shakes my hand, wrapping his other over the top and clasping it in a formal but warm gesture.

"Thank you, Peter. It's lovely to meet you," I say shyly.

Doris comes galloping around like a bloody racehorse and bangs right into the back of my legs, causing me to buckle over and stumble. She's attracting attention with her hyperactivity.

Bloody nuisance.

Peter grabs my arms and lifts me upright while Lucca shakes his head as he holds my other arm.

"Eh ... thank you."

"Hmmm, this grey ghost belong to you?" Peter asks, already knowing the answer.

"Yes, she's just a little excitable and ... well, hyperactive sometimes," I confess.

"Well, young lady, we will need to do something about this," he adds. Cameron is looking as if he's fit to burst and clearly loving watching me quiver under Peter's shrewd words because he knows how spoiled Doris is and this will be a challenge.

"What have you got in mind, Peter?" Lucca asks with optimism, grinning at him. I tighten my fingers around his hand. Nothing will be happening to my dog. She's a pet and fine the way she is, a little unruly but very loveable.

"Obedience training starts tomorrow. Excellent pedigree I must say, and by the looks, a very good breed. Very loyal dogs and unbelievably clever, but you're cutting it fine. They need to be treated firmly from the start, and it looks as if you have a playmate. Not that I'm saying they aren't great companions, but, Miss Robertson, this dog needs dominance, force at times, and a strong leader. I'm guessing she's not that old," he says, studying Doris, rubbing his hand along his chin.

I shrug my shoulders, wrinkling my nose and scowling slightly, grateful he's willing to help but not with his choice of words. It's not that I feel threatened by Peter because he's merely referring to my dog and Lucca trusts him explicitly.

Force.

Dominance.

Strong.

"I suppose she needs a little training," I mutter feeling a familiar ache in my chest.

Sensing my uneasiness, Lucca rubs his fingers over my knuckles and it slightly calms me, his small gesture sending pulsing beats straight to my core.

"A little? You think?" Cameron adds sarcastically. He gets a mighty scowl for that cheeky comment.

Doris is jumping around looking for attention from Peter, so he pats her back then places the palm of his hand on her head. She sits, tilting her head to the side. I'm amazed.

"You know these dogs?" Lucca asks.

"Yes, used to breed, show, and work them. Wait until Rose catches a glimpse of this little beauty. Although she needs a lot of work. You understand how this works, Miss Robertson, don't you?"

No, I don't understand. She's my pet and not under ball and chain.

"Where will she be sleeping?" he adds.

Lucca shrugs his shoulders as he wraps his arm around my waist. "Well, that is up to my beautiful girl." He's redeemed and about bloody time.

"She will stay with me, you know, in the house," I mutter while rubbing her ear with my free hand. There's no way I'm having her outside or in a kennel; she wouldn't know what was going on.

"Hmmm, interesting. Well let's just see how that goes, and if you need advice, you know where I am," Peter replies, giving Lucca an approving nod of his head. I watch him interact with her, and he does have a natural flare. Doris seems calmer already. Maybe Peter will be a good help after all.

"Thank you. I really appreciate it, but I hope she won't get in your way too much."

"Beautiful lady, she won't get in my way. I'm thinking about you two young love birds because they can be, shall I say ... attached to their owners." He curls his lips on one side and winks at Lucca.

Oh my goodness, I'm mortified. I think he's referring to ... bedroom time.

Fuck!

File M for mortified. Mortified, he's thinking of our sex life.

Inappropriate.

Lucca takes my hand and walks me into the house with Cameron following behind me. Peter stays outside with Doris, giving her some commands and trying to train her by the looks of it. I stop walking when my foot enters the grand hallway's black and cream, high-polished tiled flooring and slowly lift my head, taking in the magnificent interior.

Cameron strolls by me and dumps boxes on the floor near the front doors. Swallowing hard, I open my eyes wide and drink it in— the fine details, artistry, and expensive accented décor. I have the same feeling as when I stepped into the luxury suite in Florence. It's so grand.

Blinking a few times, my eyes are drawn towards the enormous crystal chandelier hanging above me. I'm mesmerised by the colours reflecting against the diamond-like pendants and droplets spinning over the room, fanning a jewelled palette of colours.

"Cameron, fix a drink. You are welcome to stay for dinner. I am just going to give Lexi the tour."

"Cheers, mate, but I'm going to head back. I've got football training," Cameron replies. Secretly I was hoping he would stay, just to make sure I settle in okay. Not that he can do anything about my lack of resilience, but it's comforting knowing he's there.

I'm lost in the amazing artwork and ornate pieces sculpted across the walls and stop listening to their conversation as I stare, transfixed on the opulent, busy furnishings around me.

"Lexi, snap out it. Did you not hear me?"

Startled, I turn to him. "Sorry, Cameron. I, um … anyway, what were you saying?"

I notice Lucca is no longer holding my hand. He's not even in the hallway. "Where's Lucca?" I ask. Have I been daydreaming that long?

"He went to find Rose. I'm heading off. Will you be okay? I'll stay if you want me to." He runs his thumb over his eyebrow and sighs then carefully forms a half-hearted smile.

"Yes, of course I'm okay. I'm just processing this. It's a big change, but I'll be fine. It's not fair for you to cancel your plans, you don't need to stay. Cameron … can you keep your phone charged? In case I need to reach you?" I ask nervously.

"Of course, but you're perfectly safe. I vetted this place out when we collected the boxes, and Lucca has a great security system and it's very private. There are cameras all around the property, and Lucca will take great care of you. Are you getting cold feet already?" He pulls me to his chest and chuckles.

I wrap my arm around his waist, lean my chin on his shoulder, and sigh. Lifting my gaze, I notice Lucca leaning on the substantial artistic banister which curls and weaves in a spiral formation.

He frowns as he pinches his forehead with his middle finger and thumb. He's concerned, possibly offended.

Shit.

Cameron kisses my forehead before Lucca walks him outside to say goodbye, then punches in the code to open the gates for him. I wave half-heartedly to him but choose to walk over and sit on the bottom oval-shaped step of the staircase, hugging my knees to my chest.

Closing my eyes, I breathe as if I'm filling my lungs with courage and strength to embrace this new reality. Lucca returns and sits beside me on the step, leaning forward and resting his forearms on his knees. We don't say anything for a few minutes in an awkward silence.

"You never answered Cameron when he asked if you were having cold feet. Will you talk to me about this please?" he asks with agitation as he runs his hands through his hair.

He drops his head, and his wavy, dark hair flops down over his eyes. He's upset with me because I haven't been honest, and he's given me ample opportunity to tell him how I feel about this move.

"I'm sorry, it's just overwhelming. I'm not having cold feet, so please don't think that. I love you, Lucca. It's just surreal being here, and it's all happening so fast. I think maybe it's because we're not still on holiday, or I feel slightly strange being here, as if I am going to wake up from a dream. Reality is hitting me hard and I feel like I don't belong here." I shrug and look down to the ground following the scrolls and intricate design of the tiles with my eyes as if I'm lost in a maze. Ironically, I know that's how I might feel in this house.

He's quiet.

"Please, Lucca, look at me," I plead, lifting his chin. "I'm sorry I'm not hanging from the ceiling, sliding down the banister, doing backflips on your front lawn, or throwing the feathers out of the pillows. It's just so new, and I don't want to disappoint you. I love you more than anything else in this world. You are my world now, but I just need time to adjust."

He grabs my face in both hands, leaning his forehead on mine as his hot breath skims my lips, and his sexy scent fills my nostrils. "I am not mad at you. I could never be mad at you, but I am worried about you. You could never disappoint me. You make me happy, so fucking happy, so stop being so critical and disparaging of yourself. I love you and I will give you all the time you need."

He puts his hand on his heart, his lips press onto my own, and he holds them there. He floods me with his azure blue eyes while breathing deeply.

I pull back, leaving a small gap between our lips. "Kiss me. Kiss me then take me to our bed. I want you to take me so badly right now," I seductively whisper then brush his bottom lip with the end of a long soft stray wave of my hair that has fallen out of place. One minute I'm cold then the next I'm roasting hot, my emotions flipping on and off like a switch.

Yanking me towards him, his tongue thrashes my mouth, assaulting my own dancing tongue. He bites, sucks, and presses so hard that my lips feel numb and bruised while I throw my head back.

He pulls away breathlessly. "I am going to have you on every inch of this house. You will remember this, I promise you, and you are going to think of tonight every time you feel lost, because I will bring you home to me," he growls possessively against my lips.

I almost combust just hearing these words. I want Lucca.

I want his love.

I want his lust.

I want his light.

I'm officially a self-confessed sex addict. I'm sure of it.

Affirmative.

I push my heavy breasts against his chest, gripping his hair at his neck, then angling myself so I can wrap my leg over his hips to straddle him. Thumping my heels into his lower back, I moan and grind into his body, pressing my throbbing clitoris against his massive bulge where I rub my damp sex vigorously against the straining fabric of his denims, causing him to fall backwards on the step.

"You trying to take me or kill me? Jesus, right now if you take me like this, you will kill me," he breathlessly stammers while he bites into the soft skin of my neck.

I actually think I might take him here and now despite Rose being in the house. I'm so undone and really don't care for anyone else but our shuddering hearts and the undulate sexual energy coursing through my veins right now.

We grip and grind as I bite on Lucca's ear and he moans with delight, digging his fingers into the flesh under my short skirt.

"Um, hey ... excuse me," a muffled voice croaks. Shit, someone is shuffling behind us near the doorway. This must be Rose and she must be mortified. I think this might be more embarrassing than when Lucca's mother walked in on me in my lingerie.

Fuck!

File P for privacy. Privacy is a luxury, and I am a shameless hussy.

I can't even bring my eyes up. My cheeks are too flamed, so I stay buried in Lucca's neck, tensing my limbs rigidly.

"Lucca, I'm so sorry to interrupt, but I'm retiring for the night. Dinner is in the kitchen for you both. I made dinner as I thought you would be tired after your trip and the packing. Miss Robertson, I look forward to becoming acquainted with you tomorrow. Lucca, please call if you would like breakfast prepared. I've stocked the pantry and the fridge, and your mail is in the study. I'll let myself out and lock the door. Enjoy your evening."

"Thank you, Rose. We appreciate it. Have I told you how much I love you and how beautiful you look today?" Lucca smoothly charms her.

She sighs. "Yes, Lucca, you tell me all the time. Now don't be going and getting Miss Robertson jealous. You need to keep all that flirting for her. I'm no spring chicken anymore, and I suspect Peter gets jealous with all the attention you give me." She chuckles.

I instantly love her.

She has the nicest tone to her voice—warm, kind and loving, and she has a great sense of humour. It's adorable the way she has a confident respectful relationship with Lucca.

Jumping up and straightening my skirt, I release my grip and walk towards her, rosy cheeked and embarrassed. "Please forgive my rudeness. I'm sorry you had to ... um, find us like this ... um, I'm Lexi. It's a pleasure to meet you. I'm thankful Lucca has such wonderful people taking good care of him. I suspect you keep him on his toes, and it's lovely to see. Peter has kindly offered to help me with my dog Doris and I'm very grateful," I ramble, barely taking a breath.

Rose has a small frame; she must be less than five feet. She has short, thick, ash-blonde hair cut in a neat bob with streaks of grey running through it. She has good skin though and looks youthful and well dressed. The hint of lilac eye shadow across her lids opens her grey eyes.

Although her blouse is smart, she wears comfortable looking beige trousers and flat shoes. There's something very earthly and warm about her, relaxed almost, as if she feels very much at home here and it swells my heart.

Unlike how I feel.

Rose holds me closer and kisses my forehead. "Finally, a beautiful, considerate young lady for my Lucca. I've heard wonderful things about you. You are such a sweet girl, and I'm thrilled to have another woman around. It also makes me very happy knowing we will have a dog again. I'm looking forward to meeting her." Normally a cuddle like this from a stranger would make me tense and back away, but I do have a soft spot for the elders. Rose had me the minute I saw the kindness in her grey eyes and heard the sweetness in her voice.

I hug her just a little too long as I inhale her wonderful scent, the smell of her perfume instantly transporting me to another place and time. Nostalgia washes over me as I momentarily cast my thoughts back to Eleanor: homemade angel cake, lavender oil, sunshine, freshly washed linen sheets, and her fresh floral perfume— coincidently the same one that Rose wears today. I smile thinking perhaps this is a sign that Eleanor's spirit and memory will be with me here.

"Are you all right, petal?" Rose asks with concern.

"Yes, sorry, I just had a familiar memory. That is all."

I think Rose and I are going to get along just fine and I like that she calls me petal; this was a name that Eleanor also used to call me.

Lucca stands and approaches me, wrapping his arm around my waist. "I knew you two would get along. I now have my two favourite women here spoiling me, and I am a happy man." He beams at Rose while his protective hand grasps my ass as he presses his hard erection into my lower back, reminding me how much he wants me.

She clicks her tongue and shakes her head, smiling at his words as she walks off. Once the door is closed, Lucca turns me around and swiftly lifts me up so I'm wrapped around his hips, causing my short skirt to ride up around my waist. He clenches my ass cheeks as he walks.

"God, I love her, but I am glad she is gone. I am so fucking hard for you right now," he growls, and my excitable butterflies have awoken once more.

Pressing my sensitive sex against the tenting of his denim jeans, I grab his hair and thrash my tongue in his mouth. "I want you inside me. Give me it right here. I can't wait." I sound very desperate, but the nervous feeling about moving in here is gone and replaced by feelings of lust and desire.

I think smelling Rose's perfume triggered happy memories for me and therefore has relaxed and calmed me. Reassuring me that I am brave and I can do this. As if Eleanor was speaking the words to me herself.

He hooks his thumbs under my lace thong and tears it off me, causing the material to burn my skin slightly with friction. Another lace thong torn and gone.

"Tell me," he demands.

I have a newfound courage in my lustful state, and I don't intend to sacrifice this feeling of desire. I want him and I know he likes to hear what I desire. "Fuck me here, on the stairs. Fuck me fast and hard, then take me to bed and fuck me again. Then I'm going on top to ride you senseless. I might even take your cock in my mouth. Then you can fuck me again."

Where did that come from? Holy shit. This is by far the dirtiest I have ever spoken out loud.

His eyes have just changed from azure blue to crystal-white blue and are the biggest and most erotically starved I have ever seen them with his pupils dilating. He hitches his breath, completely aroused.

"Fuck, you never fail to amaze me. Jesus, you nearly put me into cardiac arrest. You asked, so now you are getting, and, baby, you are not going to be able to walk tomorrow," he rasps, breathing impulsively.

Gripping me, he fumbles until he whips his jeans and T-shirt off in no time as we dirty kiss. Before I can undress, he has pushed himself into me hard, immediately taking me off guard. So goddamn hard, that I whimper in response.

"Too hard?" he groans.

Sweet Jesus. I asked for it.

"No, I want it. More, give me more!" I cry when his second deep penetrative thrust fills my sheath. We stumble back on the bottom steps of his stairs. I dig my fingers into his back as he places his knees on the stair beside my hips.

Keeping my legs tightly wrapped around his waist, I don't want to let go to this deep, intrusive pleasure. I'm aware of the uncomfortable edge of the step digging into my back, but I block it out and focus on the sublime sensation deep in my core.

Too intense.

Too good.

I want this so bad.

I lift my ass off the stair and push my hips up to meet him. When I sync with his movement, he pulls back and pounds me, and I crash into him, sending an unravelling ripple through my core, causing those butterflies to tumble.

"Don't stop, Lucca. It's too good, I need you!" I yell with utter certitude in my heady trance. My insides feel like they are shredding, and the pressure is exquisite but I need more.

Deep.

Deep penetration.

Deep delicious torture.

"Open your eyes. I need to see what I am doing for you," he demands. I strike them open only for them to roll in the back of my head, and we continue thumping and pleasuring each other with blow after blow.

Quickly.

Intensely.

Lasciviously.

Continuing to raise my hips against his primal thrashes, I'm close. He's close.

We're close.

"Let go. Come for me."

It's enough to push me into a coma of ecstasy. I give him what he wants ... and I take. I scream and scream then drop my head and bite down on his shoulder, sinking my teeth into his skin while the shock waves ripple through me. Pushing hard, he freezes, stilling himself deeply inside me.

Heaven.

"Ahh, Lexi, baby, fu ... ck ..."

He pounds another few times before collapsing on top of me. I clench for life as I allow my breathing to regulate. My heart has nearly exploded through the sheer fabric of my vest. We remain enveloped, panting in the aftermath of the spontaneous sex.

"So fucking hot ... so sexy ... so beautiful."

He doesn't let go of his grasp on my ass, burying his huge cock deep inside my sensitive sex, ensuring he's impaling me to his balls.

Intense.

I kiss his shoulder where I have bitten him, and when he finally has the strength to lift his head, he growls deeply in his throat then takes my tongue again, kissing me, licking and teasing. I feel his cock twitch deep inside me. He's revving up again, expanding to my taught muscles.

Lucca puts his strength into his strong, muscular quads, leaning his weight back onto his feet. Then, standing up, he lifts me while still buried deep inside me. I throw my head back and firm my inner leg muscles around his waist, holding on tight. He trails his tongue down my neck while I dig my fingers into the broad of his back.

"I owe you a tour," he stipulates. I wilt out some serious pleasure filled moans in agreement. "Hold on, baby, you are going to feel this. I believe you asked to be fucked."

He places his foot on the next step of the period staircase, pounding into me as he lifts then holds me in place. I rise then drop back down on his length, moaning from the deep pleasure. He places one powerful knee under my ass, balancing me before his next climb. I groan when his next step pushes me further up and down on his raging girth.

Cavernous.

Predatory.

Animalistic.

"Oh my God … Jesus," I moan against his cheek as I quiver.

I wrap my arms around his neck and close my eyes with the feel of the pressure as tears of pleasure fall. Switching his weight and feet, he climbs again, pumping me hard, and I squeal as he chokes me with his length. I'm losing sense, lost in the mind-shattering experience.

This is a completely new sensation for me, being hammered in my core in this position, like this. I hope we're not anywhere near the top yet—it's far too good, and I don't want this pleasure to end.

"More?" he teases.

"More," I beg.

He climbs again with full virility—two steps this time, and I feel as if I've been jolted to oblivion. "You are fucking destroying me. I cannot get enough of you, baby," he grinds. He has full power.

Stilling again and breathing frantically, he holds his defined knee under my ass to hold me as he throws his tongue in my mouth, moaning, hot breath to breath. My pulse is speeding while he balances me and lifts my vest over my head.

Expertly, he unhooks the front fastening of my bra then sucks my erect nipple into his mouth. Another rush cascades through my veins with the sensation.

"Please, Lucca," I beg. I'm delirious.

His hand is under my ass again, the other holding the back of my head. Another climb and I'm biting on his shoulder again to muffle my cries. He's fierce now, ramming until I cry with ecstatic indulgence. Throwing my head back, my eyes roll in the back of my head, drowning in this explosive orgasm. He takes another leap upwards, and I whimper as I shake in continual violent carnality. I ride the rippling, euphoric pleasure, thrashing my head side to side. He blissfully climbs one more time and slams into me, throwing his head backwards, pushing his chest forward, and clenching his teeth.

The veins on his arms look as if they will rip he's flexing so damn hard while pulling my ass towards him. He groans in a low roar, filling me once more. Reaching the top, he turns, stumbling back, and crashes his back harshly against the wall, bringing me with him.

He slides down the wall, taking me with him, and filling me with his slithered silk.

Stair sex. My new favourite.

His pulsing cock slams me, his root to my vulva, as I crash down on it. We fit, we warp, his steel shaft choking my sheath. I am dripping in sweat; sex hot and swollen, plunged deep in his creamy release. I can barely breathe.

As if reading my mind, Lucca places his lips against mine. "Breathe, baby," he whispers and blows hot air into my mouth. I'm heady and slightly dizzy seeing those stars again in my post-coital glow and so turned on he's giving me his air.

Filling my lungs, he repeats this several times then slides his tongue in, teasing me when I'm breathing regularly. Then he retracts slowly and puffs again, but this time he holds his lips on mine and inhales back so his own lungs are taking my air.

Hot.

Sexy.

Resuscitation.

My air. His air. We breathe.

I slam my lips against his, biting his bottom lip and allowing my breathing to slow down.

"Better?" he asks.

"Much," I reply, licking my tongue along his lips. "That was amazing. I mean I just ... never expected that. It was intense and insane."

"It was un-fucking-believable. I love it when you ask for it; I just want to give you more. I am so glad you are getting more confident because it is sexy as hell," he rasps into my mouth.

I loosen my grip, then trail my finger over his eyebrow, his feathered lashes, his lips ...

"My legs feel like jelly," I whisper.

"That was my plan."

He pushes his back against the wall, and putting strength into his legs and his heel, pulls me up with him. Not losing contact, he walks me through another grand hallway to a massive suite at the end of the huge corridor. I look over his shoulder as he walks with me, trying to absorb the exquisite décor.

I don't want to let go. This is all the space I need. Right here, pressed against Lucca.

He strides with me to the bathroom, putting the massive power shower on in the wet area. He slowly slides fully out of my sex, and I wince as he lowers me to the tiles. My legs buckle, and he has to catch me to keep me from falling.

He slides my skirt off my waist, then standing behind me, pulls me into his chest and caresses my breasts, running one hand down my navel until he reaches between my legs. He circles his fingers around my wet folds over our sexual juices, then slides two fingers inside while pressing on my sensitive sweet spot with his thumb. He slides his fingers out, dragging his sperm over my folds to my rear entrance, then pushes a finger with the lube from his sperm into the tight entrance. I moan as I throw my head back into the crook of his neck. He lets go of my breast, then torments my clitoris with his magic touch.

"Baby, do you like this?" he growls.

"Yes!" I cry, buckling under his expertise.

"I'm going to fuck that ass soon, but I want you to ask for it first."

Oh my God. *Yes!*

He pushes deeper with his fingers, and I combust in another soaring, orgasmic explosion, every bit as good as the others but different. Thrashing myself backwards to his chest, he pushes his fingers deeper inside me.

I whimper and whine, pushing my breasts forward.

Lost.

Languid.

Laced with lustful lure.

The water cascades over our bodies as Lucca removes his fingers then cups his hands full of water and cleans our smeared sex, washing the juices attentively from my sex and down the crease of my ass. Feeling his erection again, I move my arm around my back to yank and tease his hard manhood.

"Lean forward," he growls.

He keeps both hands around my breasts as the water drips off my back, and he slams and slams again, pulling me back to him and jolting me forward with each pounding thrust. I come hard and fast, trembling on my legs while my shattering orgasm courses through me.

Lucca smacks one hand on my back and squeezes one breast as he cries out my name in his own enraptured blissful release. It's a sanctuary of flapping butterflies, heady dreamy visions, and entwining undulated combined aftershocks.

I'm blurry.

I'm content.

I'm done.

As my legs give way, I slip, slide, and slither down. Lucca pulls out of me as we crash to the shower floor. He leans against the wall, pulling me into his chest, both completely exhausted and spent.

I can't move.

I can't speak.

I'm numb.

He kisses the side of my head and ear. "God, dolcezza, I love you so much."

I melt under those words when he declares them. I will never tire of this. This drugged feeling has me captivated in the best possible way.

"I love you too."

I draw little shapes on his legs like a dance in the rain as the water cleanses us, and I hold on with the little energy I have left. My eyelids betray me and close. Lucca carries me, switching the shower off, then sets me down on the double vanity unit as he wraps a towel around me. I place complete trust in him while he dries me off then carries me to bed. He places me on the master bed and snuggles his body into my side, spooning me.

The mattress and sheets feel so comfortable, soft, and divine. I think of Tuscany and Lucca's cosy bed in the farmhouse, and I sleep.

Yawning, I stretch and realise I'm still in the same position I fell asleep in. I wonder what time it is. I can see a faint flicker from a fireplace on the wall at the bottom of the bed, and I smell burning logs, freesia flowers, sweet sex, and Lucca's magnificent aftershave.

I rub my fingers softly over Lucca's knuckles. He stirs then mumbles into my neck as he pulls me tighter to him.

"Lucca, are you awake?"

"I am now. What is wrong?" he asks sleepily.

"I just wanted to hear you. I just felt because I'm in a strange bed that I ..."

"Hey, you are safe, you are fine. Were you having a bad dream?" he asks as he rubs his finger over my lips.

I turn around and press myself to him. "No, I slept soundly. I was so exhausted after all the sex. I seriously felt as if I had been drugged I was so sated, but now I'm awake, and I feel a little guilty, I suppose."

"Why? It was mind-blowing. Fuck, I am still thinking about it. There will be plenty more of that," he reassures me.

Yes, please.

"I've rudely left my dog with Rose and Peter, and I've not even seen your house properly because I was so lost in the moment and gave you the impression I wasn't going to be happy here, before I even had time to get used to it." I mention this because it looks like I have strolled on in here and jumped straight into bed with him, which is exactly what I've done. And despite loving what we shared, I will need to get my bearings to familiarise myself with my new home.

He switches a lamp on next to his bed. "Is that so bad? We had a fucking awesome time. Do not worry about Doris. She will be well looked after, as you will be, and it is home now. You have all the time in the world to get used to it." He kisses the shell of my ear, sending shivers through me.

He's right, of course. I'm worrying for nothing, and I have everything I need right here.

Him.

I spin over, throwing myself on top of him. Dirty kissing, we groan into each other's mouth. I feel his hard arousal between my legs, so I slide myself down his body and kiss every rippled section of his abs and his sexy, deep V.

"I promised I would take you in my mouth," I groan.

"Jesus, fuck ... are you for real?" he grumbles in that lustful voice.

"Mmmm hmmm, a promise is a promise," I tease, kissing towards his manhood. I'm giving it to him, raw and ravenous, fisting and pumping him in my mouth.

"Fuck, you are so good, baby. Keep going."

He grabs my hair while I take him to the back of my throat, feasting on him, swallowing his pre–ejaculation. I suck him off deep and hard, milking him and throwing him into celestial pleasure.

Swallowing his salty sperm as he shudders and bucks in his final release, he pulls me up to him, claiming my mouth again, tasting his own release from my tongue.

Italian god.

Perfection.

"You are beautiful. My something special. Have I told you that?"

Giggling, I reply, "Yes. I wanted to ride you on top tonight, but I think I might be out of action."

Panic sets in his face and he scowls his eyebrows. "What are you talking about? Why? No, what is wrong?" he blurts and tightens his grip on me. "Fuck, Doc, was I too rough? Did I hurt you?"

"No, I asked for it, remember? I loved it, and you can have me like that anytime. I think I just might be a little swollen for a bit is all. Stop worrying, it was amazing."

"Thank fuck for that. Do not do that to me. You scared the shit out of me. I know what will soothe that swollen sweetness, baby," he rasps sexily.

"An ice pack?" I guess, leaving him chuckling.

"No, my tongue."

Result!

He flips me onto my back and slides down the bed.

"Hmmm, just what the doc ordered." I seductively moan spreading my legs for him. He softly, kisses my pebbled nipples, licking my breasts and swirling his tongue gently.

He travels his slow, sensual kissing down my navel, causing the butterflies to flicker and flap gently under his soft tongue. When he reaches my sex he's careful, taking his time slowly and lightly teasing me around my sweet spot. He kisses and flicks his tongue, blowing on my wet, throbbing pulse. He has me on my clit alone, and I thrash my head to the side and softly groan, reaching my crest.

Whimpering, I grasp his hair, breathing fitfully and riding out another heavenly climax until I'm pushing my hips up to allow his tongue to tease me while I jerk with sensitivity.

Lowering my hips back down, he kisses and tantalises my wet throbbing folds, then kisses the apex of my thighs. I feel his two-day stubble tickle my skin, which I love.

Virile.

Masculine.

Smoulderingly sexy.

He repeats his kissing all the way back up my body to my mouth where I show my gratification, tonguing him back.

"Better?" he asks.

"Much. Lucca, I love you," I whisper into his ear.

"I know you do, but the love you feel for me will never come close to how much I love you." He moves a stray curl of my hair from around my cheek to behind my ear. "Are you hungry? I am starving. Let me finish the tour, then we eat," he suggests. "It is after midnight, so we will need to have a moonlit feast." I can't believe we slept that long.

He takes my hand, leading me through a door to a massive dressing room. "Where are your things?" I ask inquisitively, noticing his clothes are missing. But, I do notice there are lots of ladies' garments hanging on one of the rails and the shoe rack is stocked with lots of ladies' shoes.

"I have a walk in concealed by the wall behind the bed. This room has always been empty. I have never needed to use it, so I thought it could hold all your clothes and girly stuff. It is your new dressing room, Doc."

"I can't believe this. It's amazing. This room is bigger than two of my bedrooms put together in my house." I clasp his hand while I look around. It's bigger than *Sex and the City's* infamous dressing room.

There is a chandelier hanging in the centre, and a full-length mirror at the back. Racks, rails, shelves, and drawers all with under shelf lighting line the room's perimeter. There's a mirrored island in the centre with a massive white ornate French style mirror on it, and drawers underneath, and the most beautiful Parisian stool.

The island is covered in products, makeup, creams, and perfume—all the brands I favour. Looking up at Lucca absolutely mystified, he shrugs his shoulders.

"I had Suzanne order you some things that I thought you would like. I want you to be comfortable here." I will be in heaven putting my makeup on in here. Lucca speaks very highly of Suzanne, his PA. She made all the travel arrangements for us in Italy and last minute reservations. Now she's bought all these wonderful things for me. I can't wait to meet her.

I wrap my arms around his neck and kiss him appreciatively. "You're so thoughtful. I love it, but it's all too much, and I don't need all of this. I'm used to sharing a bathroom with Cameron and Hazel. It will take me a while to get used to this," I say, scanning the products.

A red, raw welt on his shoulder alerts me. "Oh my God, Lucca, I'm so sorry. I marked you when I bit you. I'm so sorry," I panic while kissing his bite mark.

"You are so fucking sweet, do not apologise. I like it. It is hot and sexy." He knows this is distressing me, so he changes the subject. "This room is for you. Take all the time you need. You are going to need somewhere for all the clothes I bought you, and will continue to buy you. There is a safe for your jewellery. If you want extra storage, let me know and I will arrange it."

"Wow, I love it."

All apprehension I had is almost gone. I can live with the dressing room. It's my new favourite.

"I am slightly disappointed that you never fired off and objected to this. I find it sexy as hell, and I was looking forward to taking you on that island." He runs his hand down my back to cup my ass.

"You are insatiable. Sorry to disappoint, but I'm throbbing, remember? But I will look forward to you taking me on that very island." I playfully bite the bottom of his ear.

"When you ask, you will get. You know that, right?" he asks with optimism. I widen my chocolate-brown eyes, and lift my lip at the corner in his response. I'm going to file this and revisit at my leisure.

This 'ask-get' thing might prove very beneficial.

"Let's eat," he adds, pulling me back through the bedroom.

"Hold on, I need something to cover me up. Is there a robe hanging up with all that stuff?"

"Yes, but you are good the way you are, and it is only us in the house, so relax. I do not want you covered up."

I'm not comfortable with this; Rose or Peter could see through the windows, or arrive unexpectedly. Dropping my head as I dwell on the thought, he lifts my chin to bring my face back up to meet his.

"Hey, it is okay. It is very private here, only you and me, but if you feel more comfortable I will give you one of my shirts. I love seeing you wear my shirts." The robe would have been the better option, but a shirt will do as it's a compromise and I actually do like wearing his things. It makes me feel likes he's still touching my skin.

I like it when he's not being overly persistent. "Thank you. Just for now, until I know it's okay to be flaunting about naked."

"Okay, whatever you want. It will just make it more interesting when I need to tease it off you." He chuckles. I knew he had a hidden agenda!

"You're an ass. Shirt, Romeo!" I order with a wide grin, holding my hand out. He takes my hand, walking around the bed to the opening at the other side and leading me into a walk in concealed behind the wall.

My goodness.

He has his fair share of smart designer clothes lined up, and it all appears organised and tidy, but I didn't expect anything less from him: suits, shirts, belts, shoes, ties, sports clothes, jeans, tops and blazers.

I throw on a crisp white shirt that just covers my ass, and he throws on loose pyjama drawstring bottoms that hang sexily on his hips—modestly covered, yet sultry enough to be suggestive.

Very sexy.

Casual and carefree.

I'm given the tour as I pad barefoot on his thick, luxurious carpets.

He opens the French doors off the master bedroom suite, showing me his balcony, then closes them when the cold night air penetrates through us. He opens a door to the right where there is a separate lounge area with another traditional fire, designer upholstered sofas, a round dining table, bookshelf, and a large plasma TV.

On this floor there are another five large bedrooms—three have bathrooms attached, and the smaller two have a Jack and Jill bathroom. On the third floor, there is a large family room at the end of the hallway, which has a large plasma screen, wrap around corner sofa, love seat, pool table, and a bar.

This entertainment room is very much a man's domain.

Through another door, there is a cinema room with a full-size home cinematic screen projection with sixteen leather bucket chairs and a bathroom next door. I roll my eyes. Why would he need so many chairs when it was only him living here?

"When my brothers come over with the kids we have family film days. You have no idea how many times I have seen *The Little Mermaid* and *Finding Nemo*."

I can't stop laughing. Thinking of him being the doting uncle makes me feel warm and fuzzy.

"Of course, my mates have been over for film night with a little more adult entertainment," he adds impudently.

I slap his upper arm in disgust. "Well, now I'm here, it's going to have to be Disney. No more sleazy stuff."

"I was not taking about porn. I mean action thrillers," he tries to redeem.

"Hmmm, of course you were, Romeo." I smirk, shaking my head.

Downstairs on the ground floor, I stroll through the massive open-plan kitchen that includes every possible modern convenience and gadget. There's a traditional range cooker, a huge island in the centre with two sinks at the side, granite counters, and a contrast of black hi-gloss and polished oak cupboard doors.

The kitchen boasts a large dining table and seating area with a mink suede sofa in front of a plasma TV. There is a boot room and an oversized walk-in cupboard. I make note that I can keep Doris's things in here.

Further down he shows me the well-equipped pantry and adjacent utility room with all the same fitted units as the kitchen. Through the hallway, there's a downstairs powder room, shower room, formal lounge with fireplace, high ceilings, and cornicing keeping the period features as the original part of the house.

Next door to the lounge is a formal dining room with a sixteen seated dining table and fireplace, chandelier, and massive mirror and sideboard. It's like a maze, with each room as impressive as the next.

I follow Lucca into the study and library. I could spend hours in this library; it looks so relaxing and peacefully inviting. I notice there is a window box underneath the bay window with scatter cushions; I know I'll enjoy sitting there reading a good book with a shawl wrapped around my shoulders and a skinny latte as I watch Doris run around the lawn.

Ah bliss.

There is another downstairs bedroom with a bathroom and another huge family room right at the back, which is part of the extension. I think we must be done, until he opens double doors at the back of the family room leading to another vast hallway.

With a changing area, toilets and shower room, gym, sauna, and steam room, I feel as if I'm living in a dream.

"Seriously, could this place be any more opulent?" I ask, totally bemused.

He smirks then leads me on. We face a large frosted glass door, inhaling a familiar scent. When he opens the door, I hold my hand to my mouth gasping. I stare at the indoor rectangular pool and Jacuzzi with sleek modern loungers lining the edge of the inviting pool. A table with matching chairs is situated just in front of a huge panel of glass that overlooks the back garden. The walls are coated in a pale terracotta colour giving it a sense of the Mediterranean.

"Wow, I'm speechless," I confess.

"You like?"

"Very much."

Walking over to the edge of the pool, I dip my toes in. The water is heated and feels lush on my bare feet.

"Baby, you will never get fed if you get too close to the water. It brings back memories of us in my pool in Tuscany, and right now I cannot think of any other hunger I want to fill more than having you in that pool," he groans.

A delicious shiver tingles over my full body and my nipples pebble under the fabric of his expensive linen shirt. I think the novelty of us living together is playing havoc with our temptation and libidos. I hope this feeling never fades.

"Me too. How about we eat, then if we're not tired we can take a dip. I love being in the pool with you. It's my favourite." I swish my foot against the water.

Raising his eyebrow sexily, he says, "You are on. Hold on."

He walks over to the wall and presses a button; massive shutter blinds drop down all around the glass encompassing the pool area, making it very private. He flips a switch, and Lucca changes the overhead lighting to mood lighting: twinkling, romantic and intimate.

I like this much better with the privacy. Maybe the shirt will be coming off after all.

Sprawled on a velvet throw in front of the fire, we enjoy a feast of Rose's Balmoral chicken with haggis, mushrooms, peppercorn sauce, sweet potatoes, homemade croquettes, sautéed greens, and mashed turnip—a familiar Scottish dinner.

I think of Granny and Eleanor and all their goodness. Eleanor and Rose are alike in many ways; this was one of Eleanor's favourite dishes, and she would make this for us all the time.

Lucca reheats Rose's soda bread in the oven while he pours me a glass of Pinot Noir. When he returns, I rub my bare feet along the sumptuous velvet of the throw, getting myself comfortable as I relish in the warmth and softness.

After feasting on the plentiful traditional meal, we enjoy homemade nectarine and mango cheesecake with Lucca's guilty pleasure: cinnamon gelato. Lucca presses a button on a remote control and music echoes through a home music system: Chantal Kreviazuk's "Feels Like Home."

"Doc, please promise me you will never leave me. That you will never leave here. This is your home now, and I promise to give you as much space as you need, but please never leave," he whispers, pulling me into his side. Gosh he's gotten so emotional and deep all of a sudden.

"I'm not going anywhere. This is where I belong. *With you.*"

I curl into Lucca's naked chest, drawing little shapes with my fingers in the amber glow from the flickering fire. I wrap my top leg around his, causing my shirt to ride up a little higher. Lucca feeds me a few slow mouthfuls of the cheesecake seductively then tops up the wine. Reaching over, I fork some cheesecake into his mouth, then I lean over and press my lips against his while he rolls his tongue around the citrusy sweet cream.

He groans. "It just tastes better when you share it with me."

We listen to Lonestar's "Amazed" during our soft intimate caressing. Then he lifts me up and walks me through the house back towards the pool.

I think it's going to be a late night.

Before we make it to bed, I ensure Lucca shows me how to lock all the doors and windows. He appeases me by double-checking them with me. I know Cameron said this house has cameras and it's safe, but out of habit I need to make sure everything is locked up.

Chapter 3: Old Flame – New Fire

We sleep in the next day, and the day after that. Lucca and I stop by his main office to pick up some paperwork, and he fucks me over his desk and the sofa before we leave. His office is more like the entire top floor of the building, similar to a grand suite, and even has a separate bedroom. We never made it to the bed; although we did have a quick shower after our lovemaking. He has work to catch up on this afternoon, so I schedule an obedience training session with Peter while Lucca has a meeting at Club di Energia.

The training doesn't go considerably well for me as I'm far too soft and Peter has no qualm telling me so. Rose is delighted to have a dog around again, and I catch her giving Doris treats on the fly while winking at me. We've moved Doris into the main house, but keep her locked inside the family room at night.

Peter stands firm in saying she needs to be put outside into a kennel, but Rose has a softer approach. Rose and I enjoy a long chat over tea at lunch, and she confesses that they were not able to have children of their own, hence why they bred and cared for dogs over the years.

I call Mr. Carlin to confirm everything is okay, then I call Granny and Grandpa to explain that I'm not at my house in Uddingston, but that we'll be coming up to visit them. That call was positively draining. The usual third degree came from Granny while she fired a million rhetorical questions then answered them for me. Grandpa came on the line and played his mouth organ. He told me how much he misses and loves me, which makes me homesick for him.

I call Cameron after that, then Hazel, and finally Lucy to arrange a coffee date. Mark, my work partner at the clinic, has left several messages, so I note to call him back later on, then I make an appointment with my doctor to get another prescription of painkillers for my fractured wrist. The supply I got from the hospital in Tuscany is running low.

I'm going to call my mum this afternoon, but for that I need lots of strength and courage as just the thought of it exhausts me. Momentarily, I close my eyes on the lounger with my journal and phone hugged into my chest. The hazy Scottish summer sun shines through the glass wall on my face.

Sleep.

I dream of Tuscan sun, Florence and olives, dining alfresco and blue orchid flowers, the opera and Giovanni Costanzo taking photographs ...

I'm choking, coughing, and struggling to breathe.

"Lexi, wake up. Please breathe," Lucca panics. He scoops me up and cradles me into his chest, hushing me until I'm calmer. He then walks through the house and up the stairs until we reach the bedroom. He pulls the bedsheet back, then climbs in, pulling me to his chest.

"Are you okay? Do you want to tell me what that was about?" he asks.

"No, it's nothing. I must have been dreaming."

"It is not doing any good keeping it to yourself. You need to talk to me," he pleads.

"Honestly, it was nothing, not even a deep sleep. I just dozed off."

"But—"

I place my fingers on his lips to shush him. Normally, my bad dreams relate to my past, but strangely, this dream relates to my present and then provoked awful memories from my past.

Fuck!

File P for photography. Photography is the devil.

Lucca wraps his arms around me while I drift off again. I'm so tired, but this time I don't have bad dreams because I'm wrapped in Lucca's arms. I'm safe.

"Have I got time for a bath?" I ask as I stroll into the dressing room to pick something out to wear. Lucca is taking me out to dinner with Marco and some of his closest work colleagues tonight, so I need to dress appropriately. Hanging in the dressing room is a new dress in a suit bag.

"Lucca, what's this?" I yell.

"Your clothes from Tuscany will not be here until Friday or Saturday, so I picked this for you today when I was out."

I unzip a knee length, one shoulder, midnight-blue crepe dress with a satin bow at the shoulder. It's draped in perfect crepe silk with an elegant shape to it. I look at the tag—it's a Lanvin dress.

"Lucca, how did you manage to get this? It's beautiful."

"I had Marco go to Edinburgh and pick it up from Harvey Nicholls," he replies, walking in behind me. "Do you like it?" he asks.

"Yes, I love it, but it's a Wednesday night, and it's very fancy," I add, running my hand over the material. I also wonder why he bought something new. I have garments hanging up which would have been suitable.

"Baby, it is perfect and you will look stunning in it. Hurry and get dressed because the sooner we get dinner over with, the sooner I can slide my hands under that dress and strip it off you."

"No more clothes, Lucca. I'm serious. This is your fetish, not mine. You have given me enough," I firmly declare, furrowing my eyebrows with my hand on my hip.

There's his "you are sexy and I am having you" look.

"Now we are never getting out of here because you have got me so horned up with that sexy fiery shit." He presses into me, moving my hair away so he can kiss my neck.

Folded, crumbled, and melted.

Turning around, I kiss his cheek and smile, running my fingers over his dimple then down to his lips. He has me. I walk backwards, dragging him along with me, and then it's hot, raunchy sex on that mirrored glass island top.

After our heated lovemaking, I watch the glint from the chandelier twinkle above me, reflecting sharp bright bursts of jewelled colour over my skin. Lucca brushes his thumb across the colourful little rainbow of gems on my body.

Once we're showered and dressed, Lucca sits casually on the oversized velveteen chaise lounge in his bedroom, watching me getting ready. He drapes his arms casually across the back of it and leans back, spreading his legs lazily.

This image I love—when he's relaxed, casual.

Smart and sexy.

I put the Cartier watch on and the diamond bracelet Lucca gave me in Florence. I pin my wavy hair up loosely then lean over to buckle the strap on my tan Givenchy high heels.

"Come here," Lucca says when he notices me fumbling with the strap.

I wiggle over as my shoes aren't properly secured, and he pulls me onto his lap, then lifts my leg one by one, fastening the strap buckle around my ankle.

"Better?" he asks.

"Much."

He runs his smooth fingers across my ankles then weaves them up my legs until he reaches the hem of my dress. His touch sends ripples over my body. The smallest gestures and simplicity of these touches set off amazing electricity through my veins.

"You look stunning, simply beautiful," he says.

"So do you. You look so damn handsome in your suit."

His eyes smile with gratification at my words. Once downstairs, straightening up, I look in the huge hallway mirror before lifting my Valentino clutch bag. This dress is loose but elegantly cut in a contemporary shape and fitted near the bottom. Very different in style to what I would normally wear, but I do love it. Satisfied, I take Lucca's hand to greet Marco outside. He's a very loyal friend to Lucca, and I know he thinks highly of him.

We arrive at one of Franco's brother's restaurants in Glasgow called La Tavola Italiana—the Italian Table. Marco parks the car, and Lucca leads me into the restaurant. The entire ground floor is busy with diners; even midweek, these restaurants are booked.

On entering, everyone stops to turn and stare. I suspect I need to get used to being in public with Lucca as he draws a lot of attention. He's so handsome and people just can't help themselves.

I clutch onto his hand just a little tighter. "They are staring at you because you are so damn beautiful," he whispers into my ear. Blushing, I glance around choosing to ignore his comment because he has no idea just how attractive he is to women everywhere.

There is a bustling feel to the restaurant as it isn't small and intimate like some quaint Italian restaurants. It's more commercialised, but still warm and inviting. Franco's brother, Rafaello de Santis, has done exceptionally well. He has spent fifty-one years building his empire and remains very hands on, spending most of his time in this restaurant.

Two attractive men walk towards us as we enter. Armando, Lucca's younger brother, has the same dark skin and dark inky hair as Lucca. Although it's cut shorter and has a fashionable, raised styled fringe. I can see the resemblance to Lucca and Orianna in him; although Lucca has more of Marissa's looks, but they all appear to have Antonio's crystal blue eyes.

Armando is slimmer and not as muscular or defined as Lucca. Rafaello is Franco's twin brother and could be mistaken for Franco himself if it wasn't for the brown birthmark at the side of Rafaello's eyebrow.

"It is an honour to finally meet you, Lexi. My brother Franco was not exaggerating after all. You are truly a beautiful young woman. Congratulations on your recent engagement. The family is delighted for you. We will need to have a celebratory evening to give you a chance to meet everyone," Rafaello says, holding my hands in front of him after double cheek kissing. Lucca has already told me his family and extended family is huge, a complete contrast to my small family.

"Thank you, Rafaello. That would be lovely, and thank you for your kind words. I hope to make Lucca very happy. He has such a wonderful family."

Armando smiles widely. "So this is the beautiful girl who is finally going to make an honest man of my brother, and not before time I may add. You must be very special, Lexi. I hear he is head over heels in love with you. It is about bloody time he settled down." He pats Lucca on the shoulder, giving him a wicked grin, then leans over to double cheek kiss me.

Mortified, I blush then form an unsure smile while Lucca scolds him.

"Right, Armando. Point made very well, but you are embarrassing Lexi. You need to tame that bloody tongue. Armando and Anna could have been separated at birth; they both do not know when to shut up, and they both fight like cats and dogs," Lucca informs me with sarcasm in his voice.

"Where is the little ray of sunshine anyway?" Armando enquires.

"I have no idea. Off gallivanting somewhere. You know how elusive she is."

Jumping out of my skin, I feel two hands snake around my waist and a high-pitched squeal ringing in my ears. Turning around, Anna throws her arms around my neck.

"Um, lovely to see you, Anna. We were just talking about you."

"Anna, for fuck's sake, quit that squealing. It is fucking annoying, and you are too bloody loud." Lucca shakes his head as Armando laughs with nothing but adoration in his eyes for his little sister.

"No show without punch, sis," Armando smirks, raising his brow.

"Ah there are my favourite three Ragazzi e ragazze in the world, and Rafaello, you get more handsome every time I see you, but do not tell Nonno I said that," Anna adds.

I glimpse at Lucca and he shrugs his shoulders. Anna is so like Marissa in personality sometimes, it's uncanny.

"Anna bella, come and give an old man a kiss. You are your mamma's image, do you know that? I am glad to see you are keeping the boys on their toes," Rafaello says before Anna double cheek kisses him and throws her arms around him to embrace him fondly.

"Okay, I need to get back to work. You youngsters enjoy your evening. Anything you need, we will see to it. Lucca, your guests are upstairs in the private dining area. If I get a chance, I will join you later." After patting Lucca's back and kissing me and Anna, he walks off towards the back of the restaurant.

Armando guides us upstairs. I keep a grip on Lucca's hand and Anna follows, jibing Armando about not returning her phone calls. Reaching the top, we're shown into a separate room which is occupied already with Lucca's work colleagues.

The men stand when they see us entering. Anna squawks in delight and throws her arms around a very beautiful young blonde girl whom I assume is Kimberley, the assistant.

Hmmm, not sure how I feel about this. She's very pretty and sexy. It unnerves me, I think.

"Lexi, this is one of my very best friends in the world, Kimberley Franks. I did not know you were coming tonight." Anna gestures towards her. Kimberley: petite, slim, pure blonde, very attractive, and dressed to impress. She shakes my hand rather coldly and gives me a half-hearted smile. Her taciturnity isn't lost on me.

"It's a pleasure to meet you finally. Anna has told me some very wonderful things about you," she forces through a croaked voice.

Fake. I wish I could say the same, but I don't know anything about her other than she's assists Suzanne, Lucca's PA.

"Thank you, Kimberley. It's a pleasure. So how do you girls know each other?" I ask with uncertainty while I watch Kimberley burn Lucca with a smouldering look. I've got her sussed out after only a few seconds—she is protective of Lucca and aloof towards me.

He's not hers to protect. Why is she being so hostile?

Rage.

Anna fills me in briefly that they went to university together and became very close friends.

Noted and filed. I must quiz Lucca about Kimberley. I wonder if he employed her because of a loyalty towards Anna, or because he was fucking her.

Closing the space, she turns towards Lucca and kisses him on the side of his lips, holding just a little too long for my liking. Lucca clears his throat and steps back, trying to maintain professionalism.

Fuck!

File F for flirting. Flirting with the boss will need to stop.

After Kimberley sits, the rest of the table walks around to meet and congratulate us.

Overwhelmed, I try to remember everyone's names and take everything in during the bustling chaotic introductions. I didn't get the chance to meet them when Lucca and I were at his office; they were in a meeting. Suzanne Myers, Lucca's personal assistant, is very warm towards me.

On first impression, Suzanne is sophisticated, smart, and obviously a very clever woman. She wears her caramel blonde-brown hair to her shoulders ... straight and tidy. A straight, dark grey tailored dress and fitted suit jacket looks as though it could be her business attire and flatters her hourglass shaped figure. Height wise ... I tower above her, but then I am wearing high heeled shoes. The navy blue spectacles she wears accentuates her dark blue eyes and I notice she has freckles, a ruddy complexion, and doesn't wear a lot of makeup. There's something very pretty about her because she looks honest and natural. At her greeting, I notice she has a northern rasp to her accent, very similar to my mother's actually.

Suzanne shakes Lucca's hand to welcome him and then my own. I instantly like her, preferring her use of social skills.

Appropriate.

She maintains professionalism and decorum, unlike Kimberley's flirtatious ways. I think Suzanne may be in her late forties, and I can't put my finger on it, but she reminds me of someone. I must ask Lucca about later.

She smiles at me for a long time, it's not intimidating, it's sincere and genteel because there is a kindness and warmth in her eyes. They are filled with compassion and almost appear motherly. It's weird; it's as if she understands that I'm broken. And for a moment, I think she wants to say something but hesitates.

"Suzanne, thank you for all the arrangements you've made for us. We really appreciate it," I say with sincerity because she has been exceptionally helpful and has worked hard fulfilling all Lucca's requests. I know there must be more important responsibilities to her job than making reservations. If anything, she probably delegates them to Kimberley. That thought makes me shiver. I don't like that Kimberley might know personal details about Lucca and me.

"Of course, you're very welcome. No problem at all, I'm happy to help." She smiles and places her spectacles on her head. I'm fascinated because her smile and mannerisms seem quite familiar.

Andy Johnston, his project manager, is first to make pleasantries. Andy is a slightly older man with a round face, bald head, and a well-proportioned body. His scent is distinctive—musky. He appears quiet and seems like a private person.

Lyle Graham is next in line. He has fiery-red, wavy hair, a reddish tinge to his complexion, and some rough stubble around his jaw. He wears spectacles which compliment his look. Lyle is Lucca's head of contractors and has worked for him for a long time. He has a large team working on various projects Lucca is developing.

"Miss Robertson, welcome. It's an honour to meet you." He kisses my hand, and I'm intrigued with his debonair English accent.

The next two gentlemen have clear hunger in their eyes as they rake over my body making me a little uneasy. They have both been burning me with their heated gaze since we entered the room.

Greedy-eyes introduces himself as Chris McCarron, Lucca's accountant. He has big blue eyes, shaggy blond hair, and is probably the same age as Lucca. He places his hand around my back, holding his hand just over the dimples at the top of my ass, and kisses me.

"Holy shit, you really are beautiful. Lucca is a lucky man. I hope he has you insured because he needs to protect his assets," he says assertively.

I'm sure it's meant as a compliment, but he's far too close for me, and I start to squirm. Lucca looks irate. He growls under his breath as he places his hand on Chris's upper arm to release his embrace.

"Too close, mate."

Chris immediately releases me then mumbles something as he sits down next to Lyle and Andy leaving the last and equally as lascivious man to introduce himself.

Wanting-eyes is Omari Farid, Lucca's solicitor. He strides over to me looking devilishly handsome and intrigued. He is also very attractive with dark, smooth skin, striking features, and a very good physique, evident by the way his black fitted shirt clings to his every muscle.

My heart starts racing when he approaches me. He's affecting me, and I'm sure it's his Australian accent provoking unsettling memories. He places his arm around my waist and kisses my cheek before whispering into my ear, "Hey, if you ever get tired of that persistent fucker Lucca, I'll be waiting." He pulls away chuckling before Lucca can object.

He has rendered me speechless. I know these are Lucca's friends and they enjoy friendly banter, but I'm a little surprised with how relaxed and informal they are.

"Baby, go sit next to Suzanne. I will be back in a minute," Lucca suggests to me softly, then turns around, flicking his suit jacket back as his hands enter his trouser pockets.

He is serious.

"Omari, Chris, got a minute?" There is no real question—he's demanding their time. They both follow him out of the private dining area.

"What was that all about?" Anna asks.

"I don't know." Although my suspicion is that Lucca is setting them both straight for flirting with me.

Suzanne shakes her head. "Those boys ... sometimes they don't know how to behave and when to grow up. They need to settle down and invest all their hard earned money into a family instead of this single, adventurous lifestyle they're accustomed to. They need to take a leaf out of Lucca's book. I don't know how those two get through their business. But Lucca trusts them implicitly and they are very clever boys. They are comfortable around Lucca, and perhaps it's too forward for meeting you for the first time. I can see how it would be overwhelming," Suzanne comments about Chris and Omari.

Anna laughs at Suzanne's explanation while Kimberley chokes so hard Anna has to pat her back. I feel Kimberley's eyes scrutinize my every move. I can barely bring myself to strike up conversation, and I must appear very rude. I suddenly wish this night would end very quickly. Marco has joined us, and I am glad of the distraction. It's extremely intense.

Andy, Lyle, Suzanne, Marco, and I chat while Anna and Kimberley catch up.

Lucca, Chris, and Omari return. Lucca walks around the table, takes his suit jacket off, and hangs it over the back of the chair. He sits down next to me, wrapping one arm around my shoulders as the other clasps my left hand. He rubs his thumb over the large blue diamond of my engagement ring, and I wonder if this is to remind the boys that I belong to him. Maybe it would be nice for Lucca to wear a ring from me marking our relationship, so all those women know he's taken.

Hmmm ...

Kimberley drops her face towards the table when she notices Lucca's intimacy with me. She stares at my ring then excuses herself to use the restrooms. Anna follows her. They return just as the bottles of wine are being delivered to the table. Kimberley's eyes are red and wet—she has been crying.

Fuck!

File P for predicament. Predicament to be in even before we have wine.

"Are you okay?" Lucca whispers in my ear, sensing I'm tense. His hot breath warms my neck, causing sweet flutters in my core because of his compassion and protection.

I relax, lowering my shoulders, and turn around to face him. "Yes, I'm fine. I love you," I whisper back, suddenly feeling very possessive of him in this moment. Embarrassed by my confession in such a public place, I drop my chin, but he automatically lifts it, leaning over to kiss me softly on my lips. It doesn't go unnoticed.

"You got it bad, mate," Omari says. Chris chuckles and Lucca scoffs at the two of them.

"Can you two give it a rest? Honestly, you cannot even stop touching each other at dinner," Anna blurts out, drawing attention to us.

Kimberley looks green and I'm sure I'm flaming red.

I straighten up to look at the menu once Lucca has removed his lips in his own time, ignoring Anna's remark.

After a beautiful meal of antipasto, breads, oils, Carpaccio, scallops, mushroom risotto, and a generous amount of Pinot Grigio wine, we are all more than satisfied. The conversations are in full swing, and I feel more relaxed. Kimberley has loosened up, but she glances every now and then towards Lucca and continually seeks approval. This is really irritating me, even more than Omari with his wanting eyes, absolutely intrigued with Lucca and I. Maybe Omari is just protecting his mate the same way my girls are with me because our relationship has progressed very quickly.

I excuse myself to use the bathroom, and when I stand, all the men stand with me. "Please, sit down. Thank you, but there is no need to stand," I nervously direct towards the table.

Suzanne smiles and the remaining company nod. Lucca brushes his fingers across my wrist before I walk off.

As I'm applying some gloss, the restroom door opens, and Kimberley joins me. Reluctantly, I break the ice. "Did you enjoy your meal?" I ask her.

She stares at me before answering, "Yes, and you?"

"Very much, thank you. How long have you been working for Lucca?"

"Long enough to have history," she replies dryly.

Bitch!

This is not going well. I hate history; it always has a way of biting you on the ass.

"Kimberley, I'm not sure what's going on here, and I'm embarrassed to bring it up, but I can't help notice you're uneasy and a little off with me. Have I done something wrong?" I ask with tightness in my throat.

"Nope." She brusquely passes by me to enter a cubicle. I shake my head and leave. She's not worth the effort, but she has definitely rattled my cage this evening.

Walking back to the table, I sit down next to Lucca. He moves to wrap his arm around me, but I face the other direction to speak directly to Suzanne. I'm angry and worried about Kimberley's attitude, and I just don't know what to make of it.

Rafaello and Armando join us for an espresso and dessert. I notice Kimberley orders the same flavour gelato as Lucca. I wonder if she knows cinnamon gelato is his guilty pleasure. The very thought stirs up more of this hatred I've been feeling towards her.

Lucca acknowledges it. "Good choice, Kimberley," and she brims with happiness. And now I'm livid and jealous.

She's pathetic.

I don't like her.

After dessert, there is some shuffling of seats as people leave and come back to the table, so Omari sits directly across from me now. He hands Lucca a sizeable envelope from his briefcase. Lucca nods his head and thanks him.

After chatting with Omari, I learn that he lived in Australia and moved to America thereafter to complete his law degree and now is a partner for his father's firm here in Glasgow. He actually seems very pleasant and not intimidating like my first impression of him. Noticing the Australian in my accent, he asks where I am from originally. I tense, say Victoria, and leave it at that. He tells me his sister is currently backpacking around Australia and is in Melbourne just now.

Mum.
Travel.
Backpack.
Taken.
Simon.
Michael.
Devil.
Abuse.
Fear.
Pain.

I swallow hard, inhaling very slowly to control my breathing. Having an anxiety attack after dessert seems to be a common theme, so I'm conscious of it and fighting very hard to stay in the conversation without losing composure. Lucca changes the subject very quickly and keeps a close hold around me. Omari wasn't to know and I know he was being polite, but still, it hurts to be reminded of it.

History.

Kimberley is sitting at the far end of the table nursing her wine glass and mumbling into Anna's ear. She stands and excuses herself as she has an early start at work tomorrow. Marco offers to take her home. She passively nods and reluctantly shakes my hand and then Lucca's with more familiarity. I smile, but my skin is cold, brushed with an icy chill, and quite frankly I'm glad she's leaving.

Chapter 4: Insecurities

Suzanne's husband Jonathon picks her up, and Lyle and Andy leave together in a taxi. Lucca does his Alpha male thing and wraps his arms around my waist so Chris and Omari need to say goodbye to both of us at the same time.

"Look after her, Lucca, mate. She's one to keep," Omari says, picking up his briefcase, and I blush because he says it genuinely with respect, not with the boyish banter he has been exchanging with Lucca already this evening.

He has definitely grown on me and after briefly getting to know him; I don't think he's as bad as I first thought. I was intimidated with the fact that initially both Omari and Chris appeared to be sleazy, but after listening to their friendly banter with Lucca tonight, I know it must be their way. The same way Hazel, the girls, and I would probably act together in our own comfortable girly way.

"I intend to. I am not letting her go so you two fuckwits keep that in mind," Lucca says, smirking playfully before kissing my temple.

His crude vocabulary doesn't faze me because I'm used to him swearing, and I've experienced his protectiveness. In fact, I like that he's being himself around his friends. It reminds me of the way Cameron would speak to his mates.

"Chris, still on for that game?" Lucca asks, running his hand down his cheek across his stubble.

"Hell yeah, I'll whip your ass, Lucca boy. You know nothing will keep me off that pitch," Chris affirms confidently then punches Lucca's bicep before casually putting his hand in his pocket then leans to the side.

"Chris, are you having a laugh? You're first subbed, my man, I can guarantee it." Omari scoffs, patting him playfully on the back while shaking his head. I want to laugh because the distaste on Chris's face is a picture, and he shifts his weight. He obviously doesn't agree.

"Omari, you fuckwit, I'll be man of the match, dude. It's a no-brainer," Chris chides, now slipping his arms into his blazer, then places both his hands in his trouser pockets.

"Hmmm, we will see. Lexi, why do you not ask Cameron if he wants a game with us?" Lucca suggests before pushing all the chairs in then lifting an envelope from the table that Omari gave him.

"Sure, I'll ask him. This match I would love to see. Cameron's pretty good. He played pro before going into the forces, so I'm sure he'd love to." I shrug and smile but I know I'm stirring a reaction from them. Now I have their attention. They turn to look at me with raised brows, standing more alert and enthused.

"Ha, Chrissy boy, you have just been knocked out the league, my friend. Sounds like Cameron might just show you how to play football like a proper pro." Lucca smirks. It's funny hearing Lucca using similar dialogue to his friends. Although it's the same banter, Lucca's Italian influence in his accent makes him sound very different to when his friends are sounding playful, it's actually rather cute.

"Fuck off, Lucca. I'm a force to be reckoned with. Got it all going on, on the pitch." Chris laughs with sarcasm in his voice and air kicks an imaginary ball in front of him, which results in Omari scoffing and Lucca shaking his head and rolling his eyes.

I can't help but giggle. "You really think you're that good?" I ask with some false confidence through the effects of the wine. Omari and Lucca laugh. I reach for Lucca's hand and he grasps it tightly, reminding me that he's backing me up.

"Yes, he does," Lucca adds in a more serious tone, this time insinuating he knows Chris so well he has his character sussed out.

"Well, Chris, I'm sure Cameron will look forward to it. In fact, if you are short of numbers, Cameron can bring along some of his premier league footie mates for safe measure." I lift my chin and look forward to seeing their expressions now.

"Are you serious?" Omari asks, completely flabbergasted.

"I am pretty sure she is," Lucca says. I love him for supporting me in this moment, so I squeeze his hand to thank him, and he reciprocates with a soft kiss to my bare shoulder.

"Okay, let's do it. Lucca, keep me updated. I need to do my research and suss out everyone else's weaknesses and strengths." Chris is very serious and competitive it appears.

I'm actually excited about this, and I know Hazel will combust at the thought of the competitive male testosterone during this match. She'll probably try and rope Dominic in too. Omari and Chris say a final goodbye, kissing me passively with more respect this time before heading off. Rafaello and Armando excuse themselves to attend to a matter downstairs.

Now I'm alone with Lucca. I absently glance at the seat Kimberley was sitting in before, and it provokes the tension I felt earlier on. I can't help this niggling feeling, and I have burning questions about Kimberley I'd like answered. I'm almost about to confront him until I realise we have company.

Anna returns from the restroom and wraps her arm around Lucca's shoulder. "Marco will drop you off when he is taking us home," Lucca says to Anna, which logistically makes sense since we pass her apartment on the way home.

"No, it is okay. I have a lift." She checks her phone then rests her head against his shoulder before trying to change the subject, and I can't help think she is hiding something. Lucca must be thinking the same because he looks baffled.

"With whom?" Lucca protectively asks.

"Never mind." Her head lifts straight back off his shoulder again when Lucca bristles and turns to confront her.

"With whom, Orianna?" Lucca raises his voice, this time getting agitated. I give her a sympathetic smile because I know how protective Lucca can be and I feel sorry for her being put on the spot. I'm sure she can handle Lucca and stick up for herself, but she surprises me. "If you must know, Cameron is picking me up," she snaps then warily meets my eyes, the look on her face telling me she wishes she'd never mentioned it. She was keeping that information from me, not from Lucca.

That removes the smile from my face.

I know she feels the heat in my eyes burning her, or she sees the pain flicker in them, because she nibbles her bottom lip nervously then turns her focus back to Lucca.

"Calm down, Anna. Okay. I would rather know who is taking you home, that is all," Lucca says.

"I did not want to mention it because I know how Lexi feels about it, and I did not want to upset her, and … I am an adult, Lucca" Anna adds, giving me an apologetic smile, her voice trailing off. My face drops and I chew the inside of my cheek because I'm annoyed about this; it's not what I wanted to hear tonight.

"I am well aware you are an adult, but you are my baby sister, and as your brother I like to look out for you. I love that you have Lexi's good intentions at heart and do not want to upset her, but frankly, Orianna, I am shocked that you are still carrying on this affair with Cameron when you know he has a girlfriend and how much it is hurting Lexi." He rakes his hand through his hair and places the envelope under his arm then pinches his brow with his free hand. "It is pissing me off and it should stop. It is wrong, Anna. You are both using each other."

Lucca's always been rather passive about Anna seeing Cameron because he assumed it was mindless fun in Tuscany that wouldn't continue. He's asked me not to get involved, but now they're carrying on their affair and it's changing his perception. I can see it in his eyes that he adores his sister and he's trying not to show how disappointed he is in her. If I didn't know better I'd say it's because he doesn't want to rile me up any more than I already am about it and he's considering my feelings.

Anna blushes. I'm just not sure if it's due to rage or embarrassment because I haven't seen her blush much. "Lucca! You cannot tell me what to do. Do you think I do not know this is messy? I did not exactly plan to meet him in Tuscany, but I like his company and he has feelings for me whether you like it or not. We have talked about his relationship, what we are doing, and the impact it has on everyone else. Out of respect for Cameron and his partner, I will not want to talk about what they have or do not have together. That is personal. You need to trust me." She nibbles her bottom lip again nervously.

She doesn't sound her usual brassy, confident self; her voice is breaking and she looks at me carefully, her blue eyes apologetic and pleading for acceptance. When she sighs and helplessly looks at Lucca, there's no missing she is actually hurting and troubled, and he relaxes his tense posture, softening his voice at her dismay.

"Anna, I did trust you. I trusted you not to continue this and you did. I told Lexi this was nothing and not to worry, yet you are still throwing it in her face and being selfish and immature. What would the rest of the family say? Cameron is a great guy, I am not disputing that, but you should have more respect for yourself ... Jesus." He sighs and reaches for her hand to show her he doesn't intentionally want to hurt her but has her best interest at heart.

Anna pulls her hand away, a flash of anger now across her face. "You are one to talk about respect ... trust ... being selfish and immature, especially with your history. You do not have the best track record yourself. *We all make mistakes, Lucca.* You should know that, but the thing is ... I do not see Cameron as a mistake. Very much the opposite." She raises her voice because Lucca has offended her.

My stomach knots because the last thing I need to hear is about Lucca's past. It only rekindles the anger I have been feeling about him and Kimberley tonight.

The blazing heat in Lucca's eyes tells me he is angry, hurt, shocked and ... full of regret, but it still doesn't diminish the insecurities I already have. "Okay, I deserved that. You make a fair point and I have paid, suffered, and learned from my mistakes, but I wish you did not have to drag up my past when you can see it is obviously hurting Lexi. This is about you and Cameron." Lucca reaches for my hand and pulls me into his side, wrapping a reassuring arm around my waist.

Anna panics. "Lexi, I am so sorry. I did not mean that the way it sounded, and the last thing I want to do is hurt you. I am so sorry, please forgive me. That was insensitive and rude, and I am sorry my seeing Cameron upsets you. But I ... I really connect with him and now we ... um ..." She sighs and pinches her eyes closed because she obviously is conflicted. "I am sorry. I hope this did not ruin your evening. Please try not to worry about us. I do not know what else to say other than apologise."

She reaches for my hand and I brush my thumb across her palm and hang onto her fingers to acknowledge her apology, but I'm yet to answer because I'm full of mixed emotions tonight. Although Lucca needed to confront Anna, and I'm glad for his support, tonight probably isn't the best time or place. Instead, I form a lacklustre smile and nod my head.

Lucca sighs audibly. "Thank you for apologising, but we should talk about this at another time, not tonight. I love you, Anna, I do, and I do not want you to get hurt. I need you to understand that my relationship with Lexi is my ..." He grasps my hand rubbing his thumb over my engagement ring to remind me I'm his life, his world now.

Anna's shoulders slump. "I get it, Lucca, you do not need to explain. Your relationship with Lexi is and should be your priority now. I would expect it to be, and I adore that you are settling down and being a supportive fiancé. I promise you I will not let my life interfere with yours or hurt anyone any more than I already have. Maybe I am not as good a person as you, Lucca, and I am sorry if I let you down. I never meant for this to interfere with you both."

Now I want to scream. I swallow down a lump in my throat as she clearly manipulates Lucca, and I have to look away to stop myself from lashing out at her.

Lucca lifts the envelope from under his arm, leans in, wraps his arms around her, and kisses her forehead. "Anna, please do not say that. You have not and will never let me down. Ever. Period. I love you unconditionally. I just want to protect you. I am sorry for snapping at you, but I am glad you see where I am coming from. I know how Lexi feels about it, and I have to say, I am with her on this. You need to sort this out, Anna."

She cuddles into him then leans over and kisses my cheek, rubbing her hand softly down my arm. Except I don't feel soothed, and I know that's her intention, but I'm still pissed off and feeling tense.

I don't know who I'm angrier with—Cameron, Anna, or Lucca ... for not saying something earlier to Anna, even at my house when we discovered she had stayed over. Or back in Tuscany. It should never have gotten this far. It wouldn't have been an issue if Cameron had already broken it off with Rachel.

Anna checks her text messages and exhales. "That is Cammy outside for me. Lexi, he says he will call you tomorrow. I am so sorry about everything. About tonight, for keeping secrets and hurting you. But I am not sorry for meeting Cameron. I know why you love him so much." Cameron sending messages to me through Anna only adds salt to my wounds.

We kiss her goodbye then Lucca replies to a quick message on his phone. I feel totally deflated and agitated.

"Are you okay?" Lucca asks gingerly.

I sigh then walk towards the restroom, but he follows me.

"Lexi, talk to me. I want to know what is wrong and what you are thinking."

Shaking my head, I march into the restroom, flustered and irate. I'm not surprised to hear the door open behind me. He disconcertingly walks in and leans against the door, placing his envelope on the vanity. I walk into the cubicle, ignoring him. I don't want to fight, but he waits for me because he clearly wants to chat. After washing my hands at the sink, I finally turn to look at him.

"Is this about Anna and Cameron? Or is it because she mentioned my past?" he asks.

Feeling extremely guilty for being irrational when he is at least trying to talk it out with me, I stutter, "Either. Both?" I am annoyed about his past constantly being thrown in my face, and I'll get to that, but I want to talk about Anna first.

He runs his fingers through his dark, wavy hair. "Help me out here, Doc. I do not know what you are thinking."

Is he oblivious?

Yes, apparently so.

"Okay, I'm pissed off that she seemed to saunter out of here tonight, straight into the arms of Cameron, I may add, and doesn't appear to have any regard for what you said. The minute she got flustered and appeared hurt, you backed down. Don't you realise that someone *is* going to get hurt in that mix? And it will then cause friction between us. He needs to finish with Rachel if he's going to carry on like this because I can't see Anna backing away now."

He grins at me, curling his lip and showing his cute dimple.

"Oh no, you don't. I'm seriously pissed off. I want to talk. Don't even think about seducing me," I protest, feeling my cheeks getting redder by the second. Turning away from the mirror, I press my ass against the vanity and lean back, worrying my fingers in front of my mouth in a nervous dance.

"I am not trying to distract you. I just think you are exceptionally hot when you are feisty ..."

"Lucca!" I warn him.

"Sorry. Okay, I absolutely agree that Cameron needs to finish with his girlfriend. And you need to tell me what you are feeling so I can make you feel better and we can move on. I hate seeing you like this." He sounds earnest and I do appreciate that he did try and make Anna see clearly, even if it wasn't the most successful attempt. He moves and stands in front of me, gently moving my fingers from my mouth. And instead of nuzzling into my neck, groping me, or claiming my lips like he normally does, he holds both my hands by my side, keeping some space between us to allow us to talk but tenderly holding my hands so I feel reassured by his touch.

"That is why I challenged her, Lexi. I know it is wrong and is upsetting you. You are my priority now, that is why I mentioned something, but I do not want to hurt her either. I know Anna. She puts on a brave front like my mamma, but she will have left here feeling like shit tonight, and I do not want that either. But I did feel it was time I stepped in. I will speak to both of them, if it will help." He rubs his thumb across my ring and then my wrist.

"Thank you for supporting and defending me. It does mean a lot to me." I sketch shapes on his palm with my thumbs.

"I am also so very sorry Anna had to bring up my past. I am more pissed about that right now, but she is like me that way and opens her mouth. Things can be misconstrued even with the best intentions at heart."

The mere mention of the past ignites that flame inside me that's has been switching on and off all night. "What is it? You just tensed up. Come here, baby. I am sorry." Now he wraps his arms around me, trying to pull me against him, but I snap and push him away.

"Yes, there is something else bothering me. I'm not stupid. What the hell is going on with Kimberley?" I'm back to chewing the inside of my cheek.

He stares into my eyes. "Nothing is going on. Why would you think that? She works for me." Is he for real?

"She was dry towards me, and rude, and I noticed her flirting with you. It's obvious she feels threatened or jealous." I press my thumb against my temple feeling the familiar throb of a headache starting. When he reaches for me again, I place my hand in front of him to stop him. I'm not done yet.

"Well, I am disgusted if she was rude to you. Do you want me to have a word?" After pinching his forehead, he places his hands in his trouser pockets, rocking back on his heels, and grinds his jaw. He doesn't look guilty, he looks angry that Kimberley was rude.

"No, but I get it, Lucca. I get that every woman I come across is threatened by me. I get that you have a colourful history, and I get that every woman wants to be with you. I get they have all had you first. I GET IT!" I yell, slapping my hands on my thighs.

The fury I feel about Kimberley, Cameron's infidelity, Anna mentioning Lucca's past, and Omari's comments about the backpacking have provoked a blazing fire inside me, and I've erupted.

"Jesus, Lexi." He runs his fingers through his hair and paces up and down. "Get this. I am with you, and always will be. You are going to be my wife soon, very soon I hope. Have I given you any reason to doubt that? I thought we got over this in Tuscany." He's agitated. I'm livid.

Gina and Adorna provoked the same jealousy in me, even Fran to a certain extent.

"That was different. It wasn't so close to home. I hate feeling like this. We're only back two minutes and I have the same feeling that she has been with you as well. It threatens me, Lucca, don't you understand? I have never had a relationship before, and I love you. But this ... this hurts me, and it's exhausting when everywhere we go I seem to be reminded about your fucking history with women. I hate it. I fucking hate it! There, you happy now?" I shout and cross my arms over my chest.

"Fuck ... I am not deliberately trying to introduce you to my past mistakes. She works for me. Lexi, please, I hate that you feel like this. What can I do or say to make you believe that nobody else means anything to me, that you are my fucking world and have my heart. No one else, baby." He moves closer to me, pain flickering in his eyes, and places his lips against mine, entrancing me with his charm. I pull away, not happy that there is no real closure to this conversation.

"Please, be honest with me. Have you slept with her?" I whisper, afraid of his answer.

"Yes." He clears his throat and shifts side to side.

I don't know why I'm so shocked, but I pull out of his arms. "I knew it. So why is she working for you?" I feel tears prick at my eyes, but I desperately want to hold it together.

"Lexi, please do not be disappointed in me. I had a fling with her after Fran and I split. Then I lost contact when I moved on. Anna told me Kimberley was struggling to get a job in the current climate, even as a postgraduate. She had debts to take care of, so she asked me if I would give her a position. She was over qualified to work in the back office in the club so I gave her the assistant post in my main office working under Suzanne."

I'm not comfortable with this, and I appreciate his honesty, but it has only made me feel worse, if it's even possible.

"She still has feelings for you," I mutter. How can he be so blind?

"Well, I do not have any feelings for her. I told you the type of person I was then. I never had a relationship with her or anyone else. It was simply meaningless sex. She is quick, sharp, and organised. A good employee and our history *is* long forgotten," he stresses.

History.

Fucking history.

Why can't we just fucking erase history all together? Grandpa will say it's because it defines who we are and helps us learn from our mistakes. I say it's nothing but fucking heartache.

"For you maybe, but not for her. Lucca, you talk about Anna having no self-respect, you obviously don't have any for yourself either if you think she's not into you, or for me because you're shocked I'm bothered by this. Or for Kimberley. By allowing her to work for you, you're only teasing her. If she is smitten with you, and I assure you she is, you're unintentionally leading her on." I turn away and shake my head.

Lucca looks wounded. He grabs hold of his suit jacket fisting it in front of his chest. "Are you serious? The person I do have the most respect for in this world is you. I did not know you would feel threatened by her. I would never have asked her along if I thought that. I did not think she would have the audacity to be rude to you, which is not fucking okay. Of course I respect you. I told you before, I will do anything for you. Always. But she is a good employee. Some of the arrangements I asked Suzanne to take care of for us were made by Kimberley. And I have enough respect for myself to know she is only an employee and inconsequential to me in any other sense, and I certainly do not purposely tease her as you put it. I am a fair boss."

"Was she your employee when you were fucking her?" I can't help myself; my blood is boiling. I now pace up and down, staring at the wall, but not before I hear Lucca inwardly gasp.

"No. It was before she got the job. Please, baby, come here. Tell me how to reassure you, how to make this right, and I will. I will do anything, Lexi." He begs me. I hear the fragile break in his voice.

I break.

The tears freely fall from my eyes because I don't know how to overcome my insecurities or how this will be resolved. "Don't you get it? She is always going to be a problem, and I hate that she works so closely with you. She seems to think she has some hold over you. At least your other conquests I came across in Italy accepted they couldn't have you." I know I probably sound irrational.

"Fuck!" He reaches for my hand to pull me back against him, but I jerk away again.

"Lexi, please, let this go. This was before you. She is not a threat. I promise you. Do not shut me out, dolcezza," he pleads. I hear his words, but the ache in my heart and pounding headache is causing me to lash out.

"Like you let David in Tuscany go? Or for that matter, Omari and Chris tonight?" So it's okay for him to be protective, domineering and all alpha male? If he wants our relationship to work, he has to stop his double standards and start compromising more.

"That is so different, and you know it. David was practically molesting you in his bar Tasa that night, and he is a fucking bad bastard. Omari and Chris were pushing their luck tonight because they are not used to seeing me so romantically involved. Being in love ... with you, Lexi. In love with you."

I shake my head. I have no doubt that he loves me. It's the love that everyone else feels for him that's infuriating me because I have no control over it. My past torments me enough, and I don't want his constantly dragging me down either.

"I could say the same about Kimberley," I say, walking out the restroom. I'm done for now because we are going around in circles. I'm backfiring. He's trying to pacify me with reassurances but it's not enough.

"This is not finished. We need to talk about this, but here is not the place," he whispers behind me.

Well, shit!

Lucca settles the bill. Downstairs we thank Armando and Rafaello again and promise to have a celebration with the extended family. Marco has returned to drive us home, but the tension in the car is hostile and uncomfortable.

Lucca holds my hand tightly, rubbing his thumb across my engagement ring and knuckles, but Lucca's past and working relationship with Kimberley overwhelms me. I'm restive and jealous and making it blatantly obvious.

I would like very much to sleep and forget about it right now, but chances are I won't because I am so wound up. Lucca makes small talk, and I just nod my head and impassively agree.

Chapter 5: Intrusions

Reaching *Castello di Caruso*, I politely thank Marco. I'm embarrassed he's had to witness another cold car trek home like that horrendous night in Tuscany.

I walk up to the house and dump my clutch on the sideboard mantel in the hallway then throw my shoes off.

"Can we talk properly now?" Lucca asks softly. I am glad he suggested it, because I expected to come home and have him try to distract me with his sexual talents and dismiss the talking all together.

"Okay, yes, I want to discuss this because it's festering away at me. I need to understand. I need you to understand. I just feel—"

Before I finish, Lucca wraps his arms around me, cups my ass, and holds me close, kissing my temple, nose, cheeks, and lips then strokes my shoulders nuzzles against my hair.

This isn't what I had in mind, but my body is betraying me. I sigh and relax under his gentle caress.

Fuck!

File T for traitorous. Traitorous body and mind.

"Lucca, I think we need to talk first," I softly moan through heated determination trying not to crumble, fold, and melt.

I'm nearly there.

I am there.

I'm done for.

"Okay, yes, I agree. I just wanted to touch you to show that I love you. Let me get some water for us and ensure the doors are all locked. Go upstairs and I will meet you in the bedroom and we will chat. I just need to check a couple of emails. Doc, we will sort this out, and after we do, I am caressing and tenderly loving you all night long to reassure you what you mean to me," he says, wiping underneath my eyes with the pad of his thumb before placing a final kiss on my lips.

I drop my hold on him but quiver from the loss of his touch, wanting more and looking forward to all night caressing. Like a physical prescription for the mind, it always makes me feel better.

I look down at him as I step on the first stair, and he lovingly smiles back up at me, but when he sees the hurt still written on my face he pinches his eyes closed for a moment with his own pain then looks up at me helplessly with nothing but complete love and devotion. I have faith we can work this out. We will need to come to a solution before I end up emotionally destroyed by these new self-doubts.

When I approach the bedroom, I notice a pair of black high-heels outside the door.

Not mine.

My stomach flips.

Opening the door, all I can smell is sweet perfume.

Not mine.

My stomach twists.

"About time. Fuck, Lucca, you know how to keep a girl waiting. I thought I'd drop by and surprise you since I'm in the area and you never answer my calls," I hear a woman's sassy voice. My first initial reaction is that it may be Kimberley because I've been thinking about her all night. Either way, I'm beyond furious and could not feel any more sickened.

I want to suffocate that sassy voice so tightly that she won't get any other words out. Ever.

Thud.

Thud.

Thud.

My heart labours in my chest.

Fear.

Anxiety.

Paranoia.

Afraid of what I'm going to witness, I switch on the light. "What the hell?" I inwardly gasp with shock when I see a topless blonde in my bed with massive fake breasts, lace thong, and black silk stockings writhing around on the sheets with one wrist handcuffed to the bedpost.

My goddamn sheets! My bedpost!

My heart!

Oh dear Lord, please just take me now because my heart can't handle the trauma. I clench my hands into fists and straighten my spine. "What the hell are you doing in my bed?" I ask, raising my voice.

"Your bed? It's our bed for tonight, sweetie. You're not my usual third, but if Lucca picked you, I suppose you're different and could work for me. Hurry up and get stripped, join me. He can watch, then I'll see to him, and you see to me. I've never had anyone so pretty and pure." She looks me up and down licking her lips lasciviously. "I could definitely get off with you, and teach you a few things while I'm at it. You look innocent, honey. Are you any good at oral with women? I can teach you a few things." The room begins to spin and my legs almost give way.

Bitch.

Whore.

Slut.

How dare she? How dare he? Is this the life he had before me? It would explain why he has conquered so many women in his time; maybe he fucks two a night. The thought makes me sick.

While she rubs her free hand over her breasts, teasing her nipples and licking her pouty, dirty lips, I almost vomit. I don't know what to say. I'm disgusted, angry, and fuelled with rage. How the hell did she get in here? Is this really the past Lucca had before me? Sharing himself with more than one woman at a time? I can't process and I'm repeating the same questions over and over in my mind.

"Get out!" I shout.

"Oh, a feisty one. The quiet ones have all the fire and passion. Strip."

Is she for fucking real?

She doesn't move, she just grins seductively as she slithers around.

Fuck! Fuck! Fuck! Fuck! Fuck! Fuck!

"Get out of my fucking bed! Who do you think you are breaking in here? You make me sick. Get out! Get out! Get out!" I scream then clench my jaw.

"I think you should let Lucca decide that, don't you? He never turned me away the last time." She smiles, her lewd, green eyes glazed with depravity, pouty lips smirking.

Bitch!

Tears stream from my eyes, stinging my already raw cheeks. "I swear to God, I'll drag you out of here myself. I don't know who you think you are, but this is my home. Get out! WE DON'T WANT YOU HERE!" She doesn't budge.

The fire erupts and I can't help myself. I pick her clothes off the floor and throw them at her and storm over to the bed and grab her free hand, yanking her off my bed, but I forget about the handcuff. She cries out then screams at me as her attached hand tugs hard and the cuff rattles against the headboard. With her free hand she pushes me away from her, and I stumble back right into Lucca's burly chest, taking her clothes with me to scatter at my feet. He has heard the screaming and has barged in the room. He protectively wraps his arm around me and helps me balance.

"What the fuck? What the fuck are you doing in our bed?" he rants his face screwed up as if he is disgusted. I have never heard him shout so loud or so vehemently. His eyes gloss over her then he tsks with disgust and turns around to face me. "Get yourself fucking dressed." He orders but doesn't look back over his shoulder. He mumbles and curses then softens his voice and tries to reach to cup my face to look at me.

I must look like a deer caught in head lights because I simply can't understand this mindfuck. Stepping back, I throw my hand over my mouth and almost retch against my palm.

Lucca's eyes flare with fear, with panic. "No, baby, this is not what you think. I had no idea. She has broken in. I have not seen this woman in over a year. This has nothing to do with me. I have been with you all night." He tenses and runs his fingers through his hair. So he does know who she is and has history with her. That is all I need to hear to finish me. I'm destroyed.

History.

Fucking history.

Here we go again!

"Earlier when I said you had a colourful past, I had no idea it was so vivid! You really surprise *and* hurt me at every turn." Tears stream down my face, and I use my hand to wipe under my nose. Why I'm still standing here is beyond me. Lucca pulls me into him to try and soothe me. He hears the fury and crackle in my voice and unlike earlier when the fire was lighting, now my voice is blazing. Meanwhile, sassy slut probably loves the show we are both putting on no doubt.

I push him away. "Don't you fucking touch me!" I scream at him.

"No, Lexi, no this is not what you think. I am every bit as shocked and angry as you. She needs to get the fuck out of here and we need to talk. Christ, I cannot believe I am hurting you again and not on purpose, dolcezza. I fucking hate this, hate tonight, hate myself. Lexi, please, baby. It shreds me that again you are hurt. Jesus … I …" He sounds broken. I've heard this tone before.

"We … do … not … need … to … do …anything!" I babble and curse while poking him in his chest with my finger. He doesn't flinch. He stands with his eyes pressed closed and lets me have my outburst, prodding and pressing his chest, but he's strong and barely moves. "I'm done. I can't do this anymore. I can't take it."

At my declaration he opens his stormy eyes, silently he pleads with me. He's torn and hurt himself. It's not enough. I can't forgive him for this. He reaches for my wrist when he sees me shift to move away from it all.

"Get her … out of my fucking bed! I'm not going to ask again."
I'm hysterical, shaking and feeling sick and dizzy, holding my finger
up, warning him, ready to storm out.

"I told you to get dressed. Do it now, so fucking help me God!"
he shouts over his shoulder for her benefit with a deep growl in his
throat, whereas he was softer and considerate talking to me.

"The key for the cuff is in my jeans pocket. I can't exactly reach
them." It's *her* sassy voice. She tugs the cuff to remind me. I look
down at my feet and her jeans are on the floor where they fell. I pick
up her jeans and throw them at her again, making sure they smack
her right in the face, but sigh when the key falls out the pocket and
onto the carpet somewhere under the bed and I'm not about to get on
my hands and knees to look for it.

He reaches to cup my face and winces when I jerk back. "Come
here, you need to calm down, let's get out of this room and talk.
Please, baby? You said you trusted me. Let me make this right. I am
hurting for you, Lexi, and I feel like shit. This is the last thing I want
you to see. I cannot stand seeing you like this," he begs.

Good, and so he should feel awful because that's nothing in
comparison to how I feel right now. I feel shattered into a million
pieces.

Trust? I don't know what to believe anymore; finding someone
naked in my bed doesn't really fit well in my definition of trust.
"Why don't you save your breath. I feel sick and I've had enough. I
was hurt, Lucca, really hurt earlier with Kimberley, but this is
unbelievable. Do you know what? Sort out your own fucking mess.
Un-cuff her and get her out of here, or do what you want with her," I
cry louder, holding my finger up in front of his face and having to
push him hard before he takes hold of me to calm me because I know
that's what he's twitching to do.

Not that I want Lucca to have to turn around and see her
exposed body again, but I'm certainly not helping.

"Forget her. Come to bed and let the little prude watch and learn
how a real woman satisfies a man like you." She flicks her hand at
me dismissively, her words hitting every insecurity I have. The sound
of the handcuffs clinking against the headboard goes through me like
fire, memories flash behind my eyes.

*Wrists restrained by metal cuffs, blood dripping from her wrists
and ankles, and the sheet between her legs stained with blood.*

Her insult is the last straw. Lucca tells her to shut her fucking
mouth, curses, and turns to look for the key.

I shake my head trying to dislodge the images in my head.
Disgusted, devastated, and demolished.

Fuck!

File D for disappearing. Disappearing away from this nightmare.

That's exactly what I'm doing. While he searches for the key, I turn and leave.

I storm out the room, pick one of her heels up, and throw it back against the door. I stomp quickly downstairs passing Rose on the way down. "Lexi, petal, is everything okay? I heard screaming, what's going on? Are you okay, sweetheart?" Rose asks alarmed, looking at the state of my tear stained face.

"Rose, call the police, someone has broken in!" Rose flees upstairs quickly when she hears Lucca shouting for her help. At least he has the sense to shout for Rose to take care of the naked slut and ensure she gets out.

I don't stop. I continue down stairs, grabbing my clutch and leaving the Givenchy shoes. Walking out, I press the code for the front gate, and I'm thankful that Peter and Doris are nowhere in sight. I know Lucca won't be far behind me, so I do the only thing that makes sense to me when I react to pain and suffering, the only thing that has ever kept me safe … I run.

It's fairly light outside and the streetlights are lit, so I know I'll be fine until I can stop a taxi. Adrenaline and anger have my heart pumping as I run barefoot. I run and run, fuelled with rage. It's second nature, running barefoot. I did it for the first nine years of my life when I was incarcerated. I've run in worse conditions; it doesn't faze me in the slightest.

I'm aware it's not that far until my own house, but Anna will be there and I don't want to face her again tonight. I just need to run somewhere else. Run away from the hurt and the excruciating reality of tonight, so while my blood is boiling and my heart is crushing, I irrationally decide to run to Jessica's house even though it's late, it's the next closest house.

Steve is working away on the oil rigs offshore of Aberdeen, so she'll be alone. She'll understand, and I know she won't tell the other girls of my predicament if I ask her not to.

I run and run as best as I can with a ridiculous cocktail dress on and barefooted, trying to stay away from the main roads in case Lucca follows me. My feet are numb and only just recovering from the running expedition I'd endured in Tuscany down the dark rough country road, but blocking out the pain, I really don't care about the soles of my feet. My heart is more important, and I can't stay there, not with that slut in my bed.

I feel sick.

By the time I reach Jessica's home, I'm a mess. The shaggy bun of my hair has long lost its style, and my wet curls cascade down my back, sticking to my damp shoulders and face. I hang onto the front step—sore, tired, and gasping for air. Just as I lean to rattle the front door, I hear a car quickly brake behind me.

Lucca throws open the car's passenger door and runs towards me. He scoops me up and carries me towards the backseat of the car. I try and wriggle as I'm not ready to go home with him.

"Lucca, put me down. I'm not going back with you, not tonight." As much as I will myself to forget this mess tonight and wish that I could turn back time and be blissfully snuggled in Lucca's arms without any challenges, I can't. It's too raw.

"Stop it. You are coming back, and we will talk about this. What the hell are you thinking running barefoot again? I would have thought you would have learned your lesson in Tuscany. Jesus, Lexi, look at the goddamn fucking state of your soles again," he protests.

"Lucca, I'm going to ask you one more time, put me down. I'm not coming home with you. Kimberley was enough to rile me tonight, but ... *then* I come home to discover a blonde fucking bimbo in my bed, asking me to join in on a threesome while she gets herself off fucking naked in front of me! I'm done. It's too much, and I can't handle this." Trembling, I sob against his muscular arm because I can't look up at him and have no strength to break free.

I don't want to see his eyes while I'm so furious. I'm afraid they will melt me and I'm too hurt to be crumbling just now. I think I might even hate him as much as I did immediately before my wrist operation in Tuscany.

He sighs and holds on tighter, his heart racing in a panic.

"Lucca, drop me now." He doesn't respond. "Now!" I scream. I can't even relax in his embrace because I am so wound up. Ordinarily his protective arms around me would centre me, but tonight instead of feeling cherished and protected, I feel betrayed and used.

"No, I am not putting you down until I explain. She is a trespasser and a whore and has no right being in our home. You need to believe I had no part in this tonight, and it is cutting me up that you had to witness that," he adds, pressing his nose and lips into my hair.

I'm still furious she was there in the first place. Even though Lucca played no part in tonight, it still should never have happened. I feel like I've been kicked in the stomach and tossed in the gutter. I'm sure my insecurities are contributing to my freak out, but I don't know how else to cope with this. Then it occurs to me that normally I would have an anxiety attack when I feel challenged, stressed, hurt or scared. I haven't had any chest pain because I think I am too angry to even start one; plus the adrenaline from running has my heart rate accelerated anyway. I hope an anxiety attack doesn't start when or if my blood stops boiling.

The front door opens and a sleepy Jessica comes out. "What on earth is going on?" she asks, yawning and rubbing her eyes.

"Jess, tell him to put me down," I beg.

"Lucca, please, just put her down. I don't know what is going on, but you can talk about this tomorrow or come inside. It's far too late for this out in the street." Jessica tries to reason.

"Sorry, Jessica, I am taking her home. Where she belongs, with me. We need to talk and I cannot leave her. I ... do not want to leave her." He squeezes me tighter in his embrace and lowers his voice, aware we are causing a scene and places a kiss to the side of my head.

"No, you're not. I'm staying here with Jess. I'm not going!" I shout, shaking my head side to side. Peter steps out of the car. "Please, Peter, tell Lucca to put me down. I need to stay here tonight. I'll come back, but I need time on my own," I sob, soaking Lucca's sleeve with my tears.

"Lucca, do it now, son," Peter demands.

Lucca reluctantly places me down on the slabs but grasps my hand. Breaking away, I stumble over to Jess. She puts her arm around me as I helplessly cry into her neck. "I don't know what's going on, but this is not okay," she curses towards Lucca. I cry loudly, and I'm enraged with myself for crying in front of Peter.

Jess, being a great friend, comforts me. "Go inside. You can stay as long as you need, Lexi." She strokes my hair and swings the door open fully.

"I'm so sorry, Jess," I sob.

"Darlin', don't be. You have nothing to apologise for. Go inside, please. I want to speak with Lucca." Jess sounds hard saying his name, repulsed by whatever he has done to inflict this pain on me.

Lucca is grey with anguish. He's frantically pacing up and down, running his hands through his hair and kicking anything in his way. "Lexi, please do not do this. I need to explain. I have nothing to do with what went on back there, and you must know that. She knew the code to the gate and broke in through the window in the study. Peter and Rose were in bed so they missed her intruding and the alarm never went off because she was able to open the gate. Rose has called the police. You promised you would not leave. You said you would stay. Please, baby, I love you. I love you, Lexi. Do not leave me." He falls on his knees in front of us. Breaking down.

Promise.

A promise is a promise.

I said I wouldn't leave him, and yet I'm about to turn my back on him, just as Fran had done. I do feel a slight twinge of guilt, but the hurt of being betrayed is not only twinging at my heart it's stabbing it, leaving a big empty hole.

Lowering my shoulders in exhaustion, I sigh. I need my own space because I'm so livid right now, and I don't feel like I'm breaking any promises. I'm not leaving him. I just need some time out, and I want him to realise that I'm not accepting this nonsense ... I'll go back when I'm ready but it won't be tonight. I need alone time. I glance at Lucca on his knees with his head hanging forward and the sight of him vulnerable like that makes my heart ache even more. I need to be assertive before I change my mind. Jess watches me hesitate and takes my hand.

"You're not seriously thinking of going back in that state are you?" Jess quizzes me, completely baffled. "Lex, you are too upset. You should probably stay here tonight. Let me call Hazel and have her come over."

I inhale deeply through my nostrils, wiping my eyes with the back of my hand and turn in to hug her tightly. She's right. I do want Hazel right now. "I'm so sorry to cause a scene, and I'm sorry to bring you into this. I'm not going back. I want to stay here tonight if that's okay?" I whisper so that Lucca and Peter don't hear me.

"Yes, of course it is. I love you and I want to make sure you're okay, Lexi." She strokes my arm. I sniffle back some more sobs and hear Lucca catch his breath, as if he is trying to muffle a sob of his own. Peter looks at me with sympathetic eyes, the exact same sentiment I normally share with my grandpa. This only adds to my distress because Jess is being supportive and Peter is showing that he understands why I'm damn angry.

Jess's kind words and sincerity just make me choke even more. "I know you do, I love you too. Thank you. Can you call Hazel to come over?" This time I don't whisper. I want Lucca to know that I'm hurting that much that I want my friends around me. He will know if I'm calling in Hazel that I'm a mess, and it might even hurt him that I'm seeking comfort with my friends rather than with him.

My throat croaks as she wipes more tears from my cheek. I glance at Lucca again. He's still kneeling on the concrete with his head bowed. Peter is standing next to the car patiently, shaking his head in that typical way a disapproving parent would.

Looking at Lucca like this reminds me of seeing him helpless like this in front of the altar in the cathedral in the Chianti Hills and the night at his parents' villa when he admitted he loved me.

"Peter, can you please look after Doris for me tonight? I would really appreciate it. I'll come back tomorrow at some point and get her but I'm going to stay here tonight." I take a deep breath because I know Lucca is going to object.

Lucca lifts his head and stands on full alert. His eyes are wet, and he's had a teary moment of his own while waiting on me. I knew it. He's torn and I'm shredded. I just want to throw my arms around him, but I can't right now.

"Absolutely, Lexi. Don't you worry about her, she will be well looked after. Rose and I will take her out on a long walk in the morning. You come back when you're ready. I'll tell Rose not to expect you home tonight. Is there anything you would like me to bring for you?"

"No, I don't need anything. Thank you, Peter," I say loudly, making a point that I don't need Lucca, but realistically that's exactly what I need. I need him so badly it's crushing me because I can't give in and I know it would be wrong for me to forgive him and this mess tonight. Even with the neediness I feel to have Lucca in my arms, there is no way I can back down. Not now.

"No! No ... No, Lexi, I cannot go home without you. I need to speak with you, and I do not want to leave you like this. I cannot leave you here. Please, honey, come home with me. You *promised,*" Lucca pleads. He steps forward and reaches for me because he can't help himself. I begin to rock now with my uncontrollable crying and fist my stomach.

"I can't," I sob. He takes my hand, and I know he wants to rub my engagement ring to remind me I'm his. Well, he can forget that shit.

"Don't," I snap. "I promised I wouldn't leave, but I can't stay with you tonight. I need to think. I'm so fucking angry, but you promised you'd give me my space, and that's what I need, so don't touch me. Stay away. I will come back when I am good and ready."

"Fuck!" he shouts as he kicks the step in front of him in a rage because he's completely defeated.

He runs his hands through his hair, then rubs his temple and forehead with his thumbs and middle fingers. Trying to ignore his agitation, I ask Jess to go inside and that I'll be in, in a minute, then I address Peter.

"Thank you, Peter. I'm so sorry for the inconvenience tonight and thank you in advance for tomorrow. Can you give us a minute please?" He nods and sits back in the car to wait for Lucca.

"For fuck's sake, Lexi, talk to me. I am so sorry you had to see that, so goddamn sorry. I don't want to leave without you. Please reconsider. We will talk all night until we sort this out. You cannot leave me, I love you." I see a tear leave his eye and run down his cheek.

I hate to see him vulnerable, but my emotions are past that vulnerable stage. They are at stage destruct. I try to control my own tears by calming down and lower my voice because I notice some of the neighbours have switched their lights on from hearing the racket.

"I'm not leaving you, but I need to think. I need to think about what happened and how I can move on from this, if we can move on from this. I can't be with you Lucca if I have your past thrown in my face all the time. Even with trust, because I do know you had nothing to do with that tonight. It was disrespectful and hard to stomach.

"Fuck, Lexi, no. Jesus. Please do not say that. We will move on from this. I will make sure of it. I told you I will never let you go. I am not having you doubt what we have, what we share, and our relationship over something that you should never have had to see tonight. I will make this right." He sniffles and drops his head again because I think he's trying to hide his tears, and even in his moment of weakness he still looks masculine.

"I'm more troubled by what I heard coming out of her mouth than what I saw." I'm bitter and unforgiving.

"What the fuck did she say to you?" He snaps his head back up, alarm written all over his face and an intense flicker of panic now in his cloudy eyes and voice.

"Just so you know, I'm not into threesomes if that's what you expect from your future wife, and I apologise for not being as sexy and promiscuous as all your other lady friends. I don't appreciate some random slut getting off in my bed, or asking if I'm good at performing oral sex on a woman." I spit the words at him, the whore's voice still ringing in my ears. "I'm going to bed. Don't follow me. I need space to get my head around this, and you promised …" With that, I leave him on the step outside desperately calling my name.

I trudge into Jessica's house with weak legs, sore feet, and mental exhaustion. I'm tempted to slam the door behind me, but it's her house so I don't. I ask Jess to make sure he leaves. I hear him shouting for me and approaching the front door and Peter trying to reason with him. Without looking back, I walk straight upstairs and collapse on her futon in her spare room.

Curling into a ball, I pull my knees to my chest feeling small, fragile, and weak. I cry and I cry to myself until I hear a familiar voice. Sitting up with a sense of relief, I reach for Hazel as she kneels in front of me. I wrap my arms around her and cry so hard against her neck until I'm utterly exhausted. Jess strokes my back while Hazel hushes me, calmly rocking me in her arms while kissing my head.

They haven't asked why I am upset, they just console me. "It's okay, we have you. It's okay, everything will be fine. Calm down now. It's okay," Hazel croons compassionately.

Once my tears finally dry up, I lifelessly lift my head, which now feels like a boulder on my shoulders, and thank them.

Hazel gives Jess a knowing look, and Jess leaves the room. "Okay. Come on, up you get. Let's get you fixed up. Jesus, Roo, I wish you would quit running barefoot." Hazel sighs studying my feet.

"I'm too tired, Skip. I'm so, so tired," I whisper and slump my head back against her shoulder.

"Come on, Roo. Just ten minutes. Let me clean your feet and we'll get you into bed." She stands up and lifts my hand so I'm standing.

I notice Hazel has her own pyjamas on with a hoodie over the top. She must have gotten out of bed and driven straight over to Jess's. She leads me into the bathroom where Jess has been filling the bath. "Skip, I'm too tired for a bath. I just want to sleep," I protest.

"I don't mean a long soak; I just want you to sit in it so we can clean you up. Lift your arms," she instructs, taking care of me as a mother would a small child. "Let Mamma Skip look after her little cub."

I form a semblance of a smile. "Joey, Skip, it's a joey," I correct her and stretch my arms above my head, allowing her to undress me while Jess sits fresh towels and bath products out.

Once I'm in the bath, I sit and draw my knees up to my chest and hug them while Jess turns the shower on overhead. Hazel removes her hoodie and rolls up her sleeves so she doesn't get soaked sitting at the side of the tub. After removing the pins from my hair, she washes and rinses it clean, and then washes my back gently with some body wash. I haven't moved. I'm still sitting in the same position with my eyes closed. Hazel and Jess chitchat trying to distract me, but I've zoned out and can't even recall what they are speaking about.

"It hurts so much," I mumble against my knees.

Hazel turns the shower off and kneels down beside the bath again. "What hurts? Your feet?" she asks with concern.

"No, not my feet. My heart, it hurts so much." I stop myself from saying anymore because I know I'll start bawling again. Instead, I splash my face and wash off the tear stained makeup.

"I know, Roo, I know." Hazel sighs, standing up, and holds a towel open for me.

After I dry off, she leads me into Jessica's bedroom where Jess has laid a pair of her pyjamas out for me. I dress in them and leave my hair bundled in the towel turban and climb into Jess's bed with Hazel just as Jess returns with tea and chocolate cookies for us all.

I've no idea how late it is, but I do feel better after the bath and during our tea in bed. I have relaxed somewhat so Hazel asks me if I feel up to the DBB: *drunk, bed, and bitch*. I ask Jess if Lucca left. She says it took a lot of convincing with Peter to eventually get him to leave, and then Hazel adds it's good he had just left by the time she arrived because she's going to murder him when she lays eyes on him.

I want to explain and I'd like their advice, so I tell them what happened earlier with Kimberley then about the crazy whore in my bed and how I reacted to it.

Even mentioning it flares the burning anger inside me again, and now I'm wound up and back to being tense. So many things run through my mind. I wonder if she's still there at my house ... Are the police still there? ... Was she charged with breaking and entering? ...

Why was she there in the first place? ... Did Lucca participate in threesomes? ... Is he telling the truth that he hasn't seen her in a year? ... How did she know where the bedroom was? ... Has he fucked her in the bed we share together? ... Was it in fact Rose who helped her out of her cuffs? ... Did Lucca throw her out? ... Did he go crazy when he went back home? ... Is he hurting just as much as I am? ... Is he feeling lonely? ... Is he missing me lying beside him as much as I'm missing him?

Fresh tears pool in my eyes.

"Roo, I don't blame you for being upset. Anyone would react like this and be hurt and let down. Hell, I'd castrate Dominic if I found someone in my bed ..." I hiccup and sob nosily at Hazel's words. "But I do believe he had nothing to do with tonight. And I've no doubt in my mind that he loves you. Lexi, you are his world. I can guarantee he will feel like shit, and rightfully so, but he does loves you." She passes me some tissues from the bedside table.

"Yeah, and I love him. That's why I'm so hurt. I can't give him the sort of lifestyle that he had before me. I know he's been with a lot of women, I'm not stupid, but they are fucking everywhere I turn. It's too hard. I feel so incompetent and I guess I'm worried that he will get bored with me and I will be one of those women ... you know ... used and abused as the saying goes." I brush my fingers over the suede material of a cushion, changing the textured colour from dark to light.

Dark to light to dark again.

Just like my fucked up life.

"Lex, honey, everything you are feeling is normal. Don't you ever doubt yourself. You are more of a woman than anyone else, and you would never be like those women because you are far too beautiful, intelligent, and sophisticated to ever lower yourself to their bitchy, slutty ways. It would never come to that anyway, because you love Lucca and he loves you, and I can't ever see him letting you go. I'm just so mad that you had to experience it." Jess strokes my arm and then offers me a cookie which I decline.

"Is love enough though? I do love him, but I don't even know if I'm doing this right ... the love and relationship thing. This is my first relationship and I'm so paranoid and insecure. I might even piss Lucca off. Some men hate jealous women." I snivel before another sip of tea.

"Yes, some men do. But this isn't just jealously, Lex. It's about trust and respect and understanding, and after tonight you have every right to be paranoid. You need to tell Lucca how you feel. He is probably thinking that he is fucking everything up too," Jess adds.

"Jess is right. The main thing is that when you calm down, you and Lucca need to talk. Spell it out for him. Men can be so fucking thick sometimes. Give him an ultimatum, be strong, and tell him you will walk if he doesn't listen or make any effort to reassure you. From what I gather, Lucca has only had one long-term relationship with that Fran chick, so it will be relatively new for him too. You need to work it out together, but let him stew first. Don't go back until you're ready. Make sure he knows that you are not standing for this shit and if you don't work it out, then come back home to Cameron and me," Hazel says then pulls the covers back. She edges downward to look at my feet and asks Jess for some antiseptic cream.

"Why did you not come back home to Cameron and me? I meant to ask," Hazel quietly asks when Jess is out of earshot.

"Because I thought Anna was there," I reply. Jess returns with the cream.

"They're actually not bad. You are lucky, missy." Hazel tsks, shaking her head after she has put cream on my soles.

We snuggle back into bed and my tears begin to dry again for about the millionth time tonight. "I didn't expect it to be so challenging ... you know? Falling in love ..." I say, lying back hugging the suede cushion against my chest.

"It's very hard. You need to compromise and it can be difficult. Steve and I have had lots of fights over the years. Remember the time, I went crazy because he kept getting text messages from a woman with lots of kisses at the end and it turned out to be his older sister who I hadn't met." Jess giggles and we join in.

"Yeah, I do remember that." Jess was worried sick over it at the time because it was early in their relationship.

"*And the time* ... I found lingerie in a gift box under Dominic's bed. I thought it was a Christmas present, then when he never gave me it on Christmas morning I cried and thought he was seeing someone else. Turned out it was Steve who had bought it for you, Jess, and Dominic was hiding all his presents so you wouldn't find them." Hazel laughs.

"Yeah the green satin set, that's right," she adds. I smile because I know they are just trying to cheer me up and lighten the mood.

After Jess turns the light off and we finally settle down, I barely whisper, "Jess, did Lucca say anything when he was leaving? How was he? How did he act?" I ask because I can't get the image out of my head of him vulnerable and man-crying. I know he was angry and shocked that I wasn't going home with him, but I want to know what Jess noticed about his reaction.

"He was crying, Lex, like really cut up. He told me to tell you ... 'you are the most beautiful intriguing woman he's ever met,' and that he loves you and something about you being his angel ... 'A blessing and his light,' and you've not to switch it off on him because he has you, wants you to sparkle or something, and make you feel, feel the love ... his love, yeah it was something like that." The bedroom is fairly dark, but I can see that Jess is screwing her face trying to remember everything he said.

"Oh, he said some Italian words too, and I've no idea what it was, but I think it was sweet because he had his hand on his heart before Peter encouraged him into the car." I feel the mattress shift. Jess turns on her side and wraps her arm around me while Hazel grabs my hand, clasping it and holding our joined hands in front of my chest ... *my heart.*

Nothing else is said. Nothing else needs to be said. Their touch is enough.

My stomach backflips with hearing Lucca's sweet words, because I understand each and every one of them. His words are relevant to me ... to us, and it makes me pine for him in that way that makes my heart feel empty. In my mind, I question if I've done the right thing by running away and refusing to go home. Now, I'm not so sure. I close my eyes but don't sleep, I don't even doze. Jess and Hazel fall asleep, but I just lie in the middle of them both, so tired, and so very unsettled.

By the time Jessica's alarm goes off in early hours of the morning, I feel like a train has run over me. All night, or what was left of it, I never let go of Hazel's hand, even when she stirred and moved. I squeezed her hand tightly while my head ran through everything that happened last night.

"Morning. How do you feel? Did you sleep?" Hazel asks, yawning and stretching.

"Feel like crap and I didn't really sleep," I answer.

"Lexi, I need to get up and get showered for work, you can stay here as long as you like. If you're not going home to Lucca, you're welcome to stay here, honey." Jess cuddles me before getting her work clothes organised. I apologise for keeping them both up late last night with my drama but thank them for looking after me.

Jess leaves for work shortly after. Hazel and I have another long chat in bed, just the two of us. She offers to make me breakfast but I decline. She tells me she has a class at Club di Energia but she will get it covered if I want her to stay with me, but I encourage her to go to work.

After the night I've had and feeling all the emotions I do, I decide that I want to go back home to Lucca. Not that I'm ready to talk and forgive him just yet, but I want to be near him at least, until I figure this out. It might help me achieve some clarity or closure on what happened.

"Are you sure it's not too soon or early to go back?" Hazel asks tentatively, stretching her arms overhead while sitting cross-legged at the bottom of the bed.

"Yeah, I'm sure. I want to go. There are too many things to say and too many things to share. It might not be today, but it needs to happen and I want to go now I've slightly calmed down," I reply. I'm uneasy not knowing what happened last night after Lucca left here or what he's doing and thinking just now.

Hazel says she will run me home and can come over after her classes if I want her to. I put my dress back on from last night, borrow a pair of Jessica's flat pumps since she's the same size as me, and throw my hair in a ponytail. Before going downstairs, I take one last look in the mirror, sigh, and wrinkle my nose at how ashen and tired I look. Hazel makes me coffee. I sit in silence in the kitchen sipping it, gathering my thoughts while she calls Dominic to check in with him.

"Are you ready? After I drop you, I need to go home and get dressed quickly for my first class," Hazel asks, rinsing the mugs out at the sink. She's still in her pyjamas and hoodie from last night.

"Hazel, I'm sorry you were dragged out of bed last night, thank you for taking care of me." I choke, leaning over to cuddle her, which stirs up my vulnerable emotions again and makes me teary because I love her that much.

"I love you, Roo. I wasn't going to leave you crying all night, even with Jess here. Anytime you need me, you know I'll come and get you, or you come straight back home. I mean it. I'm always here for you. If you ever need a break from your relationship, come home." She playfully lifts my ponytail, swinging and circling my hair.

"Thank you. What would I do without you?" I sob against the crook of her neck because I'm questioning if I can continue my relationship with Lucca if his past continues to haunt us.

"Hmmm, I've been asking myself the same thing. Now listen carefully. If I ever, and I mean ever … catch you running barefoot again … I'm going to throttle you!" She holds me at an arm's length with her lips pursed in a thin line.

"Yes, Mum!" I hiccup and pitifully laugh while sobbing.

"It will be you that I'll murder, not Lucca!" She smiles this time and I take her hand.

I lift my clutch bag, wipe my tears, and follow her out.

Jess wants us to lock up and put the key through the letterbox because she has a spare. I pass the key to Hazel. When I go outside, my knees almost go weak and my breath catches in my throat at the vision in front of me. Lucca is leaning against his Aston Martin car

with the same clothes on from last night. We lock eyes, both tired, weary, and pain stricken. Lucca looks lost and helpless. He cautiously smiles and advances towards me. While the earth stops spinning around us, we exchange silent words. Lucca initiates the wordless conversation by drawing me into his pleading eyes, the depth of his despair ...
I'm sorry.

I'm angry.

I'm lost.

I'm empty.

I'm desperate.

I'm hurt.

I'm miserable.

I'm destroyed.

He sighs and reaches for my hand. "Baby, please. I came back and I am not leaving here without you this time."
Reactively, I recoil again. Hazel is now standing with her hand on her hip and ready to throw some fire bombs his way. I can feel the heat radiating from her.
"Just the man I wanted to see!" She raises her voice, pointing a finger at him. He seems surprised to see Hazel here, or uneasy that I had to confide in her when I know he wanted me to confide in him. She steps forward to confront him face-to-face. Hazel looks so small and delicate standing in front of his tall, muscular body, but she's squaring up to him nonetheless.
"Good morning, Hazel," Lucca says gingerly but leans over to double cheek kiss her. He's met with a slap right across his jaw. I gasp and throw my hand over my mouth, watching Hazel wince, shaking her sore hand out.
"Shit, Hazel ...?" He moans, rubbing his red cheek with his hand and then frowns. I'm shocked; I never thought she would go to the extent of actually slapping him. Maybe he deserved it, but he's still mine and I don't know how I feel that my man has been slapped.
"Don't you, *good morning me*. Turns out, it's not a bloody good morning, because *I'm* actually shattered. I had to come here in the middle of the night and hold my best friend while she cried all bloody night long, because she was *that* upset..." Hazel rants and jabs a finger in his chest "...and all because of you. For some reason, she

84

seems to have unknowingly moved into the playboy mansion! And let me tell you this, if *you* think that it's acceptable to be treated poorly at dinner by an employee you used to fuck and *then* discover a whore in your bed, then you are delusional. Frankly, if it were me, I'd have your cards marked and send you bloody packing." She scoffs and shakes her head.

He runs his hand through his hair then gently lifts her hand away from his chest. "I agree, it is completely unacceptable and it will never happen again. Lexi and I need to talk and work this out. I know you are both angry, and you have every right to be. Jesus, do you not think that I am a mess right now seeing Lexi like this, and also infuriated about what happened last night? I hate to see Lexi hurt, and I am not giving up on convincing her that this will never happen again." He cocks his head, rubbing his hand over his cheek and chin.

"Well good. You better grovel hard and sort this shit out." Hazel softens her tone. Lucca's hand has moved from his jaw to his forehead, where he pinches his brow with his middle finger and thumb.

He turns his pleading eyes to me, "Doc, please come home with me. I am not leaving here without you." He winces before running his tongue back and forth over his bottom lip, sighs, and locks eyes with me again.

Walking forward, I reach for Hazel, hug her, and quietly talk near her ear. "Thank you for helping me, for caring, and for looking out for me. I'm going to go with Lucca, but I won't talk to him until later, once I catch up on sleep and sort my head out. Don't tell Cameron about what happened. He'll go crazy and it's complicated now that Anna's in the mix."

"Okay, I won't. You sure you want to go with Lucca?" she asks. I nod and kiss her temple. "Remember what I said. Make him stew and suffer. Phone me or text if you want me to come and get you later on."

"Okay." I squeeze her hand finally.

Without saying another word, I brush past Lucca and head towards the car, open the passenger door, and slide in. I notice his body relax with relief that I'm going home with him. Hazel gives Lucca a final grilling because I see her lips moving, eyes narrowing, and head shaking before she gets in her little Renault Clio.

Lucca slides in the car and exhales the breath he's been holding. He reaches for my face and cups it in both hands. "Lexi ... thank you for coming home with me. Fuck! You have been crying this morning too. Baby, I am ..." He pinches his eyes closed then wipes under my eyes with his thumbs. He breathes raggedly then leans over to try and kiss me.

"Don't!" Pulling my face out of his hands, I wrap my arms around my chest, turn, and look out of the window. "I never slept last night and I need more time. I'm tired and I don't want to talk just now."

He inhales deeply through his nostrils, jaw clenching, and chest expanding. "Okay. Have you eaten anything?" He asks with concern.

"No." One word that's all he's getting.

"Are you hungry?" I feel him study my body, scan every inch of me as if he is looking for signs ... damages? Cuts? Bruises? I just don't know. If he could see my heart, he'd find all the damage is there.

"No." I sigh.

He starts the ignition, the radio switching on and breaking up a certain level of hostility. "Are your feet sore? Is the damage bad? Will you let me look at them when we get home?"

"No and no." I know he's trying to care for me and strike up conversation and I'm being dry. He's lucky I'm talking to him at all. The atmosphere is thick with tension, a haunting feeling of unspoken words circling around us.

"Just drive, Lucca. I want to go to bed." He looks out his own window, staring, collecting his thoughts, then returns his focus to driving. Other than the annoying pop song on the radio, the journey is silent. The next song to play is Carrie Underwood's "Before He Cheats." I have to scoff audibly at the irony. Lucca curses and switches it off. I was enjoying it too and hoped it was making him uncomfortable. It appears it was. He leans one arm against the window resting his fingers on his tilted head.

Chapter 6: Reconciliations

Thankfully, Rose and Peter are out with Doris when we arrive home. Without another word, I storm upstairs holding my clutch bag and shiver looking at our bedroom door visualising what I found behind it last night.

I enter the second spare bedroom down the hall and slam the door. There is no way I'm sleeping in his bed after that slut has been there. I lock myself in the bathroom of the spare room, slide down the door, and lean against it. Lucca comes barging into the room, and bangs on the bathroom door, pleading for me to let him in.

"Lucca, unless you want me to sleep in a bathroom, you'd better get out of this room right now. I need space." I hear him sigh, mumble, curse, and slide down the back of the door.

I fall asleep, cold and uncomfortable against the tiles of the bathroom floor. I don't know how much time has passed when I wake up. I'm relieved Lucca isn't on the other side of the bathroom door. I stumble back to the bedroom, lock the bedroom door this time, strip my dress off, pull the duvet back, and crawl in. Hours later, a knock at the door startles me.

"Lexi, petal, I have some food for you," Rose says carefully.

"Thank you, Rose, but I'm not really hungry," I croak lazily.

"Lexi, love, please eat something. Lucca has made you butternut squash soup and a black pudding, prawn, and chorizo salad. He says you like this."

I sigh, thinking about Tuscany. *He remembered.*

"Rose, thank you for bringing it up, but I'm honestly not hungry." Eating is the last thing on my mind.

Exhaustion takes over, my heavy lids falter, and then I'm sleeping again.

When I wake, I take my pill packet from the zipper compartment of my bag, swallow my pill with tap water from the bathroom, then switch my phone on. It's buzzing frantically with text messages and about a billion missed calls. I check the time—4:30 p.m. I've slept the entire day away.

Lucca – Baby, can I come in yet? Xx

Lucca – Baby, are you awake? xx

Lucca – I love you, please talk to me? Xx

Lucca - Please do not shut me out. I love you xx

Lucca – Doc, seriously, you have been giving me the cold shoulder all day. I need to talk to you xx

Lucca - Why will you not eat anything? Ignoring me is one thing, but you need to eat. I am not happy with this. How much space do you need? Xx

Lucca - I am sorry. That was out of order, but please, baby, eat something. Come down the stairs to me xx

Lucca – I am going out of my mind down here. Doc, please. I love you xx
Lucca – Can I come in yet? Xx

Lucca – Tu sei il più bello e intrigante donna che abbia mai incontrato xx

Jess – Please text or call me. I'm worried about you. I hope you're ok. I love you xxx

Hazel – Let me know everything is ok. Does Old Ted have diabetes? Xxx

What is Hazel going on about? I will need to check in on Mr. Carlin and his home help.

Me – Mr. Carlin is not diabetic, well, not that I'm aware of, and I'm fine. Been sleeping on-off. Xxx

Cameron – When are you going to call Mum? She's been on the phone and not happy you haven't contacted her. You better make up some excuse x

Me – Ok. Fine. *No kiss* .

I don't have the energy or patience to call my mum today. It will need to wait.

Jane – Hi, hope you're well. Do you fancy meeting for lunch next week? Xx

Mark – Lexi can you call me re: rescheduling client appointments. Hope you're feeling better.

I'll have to speak with Jane and Mark at some point regarding work at the clinic. I think I might just go back early as I need some independence and normality to my routine, even if my wrist isn't up to massaging. I could sort out the administration. I could do with Mark having a go at my wrist—it's worth a try.

Granny – Hi, darling, when are you hoping to come up for a visit? We miss you and love you. Granny xxxx

Granny is so bloody persistent.

Me – I'll speak with Lucca and check when is convenient for a visit. Xx

Jess – Lex, r u ok? What's going on? Xx

Lucca – I am sorry. I am so fucking sorry, you have no idea xx

Lucca – Can I bring you something to eat? Xx

Lucca – Doris is wrecking the front lawn. Can you come and get her? xx

He's using Doris as an excuse to get me out of bed, well I'm not falling for it.

Samantha – Need to get coffee night arranged. When suits? Xxx

Rachel – Hey, would love to meet you for coffee to catch up on holiday chat xxx

Jess – Lex, let me know you're ok please. I'm worried.

Me – I'm fine. Just having a relaxing day. Sorry about last night. All is good. Thanks for letting me stay. Speak soon. Love you. Xx

Lucca – Doc, if you do not reply, I am breaking the lock and coming in xx

I know he had nothing to do with the blonde bimbo showing up last night, but he does have a colourful past and I'm disgusted, to say the least. Plus, the Kimberley situation has ignited a blaze deep in my stomach.

Me – I'm not ready to talk yet. I'm tired and still angry. *No Kiss* .

Switching my phone off, I slip back to sleep.

Rose is back at the door with food, which I turn down again.

I grab a quick shower trying to make myself feel fresher. My feet are grazed but not as bad as they were in Tuscany. When I return to bed, I try to process what has happened in the last twenty-four hours. I stare at the ceiling and listen to my playlist on my phone until sleep takes a hold of me again. The last image I must have in my mind before I fall asleep is the whore lying on my bed, cuffed to bedpost, which incites horrible nightmares.

I dream of my first memory of seeing my mum cuffed to Simon Park's bed. Mary told me to go into Simon's room to fetch something and in return, she would give me cold water from the main kitchen. She knew Mum was drugged and tied to the bed, and she wanted to ensure I witnessed it. That was her vice: she was disgustingly wicked and wanted to torment me … a child, a young, naive, innocent child. Her sinister games seemed to fulfil her with evil pleasure, which she thrived on.

Her psychotic mind was so warped, she actually smiled and laughed when I screamed and screamed. I wet myself because Mum wouldn't answer me and didn't move. Mary eventually stumbled and passed out on the floor because she was drugged herself, and I was left standing in my urine, petrified and trembling.

After Simon heard me screaming, he dragged me out of the house on sticks, threw me over the decking and onto the grass, then stormed back inside and slammed the door.

I went into shock for weeks after that brutal ordeal. I never cried, never spoke either, just hid in a quiet corner in our shed and rocked back and forth. I never told Cameron what I saw, or Mum, because I couldn't say it. Saying it was like seeing it all over again.

When I wanted the images out of my mind, I would close my eyes and try to imagine daisy chains. They were pretty. Mum and I used to make them and wear them as necklaces. They were the nicest thing I had seen at that age, and they made me feel happy. I willed myself to visualise them. Instead, the concept of the daisy chains as a necklace would evoke the disturbing scene that I witnessed in Simon's room and make me feel worse.

Mum was sedated and dressed up in a seedy costume. She had a metal mask over her face, a metal choker with spikes around her neck, which attached to a chain on a huge freestanding metal device. She was barely recognisable, but I knew it was Mum because her long hair fanned her naked shoulders. Both wrists and ankles were restrained by metal cuffs, blood dripped from her wrists and ankles, and the sheet between her legs was stained with blood. A camera sat on the bottom of the bed and a video camera on a tripod stood next to it.

I finally understood why she was always sore, bruised, and bloody. It also explained the red, raw welts on her ankles and wrists. It was shortly after that I experienced similar abuse, albeit not as explicit. Michael began tying me up and photographing me. Then a few years after, the day I tried to escape into the Australian bush ... that was the day I faced the worst imaginable cruelty. He took my innocence.

I'm trying to escape. I'm running through the Australian bush.
He's chasing me ... he's shouting at me ... my bare feet are hurting and bleeding.
It's dark ... it's hot.
I'm scared.
I can't get away.
I need to get away.

Banging on the door and shouting startles me. In a panic, I scramble off the bed and open it quickly. Lucca picks me up and carries me back to the bed holding me steady.

"Breathe, just breathe. Calm down, baby, it is okay, I have you." His voice is coarse and broken as he kisses my head and softly strokes my hair, tracing his fingers down my face and cheek. "Jesus, Lexi, you scared the shit out of me. Are you okay?"

"Yes, I think so," I pant, trying to lower my heart rate and fill my starved lungs with oxygen. He holds me tightly, kissing me continually.

Breathlessly, I whisper, "Just hold me," and he does. Stroking my hair, he presses his nose and mouth against my temple until I'm calmer.

"How did you know I was having a nightmare?" I ask once I gain some sort of equilibrium and composure.

"I have been sitting outside the room waiting on you. I must have dozed off, but I jolted when I heard you scream."

"I'm glad you're here. I need you. I need you to hold me so much right now," I sob as my tears begin. I hold onto him tightly while he caresses me with nothing but gentle, tender love.

My chest heaves while I shake, sob, and break my heart with raw, heavy tears. He squeezes me into his chest so hard he nearly crushes me. Burying his face into my neck and stroking my hair over and over, he soothes me.

"I know you wanted time and space, but I just could not handle you shutting me out like this. I am begging you to please let me back into your heart, Doc. I need you."

"I need you too," I cry with my eyes closed, thankful I feel secure in his arms right now.

"Do you want to tell me about your nightmare? Please let me help you. I fucking hate to see you like this, dolcezza." Leaning against the headboard, he sits upright and pulls me onto his lap where I nestle my head in the crook of his neck.

"The woman in our bed ... I was thinking about her and it stirred a horrible memory when I saw my mum cuffed and ..." I can't even say it. It hurts too much. I just want Lucca to take it all away, the pain, fear, paranoia, and darkness.

"Christ! It is my fault. It is all my fault that you are having dreams like this. If you never witnessed that fucking absurdity last night, you would not have had that nightmare. Jesus, Lexi, I cannot handle how much I have hurt you recently. I am so sorry. I am so sorry. I love you, baby, I love you so fucking much. You are my everything." He kisses my head hard and breathes heavily against my hair.

"I cannot endure seeing you like this, and I cannot bear that I am hurting you this much. It kills me you needed time away from me. I need to fix this, to treat you with the respect you deserve and do whatever it takes to get us past this. Tell me what to do, what you want me to do." His voice is threaded because he's hurting for me. "I love you and I promised you I would take care of you. I need your love, Lexi ... tell me what you are thinking ... we need to talk ... can you talk to me yet?" Gently, he lifts my hand to his mouth. He covers my hand in kisses and brushes his lips over my engagement ring before settling my hand on his heart and covering it with his.

"I love you too, I do, but I'm mentally exhausted, Lucca. When I saw that woman naked in our bed, I felt as if she had ripped through my flesh, taken my heart, twisted it, then left it out to bleed. I feel so scared because it's not a lifestyle I can give you, and I'm worried that I'll continue to come home to some other woman in my bed, or that I'm not enough for you," I confess anxiously.

"Christ almighty, baby, I do not ever want you to feel this way. You are so much more, so much better. I want you. I need you. Only you. Not the lifestyle that, because of last night, you think I need." He holds me tightly as I continue sobbing. "There will never be anyone else for me. You stole my heart, and I gave you mine. I have been waiting for you my entire life, and I will never let go of you. I am the luckiest man on earth to have you in my arms. Please never feel insecure again. I cannot stress to you enough that you are my now and my future. Only you. Forever, only you." His voice has faltered, and I know he's trying to be strong for me. Leaning over, he presses his cheek against mine his hot breath skimming across my wet sticky skin.

His cheeks are now wet from stray, salty tears embedded onto his skin. He inhales and continues, "I wish I could change my past, Lexi, I do. I would change everything for you, but I cannot. I can only give you my future ... my word that it will never happen again. That woman was nothing to me, and she will not be bothering us again. What can I do? Tell me what to do to make this right. I cannot stand seeing you like this." There's determination in his tone because he needs me to believe him. I want to believe him.

He pleads nonsensically. My stomach churns. What if she lives locally? What if I bump into her again?

Fuck!

File H for hibernation. Hibernation is a possibility.

"Why was she here? When was the last time you saw her or were in contact with her? How often did you see her?" I'm firmer now and try to calm my tears because I need serious answers. I swallow because I'm not sure I'm going to like what I hear. Although, I need to know. Becoming rigid, I sit up and lean back to open the space between us.

He squeezes my hand, pressing it against his chest to reaffirm he is telling me the truth and everything he says is from his heart. Meeting my eyes, he shows me he's being honest. "I have not seen or heard from her in fifteen or sixteen months. I have only ever been with her twice on the same weekend. We were in a hotel at a work conference. Both times I was drunk and it was meaningless."

"So she works with you too?" I tsk.

"No, she was with a sponsorship company but happens to know some of my employees, so she ended up sitting at our table."

"If you haven't had contact with her, then why was she here? Do they do that, the whores you've been with? Just turn up out of the blue? Help me understand this." I hit a raw nerve because his jaw twitches; he closes his eyes, opens them, and looks browbeaten.

"No, of course not. No one I have ever seen before has ever turned up and especially not in that way. I tend to only have family and my close friends here and it is by invite only. When the police interrogated her, I tried to find out why she was here. I could not understand it. I was as shocked as you. She lied and said she was invited. I barely even remember her. She told the police she was an ex-girlfriend, which is a lie. I have no idea why she would do or say that. And, she was doped up and therefore trying to play immature mind games. I still do not know why she was here."

"Well I do," I snap. "She was here for sex. Sex with you, and clearly she had some crazy idea that I was one of your other whores and she wanted me to join in. If I ever and I mean *ever* have to be subjected to that again, believe me when I say this, Lucca, I'll walk away. I'm not putting up with that crap." I turn my head and stare at the wall.

He inwardly gasps. "Do not call yourself that again. You are my fiancée, and I will do everything to make sure you know it and everyone else does too. I have no interest in anyone else but you, and I certainly would not be entertaining that behaviour in my house even if I was single. I will never let you walk, Lexi ... ever, so I will need to make it up to you and ensure you are never put through anything like this again."

I need to know, I don't know why, but I want to know. "Is that how you enjoyed sex before? With more than one woman at a time?" I'm praying this was not the case because it would crush my heart, and I might always continue to feel too inadequate for him knowing he enjoyed a more adventurous sex life.

"God no, absolutely not. I promise you. She obviously has and does, but, baby, she was doped up and completely out of it. Come here. I would never treat a woman like that and partake in something so distasteful. Lexi, you should know me better than that. I am not that type of person." If he promises me, then I believe him and I'm relieved, but still, I can't get the image of her out of my head. It's sickening. He tries to pull me back into his embrace, but I'm not finished so I remain tense.

"And then there is Kimberley. I don't like that she works so closely to you. Am I going to be introduced daily to the women of your past? Women who you have slept with, who obviously still want you. Don't you see how degrading and hurtful that is?" I slap my free hand on the mattress.

"Yes, it is degrading and I am sorry. I did not expect Kimberley to be rude or jealous. I do not and have not had any feelings for her. But you are right; she works in my immediate team, so I did not see any harm in you meeting her. To me she is just another work colleague, but I get that it was wrong of me, insensitive and thoughtless. I understand now that it is hurtful for you and that it upsets you. I will be more considerate because you are my priority, and the last thing I want to do is hurt you." His thumb brushes over my wrist. Even with the space between, us he's not let go of my hand.

I sigh because I do appreciate that he wants to protect my feelings, but she is Anna's friend and it's inevitable we are going to bump into each other again. "I feel like I am never going to get over this, Lucca. While you can try and keep me away from Kimberley, realistically, we will cross paths and I will always feel like this." I suddenly feel cold and shivery after waking up hot and sweaty.

"I am not going to lie. I cannot guarantee you will never see her again. She is Anna's friend, so she does spend time with her outside of work. Although, I will do everything I can to try and settle your worries and make you feel better. I was thinking that I could transfer her into another department so she is not working directly under Suzanne. Would that help?" He lifts my hand up and kisses my ring again and then my fingers, finally pulling me back onto his lap. I don't object this time because I'm thankful he is trying and he can now see why I'm so upset.

"Yeah, I suppose. Thank you," I answer with a sense of relief as I rest my head back on his chest.

"Lexi, baby, I am really trying here. Other than Fran, I have not had a committed relationship. With Fran it was different. Because we grew up together, she was a friend to begin with. I have told you I did not love her like I love you, and that is why it is so important for me to get this right. I feel like I constantly disappoint you and fuck things up. I am learning too. This is new to me too. I never thought I would ever be in such an all-consuming relationship, and I am so grateful that I am. I need to try and get it right, but I just keep tripping up. I cannot lose you, not now, not ever. I want to make you happy, baby." His voice is soft and sincere.

Through his sensitive caressing, I relax my tense muscles and tighten my grip on him then kiss the top of his head, reassuring him I believe him. In response to my gesture, he slumps with relief.

I don't speak as I collect my thoughts, stroking his bare chest with my fingers. I do feel better after getting it off my chest, and Lucca's promises are exactly what I need to hear right now.

"You are soaked with sweat. I am going to run you a bath then feed you. After that I will apologise some more and do everything in my power to make this right and take your worries away." Leaning over, he trails his nose over my hairline, kisses my temple and my cheek. It's not lost on me he hasn't kissed my lips yet. I've been rejecting his touch since I exploded last night so he's probably being cautious.

"Lucca, I can't sleep in that bed ever again. Just knowing she was in it and God knows how many before her ... I just can't." I stretch my legs and wiggle my toes feeling irritable with the thought of the bed she has ruined for me.

He lifts his head and stares with his grey-blue eyes; he's lost the azure sparkle again.

"I knew you would say that and I do not expect you to, so I have already taken care of it. I had a new bed delivered today, which I had already ordered for us. It was custom built and has taken a while to be completely finished. It was supposed to be a moving in gift, but it was not ready in time. I wanted us to start our new life here with something that we share together from new, a token of our relationship together. After last night, I called this morning and brought the delivery forward a few days because I thought it was necessary given the circumstances." He kisses below my ear and nuzzles against my neck.

"I thought it was the right thing to do. You might not believe me, but I have never slept with a woman other than you in this house, not even Fran." I already knew this because he said my dressing room has never been used because he has always lived here alone.

This is hurting him.

"I have a flat in Bearsden which I rent out. It is where Fran and I stayed while I was renovating this house. The woman from last night has been in the house for a New Year's party but never stayed over. Only family stayed. It was the week after that party that we ended up at the same conference in the hotel. Fuck, Lexi, I wish I could erase it all, my past."

He's desperate for my forgiveness I can hear it in his needy voice, but I'm silent and don't know what to say. I'm glad we have a new bed, but it doesn't stop my fear that she will come here again or someone else will.

"This is your home. Any changes you want, anything you need or do not like, please let me know and I will change it. I mean it, Lexi, this is our life together and you need to be comfortable and happy here."

I tilt my head up so I can see his stormy eyes filled with emotion and conflict. "Lucca, what if she comes here again? Or someone else? You know how I feel about trespassers in general, never mind facing sleazy women like her." I worry my fingers in front of my mouth.

"Lexi, it took all the strength I had not to drag her out myself and toss her. When I saw her on the bed, I was horrified. I could not find that fucking key for that stupid cuff, and then you were gone. I stormed out and sent Rose up until she was decently clothed. I have changed the code for the gates, and I am having a new security system put in. I cannot blame Rose and Peter because they were sleeping, but I need something more reliable, like sensors to also set the alarm off." I know he was put in an awkward position, but I'm glad he kept dignity and decorum and left allowing Rose to sort her out.

"Thank you for the bed. And thank you for taking care of extra security," I whisper, although I am still reeling with conflict.

"Do you feel better now we have talked?" He plays with a curl of my hair and strokes my back with his thumb.

"Yes, I do feel better. Thank you for answering my questions truthfully." I splay my hand across his abs.

"Baby, I will always be truthful. I told you that you are mine and you have me, always. Are you still tired?" he asks, tilting my head back to look into my eyes.

Sighing, I close my eyes and tell him. "I'm worried I will have the same dream if I fall asleep again. I dreamed about the day I escaped from Michael and ran into the bush. He was going to tie me up and photograph me and I hated it. I was scared. I hit him with a pot then ran. I don't even know where I was running to except anywhere away from him." I open my eyes, and he looks ashen and winded as if he's been knocked over.

"I was barefoot because we never had shoes; we walked around the shed, grass, and house like that, so I was very used to it. I crawled under the barbed wire fence then ran into the bush and faltered because I almost ran into a funnel web spider and a poisonous snake. Both would likely have killed me. I couldn't move, couldn't go forward and the only way back was to Michael. He saved me from the snake, but as a punishment for trying to run, he started his sexual abuse."

I know I don't need to tell him anymore because he's clenching his jaw and fisting his hands. It hurts him to hear this, even though he wants to help me. I've said enough. He cradles and soothes me.

"Is that the type of dream you always have during your nightmares?"

"Yes, this one the most. I'm fine when I'm not stressed or anxious, which is why I was sleeping well in Tuscany at the farmhouse. Last night was horrible for me, so it must have triggered these memories." He turns my body inward so my chest is now pressed against his.

He leans over, kissing my head sweetly. "I do not want to be responsible for these nightmares; I want to take them away. I need to understand it. Why do you always run?"

"I was angry and scared. It must be my instinctive reaction to fear, I just need to run when I'm scared and want to be safe. Mum used to tell me to run to safety when I was little." He processes what I am saying, still breathing heavily, then pulls the covers back and moves to the foot of the bed.

"What are you doing?" I ask.

"Checking your feet." He's quiet while he examines them then leans over and places small gentle kisses along the soles of my feet and my ankles.

"Are they bad? I thought it was minor grazing I had this time."

"Just some scrapes and bruising from what I can see. I will take care of them. You are going to give me a heart attack one of these days, or get yourself killed," he grumbles, furrowing his brow then continuing to kiss them attentively. I wriggle when his soft lips meet my weak spot on my sole.

He sits up on the bed, pulls me over to him, and scoops me into his arms. "So are we talking again? Do you still love me?" he asks.

"Yes, of course I love you. I never stopped. I was seriously mad at you though." I smile lethargically, glad I've been assertive and told him straight, and he broadens his grin in delight.

Chapter 7: Senses

He tells me to wait a few moments then returns and carries me into our suite, telling me to close my eyes. I can smell a familiar sweet, floral smell ... *orchids,* and hear "I Need You" by Leann Rimes playing.

"Okay, open them."

I open my eyes and look around the room. It is covered with fresh flowers, and there are fairy lights hanging over the mantel on the fireplace with lots of glowing church candles sitting on the ledge and on the bottom hearth. He places me down but keeps a tight grip on me. There are flickering candles placed everywhere throughout the room.

Romantic.

Sensual.

Warm and inviting.

The new bed is unique. It's an enormous oak four-poster, which doesn't look out of place in this monstrous suite. Carved with gilt accents, it has an antique appearance. It's draped with navy, gold, and cream velvet and covered with navy and gold satin damask bedding. There's also a sumptuous navy and gold velvet throw. But what makes my heart skip a beat is the arrangement of blue orchid flower petals spelling out words on top of the bedding.

Sposare me.

Our love.

The love.

L'amore.

These sweet words are scattered with the vivid cobalt blue coloured petals.

Looking at him in wonder, I say, "I already agreed to marry you. I want nothing more."

He now kisses me on the lips, showing his gratitude. "Good, I was worried you would change your mind. Do you like the bed?"

"Yes, it's beautiful, and the blue orchid petals are very thoughtful." I smile in appreciation.

"Look closer at the bed."

Staring at the carved panels of the headboard, I notice our names have been carved into the wood. *Gosh.* That's why it wasn't ready in time.

"I don't know what to say."

"The headboard comprises of the twists and turns of life in three separate panels. I had our names engraved in the middle panel—the "Tree of Life" panel—within the Tudor arch. The carved Baronial Lord & Lady Figures standing in the two open post arches are interchangeable by tradition to bring good fortune and to signify the bedside of the master and mistress of the house for God's blessing," he explains.

Wow, he sure put a lot of thought into this.

"It's wonderful, Lucca. I love it."

"So are you still my fiancée?" he asks.

"Of course I am. You don't need to ask me again. Although, this is really something special."

"You are something special, and I will remind you every day of our lives."

He takes my hand and leads me into the living room of his suite. In front of the large French doors is a circular dining table. The room has been redesigned like the garden of our suite in the Four Seasons Hotel in Firenze the night Lucca proposed to me.

An impressive vase of fresh fragrant blue orchid flowers dominates the centrepiece of the table, and champagne flutes and crisp white linen complete the decadence. A new song echoes from his sound system. "When You Really Love A Woman," by Bryan Adams.

He's put thought into his song choices as well.

"Lucca, it's amazing."

"I wanted to give you a piece of Firenze back, and reinforce what you mean to me. I also wanted to transform the appearance of the bedroom to make you more at ease and to make it more specific to us. I have been waiting all day for you to come back." He wraps his arms around my waist, breathing heavy into the bare skin of my neck.

I drop my head to the side to allow him access to my exposed skin, enjoying his warmth and tenderness. He kisses softly, slowly, and I quiver under his touch, but I don't think I'm quite ready to be making love to him yet. Insecurity is still burning inside me. It's still so raw.

He rubs his fingers and thumb over my bare navel. Then his hands travel to my breasts. Cupping them over my bra, I groan with delight as my body betrays me under his touch. My throbbing sex wants him badly, but emotionally, I'm not ready.

Wriggling reluctantly, I turn around to face him. "I'm sorry, I'm just not ready yet. I love what you did here, and I love you, but I just need more time. I can't relax for lovemaking while I'm still feeling insecure."

He presses his forehead against mine. "I desperately need to make love to you over and over again to show you what you do to me, and how special and beautiful you are, but I will wait. I promised you I would give you space. I am just fucking happy you are letting me back in."

He kisses my lips then moves a stray curl behind my ear. "How about I run you a bath then feed you? You must be starving."

He takes my hand and walks me into the bathroom where there are candles and flowers adorning the room. He fills the bath, adding his tropical scented oil of mango, nectarine, and papaya while I search in the fitted vanity for my products.

I lift out my packet of painkillers, but its empty and so is the anti-inflammatory packet. Lucca watches me throw the empty packet in the bin.

"What is that?" he quizzes while testing the water.

"It is just my prescription from Tuscany."

"Why do you still need them? Are you in pain?" he panics.

"I'm fine, but my wrist still hurts at times, and I need pain relief for it. Stop worrying. I can get more from the doctors."

He walks over and lifts my wrist gently, kissing all around the fractured area where the plate was put in. "After I feed you, I will go to the twenty-four hour pharmacy and get you something."

"No, don't worry. It can wait. I'd rather you stay with me. I missed your closeness last night," I confess, nibbling my bottom lip. "It smells divine in here. It smells of you."

Our communication tonight has been a small breakthrough for me, and I'm glad we talked. The effort he has gone to, his truth, sweetness, and commitment he's promised is dispersing my foul mood and softening me. His sincere confession that he is still learning at relationships and that it's new to him too warms my heart. Smelling his bath scents reminds me of special intimate moments we have shared.

"Baby, I want nothing more than to hold you close to me. I will come in the bath with you, and we will talk some more if you want to, then I will bring up food." He strips his lounge bottoms off his sexy hips, his eager erection springing free.

As if on perfect cue, his music has changed to Kings of Leon, "I Want You."

I shake my head in amusement, but I'm secretly filing a happy chapter in the library of love and lust. He presses up behind me, forcing his hard cock against my ass, and wraps his hand around my stomach, kissing on and around my ear. "I cannot be close to you and not feel this. This is for you, only you. This is what you do to me. I only need to smell you, glimpse you, and I am horned up for you. I have it bad for you, baby, and I cannot resist you," he rasps in that deep sexy way into my ear.

He has me.

"As much as I'd like to help you out with that, it won't be tonight, so you're going to have to hold me and think of something else."

"You're killing me," he groans.

"I'm killing myself," I mutter.

"Then why are you denying us? You are all I can think about. I cannot stand not having you. I just want to be inside you, feeling you and holding you close to me."

Ignoring his pleas, I remove my bra and panties and step into the water. Turning off the taps, I slide down into the warm delightful water.

Oh, that feels good.

He looks down at me, glowering with rejection, but his wanting eyes are swallowing me up.

"Well, are you just going to stand there, or are you getting in?"

He doesn't know whether to laugh or curse. Giving a playful grin, he steps in and slides down behind me, placing his legs on the outside of mine. "You are sexy as fuck when you are fiery. Have I told you that before?"

Ignored.

I'm not falling for his charms.

Wrapping his arms around me, he holds me in close to his chest and I collapse into his hold, resting my head in the crook of his neck. I feel so secure, so safe.

"Hmmm, that feels nice," I say, breathing in the sweet tropical smell and enjoying the skin on skin contact. I'm trying to ignore his hard cock at the bottom of my back. He's groaning and his chest is expanding against my skin with his heavy breathing.

"Cock tease," I hear him mutter.

I close my eyes and place my hands on his knees, lightly outlining shapes with my fingers on his skin in the flickering candle light. Feeling his two hands now kneading into my tight shoulders wakes up the butterflies and my sex for that matter.

Torture.

Bliss.

"Hmmm," I mumble.

"Nice?" he asks.

"Yes, I feel so much more relaxed already."

He bends and kisses the shell of my ear softly then moves my hair to the side and kisses my neck.

"What about this?"

Folded.

Crumbled.

Melted.

I'm wet with silky readiness, and my sex has a pulsing heartbeat in anticipation. Trailing his hands down my sternum, he pauses before reaching my breasts, which involuntarily push up to meet his cupped hands. My nipples are begging to be caressed.

"What about this?"

"Uh huh."

He massages them then tightens his fingers around my aroused nipples.

He's got me.

I'm taken.

Fuck!

File W for weak. Weak under sex duress.

"You are fucking irresistible. I want you, dolcezza. I cannot resist you. Can I have you?"

"Yes." I softly moan.

Pressing my legs together, I squirm to relieve the throbbing between my legs.

"Do you want me to help you with that?"

Absolutely.

"I need you to tell me. Tell me it's what you want. Ask and you will get." He continues to kiss my neck and ear and stroke my taught nipples.

I don't know why I tried to refuse this.

"I want you," I softly moan.

"Tell me what you want, baby."

Everything.

I push my ass against him. "I want you to touch me, I want you in me, and I want to come all around you. I can't wait. I need you."

"You are mine," he groans, sliding his hand down to the crux of my desire. He slides his fingers over my wet flesh, in between my silky folds, and slides his fingers inside me, pressing his thumb on my sweet spot. I buck and thrust up against his palm, pushing his fingers in further. He torments me with his magic touch repeatedly.

Divinity.

Tensing, I grip his arms. Climbing, I'm nearly there, then he slides his fingers out of me.

No. No. No.

What is he doing?

"Stand up and turn around, then place your legs at the side of me. I want you to come in my mouth. You will be grateful for the delay. I promise."

Oh God.

Need.

Now.

I jump up quickly, moving the water around, then stand with my legs at either side of him. He moves my legs further apart, then lifts my right leg and places my foot on his shoulder. I need his tongue so much, I'm ravenous for it. He presses his head against my stomach, his nose close to my sex. Holding my ass cheeks, he stares down at me, filling his lungs.

"Your body is amazing. The thought of never having you again nearly killed me. Fuck, I am so happy." His hot breath hits my pulsing clit.

"Lucca, please," I whine, spearing my fingers in his hair.

Andrea Bocelli's Italian love song, "Vivo Per Lei" enchantingly echoes. It's one of my favourites, but it's slow and I need a quick tempo to reach a fast climax.

He's slowly killing me.

He trails kisses on the inside of my leg, then blows where he has kissed. He's tormenting me by dragging this out. I wriggle and rock further towards him, coaxing his tongue towards my neediness.

When the music becomes more powerful, his tongue reaches my sensitivity. Hallelujah!

Swirl.

Suck.

Lick.

Kiss.

Nibble.

His fingers enter, pressing on my front wall while his tongue thrashes against my clitoris. I'm tensing, fluttering straight to my core.

"Baby, fuck my tongue and come for me," he demands.

I grind into him only with a few thrusts, and it's enough to fill me with an exuberance of pleasure rippling through my veins, my blood. I shudder with a blissful, orgasmic rush.

Continuing with his licking and kissing, he ensures I have shaken out every last electrified twitched nerve. I move his head away because I'm overly sensitive, and he laughs then slowly kisses my navel.

He lowers my leg back into the water but keeps his fingers in me. "I want you to turn around, and when I remove my fingers, slide down on my cock and lean back onto me."

With weak legs, I turn around as his fingers screw inside my sheath and his thumb rests on my sweet spot.

Sweet Jesus.

The sensation.

The music.

The amassed tension.

It's all driving me into ecstasy. I lower myself back into the water, straddling his waist. His fingers slip out of me just as I am filled with his hard, thick length.

He stills.

I still.

"Fuck, fuck, fuck," he growls. "Lean back."

I lean back against his chest, my ass sliding down his stomach, and I anchor myself on him. The penetration I feel deep at this angle is staggering. The jolting pressure of his erect cock against my front wall is making me delirious. He wraps his legs around mine, locking my feet so I don't slip. I lean my head back against his shoulder as he wraps his arms around me, groping my heavy breasts. Digging my heels under his grip, I lift slightly off him then slide back down slowly onto his length.

I scream with sheer fulfilment once I'm accustomed to the intrusion.

Our bodies glide harmoniously, raptured in the enjoyment of the sensation. We move slowly, repeating long, vaulted, deep satiated plunges, shifting the water around the tub.

"Christ, you feel amazing. You blow my fucking mind." Releasing one hand from my breasts, he teases my clitoris. I clench onto his arm, feeling his veins protruding through his skin.

"I'm so close ..." I whimper.

I feel his arms going rigid, picking up more speed, and he lifts his hips up higher, diving further into me. I don't know how long I can hold on. I'm coming undone.

Splintering.

"Now, baby. Let go."

I scream, and he shouts my name, stiffening and filling me hard as he holds me tight. My eyes roll back into my head as I dig my nails into his arms. Breathing frantically in the surrounding steam, lost and sated in my undulating orgasm, my shoulders back onto him feeling as if I have floating limbs. My head rolls side to side until the frequency of sparking electricity has surged completely through me.

"Fuck, fuck, fuck."

He's still exhilarating in his own bliss. Using his hands on my hips to lift me up and down, he pounds me a few extra times, creaming me with more sperm. He groans and melts back into the deep tub. The curls from my wet hair are stuck across my cheeks and my face, covering my chest and down over my breasts, but I don't have the strength to move them.

"Are you okay?" he asks.

"Mmmm ... hmmm," I hum. "I'm better than okay. I needed you so badly."

"Good, me too. That was fucking hot." He moves the curls from the side of my face, kissing my temple. "Can you move yet?" he asks.

"I'm not sure." I sigh with contentment. He lifts me up and I wince as I lose his girth from inside me. He spins me around and the water splashes everywhere.

"I want your mouth." He's not asking.

I kneel in the water in front of him then lean my head back into the tropical scented water completely submerging my hair, and I shake my locks, freeing them from clinging against my face. My breasts push upward with the movement, my hardening nipples surfacing from the water.

By the time I've lifted my head, he's over me, grabbing my breasts and thrashing his tongue inside me. I've missed having his tongue in my mouth. This alone could send me over the edge again. Seizing the back of my head, he hauls me towards him.

"I missed your kisses today," I pant between our assaulting tongues.

"So have I. Look at me." He's husky, sexy, and in control.

I hear another song I recognise in his playlist; it's Emeli Sande and Labyrinth's, "Beneath Your Beautiful." Opening my eyes, I see his hunger, his desire, and his passion. The exact feeling I have right now.

Without warning, he moves his hand down my saturated curtain of hair ensconcing my back then cups my ass, lifting me up. My knees and legs spread adjusting to the sides of his hips.

Sunk.

Submerged deep into the abyss, the inherent penetration back within me.

My eyes lock with his, drowning in them, and my tongue united with his just makes this experience all the more intimate while we cruise into another pinnacle of pleasure. When I can't take anymore, the current of indulgence pulls me under. We come apart, surfing to the crest of orgasm, and he fills me, spurting his release, rasping my name in gratitude.

He remains inside me, deep in my hot core, as I fall into his chest.

Completely spent and relaxed, exhaustion takes over me when Leona Lewis's beautiful voice sings "I Got You."

Kiss.

Kiss.

Kiss.

Eyes closed.

Scent awakens my senses. The lush aroma of tropical oil, fresh flowers, extinguished candles, and fresh coffee.

Sight is next sense as my fluttering lashes allow light in. A warm burst of sunlight is glowing through the window, and everything appears brighter today.

Touch—the warm, masculine touch from Lucca. His mouth is at my ear, buried in my wild bedhead hair; his hand is on my hip as we lie on the new mattress.

"Sleep well?" he says before kissing my ear then my neck.

"Mmmm ... hmmm." I stretch my used limbs.

Laughing, he says, "You are not a morning person, but you are adorable. Breakfast is in the living area on the table. You must be starving."

"I thought you were feeding me last night?" I say, turning over on my side to look at him. His crystal blues are back, twinkling in the morning light.

"I fed your hunger, but not with food. You fell asleep on me during the bath. I had to bring you to bed." He grins.

I remember our amazing make-up sex in the tub, but don't recall going to bed.

Smiling, he pulls the sheets back and takes my hand, leading me towards the delicious aroma. I grab my black silk robe from the chair as we walk by then wrap it around myself before sitting down.

He frowns as I cover up, but we're sitting in front of the French doors overlooking the front of his garden, so I'd like to maintain modesty.

"This smells divine. I'm so hungry. Did you prepare it, or did Rose?" I quiz while lifting off the plate covers.

"I did it while you were sleeping, but Rose baked some bread and cinnamon buns for us before going out."

My heels are clicking together with excitement. I love sweet pastries, especially when they're hot. I spread some apricot jam on the toasted bread. The first mouthful just feels like heaven, another sense I have awakened this morning—taste.

I drink a glass of orange juice in one go to quench my thirst. Lucca pours me another glass as I delve into a small bowl of fresh fruit and yogurt, then I enjoy Lucca's omelettes with mushroom, cheese, ham, and chives, and his homemade tomato, basil, and oregano sausages with fresh tomato, onion, and balsamic chutney on the side.

Delicious.

I even manage a sticky cinnamon bun with my coffee afterwards. I feel fit to explode but very satisfied. Lucca reads his newspaper, but occasionally glances towards me, shaking his head in amusement when I dip my finger in the apricot jam and lick it off.

"Enjoy that?"

"Yes, it was wonderful, thank you."

"I have something for you." He grins. He walks over to his jacket that's hanging over the suede sofa and lifts something small from his pocket, clutching it in his palm looking very entertained with himself.

"Lucca, you have already given me far too much and it's making me restless. I don't want people thinking we're together because I'm after you for your generosity, and the breakfast was more than a big enough treat. I'm very grateful you look after me and are such a great chef," I assure him.

"I do not give a flying fuck what other people think. I am spoiling you for the rest of our lives, and I love how appreciative you are about everyday little things. One of the many reasons why I love you." He walks around the back of my chair.

I'm expecting him to dangle some form of expensive bling around my neck, but instead he places something cold and sharp in my hand and kisses my head. Opening my palm, there are two key fobs placed in the centre. Staring while knitting my brow, I'm a little confused.

"What's this?" I ask.

"Your new transport."

"Lucca, have you bought me a car? When? And why are there two key fobs?" I ask sternly.

"Yes. If you are going all fiery on me, hurry up about it so I can take you over that sofa," he chuckles, rubbing his thumb along the bottom of his lip.

"You're an ass. Are you just trying to get a reaction out of me so you can have your wicked way?" I retort, staring at the fobs in one palm with my other hand on my hip.

Raising his brow roguishly, he leans over and presses a button on the key fobs. Beeping, squealing, and irritating car alarm sirens go off.

Sound ... my last sense this morning and shit, if it isn't annoying.

"Jesus, what's going on?" I moan, screwing my face with the impetuous noise.

"You should go outside and sort that noise out, baby. Your vehicles will attract attention."

I throw my napkin at him and pace to the French doors. Throwing them open, I walk onto the balcony and see two magnificent cars in front of the house. I squeal with delight like a child at Christmas, hopping side to side with excitement. Running towards him, I give him the biggest, most appreciative kiss I can, then run out the suite, down the stairs, and throw the front door open.

Oh my goodness.

There is a sleek, sexy, sports car and a smart looking sporty 4x4.

What the hell?

True to his word, he has actually bought me two exquisite cars.

I place my hands on both fobs to quiet the alarm sounds. Walking around the first car, I run my fingers along the pretty, sleek, sparkly sheen from the body—a deep blue colour. It's sophisticated, elegant, yet sporty. The hood is down, and I can smell the newness of the leather.

Lucca joins me, wearing just his lounge pants, as I stare in complete awe, not knowing what to do with myself. Not that I'm one for flashy or material things but wow … this is exciting and they are so impressive.

"It is an Aston Martin Vanquish Volante. I like Aston Martins and I thought you would like this model," Lucca explains.

"Wow. Oh, wow, oh, wow. I don't know what to say." I throw my hand over my mouth completely awe-inspired.

Holy shit.

"Well, stop gawking and get in. Tell me what you think."

Happy to oblige, I open the door and jump in. I throw my head back on the peacock blue leather headrest and close my eyes. My grandpa would be impressed by this car. I run my fingers over the wheel, absorbing the sophistication of the interior. There are so many buttons and gadgets.

Lucca opens the passenger door and slides in.

"Do you like it?" he asks. "It is your gift of the day."

My eyes pool with happy, delighted tears. "I love it, but I can't believe you got me an Aston Martin. This car is truly amazing. I don't know what to say other than thank you. And *you are my gift of the day.* Every day."

"Do you like the colour I chose? I thought of the blue orchid."

I think of his eyes.

"Yes, it's beautiful. I would have picked this myself." Nibbling on my bottom lip, I broaden my smile, appreciating the custom designed colour.

I throw my arms around his neck. Then, completely out of character for me, I twist and throw myself on his lap, straddling him. I'm so overwhelmed, I just want to hold him and shower him with gratitude.

I kiss him as his hands slide into my silk robe. I press my naked body against his, and he clenches my ass.

"Fuck, if this is the appreciation I get, I need to do this more often. I want to take you right now, right here."

"What about Rose and Peter?" I consider.

"Relax, they are in the village. Then they are going away for the weekend since we are having the family over."

I dive my tongue deep into his mouth and ask for it, so of course, I get it.

In the front seat of my new car. With the hood down. In broad daylight.

Car sex. My new favourite.

Leaning against his chest, I'm soaked in perspiration. Spent, happy, and content. His arms are still wrapped around me inside the silk robe; his lounge pants are dropped to his ankles. We press foreheads and caress each other.

"That was fucking amazing. We definitely need to do this more often," he says before biting my bottom lip.

"Mmmm hmmm," I mutter in my sated trance. "This is an amazing surprise."

"So was this. I love it when you unexpectedly jump me. That was hot as hell." He traces his thumb around the curve of my breast.

"And I thought you were a romantic." I smirk back.

"I am romantic, ravenous, raw, and randy as fuck. Lucky for you." He winks then darts his tongue out to slide along my bottom lip.

"You're an ass and full of yourself." I'm trying so hard not to giggle, watching him waggle his eyebrows.

"Lex, you are dying to laugh and you know that I am right."

"You missed the part about being cocky, persistent, obnoxious, confident, bossy, temperamental, and possessive." I laugh, jabbing at his chest.

"It is good to see you smile again," he sighs wholeheartedly, dismissing the character I've just gave him.

Cocky.

Persistent.

Obnoxious.

Confident.

Bossy.

Temperamental.

Possessive.

"Of course, there are lots of compliments I can give you too," I add for safe measure.

"Oh, pray tell." He moves some long, stray curls away from my face.

"Nope, your ego is big enough. Can I look at the other car now?" As I twist and slide back on the driver's seat, he playfully smacks my ass.

The second car is a black BMW X5 SUV. Lucca explains he traded his Land Rover in as he wanted a newer, durable four-wheel drive for visiting the construction sites, and I can use it for Doris, so it was a sensible decision.

This car is also luxurious, but it's a formidable family car with seven seats. It will be practical for Lucca's large family should they travel with him. After the interior tour, he takes my hand, guiding me around the front of both vehicles.

I gasp when I see the registration plates. The Aston Martin plate reads CAR US07 and the BMW reads LEX1.

OH. MY. GOD!

I have my own name on a plate, this is very surreal.

Understanding the significance of LEX1, I am baffled looking at the Aston Martin because Lucca already has CAR USO4.

Why would he need another?

"Lucca, the plates are amazing, but I don't understand why you have your surname again."

"It is your car, baby, and as you agreed to be my wife, you will have my name very soon. I spoke to the family, and as a gift I am giving you 07, the next Caruso plate. I wanted to keep it for our wedding, but since the cars were ready, I thought I would just use them. So you will have to marry me now." He exhales on his last words, awaiting my reaction.

He's nervous. He also asked me again last night with the orchid petals. It's as if he thinks I'm going to change my mind.

"Lucca, it's too generous, too much, but of course I'm marrying you. I just said that I'd like to wait awhile before we rush into it, but that doesn't mean I'm not marrying you. I told you, you are mine. *In every way.*" He trails his thumb over my bottom lip. "Are you sure that your family is okay with this? I don't have your name yet, and we haven't been together long."

"Yes, they are fine. Kate has a private registration that her father got her years ago, so she will not change it, and Sarah is not into flashy things. She cringes when she has to use Armando's car. Anna already has 06."

"Maybe the number should be kept for your nieces and nephews."

"No, you are going to be the next Caruso, so it is yours, lucky seven. I want you to have it. I am serious. I want you as my wife, Lexi."

I think this is his way of manipulating me into a speedy marriage. "Nice try. I love the cars, and the plates, but I'm happy to wait a little bit longer before jumping into the registry office." I turn on my bare heels and walk back inside.

I can hear him chuckle behind me. Damn, he's infuriating sometimes.

Chapter 8: Episodes

I dress in a designer black chiffon blouse and slim fitting capri trousers—an outfit Lucca bought me that I wore on holiday and brought back with me. I tidy up the breakfast dishes and kitchen since Lucca's housekeepers are not back in until Monday and Rose is away for the weekend. I quite like doing normal things, and it's nice having the house all to ourselves because I imagine it's going to be chaotic with the family later on.

I'm conscious of my time, so I fluff up the cushions on the sofas and arrange the flowers we brought down from the suite. Separating them into vases, I place them in the hallway, lounge, and dining room.

I have a doctor's appointment. Then I need to check on Mr. Carlin, meet Lucy for lunch, and make some calls. I call Hazel and ask her to come and pick me up to take me to the doctors as I don't want to disturb Lucca while he's working and I'm still not cleared for driving. I give her the new code for the gates after our unexpected visitor the other night. She parks her silver Renault Clio beside mine, and I hear her squawking outside. I walk out to meet her, and she shakes her head, eyeing me up.

"Aye, aye, Captain. Reporting for duty." She salutes. "How's my little cub today? Wow, you brush up well, Roo, even in plain clothes you still look like a million dollars. So tell me, are you feeling better? Did you two talk? And is the love boat calm or is it still rocking?"

"Thanks … and I'm good. I feel so much better. We talked and worked it out eventually, and I've caught up on some sleep. He knows how I feel and I'm glad I got it off my chest." I smile and twirl the button on the sleeve of my blouse.

"Well that's a relief. I'm so glad you worked it out." She cuddles me, admires the front of the house, then focuses on the garden. "Are these your new cars, Roo? Bloody hell, you'll have your own helicopter next. How exciting is this? Right, let's have the tour of the castle. I'm so excited."

"I like your jeans. Do you think I should change?" I ask her. She's wearing tight, indigo denim jeans with a pink vest top and pink lipstick. I feel overdressed now for a trip to the doctor's.

"No, you look lovely," she replies, sashaying past me.

Doris and Lucca walk into the hall. She has really settled in and seems to be like Lucca's shadow. She even lies on the floor at the bottom of his desk in the study when he's working. He's in his sexy jeans and a tight, grey knit V-neck top. I smile because his top is actually the same colour as Doris's coat.

He kisses Hazel on both cheeks and lets Doris rampage out onto the front lawn. I hear Hazel apologise for slapping him, but he says he deserved it and she agrees. I expect there to be some hostility between them, but it's not too bad. I think that Hazel has made herself clear and Lucca respects her for taking such good care of me … an understanding of sorts.

"So you look as if you're bonding well with Doris," Hazel remarks, lifting an eyebrow. She is thinking the exact same thing as me; he has fallen for the dog despite what he says about her.

"I do not know if I would call it bonding as such. It's more like she does not give me a fucking minute's peace," Lucca mumbles back, raising his own eyebrow and causing me to give him an almighty scowl. I expected him to say that. He's in denial.

"Lucca, have you got time to show Hazel around? I need to call my mum before I go out," I ask.

"Yes, of course. Hazel, are you and Dominic coming over later?"

"We wouldn't miss it for the world. What should we bring?" She pulls her hair over one shoulder and runs her hand down the length then flicks it back over again. That's the thing about Hazel; once she's said her piece and got something off her chest, she moves on.

"Just your swim gear, and do not eat dinner. We will eat later. You are welcome to stay over," Lucca replies. I'm thankful that he's making an effort and not allowing our recent drama to create any added tension between them.

She rubs her hands with excitable anticipation and smiles at his gesture.

I warn Lucca that Hazel might throw the feathers out of the pillows and slide down the banister during the tour, taking my thoughts back to my first tour with Lucca.

Stair sex.

My new favourite.

He curls his lip at one side and flashes a smouldering glance. He's having his own memory of that tour and our mind-blowing stair sex. I'm blushing when I leave them to go into the lounge and call my mum.

I take a deep breath, wondering what sort of mood she'll be in.
"Mum ... It's me."
There is a long pause for a long time.
"Alexis, sweetheart, it's so good to hear your voice." Her voice is breaking, and I can hear the distant quiver behind it. "Your brother says you enjoyed your trip. I'm glad you had a good time. I've been desperate to hear all about it. I hope you were careful. Tell me ... were you careful?"
And there it is—the paranoia.
"Yes, of course I was careful. I was very safe. Hazel and I had an amazing time, the weather was lovely, the food was to die for, and we met some amazing, wonderful people."
"Oh, you met people? *Strangers?*" She's raising her voice.
Ouch.
I pick up a loose wave from my hair and twiddle it around my finger as I slump into the sofa, feeling exhausted already.
"Um ... Yes," I say flatly.
"Alexis Evangeline Robertson, you're hiding something from me, and I want to know what it is. I did not raise you to be dishonest with me. I love you, and I'm concerned about you. Please, baby girl, don't keep me closed out all the time. I hate it. We should be able to share things. What happened to you?" Panic in my mum's voice tells me she's hysterical with worry and distraught because she's imagining the worst.
"Before I'm honest with you, I want you to remain impartial and calm. Please, just trust me. I ... I want you to be happy for me."
I'm reluctant to tell her, but I have to.
"Alexis, tell me now. You're worrying me."
Damn, I knew it. She's going to freak out. Maybe I should have got Cameron to tell her after all. Here goes.
"Mum, I've fallen in love. I've met someone, someone very special whom I care a great deal for. I love him and he loves me." My fingers tighten and my chest pounds as I wait on her reaction.
There is a silent pause—a long, silent pause.
"Mum, did you hear me?"
"Yes."
"Well, are you going to ask me anything?" I sound like a young, naive girl seeking approval, but it's because I love her and respect her.
"You've met a man? Let me just get my head around this," she finally says.
"Yes, on holiday ... well, actually, I met him here first, but then ... well, never mind. But just so you know, he loves me unconditionally and takes wonderful care of me." I plump up the cushions beside me, lift my legs, tuck my feet underneath me, and sit on them.

"You're seeing someone? Like a boyfriend?" she deadpans.

I'm not sure if her meds are slowing her down, but she sure is taking a while to process this. She's in bloody denial. It is a lot for her to process. I've never had a boyfriend.

"Yes, his name is Lucca. He's very special to me, Mum, and I want you to meet him." I twirl my hair around my fingers again and nibble my bottom lip.

"Alexis, how could you? How could you put your trust into a complete stranger? You know how I feel about that. Does Cameron know? Do your grandparents know?"

She's furious but more than that, she sounds distraught at the concept I might not be safe. She will make herself sick being frantic and I worry that this will send her into an episode. Knowing she's agitated upsets me because I fully understand why she is, and there's not much I can do to change how she feels. Her fears will always be with her.

"Yes, they know, but I asked them not to bother you with this because I wanted to tell you first. Mum, please don't be angry with me. I've never felt better. I have had a new lease on life. Lucca is caring, attentive, generous, kind, and loving, and he understands me. He's helped me to feel alive and taught me things about myself and has been exceptionally patient." I speak softly and carefully. I'm pleading for her understanding with a certain edge of cautiousness in my cadence. Often when she's frantic, I sometimes need to mollycoddle her by tiptoeing around her. Sometimes it works, sometimes it doesn't.

I bring the back of my fingers to my mouth and wiggle them around nervously. This is not going well. I'd rather she was frantic than impassive because at least I would know what she was thinking.

"Mum, say something," I whimper as tears prick my eyes.

I'm hurt.

She's hurt.

I'm hurt because she's hurt.

"You always said you wanted the best for me, that you wanted me to be happy, and that you wanted my wings to spread. I finally have all these things, and you can't be happy for me. I just want you to trust my judgement and know that I would never put myself in an unsafe environment or relationship. You know that I'm sensible and I want you to know that it wasn't a rash decision; I went through more emotions than I care to tell you while I deliberated having this relationship." The lump lodged in my throat isn't moving. I struggle to breathe and swallow.

"If it makes you feel any better, Cameron and Hazel both adore Lucca, and Mr. Carlin has warmed to him," I continue through sharp sobs.

"I don't know what to make of all this. It's very sudden. You have always been cautious and then you saunter off to Italy and return with a stranger in the blink of an eye? Am I the only person seeing sense here? You are vulnerable and have a horrendous burden to carry. You don't just meet someone and have it all go away." Her voice is high-pitched because she's so alarmed, by the time she finishes, she is breaking and tears are going to follow. I know it.

I know that only too well.

"It will never go away, Mum, I know that. Lucca has helped me in ways other people couldn't. We are very close, and I love him. He knows of my past and is understanding and protective. Why can't you believe me? If it were Cameron, you wouldn't question it." I'm restless and agitated; I uncurl my legs from under me, stretch, then kick a cushion onto the floor.

"That's different, and you know it. He's not broken like you are."

But he is, in other ways, she is just clouded because Cameron appears stronger. Why does she need to make me feel worse than I already do?

"Are you sleeping with him?" She sounds accusatory and I know she's being exceptionally judgemental before I even answer.

Oh God, this is not a question I want to answer. "Yes, I'm twenty-six years old, and we love each other." I blush because as I've never had a relationship. I've never had to have this chat with her before.

"Oh for goodness sake, you know how I feel about that. I'm absolutely shocked. Next, you'll be telling me you are running off to get married. I'm praying that you're having sex through choice and that you're not being forced. God, this is hard to understand. You're not making this easy for me. I'm concerned and I don't want you to get used or hurt." I hear her breath falter. She sounds scared, as if she's terrified for me. The possibilities she has already made up in her mind will be causing her much distress.

My stomach catapults and drops with a sudden jerk to the cave of tormented demons. I have always thought I've put her feelings first, knowing what sort of dark place she fights so hard to surface from. And it's apparently all right for Cameron to fuck every woman in the universe.

She's irrational.

I don't know what to say, so I am silent.

"Alexis, you're not telling me everything …. Oh God, please don't tell me what I think you're about to say." I can hear her voice break.

She has started crying.

Some of her crying fits last for hours, and in cases in the past, she's been sedated. I hope I've not brought that on for her sake. I hate that I'm hurting her. She has had so much hurt in her life, and she doesn't need more, but I owe her honesty.

"Mum, Lucca proposed to me. He has asked me to be his wife, and I said yes. I want to be his wife, not right away, but sometime in the future. He is the one for me. I think fate brought us together, and I need you to trust me and respect my wishes. I want this more than anything else. Grandpa is happy for me. Please, can you give me your blessing?" I plead as unruly tears cascade down my cheeks.

"I'm annoyed your grandpa is keeping secrets from me." She sobs.

"I asked him not to tell you."

"Have you completely thought this through? Do you know what you are doing? I don't know what to say." Her tone is cold and sharp through her snivelling.

"Yes, of course I do. Mum, you will love him, I promise."

I hear her grunt and scoff. "So you're actually considering this?" My stomach tweaks, because the more she asks with this doubtful tone, the more I feel.

"Where does he live and what age is he?" She croaks this time, lowering her voice with a disconcerting pity in it. Whether she likes it or not, it's happening and the more she knows the better.

"Bothwell. He has various businesses in Scotland and throughout Europe. He's very successful and has a wonderful family in Scotland and Tuscany. I've met some of his family. They're warm, kind, loving ... very hospitable and caring. He's thirty-two years old. He has two brothers and a sister." Instantly, I regret talking about his assets and his age.

"You have already met his family? It all seems a little fast, and I know how you can be in the company of strangers. I can't imagine how you can be comfortable around a new family you barely know. And I never thought you would be one to fall for someone with money. That's not you, and you know it. I taught you to appreciate life and the smaller things we all take for granted. If you're struggling financially, your grandparents and I will help you. How could you give up your principles and respect and let yourself be used, especially after our history?"

Fucking history!

Does she honestly think that I've lost respect for myself, where I came from, and my goddamn past? Does she think I have entered into this relationship lightly? Yes, she knows me, and she's right about how I would normally act in the company of strangers, but she wasn't there in Tuscany, she hasn't experienced what I have. How can I explain that it doesn't matter if it were five minutes, weeks, months, or years? It felt right. It feels right.

Lucca and his family gave me something I've never had before, the ability to trust and feel loved by people who are outside of my immediate family and small group of friends. They have given me new love and new hope. The thought of my mum never understanding or accepting that Lucca and his family will be part of my life now crushes me.

A knife has gone through my heart.

Twisted.

Severed.

Hacked.

"I'm overwhelmed that after years of avoiding contact with men, you have put your trust in the first man to woo you ... one man, and you seem to think you have it all figured out—life and love. All it takes is for one little thing to trigger your fears and you may become weak, making you even more vulnerable than you already are, therefore opening yourself to even more pain and heartache."

Mum's sobbing isn't helping. I've already felt pain, lots of it, but the love I feel is a million times stronger and it's worth it, to *feel* with Lucca.

My hot, wet tears running down my cheeks feel like blood. I am sure if I looked in the mirror I would see stained red cheeks, they're so raw.

"Is that what you think? That I'm so shallow and desperate that I'm crying out for money because money will take my fears, history, and demons away? Do you not think someone might be interested in me? Do you not think someone is capable of loving me for who I am? *And* I know I have a lot to learn and this is all new. It will take time. I never professed to be an expert. I just said that I love Lucca and he loves me." Taking umbrage, I raise my voice while crying. Jumping up from the sofa, I begin pacing around the room.

Angry.

Insulted.

Sickened.

"You're very beautiful, Alexis. I just don't want you to be taken advantage of. I know you're an adult and can make decisions, but I imagine a serious relationship would take a lot of work and commitment gradually over time. I just feel that it's too soon for you to be agreeing to marry a man who doesn't have the full insight into your past. It had taken Casey years before she truly understood you. Men are not as intuitive as women, and it could take even longer for Lucca to accept you. "

She deepens the wound.

HE HAS ACCEPTED ME!

"Lucca is intuitive. He listens. He's honest, compassionate, and encouraging. He might never *get me,* but he knows enough. I have shared more with him in such a small amount of time than I have with anyone else, and he keeps me focused. It's not been all rosy in the garden either. We've had differences of opinions and grievances, but we love each other that much that we are patient and forgiving, and more importantly, Lucca loves me through my insecurities and anxiousness. I ... can't explain it." I sigh and walk towards the window and watch Doris galloping around on the front lawn then turn around and lean against the windowsill.

Mum obviously wants what's best for me; she always does, but the fact that she's never had a *normal*, loving relationship doesn't put her in the best position to give relationship advice. I accept that it's hard for her to comprehend that I've gotten engaged very quickly, but she's never experienced the emotions I have experienced with Lucca so far. How do I say this without being disrespectful?

"Okay, fine, you've experienced a lovers tiff, but that doesn't stand for anything. Does he know about your nightmares? Does he know about the extent of your abuse?" She weeps and I imagine she's hugging her knees into her chest and nervously twirling her earrings around in her ears. That's what she tends to do when she's upset or challenged.

"Yes. He helps me when I have nightmares. He holds me in a way that calms me, and he always says the right thing." I sigh and tap my finger against the windowsill.

"Hmmm, well he would say the right things if he's after sex. Put yourself in my shoes. I'm all this way away and you tell me this, and I have visions of you being used. I've never heard of anybody falling in love so quickly and being so trusting, even without the burdens you carry. Your Aunt Eva and Uncle Jim fell in love fairly quickly, but they had a long courtship beforehand."

I'm verging on becoming furious. She doesn't get it.

"Of course you don't understand. You've never fallen in love, and you can't compare me to my aunt Eva; that was years ago. Things are different nowadays. I guess you need to trust me, but I'm sure when you meet Lucca and see both of us together, you'll change your mind." I press my thumb at my temple and rub in circles feeling the start of a headache.

"I don't need to have loved. I'm your mother. I know what's best for you." Her voice is louder, and I now imagine her pacing the floor because she sounds breathless.

I'm bypassing furious and going straight to blazing hot.

"Well, maybe if you had experienced love before, you would be a little more open-minded. You don't know what I'm feeling or what Lucca feels for me, and until you experience it yourself, maybe you shouldn't judge." I retaliate, practically shouting.

I'm way out of line.

She has every right to be disappointed in me now. That was uncalled for. My heart is racing, my head is throbbing, and I'm fit to explode with the fire that's burning me inside.

"I'm sorry, sweetheart, please forgive me. I love you, please calm down because you're making me sick with worry, and I didn't mean for that to sound the way it did. I just reacted to the shock and it's the first thing that made sense to me. "

She's pleading irrationally to me while crying uncontrollably, and I'm despicable for what I said to her. I don't want another lecture, and I most certainly don't want to hurt her anymore with my feistiness.

Fuck!

File E for erase. Erase those horrible words I just said to her.

"No, I'm sorry, Mum. I can't do this right now. I need space." I hang up on her and fire my phone across the lounge, smashing it to pieces against the fireplace.

Lucca and Hazel are in the doorway watching me. They must have heard me raising my voice so furiously, but they don't say anything. My head throbs and my chest hurts.

Sharp.

Stabbing.

Slicing.

I stare at my shattered phone, dumbfounded that I'd smashed it in anger. I scramble to my feet and run out of the room and straight upstairs to the suite.

"Lexi, wait!" Lucca yells after me.

I run into the bathroom and open my supply cabinet, searching for anxiolytics to control my anxiety attack. I can't find them anywhere, which only adds to my despair as I know I'm not going to be able to control this one without them.

I dump all the products into the sink, then lift a toilet bag that I brought from my house. I crash my hand into it, searching through my makeup and feeling for a packet of pills—any pills.

"Shit!" A sharp sting slices at my finger. I've cut my finger on a razor blade.

I turn Lucca's tap on at the secondary basin then run my finger under it, washing the blood away while my other hand presses into my chest. Lucca walks into the bathroom.

"Christ, Lexi, let me see." He lifts up my hand and shakes his head then grabs a towel and wraps it around the cut, putting pressure on it. "What is going on? What are you looking for?"

"She's looking for her beta blockers," Hazel answers, standing at the bathroom door.

I drop my head, embarrassed, while I take heavy breaths through my nostrils. Gasping for air I manage to say, "Skip, can you

... grab my ... clutch bag? It's on ...the island in the ... dressing room."

"Sure."

"Come here." He holds me to his chest, stroking my hair and rocking me side to side, keeping a grip on the towel at my fingers. "Breathe, just hold me and breathe," he whispers to my ear.

The lump lodging my throat is still there, but I'm airing my lungs with huge, slow breaths from my nostrils. After ten minutes, he has calmed me slightly, so he takes my hand and leads me to the bed.

I sit on the end as he strokes his fingers across my eyebrow, then trails a wavy curl behind my ear. He looks pained and confused, and I know he wants an explanation, but he doesn't ask. Lucca lifts the towel off my finger and returns from the bathroom with a Band-Aid.

She returns with the clutch and some water from the bathroom, and I shake nervously while I open and search through it for the pills. I find some in the zip compartment. Shakily, I pop one onto my tongue and sip the water. Hazel watches me tapping her middle finger on her chin then sits down in front of me on the carpet, crossing her legs.

"So what did Grace say to freak you out? Do you want to talk about it?" Hazel asks, rubbing my knee. I don't want to hide it from them, but I can't be fully honest with Lucca. I don't want to hurt him.

"I put her in an episode, I think," I mutter, looking down at the glass of water.

"Why?" Hazel asks, tapping her middle finger on her chin again.

"I told her about Lucca, and she wasn't exactly thrilled," I choke. Lucca runs his hands through his hair. "I'm sorry, Lucca." I'm struggling to make eye contact.

"Baby, do not be sorry. She is your mother. It would be alarming if she were not concerned about you. It is her job to protect you and want what is best for you. I can understand why she would be worried." He strokes my arm then lightly brushes my cheek with his thumb.

God, I love him.

"I tried to explain about our relationship, but she doesn't approve. I begged for her blessing and told her how happy I am. She said some things that really hurt me and I freaked." I drop my head and sigh.

"What did she say?" Lucca asks.

"It doesn't matter, just forget it. I'll let Cameron talk to her when she has calmed down, and then I'd better apologise. I might even call Casey and get her to call Mum and make sure she is okay." I shake my head, hating how I ended the phone call.

"It does matter. I cannot help if you do not confide in me. You cannot keep bottling things up." Lucca pinches his brow with his middle finger and thumb.

Hazel places her glass on a magazine on the bedside table. She shakes her head at Lucca, giving him an annoyed look. "Lucca, can you call Cameron and tell him Lexi's phone is out of action in case he tries to get her and tell him to call Casey and get her to call Grace?"

"Okay, sure, I will be back in a minute. Do you girls need anything?" I shake my head, and Hazel gives him a warm, appreciative smile, silently thanking him. I'm so glad she is here today to talk with me.

Once Lucca has reluctantly left the suite, Hazel bombards me. "Right, dish," she orders.

I spill.

"I don't want to offend or upset Lucca, so let's just leave it."

She opens her mouth then closes, then reopens it again to voice her opinion.

"Spit it out, Skip."

Tilting her head, Hazel stares upward to the ceiling while thinking, then meets my eyes. "She loves you. She's hurt that you don't confide in her, and she doesn't want you rushing into anything or getting hurt further. I understand her concerns, but I do think she's far off the mark with the gold digging. We all know that was never in the equation, and that you have no control over Lucca spoiling you. But you're also the most grateful person I know, so don't believe that statement for one moment. No one else will. She also doesn't realise that you are capable and did actually fall in love quickly. I promise she'll be feeling worse than you right now. But, Lex, she loves you, we all do." She leans over to hug me.

"Do you really think so?" I ask.

"I know so." Once we have finished our chat and she has helped me see reason and calmed me, she jumps up.

"Now, get yourself sorted so I can take you out. You're not sitting in here all day feeling like shit. Plus, I thought I could take you out in your new wheels since you're not driving yet." She beams at me trying to distract me.

Not a bloody chance.

"No, I don't want to use the new cars just now. Can we just go in yours?"

Hazel pouts. "Ahhh, spoil sport. Okay, if you really don't want to, but I think you're antagonising over her comments and I'd love to see you accept these changes in your life and enjoy your gifts. I'm sure Lucca would want you to use them, because he only wants to make you happy."

"He does make me happy. After my mum's comments, I just feel uneasy about flashing around town like the next trophy wife, especially since our relationship is still new."

Hazel says she will make tea so I get up and walk through to the dressing room. I unzip my trousers and blouse and hang them up, take the diamond earrings out, remove my Cartier diamond watch, then remove the diamond pendant from around my neck. I place them inside the safe and find an old pair of skinny denim jeans and a black T-shirt and tie my hair up.

"Why have you changed?" Lucca asks when I return to the bedroom.

"Because I'm going to the doctors and running errands, so jeans are more suitable," I reply.

He opens his mouth to say something, but Hazel grasps his arm, digging her fingers into his skin and intercepting his comment. "Well, thank goodness. I for one am pleased you now look casual because I hate walking around with you all glam like you have just stepped off a private yacht."

Lucca is shocked at Hazel, but I know exactly what she's trying to do. "Nice try." I scowl at her.

"What? I'm serious, you look like a sack of old potatoes, Roo, but whatever makes you comfortable. Right, shall we go?" she confidently chirps before sauntering downstairs.

"What was that all about?" Lucca asks as he wraps his arms around my waist.

"It's Hazel's reverse psychology. She thinks I'm in here changing outfits again, but I'm not, not today." I settle my head onto his chest.

"You are really hurting, I can tell, and if you do not want to talk about it just now that is fine, but promise me we can talk about this later. I hate seeing you like this." He searches my eyes, then circles my nose with his.

"Okay." I sigh.

"Just so you know, you look sexy and smoking hot in those jeans. Your ass is fucking amazing. Of course, I would rather see you naked, but it just adds to the fun when I have to slide them down your legs. You are beautiful in whatever you wear." He lifts my chin and kisses my lips.

"Thank you." I nibble his bottom lip.

He studies me. "Where is all your jewellery? Why have you taken it all off?"

"I'm sorry, I just—"

"Your mother thinks you are with me for my money, does she not? Is that why you are so upset and stripping everything off? You are worried about what people think?"

God, he's so intuitive.

I don't say anything. I just inhale his sexy, lingering musky aftershave snuggled into his neck.

"You do not need to answer … I know I am right, but this changes nothing. I love you and you love me, and we both know how deep our love is. One of the many reasons why I love you is because you are so down to earth, sincere, and appreciative. It is refreshing. I have never found anyone like you, and when I met you, I knew I had to have you. I would give my last penny to you, but it is not about that. I wanted to give you my love, trust, protection, and care. I will just need to convince your mother of that too."

He pauses staring at my eyes.

"I hate to think others see me as a gold digger, and now I feel guilty and unsettled, as if I don't deserve you. It makes sense that people will have opinions on our relationship and of me, but it makes me agitated. I'm sure everyone has a lot to say about me moving in here so quickly too," I confess.

"I could not give a flying fuck what anyone else thinks. I tell you this repeatedly. If I want to spoil you with gifts, I will because I can. If I want to fuck you senseless, I will because I can. If I want to romance you and make love to you all fucking night, I will because I can. I will love, cherish, and protect you because I can." He smiles confidently, showing me his dimple.

He makes me feel worthy.

Because … he can.

"I love you, I love you so much. I love everything you do for me, Lucca, but especially this." I place my hand on his heart and stare at him with nothing but love.

Smiling, he cups my ass. "Do you feel better? I do not want this phone call to affect our relationship."

Wrapping my arms around his neck, I entwine my fingers in his hair and tilt my head against his cheek. "It won't, I promise. She'll calm down, and I know when she meets you she'll fall in love with you. It's just that I said some pretty horrible things to her, but I didn't mean any of it and now I feel guilty."

"You were angry. You can apologise, and we will spend as much time with her as possible on our visit. She can even come here and stay with us for as long as you want." He thrusts his evident erection against me and grips my ass, lifting my leg up to hang around his hips.

"You would do that for me? It wouldn't be easy, and it might be a strain on us."

"It will only be a strain if you let it. We will work it out. She will need to learn to trust me, then I am sure she will give us her blessing. Now, can I slide those tight, cock teasing jeans off your ass and down those luscious, long legs?"

I giggle. "You can't. Hazel is downstairs waiting on me."

He lifts my other leg up around his waist, holds one hand in my hair, and carries me to the bed, laying me down. He steps back, looking down at me with hunger in his eyes. I'm devouring his greed and lust because I want him so desperately, especially after he helps me reason and think straight. I'm gone.

Folded, crumbled, and melted.

I stretch my hand to his chest, clenching his top, then pull him down on top of me.

"Since you have asked, you are getting," he growls sexily. He takes my T-shirt off and unbuttons my jeans in a flash, then in quick time has my bra and panties off. I'm stripped and naked for him again. He walks away, leaving me on the bed.

"Well, don't just leave me like this," I moan.

He returns from the dressing room with my diamond jewellery. "I love seeing you naked, but I also love to see this sparkle on you, so will you put these back on for me?" He leans over, teasing my nipple with his tongue.

He has never told me about the experience that incited his obsession with diamonds. In Tuscany all he told me was that they saved his life and that they remind him he's alive, and then something cryptic about thinking I'm angelic and by wearing them it makes him feel alive and he wants to give me light. I know if he wanted to tell me more, he would. I respect that we both share things that we find hard to talk about. I do think his obsession for extravagant gems is excessive but he sees it as light as opposed to the value of the stone.

"You don't play fair," I protest seductively.

My naked body and jewels make sparkly love to my Italian God.

Chapter 9: Revelations

After our spontaneous rendezvous confirming our love, I shower quickly, throw my black blouse back on this time, and pair it with my jeans then tie my hair in a wavy ponytail. He smacks my ass and smiles as I walk past.

"Nice blouse. You look beautiful. This is exactly how you looked when I first saw you in the clinic. It reminds me of that day. You are stunning, baby. God ... we have come a long way since then. Are you feeling better?" The blouse paired with jeans does resemble my outfit that day, which makes me smile. Although, this blouse is somewhat more expensive.

"Yes, I do. Thank you for listening and for making me feel special." Smiling, I wrap my arms around his waist.

I lean over and kiss him contently then look for Hazel. She's sprawled out on a lounger next to the pool with an orange juice and one of Rose's cinnamon buns. It's not like her to eat sugary carbs in the middle of the day.

"Oh, look who's back. Our next top model. My job here is done." She smacks her lips and rubs her hands together.

"Don't be a smartass. Lucca actually made me see sense, so don't think about taking the credit this time, Skippy." I lift my chin and tilt my head.

"Really? More like made you see stars. You, missy, have just been seen to, but whatever works for you." She giggles.

"Hazel!" I yell, mortified. "How do you know that?" I soften my tone, furrowing my brow, now very serious.

"You're rosy and you have that glow about you. Bless your little paws." She taps her middle finger against her chin with a smug smile on her face.

Lust glow.

"Bless my what? What are you talking about?" I wrinkle my nose, trying to work her out.

"Instead of cotton socks, paws. You know, my little cub would have paws." She takes another bite of her sticky bun. I giggle watching her. She really does make me laugh and it's not intentional either.

"Joey ... baby kangaroo," I correct her, "... I think you're in a little carb coma."

"Hmmm, I needed to release some endorphins. We're not as lucky as you to have around-the-clock sex fests. I've not had any in three days! Three days! It's sacrilege." She slaps her hand on her forehead in an Oscar-winning performance.

As much as my confidence is growing with Lucca in our sexy, heat of the moment fun, I still feel a little prudish and get embarrassed talking out loud about sex, even with Hazel.

"Oh, those cinnamon buns you're eating? Six hundred and fifty calories, three cups of sugar, twenty-one grams of fat. Shall we go?" I say, diverging from the sex chat. I never sound as convincing as her when I try and say stuff like this, but it has worked.

She nearly chokes on her last bite and spits it out into her hand in shock, but I've shut her up. For now. I turn on my heels and stroll off, leaving her dwelling on that thought.

I drop in on Mr. Carlin and check his fridge and freezer. I meet Julie, his new home help, and get to the bottom of this diabetes he's been rambling on about. I like Julie. She's sweet and has an adequate level of patience, which is necessary when dealing with Mr. Carlin.

I get him up and give him some exercises to do, then open his mail, check on his washing, and switch off the heating. I suspect this is why he likes Julie; she doesn't switch it off.

It's bloody stifling.

I leave Mr. Carlin and Julie to continue with their game of backgammon. It actually makes me a little envious she is spending quality time with him and I'm not. I go back to my own house next door and open my mail. It feels melancholy and strange; it's surreal not living here. I'm rudely awakened when I see the state the kitchen is in. Shaking my head, I march through to Hazel and give her a scolding. I've been away a few days, and she has turned my house upside down. I pick up my mail and have some words about her lack of housekeeping in the car.

Hazel drops me at my doctor's surgery then goes to the supermarket while I attend my appointment. I pick up a magazine in the waiting area and flip through, focusing on the recipe pages.

"Lexi Robertson," the receptionist calls.

I place the magazine down, and as I walk towards the door, I feel my skin shiver, so I turn briefly and tremble from head to toe, erecting my spine.

There is no mistaking the person across my peripheral vision.

Real.

Haunting me.

Oh God, I think I might pass out.

I trail my eyes from the black footwear, all the way up to a pair of ripped jeans and a fitted white T-shirt. The olive skin, unruly, blonde-streaked hair, and familiar sickening scent. I settle on uninviting green eyes.

Sly.

Sleazy.

Demeaning.

I want to run.

"Miss Robertson, this way please," my doctor impatiently says, holding the door for me.

The eyes slowly study me, crawling across my skin, undressing me and peeling me to the raw nerve. Those eyes are unknowing at first but are now clearly recognising me. A sly smile forms across the wet lips. I grit my teeth, press my lips, and raise my brow.

I turn, dazed, and walk behind my doctor. I rub my sweaty palms, chew the inside of my mouth, and try to mask my irrational breathing.

"Lexi, what can I do for you today? Are you feeling okay? Would you like some water?" Dr. Harvey asks.

Refusing the water, I stutter and stammer, but eventually I explain my recent wrist surgery in Tuscany. She checks my notes, nods, and smiles, acknowledging my injury and treatment. I ask for more painkillers and for another prescription of my anti-anxiety tablets and anti-inflammatories. After she scribbles down my prescription, she asks if there is anything else.

"Yes, I would like a more permanent form of contraception. I'm in a relationship and would like something reliable and long term," I say nervously.

"Okay, what do you have in mind?" she asks while she looks at my medical history on her software.

"I thought about the implant or Depo-Provera injection." She thoroughly goes through the benefits and side effects of both options. "Hmmm, I don't know."

"Have you considered the Mirena coil?" She goes on to explain the effectiveness of it. The description makes it sound desirable, and knowing it lasts for five years is an added bonus.

Doctor Harvey is a wise, young doctor. She took over from the retired Doctor Foster. I like her. She's patient, very knowledgeable, and compassionate, and she is sincere. She also is very hands-on, enthusiastic, and eager, whereas Doctor Foster was beginning to be absentminded in the last year before her retirement.

"When was the first day of your last period?"

I think back, counting in my head. "The thirtieth of May," I add.

"Have you been sexually active?"

"Yes." *Very much so.*

"Have you been taking your pill correctly?"

"Yes."

"So your period's due in a week if you've been regular. If you opt for the implant or coil, we'll need to refer you to the family planning clinic because we don't do it here. I can call and ask for an appointment if it's more convenient for you," she gestures.

"Yes, thank you. I'd appreciate an appointment."

She secures me a cancellation appointment late on Monday, asks about my wrist fracture, and surprises by telling me she owns a holiday home in Sienna, not far from where I vacationed. Leaving with my prescription note, I walk past the doctor's private offices and press the push bar to open the emergency exit. I'm not walking back through the waiting room to face unwelcome demons.

Hazel is not back yet, and I don't have my phone. Looking for somewhere to take shelter, I cross the road, enter the church, and lurk around the foyer as I watch behind the teak doorframe for her car passing.

It feels like hours, although seconds have passed.

"Lexi, what a pleasant surprise. I haven't seen you at service recently, is everything all right? How is your family?" It's the sweet words of Ms. Morrison, our local Minister. She is petite, cheery, and has the warmest smile. She is always welcoming and caring every time I come across her.

Ms. Morrison is very good friends with Cathy, my grandparents' minister, who is close to my family and was my local minister growing up in Aberdeen before she moved on to Grantown-On-Spey in Morayshire.

"Very well, Ms. Morrison, thank you for asking. I'm actually planning on going up north soon for a visit," I say, staring at her crucifix chain hanging from her neck. It's traditional yellow gold but has a mother of pearl in the centre. I've always admired it, and I've never seen her without it.

"Excellent. Will you be popping in to visit Cathy?" she asks with enthusiasm.

"Um ... well, yes, if you'd like me to."

"If it's not too much trouble, I'd appreciate it if you could deliver something from me."

She takes my hand and walks me through the church's right wing aisle, past the altar, to her office. The last time I was in this office was Eleanor's funeral, but it looks different, rearranged perhaps. She rummages in a drawer and lifts out a sealed jiffy bag. Placing it in my hand, she smiles.

"You're a little treasure. Lexi love, God is with you always," she says sincerely.

"I'll deliver it to Cathy for you, no problem." I smile sweetly and nod my head.

"Thank you, Lexi."

"Actually, I have something I'd like to speak to you about if you have time."

She always has time.

"Please sit and talk to me. I always have time for you."

I shift in my seat and stare at her communion service card for Sunday and some handcrafted cards made by the Sunday school children.

"I apologise for not being at church. I was travelling, and I ... um, I met someone and got engaged." I clasp my hands in my lap and look around her office admiring the changes she's made.

"I noticed your ring, but it's not my place to pry. Congratulations, that's delightful news." Her eyes widen as a genuine smile graces her face.

"I ... I've already moved in with him, and my mother isn't happy with my engagement. I love him, love him unconditionally, and I know he loves me, but I feel an overwhelming feeling of guilt as if I'm doing something wrong because my mother is disappointed in me. Ms. Morrison ... are you disappointed in me? *Is God disappointed in me?*" I whisper.

Ms. Morrison removes her gold spectacles from her face, leaving them hang around her neck attached to a neck chain, then tucks her short, brown bob behind her ears. She sits upright in her chair, pulling her shoulders back, and leans forward clasping her hands over the desk.

"Of course I'm not. I would never judge, nor would God, and you should know that. You're the same loving girl who deserves some happiness. I'm sure you're being sensible, and as much as the church has mixed views on the matter, it's changed. I'm aware of how you young ones move quickly before marriage, and it's not my place to comment. All I would advise is to do what you instinctively feel is right, and to be honest to your loved ones and to yourself. Be sensible and keep your faith, Lexi, it's very important. God will guide you, follow the light."

That's exactly what I'm following.

Ms. Morrison never remarried after her husband passed away and is devoted entirely to God. I know she talks from the heart and is extremely wise.

She places her hand over mine, and I think about Lucca and his "Luminara," his diamonds and his light coaxing me from my darkness. I smile appreciatively.

"Do I know the young gentleman? Is he local?" she asks.

"I'm not sure, but he does live locally. His name is Lucca Caruso," I softly say and blush.

She smiles contently. "Well, Lexi, that's a gentleman you do not want to let go of, and if anyone has light, it's him. He will be very good for you. He, too, is very spiritual and such a wonderful family. They attend St. John the Baptist Chapel but are heavily involved with supporting the local church's various charities. I'm thrilled for you."

I thank her for her kind words and promise to deliver her parcel.

"Tell Lucca we're all very grateful for his help at Christmas. God blesses him."

Exiting the church, I rush into the car. Hazel is beeping frantically as she parked on double yellow lines since the surgery car park was full. On the way to Bistro & Bake where we are meeting Lucy for a light lunch I tell her about my unpleasant discovery in the doctor's which gets Hazel all fired up. She wants to drive back over there and go marching in to read the riot act, but I ask her not to.

Lucy is sitting outside on the terrace, looking at a menu. She's wearing a beautiful, red sundress, tan belt, and tan wedges. She has her rich black hair styled with smart sunglasses sitting on top. I'm baffled as to why she has never met the right partner yet.

She is gorgeous, has the looks of a timeless movie star. Her dark lashes are thick and curled, and she always has red lipstick enhancing her thick, luscious lips.

"Ladybug, how are you, my darlin'?" I kiss her and notice her amazing emerald eyes have lost their sparkle.

"I'm okay. You look positively beautiful as always," she says, although there isn't a lot of enthusiasm in her voice. Hazel throws her arm around her and instantly detects Lucy is upset. She encourages her to sit and holds Lucy's hand on the table.

"We wanted to check that everything with you is okay. I'm worried about you. I noticed you were very quiet on Monday at my house, and I thought it might be due to Cameron's love triangle, which I'm sure was very obvious," I say sympathetically. I hate when my friends are feeling upset, I hurt along with them, but the topic is shamefully distracting me from my own hurt I've experienced today—another matter I've filed for later.

The waiter has placed the menu down in front of us before Lucy gets the chance to talk. We look at the menu, quickly ordering some salads, wine for Lucy and me, and water for Hazel because she's teaching a class later on.

"You remember when Rachel and Cameron went on a break in their relationship last summer? Well, Cameron and I ... we, um ..." She turns away, feeling uncomfortable.

"Oh my God, you never! I can't believe we didn't know. You kept that quiet!" Hazel blurts out completely shocked. I don't know how I feel about this, and I'm positive I might just kill Cameron for keeping secrets from me, especially regarding one of my best friends.

"It's not the first time. We had a thing briefly before he met Rachel, then we dated again when Rachel was in Paris. I don't need to tell you how I feel about him. I've always been besotted with him, you know that already, and our closeness last year just confirmed to me how badly I wanted him." My mouth is agape. Hazel reaches her hand over and taps my chin to close it. I'm shocked by her confession.

She goes on to tell us about dates they went on and how they went to a lodge up north for a weekend when Rachel was in Paris as he was on a break from her.

Processing.

I'm stunned.

When the food arrives, we barely acknowledge the waiter.

"So what happened?" I find my voice.

"We were having fun spending time together, and I thought Cameron had feelings for me, then Rachel came back from Paris and he became distant. He met me one night for dinner and told me we had to finish what we started because he couldn't give me what I wanted. He said what he had with Rachel worked for them both. Then Rachel had confessed that she'd hooked up with a boy in Paris and wanted to see him again and Cameron was desperate to get her back. I think he was jealous and wanted to reclaim her."

She takes a bite of her chicken, but I'm too shocked to move. "So, how did you feel? I can't believe you kept that to yourself for a full year. Why wouldn't you tell us?"

"Well, I was hurt and pining for him, so I went to London with work for training. I appreciated that it wouldn't be fair to Rachel if he continued a fling with me, so I learned to accept it. I thought one day Rachel would go away travelling again, and I thought she might fall in love with someone else, maybe the boy from Paris," she declares, trying to convince herself but certainly not convincing us.

"Do you love him?" Hazel asks.

"I think I did ... oh, I don't know." She takes a huge gulp of her wine, afraid to make eye contact with me.

"You're annoyed because he has completely different loyalties and morals while he cheats on Rachel with Anna." I sigh.

"Yes, they were on a break when he and I were together, but he's clearly cheating this time, and I'm hurt he hasn't given me a second thought and is acting this way." She begins to cry and my heart bleeds for her, seeing her upset like this.

I stand up and wrap my arms around her. "I had no idea. I'm sorry he's treated you this way. His behaviour is truly appalling. Lucy, please don't cry. You're going to ruin that pretty little face. Just so you know, I'm furious with him, and I do not approve. Apparently, they have an open relationship policy now—whatever that is—and see other people. Not that it makes this any easier."

This only makes her feel worse and she hiccups while sobbing. That was not my intention.

"Do you want me to have a word to him about this?" I add. I can't believe I didn't know about this.

"No, please don't. I don't want him thinking I'm a stalker. I feel as if I've been holding out for him, put my life on hold and look what's happened," she sobs, picking up a napkin and dabbing under her eyes graciously.

Hazel comments and leans over to take her hand. "Lucy, I can guarantee he's thinking with his dick and not his head. When he is with Anna, it's a bit of wild fun. I know Rachel has been unfaithful to him, so maybe you're right. Perhaps they will part ways. Remember Rachel is a lot younger than us so she's bound to want to see other guys, but you need to find your Mr. Right. You need to move on and stop feeling sorry for yourself. There is someone out there who will be perfect for you, you just haven't met him yet, so stop brooding over Cameron. He doesn't deserve you, because you, my friend, are beautiful, clever, funny, and kind."

I smile at her thanking her for giving her support. Lucy nods with understanding. I think she just needed someone else to tell her, even if it's not what she wants to hear.

By the time we change topics to discuss my new living situation with Lucca, my warm salad is cold, but I don't have much of an appetite after a catastrophic day. I play around with my food and don't eat much, but we do have another glass of cold wine.

"I think we need to have a girls' night out in town. We could all do with some dancing and fun. It's long overdue," Hazel declares.

"Yes, let's do it soon. We'll arrange with the darlin's," Lucy agrees. I give her a sympathetic smile. I know she's trying hard on the surface, but deep down, she is still hurting.

Chapter 10: Workout

I'm welcomed at the door by an energetic Doris. After petting and playing with her, I walk into the kitchen, place my bag down, boil the kettle, and look over my mail. There is a small rectangular box sitting on the counter and a note attached with my name.

Opening it, I discover a brand new smartphone. I drink my coffee as I fiddle about with the phone and instructions, but I need Lucca to help me out with it so I place it back on the counter and go and look for him.

He's in the gym pounding on the treadmill, focused and dripping in sweat. He is a vision of virile male. I admire his physique bulging through the fabric of his tight sport T-shirt.

Smoking hot.

He's turning me on as I watch how determined and effortless he works out, and how painstakingly handsome he is. I think the wine at lunch has made me slightly tipsy … *and horny.*

"Hey, baby, good day?" he pants through his pounding strides.

I can't speak.

I don't speak.

I'm entranced by his elite, competitive pace, brawny, muscled body, and his willpower. I shrug my shoulders with the half-hearted look and decide not to mention anything to him yet. I have things on my mind right now.

"You want to join me in the sauna and you can tell me all about it?" he asks as he reduces speed, preparing for his cool-down.

Yes, please! Maybe after I get what I want, I will tell him.

"What time is your family coming?" I ask.

"Not until six, so we have time. I need help with something, but I need you naked."

I raise my eyebrow and grin. "I wonder what that might be." I smile, coyly running my hand down the length of my ponytail.

He stops his treadmill, pours water over his head, and opens his mouth drinking some. The sight of him all sweaty with pure water splashing over his dark, glistening skin like this is so sensual and erotic.

I'm seduced before I touch him. I want to press my body into his, lick his perspiration from between his toned muscles, lace my fingers through his wet hair, and get sweaty.

With him.

On him.

Against him.

I lift the bottom of my ponytail and softly caress my mouth with my soft wavy hair, brushing slow, light teasing strokes across it. He puts a towel around the back of his neck and paces towards me with the predatory look, hunger blazing in his eyes.

"You have asked, baby…"

He presses his wet, hard body against my own, soaking my skin and dress with his perspiration.

"Hmmm, so what are you needing help with?" I tease.

He seductively strips my clothes off me. His eyes are gorging on me, ready to feast. He slides his sweaty hands down my back then settles to grip my ass. He forces his hips forward, moaning as he pushes his hard cock against me.

"It starts with this," he groans, strumming his tongue into my mouth. Flicking, swirling then sucking on my own tongue.

Teasing me with his delicious tongue in raw desperate kisses, he grabs my ponytail and tilts my head. I close my eyes, feeling tingling straight to my sex, a direct trigger to my most sensitive nerves. I'm throbbing and soaked for him already.

I slide my hand down his wet, fitted T-shirt, clenching his rock-hard muscles.

"Then it finishes with this."

He lifts my hand and places it on his weighty arousal. I clutch and massage his overstuffed package through his shorts, and he throws his head back.

"Fuck, baby."

I use my other hand, pulling on his drawstring of his sport shorts, coaxing them down, setting the waistband just across his hips. I run my finger along his happy trail, which leads to my desire, his desire, and where my tongue is about to follow.

"Thank you for the new phone. I have a gift of the day for you too." I drop to my knees on his gym mat.

"Fuck …" he growls.

I kiss just above his waistband, tasting the surfaced sodium and perspiration skimming his skin from his workout. Swirling my tongue, I slide my hands down his hips, yanking the shorts all the way down, freeing his erection.

His massive cock slaps against his stomach, pulsing and twitching for me. He bends over slightly and unhooks my bra, sliding it off my shoulders. My heavy breasts bounce free, and he instinctively reaches down to cup my breasts, but I lean back and sit on my heels.

"Nnm mnn." I shake my finger at him. "This is for you, and I'm in charge."

"Fuck, you are going to finish me before you even start if you keep talking hot shit like that." He grins.

I turn around on my knees and place my hands on his hips, sprawling my fingers on the smooth, taught skin of his butt and twisting him around so that my back is to the mirrored wall and he's facing it. I want him to see me pleasuring him.

"Fuck, I am getting a great view of your ass in that mirror," he groans.

"Uh huh," I tease, sashaying my ass and biting my lip. I lower myself, tantalising him with soft, sensual strokes of my tongue along the rigid shaft of his cock. Licking his creamy eagerness from the head, I massage and grip his hot sack. I take his full length in my mouth as I grasp his root tightly.

I clench my jaw around him, devouring and derailing him into an uncontrollable bliss, taking him further back to my throat. I wiggle my ass, shifting side to side and firming my knees into the mat. Circling my head, I glide him like a gear stick with a powerful drive causing him to expand in my mouth while I hollow my cheeks sucking him hard.

"Baby, so good. Let me fuck your tits."

I pull back, sitting upright, and he grabs his girth, banging and jamming between my heavy breasts, my cleavage suffocating his cock. Groaning with enjoyment, he thrusts back and forth, throwing his head backwards and pushing his hips forward. He clenches his teeth.

I manoeuvre with him, lifting and pushing forward. I place my hands on the side of my breasts and squeeze them together, encasing his cock completely with my ample cups.

"Jesus … fuck … Lexi …"

He fires me against the mirror, my back slamming against the cold sheen, then I feel the warmth of his ejaculated cream sliding between my breasts and over my sternum. Once he stills, I bend down and lick the engorged head of his cock, swallowing back his salty release. My heart racing, stomach fluttering, my sex is throbbing and pulsing with want. I need him so badly.

He slides down, kneeling in front of me and taking my mouth, biting ravenously at my bottom lip. "That was fucking amazing." His cheeks are flushed, and I find the pink tinge against his dark skin sexy as hell.

"I'm glad you liked it," I say before kissing his lips zealously.

"Baby, you ready for your workout?" he asks, pinching my budded nipples.

"Will I burn lots of calories?" I playfully ask, squirming under his touch.

"You will burn more than that. You are going need to get your blood sugar level up when I am finished with you," he says before biting my neck. I rub my clit against him with my ass pressed to the mirror.

He links his thumb under the strap of my thong and yanks hard, tearing it away from my hips. I jerk with the friction, and the lace fabric falls to the mat.

"Turn around, face the mirror. I want you to watch," he says. Erotic.

Eagerly, I turn around, still on my knees with Lucca on his knees pressed behind me. My body is sticky with his sperm smeared on me, which only adds to my sexed up tension and vibrating sensitivity in my core.

"Open your eyes," he orders.

I do and glance at my naked body, aroused and begging to be touched again, his massive broad shoulders and bronzed brawny muscles of his chest behind me. I'm so turned on by the sight of myself, the sight of him, and imagining what he's about to do to me.

"Do you see what I see?" He grabs both my breasts, kneading and teasing my peaked nipples in his hands as he smears his sperm over them. I lean my head to the side and rest on his shoulder, arching my back and moaning with long, drawn out sexual gratification while I watch him caress my breasts.

"Yes, touch me, Lucca, please," I beg, running my tongue under my top lip, pushing my ass against his cock.

"I will, but I want you to touch yourself first."

Sweet Jesus. I was not expecting that.

Oh my God. This is very dirty and completely out of my comfort zone. I want to please him and I need him desperately, so finding an inner courage, I try to forget my inhibitions. Placing my hand on my stomach, I pause. I stare at Lucca's eyes in the mirror, waiting for reassurance, guidance of some sort.

"Lexi, I promise you will like watching yourself, and it is such a fucking turn on for me. I want you to know how I feel about you. Imagine it is me touching you." He teases me by brushing his thumb across my navel.

I look at my big, chocolate-brown eyes, my perky nipples, large, sticky breasts, and flat stomach down to my mound. I wrap my hand around my back to grip his semi-erect cock, then with my other, I trail my hand down, barely touching myself.

"Touch ... for me," he rasps.

I slide my hand, cupping my sex, then move my fingers around, sliding over my wet cleft and stimulate my clitoris, all while watching myself in the mirror and stroking Lucca at the same time. I can't believe this siren has taken over my body. I think I like her.

He's right. I'm helplessly turned on.

"That is it, baby. Imagine it is my tongue sucking that sweet fucking pussy."

I feel dirty, but I'm so stimulated that I want to do this and his dirty words are adding to my arousal. I find it insanely erotic.

"Sexy as fuck ... Jesus, keep going, baby, you are hot. I am trying so hard to refrain from touching you right now because I want you to experience this. It is doing crazy fucking things to me, baby, watching you," he says, towering over my shoulders.

I feel as if I'm starring in a pornographic movie—sexed up and horny as hell.

"Fuck your fingers," he demands.

I stroke, rub, then push my fingers inside my reverberating entrance, causing Lucca to gasp at the vision. I hunch forward, then draw myself back, exhaling seductive, quiet whimpers. With my fingers encased in the heat of pulsing muscles, I torture myself with the same technique Lucca would use, albeit it's not as deep, then fall forward, freeing my grip from his cock.

"Lucca, I want you. Please, touch me," I plead.

He pulls my shoulders back towards his chest and trails his hands from my breasts down towards my begging sex, then pulls my wrist. He lifts my hands and sucks my fingers, licking my juices.

Oh my God.

I'm nearly combusting with the sight of his suggestive gesture. I can't wait. I grab his hand and place it between my legs, then move my knees further spreading them wider.

With his expertise, he has a couple of fingers in me with his thumb strumming my clit. I toss my head back but keep my eyes open and watch as I chew the inside of my cheek. I smash towards the heel of his hand, and it's only seconds before I cry out and buckle in spasms under his magnificent caress.

I push forward and back, banging my ass against his hard erection. Teasing my breasts and puckered nipples, I thrash with erogenous pleasure, crying out his name. I continue to quake in tremors when he removes his fingers, sliding my arousal over my sleek folds.

He sits back on his ass, adjusting his legs so that they are at either side of me, his legs bent and feet touching the mirror. He lifts me up. "That was unreal. Sit back on me and stretch your legs to the front," he demands. "I want you to watch your sweet pussy when I fuck you. I want you to see when your sexy pussy becomes swollen and milks me."

Holy shit.

My feet touch the mirror, my legs widely parted, and I get a full view of my throbbing, pink sex. He picks me up and slams me down onto his huge hard-on, filling me to my core. He leans back on his elbows, straining his hips up and pulling me up and down on him. It's a similar position to the make-up sex in the bath, except I can see his cock ramming into me, his sack tightening. We're exposed, and it's raunchy as hell. I press my feet on the mirror for support then slide back up and down, thrusting, grinding, and compounding his rock solid cock in the heat of my sex.

It's too much.

It's not enough.

I need more.

I can't take more.

Intense.

Erotic.

Inconceivable.

"Baby, watch me ride you, feel me pump you. Fuck, I need to pound you senseless ... tell me what you see." He groans. "You are my eyes, baby, tell me," he demands between grunts and breathless gnarls. After pleasuring myself in front of him, telling him what I see doesn't faze me. I'm excited to say the words because I know what it's doing to him, what it's doing to me.

"Your cock, hard and big, slamming into me. It's enraged!" I bawl when another forceful pound shafts me.

"What does your pussy look like?"

"It's swollen, pink, pulsing ... I'm so nearly there. Fuck, holy shit!" The sounds of these words coming out of my mouth is enough to send me into a splintering orgasm. It's seconds until I scream and scream as I detonate into an astonishing, heady explosion.

He roars deep in his throat, stiffening, powerfully firing up into me and filling me with his release. Blazing wet heat in my sheath, he sprays my insides then collapses. My back smashes against his chest.

Spent.

Impassioned.

Sensitive.

Blissful.

"Doc, are you okay?"

"Mmmm," I mumble.

"Christ, Lexi, that was unbelievable. I love you." His arms wrap around me, hugging me tightly across my chest as we get our breath back to a steady rhythm. He kisses the side of my head over and over. "I will need to send you away for lunch more often if that is how horny you come back to me."

My new confidence today maybe stems from Lucca helping me earlier when I fretted about my phone call with my mum, the wine at lunch, or running into a face I'd rather forget at the doctor's. It's perhaps all three and I feel very satisfied I experienced this with Lucca today.

I feel cherished.

"Uh huh," I softly whisper. He kisses my temple, and my eyes close in my post-coital glow. I'm worried I'll spin in a daze when my eyes finally open.

Once he's upright and has peeled his sweaty back from the soft mat, he brings me into the showers outside the pool area and washes our lovemaking fluids away. He grabs fresh towels and carries me past the pool into the sauna.

Sitting with his back to the wooden wall on the bench, he pulls me into his chest, placing a towel underneath me and wrapping me with his thick, muscular arms. I inhale the hot, dry heat through my nostrils at first, then realise it's burning me, so I open my mouth. I'm languid and limp as I relax against Lucca's body.

"That was amazing, Lucca. I'm so exhausted, but in a nice way." I trail my fingers gently over his hands and arms.

He kisses my head. "I was worried, you were so quiet."

"I loved it. My body is still trembling." I sigh with contentment.

"Good, I fucking loved it too. It just keeps getting better, baby. I wanted you to see just how sexy and hot you are. Jesus, that image will stay with me forever. We will definitely be having more mirror sex." He caresses his thumbs along my arms and chest.

Mirror sex.

My new favourite.

"So can we chat now?" I ask, because I got what I wanted and I'm ready to talk. This seems to be a common theme, after sex we open up to each other, or sometimes even before sex depending on our mood.

"Of course. Tell me what is on your mind." He sits upright, lifting me further up against his chest.

"I met with Lucy and discovered she had a relationship with Cameron, and she's really hurt now. I feel awful." Normally these type of chats I keep for my DBB talks with my darlin's but I trust Lucca and feel comfortable talking about my feelings regarding my close relationships, and he always gives me level-headed advice.

"I am so sorry, baby, that Cameron is causing you stress, and I hate that this situation is making you upset. I called Anna today to ask her if she thought about what I said the other night. She feels awful about upsetting you and wants to make this easier on all of us. She is falling for Cameron, Doc, and I cannot change her mind it appears. Anna confirmed what you said, about Cameron and Rachel having an open relationship. I just hope they know what they are doing, because I hate to think of Cameron treating my baby sister like that." With his arm around my chest, he strokes light caresses over my shoulder and chest.

"I just don't want either of them to get hurt or this to get out of hand, and I agree, they better know what they are doing." I press my lips together in a firm line.

"Anna said he is finishing with Rachel for good because he and Anna are serious about one another. If that is true, and he promises to treat Anna well and stay committed to her, then what can we do? Anna also asked me for permission if Cameron can come as her partner this weekend, but she is worried about what Savio and Armando will make of it, so she is nervous. I was not sure what you would think, and I wanted to ask you first." He presses his nose to the back of my hair and places a soft kiss on my head. I sigh and chew the inside of my cheek because as much as I try and deny this, it is actually happening. They want to be together and no matter what Lucca, I, or anyone else says, it's inevitably going to happen.

"At least she had the decency to ask. Both of them will be here regardless; they may as well come together. Your brothers are going to find out about them soon enough. I just hope he does not screw this up." I shift a little starting to feel the heat of the sauna now. "I do want to talk to him again about this," I add, peeling my wet hair away from my moist skin.

"Yes, if it puts your mind at ease, you should. When I called Cameron to tell him about your misunderstanding with your mum, I had a thorough talk with him. I am sorry, Lexi, I might have come off a bit sharp giving him a grilling, but I want him to know that I have Anna's interests at heart and that he better do the right thing by her and treat her with respect. He would do the exact same thing if it were you, I am sure."

"Yeah, he would." I know Cameron would do the same. When Dominic told him about Lucca and me, he made it his priority to get one of his internal investigator friends to find out everything he could about Lucca.

"Please do not think that is a reflection on how I feel about Cameron. He is a great guy, and I would rather see her with him than someone else if he treats her well. But as her brother, I need to look out for her, that means being protective."

Dipping my head sideways, I look up at him and smile. I don't feel offended, I feel relieved that he's protecting Anna. I would expect this from him, and given how I feel about the situation, it relieves me he's now taking it very seriously.

"Lucy will get over it. She is young and attractive, and she will meet someone else. They must have known what they were doing and it could not have been that big a deal or you would have known about it by now," he adds, sounding very level-headed.

"Hmmm," I muster. I know he's right, but I can't help feel a pang to my heart for Lucy. I know men don't tend to get the same level of emotions we do over friendships. I know this because although Cameron has close friends, he would never be as deep and sensitive as me.

"Is there anything else that is worrying you? You seem deflated and out of sorts," he asks. Tensing up, I rub the sole of my foot on top of the other and feel thankful they are only scraped and don't have the same abrasions as I had in Tuscany.

"Yes, I had an unpleasant experience in the doctor's clinic." I grind my teeth and flex my muscles.

"Christ. Why did you not tell me? Baby ... what is wrong?" He panics, leaning over to nuzzle his face into my neck and grip me tighter.

"I've been putting off telling you because I knew I'd end up tense and angry about it. I ... I'm just so exasperated thinking about it, never mind having to face it." I'm overwrought; Lucca takes his hands to my shoulders and begins to knead them, freeing some tightness in my muscles.

"Tell me, dolcezza. You are worrying me. What did you face at the doctor's that has gotten you so wound up? Are you pregnant?" His voice sounds buoyant. I wish he'd drop that hope. Why would he think that? I have not given him any indication that I am. And I've been drinking wine today; does he think I would be that careless if I were? *Sheesh.*

"Absolutely not. I'm not pregnant, nor planning to be. Do you want to know or not?" I snap, slightly pissed off because I have something serious to tell him and if I were pregnant, I think I'd have more respect for him and tell him right away ... not pitter-patter around the truth.

"Of course I do. I am sorry, I do want to know. I only asked that because it is the first thing that came into my head. Doctor's ... women's issues ... pregnancy? And you do want to talk. I am sorry, I should not make assumptions." He does sound apologetic.

"No, you shouldn't. I was there for prescription meds for my wrist." I chew the inside of my cheek, I wasn't even going to tell him about the painkillers but he needs set straight, he has far too vivid an imagination.

He sighs, leaning down to kiss under my ear then rubs his fingers over my wrist, lifts my hand to his mouth and kisses my wrist sweetly. "I ... am ... so ... sorry." His tone is soft and gentle and it's not lost on me that his apology is deeply sincere and from his heart. "Please tell me what happened," he adds after caressing my wrist.

"I saw her, the woman who was in our bed. She was in the waiting room and stared right at me." I sigh. Subconsciously, I draw my knees up to my chest, feeling the familiar insecurities I did the other night. This is why I tried to avoid talking about it, because I don't want to get flared up before Lucca's family arrive.

"Did she say anything to you?" he panics and tenses.

"No, but if looks could kill ..."

"Fuck. I am sorry. I would gladly make her disappear if I could. Unfortunately, she does not live far from here, but please do not let her bother you because I know she got the message. She knows not to cross the line, to stay away, and what you mean to me. I have made that pretty clear. If she threatens us, trespasses again, or commits any other sort of unsavoury acts, then I might be able to get a restraining order set in place. She was charged with breaking and entering, so I imagine she will try and avoid us." He kisses just below my ear then pauses holding his lips still, breathing heavily against my skin.

"What's her name?" I ask. I'm curious and I never even thought to ask after the drama of that night.

"Why do you want to know? What does it matter? I would rather not cause you any more distress and unwanted thoughts regarding that awful night." I feel his chest expand and lift as he stretches, running his fingers through his hair.

I'm silent.

"It is Leila," he whispers, sounding like he's ashamed or even hurt to say her name.

Now I'm being mentally vindictive to Leila. Leila the slut, bitch, whore. At least now I know, not that it makes a difference, it's just another name to add onto my list of Lucca's exes.

Trying to change the subject because I feel he has become uptight since I brought her up and I don't need any more tension today. I tell him about the church and Ms. Morrison sending her wishes. I then ask him about Suzanne because it has been pressing on my mind since we were out for dinner.

After a pregnant pause, he answers. "Suzanne is Casey Huddersfield's sister."

"Casey? Our therapist?"

"Yes, they are very alike."

This explains the resemblance and that's why she was acting very motherly and caring. I wonder if Casey has told her about my past, but then she is professional and follows a code of conduct with disclosures. Suzanne must know my mother then? I wonder if that is why she has been going out of her way to help Lucca and me. Obviously it's her job but I sense she is being extra compassionate to me and loyal to Lucca.

"Actually, I called Casey today and explained about our relationship and asked her to call your mum and check on her as opposed to Cameron calling her."

"What did she say?" I swallow, my mouth feeling parched and rough as sandpaper.

"She is happy for us and was surprised to find out we are together, but definitely delighted and said she will call your mum.

Casey mentioned she is going up north fairly soon to her cottage so she will drop by and see your mum as well."

This is a relief. I know Casey will always say the right thing and help Mum focus. The fact that she knows Lucca well is a bonus; maybe she will say good things to assure Mum and help put her mind at ease. Thanking him, I reach up to kiss his jaw then think about the winter day a few years ago when I was in Casey's office for a session and bumped into Lucca by chance.

Fate.

Destiny.

Future.

"There's something I want to speak to you about," he adds, bringing me out of my musing.

"Oh."

"Next week, I need to work in London for some design briefs on a development I am working on, and I have a very important meeting I need to attend. Then I need to go to Sardinia to finalise my contracts on the Porto Cervo renovation. I want you to come with me because I do not want to leave you here alone."

"I'll be fine by myself. I have Hazel, Cameron, Rose, Peter, Mr. Carlin, Doris, and my girlfriends," I reply, although I don't really want him to go. When we left Tuscany I knew Lucca's work played a huge role in his life. He's a very successful businessman and has obligations. I guess I thought we would live in our blissful holiday stage a little longer before life intervened.

"No, I want you with me. Also, I wanted to tell you Francesca has been in touch." He slides his hand down my arm which is coated in droplets of perspiration from the heat of the sauna. I notice both our bodies are wet and reddening in colour with the heat.

He has my full attention. "How is she recovering after her overdose?" I ask, genuinely interested in her wellbeing.

"She is doing much better. She has asked me to consider sourcing her fashion company's new premises in Milan as they are expanding and need a bigger property. She is aware Osurac Industries owns a few buildings in the city, but I wanted to speak to you about it first."

He sounds cautious seeking my approval. I think the heart-to-heart we had the other night has made him more sensitive and considerate of my feelings.

Dear Lord, this day is just getting more challenging by the minute.

History!

Fucking history!

Fran is always going to be a part of Lucca's life, but he lost contact with her for over two years and now after her suicide attempt in Tuscany, I think he feels indebted to help in any way he can. I believe it's honourable of him to want to help her, but it's thrown me off as I didn't expect her to be in touch so soon. I thought she would be recovering and work would be the last thing on her mind.

"Well, are you going to?"

"Not if you do not want me to, and I would understand if you object. It is just that I feel as if I need to help her progress in her career because it is the only thing giving her hope and focus at the minute. She is not back at work yet, but she would like a transition before winter."

He confirms exactly what I was thinking and has the decency to ask if it bothers me. I like that he's respecting me. I'm not entirely sure how I feel about Lucca being back in Francesca's life; they have so much history together, but I hate to see anyone suffer like that. If her career gives her escape, then I want him to help her. Distraction has always worked for me and maybe it will be good for her as well.

"Okay, I want you to help her. I trust you." I tilt my head to the side and gaze up to search his face for signs of conflict. All I see is warmth in his soft, loving eyes looking down at me.

He leans over, placing a kiss on my neck. "You are so special. There is no one like you." He finishes on my lips. We kiss for so long I barely notice the sauna's temperature increasing. When we part lips, I struggle to get a breath.

Dizzy.

Hot.

Dehydrated.

"Lucca, I need out," I panic feeling light-headed.

He lifts me to my feet and opens the door. The cool air brushes my stinging skin and fills my rasping throat and empty lungs. It's heavenly.

Chapter 11: Famiglia

After showering properly and washing my hair, I walk into my dressing room and discover boxes and cartons littered all over the floor. My clothes from Tuscany have arrived. Looking through it, I try to find a suitable outfit for tonight. Even though the dressing room is stocked with clothes, I want to ensure I get the wear out of these clothes first; it seems like such a waste otherwise.

I choose the black and gold braided miniskirt and black chiffon vest top which I wore when I left the hospital after my wrist operation. I moisturise with my Brazil nut body butter, put leave-in conditioner in my hair to let it dry naturally, then apply some light makeup. I put my jewellery back on before I go and help Lucca in the kitchen.

Lucca has everything under control and won't let me help much. He has fresh ingredients everywhere, the pantry is stocked, and the fridge is filled with alcoholic beverages. I lift a carton of orange juice out of the fridge then pick up some kiddie fruit smoothies and yogurts and grin at Lucca.

"Roberta loves those shake things, and A-Jay and Emilio love those fromage frais pots." He shrugs.

Endearing.

I think it's very cute. His thoughtfulness is very sexy.

I place them back in the fridge.

Hmmm. It gets me thinking. I imagine Lucca would be a doting father.

I jump onto the kitchen island and sip my fruit juice as I watch him. He's a natural with food and hospitality. "Tell me about the hospitality business you own. I know you said you were a silent partner but you never told me anything about it."

"I own several restaurants but choose to focus on my property development and my health clubs primarily." He stands between my legs and wraps his arms around my waist. I link my feet behind his ass.

"Do I know the chain?" I ask.

He takes a drink of my orange juice, then kisses my wet lips. "Luminara."

I'm left speechless.

"What? As in *the* Luminara? You own that chain?" I'm dumfounded. Actually, I don't know why I'm that surprised. I now understand his passion for light, and why he proposed to me the night of the Luminara festival.

Luminara is rustic, authentic, and a little quirky. It's a renovated church with all the original features. It boasts heavy wrought iron chandeliers with candles, impressive artwork, and private seating areas with red roses and purple velvet curtains and drapes separating the areas. I can see Lucca's stamp on it because it's very opulent. It's known for being a one-stop socialising spot, with a restaurant, bar, nightclub, and function suite.

Lucca washes the different tomatoes and separates them for the various dishes he plans to cook. "Yes, that is the one. I hope to take the chain to Tuscany and surrounding areas. Of course, it is early days, but it has been very successful so far. I have a professional management team and an incisive club manager. Giorgio is great, very hands on, and a clever guy. We have had our moments in the past, especially regarding the chain and my land in Tuscany, but that is all water under the bridge and we work well together."

I wonder why Giorgio was not invited to the meal the other night if he is one of Lucca's managers; I guess he would have been working himself. "We had our Christmas night out last year in Luminara. I stayed for the meal and a few drinks, but never went down to the club for the dancing."

"Good, I am glad you are not in clubs on your own. I will take you when you want to go. After that night in Firenze, I am not sure I ever want you in a club again without me," he says protectively as he dices vegetables. He's oblivious to how possessive he sounds sometimes. I tut, shake my head, and roll my eyes. "What did you think of the food?" he asks curiously.

"It was beautiful from what I remember. I think I had the steak." I wrinkle my nose, tilt my head, and look up at the ceiling trying to remember.

He smiles at me. "Good. Well, I will take you one night, and if you want any changes made to the menu, let me know and I will arrange it with Giorgio."

Lucca's phone starts ringing. It's Savio, Lucca's older brother by one year, looking for the new code to the front gate. We walk out the front to greet Savio. Again, like Armando, he has the inky black hair and eyelashes and deep olive skin and has their father Antonio's appearance.

Savio has short neat hair, wide eyebrows, and is slightly wider in the face and jaw than Lucca. He's dressed in a smart looking pair of grey, washed-denim jeans and a fitted, white shirt. When he places his hands on my shoulders to kiss both my cheeks, I smile because it feels familiar.

Similar to Lucca's gesture that I've grown fond of.

Kate exits the car with their two children running around at her feet. I'm entranced by her beauty. Her white-blonde, thick, wavy hair sits just below her shoulders. She wears thin braids at either side, pulling her hair back in a half-up fashion, and she has a thin, printed blouse on and skinny leather jeans. She looks beautiful—very fresh and modern.

Kate rounds up her two children, who are adventuring towards the water fountain centrepiece in the garden. Lucca strides down the steps, and a huge squeal escapes the beautiful blonde girl.

"Uncle Lucca!" she yells as she runs towards him. He gracefully picks her up and cuddles her, spinning in circles.

"There is my favourite girl. How are you, my little princess? I have missed you." He gives her a kiss, and she giggles and swings her legs.

My stomach jitters at the sight of Lucca's effortless, carefree love. Lucca has already told me Roberta is nearly five years old, and that she was named after Kate's father Robert.

Savio and Kate also have a young son named Emilio. He is three years old and very much a little character. Lucca mentioned he's very mischievous and has lots of energy. He scuffs his feet around the gravel, and his brown curls bounce and bob as he fidgets around.

"Unkie Wooca, can I play in the pool?" he says.

Lucca places Roberta down on her little pale pink ballet pumps and strides over to him. "Absolutely, buddy. Have you been a good boy for your mamma and papa?"

Lucca scruffs his hair, treating him like a big boy, and Emilio peeks down at his feet. I find it very amusing. Cameron used to do this when he felt guilty about something. Actually, he still does it as an adult. I smile watching him.

"Me been good boy. Me got gold star at big boy schwool." He beams up towards Lucca.

"Well done, buddy. That is brilliant. Have you been playing nice with your sister?" Lucca inquisitively asks, knitting his brow.

"No, he's bad. He stole my sweeties and my teddy bear and pulled my hair," Roberta gripes. Lucca stares at her with the soft, loving glance he often gives me. Oh my goodness, she is four – nearly five years old and has him hooked around her little pinkie. Emilio starts sobbing and stamping his feet.

"I never. I pwomus I never, Mummy." He must know he is about to get into trouble.

Kate picks him up, shaking her head, calming him down. She walks over, introduces herself, kisses me, and then kisses Lucca. She passes Emilio to his father's arms, and he buries his head in Savio's chest. Both Kate and Savio congratulate us on our engagement as she admires my ring.

I make small chat with Kate but crouch down when I notice a huge pair of blue eyes scrutinising me as Lucca holds my hand. "Hi, I'm Lexi. I'm so happy to meet you, Roberta. I love your dress. It's very beautiful." I smile.

"Why are you holding my Uncle Lucca's hand?" she asks.

"Roberta, don't be rude," Kate scolds, knitting her brow just like Emilio did moments ago.

I don't know what to say. I'm being challenged by a four year old. Lucca leans into my neck and whispers, "You have your work cut out there, baby," he chuckles.

I smile broadly, matching her confidence. "I'm your Uncle Lucca's friend," I say, hoping this explains our relationship.

Lucca nearly chokes. "Lexi and I are getting married. She is going to be my wife and then she will be your aunty."

Savio finds this amusing. "Ah, Lexi, you might have a fight on your hands for Lucca's attention."

Roberta crosses her arms over her chest and scowls her little forehead and pouts her lips. "Are you going to have a big princess dress?" she asks.

"No, I probably won't, but you can. We'd like you to be a flower girl and wear a pretty dress and carry flowers." We spoke about this on the flight coming home from Tuscany. Family is very important to Lucca; he very much wants the kids to be involved when we get married, and I can see why. I notice her expression change from sceptical to inquisitive.

She thinks about it. "What's a flower girl? I don't want to dress up as a flower. Everyone will laugh at me," she whimpers.

I hold her hand, trying not to giggle. "You won't be a flower, and no one will laugh. They will think you're beautiful. You'll be a helper and get to wear something very fancy and be my special little princess fairy girl." I hope this wins her over.

"I love fairies and princesses and castles and rainbows and unicorns and teddies and queens and crowns. Mummy, can I? Can I be a princess and have a big fancy dress?" She twirls on the spot and looks up at Kate who smiles adoringly down at her.

"Yes, honey. Princess it is." Kate sighs with a hint of a smile.

Lucca picks her back up, tickling her, sending her into playful giggles. "You already are a little princess."

Once in the house, the kids go exploring. Lucca helps Savio in with the bags then parks his car around the back next to the guest accommodation. It gives me a chance to talk with Kate and get to know her.

I pour us both a glass of wine as I learn that Kate helps Savio with the restaurant part-time. She tries to split her time evenly between being a mum, wife, and business owner. I like Kate. She appears to be friendly and ambitious—not what I expected.

"So when are Armando and Sarah coming?" I ask her.

She rolls her eyes. "God knows. Those two are late for everything. Sarah has her hands full with Antonia. She's only eight months old and teething, so she's restless and into everything. She's very inquisitive." She then asks me about our trip in Tuscany and how I enjoyed it.

Lucca returns with Savio, Armando, and Sarah. A-Jay is pulling at Sarah's legs, and Antonia is snuggled in her arms.

Sarah has beautiful hair, almost pre-Raphaelite with its warm-red colour and shiny condition. She has a pale skin tone with minimal makeup on, naturally pretty, and is wearing a green short-sleeved blouse, tight jeans, and flat pump shoes. Antonia has a head of thick chestnut hair and bright blue eyes. She's very pretty, like a little doll with her fat legs and chubby face. She's wearing a cream linen dress with a lilac sash and bow and a little lilac flower clip holding her hair back from her face.

Little A-Jay has darker hair than Antonia and warm brown eyes. His hair is styled short and spikey at the front. He has on denim cargo shorts and a white T-shirt with a purple knitted V-neck tank over the top. A-Jay is the same age as Emilio; there are only six weeks between them, so they are very good friends. He slides along the kitchen floor on his knees pretending to be a Ninja Turtle.

Armando kisses me then helps Sarah with the baby bag hanging over her shoulder. Lucca kisses Sarah and lifts Antonia straight out her arms. She uses the opportunity to congratulate us and admire my ring.

"A-Jay, come here please and say hello to Uncle Lucca and Aunty Lexi," Sarah says.

"Helwo, whares Emo?" That's all we get.

I chuckle, watching him run away. It's strange being called Aunty Lexi. I've never really been around children much before now, and I've been welcomed into such a large family. It feels warm and nice.

I watch Lucca kiss and coo at Antonia, making her giggle at his funny facial expressions. She tugs on his long, wavy hair at the back of his neck. "Ouch, missy," he says, and she chuckles even more.

"Would you like wine, Sarah?" Kate asks.

"No, I'm good, thanks. I'll wait until after Antonia is down," she says, rummaging through the baby bag.

"Do you want to meet your Aunty Lexi, wee cheeks?" Lucca says to Antonia then places her in my arms. My goodness, she's a heavy little lump.

She puts her fingers straight in my mouth, pulling on my lip, and I rest her on my hip and kiss the side of her head. She gargles and goos and swings her chubby legs around.

"I think she likes you. Looks like you have a night off, Sarah," Armando says, placing baby bottles in the fridge.

Sarah puts the kettle on. "I'm going to find the boys and make sure they are behaving then I'll bring their things in from the car. I'll be back in a minute. Lexi, are you okay with her?"

"Yes, we're fine. Aren't we, honey?" I reply, looking down at her big blue eyes that could melt a thousand hearts.

"You better watch out, Lucca. I think Lexi is getting broody there." Kate chuckles.

Lucca just smiles but watches me contently. He's giving me the look. Soft eyes ... dimple smile ... biting on his bottom lip.

Absolutely not happening.

"Don't give him ideas, Kate. Let's find your cousins, baby girl." I walk out the kitchen into the family room with Antonia on my hip and pause in shock, hardly believing the sight in front of me.

Oh my God, I forgot all about Doris.

Astonished, I watch Doris sprawled out on the carpet as Emilio pulls her ears, Roberta cuddles her face, and A-Jay sits on top of her.

She loves it. Doris is in doggy heaven getting lots of attention.

"Kids, just be very careful. She's a big doggy and if she gets excited she'll knock you over. Don't place your hands near her mouth in case she snaps." I frown, watching Roberta pry her mouth open and count her teeth. Hmmm, looks like she won't be snapping after all. Her tail is wagging frantically.

"What's the doggy's name?" Roberta asks.

"Doris."

They all giggle.

"That's a fwunny name," Emilio says, looking in her ear inquisitively.

Sarah walks in and gasps at the sight of them snuggling into Doris. "I think they're fine. She's very soft and protective, but I'll take her out if you're worried about the kids being around her," I gesture.

"It's not the kids I'm worried about. They seem fine and they like animals, but your poor dog will be face painted and dressed up soon. Beware," Sarah says. We both start laughing. "I'm going to heat up Antonia's milk. Are you okay with her still?"

"Yes, off you go. I'm fine."

Doris runs over to me and paws at my legs, nudging me off balance. I believe she's jealous that I'm holding a baby. I've seen it all now.

Peter was right. Doris is far too spoiled.

Roberta kisses Antonia's hand as I hold her. "That's nice, Roberta. You must love your little cousin, so sweet."

"She's just a baby, Aunty Lexi, and I am a big girly," she says in a sing-songy voice.

I chuckle. "Yes, you are."

I walk back through to the kitchen area, Antonia on my hip, Doris following me, and Roberta holding my free hand. I ask Lucca to put Doris outside so the kids can play. I don't want to leave her unattended with them in case anything happens.

"Lucca, is the pool door locked?" My mind is now running wild because I want the kids to be safe and to ensure the house is child-friendly for them.

"Yes, baby, it is locked." He wraps his arms around me, settling his chin on my shoulder. Antonia looks up at him and gargles. He runs his hand over her hair and rubs her cheeks. "You look very comfortable. You are a natural," he whispers into my ear.

I press my finger on Antonia's button nose. "Your Uncle Lucca thinks I'm going to fall for that. Well, little honey, he's very much mistaken." She sings out a long tune, and I agree with her, smiling and nodding my head. "I know, that's what I think," I say in an animated voice.

"I will just need to convince her one day, wee cheeks," Lucca says. He kisses my cheek before helping Savio and Armando into the kitchen, which leaves me with fluttering butterfly wings at his sincerity and gentle touch.

I fasten Antonia in her high chair just as Sarah comes with her food and milk. Then I head upstairs. In one of the spare rooms upstairs, I find the gifts we brought back from Tuscany for the kids.

"Aunty Lexi, can you put makeup on me?" Roberta's little voice says behind me. I think she is going to be my shadow tonight as she has followed me.

"I don't know if your mummy would approve, princess."

She looks upset.

Folded.

"Okay, how about some pink blush and gloss to match that pretty dress, and then we will do your nails? I will tell your mummy it was my idea."

She claps her hands and hugs my legs. I sit her up on the Parisian stool at my dressing table in our suite and pamper her. I let her open one of the gifts, which is a little silver bracelet with a diamond set heart charm on it and matching necklace.

"I love it! Do I look like a princess?" she asks, swaying in front of the mirror.

"Yes, you do. Shall we go and show Uncle Lucca?"

She throws her arms around my neck and kisses me. "I love you, Aunty Lexi. You're my new bestest friend. Well, you and Millie from my nursery."

I smile and love how innocent and sweet she is. Always room for more bestest friends, especially sweet ones like Roberta.

When we get downstairs, Hazel, Dominic, Anna, and Cameron have arrived and greet our other visitors. Roberta squeals when she sees Anna and jumps up for a hug. I give out the other gifts to the kids and leave Antonia's next to her baby bag.

Sarah has sweet potato splattered all over her blouse. "I'm going to change my blouse. Will you give her the milk for me?" she asks, looking down at her blouse. Antonia bounces up and down in her chair, swinging her legs.

I lift Antonia from the high chair and sit on the sofa, cuddling her into me as I give her the bottle; she wraps her arm around my back and fiddles with my hair sitting across my chest with the other hand. I gaze down at her and feel a rush of warmth at how effortless and nice this feels.

Lucca watches me from behind the kitchen island, glancing and smiling with adoration while I feed Antonia. Roberta jumps up and walks over to tug at Lucca's hand.

"Thank you for my presents, Uncle Lucca." I'm impressed with her politeness and good manners.

Placing his oven mitt down, he lifts her up. "You are very welcome, baby girl. I am glad you like them. Have you got lipstick on?" he asks with a cadence of amusement.

She giggles.

"This better not be for the boys. I hope this is just for Uncle Lucca." He kisses and tickles her.

"It's Aunty Lexi's," she blurts out, squirming around playfully.

"Oh, is it now? Well, let us see if she has got it on too." He carries her over to the sofa, places her down, then leans over me, kissing my lips and holding just a bit too long in front of Roberta. "Yep, it is definitely Aunty Lexi's lipstick, watermelon flavour. Yummy."

"You're funny, Uncle Lucca." I smile, rolling my eyes at him, but deep down I have so much love for him right now. He is melting my heart.

Once the food is ready, we go into the formal dining room and set the buffet style platters down for everyone to help themselves. It looks and smells divine.

Savio and Lucca pour champagne for the adults and give the kids fruit juice cartons. I notice Sarah passes on the champagne. Cameron sits across from me, but I purposely don't make eye contact with him. I don't want to talk to him in front of the others in the event I get angry with him. I'm still pissed about him hurting Lucy. Savio and Armando politely chat away with Cameron and Dominic getting to know them, which gives me a bit of a breather.

"Lex, can you pass down some bread please?" Cameron asks. Not lifting my head, I pass the platter. He looks at me with the blank expression on his face and shrugs his shoulders, obviously wanting to know why I'm so cold towards him today. I narrow my eyes, silently telling him we will talk about it later.

I'm about to bite into a piece of sautéed king prawn when I hear Antonia crying and think of Sarah. I place my fork down and excuse myself. I have an idea.

Sarah is trying to shush Antonia, pacing the floor with her. "It's normally her bath time, so she is all out of sync. I'm going to bathe her and get her down, and then I can relax. I'll heat my dinner later." Sarah passes her from arm to arm, patting her back trying to calm her sobbing.

"Look, I was out for lunch today and I'm not that hungry just now, so you go eat and enjoy some food. I'll put Antonia in the bath if you'd like. I can reheat something up later if I'm hungry," I offer, because she does look tired and flustered.

She takes a moment then sighs with exhaustion. "Thank you, but it's fine, really. I'll do it." I think she is only trying to be courteous, but her tired eyes tell me she would probably welcome the help and a break.

"Sarah, I'm fine, honestly. I wouldn't offer otherwise. Please, go back in and relax, and I'll take good care of this little girly." Antonia stops crying when she sees she's getting attention from someone else.

"Okay, if you're sure, that would be great. All her things are in the baby bag, and there is a monitor already on in the first spare room. Her travel cot has been built already should she fall asleep. Her soother should be in the cot." She kisses Antonia's forehead and hugs me, passing me her daughter. "Shout if you need anything," she adds, kissing Antonia before she heads off.

I smile then walk with Antonia and the baby bag up into our suite, leaving them all to enjoy their food and company downstairs. I sing and play, trying to distract her as I run the bath. Not that I've done this before but Lucy has a niece and I've watched her do bath time when her niece stays over. How hard can it be? I strip her clothes and diaper off since she's a lot calmer and not wriggling as much. Then I sit her on my knee, putting my elbow in to test the water. I make bubbles with her baby bath oil, and once she's in, I let her splash around while keeping a grip on her.

"Hey," Lucca says as he bends down to the floor and wraps his arm around my waist, kissing the side of my head. "This is a really nice thing you have done for Sarah. I do not think she has sat down properly with Armando for a meal at a normal time in ages."

"Honestly, it's fine. She looked tired and I'm more than happy to help. Plus, this little girly really likes her Aunty Lexi."

I really like her too.

"I'm glad at least one of her aunts is sensible. Kate and Anna are opening another bottle of champagne." He laughs.

"Look, Antonia, Uncle Lucca has come to play with us," I sing to her. She gurgles and coos, then kicks her legs with excitement in the water and both of us end up soaking wet because we are leaning over the tub.

"Cheeky," Lucca says as he strips his top off.

"She really is adorable," I say, watching every expression she makes. It amazes me.

"Hmmm, so are you. You look so sexy right now. I am picturing you doing this for our kids. I know I said it earlier, but you are very good with them. You are a natural." He smiles contently and looks so carefree washing Antonia, as if he's enjoying the experience of bathing the baby.

Fuck!

File M for maternal. Maternal denial.

"This is different. It's nice to enjoy other people's kids, but you know I'm not in a good place emotionally to be a mother. I am too insecure, and it wouldn't be fair. Besides, I want you all to myself." It's probably not what he wants to hear, but it is the truth.

"Hmmm…" He presses his bare chest into my back and kisses my shoulder. I quiver under his touch, feeling a light tempo beating in my stomach.

"Lucca," I whisper when I feel his hand slide under my skirt. He strokes between my legs, then cups my sex. "Not in front of the baby, because you're getting me revved up and core teasing me," I moan, trying desperately to block out the pleasure he's showing me.

He groans, then laughs. "Okay, let's get her out and dried. You ready, wee cheeks?" He trails his hands up and gropes my ass cheeks, teasing me.

Antonia smashes her thick legs in the water, splashing both of us again. Hopefully, that will cool him down. Once she's out, I dry her on the bed with a big fluffy towel. Then Lucca puts her diaper on and buttons her into her pink romper suit. She rubs her eyes and yawns.

"You change your clothes while I try and settle her," he says.

When I return from the dressing room in my pink lace lingerie, I admire the most breath-taking sight I've ever witnessed. Lucca is lying on his back on the bed still bare chested in his jeans with his legs sprawled out, and Antonia is sleeping across his chest on her front, her face snuggled just below his neck. Lucca has one hand cupping her little bottom, and the other resting on his chest with Antonia's little chubby fingers curled around his.

Two angels.

Her pale pink romper against Lucca's deep coloured skin is a pretty picture.

Lucca's body is so brawny and muscular that Antonia looks like a little light pink feather against him. It's the sweetest vision I could imagine. It's doing nothing for my maternal denial. I'll need to file that thought.

He glances towards me smiling. "Come here," he whispers.

My heart drums.

Thud.

Thud.

Thud.

I walk to the bed and curl into his side, wrapping my arm around Antonia's back and across Lucca's chest. There is something so warm and lovely about this feeling. I close my eyes, enjoying the closeness and intimacy as Lucca kisses the side of my head.

"Lexi, we should put her down." Lucca's hot breath against my head causes me to stir as he moves a stray curl from face.

"Did I fall asleep?" I ask, yawning.

"Yes, I have been watching the two of you sleeping on me thinking how lucky I am."

"How long was I sleeping?"

"Maybe thirty minutes."

I unhook my leg from his, sitting upright, then lift Antonia from his chest and cradle her into me. She's in a deep sleep, a heavy weight in my arms as I walk towards the spare room and place her down. Lucca's body heat presses right against me and his hands splay over my hips.

I lean back into him, moving my head to the side. He kisses my neck softly then trails his hands up and over my breasts, running his finger across the pink lace. My chest is rising with anticipation and my nipples strain against the lace fabric.

"That was a really special moment in there. You have me, Romeo." I turn around and jump up wrapping my legs around his waist and kissing him desperately. He groans and walks me back into our suite and closes the door, forgetting about our visitors.

I'm his.

He's mine.

And nothing else matters.

We change our clothes after some quick fondling, check on the baby, then walk downstairs.

Strolling into the downstairs family room, everyone turns around and we get whistles and claps from Savio and Armando. Lucca scowls at them, but I'm sure I hear him roguishly laugh under his breath. I'm mortified and blushing a shade deeper than my pink vest. I tighten my grip on Lucca's hand.

"You two are supposed to be babysitting, not baby making." Anna chuckles.

Oh my God.

Please subtract me from this equation. After some banter back and forth, we manage to change the subject, thankfully.

Cameron shakes his head then carries on with his game. Cameron and Emilio are playing against Dominic and A-Jay on some guitar game on the Wii console. Roberta is hanging over Doris putting her dolly's hairbands on her, telling her she's her new pony, and Sarah looks like she has relaxed as she hugs a wine glass.

"Thank you, Lexi. I really appreciate it. Is she settled?"

"Yes, she's fine, out cold. She soaked us with the bath water. That's why I um … um … changed." I blush again looking down at my top, I feel like I need to give an explanation and remedy their ideas of what were up to.

"Lexi, we left you a plate of food," Hazel says. I walk back into the kitchen to heat it up. Lucca follows me, grabbing a beer from the fridge. I sit at the dining area next to the kitchen, and Lucca sets a large glass of wine down in front of me.

Hazel comes and sits next to me with her own wine. "Did you idiots know the baby monitor was on in the spare room?" She laughs, wrapping her arm around my shoulder.

"Oh my God," I drop my fork, suddenly feeling humiliated all over again.

"I had to stop Roberta from coming up," she adds.

Fuck! It's only getting worse.

Lucca leans against the counter, holding his Peroni. "Relax, Lexi. Roberta will not have a clue, and we were only in that room a minute. It's all clean. They would not have heard us in the suite."

I take a huge swig of wine, followed by a bite of lasagne, and realise I've worked up an appetite. I'm starving and I never ate lunch today either. I know I need to get something in my stomach. The last time I starved myself and drank alcohol, it didn't go well.

Cameron walks through, very chuffed with himself. "Team Emo, victory," he announces, fist in the air, then grabs a beer. I don't make any eye contact. "So you going to tell me why you're so pissed off at me? What have I done now?" He leans against the kitchen island, flipping his beer cap off.

I ignore him and continue to eat. I know I need to speak to him, but I don't know how to address it without it sounding too abrupt.

"Lucca called and told me about your argument with Mum. Is that why you're fuming?" That's it, the trigger.

"Hmmm, let me see. Mum thinks I'm some sort of gold digger and with Lucca for his money. She doesn't approve and is disgusted with my behaviour because she says it's too soon to fall in love, yet she dismisses your man-whore tendencies. But then there's also the fact that my best friend is hurting badly, and the funny thing is that it's all about you, Cameron. Were you ever going to tell me?"

He sighs and shrugs his shoulders.

Not good enough.

"It's not a big deal. Lucy and I had a thing, but I always wanted Rachel deep down. Lucy knows it would never be anything serious, and before you ask, yes, Rachel knows I've been with Lucy. I don't know what the big deal is? Lucy and I had fun, that was it, nothing more, and Rach doesn't want to settle down with me." He absently munches on some tortilla chips and salsa.

"Hmmm. It is a big deal, a massive bloody deal, and Rachel, Anna, and Lucy don't deserve this treatment," I spurt.

"I'm going to finish with Rach. She wants to go travelling again, and it's not working. We're drifting in different directions. Plus, I know she's not been faithful to me recently; she just hasn't got the confidence to dump me. I'd be doing her a favour. It's the right thing to do. She's been back in touch with that guy from Paris," he says with certainty, his fingers raking through his hair and musing his waxed shape.

"Well, good. Finally. Do it soon, Cameron, please. I'm supposed to be meeting her for coffee, and I don't want to feel awkward." I turn around in my chair and face him.

He walks over to me and wraps his arms around my shoulders. "So are we good?" he asks. I smile because I'm happy he's finally doing the right thing, but I want him to sweat a little longer.

"I suppose," I mumble.

"If I speak to Mum for you, will you drop this Lucy thing?" he asks.

"What Lucy thing?" Anna asks as she walks in for some drinks for the kids.

Oh God, this just keeps getting better. He should be doing the right thing and telling Rachel, Anna, and Lucy where they all stand in his screwed-up love triangle thing he has going on.

I take another gulp of wine. I have no intention of telling Anna about Lucy. That's up to Cameron. "Will you take Doris out for me? I want to spend some time with Kate and Sarah. I've barely spoken with them all night," I say, hoping he takes the hint.

"Sure. Anna, come outside with me. I want to talk to you." He cocks his head and reaches for her hand. Anna looks nervous. She might be thinking he's giving her bad news considering he and I were talking a moment ago. Although, Cameron just stares at her and smiles with a look of adoration, and I see Anna relax and return the smile.

He whistles and Doris gallops through, I still haven't mastered that whistle. Anna takes his hand and follows him. I give him a sympathetic "thank you" smile, thanking him for doing the right thing.

Hazel and I catch up while we're on our own and she asks if I feel any better about my phone call with my mum. I then decide to discreetly tell her about Leila being charged with breaking and entering and how serious Lucca has taken it.

She listens, intrigued, tapping her middle finger against her chin, then comforts me the way she always does by being understanding and supportive. It prompts me to tell her that the bed is new and it's a good job too. Then she cracks jokes about it afterwards which makes me laugh.

"Roo, it has taken you years to let one man in your bed, never mind a threesome, bloody hell that would throw you over the edge. And with a chick? If that ever happened, the earth would freeze over." I almost choke on my wine from laughing that much, watching her raise her eyebrows. She's right of course, plus the thought of sharing Lucca would destroy me. Typically, I blush and she gives me a cuddle. Then we join the others.

Sitting on the sofa in the family room, Roberta stands behind me and plays with my hair.

"Mummy, when I'm big I want long hair like Aunty Lexi."

Kate smiles. "Be gentle, Roberta, don't tug too hard," she says when she sees my head being yanked backwards.

"Right kids, bedtime," Savio announces.

"Noooo!" the three of them shout in unison.

"It is bedtime. If you go to bed now, you can go swimming and watch a movie tomorrow." Savio lowers his voice sternly. They all cheer and jump up.

"I want to sleep in Uncle Lucca's bed. He has a big castle bed. Mummy, can I?" Roberta pleads.

"Oh, I don't know. You need to ask Aunty Lexi," Kate replies cautiously

"Yes, of course you can, but your Uncle Lucca snores." I say, smiling.

She giggles.

"I do not. Roberta, that is fine, princess. I hope you are not going to snore," Lucca adds.

"Nah." She giggles again.

"I'll go up and get them settled then check on Antonia. Is it okay if they stay upstairs instead of the guest house tonight? Saves lifting them over," Sarah asks.

"Yes, you can all sleep here. Makes no difference," Lucca replies.

After everyone has had a goodnight kiss from the kids, and Kate warns the boys to behave and not to go near the top of the stairs, Armando and Sarah take them upstairs to settle them. Lucca fills everyone's wine glass and grabs beers for the boys then comes and sits on the sofa, pulling me into his lap.

Bliss.

Anna and Cameron return holding hands. They look happy together.

Savio, being the eldest, has been studying Cameron all night. I imagine he is protecting his younger sister and trying to get to know him. Anna was right to be nervous about what her brothers would think.

Everyone is getting on and enjoying their night with lots of various conversations on the go. Armando and Sarah join us again. He slumps down on the sofa and pulls Sarah onto his lap, kissing the side of her head. Sarah thanks me again for helping tonight with the baby. It's lovely to see her finally relax.

"So what are your plans for the wedding?" Kate asks.

I shrug, not knowing the answer because we haven't discussed it much or made solid plans. Lucca strokes my arm.

"Mamma has been on the phone. She would like to know a date as she is twitching to get her teeth into it," Lucca says. Everyone laughs.

"Good luck with that," Armando adds, rolling his eyes.

"Well, you know I will love to help co-ordinate," Anna adds.

"We want it stress and drama free, Anna," Lucca announces, and Kate nearly chokes on her wine as if recalling some of Anna's past efforts.

"He has a point, Anna," she says, finding her voice.

"I will have you know I am quite a good planner and have impeccable taste." She waves her fingers around in the air making her point.

I can sense Lucca rolling his eyes behind me. I feel his body shift and hear him grumble low in his throat.

"You and Mamma are carnage together, Anna, no offense," Savio adds diplomatically before drinking his beer.

She pouts her lip and looks at Cameron. "I think you would be a great organiser, honey," he says. I have never heard him call her this before. Maybe they are getting more deeply involved and I've not paid much attention.

"Thank you for having faith in me, Cammy. You lot underestimate me," she chides then blows Cameron an air kiss. He winks at her with that roguish look of his.

"Heads up, Lexi, she had me on constant speed dial before we got married. I had to put an out of office message on my emails because she was hounding me," Kate says playfully, nudging Anna in the arm.

Sarah nods. "Yep, me too. And it was especially hard for me as I wanted everything simple and plain." Armando leans over and kisses her forehead in a sweet gesture, as if appreciating her simplicity.

"Admit it, Sarah, it was an amazing day," Anna retaliates.

"Okay, but it was stressful leading up to it." Armando nods his head in agreement.

I want to run away to marry Lucca and circumvent all of this drama and stress that's been mentioned. Do I need more drama in my life? No, definitely not. Hazel saves the day by talking about plans she and Dominic have discussed for their wedding to take focus away from me. I mouth a silent thank you.

We can hear Antonia stirring from the baby monitor and Sarah sighs. "She might need a bottle to settle her down again."

Armando kisses her head. "I will go and see to her." Sarah lazily reaches up and kisses him on the lips to thank him. It gives me an idea.

"Armando, why don't you move the travel cot into the suite and she can sleep with us tonight? Roberta is there anyway, and it will give you two a night to yourselves."

Armando looks at Sarah for approval, and she smiles at me with big, bright, excited eyes. "Really? That would be great. I can't remember the last time I slept through the night. Armando, will you give her a bottle and some teething gel and get her settled in the suite?"

"Sure, honey."

Lucca leans down and kisses my lips chastely. "One of the many reasons why I love you," he says in his husky voice.

"Give it a rest, you two," Anna gripes, and Cameron chuckles. He watches her interact with her brothers and I see a sparkle in his brown eyes; he's admiring her. Oh! ... I realise he might actually be falling for her.

After another hour, we all head to bed. I make sure Doris is locked in the family room and switch off the baby monitor. Then Lucca and I check all the doors are locked. After checking on Antonia and Roberta, we go into the bathroom, shower quickly and quietly, then dress in modest nightwear and quietly slip into bed. I move Roberta over, leaning on my side and snuggling into Lucca.

He kisses my head, nose, cheeks, and lips. "Have I told you lately that I love you?"

"Yes, I love you too. Thank you for everything today," I whisper.

"Thank you for being you and so goddamn special to me," he whispers back, then I allow my head to rest on his chest and fall off to sleep.

Chapter 12: I'm sorry

"Mummy, when I'm a big girl will I have long hair like you?" I ask, sitting cross-legged on the ground of our shed waiting for Mummy to do my hair.

"Yes, I hope so, Alexis."

"Mummy, why do you squeeze milk out of them? And why do I need to drink it?" I ask.

"It's good for you, and it will make you big and strong," she replies as she uses her fingers to comb through my hair.

"Like Cameron and Michael and Simon?"

"Yes, I'm going to squeeze milk for you now. Can you pass me that tin cup, Alexis?"

I can because I'm a big girl. I jump up, leap towards the shelf, and reach for the tin cup. "Mummy, what's a peetsa?"

"Where did you hear that word?" Mummy sounds mad.

"Michael said if I do what he says, he will give me some peetsa to eat. Does it make me big and strong like my milk?"

"No, sweetheart, it's not good for you. Please, just ignore him and say no thank you."

"But, Mummy, he said Cameron gets it on a Sunday for helping to lift wood. I want it too."

"You don't need it, and he will be bad to you if you say yes, so please say no."

Mummy lifts her white nightie up and fills my cup. I wait forever and ever, and I am very thirsty.

Once I've finished, I ask Mummy what she is going to drink and she says water. I think that's boring because it doesn't taste as nice as my creamy milk. Mummy feels tired, so she cuddles me into her side then falls asleep. I need to pee but Mummy is still sleeping, so I get up and sneak outside.

Cameron is lifting big silver metal things for Simon. I walk around back and pee into our hole in the ground, then use the bucket and pour water in just as Mummy showed me.

"Cameron, I want to play."

"You can't just now, Alexis. Go to bed with Mum."

"Hey, Alexis, I have a game for you. Do you want to try some pizza?" Michael says.

"Mummy says no."

"Well, your mummy is sleeping and won't know. I won't tell her."

"Don't!" Cameron shouts at me.

Michael punches Cameron in the tummy, and he yells and falls on the grass.

"Say a word and I'll use that metal to cut your throat, little boy."

Michael is mad with Cameron, and I want to hug him because I feel sad. Michael grabs my hand and pulls me into the big house, the one on sticks.

It's high so I need to take five big-girl steps onto the deck. He drags me around the back of the big house and opens the window. He slides it open, picks me up, and throws me in. I hurt my arms and knees when I fall on the carpet.

We don't have a carpet in the shed; we have ground.

It smells of something like food. There is a big, square, brown box on the end of bed. My tummy makes a funny noise. Michael opens the box, and there are big triangles in it—red, orange, and yellow.

He picks one up and bites it. He likes it because he licks his lips, and I want to bite it too.

"Mmmm, tastes good. This is pizza. If ya want to taste it, ya need to watch me. It's a game. You sit on the end of the bed."

I want to taste pizza.

I walk up and sit on the bed. It's hard to climb because we have flat beds on the ground, and he has a big, high one.

"Now, take your dress off. Sit on the bed and watch me. Then ya get to eat the pizza, and that rumbling in your tummy will go away. It's yummy," he says.

I'm not sure because my mummy will be mad. I want Cameron to help me. He leans over and places the pizza on my lips. It's cold and bumpy.

"Lick it," he orders.

My tongue licks it. It's nice and tastes different. I like it. My tummy is making funny noises.

"Now take your dress off. It's okay, I promise. All you need to do is watch."

He never keeps his promises.

I don't move because I know Mummy will be mad. He gets angry and pulls my dress over my head. Then he leans back on the pillow and stares at me. He has green eyes like the grass.

He places his hand on a lump in his shorts then puts his hand inside.

He moves his hand fast, making funny noises, then he makes a loud, weird noise and falls onto his big bed. He lifts his hand out and shows me. He has slimy milk on it. He rubs it on his top.

"Good girl, now you can get pizza," he says. I'm happy because I want to have it in my tummy before Mummy wakes up.

He kept his promise today.

He never keeps his promises.

I bite it but just swallow. "No, ya silly freak. You need to chew it," he says.

I try but my teeth are banging together. It is hard to chew.

"That's it, keep chewing. Next time ya get to chew this, and I'll give ya candy." He puts his hand on his lump in his shorts. I like pizza but it takes me a long time to chew it. I feel thirsty so Michael hands me a cup with black water in it. It's hot and fizzy.

"It's coke, drink it."

"I only drink my milk!" I cry.

"Drink it!" he shouts.

I drink it and it's yummy. "I want my mummy," I cry because I've been bad.

He's mad but he thuds his feet and puts my dress back on me.

When I go back into the shed, Mummy is gone.

"Shhh, Simon has taken her to the house. Go to sleep. She will be back soon." Cameron cuddles me and I fall asleep. When I wake in the morning, Mummy is very sleepy. She talks funny and sounds strange.

After a while, she wakes up and pulls me into her, holding me tight. "I love you, I love you, are you all right?" Then she hugs Cameron and cries as she holds him. I hate when Mummy cries. She cries a lot.

Cameron goes outside to pee, and I watch him kick a stone.

"What's that on your dress?" she asks. I swing my legs, and look at the ground. Mummy smells it. "Did you eat pizza?" she says. I stay quiet and move a stone around on the ground. "Alexis, did Michael give you pizza?"

"Mummy, I so sorry but he made me," I cry.

"I thought you were a big, brave girl. I'm disgusted that he forced you. If he bullies you again, please try and run away. Just run or shout for help." Mum is sobbing, she is upset.

When Cameron comes back, he has cut his lip. It's bloody and he has marks all over his face.

"Stay away from Michael, Cameron, I don't want him hurting you."

"Mummy, I sorry, I sorry, and I sorry ..."

Chapter 13: Dream a Little Dream

I thrash my legs around.

"I'm sorry, I'm sorry," I mutter. I shoot upright, whimpering in panic. I'm suffocating.

Lucca grasps me. "Lexi, breathe, baby, calm down. I have you." He throws the covers off me to give me air and strokes my arm. My back presses into the mattress as my chest heaves up and down with the panic.

He blows on my face then turns my head to face him. "Bad dream?" he asks.

Roberta stirs. "Aunty Lexi, what's wrong?" She whimpers, rubbing her eyes. I've startled her and now my stomach twists with the worst possible feeling of guilt. I'm distressed because I've alarmed this innocent little girl. She was blissfully sleeping until my restless nightmare panicked her. The thrashing of my legs and mumbling has woken her up and scared her.

She sits upright, curls her fingers around my arm, and grasps onto me tightly. Instantly, I pull her onto my lap and cuddle her, rocking her back and forth in my arms and quietly hushing.

"Nothing is wrong, baby girl, everything is fine. Go back to sleep, angel." I kiss her on the head, smooth her hair, then climb over Lucca and walk into the bathroom shaking. I find my anti-anxiety pills and place one on my tongue then inhale long, slow, steady breaths before the chest pain becomes too sharp.

He follows me a few minutes later. "I have settled Roberta. Jesus, what is wrong?" He moves my hair away from the beaded line of perspiration around my forehead and cheeks then runs his hand through his hair. "I hate seeing you like this. Let me help you, Lexi," he pleads.

I slump on the floor leaning against the bath edge. "I had a terrible memory. I think being around the kids has provoked my memories. I think I'm four in the dream, maybe five, and my mum was disappointed in me. I think my fight with her this morning has brought some things back and having Roberta playing with my hair, triggered a memory." I chew the inside of my cheek then worry my fingers in front of my lips.

"Tell me about it," he says softly, sitting down beside me. I know some things I share with him tear him up, and it's hard for him to listen to, but he's trying so hard and he desperately wants to help me.

So I do. I explain the dream, while I pick the skin on my hands. He places his hand over mine to hold me still, patiently listening.

"Lexi, you are having so many nightmares and I worry about them, about you. I think it might be a good idea to go back and see Casey Huddersfield. I can come with you ... come here." I lean into him, wrap my arms around his waist and neck, and he pulls me onto his lap.

"I'm so sorry. Certain things trigger them," I sob.

"Sorry for what? It is hard for you to control, no need to apologise." He rocks me gently in his arms, the same way I did for Roberta.

"Waking you up and disturbing Roberta. I told you, I'm not cut out for having kids. I can't even keep myself sane. That poor girl will be traumatised in the morning. Lucca, I know you're only trying to help, but you've been the best therapy for me. I love the kids, but spending time with them is triggering so many memories. What if I had kids and I'm still like that around them? I'd be a basket case and have nightmares which would continually upset them." I try to reason with him.

He kisses my head then my lips. "I love you so much."

A sleepy looking Roberta walks into the bathroom, yawning and rubbing her eyes. "I need a pee-pee," she says, looking a little scared. Then we hear Antonia crying from her travel cot. The full house will be up next.

"I will get the baby, you stay with Roberta," Lucca says.

After helping her to wash her hands, I splash my face then carry her back to bed. Lucca is on the bed with Antonia leaning on his chest, the skin on her cheeks red and inflamed, and she's gnawing at her knuckles. I tuck Roberta in and kiss her head, having to hold back tears that I've had to settle her, and try to remain strong as if everything is alright because I don't want to upset her.

"Sweet dreams, angel," I whisper. Then I walk around towards Lucca and take Antonia from his arms.

"Uncle Lucca, I'm not tired. Can you tell me a story?" Roberta says, peeking up at him. I smile at him adoringly as he cuddles her into his side.

"Once upon a time, there was a prince named Lucca who was very lonely, so he was searching for the love of his life." I smile at his sweet story, albeit a little corny. "Destiny and fate plays a big part in this story as Prince Lucca meets his Princess Lexi."

Roberta yawns and falls asleep during Lucca's retelling of the garden of paradise wedding proposal.

After soothing Antonia's gums with her teething gel, I sway her in my arms and sing "Dream A Little Dream" to her— the same song my mum hushed to me. Closing my eyes, I recall many nights lying on the dirty mattress in our shed after Michael bullied and tormented me, and Mum would calm and soothe me with her sweet singing.

After the terrifying ordeal when I found her tied to Simon's bed for the first time, and I went into shock, it was Mum singing "Dream A Little Dream" that gradually helped me. At first I liked the softness in her voice. I responded by tapping my fingers against her arms. Then I'd sway along with the melody. After a few more nights, I really listened to the words and associated this song with Mum loving, protecting, and cherishing me. I would then hum along ... until I eventually began singing some words along with her. Several weeks passed and by the time I sang the full song with her, I was fully communicating again in speech and showing various emotions.

I can feel myself becoming very emotional. Although this song was always a successful way for Mum to soothe me, it also brings back memories that disturb me. The night we got away and escaped, Mum had to soothe me for several weeks afterwards when I was in shock again by singing this very song, day in day out.

Fire.
Screaming.
Yelling.
Blood.
Tears.
Moss.
Dirt.
Dig.
Escape.
Gun.
Shoot.
Bang.
Panic.
Run.
Free.
Breathe.

I feel a sharp pain in my chest, and I force myself to fight it, to be strong, because I don't want the baby picking up on my tension. Closing my eyes, I breathe slowly with control and pick another song.

Antonia is fighting against sleep, so I swaddle her in my arms and sing Eva Cassidy's version of "Somewhere over the Rainbow," another one of Mums favourites, but I associate it with happy memories because Grandpa plays this tune on his harmonica. Lucca slides out of bed and wraps his arms around my waist, swaying with me side to side, and despite the haunting memories I incited tonight, I don't want this moment to end.

When her little eyelids close over, I kiss her then place her down in the cot, wrapping her blanket around her. Lucca turns me around to face him.

"That was really precious. You are gifted, Lexi, and a real natural with her. Thank you," he whispers. Then he sways me and sings quietly, "Dream A Little Dream" into my ear. He's trying to settle me peacefully as I have just done with the baby, but given my latest vision, the night that we escaped, I begin to cry. Hearing the words sung back to me has broken me. As quietly as I can, I shake and sob against him. Lucca guides me into the living area of our suite so we don't disturb the girls anymore.

He doesn't bother putting the light on. He sits on the sofa and pulls me onto his lap. I'm so emotional and want to clutch onto him as tightly as I can. I turn around, kneeling at either side of him, and envelope myself around him like a monkey hugging a tree. I need this closeness and it's not even close enough. My shoulders jerk, body shudders, and chest aches while I cry hysterically against him.

"Jesus, baby, shush now, I have you. It is okay." Lucca rocks me back and forth while I practically strangle him—I'm gripping that tight—and rubbing my nose beneath his ear.

"It's the song, I thought it would help calm Antonia. Mum used to sing it to me; it soothes me, but tonight it elicited some bad memories after the dream I had. I'm such a mess." I cry and cry.

"Do you want to tell me about it?" he asks attentively, giving me considerate caresses, tender kisses, and wipes my tears away, showing me nothing but love. Eventually once I'm more composed, I tell him snippets about the mattress on the ground in the shed and Mum singing to me at night time. He asks about why that particular song set me off tonight, so I tell him vague scraps about the night we escaped, deliberately leaving some vital information out.

"Christ," he gasps, sounding crushed listening to me. With one hand around my waist, his other hand rubs my back over my pyjama top then slips into my hair where he entangles some hair between his fingers and holds my head. "I want to *soothe you now*, make you relax, and take away those awful memories. I would love you to have good memories and think about a happy time before you fall asleep, it might help, si?"

I snivel and sigh, keeping my eyes closed, "Maybe, but I can't think of much right now." I sob. It's too exhausting having to pull up years of mental files and search H for happy. Perhaps if it weren't so late and I wasn't as distressed, I would be able to think clearly. It appears Lucca has other ideas to rekindle my happy thoughts.

He sings Andrea Bocelli's "Because We Believe" in Italian and English softly to me, reminding me of the happiest time of my life … when he proposed to me in our *garden of Eden* in The Four Seasons Hotel in Firenze.

Our song.

I smile against his chest and place a soft kiss on his neck. Standing up, we adjust, and I straddle his waist keeping a tight grip, ensuring I'm wrapped around him. Singing quietly, he paces the living room of the suite with me engulfed tightly around his body, soothing me … *reminding me* … until I'm relaxed and focused on my happy memories.

Our past.

Our future.

Our memories.

I wake in the morning to the sounds of giggles. Roberta is sprawled over me, playing with my hair, Lucca is bouncing Antonia up and down on his chest, and Emilio and A-Jay are under the covers at the bottom of the bed, playfully wriggling around. Lucca was right last night by saying she wouldn't remember a thing. I'm so relieved.

"We seem to have acquired a few more children," Lucca says. He looks so happy and spirited right now and very content with all the kids in the bed. I don't even need to imagine, I know this is what Lucca would like for his future.

"I see that." I smile. Roberta and I go under the covers and tickle the boys who are screaming and laughing.

"Is it musical beds? What is all the noise? We heard you from down the hall," Anna grumbles, yawning and stretching as she enters the suite with Cameron following close behind.

Walking over to the bed, she lifts Antonia off Lucca and sits on the chaise lounge with her.

"Hey, wee cheeks. Were you a good girly last night?" Antonia gargles, giggles, and pulls on Anna's hair.

Cameron takes a shot with Antonia, and she pulls his bottom lip and puts her fingers straight in his mouth. Anna watches and smiles then leans over and kisses the tattoo on his upper arm

Hmmm …

As Savio and Kate prepare breakfast, Dominic entertains Emilio and A-Jay, and Cameron and Anna take a turn looking after Antonia. Roberta and I sit on the sofa in the open plan kitchen area where I brush and braid her hair and play *"houses"* with her little wooden doll figures. I watch Hazel tie her trainers with her fitness clothes on and head towards the gym.

Shit.

I've got sweaty palm prints smudged all over the mirrors.

I haven't had a chance to clean them, and the housekeepers aren't due until Monday. Not that Hazel would mind, but I don't want people thinking that way of me. I hope it's not too obvious.

While Savio and Kate have breakfast underhand, I head back upstairs to our suite, make our bed, then join Lucca in the bathroom.

"Are you okay?" Lucca asks, leaning over for his shaving foam.

"Yes, I'm good. I've enjoyed spending time with the kids. They're great, but I'm just feeling tired. I don't know how Sarah does it every night. Lucca ... about last night, I feel so bad about waking the kids up and scaring Roberta. Do you see why I wouldn't be a good mother? The poor girl shouldn't see that, and let me tell you I witnessed my mum having nightmares, horrendous ones and it's traumatic. I remember some of them," I say, wrapping my arms around his waist, resting my chin on his shoulder.

He moves my hair to the side and places soft kisses on my neck. "Lexi, you were not too loud and did not say anything remotely scary, and Roberta is too young to comprehend. I knew she would wake up and forget what happened so please do not feel bad." He stares in the mirror with reassuring warmth in his eyes.

"Yeah, maybe." I sigh, watching him rinse his razor blade underneath the tap. "I just think I caused more harm than good. All I wanted to do was help Sarah and Kate but I ..."

"I am sure Sarah appreciated your help. They have all told me they love you, and I know the kids adore you. Sarah and Kate said you were a natural. It makes me so happy to see you bond with them. Please do not doubt yourself; you were great with the girls last night." He kisses me then begins his shave. This leaves me with a lot to think about.

After breakfast I take Doris out for a walk with Cameron to Bothwell Castle grounds and have a long discussion about his love predicament.

"So, you and Anna. Is it serious? Lucca seems to think it is," I ask, tossing up some leaves with my feet. He picks up some sticks to throw to Doris, and then we sit on a bench overlooking the river. "Anna isn't like anyone I have ever met before. She is so different. When I saw her in Tuscany I was instantly attracted to her. How could I not be? She's gorgeous but it's more than that. I love her sass, tongue and cheek, and smart mouth."

He runs both hands over his hair shaping it up at the front then shakes it out. I did see something in his eyes last night that told me he was falling for her. Perhaps their relationship is as deep as Anna was trying to make out.

"I mean, she's ballsy and confident and full of life. She has a mind of her own and she's not the clingy type. She's independent and knows what she wants. I like that she's decisive. Also, she makes me laugh, apart from the fact she's shit hot, it's like hanging out with a dude. She has a wicked sense of humour sometimes. We've had a great time together." He cocks his head, taps his feet, and waits nervously on my response.

I think about what he's said and maybe he is right that they might be compatible. The last thing Cameron needs is someone who's needy and clingy around the clock, especially when he works crazy shifts.

"Oh, I never realised how much you actually do care for her. I thought you were just having a bit of fun." I walk over to Doris and help her find the stick she's been looking for then throw it in the shallow river, and she frantically gallops in splashing around the water.

"It started as fun but the more time I spend with her, the more I feel for her. It's not like we're going to settle down, but shit, I can't stay away from her. She has helped me, you know. When I came back from Tuscany I was fucked up a bit, because of you telling me about your abuse. It got me thinking about my own abuse and my mind was all over the shit. Anna was patient, she helped me … showed me lots of compassion, and we shared something special. I've never had that before with another woman. Rachel is as deep as the ocean, and you know I am too, so neither of us truly opened up to one another, but with Anna … I don't know, she has a way of encouraging me to open up and talk, and surprisingly it felt good."

He sighs staring out at the river with one hand wrapped around the tattoos on his arm.

I walk back to stand in front of him. I do understand his words because Lucca does the same for me; perhaps it's a talented Caruso family trait … *counselling*. I know that those two are in deep together. "Don't you think people will think it's weird that we're brother and sister and so are Lucca and Anna?"

He quirks his lip and grins. "Lex, you are so naive sometimes, it's unreal. I don't think there are any rules. We are individuals and so are they, and nobody is going to judge us."

"Hmmm, I guess. Does that mean you *are* officially going to be a couple?" I chew the inside of my lip. "Look, I'm worried, if you screw things up with her it will cause problems between Lucca and me." I kick a stone and nibble my bottom lip.

"C'mere." He jumps up, puts his arm around me, and hugs me. "I wouldn't do anything to hurt or upset you, and you will always come first. *Always.* The only reason I'm telling you this shit about Anna is because I know you don't approve, and I'd like you to get it. But, you have nothing to worry about. I promise you."

Promise.

A promise is a promise.

I believe him.

When I broach the subject of Lucy, he tenses up rigidly, looking down, and runs his hand through his shaggy hair messing up his unruly style again. Although he has opened up about Anna, I think he finds it hard to talk about Lucy because he knows how protective I am of my friends.

"You know, Lucy still has a lot of strong feelings for you, Cameron. She can't move on while she's still hankering over you. I feel so sorry for her, and it pains me to see her upset. Do you still have feelings for her?" I ask as we start walking back.

"It was a while ago. I like Lucy a lot, and I had an amazing time with her, but the timing was off and ... oh, I don't know. I will put this right, Lex, I know how you feel about it, and the last thing I want is to give Lucy any false pretence and lead her on. She deserves someone better than me and should move on. I don't want to hurt her either." He scuffs some pebbles on the ground.

Got it loud and clear. He does have feelings for Lucy deep down.

Fuck!

File L for love. The love triangle Cameron is messed up in.

I decide to drop it because he obviously doesn't want to tell me too much about Lucy. On the way back to the house, I ask, "Have you thought anymore about going to see Casey?"

He shrugs and says, "I don't feel like I need to."

I was shocked to discover Cameron had also been subjected to sexual abuse when we were held captive. "I'm still having night terrors. Lucca wants me to go back and see her," I say before we approach the house.

He stops, places his hand on my shoulders, and turns me around, looking at me with warmth and sincerity. "Well, then you should. You trust her and it wouldn't do any harm. I'll come with you if you like, but shit, Lex, don't ask me to go in for a session. I like dealing with it my way, and Anna has been good for me. You definitely should though."

I smile half-heartedly because I appreciate his gesture, but I can't help feeling he's in denial and afraid to admit he might need to talk about his experiences. If I didn't know him any better, I'd say it's because he probably thinks it's a chick thing to do. He hates not appearing macho. Doris gallops into the living room and slumps on the carpet against the sofa, thoroughly exhausted. The front of the house is quiet. I walk through to the pool area and everyone is in the water.

Chapter 14: I'm all his

The kids look adorable in their armbands and swimwear. I sit on the end of a lounger waving to the kids and smiling at them, encouraging them to have fun. Lucca places his brawny arms on the pool edge then lifts himself up, looking very much the Italian god I've fallen in love with. He strides over to me, lifting his hands to sweep his wet hair back, exposing his ripped abs.

"You coming in?" he asks, leaning over and kissing me, saturating me with his dripping body.

"I'm not sure."

"Puhweese, Aunty Wexi. I can swim, wook at me!" A-Jay shouts while trying to paddle in Armando's arms, splashing everywhere.

"What's wrong?" Lucca quietly asks me, slowly moving my chin forward so I'm looking straight into his eyes.

"My scars," I whisper on a shiver then rub my thumb across my brow.

"Baby, no one will even acknowledge them. The kids might say something but they are too young to know any better. If you would feel better, wear a vest over your swimwear. This is your family now, and nobody will judge you. Please do not shy away. You are beautiful, and you have nothing to worry about. I do not even notice your scars. All I see is your beauty." His eyes are soft and earnest, as if he's pleading with me. Roberta paddles across the pool, splashing her legs, then rests her chin on the side.

"Aunty Lexi, can you come and play with me?" she begs.

I can't say no to that sweet face. "Okay, okay. I'm going to change. I'll be down in a minute."

"Good girl," Lucca says then kisses me before jumping in the pool and sending the children into fits of giggles. Walking past the steam room door, I can vaguely see Anna through the cloudy glass. I pass Cameron on the way up to the suite, and he's got a towel around his waist.

"Anna's in the steam room," I say, and he smirks at me with his boyish grin. I perish that thought and shake my head.

After I make a quick call to Mr. Carlin to check on him, I put on a ruched, deep-purple bikini with a gold brooch to the centre of the bust and at both hips, then slip a sheer, purple and gold trimmed kaftan over the top. I roll a towel under my arms and head towards the pool, opting to leave my hair down so it covers my back.

Lucca watches me from across the pool as I slip my kaftan off. I slide into the pool and notice a dark shadow under the water swim towards me. Lucca takes hold of my hips then emerges from the water, sliding up my body and pressing his taught body against me.

"Nice bikini. Can I rip it off you later with my teeth?" he asks as he discreetly slides his thumb under the elastic waistband at my hips.

My skin convulses with his small touch. We don't usually swim together clothed, we're normally naked, but this just adds to the suspense and excitement. I drag my bottom lip under my top teeth.

"I need to speak to you about something, when you were upstairs … we …um …" He frowns and pinches his eyes closed, as if he is in turmoil about telling me something bad or something I won't like. Now he has me panicked.

Ready to ask what's wrong, I'm shaken straight out of that thought when the kids giggle and splash towards us. Roberta paddles towards me in her cute, red bikini, armbands on, and jumps up on me. I swirl her around the water while she holds her head back, her blonde hair floats in the water around her.

"You look like a mermaid, Roberta," I say, leaving Lucca to lean on the poolside edge rubbing his thumb over his eyebrow.

"Lexi, we need to …" he reaches for my waist under the water to protectively pull me closer to him while I try and entertain Roberta.

Pausing with my water play, I notice Anna is not alone as she exits the steam room—Kimberley is with her in a shimmery-gold, slinky bikini that barely covers her ass, strutting like a catwalk model.

Bitch!

Fuck!

File S for stop. Stop stalking our family time. Why is she even here?

Lucca lifts Roberta off me and swooshes her through the water towards Kate's arms. He frowns as he turns to face me looking cautiously with a flicker of pain in his eyes.

"Why is your assistant, the one you used to sleep with, at your family weekend in a bikini, strutting around your pool?" My tone is cold and sharp, body rigid.

He sighs. "I was trying to tell you. Anna invited her. She is her best friend, and they normally spend weekends together, and we are at a pool so she is in a swimsuit. I am so sorry. She just turned up when you were upstairs. Anna arranged it with her and thought nothing of it because she does not know how you feel about her." He sighs, knowing how I will react and he would be right.

"So she hangs around here a lot, then?" I snap with sarcasm, turning my back; he swirls me back around as quick as I turned.

"Baby, please, do not get upset. I know you must be angry right now, and I understand why. She is Anna's guest, not mine, and given how you feel about Kimberley, she is the last person I would invite to something like this. I cannot very well tell my sister to un-invite her best friend when she was already standing here with her swim stuff, but I will make sure that Anna knows I am not happy about it and ensure this never happens again. It is your home and if you do not want Kimberley here, then I promise she will never be invited again," he says sincerely.

"I thought the talk we had the other night would make me feel better about this, to a certain extent, but now … seeing her here like this has made me feel worse, adding more salt to my wounds," I complain quietly.

I lean on the side of the pool and pull myself up then reach for my towel. I wrap it around me and walk through the spa area towards the family room. I storm upstairs into the suite and slide my wet bikini off, patting dry my skin. Wrapping my robe around me, I twist a towel over my head then pull back the covers and climb into bed in a stupor. I'm infuriated and enraged with jealously. I don't want her here because she's rude and vindictive.

Moments later, Lucca is standing at the bottom of the bed with a towel around him. "Are you ready to talk about this?" he asks. I fidget with my robe and don't answer. "Baby, I know you are angry. I am so sorry you feel like this. What can I do other than ask her to leave? But Anna is going to wonder why, so we will need to tell her. I know it is awkward and unpleasant. Fuck … this is such a mess." He groans and shakes his head.

Standing at the bottom of the bed, he cocks his head, silently pleading with me to calm down. Turning up for lunch fully clothed would be one thing, but to see her flaunt around in sexy swimwear like that fucking infuriates me. She is deliberating trying to make me jealous. It's not fucking okay. I wonder if Hazel has seen her yet. Maybe I should just brush it off because I know by the time Hazel finishes clawing at her, she'll be left feeling raw and wishing she never showed up here.

Lucca looks down at my wet swimwear on the towel. "Are you annoyed she is in the pool? Spending time with the family or here in general? Help me understand what you are thinking. I want to make this right. I promised you I would do what I need to, to consider your feelings and talking about it the other night helped us." He wipes at some droplets of water on his face that drips from his hair.

"Are you seriously asking me that question? You're just about as intuitive as Cameron. All of it, the pool, the family and the fact she is in your home when she is supposed to be a fucking employee. It's wrong ... and a swimsuit? A slutty, fucking gold swimsuit? She wants you to notice her parading about like that. I'm so goddamn furious." I raise my voice, tsk, sigh, and look away.

"Is that worrying you? Jesus, Doc. I have told you a million times that I can never look at another woman when I have you. I do not need to. My eyes are for you and only you, and if I need to remind you how goddamn sexy, beautiful, and attractive you are to me, then I will do it every minute of every day by telling you and showing you." He softens his voice, still husky but much more considerate.

"Your lovey-dovey words, Lucca, can't make my insecurities go away or change how I feel." I moan and slap my hands on the mattress in a mini tantrum.

"That is just it. I need to make you feel, feel us. I need to remind you how we feel together and how much I want you. That fiery shit is turning me on. Keep talking, baby," he says, untying his board shorts and letting them drop to the floor, his massive arousal springing free. I can't help but stare directly at him.

"Oh no, you don't. You're not distracting me. I'm serious, Lucca. I'm pissed off, and we need to talk about this," I protest.

Blatantly ignoring me, he pulls the covers back, climbs on top, and unties my robe.

Sexy bully.

My breasts are still cold from being wet, and my nipples pucker as soon as the air brushes against them. Groaning, he lifts my feet.

"Would you be more relaxed if I do this?" He kneads the soles of my feet, and it feels like heaven. I begin to relax. Then he kisses the bottom of them, and I squirm and giggle. He continues his magical touch along the inside of my legs, stroking, pressing, and kissing. I'm done for.

Folded.

Crumbled.

Melted.

"We need to talk," I stifle, infuriated my body is betraying me.

"You talk, I will play, then we will talk together afterwards," he says before his tongue caresses my pulsing sex. The only talking I can manage now is the letter O in the form of deep, sensual groaning.

Completely sated and thoroughly exhausted, I stretch on top of Lucca at the bottom of the bed with my forehead against his, my sensitive breasts pressed against his quickened heartbeat and my legs languidly straddling him.

He's managed to do it again—relax me, bringing me back to rational focus. He runs his thumb and fingers down my back and over my ass, softly stroking my skin with his fingertips.

"Are we in love again?" he asks, nibbling on my bottom lip.

"Yes, I'm always in love with you, but I need to tell you how I feel, and you keep distracting me. I know how you feel about me, but I also know how she feels about you and I don't think she can be trusted." I'd welcome this distraction anytime because he makes me *feel*, but talking is a must or else I'm going to explode today.

He rolls me over onto my back then leans on one arm at my side, placing his other hand on my navel. I take a huge breath. I need to be honest about my feelings or they will fester away at me.

"I'm jealous. There I said it. I'm jealous of her." I focus on something on the ceiling because I'm embarrassed by saying this and don't want to look him right in the eyes.

He studies my expression with genuine concern. Moving a tousled wave from my eyes, he skims over my cheek with his thumb then over my lips. "The last thing I want is you being uncomfortable or jealous. You have no reason to be. You are mine and I am yours. You are all I will ever want or need. You need to trust me but I am glad you are being honest with me. It is killing me, Lexi. I do not want my fiancée ever to feel jealous. Promise me you will listen to me when I tell you how much you mean to me. I cannot handle the thought that you feel envious and especially of someone like Kimberley." He leans over to kiss me all over with nothing but sweet, tender, loving care.

My stomach churns and I feel an awful weight tugging inside my core. It's the dreaded guilt pulling me towards that black cave. *Darkness.*

"You have nothing and no one to feel envious of. If anything, Kimberley most likely feels more awkward than you do. She has never seen me in a relationship other than with Francesca, and if she has feelings towards me like you say, then she will be hurting because of the love I have for you and only you. She is making a fool of herself if she thinks for one moment I am going to pay her any attention. If anything it makes me lose respect in her even more." He nibbles on the shell of my ear.

I twirl his wavy, wet hair with my fingers from one hand and stroke his chest with my other. "I spoke to Suzanne yesterday about moving Kimberley's position. Suzanne is fine with it as long as I find someone to fill Kimberley's post to help Suzanne with her work load."

"Oh … I know you talked about it, I didn't think you would actually move her job." I am so relieved he is taking this seriously.

"Yes, of course I am. I said I would and I made you a promise. I actually was thinking she could work in the admin office in

Edinburgh Club di Energia. That would get her far enough away. If she moans about the travelling, then she has a choice to make: stay or go. I love you, dolcezza, and will do anything it takes to make you happy."

I tilt my head to the side, nuzzling into his chest, and he protectively pulls his arm around me, enfolding me in his grip. "I know you do. Please, don't mention anything to Anna until later. I don't want to be seen as the insecure new girlfriend while Kimberley is still here or give her the satisfaction that she is getting to me." I sigh.

"*Fiancée*," he corrects then adds, "Whatever you want. I will make sure she leaves after lunch. She has wasted enough of our family time today."

"Are you mad at me for storming away?" I gingerly ask.

"No, how could I ever be mad at you? You are too fucking adorable." He leans over and places soft kisses on my swollen lips.

I find dry swimwear to put on. This time I choose my emerald green bikini. It will be obvious that we've been preoccupied with each other, but the other swimwear is wet and cold and would be too uncomfortable against my skin. After the baby monitor incident last night, nothing could be as mortifying, but I actually would love to make a point to Kimberley.

Lucca fastens the bikini strap at my back. "Hmmm, this makes me think of the day I stripped this off you at the farmhouse," he rasps in my ear then places gentle kisses on my shoulders. He grasps both my breasts, rubbing his thumb across the edge of the bikini, and adds, "We also need to discuss next week. I have to work away, but I want you with me if you are going to continue to have nightmares." We touched on this but never came to a conclusion about it.

I turn around, wrapping my arms around his neck. "Thank you for looking after me, but honestly, I'll be fine. I'll have Hazel, Cameron, Lucy, or Jess come and stay with me. I have an appointment at the family planning clinic, and I've made arrangements with Mark to go into the clinic for a day. I don't want to leave Doris again after just getting back, and I've promised Jane I would meet her for lunch."

Choices.

I've made my decision. As much as it pains me to be separated from him, I have obligations and I need to stay here.

He tenses and clutches at my shoulders, piercing me with despondent eyes. "Firstly, I am not having you go back to work yet, and definitely not while you are still recovering. Secondly, you never told me you had an appointment at the family planning clinic." He's not enthused. I knew he would react like this. That's why I never told him.

"I told you that I wanted a more permanent form of contraception in Tuscany. You don't want to wear condoms, and there is always a chance you might have to if I miss a pill."

"What do you mean permanent? You are not considering some crazy shit like getting sterilised, are you?" He's panicking now.

"No, just something like an injection. I can get one every twelve weeks, and then I don't have to worry about taking the pill. It's completely safe, and fertility normally resumes afterwards. It's just a consultation," I explain.

"Lexi, I think we need to talk about this further. I want to have a family with you, and don't want to wait years to do so. This sounds like an extreme option." He pinches his forehead with his middle finger and thumb in agitation.

"Lucca, stop pressuring me. It's my body," I protest. I wasn't able to have control over things that happened to my body as a child, so I most definitely will make sure I do as an adult.

He looks anguished, dropping his hands from my shoulders and slumping his own shoulders, completely deflated. He looks down and is momentarily silent.

"I'm not ready to have kids yet, so please just accept that the contraception is only temporary until we decide the time is right to try," I add, because even though I'm making choices regarding my body, I am willing to compromise, especially after the time I've spent around the kids. It's got me thinking about the concept of having kids at some point, especially with Lucca. This is something I would never have considered, ever, but I am warming to the idea.

He looks up at me with huge hopeful eyes and a massive smile. "Are you telling me you have changed your mind and that you do want to have a family with me?" He places his arms around my waist, pulling me in close to him.

"Yes, I've been thinking about it … how good you are with the kids and with Antonia, and how much I wanted to nurture and care for her. I never thought I would have a maternal instinct, but I enjoyed it. It felt natural. I loved watching you be so soft, caring, and attentive with them, especially the baby. It warmed my heart."

He picks me up, holding me tightly to his upper body and wrapping my legs around his waist, then kisses me fervently. "You have made me very happy indeed. God, I love you. You will be an amazing mother."

Once he has left my mouth to let me breathe, I add for safe measure, "I'll definitely consider it, but not until after we're married, and it will depend on my emotional state as well. It's only fair."

He smiles in acceptance. "Okay, I will take it."

Holding hands in serenity, we walk back through to the pool to find chaos. Hazel is sitting in the Jacuzzi with Dominic, Anna, and Cameron. Kimberley is sitting on the ledge, dangling her feet into the water. Trying to keep my composure, I walk around the ledge and reluctantly welcome Kimberley.

Hazel presses her lips in a firm line and raises her eyebrow to Lucca and then nods towards Kimberley. She is letting him know she is not happy with Kimberley being here either, it appears.

"You two are unreal. Another quick change? Can you not keep your hands off one another?" Anna giggles.

Kimberley clucks her tongue then slithers down, submerging herself into the Jacuzzi to join them. Hazel smiles, pleased that unintentionally Anna has pissed Kimberley off. I feel satisfied Kimberley knows exactly what Lucca and I have been up to. Hazel taps her middle finger on her chin, and I know she's contemplating something.

Excusing myself, I go back into the pool to play with the kids. Kimberly has a full view of my back and will undoubtedly see my scars, but I'm going to try to dismiss that anxiety, thinking of Lucca's kind words and reassurance.

He likes me confidant. If she can show her body off, then so can I—scars as well.

"Ewww, what's that on your back?" Kimberley blurts out for all to hear, drawing attention to me.

The kids have now noticed, and while I explain to them it is just some marks and convince a worried looking Roberta that it isn't sore and I can't feel them, Anna has scolded Kimberley for being rude. Kate and Sarah take the kids and move them to the far side of the pool.

"Kimberley! That was uncalled for. Why do you have to be so rude?" Anna says, totally shocked and seems flushed with embarrassment for Kimberley's outburst. Cameron tenses, filled with rage, as does Lucca.

"What? I'm only asking a question," Kimberley says but doesn't even look remotely apologetic.

Hazel sees me flustered and clenching my jaw. "You know what, Anna, I don't care much for your friend and maybe now you might start to see how much she is deliberately trying to annoy and hurt Lexi. In fact, Kimberley, I'm done sitting in your company. It has been very unpleasant and it's unfortunate, because it was such a great day until you arrived to try and ruin it," Hazel says, leaving both Kimberley and Anna gobsmacked. She gets up and walks towards the steam room, followed by Dominic.

Lucca leans on the ledge of the Jacuzzi and tells Anna in a flat but firm tone that they need to talk later. Kimberley bristles and rolls her eyes. He completely ignores Kimberley and doesn't make any eye contact. Cameron looks at me wondering what the hell is going on and shrugs. Then Lucca strokes my back and moves me away towards the kids, who thankfully were splashing around and didn't pay any attention to the exchanged words.

Sarah thanks me profusely for the babysitting duties and says she's never felt more energetic after having a good sleep. Putting a brave face on, I put my arms out to Antonia to take her for a while. I'm ecstatic that she giggles and practically jumps into my arms, splashing her chubby, little legs eagerly as she tries to climb into my embrace. She looks adorable in a lemon and pink frilled swimsuit. I kiss her plump cheeks then wade around the water with her.

"Wook, Aunty Wexi, I'm a shark!" Emilio shouts.

"Wow, that's great, Emilio," I praise as I watch him put his face under the water. Roberta has leaped on my back, wrapping her legs around my waist and her arms around my neck as she enjoys a piggyback ride through the water.

After smiling and watching me closely, Lucca finally joins us to take Antonia from my arms, noticing I'm being weighed down with the other kids. She puts her hands straight in his mouth, babbling and blowing bubbles. There is something very sexy about him holding the baby.

It's endearing. My heart picks up a staccato rhythm watching him, and I ruminate about our future. I think I could actually do this for him after we're married. When I know no one can hear, I kiss his shoulder, resting my chin there and whisper, "If you're going to be that sexy and handsome with our baby one day, we might need to get married as soon as possible." Jesus my emotions are all over the place. One minute I'm so opposed to the idea and the next I warm to it. It's mentally exhausting.

"Antonia, do you know how much I love this woman?" he says in an animated voice. She chuckles at him, rocking in his arms. Armando takes Antonia to get her dried off for her lunch, and Lucca pulls me to him, kissing me heatedly.

"Ewww!" the boys squeal when they see us kissing.

"Give it a rest," Cameron groans.

Kimberley glances towards us very icily. Then she slinks off to the sauna with Anna to probably gossip about what was said earlier. I hope Anna puts her in her place. Cameron is unbelievable. I need to watch his flirtatious ways and sexual gestures, but it is not appropriate in front of the kids so I take the opportunity to splash Lucca playfully then mingle with Kate and Sarah.

After another delicious family lunch, I ask Hazel to help me clear up in the kitchen to give us some privacy to talk while Lucca is talking with Anna in his study. Cameron and Dominic are outside with Doris and the boys, kicking a ball around, while Kate, Sarah, Armando, and Savio are in the family room with the girls.

"Thank you for sticking up for me earlier," I say, putting the milk back in the fridge.

"You're welcome. I was not having that devious little bitch speak to you like that. She was trying to get a reaction out of you. You did the right thing by ignoring her. I think that annoyed her more. I probably pissed Anna off, but no wonder. Does she honestly think her best friend is a nice person?" Hazel scrapes some plates and puts them in the dishwasher. "I take it you never knew she was coming?"

"No, I didn't. Apparently Anna invited her; Lucca is having a word with her now. I swear she bloody infuriates me," I curse, rinsing some glasses.

"Roo, I'm telling you that girl is trouble. You were right to pick up on something the night you met her at dinner. I don't understand how she and Anna are friends, because they're so different. Kimberley is riddled with jealously, so you're going to have to be careful. She feels very threatened by you; even Dominic picked up on it. Before you and Lucca returned, she was being manipulative, asking Anna things about you until I eventually butted in and said if she wanted to know anything to ask me. After all, I was sitting right next to her."

Hazel follows me into the pantry where I place some ingredients back on the shelves.

I shrug. "I don't know what to do about her. I'm not happy that's she's here. In fact, I'm pissed about it, and it's been annoying me all afternoon."

"You need to tell Lucca and keep her at a distance. There is just something I can't put my finger on. She's not trustworthy." Hazel is very serious, and I trust her instincts because she is a good judge of character.

I drop my dishcloth and hug her. "I did, we chatted about it. I think he's going to shuffle her to a different position, but don't mention anything. Thank you for looking out for me. I love you." I step back, holding her hands. "Do you know she has a history with Lucca?" I think this is what is getting to me more.

Hazel lifts her eyebrows and puts her hands on her hips. "Do you think I'm stupid? She still wants him, Lexi, and I wouldn't be surprised if she's using Anna to get to him." Hazel nods her head with a knowing look.

Lucca brings his laptop from the office to the open living area of the kitchen and sets it up.

"Did you speak to Anna?" I ask, gathering the place mats from the table.

"Yes. She had no idea that Kimberley has been so rude to you and how you feel about it, and she said she never would have invited her if she knew it was going to upset you. I have asked her not to invite her back." He lowers his tone so no one overhears. Hazel on the other hand doesn't seem to care who hears her.

"Well good. Having your past continually thrown in Lexi's face is pissing me off. An employee should not be hanging out at your family home, never mind one of your exes who obviously has it in for Lexi. I'm surprised you never threw her gold slinky ass right out the pool. If I were not a guest here, I would have dragged her out. Are you going to invite Miss threesome around for a splash as well?" Hazel rants with her hand on her hip.

Lucca sounds offended and hurt with her words. "Of course not. I agree she should not be here, and quite frankly I am fucking pissed off too that she is. Anna is talking to her just now. Lexi, are you okay, baby?" He sounds exasperated and genuinely annoyed. He cocks his head, looking over Hazel's shoulder at me.

"Yes, I am just ..." Hazel nudges me in the waist to warn me that Anna and the others have returned so I keep quiet and we change the subject.

Lucca Skypes his parents. Antonio and Marissa have his grandparents over visiting, allowing them to speak and see the family through the webcam. Marissa, looking smart and beautifully tailored with her hair styled in place, weeps as she speaks to her grandchildren. She's overwhelmed with longing and emotion, missing them all very much. We catch up on lots of various topics and have a nice time speaking with them.

Marissa takes the opportunity to ask if we are any further with the wedding plans, to which I try to change the subject. Sarah giggles and nudges my waist discreetly so they can't see, but Lucca notices and he grins at our harmless fun and shakes his head, knowing how overbearing his mother can be, although she means well.

Antonia gets a little restless biting on her toy and Marissa notices. "Sarah, I was thinking I could come over and help you with Antonia when your maternity leave is finished. Poor darling's little gums are bothering her, and I hate the thought of her going into a nursery."

Sarah gasps and I prod her in the waist, returning the little joke we are sharing. Put on the spot, Sarah adds, "Um, thank you for the offer, Marissa, but honestly it's okay. I am extending my maternity leave this time. I like being at home with them, but it will be lovely to see you when you're home. The kids will love that."

I quietly giggle. Kate smiles as Sarah is cornered, and I am thankful the pressure is off of me.

"Plus, Lucca and Lexi are great with Antonia, so I know where to come if I need extra help." Sarah turns and gives me the cheekiest grin, and I have to look away to save myself from bursting into loud laughter.

"Well excellent, I am glad. Those two need lots of practice for when they give me more little darling grandchildren," Marissa enthusiastically says. That wipes the smile off my face quickly.

Antonia is getting more restless, so I take the opportunity and let everyone continue chatting as I walk with her into the living room and find Kimberley sitting on the sofa dressed in a skin-tight, cotton maxi dress that hugs her slender frame. She glances up towards me then drops her head and continues to scroll through her phone, not making any effort to speak.

Why is she still here?

I feel I need to be the mature person here. "So have you enjoyed your day so far?" It's the only question that comes to my mind.

"Yes, I used to spend a lot of time here on the weekends with Lucca, so it's nice to be back." She smirks.

Liar!

That's not even being filed. It's going straight in the shredder.

"Well, of course, you know I live here now, so if Anna is planning on coming over or inviting guests, she will need to check with us first to make sure it is a convenient time. Today perhaps was not the best day for her to invite you." It's abrupt but the most diplomatic way I can warn her off.

"It was never a problem before. In fact, I had my own key. We had an arrangement." Speaking casually, she continues scrolling through her phone, not even bothering to look up.

"You had an arrangement?" I interrupt. Now she looks up with a small smile.

"Maybe I'll just come over when you're not at home. We'll get more business done and it will be like old times. He'll probably be glad of my company because we're so good together." She's pressed a raw nerve with that comment.

"Kimberley, I don't know why you're being such a bitch towards me, but I've got no time for your juvenile behaviour. I don't appreciate your tone or remarks, and I'll make sure Lucca knows exactly what you're doing. I'd be careful if you value your job and your friendship with Anna. I'll tell everyone you are just leaving." Thinking I have the upper hand, I turn around, stepping towards the door as I carry Antonia on my hip.

"I don't give a shit about what Anna thinks. I care about Lucca. He's going to get bored with that goody-two-shoes, little-miss-perfect act you're putting on. He's wild and adventurous and likes his women with more confidence. When he dumps your ass, I'll be there for him just like I was when Fran bored him. I know exactly what he likes and needs." She twiddles her hair, sounding very smarmy and sure of herself.

Fire erupts from the deepest cavity in the black cave of my core, and I turn back around. "Kimberley, you're not welcome here. You don't threaten me in the slightest. Actually, I pity you because you're pathetic and you make me sick. You really are a spiteful little girl and need to get a life of your own." My temper is flaring. Fidgeting, I juggle Antonia back and forth between each hip because I'm agitated then pace the floor towards the sofa.

"Oh right, just like you have? Playing the helpless, innocent card and sponging off Lucca's money? Only difference between you and Fran is she had her own money and two normal parents that loved her. It's clear you're crying out for attention and love, and Lucca is an easy target, but that emotional crap is not the love he needs. He needs passion without emotion."

Stunned.

Speechless.

Shocked.

"How did you get on with your little threesome the other night? I meant to ask. Did Leila teach you a few things, or did you run a mile and let Lucca have her all to himself?" she asks nonchalantly, staring at her polished fingernails admiring them. If I weren't holding this baby I would get my nails right into her skin and rip her to pieces.

Fucking spiteful little bitch!

"How do you know about that? You conniving little ..." I spit, absolutely fuming.

"How do you think she knows the code for the gate? Hmmm?" She tilts her head and smiling and raising her brow.

Lucca storms in, strides past me, and pulls the baby monitor out of the socket next to the fireplace and places it next to Kimberley on the sofa. They've heard everything, and in this moment, I'm grateful.

"That is enough, Kimberley. That was uncalled for. Do not ever judge or speak about Lexi like that ever again, got it? I am so goddamn angry with you. I should have known you would be a problem. You are no longer welcome here ever again. I do not want anything to do with you. You are finished and you disgust me."

Lucca is enraged; he's clenching his jaw and running his hands through his hair. I watch as he fists his hands by his sides, causing the veins on his arms to surface with his muscles contracting so tensely.

Cameron is standing behind Lucca with the same angry, offended look and stance. I notice Hazel and Anna both standing and staring, completely appalled. I strap Antonia in her stroller with shaky hands then pass her to Hazel. She curtly nods and walks away with her but returns moments later.

Lucca's not finished scolding Kimberley yet. "How do you know about Leila? I swear to God, Kimberley, if you had anything to do with that I will see to it that your CV is so fucked up you will never get another decent job, not to mention I might be able to have you charged with conspiracy to commit unlawful entry." She clears her throat, bristles, but doesn't answer.

"I am not even interested. You have said enough, now fucking apologise. I am waiting." She's silent and can't make eye contact with any of us after her outburst. "Kimberley, you better fucking apologise so help me God ... and get that fucking idiotic fantasy out of your twisted head. I belong to Lexi."

"You deserve more," she replies.

Bitch!

"You are nothing to me, and you never will be. Lexi is fucking everything. How do you not understand this?" Lucca snarls, pacing up and down.

Anna stumbles forward, looking traumatised. "You were just using me to get to Lucca? All those years I confided in you, sacrificed, and put my neck on the line for you. I cannot believe you could be so conniving and devious." Anna's voice breaks, and her eyes fill with tears.

"Apologise to both of them!" Cameron shouts at Kimberley.

Fuck!

File C for catastrophe. Complete fucking catastrophe.

Anna takes Lucca's hand and leans into him. He comforts her by kissing the side of her head and rubbing her back. I still haven't moved. I'm alarmed and cold, my head is pounding, and I feel queasy, but I don't cry. I won't allow it. I want to stay strong for Lucca and for Anna. It's Hazel's turn. She pushes past us and heads to the sofa, pointing her finger right in front of Kimberley's face.

"I fucking new you were a horrible little cow. I was being exceptionally polite earlier, and honestly, I'm glad you showed your true colours today. Now everyone knows what a back stabbing little whore you really are. Don't ever ... and I mean *ever* interfere with their relationship again. Stay away, because if I find out you are playing games and meddling, you'll wish you had never met me." For someone so petite and dainty, Hazel can look determined and intimidating when she gets on her high horse.

"Kimberley, how could you? I am supposed to be your friend. This is my family you are messing with, and Lexi is family now. I am so fucking angry at you for upsetting her and hurt that you would use me like this. I cannot believe you would do this. You have absolutely maddened me today, and I do not think I can forgive you for this." Although Anna stays close to Lucca's side, she is beginning to break and hold back her tears.

Kimberley tsks, stands up, and moves past me, pushing me brusquely with her shoulder as she does. Before she makes it to the door, Lucca grabs her arm and leans close to her ear. The look on his face leaves no doubt that the words whispered in her ear are a threat. Her face is scarlet, and she looks as if she is about to cry, but she isn't given the opportunity. Cameron clutches her upper arm and pulls her to the living room door.

"Please, let me do the honours," Hazel chirps, grabbing at her wrist to drag her out, watching from the front door until she exits the main gates.

Anna is a blubbery mess. "I am so sorry. I do not know what got into her. I have never seen her like that before," she whimpers.

Lucca kisses the side of her head and warns her, "Anna, stay away from Kimberley please. Your friendship with her is not worth the heartache." She sniffles and nods. I give her a sympathetic smile, pressing my lips together.

"I'm sorry, Anna. I'm sorry you had to witness that," I mumble. She nods her head as tears flow down her cheeks then hugs me in such a warm, affectionate embrace, I melt into her.

"No, do not apologise, it was my poor judge of character. All this time she has been using me. I am so sorry, Lexi, please forgive me. I cannot apologise enough. I feel awful that you have had all this going on. I had no idea she was playing games, and I did not know she was rude to you the other night either. I would not have asked her here otherwise. You must think I am an insensitive bitch. I am so sorry." She sobs against my shoulder.

"No, I don't. I'd never think that. It's not your fault. At least you now know she was using you. Lucca is right, don't waste any more time on her," I reassure her, trying to comfort her because she's taking it bad, the embarrassment and the guilt.

Cameron takes Anna's hand, kisses her lips, and wipes under her eyes. "Come with me a minute," he says to her softly.

I like to see him caring and compassionate. I feel proud of him, and it's the first time I'm actually pleased to see both of them intimate with each other. Once Cameron and Anna have left, Lucca shuts the living room door and strides over to me. Wrapping his arms around me, he walks us back towards the sofa and collapses on it, taking me with him.

Lifting his chest, he inhales a long deep breath then exhales, burying his head into my soft, tousled hair. "Baby, I am so, so sorry. I should have listened to you and trusted your instincts. Are you okay?" he asks, running his hands under my top at the back, skimming my bare skin.

The heat of his hands is warming my skin and feels lovely. I relax and sink into his chest. "Yes, I'm fine," I whisper.

"Please, do not take anything that she said to heart. She is clearly twisted and being irrational. It means nothing. It is obvious she was trying to hurt you and succeeded. At least we now have some sort of explanation as to why Leila randomly showed up. Kimberley must have sent her."

I'm angry that Kimberley instigated that horrendous scene with Leila in my bed, but I'm also relieved that I know now that she didn't casually turn up here by chance. I glance up and he takes my face in both hands, kissing my eyebrows, then my eyes, nose, cheeks, and lips, lingering softly on my lips.

I no longer feel lost or empty.

"She was interrogating Hazel earlier and mocking me, so I was prepared for her backlash. It's okay, I won't take any of it to heart, I promise. I'm only sorry Anna was hurt by her."

"Cameron is a good guy. He will make sure she is okay. You are my priority. Please tell me you will be okay," he pleads, searching my eyes.

"I'm okay, honestly. I knew she was going to try and interfere somehow. I'm not affected by what she said, and I'd never let her have you anyway."

He chuckles. "Good, I am so proud of you and the way you stood up for yourself. God, you are so special to me. Have I told you lately that I love you?" He smiles, then skims his tongue along my bottom lip.

"Yes, you tell me all the time. I love you too, and just so you know, I wasn't prepared to let her anywhere near you. She says she has a key?" I ask inquisitively.

He runs his thumb over my bra strap causing me to tremble. His tone is sincere. "Not anymore. I had new doors put in last year. She only had a key because while I was in Naples working, there were renovations getting done at the main office and I allowed her and Suzanne to work from my study here while my other employees were set up in temporary offices. I have never been with her here in this house. She was trying to get a reaction from you."

I believe him. He did mention this before and I know Kimberley is a liar. "Did you hear the full conversation?"

"Pretty much. The baby monitor was on."

I rest my cheek on his chest. "Remind me when we have kids to be cautious of the baby monitors."

"Baby, let me see your eyes," he asks so softly that I smile.

He slides me up so he can look straight in my eyes again. His hot breath skims my bottom lip, and his beating heart pounds against my own chest. He doesn't need to say anything—he thanks me with his eyes and his tender touch.

I'm all his.

Chapter 15: Dark Black

We bury the Kimberley ordeal and head into the cinema room. The kids are jumping from seat to seat on beige, leather bucket chairs in the front row. Emilio and A-Jay being warned by their mums. They might get separated if they can't sit still. Anna looks a little weary from all her crying but much better than she was earlier. Cameron has shown her great comfort. He hasn't let go of her since Kimberley left, and it leaves me thinking that maybe they would make a good couple.

I smile, showing him how much I admire him right now.

He smiles back.

I take a seat second row from the back, and Roberta sits on my knee. There are many spare seats, but I think she likes the comfort. I braid her hair as she plays with her doll on my lap.

Hazel is in the row behind me. She leans over, and whispers, "What happens in the back row stays in the back row." Dominic shakes his head, nudging her.

"You're unbelievable. There are children here," I gripe.

"Oh relax, I'm only joking."

I'm not so sure she is.

Lucca and Armando return with a box of ice-cream tubs, chocolate, and drinks. Once everyone is sitting, the movie starts to play. Lucca takes his seat next to me, wrapping his arm around my shoulders.

It's the all-time classic, *Beauty and the Beast*. Roberta is thrilled because she loves anything princess, but the boys aren't so sure. I fall asleep just after "Be Our Guest," closing my eyes on Lucca's shoulders.

"Baby, wake up," Lucca whispers. My eyelids flutter open and it's dark and noisy with only the movie credits flickering on the screen.

Everyone is shuffling out of their seats. The adults go to the bar area, and Savio fixes everyone drinks while the kids run around the open plan attic family area next door to the cinema room. Lucca puts his surround sound music system on, and Snow Patrol's, "Chasing Cars" fills the room.

I sit on the corner sofa and bounce Antonia on my lap. She presses her feet into me using all her strength to straighten her legs so she can watch the boys drag some toy cars across the carpet. I place Antonia on the floor with the boys, and she's off, crawling and trying to pull herself up on the opposite sofa.

Hazel has sprawled out over the other sofa and looks very relaxed. The music changes to The Lumineers' "Ho Hey." Savio picks Roberta up and twirls her around the floor. She giggles and throws her head back, allowing her hair to flow down her back.

Sipping my fruity iced drink, I look over to Lucca behind the bar. His shirt sleeves are rolled up as he mixes drinks. Damn, he knows that sight makes me lose control and has a direct line to my sex. It's far too distracting and utterly hot. He winks at me, then leans over the bar, placing an umbrella in a fruity concoction.

The men go downstairs to prepare dinner, and Kate and Sarah ask what happened this afternoon. Anna and I explain quickly, desperate to put it behind us. By the time the boys have brought homemade pizzas from the kitchen, we're on our third cocktail and giggly.

When I see the huge pizza platters, I suddenly lose my appetite, thinking about last night's dream and the first time I tasted pizza. I choose to entertain Antonia while the others eat.

"Why are you not eating?" Lucca asks.

"Oh, I'm just not feeling like it right now," I passively reply.

"You should eat. I am worried that you are fretting over today."

"No, I'm fine, and I haven't given it another thought, honestly. This little madam is keeping me distracted. I'm good, so please eat yours, and I'll get something if I'm hungry," I reply more assertively.

"I thought you loved pizza?" I did tell Lucca about my nightmare last night, but it was more about how Michael manipulated me and made me watch him pleasure himself. I never mentioned the pizza. I thought it was irrelevant until now.

"I do, but I'm just not in the mood right now. I'm sorry." I shrug and sit on the floor, crossing my legs Indian style with Antonia between them climbing over me.

"You know, you think you've tasted pizza, but not until you've tried Savio's. His are to die for, even better than mine," Lucca says with a boyish smirk. He lifts a slice of pizza, takes a bite, then leans over me and holds out the slice to my mouth.

"Okay, I'll try it." Ordinarily I love pizza and it does smell great. I bite into it, closing my eyes with mixed emotions, but what's more empowering is the fusion of flavours, the texture, and the hot, soft, thin base.

It's divine.

Closing my eyes, I don't realise I'm making a low humming sound.

"Christ, you look sexy as fuck. Who would have thought pizza could be so orgasmic." He chuckles.

Instantly, I drop the pizza base on the platter and swallow a long, hard gulp, trying to pass it by the lump in my throat. "I'm done," I say sharply.

"Why? What is going on with you? Have I said something wrong?" Confused, he knits his brow then tilts my head up. I know he had no way of knowing and it wasn't intentional, and now he looks upset that he's hurt me.

"I'll tell you later, but please don't make a scene." I sit Antonia on her play mat, supported by cushions, and he takes my hand, excusing us as he leads me down the two staircases to the kitchen. He lifts me up onto the counter then places his hands on either side of me.

"Okay, talk. I am listening."

Sighing, I relay my nightmare to him in full this time—the first encounter with Michael Parks involving the pizza. He releases the air he has been holding then strides over to the fridge. He opens a bottle of Chianti and pours us both a glass of wine then lifts a ciabatta loaf and slices it. After rummaging around in the fridge, he places ingredients down on the counter.

"What are you doing?" I ask. He hasn't even commented yet and his behaviour is worrying me.

"I am making us a little something. It is not the right night for pizza, so I will muster something else up because I am not having you starve yourself."

He spreads leftover homemade pesto on the bread with salami, parma ham, sun dried tomatoes, basil, and mozzarella, then places it under the grill. He washes the board down with his back to me. He isn't looking at me, and he isn't asking any questions. He's angry.

"I shouldn't have told you. I'm sorry," I whisper.

Turning around, he shakes his head then runs his fingers through his hair. "No, I want you to tell me. I want you to be honest. If I am going to help you, I need to know about your nightmares, but it pains me to think of what that evil fucking monster did to you. It hurt last night when you told me, but I wanted to be strong for you, but now this, Lexi. It tears me up that he ..." He punches the pantry door in rage.

"Come here," I say cautiously, because he's going to breakdown. In role reversal, I need to be compassionate and reassuring towards him. Comfort him. I take his face in both my hands and kiss him softly. "I'm here, right here, and I'm not going anywhere. It's all in the past, Lucca. He can't touch me or harm me. I have you and you take it all away. You make me feel whole. Please don't be upset or feel guilty about what you said. You couldn't have known the pizza would upset me. I need you to be strong and forget about it all. Love me right here and think about our future. Please, calm down ... for me."

He closes his eyes, taking long, slow, steady breaths. "He is still fucking harming you, Lexi ... your mind. You are having nightmares about it, and I wish I could take it all away." His voice is broken.

I hold him, tenderly caressing him the way he does for me. I discover it's great therapy being the giver of comfort, and it relaxes me too. We sit on the kitchen floor, barefoot in our denim jeans with our wine, and eat our toasted ciabatta bread. There is something powerful and special about this moment binding us together.

Simple.

Forgiving.

Honest.

Relaxed, I rub my bare feet along Lucca's exposed ankles and lean my head on his shoulders, contemplating the last few weeks. I'm grateful.

"You know I will do anything for you, and I will give you anything. I just want to take it all away," Lucca says, slumped against the kitchen cupboard.

Sitting my plate down, I turn to look up to him. "I know you would. You've taught me to trust, to love, and to be loved. I've changed, Lucca, and I'm different. I have more confidence, and I'm not as paranoid. I'm stronger and better because of you."

"Jesus, I love you more every fucking day." He presses his nose on my shoulder, kissing my skin with his moist lips.

The party in the attic room is in full swing.

Cameron has his guitar, the kids are in bed, and Antonia is sleeping in the travel cot in our suite.

Lucca fixes drinks behind the bar as I slump on the sofa next to Anna and put my arms around her shoulders. I kiss her on the side of her head, then grasp her hand, and she grips my hand tightly before Cameron plays his next piece.

He's sitting on the snug chair with his leg crossed over the other knee looking very much the rock star. He strums some chords playing "The Cave" by Mumford and Sons and sings along with lyrics. The tone of his raspy voice is spot on, and his tuning is impeccable.

Anna's eyes become alive. She's captivated with his talent. She sits upright, entranced watching him, and in this moment, I'm so proud of my brother. I've chosen to forgive his flaws over the last few weeks and accept that they are falling in love with each other.

His next song is John Legend's "Ordinary People." Then he wows everyone with his version of "Iris" by the Goo Goo Dolls. Anna looks fit to be undone. It's the quietest I've ever seen her.

"You know, he is really talented. Plays great and has an amazing voice," Lucca says. Then he turns to me with his "light bulb moment" look.

"No way! Not a bloody chance. Forget it," I protest.

"Baby, you have an amazing voice. I have heard you sing. You and Cameron surely must sing together," he says enthusiastically.

"We did, but in private." Lowering my voice, I drop my gaze, shift with uneasiness, and set my drink down on the table.

"Lexi, this is your family now. I do not know why you would be bashful singing in front of us because you sing like an angel."

"No, Lucca, drop it."

I excuse myself to use the bathroom. On return, Cameron has the glint in his eye, the mischievous one, which means this has all been discussed while I was making myself scarce. Lucca walks over and takes my hand leading me to the sofa.

"Come on, Lexi, just one song. We will all take a turn if it makes you feel better," Anna suggests.

Cameron shifts in the snug chair. "What do you say, baby girl?"

"No." I scowl.

"Well, if you are not singing, then I am going to," Lucca says.

Oh shit.

Not that Lucca has a bad voice, but it's not brilliant either, and I would rather he kept it only for me in private. I have memories of him singing romantically into my ear after we danced with the baby, and when he proposed to me in Firenze, dancing around the private garden of our hotel suite, and it was lovely. I'd like the memory to stay lovely.

Hazel chirps, "She's not that good anyway, Kate. You'd need to cover your ears because she can't hold a tune and she'll crack that glass table." Hazel knows exactly what she's doing.

Fuel to my fire.

Heating up, I let go of Lucca's hand and stride towards Cameron, whispering in his ear. Then I sit next to him and singe Hazel with my eyes. I don't care for her mind games. Damn, she gets me every time with that reverse shit.

I'm so goddamn weak.

Cameron starts strumming, finding his chords, and once he has the rhythm, my nerves truly kick in. I rub my sweaty palms together, swallow, then close my eyes and begin to sing Kristina Train's "Dark Black" quietly until I reach my upper register in the chorus. I keep my eyes closed. It's a harrowing song with deep emotion, which is why I coast it effortlessly.

I'm pouring my heart into the dusky, moody melody, subtly staying true to the melancholy, pain, and anguish behind the lyrics. When I finally lift my head, opening my eyes, everyone is still, poised, entranced, and completely silent. It's like watching a silent movie and only I can hear my voice, but it's a distant echo and someone else is singing it to me. Like an out of body experience.

Humming at the end of the song, I shake with nerves, wondering how it's received and if I made a complete fool of myself.

Most likely.

I've never really sung in front of a group apart from when I was drunk, and I slurred some songs to the girls hugging an empty bottle of wine right before they hauled me into a taxi, but everyone jumps up off their seats to applaud me. I smile and blush. Lucca is captivated. His eyes thank me, and he blows me a kiss and winks.

"Wow, that was incredible," Sarah says.

Kate hugs and praises me. Armando, Dominic, and Savio are still applauding. I'm trembling. I can't believe I did that!

"My work here is done," Hazel chuckles. "Turns out you're not so bad after all," she adds then gives me a knowing nod of her head, as if to say well done.

"You have a beautiful voice, Lexi. You do not know how talented you are. A model and a singer!" Anna praises. "Oh my gawd, you need to duet together. Do something else," she demands.

Cameron smiles roguishly then whispers in my ear, but I'm not sure. I've heard him singing in the house, and I've sang it in the car and out walking Doris in the woods with my earphone's in, but we've never sang it together.

"We can do this. I'll come in and follow your lead. Just pretend no one else is here," Cameron suggests. He nudges his knuckles lightly across my chin.

"Okay, let's do it." I don't know where all this confidence is coming from, but it's impressing Lucca. I can feel his enthusiasm.

"A Martian invader from outer space has landed and switched bodies with my good friend here." Hazel smirks at Dominic. He pushes her shoulder, shooing her sarcastic comment.

"Ready?" Cameron asks me.

I nod, although my legs are quaking and I'm fighting hard to keep my head above the water before I drown.

After his intro, I compose myself and prepare to sing Pink's "Just Give Me A Reason." I keep my eyes open this time, staring into the azure blue pool of Lucca's eyes and swimming towards him with my words.

Floating.

Adrift.

Cruising.

I imagine his eyes as a white-washed illusion of an ebbing crystal tide softly rushing over my body. He leans back on the sofa, placing his arms behind his head, not taking his eyes off me. I'm not singing this for him. I'm singing this to him.

Finding my vocal strength, I lift higher in the chorus with more confidence. Cameron joins in with Nate Ruess's lyrics, but in his own alternate rock husky tone. I soar, and when we sing together in harmony, everyone gasps as we complement each other's registers. I lose myself, tapping my feet on the floor.

I hear myself. For the first time, I actually hear myself. I come alive, my wings take flight, and not in my core. I've literally lost all gravity, and then I escalate upward on the bridge of the song. On our last note, I smile, biting the bottom of my lip demurely and pleased with our first effort.

Lucca approaches and kneels in front of me, breathing heavily. Taking my face in his hands in front of everyone, he kisses my lips, pressing hard and long. I'm breathless when he pulls away. Cameron smirks at Lucca's appreciation of my singing and begins to play Lady Antebellum's "Singing Me Home." It's light and uplifting, so we have everyone join in.

Music was a form of therapy for Cameron, and I suppose it distracted me too. After a great reception, we sing Kid Rock and Sheryl Crow's duet, "Picture." Cameron lowers his tone; he's raspier and it harmonises well with my soft voice in this song. Once we're finished, I give Cameron a kiss and tell him I'm going to get a drink. Cameron takes a break from playing as well and disappears with Anna.

Lucca's enthusiasm looks deflated. Standing behind the bar, I ask Lucca why he's frowning.

"You were amazing, baby ... fuck, you just keep surprising me. That was breathtaking, and you truly sounded like an angel. I wish you would believe in yourself more."

He runs his hand up under my vest, running his thumb along the bottom of my bra. The touch of his hand against my fired up skin, combined with the adrenaline rushing through my body, sparks shockwaves of electricity.

"Thank you, but I'm a little embarrassed. I admit I enjoyed it after I got into it." His expression becomes conflicted and he digs his fingers into me. "I can tell something is wrong, Lucca. What's the matter?"

He sighs, pressing me against the bar counter and holding onto one hip with the other against my bra strap as he leans his forehead against mine.

"You have an amazing tone, and you are very gifted, baby, both of you are. But it pained me when you sang about the dark because that is all in your past. I would love to hear you sing about the light someday, something to symbolise your freedom from that dark. The last song about the pictures ... it just got me thinking about your insecurities and your distaste of photographs. I would love to help you with that."

"Is this about Giovanni Costanzo?" I ask. We have not spoken about this since the well-known photographer offered me a modelling career in Tuscany. Lucca seemed to have the notion it would help me lose my insecurities if I saw pictures of myself.

"God no, but I do wish you would consider that offer. It would help if you had more self-assurance. You need to have faith in yourself. Faith in your beauty, your talent, and your warm heart." He places his hand on my chest and smiles showing me his dimple smile.

"Don't you think I'm getting better? More relaxed?" I have a moment of hesitation. This was a big deal for me tonight, letting go like that.

"Of course I do. You have made so much progress, but one day it would be nice to have pictures and memories of our own. You know, when we get married, people will want to photograph us ..." He moves some hair away from my face and brushes his thumb over my cheek.

He's right. I've never thought of that.

"Well, I'm sorry ... I'm trying." I drop my head with disappointment.

"No, dolcezza, do not feel bad about this. I just want to help you, and I think I know how. Leave it with me." He lifts my chin, tilts my face back, then kisses me, and I explore his mouth, marrying my tongue with his. I absolutely love him with every beat of my heart.

The rest of the night is light-hearted and lively. I decide to lay off the cocktails and opt for juice as Antonia is sleeping in our room again and I want to keep my wits about me.

After Anna checks on the kids, she returns with a game of Twister.

Hazel's eyes come alive. "Oh, have you seen my body balance poses? This should be fun!"

I swipe the cocktail from her hand. "Behave," I warn her, but when I see her pout, I can't contain my laughter. "Okay fine, you have fun. Just don't dislocate anything." I giggle.

The game is hilarious. Everyone has had their fill of alcohol, so they fall on top of each other buckled in hysterics. I don't participate because I can't put too much weight on my wrist yet, but I enjoy watching them fall on their asses.

While everyone is entangled in a mess on the floor, I take some empty glasses to the sink in the bar. Lucca thrusts against my back cupping my ass and pressing against me. "I'm glad you were not playing. The vision of that perfect, sexy little ass in the air would have me so fucking hard I would find it difficult not to take you there on the floor," he rasps.

"Hmmm ... well, maybe when my wrist is better we can play strip twister, just you and me."

He growls, taking his hands off my ass and pressing his erection against the bottom of my back, then coiling his fingers around my hips and tugging me towards his manhood.

"How about I twist, bend, and shift you into position then fuck you shamelessly over my desk downstairs?" he growls in my ear.

My cheeks redden and my heart rate quickens with his crude suggestion. My throbbing sex is begging for just that.

"Let's go and make some moves, Romeo." I grind my butt against the bulge in his denims as my hands wrap around his hips.

I squeeze my legs together as excitement flares inside me. We sneak out, frantically kissing and groping at every corner, stair and doorway we pass until we reach his study. Once inside, he kicks the door shut, then locks it. I eye up the desk with devilish eyes, my chest shuddering against my blouse with anticipation.

"Tell me how you want it ... ask, baby."

He pulls his clothes off, and I strip my vest and jeans off nearly as fast, hooking my thumb under the string of tiny lace thong, teasing him, then brushing a loose soft curl of my hair against my lips suggestively.

His wanton eyes nearly catapult out of his sockets while he strongly bangs me against the door with his body. After overcoming my fear with singing, my bravado has taken over.

I tell.

I show.

I beg.

And I ask for more.

He gives it to me.

I take.

Take.

Take.

Maybe music is good therapy for me after all.

Losing count of my orgasms and Lucca's perpetual climaxes filling me, I collapse. I've been thoroughly twisted inside and out until I'm so spent and lethargic I need Lucca to help me redress and carry me back to the suite.

After checking on the baby, he pulls me into his side, tightening his arms around me. "Okay?" he asks.

"I'm better than okay," I murmur through sleepiness.

"I love you, dolcezza." He kisses the side of my head.

My last thought as I close my eyes is that I love that game a lot. Twister sex is my new favourite.

Chapter 16: Compromises

The sun shining brightly through the French doors is a charming vision to wake up to.

Not as lovely as the illuminating golden Tuscan sunshine that I still fantasise about, or a certain Italian god and an adorable baby girl smiling over to me for that matter.

"Morning, beautiful."

Lucca has his arm around Antonia's waist while she bounces up and down on the mattress between us. He reaches over kissing me.

"Hmmm … morning yourself, handsome," I mumble, yawn, then smile with loving eyes.

"Aunty Lexi is not a morning girl, Antonia. She is a little bit grumpy," he chants to her. She chuckles.

Rolling my eyes, I hold my arms out to her and cuddle her into my chest, kissing her lips, cheeks, then forehead. She smells of baby bath and powder. It's just lovely. Lucca leans on his side, propping his head up on one hand and resting on his elbow as he plays with my hair.

There is no television or music on this morning as the adults of last night's party are feeling rather delicate. After a sleepy, quiet breakfast, everyone slowly starts moving, trying to hush the noise from the excitable children. Everyone is feeling the effects of last night's alcohol, and we're not as energetic as we were yesterday morning, but we all agree it was a great night and we must do it again.

As Lucca, Savio, and Armando cooked breakfast, Dominic and Cameron offer to clear up the kitchen, leaving Sarah and Kate to get the kids washed and dressed. I have a long shower and worry about Anna. Being used by your best friend must be soul destroying.

I take out a designer grey and black fitted dress with a thin belt for later but dress in yoga pants and a hoodie to take Doris for a walk on my own.

Walking through the park and reflecting on my week ahead of me, I'm sad to think of Lucca leaving me for a few days while he works. We've been together every day, but I suppose it's healthy. We need our own space too. I'm used to being independent, so surely I will manage on my own.

When I return to the house, the girls decide they are going into Glasgow to shop, and the boys make plans to take the kids to the park before stopping at the garden centre in the Clydeside to pick strawberries and then for ice cream. Lucca's face is electric at the thought of gelato. He's more excited than the kids.

"Are you looking forward to going out with the girls?" Lucca asks, upbeat, watching me get dressed in the grey dress. It has a racer back so I opt to leave my bra off and the weather is mild today so my shoulders won't be cold.

Placing the back of my hand to my mouth, I worry my fingers around in a nervous dance that tells Lucca I am thinking carefully. "I'd rather spend today with you since you're going away this week. I don't want to waste any time we have before tomorrow morning."

"That is why I want you to come on my trip. It is not too late for me to arrange. I will only be in meetings during the day in London, and when I am looking at the properties in Sardinia and Milan, you can come with me. If I have time we can sightsee. I have an appointment I cannot miss, but then we can spend time together." He moves my fingers away tilting my head up with his thumb then kisses my lips.

A twinge of nerves reverberates in my stomach from his soft kiss and I release a low groan, relaxing my muscles. I actually do feel helpless and nervous about him going away, but I need to keep some sort of boundary and independence. "If you keep kissing me like that, I'll drag you in the hotel room, and you won't make any of your work appointments."

"Fuck, do not make this any harder for me. Please reconsider, Doc. I am not happy about this either, and I know you do not want to be here on your own. Your eyes have just confirmed how you truly feel about it. Si?" His tongue darts out to moisten his lip as he rubs his thumb across his jaw.

God, he's good.

"Lucca, I can't go with you. I don't want you to go either, but I'm a big girl and I need to keep my plans for this week. My girlfriends all have time away from their partners, and they say it's healthy. I'm worried I'm going to become too dependent on you emotionally. It took me a long time to move away from my family to start a new life, and I'm afraid to be on my own again. Can you understand that?" Sighing, I nibble on my bottom lip then straighten his collar.

"Okay, I will try and understand, but it is killing me and I am not happy about it one bit. However, I respect your wishes. I would have you with me 24-7, but I get that you need your space too." He presses his lips together and exhales in a long sigh.

He runs his fingers down my jaw and throat then softly kisses it and rubs his thumb over my diamond pendant. Moving my head to the side and closing my eyes, I groan, basking under the heat of his tongue on my flesh, hot flutters across my skin.

"You know, there is something good about this though," I seductively whisper as I follow the contours of his biceps with my fingers.

"There is nothing good about being separated from you, from this ..." His hands travel to the swell of my breasts.

"The girls tell me that the sex before and after separation is hot as hell." I absently brush the bottom of my hair over my lips.

He pushes his body against mine. "Do they now? What else do the girls say?"

"Hmmm ... that it's steamy, raunchy, and sexy as ever." I bite down on the flesh in my mouth on the inside of my cheek, nervously feeling like a temptress.

"Lexi, it is all of that with you and more every time. You have no idea. I am looking forward to lots more of it tonight and when I get back from my trip." He cups my ass and presses his arousal into the bottom of my stomach.

I wrap my hands in his wavy curls then assault his tongue with eagerness, but he pulls away.

"Baby, you will have me slamming into you and I want tonight to be special. They are waiting on us downstairs. Can you hold off? Have fun with the girls today and we will have fun tonight. *Lots of fun.* " He smiles showing his sexy dimple.

Highly unlikely I can hold off. Not now.

Bloody core tease.

"Fine. If you're not taking me right now, I'm off to spend all your money with the girls." I turn around and pace into my dressing room, leaving him laughing hysterically.

He walks in, wiping some laughter tears from his eyes. "Nice try, Doc. I know you are trying to throw that fiery stuff at me thinking I will take you now, but I am holding out for tonight." He chuckles.

"I have no idea what you're talking about." I open the drawer to my dressing table, rummaging for a nail file, keeping my back to him. Picking up my phone, I read my text messages; conscious he's watching me the entire time. "The girls are going to the movies tonight and have asked if I want to go."

"Well, tell them no. You will be busy tonight."

I turn around; sitting on my stool and crossing my legs, then look downwards as I file my nails. "Hmmm ... I'll think about it."

"I am serious. I need you here." He fiddles with the bottom of my hair.

Sighing, I turn to face him. "Lucca, I was never going out tonight and have no intention on spending your money. You know that, right?"

He laughs. "Doc, I knew you were jesting about the shopping, but I panicked at the thought of you going out tonight. It is not an option. I am sorry, honey. Normally, I would not mind at all, but your friends will understand it is for the hot sex before our separation. I have an idea how I can make it up to your friends."

"Thank you."

He looks puzzled. "Thank you for what?"

"For being you. For putting up with me." I rest my cheek on his chest.

"I love you and I am the fucking luckiest man alive. I am not putting up with you as you put it. I am living it up with you because I love you."

He leaves me so I can finish getting ready. Then he returns smiling.

"Change of plans. We are all going into town now. Savio has an appointment he is going to fit in, so we will grab some lunch and you girls can shop while we entertain the kids. It suits everyone, and I promised the kids a bear from that factory place they go on about."

"Come here." I yank at his shirt and pull him towards me. "I love you so much it hurts." I passionately kiss him until I hear giggles and rowdiness, and the kids interrupt as they bounce up and down on the bed. Thank goodness, we're decent.

Dominic and Cameron help Savio and Armando pack up their cars with all the luggage and kids toys and equipment. I'm looking back and forth like I'm watching a Wimbledon match, and it's exhausting.

I take Antonia from Sarah and search for Lucca. He has just put Doris in the downstairs family room and is locking up. "Hey, my favourite girls." He kisses Antonia then kisses me with warm appreciation, giving me a roguish grin.

"I was thinking we could maybe buy some toys and things at some point for when the kids come over and stay. You should see what's getting loaded into the cars. It would make it easier on Kate and Sarah so they don't have to bring all their stuff with them every time they visit."

"Antonia, that is why I love your Aunty Lexi; she is so thoughtful. Would you like to come back and stay with us, baby girl?" He takes her out of my arms, and she kicks her legs with excitement and buries her head into his chest, gargling and humming.

I chuckle. "Um, Lucca, she's soaked your shirt with drool. Her gums are bothering her."

He looks at his shirt and laughs. My heart melts. He is just perfect to me ... *perfect for me.*

I've no doubt that he will be a wonderful father. I take him by the hand, and we head out to the cars, agreeing to meet everyone in Glasgow as all are leaving in their own cars.

"I'm going to start driving tomorrow. I've been doing my exercises and the new painkillers I have are much better, so I should be fine." I sigh, watching Lucca open the passenger door for me.

"You are not ready to drive yet," he gripes.

"Lucca, I'm a Physiotherapist. I know my body."

He stares at my wrist and frowns. "I am not comfortable with you driving yet. What if you cannot manoeuvre the wheel properly and have an accident? Lexi, I would rather you held off a little longer before driving."

Staring downward and shrugging, I rub my fingers over my wrist and subconsciously let out a sigh. "You bought me the cars, Lucca." I grumble.

He lifts my hand kissing my wrist repeatedly. "Okay, I will let you test drive around the streets, and if you are okay and pain free, you can drive today," he says reluctantly because he's still not convinced.

I screech with enthusiasm and pitch my arms around his neck, kissing his lips. "Thank you, I love you." I'm excited to be getting control of my new car.

"Hold up, you are not driving in those." He gestures towards my five and a half inch Louboutins.

"Why?" If he is referring to my grazes on my soles, he needn't worry. They are just minor scrapes.

"Because, it is not safe to drive with high heels like that. I would prefer if you wore flat shoes when driving."

I agree, but only because I want to meet him in the middle. I return to the house, grab a pair of black, patent, Lanvin ballet flats and put my heels in my tote bag.

My new Aston Martin Volante drives like a dream—smooth, dynamic, and sleek. It has the sporty but functional specifications and interior. Cruising this sophisticated flash car feels effortless, as if I'm gliding. I could get used to this.

"I need to give her a name," I say, tapping the wheel.

"Nervous fucking wreck, how about that?" he says, watching the side mirror.

"Very funny. I'm calling her Chitty."

"Whatever you want, Lexi, just keep your eyes on the road." He rolls his eyes at my playfulness. I always loved that film in my early teens at Granny and Grandpa's. I slip onto the motorway. This is an experience, so I am going to enjoy every minute. Lucca relaxes only slightly when he knows I can manage this until I put my foot down to accelerate and nearly throw us back through the seats.

"Jesus, calm down. It is powerful and you are speeding. That was careless." He's not amused.

"Okay, I was only testing her." I pout.

By the time we approach Glasgow, I have successfully managed to work the loudspeakers on the acoustics to blast out a remix of Rihanna's "We Found Love," which I find quite fitting given the circumstances. I tap my fingers on the wheel, smiling enjoying the beats.

Lucca turns it off and he's back to being fractious. "Concentrate, Lexi ... I have just found *you* and I do not want to lose you. Fuck, watch the lights, slow down!" he shouts, running his hands through his messed-up sexy hair.

Spoil sport.

I've had endless fun, so I'm disappointed when our short journey has ended. Once I reverse park, I turn around to Lucca and take his face in both hands kissing him. "Thank you, I really do love it, and it drives like a dream." He looks chalk white. "Lucca, what's wrong? Are you sick?"

"You could say that. Lexi, you are too easily distracted, you do not concentrate, and stop that freaking dancing and singing at the wheel. I am serious, Doc. You were careless, and I am not sure I want you driving this week when I am away in case you get carried away."

"Are you serious? You buy me a car like this, but you won't *allow* me to drive it?" Fire is burning at the back of my throat.

"I did not say that, I just do not want you driving alone. I want you to enjoy it, but I want you to be sensible. Marco can use the company cars and drive you anywhere you need to go," he suggests.

"Are you done with the lecture?" I scoff.

"Please, do not be upset. I am concerned and a little traumatised with your driving. That is all." He softens his tone.

"You're being ridiculous. We were perfectly safe. I always drive like that, and I've never had an accident." I'm firm reprimanding him looking out my window rolling my eyes.

After a few moments of silence, he sighs. "You look sexy as hell behind the wheel." He reaches for my face. With his fingers under my chin, he turns my face around.

"You've changed your tune," I whisper with an almighty scowl on my face.

"Come here." He places his hand on the nape of my neck and kisses me. Once I've relaxed under his tender caressing, I show him my appreciation and lasciviously kiss him back. Outside the car, I slip my ballet flats off and put my heels back on, drawing a lot of attention from pedestrians and moving vehicles.

Lucca shakes his head, coyly smiling. "They're watching you, not the bloody car. You're going to give me a heart attack." He has been so worked up since I sat behind the wheel today, and it's made him on edge. I've no idea why he's paranoid about my driving.

Chapter 17: Gifts of the day

We decide to eat in Princes Square so that the kids can run around the huge circular floor space in the centre of the Upmarket Shopping Centre. After dolci, gelato being Lucca's preferred choice, Hazel, Anna, Sarah, and Kate head to a boutique across from the restaurant. I choose to stay, play with the kids, and spend as much time with Lucca as I can.

Roberta has a little doll stroller with her and Emilio and A-Jay are scurrying around the floor racing cars. They seem to have made some little friends as well, which is adorable. A little redheaded girl is sitting next to Roberta sharing her sweets and nursing her own little dolly.

Watching them contently, I think about how different my childhood would have been if it were normal—whatever normal is.

I wonder what it would have been like if I'd had friends and had experienced other situations and circumstances.

When I was a child, my life was normal to me. It was all I'd ever known, and I'd had Cameron who was my life. I was blissfully unaware of anything else. It wasn't until we escaped and were gradually introduced into society that I became aware. That was when we knew we had missed things. We were encouraged to learn how to build relationships, to be involved, to discover, to trust, share and accept through role-play, therapy, and various games.

After many endless counselling sessions, which never made a difference for me, Mum helped Cameron and I both realise that although we missed fundamental things, we'd never missed out on love—nothing but unconditional love from our mum.

I do have a massive amount of respect for my mum for having to raise us in the circumstances which she had to. It's a challenging job in today's society, and my mum was alone without love or support.

With only hope and promises.

Processing this thought, I startle from my reverie when Roberta takes my hand and asks me to play with her and her new friend Melissa.

I twirl the girls around and around on the marbled circle floor that is centred within the spiralling rows of prestigious shops, bars, and restaurants. They skip, dance, and hop so innocently. I'm thinking I should have kept my flat pumps on now—high-heeled shoes don't seem that appropriate. The place is buzzing with lots of children, parents, and grandparents sitting on the wooden steps edging the circle. Weekend shoppers are hanging over the light oak and gold railings as they people watch.

Lucca doesn't take his eyes off me. Even in conversation with the others, he is smiling at me adoringly. I notice Cameron standing talking to a group of handsome, smart men who are now sitting at the table next to us—his premier league football mates. They often can be spotted in this square on weekends as well as their wives and girlfriends. I don't spot any females today. I do recognise a few of the boys though.

Cameron turns around to me smiling then continues his conversation with them. I'm sure he's telling them who I am or reminding them as I have been introduced before but have never really paid attention. I've never been sucked in by the cliché attached to the celebrity status they have acquired through their football publicity, and Cameron didn't bring a lot of his mates by the house we shared because he understood that I didn't like strangers there. I've met them at charity events and in the local bar and at one of Cameron's birthday nights.

Jackson always came across as rather sleazy; he knows he's extremely attractive and uses it to his advantage and is notoriously popular for it. They sit back in their chairs, leaning on their arms, studying me. It's making me uneasy. They have a reputation for being unfaithful and very much 'players' on and off the pitch. I wish I hadn't worn such a revealing figure-hugging dress now.

"Lexi, come here a minute," Cameron shouts over.

Oh dear Lord. Not the introductions again.

I tell Roberta to play and I'll be back in a minute. I drop my head blushing, reluctantly pacing towards Cameron, but I feel two hands grip me around my waist, an intense body heat against my back, and I smell that sexy scent. Lucca turns me around and graces my lips then moves my hair over my shoulders and kisses my neck.

"Thank you," I whisper.

"You are not going over there on your own. You have every fucking cock at that table hard, baby. Trust me. They are eyeing you up as if you're a piece of hot new ass, but you are my hot ass," he groans.

I chuckle. "You're a caveman, but my ass is all yours, *Romeo.*"

"And I would like to keep it that way, dolcezza."

He takes my hand to approach the table where six handsome, horny men burn me with their shameless, roaming eyes. They are undoubtedly attractive, and I wouldn't be human if I didn't notice them, but they are known for being in love with themselves, and their reputation is despicable.

Actually, I shouldn't judge as I know Lucca had this exact reputation prior to meeting me.

The fact that I'm hanging onto Lucca's arm doesn't seem to deter their eagerness at all. In fact, I'm guessing it piques their interest. They sit up in their chairs, drinking me in and scanning my body, making me feel exposed before them.

Bare.

"Lex, you remember Jackson, Jordan, Adam, and Ben. This is Ethan and Tyler, the new transfers. Lads, this is my sister Lexi and her fiancé Lucca."

I'm grateful he uses the word fiancé to set the scene. He gestures his hand around the table then back towards Lucca and me.

Jackson, being the first to stand, closes the space with sexy confidence. There is boldness in his posture as he kisses my cheek, holding onto my upper arm with hot hands, trailing his fingers down my exposed arm cascades nervous tremors over my skin causing me to slightly tremble.

Damn freaking body is a traitor.

"Pleasure to meet you again, Alexis. You look great, absolutely stunning," he whispers.

Lucca grumbles and clears his throat. Blushing, I politely thank him modestly and smile at the rest of the group. Lucca growls again and tightens his grip on me. He inhales and expands his brawny chest, protectively towering behind me and reminding them I'm his. With reasonable manners, Lucca leans over and shakes all their hands in turn then pulls me back against his chest, firming his fingers over my hip and shooting Jackson a look of warning that only men understand.

"Lucca, mate, you are a lucky man," Jordan says as he leans over to shake my hand.

"Thank you. I am extremely lucky and very grateful that this beautiful girl is all mine."

Okay, he's confirming his ownership and not messing around either, which I appreciate in this moment. Cameron has noticed it too.

"Lexi, you look great. It's been like what two years?" Jordan says before sitting back down.

Lucca snorts and tenses. I believe he's jealous.

"Hmmm, I'm not sure. Something like that," I reply absentmindedly.

"What have you been busy doing?" Adam asks with interest in his voice.

I don't know what to say. What should I say? Up until I met Lucca, life was fairly uninteresting.

Orderly?

Paranoid?

Insecure?

Dark?

Yes, all of the above.

"I'm a self-employed physiotherapist now," I confidently reply. *None of the above*. Definitely not. Not anymore.

"Wow, that's great. You know, we could put a word in. The team is looking for a new sports physiotherapist," Jordan adds.

Before I reply, Lucca charges in, "Sorry, boys, thank you for the offer, but she is not practicing just now. She has an injury." He sharply inhales a long breath, stroking my wrist. I grit my teeth and bristle so he knows I'm pissed at him for this and I'll be having words with him about it.

"That's a pity. I hope you recover soon. Keep it in mind and be sure to let Cameron know when you're back practicing and we can make arrangements," Ben adds.

Jackson leans back in his chair, studying me. Lifting his athletic arms, he runs his hand through his hair, holding on the back of his neck while the other traces the rim of the glass with his thumb. He's trying to distract me, but I'm more distracted by Lucca's fingers gripping my hipbone.

"Jackson has moved from Newton Mearns and bought a house in Bothwell," Cameron says, moving on from the physio topic because he can see it's pissing me off.

Well shit. Discovering Jackson will be living close by has me flustered. Not that I plan to see him, but it's because of the perception I have of him. I'd rather not bump into him, even if he is Cameron's friend. This will have Lucca going batshit crazy and he'll probably put his house up for sale, knowing he is a neighbour.

"I think you live near Lucca and Lexi actually," Cameron adds.

Yep, I better get packing boxes. We'll be on the move. Shit!

Jackson's eyebrows lift, piqued by curiosity. "Where are you, mate?" he asks.

Castello di Lucca.

I hear Lucca's low muffled groan. "The Smithstone," he retorts.

Jackson seems surprised. "Yes, I know where you are. Great property I hear. We're in the next street," he advises.

"Such a small world. That is great, it is a lovely area," Lucca scoffs.

I'm relieved. "We," as in plural, as in not just Jackson, so he must have a girlfriend.

"Cam tells us you have a footie match on the horizon," Jackson says.

"That is right. I enjoy a game, but my mates, Omari and Chris, think they are shit hot." Dry and cold. I'm not mistaking it. Lucca normally is much more pleasant and has better social skills.

"Well, we'd be happy to get involved. I'll speak with management. You ever considered doing a charity match?" There is a softness and slight enthusiasm to Jackson's tone.

That gets Lucca thinking. He relaxes in his tight grip. I remember my conversation with Ms. Morrison about Lucca's contribution to charities through the churches, so maybe Jackson has won him over. He has definitely chilled out.

Phew, there will be no blood spilled today.

"So what do you do, Lucca, if you don't mind me asking?" Blonde haired, blue-eyed Ben asks in interest.

Fair question, I suppose, but I also know how modest Lucca can be.

"Lucca owns Luminara," Cameron butts in.

Idiot of a brother.

"Wow, we often have nights out there. Great place. We actually have a team night out booked there soon," Adam adds.

"Great, well, I will make sure you boys are looked after and have a good night. I can make arrangements for you to have the club exclusively." Lucca's business head has taken over.

"Excellent, mate. That would be great." Jordan is enthusiastic.

"Lucca is CEO of Osurac Industries as well as owner of The Club di Energia chain. Luminara is only a small part of that," I blurt. Me and my big bloody mouth. I feel as if I want to place my man on a pedestal—to praise his worthiness, his achievements and assets and to crush their ever-growing egos.

Lucca leans in and whispers in my ear, "Cavewoman." Curling his lip, he smirks at me, and I hold my laughter back.

"Our girlfriends and wives are all members at your club," Jordan adds.

"Yes, I am aware. I hope they are happy with the facilities." He's definitely not as brusque, and there is no sharp edge in his tone. He's probably more relaxed talking about work and that I'm not the topic of conversation. I backtrack with his last comment.

How does he know their wives and girlfriends? Obviously he owns the club, but he's never there because he's normally at the main office. And does he make a point to get to know every single member on the database?

Hmmm… sorted and filed. I'll be turning this page back later. I decide to go before I blurt out anything else silly or before the conversation comes back around to me.

"If you'll excuse me, gentlemen, it's been a pleasure to meet you again. Good luck for next week's final. Ethan, Tyler, I wish you all the best settling into your new team. I'm sure you'll do great, and

Cameron will keep me informed, I'm sure." I smile before moving forward.

I politely shake Ethan's and Tyler's hands, causing all the men to stand. I repeat the gesture with the other four, and it's not lost on me that there is no cheek kissing this time. Lucca has conquered that notion and I'm glad.

A few months ago, the thought of standing in front of a group of men like this would have petrified me and there is no way I would have moved forward to offer hand shaking the way I just did. The fact that they are Cameron's friends makes it easier and also that Lucca is holding me tightly. After socialising here and in Tuscany with Lucca's family, I am becoming more relaxed. It's not the thought of this group or the fact they are men that's making me restive; it's the way they're looking at me. I don't remember them looking at me like this before, or maybe I was just not aware of it.

"I'll leave you boys talking football. I'm off to find the girls."

"Excuse me just a second, boys" Lucca takes my hand and walks me away from the table towards the circle floor area. "You are so fucking adorable. I love how you claimed me and bragged, but you did not need to do that."

"You're mine and I'm proud of you, so you deserve a little bragging," I relent.

He wraps his arms around my waist and kisses my lips chastely. Closing my eyes, I forget where we are for a moment. He parts his lips from mine, keeping our foreheads touching. Inhaling his intoxicating scent and filling my lungs, I sigh. Then catch a glimpse of Jackson curiously watching us. Lucca's hand comes up and places a loose curl behind my ear.

"You don't like him, do you?" I ask and don't need to say who; he knows I'm referring to Jackson.

"Nope, not one fucking bit. He has it bad for you. I will be civil for now as he is Cameron's friend, but I will be watching him." His body is tense and rigid. He's serious in his alpha male stupor. "He makes you uneasy." It's a statement but he says it in a way he's asking me.

"A little," I reply, briefly glimpsing over to him.

"Stay away from him … for me? He has a reputation." He's sincere and gentle.

"Of course I will. You don't have to ask, but I don't want it to interfere with an opportunity for charity football. Omari and Chris would be thrilled, and it could be good publicity for your business as well as a brilliant opportunity to contribute to charity." I nibble my bottom lip and smile, watching the kids playing on the circled floor area.

"Perhaps, I am not sure now. I will chat to the boys about it. Here, I have something for you. Give me your hand." I hold my palm out and he puts his hand in his blazer pocket and places a plastic card in my hand.

"What's this?"

"It is your new bank card."

"But I don't bank with this chain." Then reality dawns on me as I look up and sigh, not amused in the slightest. "This is your bank?" I lower my tone.

He kisses me. "Yes, I have added you to my accounts. The pin number for this account is in your phone, but once you have memorised it, please delete it. The sooner we get married the better. I would like to be placing Mrs. Caruso's new card in her palm."

I'm speechless. It takes me a moment to shake off my stunned expression. "You can't give me access to your accounts. It's not my money. I have a wage and I can survive. Actually, that reminds me. Why did you tell the boys I'm not working? I didn't appreciate the way you barged in and answered for me. I *will* be going back to work, Lucca. I trained for years. I'm good at what I do, and I enjoy my job. It is not your place to tell me if I can work or not. And Mark is my business partner. It's his lively hood too, so my contribution and any patients I bring in affects the success and reputation of the business and his financial security." I cross an arm over my chest and rub my arm.

"I know it is, and I know your work is important to you, and I get why it is important. You like to help people and you like your independence. I said that because I do not want you to work anywhere you feel uncomfortable, and in a football club full of men …?" His eyes search mine. "I know I would not be comfortable with it, and you definitely would not either. I was thinking, if and when you want to go back, I would like to invest in your business. We could source premises for you and Mark, so as opposed to hiring the room at the club, you would have your very own practice. Something stable and permanent." His brilliant smile shows he is deadly serious and it's well thought out.

"Wow, I was not expecting that. I thought you were going to try and convince me not to work," I say, wide-eyed and smiling. Investing is so much different than just buying me something.

He cups my cheek with one hand. "You do not need to work, and I would love to take care of you and give you all the things you deserve, but if it is that important to you, then I would love to help any way I can. It will give you a sense of achievement by helping others, and it will help Mark out financially if your business grows."

He presents the card to me again. "For now, I want you to take this bank card."

"No, you can't give me that, but I will definitely consider a business proposal, to help grow our physio business." I know when he gets persistent there is no reasoning, but perhaps by me accepting his help with my work, he'll compromise and accept I'll live off my own earnings.

"Yes, I can. Everything I have is yours now." He lifts my hand and places it on his heart, the plastic card stuck between his shirt and my hand. His blue eyes sparkle like they did when he gave me my first gift ... the Cartier watch.

"And what if I run off into the sunset and bleed you dry?" I'm being sarcastic.

He starts laughing. "Do not make me laugh. Lexi, it is not in your nature. Plus, I know you hate shopping. I want you to be secure, and if I am at work and there is something you need, you can have it. I do not want you to want for anything in life ever again." Pain flashes through his eyes. He presses them closed tensing his jaw.

"If this is about me telling you why I run barefoot and my nightmares about the bush, Lucca, you don't need to give me access to your money because of something that happened when I was a child. I don't want for anything. I'll never be hungry and I have your love. That's what's important. Lucca, look at me." I need to see his eyes the same way he does when I'm conflicted.

He opens his eyes, his breath ragged. "Lexi, I want to do this for you, to take care of you. I told you that in Tuscany even before I learned of your misfortunes. I need you to take this. It is my responsibility to take care of you, and I want to very much. Please, Doc?"

Thanks to these ridiculous shoes, I am able to lean my head on the front of his shoulders. "Thank you, I do appreciate the gesture, but no." I remove my hand and place the card in the back pocket of his jeans, keeping my hand there a little longer than necessary and groping his amazing butt cheek.

"We are not arguing about this here. Take the card back," he demands, shocked I've refused it.

"No." I slip my hand out his pocket, stand back, and press my lips together, knitting my brow.

"Why?" I can see his jaw twitch. He's trying to keep his cool, but I know he's getting irritated. The more I refuse him, the more frustrated he'll get, so I try and sound convincing with control in my tone to make him see reason.

"Because I just want *you*. I don't need anything else." Crossing my arms over my chest I watch him sigh and shake his head. Why does he not believe me? I've always told him *I just need him.*

"Is this because of what your mother said?" Grabbing his bottom lip with his middle finger and thumb, he pinches and pulls it then rubs his jaw. I'd say he is beyond frustrated now and here is not the place for me to talk about it and get him worked up.

Yes. I don't respond. I look down instead.

"Doc, please take the card." His steps towards me, sighing in exasperation.

"No, I don't want it." I'm not backing down. I raise my voice and mimic his loud sighing so he knows I'm angry.

"For fuck's sake, you are driving me crazy. Stop arguing with me and take the goddamn card, or I will pick you up in a fireman's lift and walk with you into every fucking shop in Glasgow and make sure you use it." His posture has become tense, and he sounds deadly serious. His eyes narrow on me and his jaw twitches.

Shit.

He runs his fingers through his hair.

I unfold my arms, hand now on my hip, and step back evaluating the seriousness of his threat. "You wouldn't dare."

He exhales in exasperation again, a flicker of certainty in his eyes. "One last chance," he warns.

The football team boys are all witnessing this. "Lexi, you might want to reconsider that," Armando adds. He has left his table and is playing with the kids on the floor space behind us.

I ignore him. "I'll be back shortly. Go and talk to the boys and keep your eye on the kids." I turn on my heels and walk towards our table to retrieve my handbag. Savio has just ended a phone call and watches me approach, looking flushed with anger. I only make it a few steps before I squeal as my body is swiftly lifted off the floor. I'm hanging over Lucca's shoulder leaving everyone chuckling at Lucca's exhibition.

"Put me down."

"No."

"Lucca Caruso, put me down right now!" I yell and try to wiggle. His grip only holds me tighter. My cheeks are red and my long, brown, glossy locks are hanging down past his butt. His hand is splayed across my ass in my tight figure-hugging dress in an attempt to preserve my modesty.

Oh dear Lord. Beam me up because I'm mortified.

"I think we will go to that boutique in the corner since we need to get new lingerie. I keep tearing all the others off you," he says loud enough so everyone hears.

Bastard!

The entire table of boys have overhead and will love to relish in the details.

I smack his back. "Lucca!" I scold him. "Cameron, tell him to put me down!"

"Sorry, Lex. I'm actually finding this rather amusing."

Bastard!

"Lucca, drop me right now," I bark, then I ruffle a sigh as I know he's not going to when he starts walking with me. "

Will you accept?"

"Yes, just let me down," I moan.

Folded, crumbled, but definitely not melted.

Not under these circumstances.

Slowly, he slides me down his body in a tight embrace. I rub against every toned ripple of his eight pack abdominal muscles then his hard bulge. Oh God, it's turned him on.

Bloody horny asinine arse.

My hair is all over the place, so now I actually do look like his cavewoman. Sniggering, he moves it away from my face. I'm breathing frantically and very hot. He kisses me in apology, but I press my lips firmly closed, not returning the gesture because I am so pissed off.

"Will you accept the card?"

"Yes, but that was uncalled for," I snap, jabbing my finger in his chest.

"Please, be reasonable. It was just a bit of fun, and you will be my wife soon enough, so I want to share everything with you. It is important for me to take care of you." He places his arms around my neck and pulls me in closer to him so our foreheads touch.

"Lucca, you embarrassed me, and everyone is staring at us."

"Fuck them, let them stare. I just need you to do this for me. You really are stubborn, Miss Robertson, but I fucking love it," He says, grinning with his wicked smile.

I sigh, rolling my eyes. "Give me the card before I faint, and if you don't see me again … I've run away," I jest in surrender.

His eyes burn me. He's not amused. "Do not say shit like that. It is not funny. You promised not to run again."

"I'm sorry, I didn't mean it literally," I mutter, lowering my head, but he lifts it up gently. I said it without thinking.

"No, do not dare apologise. I over reacted. I am sorry. Kiss me, dolcezza."

His hot breath on my lips has me rattling at the knees and elicits a flutter deep in my stomach. He moves his hands up, grabs the back of my head, entangling my wavy, long mass in his hands, and I close my eyes, kissing him indulgently without consideration for anything else round about me.

Tongues circling.

Clashing.

Caressing.

"I am looking forward to ravishing every inch of this glorious, sexy body tonight."

And now I'm melted.

Into him.

For him.

Liquid love.

I'm damp between my legs, sensitive and twitching to have him on me, in me, and around me, but I need to compose myself and wait before I drag him into the restrooms and allow him to do just that right now. God! He does it to me every time.

"You have a lot of making up to do for embarrassing me. I will expect complete attention all night long." I run my fingers through his curly jet-black hair. I'm not asking, I'm telling.

"Fuck. Oh, I plan on doing nothing else. Do you still love me?" He smirks, running his tongue along his bottom lip. Every time he does that he looks vulnerable but ever so sexy.

"Yes, I love you. Can I go now?" I grumble because I'm exasperated with this little performance.

"Yes, keep your phone on and remember your pin is stored in it." He places the card back in my hand and walks me to the edge of the tables to get my bag. Everyone claps and cheers.

Ugh.

"And that, boys, is my sister." Cameron directs to the table. "I'm glad you made up because I'd get her moaning shit later if you hadn't," Cameron jests towards Lucca.

Fuck!

File F for fireman's lift. Fireman's lifts are so goddamn humiliating.

I blush, fluttering my lashes and forcing a smile towards our local celebrity boys who are mesmerised by my antics. Lucca smacks my ass playfully before sending me on my way.

Roberta pulls at my dress. "Aunty Lexi, were you naughty? Why was Uncle Lucca lifting you?" Her big, blue, innocent eyes are staring up at me. Everyone chuckles at her question.

"Yes, she was naughty, Roberta," Lucca answers for me.

I'm rolling my eyes but certainly not entertaining that comment. "Princess, I'm going off to find your mummy. I'll be back soon. You have fun and pick a nice teddy bear out." I bend down and kiss her forehead.

Lucca watches me, smiling fondly, but I'm also aware of Jackson devouring me with his eyes. I choose to ignore that look.

File.

Ignore.

Denial.

The order of my life.

I have no intention of spending Lucca's cash on myself, but I do have some gifts I'd like to purchase, so my first stop is the Swiss pen shop within the indoor centre. I don't want Lucca to see where I'm going so I take the elevator and walk around the first floor. I bought him a sleek ballpoint pen in Tuscany, so I opt for a fountain pen this time—more of a keepsake rather than an everyday use pen.

I don't have time to get this one engraved, so I have the Diamond Le Grande fountain pen wrapped, knowing he loves anything with diamonds. When I slot the card in the chip and pin machine, I feel sweaty and nervous, as if I'm doing something wrong. I feel guilty using his cash instead of mine, but this is for him so I can just about justify this.

I'm going to marry Lucca, and I know he will appreciate my gift and will not think twice about the money. My stomach backflips in case it's the wrong pin or it doesn't work, but then I know enough to realise Lucca's bank account is financially secure.

When the helpful attendant smiles and tears off the receipt, I relax my shoulders and breathe. Feeling relieved, I call Hazel and find they are in Buchanan Galleries—a large, indoor shopping centre ten minutes up Buchanan Street. I tell her I'm going to House of Fraser department store and I won't be long.

I know exactly what I am going to purchase.

I walk straight past the cosmetic counters. Although, I kick myself as this is my own guilty pleasure. I adore make up and skin products, and I could go absolutely mad in here buying pretty powders and glosses and sweet smelling creams, all of which I don't need right now. It's not about me today.

My mum thinks my desire for them is because when I was younger and trapped, we only had running water from an outdoor hose and that was it. No soap or toothpaste or general toiletries. I remember my mum on her monthly cycle using a rolled up face cloth to absorb her blood, then she would rinse it outside in a bucket. I'm lucky that my cycle didn't start until we escaped.

I feel self-conscious about the scars on my back. It's all in my mind, but without cosmetics I feel stripped bare and it makes me think of being naked, scarred and … *ugly*. They've always made me feel ugly, and using cosmetics, even if it's just the hint of a little blush on my cheeks, makes me feel less bare and exposed.

I continue my wandering until I reach the lingerie department. The efficient attendant approaches me and asks if I need assistance. Of course, I'm mortified. I politely refuse and peruse the rails of designer underwear on my own. Again, this gift will be for Lucca, and I plan to wear it when he gets home next week. The thought of it sparks my intense, raging desire for him. I find what I'm looking for, and it's wrapped and bagged.

I meander towards Buchanan Galleries slower than normal due to my high heels' height, just enjoying the day.

Once I reach the Buchanan Galleries shopping centre, Hazel texts to say they are all shopped out and in Starbucks having coffee. I tell her I will join them shortly and venture towards John Lewis department store to purchase a few more small gifts for all the people in my life now. I have no hesitation over spending Lucca's money on his family. The thought makes me smirk to myself as I repeatedly hand over the shiny little card.

I have gifts for my mum and grandparents from Tuscany, but I'm feeling horrible after my fight with my mum and would like to purchase her something special. I know exactly what I'm going to get her—something that has changed my whole life, and something I should have done earlier when my therapist Casey recommended it. Something that Lucca introduced to me for which I will be entirely grateful because it has been so special to me.

A journal.

My last stop before meeting the girls for coffee is the kitchen and housewares shop. I've found the perfect third gift for Lucca. Just as I pay for an ice-cream maker, my phone chirps.

"What are you buying for the kitchen? Rose would have taken care of that. You should be buying yourself something nice." I turn around looking for him and don't see him anywhere.

"How did you know I'm in here?"

"We saw you go in. We are next door stuffing teddy bears. You want one?"

I chuckle. "Lucca, I think I'm a bit old for teddy bears."

He laughs. "Okay, come and get us when you are done." The thought occurs to me that I've never actually owned a teddy bear or cuddle toy ever in my life.

I walk in and see the kids having a ball picking outfits for their new teddy bears. Lucca pays and the kids all hang off his legs thanking him, showing lots of appreciation.

Once inside the coffee shop, I dump my bags and turn to talk with my handsome fiancé while Hazel orders an espresso for Lucca and a skinny latte for me.

"Good time?"

"Yes, it was productive," I reply.

"Did you get something nice?"

I picture the lingerie, which is giving me sexy chills thinking about it and how nice it will be for both of us.

"Yes, I bought gifts actually and something very nice for you."

He holds my hips and kisses my nose. "You are so thoughtful, and I love that you are, but if you are not going to treat yourself I will need to continue to spoil you anyway I can."

I hope he means in the bedroom.

"You can spoil me tonight," I whisper, stroking the end of my hair across my lips.

He mutters with a low groan and adjusts his jeans. "You have me twitching for you. You need to stop seducing me in public or we will not last until tonight, and I will need to take you into the restroom."

After the fireman's lift, I've no doubt in my mind he would as well.

I grin, knowing I'm being a tease, blithely running my teeth across my bottom lip. Lucca sharply hisses through clenched teeth, and I need to pull away before things become very heated.

I pass the bag containing a dress for Antonia over to Sarah who's feeding her some soup in a highchair.

"Lexi, that is so thoughtful. Thank you so much. You're very kind and it's beautiful. Look, Antonia, at your pretty new dress," Sarah says, holding the dress up to show Armando, keeping it away from the soup.

"Mummy, wook what we got!" Emilio holds his bear up to Kate.

"You are very lucky. I hope you all said thank you."

"Skip, what did you get?" I ask.

"Just a new sports bra and running vest for work. Dominic has curbed my spending so we can save for the wedding." I rub her arm and wish I could help her out more. I know she's saving, but she's not mentioned she's struggling for money.

"Hazel, we will need to save for twenty years if you keep spending," Dominic gripes.

"Well, maybe your boss needs to give you a pay increase." I smile at Lucca and he nods.

"I will see what I can do." I squeeze his hand tightly to thank him.

Hazel silently mouths a thank you then blows me a kiss; I catch it and give her a wink.

We kiss everyone goodbye then head for home with my bags of gifts I've purchased.

As we walk I yawn and lean on his shoulder, slumping downward. "You are tired, baby. Let's go home."

It has been a hectic weekend and I'm feeling sleepy now. "I'll need to call my mum later and apologise." I yawn again and rub my eyes.

He stops walking and turns me around, leaning me backwards in a dip. He kisses me so sweetly on the lips and neck that I could stay frozen in this position forever. "Your mother is very lucky to have you. I am very lucky to have you."

He opens the passenger door for me and gestures for me to get in.

I suppress a yawn by trying to clench my mouth closed while I'm rummaging for my keys in my hand bag, surrendering them to him without argument. I'm just too tired.

"Save your energy for tonight. You will need it." His lips marry mine to silence any objections I may have. A shiver runs through me at the promise in his voice.

Chapter 18: Trust Me

Closing my eyes on the way home, I feel rather drained after a few days of entertaining and babysitting. After a seemingly smooth journey, I flutter my eyelashes when I'm carried through the front doors of *Castello di Caruso* otherwise known as "The Smithstone."

I blink, noticing the crystal of the chandelier above me, the glass twinkling bright 3D colours overhead and I can hear Doris distantly barking from outside.

Flinching at the sound of the door closing behind us and my shoes clattering on the marble tiles I murmur, "Hmmm. I must have fallen asleep." His hot breath and tongue flickering over my neck has sparked me back to life. Curling my hand around his neck, I pull him in closer pushing my chest forward and groaning into his ear.

He starts lifting me up the stairs. "You are shattered. You need some sleep."

I clench my hands on his brawny, defined biceps. "No, I need you. I'm awake and you promised to spoil me, Romeo. Spoil now. Sleep later." I pout my lips.

"Are you up to it? Because you will be numb and exhausted when I am done with you," he asks with concern walking into the suite.

Oh, numbness is good. I think I can manage that.

"Of course I am. I want you to take me, claim me and have me. I don't want to waste any time tonight. I've been craving you all day."

He sits me on the edge of the bed, kneeling between my legs, then slowly unzips the side zipper down on my dress. Before removing my dress, he traces his thumbs over my nipples, causing them to pebble under the stretchy fabric.

He skims his hands over the material, touching all my curves, then tugs my dress up, pulling it over my head. He hisses a sharp breath, clenching his teeth at my exposed breasts, running his gaze over me. He brushes his thumbs across my nipples which are begging for his moist tongue, and he obliges by swirling over the perkiness with light torment.

"Jesus … I fucking love your tits, Lexi." He growls his desire, which is emanating deeply from within his raspy throat.

I weave my fingers in the wavy hair at the nape of his neck. "You need a haircut soon, Romeo."

I moan with pleasure when he nips and bites. "I like you to have something to grip and yank when I am buried deep inside you, making you scream my name."

Sweet Jesus.

I almost combust with rapacious need burning through me.

"Lucca," I moan.

His tongue travels in wisps of feathery caresses over the curve of my breasts and down my flat abdomen. Then, stroking his thumb over my panties, he pushes me backward on the bed. Leaning back on my forearms, arching my back, I attentively watch his eyes streaming over my body.

The vision of his desire for me is undoing me as his virile hands explore my body.

Sensual.

Alluring.

Hypnotic.

He strokes the insides of my sun-kissed legs, teasing ever so close to my damp core.

A little higher, Lucca. A little higher.

His masterful fingers enticingly spiral down my legs, pressing towards my feet where he stops, and his hands massage both soles in turn.

"Hmmm, that feels nice."

"I am taking it slow tonight. I want to make endless, gentle love to you."

He can have any speed of love and sex he likes as long as I get him. All of him. He usually tells me to ask for it, but I think I have made myself pretty clear. I want him to work his magic and have teased him enough about it all day.

He kisses the soles of my feet, kneading on my weak spot and causing me to buckle into a sensitive squirm. Then he slides his hand under my lower back and lifts my upper body so that I'm facing him.

"I was enjoying that."

"Do not worry. I am going to massage every inch of this glorious body tonight. I hate that you are not going to be with me next week. I need my hands on you for as long as possible." He'll have me all anxious again, bringing our temporary separation up.

He nudges my legs further apart and pulls me down towards him so my ass is sitting on the edge. I slowly undo his shirt buttons and brush his shirt gently down his arms, closing the space between us.

This is going to be intimate, and I need it so much. I loved last night's ravenous, carnal passion, but there is something so endearing about being preciously indulgent.

Close.

Considerate.

Special.

Laboriously, my heart beats against his every chest in a staccato rhythm. With two fingers, he lightly taps under my chin and tilts my head. I blithely run my upper teeth halfway along my bottom lip while the tip of my nose skims across his, catching his warm breath across my lips.

Dipping my head down to the side, I give him full access to my throat and neck.

Sucking.

Teasing.

Nibbling.

My hands lace through his hair like silk weaving through a threaded web, and closing my eyes on a humming mumble, I enjoy his sleek strokes and kisses across my collarbone, shoulders, crook of my neck, and below my ear. I slide my hands down over his shoulders, needing to feel more of his body. I stretch them out, splaying them across his wide, bulky chest muscles clenching his huge pectorals in my palms.

Trailing my fingers over his ripples, he mimics the gesture and moves his hand slowly towards my breasts. He teases me with his featherlike caress, and I plunge forward, asking for his virile hands and his tongue again.

Soft.

Slow.

Seductive.

Throwing my head back, I disappear into a world of lazy pleasure. The dampness between my legs is increasing, soaking the sheer fabric of my panties. The tingling of my skin is tweaking and pricking—soothing but powerfully erotic at the same time.

"Nice?"

"Hmmm … very."

Still with my eyes closed, I hum when his mouth takes my pebbled bud. His tongue doesn't assault, bite, or thrash now; it merely twirls around and wisps over my beaded nipples barely touching. Now he softly blows air across the wetness of my aroused nipple and repeats the action on the other.

Delicious.

Divine.

Decadent.

"God you are perfetto, dolcezza. Mi manchi gia."

His husky bedroom Italian words cause my world to spin.

His masterful tongue licks along my lips, settling on a long seductive kiss.

Standing up to slip his belt off, he bores his crystal-pooled eyes into mine.

Hot.

Smouldering.

"Let me do it."

His illuminated azure blues coax me into his calm waters.

I unbuckle him slowly, sliding his belt through the loops. I'm so close to his ripped abs that I have to kiss them, softly and tenderly, the way he has been with me. I inhale his unearthly, rich, masculine scent, which blissfully transcends me. He straightens his back, filling his lungs and entwining his fingers through my long, soft, curly hair as his body stiffens under my tender caress.

I love how he towers above me, watching and guarding. It makes me feel protected and safe, and the way he lusts for me has me encompassed in complete love.

I slip my thumb down his happy trail and under the waistband of his jeans. I lightly skim my fingers then stop momentarily, pressing my lips to his defined obliques. Inhaling the divine tropical scent of his skin, a rush of warmth cascades over me. I never want to let go of his body, his heart, or his mind.

Breathtaking.

Handsome.

Glorious.

"Are you okay, baby?"

"Yes, I'm just enjoying you, all of you, and thankful I have you," I say against his taught muscles before looking up towards him.

He trails his thumb across my cheek then traces my lips with it. "I am never letting go. I am yours, only yours, forever."

I press my forehead against his sculpted abdominal muscles. Finding his button, I undo it then slide his zipper down, breathing heavy against his pelvis. I place my hands on his hips inside of his jeans and slowly hook my thumb under his boxers' waistband. His hard arousal is bulging in his tight fitting boxers, and I can smell his sweet pre-cum dampening them already.

I'm so tempted to touch, to ravish him, but I'm too engrossed with our slow pace. Gliding my hands down the inside of his jeans, over his hips and inside of his legs, I tempt his jeans slowly down his legs. Taking a grip of the soft denim fabric, I slide them down further until he steps out of them, kicking them aside.

My hands trail back up to clench his butt, then I kiss lightly on the waistband as I inhale the sweet smell of sex again.

Having no restraint, I kiss his hard cock over the top of his boxers, closing my eyes and wishing my tongue was washing that sweet sex down. He hitches his breath and grips my hair, then gently takes my hand and lifts me up. I press my body against his, but I allow him to take his time and relish in the conquest of exploring one another seductively and lazily.

Pushing my hair back over my shoulders, he kisses my lips gently, trailing his fingers down my spine to the hollows of the dimples above my ass then over the satin of my panties, cupping my ass, lifting me up. My legs wrap around his waist, encouraging his engorged head to probe my sensitive spot.

The pressure floods and soaks the sheer fabric rubbing against my clitoris. Rolling my hips gently back, I shudder forward and rotate my pelvis to give my throbbing spot some friction.

"Look at me." he directs.

Fireworks.

I gaze into his eyes, pleading to him with my desperation almost exploding. "I can't wait ... I need to ..."

"Shhh, look at me. You can control this. You need to slow down, baby. I need you to be patient because I will have you so ready for me that when my cock delves into that hot, wet velvet pussy of yours that I will blow your beautiful mind."

Sweet Jesus. Holy shit. Please do.

"I don't think I can wait, Lucca. I need you inside me now." I grip his back and wriggle in his embrace, thrusting against his bulbous knob. "Please, Lucca, I can't wait." My voice falters.

"I want to appreciate every last inch of your body first. Can you give me that?" His voice is so smooth and candid that he's delivering an honest promise to me even though he's asking.

Anticipation.

Vulnerability.

Unconditional love.

"Yes." I inhale deeply.

"Good girl. Let me tenderly love you."

I close my eyes, breathing heavily to cool my scorching passion. Walking to the top of the bed, he lays me down on my back.

"Dolcezza, turn around." I slowly roll over, lying on my stomach. "Wait here."

"Where are you going?"

"Do not panic, just the bathroom."

Settling, I throw the pillows and cushions off the bed and lie flat on my stomach. I try squeezing the pulsing desire between my legs, pushing forward into the mattress to rub my clit against it, but it's just not giving me what I need.

I hear Lucca closing the heavy designer drapes across the French doors, and then soft music from his surround system echoes. Shania Twain's "You've Got A Way With Me."

He kneels at either side of my body, dipping the mattress as he straddles my waist. Leaning over me, his warm heavy chest presses against my back, and his hot breath is close to my ears.

"Do you trust me?" The undertone of his voice whispers in my ear before he presses his nose to my hair and inhales deeply. The sound of his soft, sensual groans and feel of his hot breath against my neck makes me relax underneath him.

"Yes."

He kisses my cheek and neck tenderly. "I am putting something over your eyes, but do not panic. Just close your eyes and breathe. Remember this is me and I am about to cherish and worship you. I will take care of you. Even though you will not see anything, you will feel me, do not be afraid. Think of our light baby."

Wait.

Why?

What?

I'm tense and gripping the sheet, but my heated, damp sex is screaming to allow it.

"Lexi, baby, are you okay? Please relax. Do you trust me?"

"Yes, I trust you." I try to mask my quivering hesitation because of course I'm apprehensive, and my heart is beating fast, but I also feel a surge of excitement and anticipation because of the things Lucca makes me feel. His words, his promises, his touches. I am completely safe.

He places a dark, soft satin blindfold over my eyes, and my breathing becomes short and ragged.

"I will never put you in danger. I will never hurt you. I want to protect you because you are my something special, so let me give you something special. I think this will be good for us and help you with another level of trust."

"Lucca?" I quiver; I just don't know if it's through nerves or desperation.

"Hey, I am here, right here. It is you and me, and nothing else. You will only feel these." His hands softly massage my shoulders. "And this." His lips press under my ears, his tongue writhing across my heated skin.

Long, slow, deep breaths help me to relax. His touch is heavenly and does put me in a trance, so I refrain from fluttering my lashes against the soft fabric covering my eyes and allow my lids to clamp heavily together. I'm calm.

"Okay?" he asks.

"Uh huh."

"Good, I am not going to talk. Just listen to the music and relax, enjoy my touch. I am going to touch you everywhere." His words sexy, voice husky.

The pressure is building in my sex, and my panties are now saturated with the leaking dampness of my wetness causing an impatient stirring of fluttering wings in my abdomen.

The next song to play is Kristina Train's "I'm Wandering."

I hear the noise of a lid being placed back on a bottle and instantly smell the sweet aromatic calming massage oil.

Hmmm, I think I like this mysterious seduction already.

After placing soft kisses along my shoulder blades and over the weaving scar marks on my back, I surrender my tight muscles under Lucca's heated, oily hands. They start slow, circling, kneading, stroking and pressing every knot and tense muscle in my shoulders with just the right amount of pressure to unravel my last few days of chaotic stress.

"Hmmm, it feels so good." I murmur, slumping deeper into the mattress. Then I continue to contently hum and sigh, thoroughly turned-on and unwound under his wandering expertise.

He works his way to my right side, wrapping his large hands around my shapely, thin arm and massaging all the way down to my wrists. Then he smooths his palms over my hand, sliding and pressing each finger to the very tip. He's being very attentive as he repeats his technique on the other arm. Once my fingers have been precisely touched to my manicured nails, he lifts both my hands and places them above my head.

"Come Away With Me" by Norah Jones smoothly chants as he gently strokes under my arms and down the side of my breasts, following the natural curve of my body until he focuses on the middle of my back, then my lower back, showing careful respect down my spine to my dimples above my ass.

I lose his touch and wonder where he's going to travel to. Leaning over me, he kisses the dimple at the top of my ass then hooks his thumb under my panties and slides them down my legs.

Eureka!

Just as I hoped, he's heading straight for my sleek sex folds.

However, he surprises me by taking my toes of my right foot.

With more oil in his hands, he follows the same special procedure. Each little toe is stroked, pressed, and pulled. The soles of both feet and ankles get some extra attention and in equal measures.

He uses more compression on my calves, lifting my leg away from the mattress so he can wrap his hands around and work the front. As his hands climb towards the top of my legs, I spread them wider, hoping he'll understand my urgency, but he pauses at the bottom of my ass, murmuring his own amorous words. Caressing my hips, he repeats on the other side.

He's torturing me and dragging it out. It's pleasurable, but I know what would please me more. Something closer.

Wriggling when he trickles some oil directly onto the bottom of my back this time, I hope he's taking his tender caress somewhere else. No lubrication required. I'm soaked. He places his thumbs at either side of my dimples at the top of my ass.

I twitch and subtly sashay my ass, desperate for his touch. As he holds his thumbs in place, his fingers tap and dance on the oily flesh around the top of my ass.

So close. Almost there.

Gruffly, his breath catches his throat when his hands start to manipulate the swell of my ass cheeks. I tilt my pelvis and roll my hips, lifting my ass just slightly, and he groans at my suggestive position. Norah Jones's "Turn Me On" plays, which only adds to my desperation to have him inside me. The sultry words are liquefying me.

"Lucca?"

He doesn't answer, and I've lost his touch again. He's seriously frustrating me now. I feel the mattress move, and I suspect he's sitting back on his knees. What's he waiting for?

"Lucca, what's wrong?"

"It is okay, baby, nothing is wrong. I'm just admiring your glowing skin, perfect body, and sensational ass. You have me so fucking hard right now."

Good. Get on with it.

His hands return to my inner thighs, and he nudges my legs apart further, but just as I think I'm about to delight with his fingers between my legs, he leans over and places soft kisses on the inside of my legs. His shaggy hair brushes lightly across my skin, and his stubble grazes my inner thighs.

I finally feel his hot breath travelling close to my sex, and his tongue is on me, licking, weaving against my moist folds, then slipping into my core opening just as his oily thumb presses on my sweet spot.

"Oh good God," I moan softly.

My fingers grasp onto the sheets as I get up on my knees, lifting my ass higher and spreading my legs wider, giving him better access.

"I love how wet you are for me. I told you the wait would be worth it."

The intense heat building inside me is escalating. I thrust back, looking for more. I need him to move with me, but he's still. The sleek, quick movement of his tongue stops again. Jesus, it's driving me crazy. Two fingers enter me as his tongue flicks on my clit.

Utopia.

I'm inwardly gasping and tensing my muscles, preparing for a storming climax. "You are close, baby, do not come yet. Control it and just breathe. I need you to wait." There's a rasp in his voice as his hot breath skims my wet, pulsating core.

"I can't …" I whimper.

"You can. You are fucking amazing. Just hold off a little longer. I want you to come apart when I am buried inside you."

"Lucca, I'm close. Don't stop," I pant.

"Inside."

I'm enjoying the build-up, but I need release. He needs to take me before I explode. I'm ready for detonation now. He removes his fingers, but keeps his tongue swirling and teasing in and out of my core opening.

I'm losing control soon, and he knows it. He removes his tongue.

"Take me," I beg. "I've been more than patient. It's time to deliver that promise, Romeo."

After his boxers are off, he kneels back on the bed behind me and wraps his hands around my waist, pulling me upward so my back is to his chest. "You ready?"

"Yes, hurry up. Get inside me before I explode!"

He stifles a laugh. "There is my fiery girl's mouth that I cannot resist. You are goddamn irresistible when you are angry."

He sits back on his heels, and I straddle him with my back to his chest. I'm still in the dark, but I know his body well enough to comprehend that's our position.

His sleek, engorged head teases my clit before he thrusts up driving into me.

"Fuck," he grits through clenched teeth.

The turmoil in my stomach is peaking towards a storm, the wings fluttering, heading south, and blood pounding in my ears. I throw my head back, enthralled under the rooting pleasure.

We are still. His shaft is impaling and stretching me as I clamp around him. He wraps his protective arms around me and grasps my breasts.

"Christ, you feel so good. Your damp, tight pussy is fucking unreal. Move with me," he adds with a deeper rasp.

Tightening my inner leg muscles against his toned quads, I lift and he lowers me slowly onto his long hard girth. Not all the way down to his root, but just enough to pleasure me, and I bask in the glory of it. We repeat this thrust several times slowly, then he stops, leaving me antsy and panting.

"Ready?"

"I need all of you. Now!"

We are so comfortable now with one another sexually that I understand what his intention is. After the teasing, he now needs to fuck me harder, and I want it so badly.

Grasping my hips, he lifts me higher and pistons his hips to shoot up into me harder with fierceness, with more rage. Anger, friction, and desire. His power emanates, propelling him into overdrive, and he thrashes up. Soft cries escape my mouth from the sheer delight and pressure.

"I have waited all fucking day for this," he claims as he shudders into me repeatedly. He releases his massaging hands on my breasts, and travels towards my abdomen.

"Lexi, baby, I'm nearly there." His fingers find my clit, moving in small circles.

"Ahhh," I moan repeatedly, succumbing to my heightened prolonged climax.

"Come for me, baby."

I come hard and fast. I detonate into an earth-shattering, intensive climax, crying and screaming as it tears through my body ripping at my core and shredding my nerve endings.

The room spins, my body quakes, my eyes roll, and I grip his hair as he slams into me again, aggressively yelling out my name then biting my shoulder, filling me with his hot fluid. I float on an echelon that's blissful hedonism. I've lost all control of my senses. It's tumbling around my body in my heady trance.

His heart is pounding against my back, his fingers dig into my hips, but I can feel only incessant pleasure. Becoming limp, I drop my arms from behind his head, covering his hands on my hips.

"Fuck, that was sensational. Shit, Lexi, did I hurt you?" He kisses my shoulder, loosening his fingers and wraps his arms around me, kissing my cheek as our erratic breathing starts to stabilise.

"No, it was amazing."

"Was it worth the wait?"

"Yep, it sure was, I've never come apart so intensely with the build-up. That was hot. I love you." He rocks me, caressing my skin, still buried inside my sheath.

Massage sex.

My new favourite.

"Hmmm, we must have delayed gratification more often. Fuck me, you felt so good," he says, still kissing my shoulder.

"I think my legs are dead, completely frozen." I giggle.

Lifting me off him, he turns me around and places me gently on the bed before removing my blindfold. Fluttering my lashes, getting used to the dim candlelight, I stare at his loving, appreciative eyes. He rubs my legs, kneading into my muscles with his thumbs and fingers.

I take his face in both my hands, kissing his lips until our tongues have tangled against one another, and we're lost in our sensual, dirty kissing. He leans over and takes my nipple in his mouth while nipping the other. Parting my legs, he hovers over me.

"I told you this was going to be a long night." I smile and bite on my lip. "Now, I want to look right into those big, beautiful eyes when you come apart again. Right here, baby, in my eyes."

Holy hell.

Grabbing his butt, I pull him towards me, wrapping my legs around his waist. He delves straight back into me, claiming me all over again, and I'm very willing to give.

After our missionary lovemaking, he carries me to the shower and fucks me against the vanity unit then in the shower one last time for safe measure.

Insatiable.

We wash every inch of each other's bodies with a soft sponge soaked in his tropical body gel under the hot spray of the powerful jets. Feeling absolutely exhausted and completely spent and relaxed, I'm barely able to move my floppy limbs.

Closing my eyes, Lucca towel dries my hair and body. Then I slip one of his shirts on without underwear, just enough to cover my ass and no more.

"You are glowing, Lexi," he says, running his fingers over my cheeks.

Lust glow.

"You're insatiable and sexy," I lazily reply.

Lucca puts his lounge pants on and takes my hand, leading me downstairs to the kitchen to see what delight Rose has prepared and left for us. There is a note to say they have taken Doris for a long walk to give us some privacy tonight, and they'll keep her in the coach house.

They really are great people. Lucca is very lucky to have them.

After a cosy, relaxed dinner of roast lamb and all the trimmings with a glass of Pinot Noir, we follow with a slice of Rose's pineapple upside-down cake. It reminds me of Lucca's present, so I send him out to the car to pick up my bags. I show him all the gifts except the underwear and fountain pen. He is thrilled with his ice-cream maker.

"So if you make gelato for me, I am going to have to smother it across your body and enjoy my dessert from your skin. Win-win. Cake and eat it?"

Chuckling, I tell him that is exactly what I had in mind.

While he packs his bags, I load the dishwasher and then make my note to accompany the fountain pen gift since I never had time to get it engraved. I head into his study and rummage in the drawer of his desk. Placing my hand on a notepad, I lift it out and stare at a bunch of invoices held together by a clip.

Lucca's business and finances are none of my concern, and I shouldn't pry, but I can't help lift the bundle of paperwork and stare at the heading. It's for a clinical research programme for a cancer trust.

Scrolling across the pages, it's clear the payments have been going out from one of Lucca's accounts to this clinical research company. Lucca is generous and kindly helps charitable organisations so that would explain it, but why this type of cancer?

Filed for later.

I place the bundle back in the drawer and open Lucca's new fountain pen to scroll on the paper.

'When I can't be with you to brighten your day, I hope this diamond set pen brings a sparkle to your genius and gives you inspiration.'

'Tu sei il mio qualcosa di speciale. TIii amo ora e per sempre. Lexi x.'

'You're my something special. I love you now and forever. Lexi x.'

This is the same message I had engraved on the expensive pen I gave him in Tuscany. After running my fingers along the pen, I place it in the navy blue box and use the note as wrapping paper. I tape the edges neatly but ensure the scrolling message is decipherable on the top of the rectangular parcel.

Leaving the study, I discreetly place it in Lucca's briefcase.

I decide to call my mum. It's time I apologised and mentally note that I must ask Lucca about the cancer research trials as I am genuinely interested, but it's not important so it can wait.

Flat out across our bed, I watch Lucca go back and forth with various ties and shirts. He holds up a lime green tie and I shake my head wrinkling my nose. Rose had the housekeeper wash and iron our clothes today while we were out, and she organised Lucca's work wardrobe, so he just needs to decide what to take. We've topped our wine glasses, and I'm grateful for the little buzz-kicked courage I have.

"Mum, it's me."

"Alexis, sweetheart I'm so happy you called. I was so unsettled the way things were left on Friday. I tried calling you back ... I—"

I interrupt her. "Mum, I'm so sorry. I was just so mad, but I should never have said those awful things to you. I'm so sorry." Twirling the back of my hand and fingers near my mouth fractiously, I hold the phone to my ear with the other.

Lucca looks at me, winking proudly with his sexy dimple smile, which relaxes me a little.

"Alexis, sweetheart, please don't. There is no need. It's I who should apologise. Cameron called and enlightened me of your relationship, explaining how safe and happy you are, and confirming your happiness to me. But I have to say it was speaking to the charming Mr. Caruso himself that reassured me. I now know you are loved, safe, and protected. He sounds like a true gentleman. You're very lucky, Alexis."

"Wait, you spoke to Lucca? When?" My eyes burn right through him, and he playfully lifts his eyebrow and one side of his lip revealing the devilish dimple again. Sitting upright now, she has piqued my interest.

"He called me on Friday when you went out with Hazel. Cameron gave him my number. Anyway, no matter. The point is I had a long chat about him with Casey, and then with Lucca himself, and I feel so much more at ease with your situation. He seems to be a sensible man and he sure as hell loves you. I'm looking forward to meeting him, and of course, seeing you, my darling girl. I have to say I did feel sick to the core wondering what sort of mess you have gotten yourself in, but as it happens, Lucca put my mind at ease and Casey helped too. She has nothing but great things to say about him."

Direct, clear, and concise. This is not my mother.

"Oh did he now?" I crease my brow and firm my lips to form the "I'm not surprised" look towards my charming Italian god, who never fails to amaze me.

"Yes, he did. Such a wonderful man you have there. I have some reprieve from the clinic, so I'm staying back at home with your grandparents while I finish my art course. I want to spend as much time with you both as possible."

"Mum, is that such a good idea? I mean, I want to see you, but maybe it's not a good idea having so much time away from the clinic just in case ..." Propping myself up, feeling nervous, I reach over and swirl my fingers over the embellished design carved into the headboard.

"Just in case what, Alexis? Spit it out. You think I'll have an episode, don't you? Are you ashamed of me?" Panic rising in her voice causes me to stop tracing over the wood.

"No, I'm not ashamed of you. I love you. I just worry about you." I twirl my hair around my finger and chew the inside of my cheek.

"Well, you need to stop fretting. Casey is coming to visit soon, so I will be able to talk to her, and it's my job to worry about you, not the other way around. You'll make yourself ill worrying about me."

Ironically, she has a point, but I feel responsible for her wellbeing. She's much more vulnerable and fragile than I am. We chat a little longer than we usually do because I have her in a good mood. I ask after my grandparents and she tells me about her painting classes. After telling her I love her and will see her on the weekend, we hang up.

That wasn't as bad as I thought.

"Lucca, can you come here a minute?" I call to his dressing area as he saunters through.

"You and your mum okay now?" he asks, rolling a belt up and slipping it into his case.

"You know fine well we are, so spill." Lifting my brow, I cross my arms over my chest and tap my upper arm with my index finger.

"Spill what?" He's masking the amusement in his voice.

"What did you bribe her with?" I ask sternly.

He laughs, grinning widely, and puts his hand on his heart. "I am wounded."

"And I'm serious." I sit upright moving to the edge of the bed.

"I did not bribe her. I convinced her how much I love you and how good we are for each other. It took a bit of work, but I did not want you going up there feeling the way you did. I also spoke with your grandpa, and I can see why you adore him. He really loves you, but you know that, right?"

He has me smiling again.

"I do know, and I love him too. You'll have some competition when we go up there because I don't leave his side." I smirk.

"Well, I love a challenge." His hand travels under the shirt I'm wearing to cup my ass, pulling me in closer to him.

"I love you so much, thank you for speaking with her. I think I might call Casey at some point just to ask if she thinks it's a good idea her being back at home."

"I would do anything for you. You make everything worth fighting for in my life and keep me very much alive." He places a loose curl behind my ear while I lazily yawn. "Hmmm ... you ready to go to bed?"

He pulls the sheets back and slides me into bed. Locking up and turning the lights off, he climbs in beside me, spooning me so close and gentle that I drift off into the most relaxing sleep I've had since being in the farmhouse in Tuscany.

A featherlike stroke over my navel to my groin wakes me up out a deep sleep. "Hmmm ... what time is it?" I groan.

"Early, but I need to go to the airport soon. Marco is picking me up."

Sighing, I've become very needy with his inevitable departure. "I was hoping we would have an extra few hours together before you need to go." Turning around, I wrap my arms around his neck, still wearing his shirt from last night.

"I woke you up a little early to give me time ..." he kisses my forehead, cheek, and lips "... for this." He rolls me onto my back and trails his hands up my inner legs followed by his lips, kissing my hot skin until his lips meet my pulsing sex.

He makes sure I remember his touch long after he has to go.

After an amazing early morning orgasm, he lifts the shirt off me and keeps my arms above my head as he presses his body to mine, entering deep inside me.

Horny sleepy sex.

No asking.

No begging.

Just claiming and delivering, until we release together and hold onto to each other, calming ourselves quietly. A stray tear escapes and rolls down my cheek. Lucca wipes the tear with his thumb.

"Hey, it is only a few days. Then I will be back before you know it."

"I'm just going to miss you. I thought I would be okay with this, but now I wish I was coming. Although, I do like all the sex you've treated me with."

"You would be getting the sex regardless, baby. You will just need to stay busy until I am back. Suzanne might call you to check if you need anything. Keep your phone on so I can speak to you every day. I would rather you did not drive, so Marco or Peter will take you anywhere you need to go. Remember to call Mamma back about the wedding plans and think of a date while I am away. The sooner you become Mrs. Caruso, the better."

I shower with Lucca, even though it's early, then I watch him get dressed in a sharp, black designer power suit. The quality material fits his broad shoulders and muscular body superbly and does nothing to contain my need for him right now. His dark, wavy hair curls at the edge of his crisp white shirt collar. His eyes are electric, and his long, black eyelashes compliment the deep tone of his suit.

He fixes his cufflinks and tie, and when he turns around fully, my mouth nearly drops to the floor. "What's wrong? You do not like it?"

"Hell no, I love it. You look very sexy and hot. Hold on a minute."

I walk into his dressing area and come back with a different tie. I kneel on the end of the bed and unravel the beautiful pale blue silk tie he's wearing, then wrap a black, grey and pink striped tie around his neck and begin to knot it.

"What is wrong with the blue one? It is my favourite."

"It's my favourite too, but it accentuates your beautiful crystal-blue eyes, so you're not wearing it," I say earnestly.

Catching him off guard, he laughs. "Really?"

"You know fine well how much I love your eyes, and paired with that tie you're mesmerising, so I'd rather you keep this one and wear it just for me." I'm turning into a possessive freak.

He leans over and runs his fingers through my hair, clenching a handful before kissing me passionately. "Deal, but I promise my eyes are just for you."

Inhaling his sexy masculine scent of musk, wood, and citrus, I'm regretting my decision to stay here. I hate the thought of him being around other women—professional women who are powerful and sexy.

Oh God.

On our final kiss in the hallway, I jump up and straddle Lucca's waist, hanging onto his neck at the front door. When I hear the car door open and realise Marco is standing there grinning at us, I slide down and try to look decent.

"You keep that bed warm for me, and keep your phone on. I love you, dolcezza. Please stay safe for me." He rubs his thumb across my swollen lips from where he has been kissing me this morning.

"I love you too. Safe flight, hurry back to me." Moisture coats my eyes as I watch him walk off.

Lifting his bags, he winks at me and then he's gone. I'm all alone again. Wrapping my arms around me, I wonder how the next few days will pan out without him here. I close the front door, lock it, and head back to the bedroom. I can smell his lingering aftershave all the way upstairs into the suite, and it's intoxicating. I fill my lungs with his scent.

I decide to go back to bed and sleep for a bit, still exhausted from our busy weekend. Leaving my robe off, I put his shirt back on just to feel him near my body then cosy under the covers like a lovesick teenager with his blue tie sitting on the pillow next to me.

Chapter 19: Uprising Michael Parks

Rubbing his temple, Michael checks the departure board and curses.

He missed a flight from London Heathrow to Glasgow International. Although they are frequent at this time of the morning, he hasn't booked a seat, hoping he'll be lucky.

Michael decided it was time to change his appearance, so his crooked teeth have been replaced by a not so respectable backstreet dentist. He paid cash with the drug money his mother Mary stashed away for him to have a complete new set of teeth implants, which he wouldn't have bothered with before but he's reluctant to leave any trace of his old self other than his scars caused by Lexi while trying to escape all those years ago in Australia.

His evil green eyes have been temporarily camouflaged by tinted grey contacts. It's been a busy week since arriving in the United Kingdom with a lot of seedy prep work being done as far away from the public eye as possible.

He has managed to transform his facade and looks almost like any other business traveller. Keeping tinted glasses on, he approaches British Airways first and to his surprise, he has the last available seat on the next flight.

Handing over his fake passport under the name of Kyle Saunders, he pays for the flight with cash. He could easily undress the sweet smelling red-lipped busty blonde with his natural greedy green eyes, but he doesn't want to draw any attention, so he barely makes eye contact as he adjusts himself behind the desk.

He orders a black coffee, a muffin, and a bacon roll for breakfast then wanders into the nearest kiosk to purchase a newspaper and painkillers. He pulls his suitcase behind him.

Picking up a newspaper and turning the first page, he's not watching where he's walking and collides with the hard chest of a tall, dark gentleman dressed in a striking designer suit and a pink and grey tie.

"I do apologise, please excuse me," The smart looking businessman gestures in an identifiable Scottish accent with Italian flavour.

"Watch it, man," Michael hisses in his Australian accent. He barges past the businessman to pay for his goods before checking his luggage in. The businessman shakes his head at the stranger's rudeness but continues onwards to meet his driver and phone his girl who he left just a few hours ago.

Once seated on the flight, Michael lifts the manila envelope from his hand luggage to scan over it again. Satisfied no one is paying attention, he discreetly scrolls though all the facts that Damien Thomson, the unconventional investigator, filed for him.

There is enough information on Grace Elizabeth Robertson to know where she is situated in Scotland. His intention is to hire a car under the name of Kyle Saunders. Then he'll purchase a used car by cash under the name of Uuka Benadi. Uuka is a South African name meaning "uprising," which Michael deems appropriate considering his intentions.

Frustratingly, he still can't find anything on Alexis, Grace's daughter.

The girl will be alive, he knows this for sure. She's smart and will be staying away from the public eye, living a private life, as will the brother, Cameron. They were smart as children and if they have any sense, they should always feel threatened, especially if they have received any prior warning about his release. Michael scratches his nail over the scar on his wrist in contemplation. If they have sense, they should be hiding, he imagines.

This journey may be a lot more challenging than he initially thought.

Weighing his options, he toils with the best approach. He could approach Grace Robertson for the information he needs or have Alexis lured to him like blood to a shark. In Grace's case, honey to the bees, but he would jeopardise his operation and chance to take Alexis.

Grace is not his priority and she would recognise him, even cloaked behind his new appearance. Then there is his obvious Australian accent.

Sharing a cell for many years at the Australian prison with a South African immigrant has become useful. He has managed to copy his accent successfully, and he can easily pass for South African as a result.

He needs to keep a low profile and be clever and patient. There is also the boy to consider, the brother who again has been difficult to trace. He wonders if their names are changed by deed poll perhaps, or they have had legal representation helping to maintain their privacy.

Closing his eyes and grinding his new sensitive teeth, he brings his focus back to the inevitable. The time has come to stalk his prey, claim his worth, and reincarnate demons past. Revenge is sweet. He can almost taste it as he runs his tongue across his bloody gums.

Damien was asked to go over and above his initial agreement for this private investigation brief for a substantial monetary increase. He has proved his worth and earned his respectable fee by setting Michael up with a casual job interview, a local job in the area he wants to survey.

Working underground, Damien also managed to arrange the required weapons, various drugs, another fake passport and credit cards, two new mobile phones, a tracking device, and various tools Michael requested, all of which will be awaiting him in a safety deposit box in Glasgow Town Centre. It's a pity Damien won't enjoy his respectable fee—he knew too much and had to be taken care of ... permanently.

The headlines in London yesterday claimed Damien's recent death to be a suicide. He was notorious for being involved with illegal drug smuggling and underground gangs were hunting him down. Although a post-mortem has not been carried out and investigations are underway, the police have made a statement saying nothing has been confirmed yet.

He was found dead in his car by a riverbank, and further investigations are underway. They're hoping to fit another jigsaw piece into the on-going perplexed puzzle of one of the UK's biggest drug trafficking operations. Damien is a little fish in a big pond, but they're hoping to find some links to the untouchable underground group.

It was just by chance Michael met a few of the gang members associated with the underground drug scene when he had his second visit with Damien in a dark alley outside of a strip club in London's Soho district. When Damien was called away to deal with an uncooperative client, Vladimir the Russian—who delivered a parcel of crack to Damien—was kind enough to enlighten Michael of the danger surrounding Damien. In regards to the close watch on him by the police, it was risky for Vladimir being there doing business with him.

It was then Michael had the foresight to use Damien for his contacts, but paid Vladimir a substantial amount to take care of him and make sure it looked like a suicide, keeping it clean without a trace.

Vladimir accepted the money and the job as nothing fazed him—it wasn't the first time he would wash blood from his hands. Damien was drugged with sleeping pills then placed in the driver's seat of the car. He suffered carbon monoxide poisoning and there was no sign of struggle.

At Glasgow International, Michael picks up a rental car under his temporary name of Kyle Saunders. Programming the GPS for Glasgow, he then pulls out the crumpled photograph of the brown-eyed girl. It's one where she is tied to the bedpost in Simon Parks' room.

The picture depicts a young Lexi, helpless, petrified, and innocent with a torn vest and no panties. Time is near. Not being able to help himself, the strain of his erection in his black trousers has distracted him. It's a weakness he has never been able to contain when thinking about her and the unimaginable cruelty he bestowed upon her.

Sitting behind the wheel in the multi-storey car park, he masturbates while staring at the picture. He throws his head back and clutches the wheel with his hand. It won't be long until Michael has Alexis—he'll come all over her face before scarring her and doing inexplicable things. He'll leave her to suffer after torturing her and violently taking her life, like she took another's that wasn't hers to take.

Chapter 20: Runner

I sleep so long that my phone buzzing wakes me up a few hours later. Smiling, I answer Lucca, who is calling to say he's landed in London and currently being driven to the hotel for the conference. When I tell him I'm back in bed, he groans quietly down the phone and tells me he misses me already and that he wishes I was lying beneath him.

I need to press my legs together with that familiar pulsing listening to his sexy voice. I wish him good luck with his meeting and tell him my plans for today. After a quick shower, I slip into my fitness bra and tank, short black running shorts, and running shoes.

I strap on my iPod armband, pull my unruly, long, soft brown hair into a ponytail, shuffle around with my playlist, and grab my earphones. Running with earphones in isn't something I used to be able to do. It's only since I got Doris that I'm able to. She alerts me if there are any intruders or strangers and keeps me safe. Sitting on a wooden chair on the back pergola area just outside the indoor pool section, I drink a bottle of water and enjoy some south facing sun beating against my legs.

I send out my texts for the morning.

To Lucca – I miss you already. I love you, Romeo. Have a good day. Xxx

Lucca - It is driving me mad not having you by my side. Have fun this week. I will call you later. Keep your phone on and be careful. Miss you. Romeo. Xx

To Cameron – Thank you for speaking to Mum. I owe you. What shift are you tues/weds night? Can you stay with me? Xx

To Hazel – Can you check in later? If you pick me up, I will come to class with you. Xx

To Jess – You ok to stay with me 2nite? PJs, dinner, and movie? Xx

To Lucy – Are you ok? Lucca's away so I'd love your company. You can stay Tues/Weds night whatever suits. Xx

To Jane – Still ok for lunch tomorrow? I hope baby hippy is behaving xx
To Rachel – Sorry haven't caught up with you yet. It's been a busy week. Let me know when you're free. I could do Weds 4 coffee xx

Then I send a group text to the girls …

The Darlin's - Coffee night Weds at Castello di Caruso, my darlin's. Bring your suits 4 a swim. Xx

Samantha – Fuck the coffee, Frozen Margaritas senorita? xx

This makes me smile—any opportunity to relieve the work stress.

Welcomed by a refreshed Rose and Peter after their weekend away. I give them their gifts. They are overwhelmed by my thoughtfulness, and I'm thrilled they like the things I picked out. I truly feel comfortable around them both.

Doris nearly knocks me over in her excitement. She spies the running shoes. Her almost human eyes roll in her head, and then she does her hyperactive dance and sprints to the front gate. She knows we're going for a run, and as always, she's one step ahead.

Peter is on the phone talking to Lucca's security firm about fixing the side camera around the house, so I politely wave and head off. I just manage to get the leash around Doris before she drags me off my feet.

Walking briskly at first, I start to jog, listening to my power fitness tunes courtesy of Hazel. As I jog through the Victorian streets, I watch the sun bursting little streams of light through the sprawling branches of the tall maple trees adorning the narrow pavements and shadowing the red sandstone walls. I jog past the boutiques and restaurants on the main street and ignore the stares as I continue onwards and head to Bothwell Castle grounds.

In my training zone now, I'm breaking sweat just controlling my rapid breath while Doris looks as if she's meandering slowly by my side. I pound up the narrow pathway overgrown with green hedges listening to my music, hammering my frustration of all my worldly worries on my steps. I turn my music up when I get into my training zone. I'm deafened by my music as it's so loud ...

But I sense something.

I sense someone approaching

I feel goose bumps, shivers under such hot, sweaty circumstances. My heart rate increases and the blood drains from my head and thumps in my ears. Doris glances up to me in mid-stride and closes the space between us, ensuring her grey velvet coat brushes my legs as we move together. This is the reason I picked her—her protection and loyalty. The burn in my stomach and thumping heartbeat drives me to accelerate.

A shoulder comes parallel to mine.

Intruder.

I don't turn to look.

Increasing my already rapid pace, I yank at Doris to inform her we are on the move. Whether that's in front or on a detour, it will definitely be away from this stranger intruding our space. My clothes are so damp with sweat, that they cling to my body. The salt from my perspiration is lining my lips and coating my skin's surface. My eyes sting with remnants of yesterday's mascara, but through the sweaty, stingy, hazy blur, I pound through it because getting away from the stranger is the priority.

Gasping.

Panicking.

The stranger keeps up, side by side. It's definitely a man—an athletic man, but a man just the same. I can't bring myself to look because I might falter or panic. If this person is a threat, Doris will let me know. Focused straight ahead, I pass creeks, bends, and potholes, powering up steps up and over a bridge and down the steps at the other end.

Panting.

Gasping.

Burning.

The stranger has the edge. He picks up speed and strides in front of me, and I catch a glimpse of his back and biceps from the side through my wet, salty lashes.

The path bends sharply in the corner, so I prepare my body to swerve, leaning to the side. As I lean inward, I stumble over a broken branch on the dirt track, twisting my ankle and knocking me to my knees.

"Ouch!"

Doris barks loudly and my earphones fall from my ears landing somewhere beside me in slow motion.

My hands have scraped across the gravel on the fall, so I try to protect my fragile wrist by leaning on the other arm, grazing my skin in several places, and my knees hit the stones as I stumble. I don't need to look to know I'm cut and bruised from my tumble.

I can feel the stinging sensation to my skin.

Then it hits me.

The pain.

I fall over onto my side in aching despair and scream in agony. Doris pounds on top of me, which only makes me worse. I'm suffocated. I can barely breathe, and I need to push her off.

"Oh my God ... fuck, are you okay?" A fast, panting, deeply masculine voice asks. He's on his knees.

"My ankle. Shit, my ankle. I went over on it." I try to stretch my leg and wiggle my foot side to side. Heart racing, chest heaving, blood pounding in my ears.

"Don't move," he instructs.

Not that I can with a massive Weimeraner gun dog hovering over me. Doris eventually moves away and lies by my side, so now my whole body is exposed to him.

A smooth masculine hand moves over my wet, sweaty leg to my ankle sending shivers over my body. I flinch. I wish Lucca were here.

I try to sit up to face the runner, but I slump on the gravel, having an urge to turn my head. I need to vomit. "Oh my God, I'm going to be sick."

Leaning away, the runner puts a hand on my hip and the other on my shoulder to hold me. I curl my body to vomit at the side of the path in the most un-ladylike fashion, wrenching repeatedly and gasping for air.

Taking deep breaths after I've emptied my stomach, I'm shaking all over and embarrassed as my stomach catapults. I always react to pain by vomiting, ugh!

"Are you better?" he asks.

"I'll be fine. I'm sorry, it's just a reaction to the pain." My face is scorched red from exhaustion and embarrassment.

"Don't be sorry as long as you're okay. Are you going to be sick again?" I still haven't glanced at the man offering to help me, but Doris is surprisingly calm and his voice is soft, sincere, and steady.

"No, I think I'm good. I haven't had breakfast and I'm a little shaky. It's a miracle I didn't faint. That's my party piece apparently." I try to make light of the situation.

Still fixing my gaze on the path, I can't look up as the blood draining from my head will make me dizzy. Crouching in front of me, two sweaty hands cup my face and a familiar pair of eyes bore into mine—rich, chocolate eyes. I was about to jerk away but I'm stunned.

Jackson.

Why would someone of his calibre and reputation be out running solo on a public path anyway?

"Oh God, Jackson, I'm sorry. I've overdone it, and I think I've hurt my ankle. I must be a state. I'm sorry. You must think I'm ..." I ramble, because I'm so embarrassed but relieved it's not a complete stranger.

I don't know why I'm worried about my appearance and what he thinks as he intimidates me slightly, but strangely, I do worry about what he thinks. He stares into my eyes, his brown eyes meeting mine softly.

He seems genuinely worried. I feel the heat of his athletic body towering over me and the soft touch of his hand here and there on my red-hot skin. He is every bit as handsome as he was yesterday.

Before I met Lucca, I could not have had contact in such a close proximity, but I now know that not everyone is sinister and corrupt, willing to hurt. Jackson's touch is a welcome relief in the absence of Lucca's caring hands.

I genuinely think Jackson wants to help even though I'm still slightly intimidated by him. Or am I? Oh Jesus. I'm so confused.

"Christ, Alexis, I could barely keep up with you. You're fast. That was a bad fall you had there. Is it broken?"

I move it from side to side, wincing with the strain. Leaning over, I untie my lace creating room to breathe. "I think it's sprained ... I need to get my sock and shoe off to assess properly, but it's not broken. It just hurts like hell."

Jackson sighs and loosens the laces then runs his hand across my cheek and removes a little piece of bark clinging to my hair.

"What are you doing running out here? Doesn't it bother you that people will know who you are?" I ask.

"I have a gym in the house, but I like to get out in the fresh air and have some normalcy about my life. I park my car outside the castle ruins so I don't need to venture onto the main street. I didn't know you could run like that. Fuck, you're good," he says, running his thumb gently over my ankle.

"Not anymore by the looks of it." I nod towards my ankle. "I used to run a lot, but I'm out of condition as I was abroad then suffered another injury."

"Is that why your skin is lovely and bronzed? Were you somewhere nice?" He shifts, unsure whether to help me up or not yet.

"Italy," I reply, adjusting myself as I try to stand.

"With Lucca?"

Why does he want to know? What difference does it make, surely it's obvious.

"Yes."

He lifts my earphones and passes them to me but does not comment further. "Can you stand up?"

"Yes, I think so." I stand then stumble into him leaning on my stronger ankle taking pressure off the other.

"Here, wrap your arm around my shoulder. I'll help you walk back." Doris is circling then sniffing him and rubbing her head off his thigh, but she's not barking so I know she trusts him.

"Doris, stop it." I giggle.

"She's okay. I have two Dobermans so she probably smells them, and Shawna has one of those white fur ball things that sits on her fucking lap all day like a toy fucking trophy. The Dobermans hate her."

I laugh and form a smile amidst my cringing with mortification. "Shawna or the fur ball?"

He grins. "Um, both actually." He laughs light-heartedly.

"Jackson, thank you for your help, but honestly, I'm fine. I think it's a sprain. I'll manage back. You go on with your run. It's not good for you to stop like that while training. I'll call Cameron to come and get me."

Shit.

I don't have my phone. Only my iPod and looking at Jackson in his sports kit, he doesn't look to have a phone either.

"Cameron? Why not Lucca?"

"He's working away this week." I look towards my ankle and sigh, wishing Lucca could scoop me up in his arms the way he normally does and make me feel better.

"I'm not leaving you on your own. I'll make sure you get home. Cameron would never forgive me if I left his baby sister in pain like this." He holds a hand on the back of his neck and nods towards my ankle.

Rolling my eyes, I sigh. "Okay, thank you."

Putting my weight onto his side, he wraps an arm around my waist firmly. Flinching under his touch, I manage to hobble a few steps.

"You need some water and something to eat. Then you need to get ice on that ankle and get it elevated."

I smile at his instructions. This is exactly the advice I would give but I don't mention it. I'm well aware of how to look after sprains; he's only trying to help. "Yes, sir."

I hobble another few steps but close my eyes and grit my teeth, grimacing from the pressure and pain. Before reaching the steps of the bridge, he surprises me by lifting me up and cradling me into his chest. My arm automatically wraps around his neck as he carries me over the bridge. I'm flooded with feelings and mixed signals.

Lucca's arms are the only arms I want to be in and a stranger touching me, never mind carrying me, would normally have me hysterical or cause me to run. I'm in so much agony and it's not as if I can run anywhere. I need his help but it doesn't stop me from feeling tense and nervous.

One arm around my back the other under my legs, his hand is close to my ass, holding me to him. The same hand is splayed over my tight running shorts, which barely cover my ass and the skin at the top of my legs. His hold on me is close, but it's the only way he can carry me without a fireman's lift or me straddling his waist, which would never happen. I'm about to protest, but I know it would take me ages to get over the steps, even if I could, and I feel secure strangely.

Folding ...

At the other end of the bridge, I expect him to put me down, but he doesn't. He continues to carry me as he makes small talk. Leaning against his chest, I inhale the sweet scent of fragrant flowers and oranges and musk mixed with sweat.

Now my chest is heaving a little again while my pulse quickens. He stops and looks down at me. "Are you okay?"

I'm not. Anything but. Jackson scents remind me of Lucca's tropical body products and the musk in his aftershave, which makes me pine for him, and I'm missing him terribly. It's adding to my unease.

I'm getting anxious. This is inappropriate. I wonder what Lucca would make of it. He warned me to stay away from him, but it's not as if I've had a choice.

Guilty ...

"Yes, I'm fine. You can put me down if you like." I suggest even though I know I wouldn't get very far on my own right now.

He continues to walk, ignoring my suggestion. "We're nearly there. I want to do this to help you, and besides, you're light as a feather, so it's no hassle. You know, Alexis, you're not like other women."

What's he going on about? How would he know?

"You're beautiful and sincere, but I'm sure Lucca has already told you that many times."

Fuck!

File P for panic. Panic attack flaring up, just directly.

"I'm not going to lie. Most girls throw themselves at me, and will do anything to get my attention as they strive to be the next chick hanging on my arm. It drives my current girlfriend crazy, but she was one of those girls before ..."

I take a deep breath with his next stride. Where's he going with this?

"Yet, here you are in my arms, and you couldn't care less. You're different."

I wouldn't say I couldn't care less. He has rendered me speechless. All the years I could have been in the arms of a man before I met Lucca I didn't want to. Now I don't want to because I only want to be in Lucca's.

"I watched you yesterday, and I know the other boys did too, but I was intrigued." He tilts his head down angling near my head, his words close to my ear, giving the impression he wants me to hear him. Really hear him.

I'm aware I was under surveillance yesterday, but I'm not letting on. "Why are you telling me this?"

Halting his steps, he readjusts his arms slightly. "You're the only woman I've ever met who really fascinates me. You don't seem fazed at all about my celebrity stardom, nor are you throwing yourself at me trying to impress me. It's refreshing to meet someone so down to earth with natural beauty. Lucca is very lucky to have you," he says casually.

I'm not sure if it's a compliment, an act of sincerity, or an attempt to chat me up, but he's succeeded in making me quiver ever so slightly, and oddly, he doesn't seem to intimidate me, especially not the way he did yesterday.

Is it too early for wine?

He tenses a little. "Are you intimidated or appalled by me because I have a reputation for being a womaniser?"

"What? No, I mean I'm not intimidated or appalled. Why would you think that?"

He sighs. "I see it in your eyes."

Lucca tells me this often. "Okay, I admit I did have my opinions of you, and if I'm honest, they weren't favourable ones, but I didn't know you. Right now, I don't have any feelings other than embarrassment about the state I've got myself in today and thankful that you're kind enough to help me."

I lie.

Stopping at a bench in the narrow dirt path surrounded by overgrown wild greens, he sits down to take a rest but keeps me on his lap. I shuffle over so that I'm sitting on the bench by his side stretching my legs and rotating my ankle slowly. Doris lies at my feet. Jackson watches me stretch out, narrowing his eyes over my bronzed legs.

There is an awkward silence. I know he's waiting for me to say something, but all I can think about the pulsing throb at my ankle and the fact that I think Lucca will be furious when he finds out I'm spending time with Jackson. I know his intention is to help me, and he isn't threatening me in any way, but Lucca won't see it like that. He'll assume Jackson's trying to flirt with me and for that reason alone, I should ensure I put Jackson in his place.

"I'm not fazed by stardom, money, or status. It doesn't impress me. People probably think that I'm with Lucca for his money, but I'm not. I love Lucca for who he is, what he is to me, how he makes me feel. I'd still love him if he were penniless because money can't buy you love or happiness."

I pick a piece of broken bark splintering from the bench and twist it until it breaks off. This is the same bench that Cameron and I sat on when we were having our chat yesterday morning. I wonder what he would make of this. I know he thinks highly of Jackson and that gives me some comfort.

Jackson drops his head, leaning his arms on his legs, and holds his hands in front of him. "That's what I mean. You're honest and sincere. Not like the women I've been linked with who have no interest in getting to know the real me. All they care about is the image, the money, and the stardom. It's hard to convey a true picture of me when the press tarnishes my reputation at every opportunity." He sighs and shakes his head.

There is gentleness in his tone that tells me he is telling the truth. That he's not the smarmy, unfaithful man the press makes him out to be. He doesn't seem audacious or over-confidant. There is a definite vulnerability there in his face, voice, and actions.

"I would hate to be in the public eye like that. Having people judging and criticising my every move." I mean it too; it must be awful. I love my privacy and the thought of being exposed like that must be soul destroying. I guess some people like being in the public eye, but it can't be easy.

He looks up, cocks his head to the side, and smiles his sexy smile. He runs his middle finger and thumb over his stubble of his jaw. "So you understand that I'm not the person your eyes told me you thought I was?"

"Yes, I suppose I do now. Jackson, if you're not happy, then I'm sure there is someone out there for you. Someone who is interested in you and not your status or money. You just haven't found her yet."

He rubs his thumb over my hand. "I just did, but she's taken."

Bloody hell.

I pull my hand away and almost choke sucking in a huge gulp of air. My cheeks are flushed and head is starting to throb with an imminent headache. He doesn't even know me, how can he say such a thing? I can't say anything. I'm lost for words.

Three things strike me. Firstly, I know Lucca will go caveman if he heard this. Secondly, I know for certain Jackson would never try and hurt me after his confession; he's too sincere and honest, therefore I'm safe. Thirdly, what now? I know where I stand, but he clearly doesn't, and that I need to address properly when I find the right words.

"Come on, let's get you home." He stands and scoops me up in his arms again. I'm not aware I've been holding my breath until I gasp for air and sag against him. Nothing will ever happen between Jackson and me. Ever. My heart is with Lucca, and he knows it, but I'm still flattered and confused by his compliments.

We're quiet until we reach his car. No surprise, it's a ridiculously expensive, black Rolls-Royce. Rolling my eyes, he catches me and smirks. He places Doris in the back then helps me sit me in the passenger seat.

"You're lucky I've not got the Bugatti today. The dog wouldn't fit." I want to laugh, but I shake my head. "Oh sorry, I know, it doesn't impress you," he adds, not with sarcasm but with a general apology.

I give Jackson the code for the gate so I don't have to get out and walk around to the panel on the driver's side. I think I trust him enough to know he won't be breaking and entering.

Parking in front of the water feature, he eyes up our cars and raises an eyebrow. Both Aston Martins and my BMW are here, along with Lucca's Bentley classic car that Peter has obviously been working on today.

"What?" I ask him as he studies me quizzically.

"Nothing." He tilts his head to the side and coyly smiles.

"They were a gift, of course." I blush looking down.

"Of course," he adds mockingly and smirks.

Unclipping my belt, he picks me up without asking then climbs the steps and opens the front door. Rose must be inside because the door is unlocked.

"Nice house."

"Thank you." I refrain from saying it's actually Lucca's house because I need to reiterate my place. I belong here. With Lucca.

Lexi and Lucca.

The Italian god and I.

Us.

Together.

Castello di Caruso.

He asks which way and I point in direction of the kitchen because it's a neutral space. Bedroom too intimate, lounge too cosy, family room too inviting, dining room too stuffy. He strolls into the kitchen area and sets me on top of the island in the middle of the kitchen.

"Thank you for bringing me home. I'll be okay, honestly."

He stares at me and moves a stray curl from my face behind my ear, lightly brushing his thumb across my cheek. I shuffle, letting him know that I'm uneasy with this level of intimacy and shift away.

"Right, let's see what the damage is." He carefully slips my shoes off, but I wince a little. "It's bruised," he says while frowning. It will be highly inflamed and bruised. Just another minor setback to add to my many injuries, but it does feel like instant relief getting my shoe off.

He traces over the swollen area with the pad of his thumb. I wiggle and rotate it then do the squeeze test compressing the tibia and fibula. I then do an external rotation stress test, keeping my leg straight as I stress the deltoid and syndesmosis.

"Yes, it's just a sprain, thank goodness. I should be good in a few days, but another six weeks of recovery possibly, depends how quickly it heals." I sigh.

Satisfied, he lifts a glass tumbler from the cabinet and fills it with water. "Drink up," he says. I do then I realise he must be thirsty also.

"The drinks fridge is full so help yourself to whatever you'd like."

"Water is fine thanks." He reaches up for another glass flexing his toned muscles in his arms and back that I need to look away from to distract myself. He is not as muscular or defined as Lucca, but still, his body is impressive. I quickly draw my eyes away because it doesn't feel right that I should even notice such a thing.

"Do you have a first aid kit?" Jackson asks after filling his own glass up.

"Yes, why?" I wrinkle my nose and chew the inside of my cheek.

"I'm going to clean up those cuts on your hands and knees." He leans back against the counter top and points towards my skinned knees.

"No, it's okay. It's fine. I'm just going to jump in a shower." I know he means well, but it's too much to have him tend to a cut on my knee. I'm a grown woman; I'm more than capable of doing that myself, unless it was Lucca. I'd gladly allow him to treat my cuts because he cares for me so tenderly.

"I'd like to tell Cameron I never left you battered and bruised. He'd annihilate me if I did, and he's too good a mate to lose. Plus, if it were someone I cared about, I'd expect them to be looked after, so let me do it." He raises his brow so that his statement appears more as a question as he's waiting on the okay.

Chapter 21: Guilty as Sin

My brain is telling me not to entertain this, but my logic isn't cooperating today. "There's one in the third cupboard in the utility room I think." I sigh and succumb. Doris bolts into the utility room for a drink from her bowl. Jackson returns, setting the kit on the counter, then fills up Doris's bowl with fresh water and places it down for her then pets her.

"Thank you."

"No problem." He shrugs as if it's nothing.

Doris is thirsty. After her drink, she lifts her head and points her nose towards the counter, sensing some of Rose's fresh-baked goodness sitting up there. Reaching over, I lift the lid off the tub, and the sweet smell of cinnamon fills my nostrils and my stomach rumbles.

I hope Jackson didn't hear that.

I throw Doris a bun and she gallops away, knocking over a basket of clothes on her way. Picking up the basket, Jackson then opens the first aid kit and grins at me.

"You have her spoiled, but she's a great dog."

"Yes, she is. She loves Rose's baking. I know I shouldn't but—"

"They do smell pretty good." He lifts his chin and peeks over into the tub.

"Help yourself. I think there's a banana loaf and cinnamon buns by the look of it. She's an exceptional baker."

"You should eat. You've been running on low fuel and have been sick, so no wonder you're shaking." He trails a hand down my arm and settles his hand on my wrist which is now gripping the counter top.

I'm shaking because a premier league footballer, a very handsome one at that, is about to clean my cuts.

Someone who my fiancé warned me to stay away from.

Someone who my friends would drool and die over.

"I'm going to refrain from the baking. I'll end up too fat but please have some. Help yourself."

He stops then looks over his shoulder to locate the kettle and switches it on. He asks where he can find a clean cloth, and I send him to the downstairs bathroom. Staring at my hands, I turn my sore wrist inside the claw of my other hand, massaging it a little with my thumb and middle finger as the fall did put strain on my wrist fracture. How am I going to explain this to Lucca? Not that I'm doing anything wrong, but he will fret.

Explode. More likely.

Returning, Jackson puts his own hand lightly over my delicate wrist, and I tremble with the unfamiliarity of his touch.

"Is this the injury you were referring to?" He sounds concerned, turning my hand around, and looks at the small thin scar on my wrist then shakes his head.

"Yes, I fractured it in Tuscany. I had surgery and had a plate put in."

"Oh, shit. Is it okay? Did you hurt it when you fell?" He slackens his grip on my hand, frightened he might be causing any more pain.

"It's fine, just tender."

"How did it happen?" He frowns.

"I fell." Then I snap my mouth shut because I'm not telling him how. That's a need to know.

He chuckles. "Funny that, you have a habit of falling." He sniggers and I'm glad he doesn't probe any further.

If he doesn't open the space between us, I'll be falling off the counter in a fluster.

Smiling at his light-hearted comment, I relax my muscles and shoulders. Dropping my wrist, he runs the tap, soaks the cloth, and starts to dab my knees with the warm, damp cloth, carefully removing little shards of grit and stones clinging to the dried blood. His touch is every bit as sensitive as Lucca's but different.

Fuck!

File T for traitor. Traitor because I can't believe I'm allowing another man this close to me.

The housekeepers from Lucca's cleaning agency have finished for the day and enter the kitchen to say goodbye and tell me Rose is away to do the food shop for the week. I thank them and ask if they can leave the gates open for now.

"Ouch," I protest when Jackson dabs antiseptic on the cuts because it does sting. He then repeats the same process on my hands, being very gentle around my wrist.

"Stop being a baby." He chuckles because I'm screwing my face up.

"I'm not being a baby. It stings." He laughs louder. "What's so funny?" I scold him.

"You, the way you bite the inside of your cheek and furrow your brow when you're concentrating."

"Stop trying to distract me."

"Well, is it working?"

Oddly, it is.

"No."

"You should put some of this antiseptic cream on when you come out of the shower, and I'd leave the cuts open, let the air get to them."

· "You know a lot about cuts," I say.

"I've had my fair share of grazes, strains, and injuries on the pitch."

He lifts my wrist up to examine it with his chocolate eyes, skimming my skin, lifting my hand towards his mouth as if in slow motion. Gasping, I hold my breath because I think he's going to kiss my skin.

He doesn't.

Thank goodness.

"Good as new. Well, almost. You need ice on your ankle, and you need to eat. I'm not much of a cook, but I can make you a sandwich or something so you don't need to be on your feet."

I don't catch much of what he's saying because I'm still thinking about how he almost kissed my skin. His lips were so close that I could feel his breath skim across my wrist.

"Alexis, breathe … Jesus."

Coughing and choking, I'm embarrassed. "What?" I sputter.

"Sandwich?"

"What about a sandwich?"

"Were you even listening to me?"

"Um, I …" Oh God.

Doris starts barking and I hear the doorbell. *Saved by the bell.*

"Wait there, I'll get it."

Before I can say no, he's confidently striding to the front door. I hear talking from the hall, then he returns with Omari. If I wasn't heated and flustered before, I definitely am now.

"Omari, what a surprise. Lovely to see you again. Lucca isn't here I'm afraid."

He's dressed in a smart, tailored suit, looking devilishly handsome and well groomed with a deep purple tie on which complements his dark skin tone.

"I know Lucca is out of town. I'm here to deliver documents he asked for. They're for you, actually. You can look over them and let me know if everything is satisfactory at a later date in case you want to go over anything with Lucca first."

he set the document folder on the

"Okay." I smile watching him set the document folder on the counter. I hope it's not one of those prenup things, but I suppose he'll want to protect his empire, and rightly so.

"I hope I'm not interrupting anything." Omari inquisitively lifts an eyebrow, obviously wanting to know why I'm hanging around in my kitchen half-dressed with Jackson looking as if we've been tumbling around in the bushes.

"I'm sorry, Jackson, this is Omari Fayed, Lucca's very good friend and solicitor."

"Omari, I've heard a lot about you." Jackson sounds upbeat, taking Omari's hand which throws Omari off. Then reality dawns on him when he realises who Jackson is.

"Really?" Omari looks at me and I shrug, not knowing where this is going.

"Yes, Cameron introduced me to Lucca yesterday. He mentioned you're a keen footballer, so I suggested we should get a charity match organised."

Omari looks absolutely thrilled. "That would be great. I love a good game, but I admit I don't get the time to play often. Our mate Chris is diehard. He thinks he's shit hot, but he's not. He's a delusional idiot."

Jackson laughs. He has a rather cute laugh.

"Well, I'm sure we can get something arranged and all for a good cause." Jackson nods his head.

"One of Lucca's interests is supporting the drug trials for treating certain cancers among many, but I'll let him talk to you about that. I'm sure this will excite him," Omari adds then backtracks when he sees the blank expression on my face.

I wonder what Omari knows about it. I am curious. I remember the invoices I found in Lucca's study. I had forgotten about that until he mentioned it.

"Shit, Lexi ... what happened?" Omari's eyes trail down my legs to my knees. Jackson lifts some mugs from the cupboard and holds one up to Omari, moving around my kitchen as if he has been here forever.

"Coffee for me, thanks. Are those Rose's cinnamon buns I smell?" He walks over to the tub and lifts a bun out. "Hmmm, Lucca is one lucky son of a bitch," Omari says before scoffing a bit of bun.

Jacksons chocolate eyes meet mine. "Yes, he is," he adds then turns around to make the hot drinks. My heart skips a beat.

Fuckity-fuck.

"So what happened?" Omari asks, pointing to my legs.

"Oh, I was out running and went over on my ankle and fell. Jackson was out running too, so he helped me home as I could barely walk on it." I lift my ankle so he can see the swelling and start of the bruising.

"That's a nasty bruise you're going to get on your ankle." Sighing, I shrug nonchalantly. Bruises fade; I've had many so they don't really faze me. It's the damage inside that stays with me forever. "Have you told Lucca yet?" he adds.

"No, I'm just home and I didn't have my phone with me. Why?" I sing and drag out the end because I'm curious what he's going to say, but I think I have a pretty good idea.

The shaking of Omari's head confirms to me that Lucca will be pissed. "He'll be on the first flight home when he finds out. Oh actually on second thought, he can't. He has an obligation he can't miss. Shit that'll piss him off even more. You here and hurt, him over there. Yeah, good luck with that." He lifts his brow as if to warn me.

I bristle at his suggestion but tap my fingers quickly on the counter. "I'm absolutely fine, and I wouldn't allow Lucca to fly home because I have a stupid cut to my knee and a sprained ankle. Omari, please don't alarm him with this. I'm sure you know how protective he is, and there is nothing to worry about."

"Sure, I realised that the other night at dinner, but I'm just warning you." He loosens his tie a little at the neck and leans against the opposite counter.

"Thank you," I whisper.

Jackson puts out coffee for all three of us then enjoys one of Rose's buns as Omari has another. I sit like Humpty Dumpty in the middle, sipping coffee, listening to them talk about football.

Just as I'm about to hobble off the counter to check what's in the fridge, Cameron strolls in, eyeing Omari's hand which is resting on the counter near my ass. Cameron shakes Jackson's hand and pats his shoulder, surprised to see him here, then turns his gaze back to me then over towards Omari.

"What the fuck have you gone and done now?" he scolds. Narrowing his eyes, he points to my knee and ankle.

"Stop shouting at me. Why are you here?"

"Because Lucca has been trying to call you. Your phone is off, so he is worried about you. You look as if you've been dragged through a hedge backwards. Dish. What did you do this time?" He lifts my leg and shakes his head. Jackson smirks listening to the two of us snark at each other. It occurs to me Cameron doesn't even ask Jackson what he's doing here.

Sighing, I ignore his question and introduce him to Omari. He shakes Omari's hand and apologises for his irrational tone and bad manners then lifts a bun from the tub.

"God, these are good," he says after chewing a few mouthfuls. "So?"

I'm so angry with his abrupt tone that I slither off the counter, wincing when my feet hit the tiles with my weight on my ankle. The three of them stare at me, noticing my discomfort.

"Jackson, thank you for helping me home. I really do appreciate it, and thank you for tending to the cuts. Could you fill Cameron in before he has an aneurism?" He smiles and nods.

"Where are you going?" Cameron gripes.

"I'm going to shower. I have an appointment."

"You're not seriously going like that, are you?" Jackson asks, sounding alarmed. I detect a hint of genuine concern and warmth in his eyes.

"Yes, I have to." I hobble across the tiles.

"Forget it, mate, there is no reasoning with her when she gets something in her head. Her and those two fucking left feet," Cameron adds, scoffing another bun down and opening a carton of orange juice from the fridge which he drinks in a long gulp from out of the carton. Ewww gross.

"Omari, if you could leave the documents there, I'll have a look at them later. If you're not here when I come back down, I'll get Lucca to call you," I say, looking at the documents.

"Sure thing, Lexi." He smiles like someone straight from a male calendar with his deep eyes, beautiful chocolate skin, and well groomed looks.

"Boys, I won't be long so help yourselves to anything," I say, holding onto the door.

"Thank you, Lexi, but I really do think you need to eat too," Jackson says with concern before I leave.

"I will when I come down." I look over my shoulder to smile and I'm positive Omari and Jackson are eyeing my ass.

Perverts!

I don't know if it's because Cameron is here, I feel a little more comfortable about both Omari and Jackson, or it's because the words and interaction I've shared with them has helped me relax. Ironically, my first impression of them both wasn't favourable, but getting to know them and giving them a chance, like the way I gave Lucca a chance, has made this easier for me.

I have choices to make and my choice is to trust them.

The thought of them staring at me isn't making me as self-conscious or anxious as it normally would. Ordinarily this would freak me out and make me panic, especially if it were complete strangers doing this. But I don't feel as if they are total strangers because Omari is close to Lucca and Jackson is close to Cameron and there is a definite connection here, an understanding of trust, boundaries, and respect. Being in groups, mixing with men who aren't threatening, is teaching me to trust, undeniably helping me be more accepting and stronger.

When I reach the suite, I want to slump into bed and pull the covers over me, but I can't. I need to keep my appointment at the clinic and visit Mr. Carlin. I take the painkillers I use for my wrist as these will help with my ankle ache. Standing under a hot shower, I recoil a little when the water reaches my cuts and stings the open wounds, but I grit my teeth and it passes very quickly until it feels numb.

Blowing my hair dry, I run my fingers through the natural waves so it's soft and bouncy. Lathering myself in my Brazil nut cream, I throw on a bright-coral silk vest top and tailored white shorts. I put on my diamond stud earrings, Cartier watch and pendant, then skim some bronzer over my cheeks, touch up my mascara and gloss, and spray some perfume. I put my gold gladiator sandals on and grab my gold clutch bag.

When I totter downstairs and find the kitchen is empty, I'm relieved. Maybe they did decide to leave after all, but I wander slowly through to the family room, balancing on one foot, and find Cameron, Omari, Jackson, and Doris watching the highlights from Jackson's last game.

No such luck.

I laugh at Doris sprinting from side to side as she watches the football on the big screen. Jackson and Omari lift their eyes and stare at me, clearly admiringly. Omari is the first to drop his gaze, focusing back on the game, but Jackson holds his a little longer, giving me a gentle smile and sweeping his eyes across my body.

Feeling awkward with the atmosphere in the room, I break the silence.

"Cameron?"

Nothing.

"Cameron?"

Still nothing.

Jackson nudges him, taking Cameron's focus away from the TV.

"What's up?" he asks without interest.

"Can you drive me?"

"When's your appointment?" He still doesn't take his eyes away from the screen.

"Three."

"Sorry, Lex, I can't. I'm late shift. Can Peter or Marco take you?" Jumping up, he shouts something obscene at an attacking player who missed the shot and rakes his hands through his hair. Omari and Jackson shout out in unison following Cameron's outburst.

I cross my arms over my chest after their rowdiness quietens. "Peter is out, and I don't want to bother Marco. It's okay, I'll get a taxi or call Hazel."

Cameron starts shouting at the referee on the screen and running his hands through his hair again, even though he has seen this game and knows the score. When he starts swearing at the TV, I sigh and head for the kitchen.

I open the fridge to see what I have left after the boys raided it since we must be low if Rose is doing a food shop. Smiling, I reach for the soft cheese and smoked salmon on the top shelf, but I stop when I sense someone close behind me. I know it's not Cameron.

"Here let me."

Jackson.

He takes the food down but stays close to my body, his face near my hair inhaling my scent. "Hmmm, you smell nice," he whispers and ever so slightly moves my hair over my shoulder so that his hot breath is close to my neck.

Gasping, I flinch, straightening my spine, and try to ignore his subtle flirting. I take the food out of his hand and then walk to the island to make myself a sandwich. "Thank you. Do you want one?" I ask sharply without looking upward.

"Depends what you're offering me." He smirks. Impish humour graces his handsome face.

Oh my God.

"I meant a sandwich," I say bluntly because I'm horrified.

He laughs. "I knew what you meant. I'm good. Cameron brought us food."

Relieved and giggling, I ask, "What was it, takeaway pizza?"

He joins me in my amusement. "No, just some chicken salad rolls and potato chips."

"That's Cameron's culinary masterpiece because he can't cook," I add.

"Nothing wrong with that, neither can I, but I get by. Look, I'll drive you to your appointment." He raises his brow as if asking another question.

My body pricks with a nervous energy running through my veins.

Once I've spread my bread, I hobble to the pantry for a lemon. Jackson frowns as he watches me limp about. "Alexis, I'll take you. I'm off today so it's no problem. I want to help."

He reaches over and places a hand at the small of my back. My skin pricks with nervous goose bumps so I break the contact to move to the fridge. Keeping my distance, I take a seat on a bar stool at the island and cross my legs then think better of it when my grazed knee chaps off the skin behind the other leg.

"So I'll take you, Alexis?" I hear him but my thought process is slowing down. I do notice that he always uses my full name. I'm not sure if it's through politeness or unfamiliarity. I'm hoping it's through politeness.

"Thank you, but no, it's not a good idea. I really am grateful for everything you've done today for me, but I think it's better if I go alone." I chew the inside of my cheek and furrow my brow.

"Okay, I'm sorry if I overstepped the mark. I was only trying to help." He sighs and holds his hand to his nape.

Now I feel awful.

Keep composure, Lexi!

"No, I'm sorry. I just think it's maybe best if we don't ..." *Spend any more time together because Lucca is going to flip.*

I'm hoping he takes enough out of that to realise I'm insinuating nothing will ever happen between us. He reluctantly nods in agreement then traces his fingers across his sexy stubble, deep in thought, the mirth in his eyes subsiding.

"You look beautiful, by the way. You wouldn't know you had twigs in your hair a short while ago and looked like Jane of the Jungle." He smiles and it's so cheeky yet friendly I can't help but smile back.

I smack his arm playfully. "Very funny, smartass," I chide. He's likeable. Would definitely make a great friend. I can see how he and Cameron are good mates; they have a similar sense of humour.

"No, really, all joking aside, you look lovely. Did you put the antiseptic cream on?"

Frowning, he knows I haven't so he lifts some out the first aid kit and starts to rubs it into my knees. Inwardly gasping, I can't concentrate on eating, not when the UK's number one sexiest male footballer is touching me. I drop my sandwich on my plate and hold my breath until I'm interrupted by Cameron.

Praise the Lord ...

"Lex, Lucca is on the phone. He's not a happy chappy, and he's worried. Sounds a bit pissed, so you need to speak to him. Everything okay here?" He looks at me with his protective look, glances at Jackson and back to me, then nods.

"Yes, fine, give me the phone," I answer, slightly agitated, not purposely with Cameron but more at the thought Lucca being pissed.

Cameron passes me his phone, taking it off silent.

I breathe deeply to prepare myself and shift uneasily, but it doesn't discourage Jackson. He continues to apply cream to my sores. Cameron looks at me again for a reassuring sign, I nod flicking my hand so he know it's fine to leave then heads back off to the family room to zap back in front of the plasma like a firefly buzzing amidst a flickering candle. Engrossed.

"Hey, honey," I chirp, hiding any anxiety in my voice.

"What the fuck is going on? I am only away a few hours and you are injured, stranded, and a fucking footballer is swooning over you who I would rather not be within a mile of you. Jesus, Doc, I am out of my mind with worry. Why did you not take your phone? What the fuck were you thinking? And why the fucking hell is he still in our house?"

Pissed?

Understatement.

I need to lift the phone away from my ears; he's so loud and swearing so badly.

I'm sure Jackson heard Lucca's rant. Blushing, I move his hand from my leg, wriggle off my stool, giving him an apologetic look, and go into the lounge and shut the door.

"Lucca, please calm down." I hobble to the sofa and slump down.

"Calm down? Baby, I want to come home and I fucking cannot right now. I knew I should have brought you."

"No, Lucca, don't be irrational. I was running with Doris, and I didn't take my phone. I tripped over a branch and fell over on my ankle, but it's absolutely fine. I was lucky that Jackson was out running because he helped me home. I know how you feel, but if it weren't for Jackson, I'd probably still be stuck there. Please be reasonable. I promise you with all my heart that this is innocent, and I'm in one piece." I sound snarky, leaning over to examine my ankle again.

"Baby, it is not you. I trust you, sweetheart. It is that bastard I do not trust. I want to be there for you, not some stranger looking after you. Did he touch you? Did the fucker place his hands on you?"

I lie. My heart beats out of control, and I feel a rush. It begins with tingling then ends in numbness. I hate lying, and especially to Lucca, but I'm afraid it will hurt him if I tell him the truth.

"No, he never touched me, other than to carry me to the car because I was hobbling. He dropped me off and stayed to make sure I was okay and looked at my cuts. Cameron is here looking after me now, so you don't need to worry." I hear Lucca suck in sharp breath then hiss.

Exaggeration.

Jackson's hands have been touching, cleaning, and stroking my skin, and Cameron's more focused on the football match, but I'm not telling Lucca every last detail. It will send him into a seizure.

There is silence on the line and heavy breathing. "Lucca, talk to me." He's still silent. Faltering, my voice breaks. "I'm sorry, it was an accident. I can't help who helped me, Lucca. It was coincidence." After the coincidence of Lucca and I bumping in to each other in Tuscany, he should know fine well these things happen.

"Fuck, Lexi, do not dare apologise. I know, baby, I know. I just hate that he is with you and I am not. I saw the way he looked at you yesterday, and I know he wants to fuck you."

I don't know if it's guilt, but suddenly I feel like I'm getting a scolding, and a few tears escape my eyes tricking down my cheeks. I hold it back but Lucca knows me so well, every emotion I have shared with him has him so attuned to me.

"Are you crying?" He softens his tone and curses. I think he's angry with himself for hurting me.

"No," I silently sob, muffling my sniffles.

"You bloody well are. Please, baby, do not cry. I am sorry. I am so sorry for shouting at you. I just love you so much and want to care for you. It kills me I cannot do it when I am not there."

I swallow a lump at the back of my throat. "I just twisted my ankle and it's nothing, so please focus on your work. Jackson just brought me home, but he's leaving, and I need to go to an appointment at the clinic."

"Good, I am glad he is leaving. I will have Marco come and pick you up. I am sorry, Lexi. Please, do not be upset. If I could, I would be back home in a few hours."

I know he would and I'd love him to be back here with me wrapped in his embrace, but that's ludicrous and he has obligations as do I.

"No, I'm fine. I'd be annoyed with you if you left important business to come home. I'm missing you and of course I can't wait to see you but I'll cope. I'd rather you concentrate on your meetings and work." I'm fighting to hold back my tears, but it really is obvious I'm upset.

We bicker back and forth until I've convinced him to be reasonable and not to worry and that I've already made plans with the girls anyway so I won't be on my own.

"Are you okay?"

"Yes."

"Really, Lexi? Do not bullshit me. Are you okay?"

"Yes, I just don't like upsetting you."

"Baby, you could never intentionally upset me, you know that, right? I fucking love you. I will make this up to you, I promise. I am so sorry for shouting at you, and I am so sorry I am not holding you right now. I would tenderly kiss you then bury myself so deep inside you so I could take all your pain away and give you nothing but pleasure, love, and devotion."

Emotional.

Again.

His voice is breaking, and I'm having to press my legs together to quell the raging throbbing desire in my hot core. His sensitive words hit me every time, mind, heart, soul, and sex.

"It's okay, I knew you'd be mad. I'm upset because I'm premenstrual and my hormones are all over the place. I'm not upset with you, but I will definitely take you up on the pleasure and devotion. That always makes me feel better."

I refrain from telling him I'm in pain, feeling sick and dizzy and don't have an appetite, which will have him checking into departures quicker than I can drink a glass of wine.

"I got your gift. I love it, dolcezza. That pen will light up my week without you. You are so goddamn special and kind. I love you. I cannot wait much longer until you are my wife, Lexi. Please think of a date and we will talk about something for our engagement when I get home."

Folded.

"I'm glad you liked it. I thought you hadn't seen it." I smile, thinking of him opening his gift, and it makes me feel warm and fuzzy.

"That is why I was trying to phone you, but I freaked when your phone was off. I am going to spoil you rotten when I get home. I have a few gifts for you as well, dolcezza." His tone is more relaxed than it was, and he sounds mysterious now, to the point I find it exciting and uplifting.

"You already spoil me rotten."

"Not enough. Thank you, Lexi, for the gift. I love your thoughtfulness. I am going to send Marco for you shortly. Can you put Jackson on the phone, baby? I need to speak to him."

Oh God. My stomach is back flipping.

"Please don't go all alpha male on me. You should be thanking him because he genuinely looked out for me and was a perfect gentleman." Now my mood is shifting from excitable to nervous.

"Lexi, the fucker intimidates you."

"No, he doesn't, not anymore. It's all an image the press has portrayed. He actually is an alright guy, and he said he wanted to help so Cameron wouldn't get pissed at him for leaving me. I can see how they're friends because he is really down to earth. He's been extremely obliging by bringing me home. Please don't give him a hard time. He's done nothing wrong."

He moans then hisses through his teeth and sighs, contemplating it. "Lexi, just put him on."

"Please, Lucca, are you even listening to me? Promise me." I sound like I'm pleading because he's worrying me. It's obvious he's going to be rude, and I hate bad manners, even if he is protecting me and has my best interests at heart.

"Fine. I love you, and I will speak to you later." There's no mistaking he's sharp and to the point. I don't think he has any intention of being civilised.

Hobbling back into the kitchen, Jackson is leaning against the counter drinking a fruit juice, gauging me. Biting the inside of my cheek, I pass him the phone nervously.

"Lucca wants to speak to you." My arm is stretched fully, and I keep my distance. It's as if hearing Lucca's voice he has me believing he's watching me.

Using the pad of my thumb, I dab under my eyes wiping the last of my stray tears away. Jackson cocks his head, watching me while listening to Lucca. Aware he's looking at me, I turn my back to him, lifting a hankie to blow my sniffling nose. I place it in the bin, wash my hands, then load the dishwasher with the plates, tossing my sandwich in the bin having lost all appetite which he notices also.

Listening to Jackson, he's calm and collected and sounds understanding, but I can't hear Lucca, so I've no idea what he's saying. Jackson is telling him there's no need to thank him, it was no problem, and that he would have done the same. I also hear Jackson reassure Lucca that I'm fine and not to worry. All the while, Jackson's watching my every move.

When he hangs up, Jackson tells me Lucca thanked him and that he was grateful for his assistance today in his absence, so I relax my shoulders, forming an unwavering smile and I'm relieved.

"You still haven't eaten anything," he points out.

"No, I'm really not hungry anymore."

"Have you been crying?" He places the phone down on the counter and tilts his head, studying me

"No."

There is an unsettling tension in the atmosphere, a thick foggy air that surrounds us both.

"Alexis, I should go soon. Lucca did thank me, but he also gave me a strong warning to stay away from you when he's not around, and I need to respect that." He shrugs his shoulders nonchalantly. The change is night and day. One minute he wanted to run me to my appointment and now Lucca has warned him, he wants to rush off.

Hot and cold.

Lucca - Caveman!

Shaking my head with realisation I whisper, "I'm sorry, he's a little protective."

"No, don't be sorry, I get it. If you were my girl, I'd do the same. And you're not any ordinary girl, so it's no wonder he feels as if he needs to protect you from douchebags. Guys like me." He holds one hand on the nape of his neck in an exasperated sigh.

I sincerely hope Lucca never called him a douchebag or I'll be even angrier.

I turn around, and he catches my sad expression. I sense he's putting himself down because of the bad boy image portrayed, and I feel as if I need to remedy his doubts.

"Hey, you're not a douche, you're a great guy and misunderstood," I reassure him.

His lip curls.

"Don't be mad at him, he's just looking out for you, he really loves you. He's got absolutely nothing to worry about but I'll respect his wishes. He seems like a great guy."

He leans towards me, closing the space ... his lips near mine ... my pulse quickens, my heart pounds and I feel hot and flustered again. I can't look in his eyes, knees trembling, body shaking in fear. Quickly, I tilt my head to the side dipping my chin. Just when I think he's going to try and kiss me, he nudges his fingers lightly across my chin playfully.

Something Cameron would do.

"Look after yourself, Alexis, and that ankle and wrist and cuts and whatever else is going on because of your two left feet."

I laugh.

"I'll try, but I'm a calamity, so it's going to be a challenge."

He wipes a tear softly from my cheek. I know this is wrong, but I find comfort in it.

When I open my eyes, he's gone and I furtively breathe as I hold onto the warmth of my cheek where his hand was.

Moments later, Omari politely kisses the same cheek as he prepares to leave.

"Omari, did Lucca give you a grilling?" I ask gingerly before he does go.

"Hell yes, but what did you expect? He was frantic. He wanted me to wait until after Jackson left to ensure he wasn't left alone with you. It's funny as it's always been me he doesn't trust. I suppose I'm the good guy now." He smirks that devilish sexy grin.

Fuck!

File G for guilty. Guilty as sin.

"I suppose you are," I reply, sounding lifeless with little enthusiasm in my voice giving Cameron the eyes.

Once they leave, I slump on the sofa in the living room, totally bewildered and feeling awful. Doris jumps up and snuggles in, burying her head into my neck sensing I'm upset. Cameron left with Omari to get ready for work. He said he'll check in tomorrow, satisfied that Jess will be staying with me tonight.

I could curl up and sleep now, but I have obligations.

Chapter 22: The colour Blue

Marco kindly waits outside the family planning clinic for me in Lucca's black stretch limo. Of all the cars, he has to have me driven around like a blooming gala queen. I would have gotten here just fine in my little Ford Focus.

Ridiculous.

Going through all the contraception options, I make a last minute decision change. Initially I wanted Depo-Provera, but I can't be bothered with going to the surgery every twelve weeks to get the injection, so I decide to go for Nexplanon, the contraceptive implant which will be inserted under the skin of my upper arm.

I won't need to worry about the risks when accidentally missing my pill, and after we are married, when the time is right and I'm emotionally in a better place, I can have it removed anytime and fertility should resume.

Ideal!

The young, helpful doctor thoroughly goes over the pros and cons. She mentions the side effects, a few being sickness and feeling light-headed, but that doesn't concern me. I'm used to feeling like that. The main benefit for me is that I'm covered and will not need to worry about it, and chances are my periods may become lighter or irregular or may disappear altogether.

She pulls up my medical records and goes over everything thoroughly, checks my blood pressure, height, and weight. When she asks me the date of my last period, she gives me a pregnancy test stick to just to be sure I'm not pregnant before carrying on with it.

I've never done a pregnancy test before, but she explains to me its procedure, common practice, not to panic, and how it works. I use the public toilet to pee on the stick, and then the doctor comes back for me to enter the room almost right away. I'm thankful as I'd hate to be sitting in the waiting room pondering over the fate of my future.

Not that it would be a catastrophe, but I'm not ready at this period of time in my life, and while I'm here alone without Lucca is not how I imagined taking a pregnancy test to discover said fate.

My stomach is in turmoil, and I'm rubbing my hands nervously picking at my skin.

Please be negative. Please be negative.

My throat is dry and I do feel queasy, but that's lack of body fuel and possibly dehydration. The doctor looks at the stick then turns around to her metal table and tears a white packet open.

Why is she not talking? What is she going to do?

She politely smiles. "Lexi, you're not pregnant, so let's prep to insert your implant. I need to use a local anaesthetic to numb the area. Are you okay with needles?"

Relief?

Yes.

Needles?

Not so much.

"Yes."

Turning away, I hold my breath and let her carry on. I'm so relieved that I'm not pregnant, now is not the time. I can't even get through one day without drama, never mind a baby to consider. I know that I love Lucca, and after the weekend with his nieces and nephews I know I'd like kids ... babies. Just not now.

I breathe and after the quick procedure she keeps me seated until she's certain I'm not going to faint or be sick then checks my blood pressure again. Happy with her results, she advises me, I will need to use condoms for the next seven days for further protection.

I smile respectfully, knowing that will never happen, so I'll continue to take my pill for another week instead. Quickly she reminds me my next cervical smear test will be due in a few months.

Already?

They always get that in at the end of an appointment. *Karma crushers.*

My phone rings. It's Lucca, but I ignore it. I'll call him when I'm outside.

When I step out of her office, I need to hold onto the wall. I don't want to draw attention to myself, so I slip into the toilet. I do feel rather faint. I splash my face and sit on the stool next to the sink. I need to eat, and the needle phobia has not helped that situation.

Sitting with my head in my hands has helped. Once I'm steady, I head back to the limo, slowly bearing weight on my better ankle, thankful that there has been no fainting today.

I slip in the back. "I'm sorry, Marco. It took longer than I thought."

"No worries, Lexi. Lucca is on the line and he wants to speak to you."

Persistent bloody pest!

Marco passes over his phone.

"What happened in the clinic?" No hello, hi, or hey, baby. He sounds abrupt.

I'm not sure I want to divulge personal information in the presence of Marco or wait until later.

"Everything is fine. Can I call you later?"

"Pass the phone to Marco."

Insufferable.

I give Marco the phone.

He nods then hands it back as he presses a button. A privacy screen rolls up and completely separates us. He won't witness me rolling my eyes then. Is this for real?

Ridiculous.

"He cannot hear you unless you press the buzzer for the intercom, and he cannot see you either, so tell me what happened. I want to know because you are mine and I hate not being at these things with you. It crushes me." He sounds flustered and he's breathing awfully quickly. I imagine him raking his hands through his hair or pinching his brow.

I remember Lucca telling me how he missed the ultrasound when Fran was expecting his baby, the day Fran was in a tragic car accident which killed her father and their unborn child. It's understandable he is concerned and protective about these things and doesn't want to be shut out, especially when it involves him.

"She made me take a pregnancy test."

"Fuck, Doc, and I was not there." This is not going as well as I'd hoped. He sounds hurt, as if he has let me down, his voice is broken. I'm silent, other than my breathe exhaling on a soft sigh.

"Baby, are you …?" He sounds more upbeat and optimistic. I look at the small square dressing on the inside of my arm.

Ironic.

He's hopeful. I wasn't.

After our chat in Tuscany and our recent discussions, I know he wants this badly for us, soon apparently.

"I'm not pregnant, but I did get an implant in my arm. I can get it out anytime for when we start family planning."

"Oh."

"What do you mean oh?" I snap. I was expecting some support.

"Nothing, it is fine. How did they get an implant in your arm?" He sounds pissed off now.

"They gave me anaesthetic, numbed it, and made a small incision in my skin and inserted it." I thought that would be pretty obvious but maybe not to a man.

"Lexi, do not tell me anymore. I cannot handle it." Why is he acting so irrational?

"Handle what? You're freaking me out here and sound absurd." I begin to raise my voice. He can't wrap me in cotton wool all the time. This is life, whether he likes it or not. I am upset and agitated from tiredness and hunger, and Lucca is getting the brunt of it.

"They cut your fucking skin? Why would you get that done after all the fears and phobia you have regarding your skin?" He shouts. Either he thinks it's bigger a deal than it was, or he generally is squeamish and the thought disturbs him. I know it troubles him looking at the small scar on my wrist, but that's more through guilt rather than the concept of the procedure.

I'm exasperated, but there's no reasoning with him. I need to learn to keep quiet if he is going to freak out if a feather or snow flake or petal bloody lands on my skin. Heaven forbid.

"Lucca, it's a method of contraception, a very reliable one, and they insert these in thousands of women every day. It's a nick in my skin. A tiny little nick." Slowly and calmly, I try to make him see reason, as if I'm talking to an unreasonable child.

"What is wrong with your pill?"

"Nothing, but it's not reliable enough with my track record of being sick and dizzy episodes." I need to win this battle and quickly, as he's giving me a headache. "Lucca, this means no more condoms, ever ..."

"Well, why did you not say so?" He sounds sarcastic but I don't think that's how he meant it to sound.

Insufferable.

"I am serious now. When I tell you I want you to get it out, I will be there with you, but when I want it out, baby, it is coming out." It's his turn to sound slow and calm trying to convince me.

How dare he?

What the fuck is it with his obsession to have a baby? And this controlling is not on. I will not stand for it.

"Lucca, it's my body, I will get it out when I'm good and ready. Don't you dare try and control me. I've had a lifetime of it already. It's my decision to make, not bloody yours." I'm crass and don't care how tactless I sound. I'm so angry with him and ready to explode. I like his protectiveness, and I like his possessiveness to a certain extent. It reminds me I'm his, and he's mine but this level of controlling is not fucking on.

Rage.

Fire.

Burn.

I'm flustered now. I need to put my window down I'm feeling so hot. He is lost for words. For once.

"God, I am so sorry. I did not mean that the way it sounded. I just mean ... I hope it is not forever. You already said you would try as soon as we are married. I panicked because at the weekend you expressed having a family is something you would like for us. And it made me so fucking happy, you were coming around to the idea.

Then you choose to have something long term like this thing in your arm without mentioning it," he whispers.

"I ... I do not want to control you, or upset you. I am sorry, Doc. I am sorry for the way that came across. I just love you and want to spend the rest of my life with you and family is a big part of that for me, for us." He sounds sincere but I'm so mad at him still. I worry my fingers in front of my mouth in fast, quick, agitated movements because I'm irritated.

"Yes, and I agree, but not until I'm ready, so stop pressuring me. God, you sound worse than my mum right now, if that's possible. Or worse, *my granny*. If you keep going on about it, I'll never get the bloody thing out," I yell.

I could cut through the air with a sharp edge right now. He doesn't know what to say. I've shocked him and he's speechless that he's hurt me or angry with my yelling. I know he's thinking of apologising because I can hear him suck in a huge breath, as if he's gasping and preparing himself for a long speech. I don't want to hear it. Then he exhales the breath he's been holding onto.

I'm aware I'm snarky and irate with the lack of food today and my exercise exertion, but he's seriously pissing me off.

"Lucca, I need to go. I'm visiting Mr. Carlin, so I'll call you later."

"Okay."

I was expecting an apology of sorts, but I don't receive it. I've had enough now.

Blazing anger heats my body. Inferno.

"Okay," I bluntly reply. No goodbyes.

Cutting the line dead, I press the buzzer and ask Marco to lower the screen and hand the phone back to him.

I'm not in the mood for any of Lucca's lovey-dovey nonsense or complete, possessive alpha male shit either.

"Marco, can you take me to M&S food so I can pick something up, and then to Mr. Carlin's please?"

"No problem. You know, Lexi, it is not any of my business, but he really loves you. I have never seen him so in love or intense, and he is a different person around you. It is endearing to watch him flourish and enjoy his love for life again, and you give him hope for his future."

Why is everyone talking in bloody riddles today? His future? What about my future? And the present, hope for today? I slip back into the frame of mind I frequently used before meeting Lucca, that I should take each day as it comes, and if I get through it without falling apart, then I'm grateful for life, here, today in this moment.

"Thank you, Marco, I appreciate it, I do. We'll work it out. It's just so new to me, I suppose. I really have never had so much—"

Protection.

Love.

Passion.

"Give him time and give him a chance. I have known him a long time. We grew up together, and his relationship with Francesca was more of an obligation, but with you it is as if his life depends on you. He adores you. He has had a challenging morning today, and he is not himself. He is stressed." He looks in the rear-view mirror giving me his attention.

So have I.

"Thank you, Marco. I do appreciate your words. I love him too, more than anything else. I'm also out of sorts today, and he's being overly protective. You know, the funny thing is, I've always needed someone like Lucca to secure himself around me and protect me as much as I tried to deny it before, but yet here I am being suffocated." I worry my fingers in front of my lips slowly and lazily this time in contemplation.

He nods his head in acknowledgement and continues driving. I wonder why Marco doesn't have a girlfriend or wife. He'd make someone very happy, I'm sure.

I'm not comfortable enough to ask him, but maybe one day I will. I want to call Lucca, to reassure him I'm not mad at him and I forgive him. I lift my phone from my bag and scroll over his name. I think about my mum not having any choices, having to be silent and submissive, and I realise I don't want to be subjected to similar misfortunes. I need to be in control of my life.

I throw my phone in my bag and look out the car window, feeling remorse about my tension with Lucca, but equally happy I have taken it upon myself to be decisive about my body and the family planning issue.

Chicken, pasta, basil, tomatoes, chili, and mayo—great comfort food. I devour every bit in the back of the limo. I couldn't wait until we stopped, I was that hungry. I feel better for eating but hope it doesn't later put me in a carb coma.

I bought Marco a salad and a sandwich and some double chocolate brownies for putting up with my PMS tension, he's thrilled I think, but says he'll have it when he stops driving.

When I arrive at Mr. Carlin's, I invite Marco in as I don't like the thought of him sitting outside too long. Mr. Carlin is in his usual chair doing the newspaper crossword, and the heating is on full blast as normal.

After the introductions, I storm into the kitchen to turn it off. He doesn't make eye contact with me. Sheesh, he's in a foul mood. He continues to grill Marco until he knows everything except his national insurance number.

I make them tea, check his fridge and freezer, and stock it with the niceties I purchased, feeling guilty that I haven't been cooking. I bring his washing in limping on my better ankle and put another load on.

"Well, are you not going to speak to me?" I ask, finally joining them.

"Hmmm … what's that? I think there is a stranger in the house, looking for my attention," he grumbles. Rolling my eyes, I sit on his coffee table, crossing my arms.

"I'm sorry, it's been a busy week, and I had to settle into the new house. I know you were well looked after with your home helpers, but it's no excuse."

"And so you should be, lassie. I've not seen you for a full week, and your grandmother is asking all sorts of questions on the phone. Elizabeth is not one to be ignored. And, I like the way you make my tea." He dips his head, his spectacles dropping low on his broad nose, then points to his mug.

"I said I'm sorry. I'm here now, so stop being stroppy and tell me what my granny said." I look at Marco and subtly roll my eyes. He forms a smile and has humour etched all over his face and tries to look impassive.

Mr. Carlin goes on to tell me about my bossy, temperamental firecracker of a grandmother. Although her heart is in the right place, she's suffocating most of the time. If I don't answer her calls, she tries Cameron, and if he ignores her, she tries Mr. Carlin.

"Okay, get up. I'm taking you to Lucca's house to show you around. You can meet Rose and Peter and have some dinner with us. I'll get Marco to drive you home," I say, looking at Marco for approval. I feel guilty for neglecting him all week.

"Yes, of course, it is no problem."

He picks up the newspaper and flips to the front page as he adjusts his glasses. "Well, I'm not fussed," he mumbles cynically.

Putting on a fake smile, clenching my jaw, I ask, "Why ever not?"

"Hmmm … well, I like my home comforts and it's inconvenient tonight." He harrumphs and pings his suspenders. I'm dying to laugh.

"Have you someplace else you need to be?" I lift my eyebrows with my hand on my hip.

"No, but I'm old and can't be bothered."

Sighing, I give Marco a look of exasperation, exhaling and rolling my eyes. Mr. Carlin is sucking the life out of me here. Being in the ornery mood I'm in today, I'm not accepting his petulant grumpiness.

"Fine, don't come, but Peter will be disappointed as he enjoys a single malt dram and loves a game of chess. He was looking forward to the challenge. Marco, you ready to go?"

Mr. Carlin raises his bushy eyebrows and lifts his walking stick from the side of his chair, pointing it at the hallway. "Son, be a gent and lift that grey jacket for me," he directs at Marco, who's happy to oblige.

Satisfied he's coming, I nip next door to my house and pick up my mail and briefly tell Hazel about my day so she doesn't expect me at her classes this evening. She can't believe me, her mouth has dropped to the floor when I tell her who helped me, and I wonder how many flies she has caught. I tell her I'll give her the detailed version at the DBB, when she stays over this week.

After a quick assessment of the rubble, I warn her to get the house work done as it looks like an explosive mess. She humours me and tells me to relax, she's doing it today. Distracting me from my nagging, she enlightens me that Rachel was over last night and left crying, that Cameron finally broke it off with her. I wonder why he never said anything about it today when he was over.

He seemed pretty emotionless to me. I never know with Cameron; he's very good at hiding his feeling sometimes. Bloody mystery.

After all the formalities, the house and grounds tour and the million questions that come with it, I leave Mr. Carlin in the good hands of Peter on the pergola area outside the pool at the back of the house. Rose checks on the dinner, and I excuse myself to call Jess to make sure she's still coming over.

"Oh, Lexi, there are parcels for you. They arrived when you were out. They're in the store cupboard." Peter says while straightening some ceramic pots on the patio area.

"Thank you, Peter."

I find five large boxes covered in brown paper with traditional string wrapped around them and a little gift bag with a blue satin ribbon tied around the handle. Dragging them into the living room, I peel the brown paper to find rectangular boxes covered with ordinary white poster paper and Italian words scrolled all over it. Lucca has elaborated on my quirky idea of writing on the paper to use it as gift-wrap. It's cute and very original. How did he manage this?

I'm touched.

Inside the gift bag, I find a card and a smaller box under blue tissue paper. Opening the card I discover it's not a shop bought card, it's expensive high quality thick cream card, on the front it says:

'Soon to be Mrs. Caruso.'

'Doc, since you do not treat yourself, I am ensuring that you will be treated always and forever. Open the small box last and wear them for me for when I get home. I will be able to think of nothing else except how beautiful you will look with these against your skin.

I fantasise about your naked body glistening in diamonds when you are wrapped up in my embrace.

Keep them safe. You told me you are mesmerised by my blue eyes, which are for you and only for you. I am mesmerised by you, all of you. When you wear these for me, and only for me, my blues will be gleaming in yours, joining your sparkle to mine.'

He is referring to the blue silk tie I asked him to wear for only me as it accentuates the bright crystal azure colour of his eyes.

It appears I won't be wearing the sexy lingerie I bought for him after all.

'Il colore blu è quello di fiducia, lealtà e onestà. Blu è un donatore non è un introduttore alla ricerca di tranquillità, pace e tranquillità. Blu è conservativa, prevedibile e sicura. Blu è idealista, affidabile e responsabile. Blu è il colore di spirito, il nostro spirito.'

(The colour blue is the one of trust, loyalty, and honesty. Blue is a giver, not a taker searching for peace, calm, and tranquillity. Blue is conservative, predictable, and safe. Blue is idealistic. It is reliable and responsible. Blue is the colour of spirit - our Spirit.)

Blue is definitely our colour from his eyes, to the blue orchid and whatever surprise he has for me in here. He is the most thoughtful person I've ever met. I love his romanticism, and everything he does is from his heart. He makes me feel complete.

'There are five other parcels—a gift of the day for every day we will be apart this week. Enjoy your gifts, Dolcezza, I hope you like them. I miss you, sweetheart, and I love you. Please keep the bed warm for me.

All my love,
Lucca xxx'

The first box I pick up has the words *L 'amore* sparsely scribbled across the makeshift wrapping paper. Inside is a cobalt blue crepe dress with a matching bag and shoes, and a Caspian-blue chiffon strappy top with a black leather A-line miniskirt. Holding the dress up to my body, I'm once again blown away by Lucca's impeccable taste and generosity.

The next box has the words *Virilità,* meaning virility. Opening the box, I gasp, peeling back the blue tissue paper to reveal an elegant, strapless marine blue chiffon full-length cocktail gown with a lace panel around the corset. The front has Swarovski crystals encrusted on the lace of the bodice. The internal corset has ribbon weaving across the back and is just simply stunning, very exquisite and unique.

It's another beautiful gown for a special occasion and comes with a silver clutch and amazing killer high-heel shoes. I hold it to my chest and close my eyes. I can imagine wearing this on Lucca's arm again, complementing his beautiful, bright blue eyes.

Then I think of poor Hazel trying to save for her wedding and here I am lavished in gifts costing a small fortune. Frowning, I place the dress in the box, and not because I don't appreciate these wonderful things, I do. I just wish I could help Hazel more financially, but I don't want to ask Lucca for any of his money. He's earned it and it belongs to him.

The next box is scribbled with *Sessualità,* meaning sexuality. He is quoting me his interpretation of our flower, the blue orchid.

Inside has five expensive lingerie sets, all in various colours of blue. One set is very racy; it's sky blue satin with black lace and a matching thong and garter. One is navy blue fine lace, and another is electric blue silk under black mesh with large motif flowers on the straps, very much like the orchids. Another in cornflower blue with a ribbon that ties at the bust and the matching panties tie at the side with a ribbon also.

Then there is an ice blue long satin nightgown and matching robe. The final piece is a short, sexy, blue chiffon baby-doll nightdress, which is completely transparent, and a matching thong. He did promise to buy me new underwear, as he's been ripping them off me of recent. He must have picked every blue piece in stock.

This lot will only last him a week.

If I'm lucky.

The fourth box reveals the word *Fertilità,* translating as fertility. The irony isn't lost on me after the eventful day and discussions with Lucca. Laughing, I lift out a new pair of blue denim jeans, a fitted, blue tank, a long, oversized, ecru wool cardigan, and a pair of skydiver blue Converse trainers.

This is by far the most suitable of gifts for me when I love to have my dress down comfy days. I try one Converse on and immediately fall in love with them. I'm sure I will get lots of wear from these.

The fifth box is of equal size with the last word *Dolcezza* scripted on the white poster paper; Lucca's word for me meaning sweetness. Inside, there is a white candle in a glass jar and a blue card. Smelling the fresh linen scent of the candle, I look at the card.

'The candle represents my light for you, our "Luminara." I have arranged a treat for you and the girls on Wednesday night. Have them all come to the house for 6:00 p.m. for a night of pampering, spa treatments, and relaxation. All they will need is swimwear. I have taken care of everything else. I have arranged cover for Hazel's classes at the club for that evening. Enjoy, baby.

Love,

Lucca xxx'

Squealing in delight, I can't wait to tell the girls and have them over for a pamper night. He has absolutely outdone himself this time as he always does. All my previous premenstrual tension is dispersing, and I have new found love for his lovey-dovey sweetness.

I'm about to text the girls when I remember about the smaller gift in the gift bag. Completely overwhelmed, I wonder if this is what it must have felt like being a young child excited at Christmas time waiting on Santa.

Not being able to contain my curiosity, I open the box and stumble backwards having to hold onto the edge of the sofa, blinking in sheer disbelief. Diamond stud earrings again, but this time in a unique beautiful blue diamond colour matching my engagement ring with diamonds circling around the blue stone. They look very rare and collectable. I can't quite comprehend such a treasure is in my hands, and that Lucca has gifted these to me.

Shaking, I lift them out their box and marvel, dumbfounded by their beauty. I take out my own diamond stud earrings and replace them immediately with the blue ones and look at them in the ornate, gilded mirror over the fireplace. My legs are quivering, and I feel tiny, fragile, and delicate. These stones could easily be Lucca's crystal eyes staring back at me.

Neatly placing my original earrings in the box, I call Lucca. He answers on the second ring.

"Hey, I've just opened your gifts, and I don't know what to say. I'm overwhelmed. Lucca, these blue diamonds are just the most precious thing I have ever seen. It's unbelievable, but it's far too much." Tears are threatening to break and my voice is choking with his thoughtfulness, and I'm still plagued by guilt for my abominable mood earlier.

"I am glad you like them because they are yours and I want you to have them. Lexi, I am sorry about earlier. The last thing I want to do is control you. I hate when we fight. Will you forgive me?" He sounds anxious but at the same time relieved to hear from me.

"Of course, I already have. I'm the one who is sorry. I was just tired and ratty, but I shouldn't have snapped at you."

"No, baby, you have done nothing wrong. You were being honest and I was being unreasonable. I just want to protect you because I love you so much, but I got carried away. I fucking hate that you thought I would ever control you like that. You are my world now, my life, and I just want you to be happy and for us to fulfil our lives as best we can and live without having any regrets. I am so fucking sorry I hurt you." His voice is broken.

Fingering the earrings in my ears, I am pining for him all over again. "I am happy. I have you, and that's all I need right now. You don't need to shower me with gifts. I love them, I do, but I love you more." I know he genuinely does feel remorse about how we left the situation, but I feel as if I need to address the baby topic again to settle this. "You know, I'd rather we get married first before we talk babies." I mention it like this so he knows I'm not opposed to the idea but I do need to settle this.

"Thank God you are still considering it, Doc. Yes, of course, whatever you want. I would never make you do anything you did not want to do and I respect you too much. I would never control you like that, baby. I just want you to know how much I would love that for us. I was worried you would be angry at me, and it would put you off." His guard is down, and he sounds more relaxed.

I can't stay mad at him. "No, I just don't want to feel pressured into it by you and your entire family, can you understand that? This isn't a small decision. It's life changing and it needs to be when the time is right."

"Yes, of course. I was an asshole earlier and should never have spoken to you like that. You tell me when you are ready. I will wait and respect your wishes because you are my light and I never want to abuse your trust or control you." I feel so relieved we have had the chance to speak about this and clear the air.

He means it too. Although we rarely exchange heated words, we both seem to find a way to forgive and forget and make it work after explaining and reasoning.

"Thank you. I am so glad you understand and we sorted this out. Lucca, I do love the gifts, thank you. How did you manage this? I can't get my head around all this. You must have super powers," I say, staring at everything on the floor.

"Suzanne helped me. That woman needs a raise. I especially liked the lingerie and cannot wait to rip those off you." His sexy rasp is back.

He's unbelievable, but I agree. I'm excited about him doing that also, feeling a tingling of excitement in my core just thinking about it.

"How did you manage the writing on the paper?" I ask curiously because it's definitely his writing.

"You inspired me with your note on the makeshift wrapping paper. I found the pen last night when I packed, but I did not want to tell you. I left early on purpose before my flight so I could go into the office and write on the poster paper and cards with the fountain pen, as I wanted to personalise it.

"How did you acquire the blue diamond earrings?" There's no way Suzanne picked these, because they match my engagement ring.

"I brought them back from Florence. There are only five of this particular set in the world, and they are very valuable. I bought them the same time I got your engagement ring. After you mentioned the colour blue, I thought now was the time. I was going to wait, but being away from you is driving me crazy, and I wanted me to still be with you somehow."

"I just don't know what to say." I stutter with amazement.

"Thank me with your lips when I get home. I cannot wait to see you wear the earrings. How is your ankle? Marco said you looked unwell when you came out the clinic?"

"It's fine. I was just a little dizzy but was good as new after my lunch." Said ankle is actually okay, not too bad at all until I put pressure on it or move it, but I'll omit that little detail.

"Baby, I need to go back into my meeting. I will call you later on tonight. Keep your earrings in the safe when you are not wearing them. I love you, dolcezza."

After transporting all the gifts upstairs into the suite, I place my original earrings in the safe with my other jewellery and keep the blue diamonds in.

Jessica arrives just as Rose is serving dinner. She admires my earrings and I give her a quick tour. Since it's a lovely evening, we sit outside on the pergola. We enjoy a starter of asparagus and stilton soup then chicken and mushrooms in a white wine sauce, crispy garlic-rosemary potatoes, and various dressed greens, parsnips, carrots, and squash. We finish our meal with a slice of Victoria sponge cake and tea that Rose prepared this afternoon. Marco joins us for his meal but then pardons himself to work in Lucca's study.

Mr. Carlin is in heaven. We won't be able to get him home at this rate, and I see Rose has made a little extra effort for him.

I smile watching him relax and enjoy himself. Rose has been very attentive. I think she feels sorry for him as he's on his own after losing Eleanor.

Jess and I clean up and load the dishwasher to allow Peter and Mr. Carlin to continue their game of chess with their dram of whiskey. Doris nearly knocks Mr. Carlin off his chair she is so excited to see him. He shoos her away impatiently with his walking stick and pretends he has no interest in her, but I did notice him slipping her some potatoes when he thought no one was paying attention. That man is too stubborn for his own good.

He gives me the run down regarding the home help, and after some truffles and a dram of whiskey with Peter, I catch him yawning so Marco obliges by running him home. I text Hazel and ask her to go in and ensure he doesn't put that blooming heating on again.

I feel compelled to apologise to Marco for my temper earlier before he leaves, but he smiles and reassures me I have nothing to apologise for.

Bidding Rose and Peter good night, Jess and I put our pyjamas on and cuddle on the sofa for a long overdue chat, a DBB, but on the sofa instead of the usual bed. I haven't had the chance to speak to Jess since my disastrous night turning up at her house after finding an intruder in our bed. I assure her everything is okay, that Lucca took care of the situation and we talked about it.

I give her the tour of the rest of the house and dressing room and show her the gifts I received today. She rubs my arm and hugs me, saying she is absolutely delighted I have found happiness and security and that she wants nothing more for me. Jess says she knows Lucca loves me and will take exceptional care of me. I believe her sincerity because she's honest and very caring.

After locking up and bringing Doris in, Lucca calls to check in on me. We talk for almost forty minutes. He's leaving London early tomorrow for his flight to Olbia, Sardinia, so he's advised he'll call when he can. I refrain from telling him I'm going into my clinic at the club tomorrow because I know he'll object, especially after he stressed I should be recovering still before going back to work.

When I return upstairs, Jess is sound asleep in my bed. I'm comforted knowing she's here. Like old times.

Chapter 23: Men in Black

Jess is leaving early for work after some croissants, fruit, and coffee. She is driving to Newcastle today for a sales conference. In the fridge, I find a packed lunch in a brown paper bag for her with a post it note.

For your trip, Jessica. Enjoy.

It could only be Rose.

God bless her. She truly is remarkable. She must have come in early to prepare it and has left some sweet niceties on the work top, which I shove into Jess's handbag. After an early breakfast, Jess promises me she will be back at 6:00 p.m. sharp Wednesday evening. All I tell her is to bring her swimsuit, deliberately not divulging the details of Lucca's treat wanting to keep it a surprise for all of them.

After a hot shower, I'm amazed that my ankle feels less swollen and tender today. Dressing, I opt for pleated, above the knee, black chiffon skirt and black fine knit tank top and wear black ballet flats since I'm going into the clinic today. I throw my hair in an undone bun, apply minimum makeup, and then walk Doris. I call a taxi to pick me up because I'm not having Marco drop me off in a limo at the club. That would raise eyebrows and the gossip is most likely circulating about Lucca and me already.

It seems like forever since I have been in my physiotherapy clinic. Walking past reception, I have an unnerving feeling everyone is watching me, their eyes are following my every move. Some people I know, some I don't, and it makes me restless. I don't recall them watching me like this before.

There is only one explanation – Lucca.

They've heard we're engaged, and the women are most likely very curious about what's going on, or envious as I've claimed their Italian god as my own. I carry on past the bar area with my focus straight ahead to the wooden doors, avoiding all eye contact.

As it's summer and the kids are off school, the racket club and various other sports' clubs are bustling with families. It's packed today, and I feel almost claustrophobic. I arrive at the clinic upstairs thirty minutes later after meeting absolutely everyone with nothing short of a million questions.

Word travels fast around a club like this, and I'm sure I'm not flavour of the month.

Mark and Jane are waiting on me in the clinic. They both congratulate me with a huge hug. I can't believe how much Jane's baby bump has grown since I last saw her. It's amazing. She looks like she's glowing and flourishing with her pregnancy.

Her busy green and purple flower power tunic complements her unruly, fiery hair, and I see the toes of her biker boots from under her maxi gypsy style skirt. Some things never change. I love that she stays true to herself.

I keep my phone off to give Mark the courtesy of my full attention during his debrief as we have so much to cover. I don't mention Lucca's proposition about sourcing and funding us our own practice, because I'd rather wait until it's been further discussed and possible first.

Having missed my independence of working, I'm eager to get my teeth back into it. Mark has a look at my wrist and my ankle, spending some time manipulating the areas which does help considerably. I'm thankful I still take the heavy duty painkillers for my wrist, as it's also serving the ankle pain.

We have lunch in the bar area. Rena the chef makes me a lovely prawn sandwich and small minestrone soup. Jane shows me her baby picture scan and tells me all about her plans for the nursery. Mark says that the membership client base has increased dramatically, and they have all asked for appointments with me personally, so I have a massive waiting list.

A waiting list?

That's strange because Mark and Jane both are very competent and highly regarded, and if their pain and injuries were causing grief, then surely they would want to be taken as soon as possible. His theory is that they have found out about my relationship with Lucca and want to get to know the woman who has finally stolen his heart. I shuffle around, feeling slightly uncomfortable with that thought, but he has a point. He also adds that the majority of these clients are female, so it does add up.

I expected this to be difficult as Lucca owns the club, and it's inevitable I will experience challenges because of this and his history with women, I just didn't expect my personal space to be invaded by a club full of desperate cougar wives all after my man.

Hazel runs by and stops when she sees us. "Jane, you look amazing, honey. I love your tunic! Is it new?" She smiles and winks at me.

"Shut up, Hazel. Stop being sarcastic. It's actually maternity wear," Jane bites back.

"Oh, I can see that." Hazel giggles.

Mark stifles a laugh at Hazel's mockery. Rolling my eyes, I ignore their tete-a-tete and smile apologetically at Jane then warn Hazel with my eyes to be nice.

"Skip, make sure you're at my house tomorrow for 6:00 p.m. Lucca has arranged cover for your classes."

"Excellent, I'll stay over then. I need to dash, I'm late for my class. Addio amici. " I watch as she runs up the stairs.

We are gathering ourselves to return to the clinic when the club's temporary manager interrupts us. "Excuse me, Miss Robertson. I have Mr. Caruso on the phone for you in the office, and he would like to speak with you. This way please."

I follow him into his office and realise I've had my phone off all this time. He's probably been trying to get me, but how does he even know I'm here?

Stalker.

"I'll give you some privacy." The manager closes the door behind me.

"Hi, honey, how did you know I'm here?"

"I own the club, Doc. Peter said you left in a taxi, why? And why have you turned your phone off? I have been trying to call you. Why are you back at work? I told you not to go back yet. You are not in a position to be practicing, and I am not comfortable with it. I want you home."

I press my lips together in a firm line and keep silent, processing his irrational questions. He told me yesterday he wouldn't try to control me, yet here he is being domineering again, and I don't like his tone.

"Lexi, talk to me," he demands.

Irrational bloody pest.

"I'm here because I work here and have a lot to catch up on. I took a taxi because I don't want to be driven to the club in a limo or bother Peter. I have my phone off because we were having a meeting, and I'll decide when I'm good and ready to be back at work. Now is there anything else you want to scold me about, because I don't appreciate you hounding me. You said you wouldn't control me, yet here you are suffocating me again," I bark.

He sighs before answering. I can tell he's stressed, but he's being irrational. "I am sorry. Shit ... I truly am sorry. I do not want to control you and make you feel like that. That is not my intention at all. I just believe it is in your best interest to stay off work. You are still recovering from an injury, and I would prefer it if Peter or Marco drives you anywhere you need to go so I have peace of mind knowing you are safe if I cannot be there to protect you myself." Jesus, I've never heard him so wound up. He sounds a thousand times more frantic and stressed than yesterday.

"Lucca, I love that you want to protect me, I do, but I need to live my life as normally as possible. I'm not going to break in two, and you can't keep me wrapped in cotton wool." I stress the last few words
"I just need you to trust me and do as I ask. I want you to go home with Marco. He is waiting outside." He's ruffling my feathers with this petulant dictating.

"No, I have to finish my work. Hazel is here, so I'll have her drive me home when I'm finished." I'm firm.

"Damn it, Lexi, just do what I am fucking asking. I need you to go home. I need to keep you safe. Stop objecting and just get in Marco's fucking car."

What? He never swears directly at me, even when he is being persistent, petulant, or bossy. I hear him swear all the time, but not like this. It's out of character for him to speak to me this way. I definitely think something is wrong. He's not himself.

"Stop shouting at me. You're scaring me. What's wrong? Something isn't right. Why are you being like this? Lucca, this is me, what I do. If you want to marry me, you need to accept who I am and stop trying to control me. Is this how you were with Fran? Did she do everything you ordered?" I'm sharp and expect to have pushed his buttons; instead, I've wounded him with my questions.

He sounds breathless on the other line and very strange. "Fuck no. I love you exactly the way you are and would not want to change you for the world, Lexi. Fran and I did not have a relationship like we have. I have told you that. I did not control her nor had any want to. She is not you. You are everything, Lexi, and *mine*."

"So it's just me you want to order about because I'm a pushover!" Feeling hot, I yell, face fuming and fold my arms over my chest.

"I am sorry, I do not want to scare you or push you. That is the last thing I want to do. There is nothing wrong. I would just feel better if I know where you are. Please, baby. I just want to protect you."

For goodness sake, next he'll be tracking my mobile phone, or better yet have someone follow me. "You know I'm here. Isn't that good enough?"

"No, not when I cannot be there with you. Fuck, just do it, Lexi."

He's losing his mind, going all crazy on me. If this is what he's like when he works away, I'll definitely be going with him next time rather than put up with this nonsense. That's if I even excuse his poor behaviour and we get past this. I never experienced any of this irrational behaviour in Tuscany, and ever since we got back, all we've done is fight, argue, and cry. Life is proving difficult right now and having a relationship is a lot harder than I could ever imagine.

"I have just had a difficult morning that is all, nothing for you to worry about. Please, Lexi … Do you trust me?" He softens his tone.

"Yes, of course I do, but you're scaring me."

Groaning he adds, "Mamma wanted to Skype you, something about wedding chat." He's lying.

"Lucca, that's a lame excuse to get me home. I can call her anytime." I chew the inside of my cheek and fidget with a paperclip on the desk.

"Okay, you are right. Yes, it is." He sighs.

"Can you be honest with me then? Why do I need to leave here so desperately? Give me a good, valid reason and I'll go, but not until you explain yourself because you sound absurd." I doubt there will be any rational explanation that will make me leave my work today.

"Okay, I am only thinking about you."

"Lucca, spill." After I've bent the paperclip through frustration, I pick another and started twisting it.

"Kimberley is in the club, and I would rather you not run into her."

"Is she in the gym? I haven't seen her," I ask.

"No, she is in the conference suite with Suzanne and some of my staff working on the projections for the Edinburgh launch. I have been on a conference call with them this morning from Sardinia."

"What?" I screech. "Why is she still working for you? Why would you not tell me this?" Is he out of his mind? I thought after her episode at the weekend he would have well and truly fired her ass.

"Calm down. I knew you would react like this, so that is why I did not tell you."

"Answer my question, Lucca!" I snap and flick the paperclip right across the desk.

"I cannot fire her. She is in the union and has a representative, so she has sought legal advice. She also has consulted with HR claiming unfair dismissal, and I have no valid grounds to dismiss her other than personal grievance. I need to wait until she fucks up from a business perspective. It does not look good for the company or my image, and there will be disastrous consequences if I do. I have set up her transfer to the Edinburgh club in the meantime, but it is a lengthy process." He sounds exasperated. "I have been working through the night with Omari and my reps to resolve this, but unfortunately, I need to keep her in a position just now, not through choice but because I have to."

My heart is breaking for him now as I know this is out of his hands and it would explain why he's stressed and why he wants me out the club, away from her, even if he was demanding and out of order the way he spoke.

"What are the consequences?" I ask.

"Well, apart from bad publicity and a probable unpleasant threatening lawsuit, there is something else. She has something over me which I do not want to burden you with."

"Please, tell me."

He sighs and I hear him groan deep in his throat. "Fuck ... she has a video of sexual content in her possession and is threatening to release it if I dismiss her."

"Are you kidding me?" Jumping up in a panic, I place my hand on my chest, feeling my knees tremble, and stare at the door, expecting to be confronted with her. I need to sit back down because I'm worried my legs will give way.

No fucking way! I can't take much more of this crap.

"No, I wish I were." He clears his throat.

"That little twisted bitch. She's poison. I'm disgusted, but not surprised. I assume you're in the video?" I'm hoping he says no, but his outburst speaks volumes now, and I understand why he would want to protect me.

History!

Fucking history coming back to bite us on the ass again. I know he can't change his past, but it's grating on me now. First Leila in my bed and now this. What else will she try and do to get back at us?

"Yes, I am. I am sorry, baby. It was a long time ago. It is her and me here in the club after hours one night. I had the security tape destroyed, and I do not know how she managed to retain a copy, but you understand I cannot allow it to be released. I cannot have you hurt and disrespected like that, and it would crush my business reputation." His voice is soft and filled with sincerity.

"Is this about money? I can't believe she is blackmailing you." I press my thumb on my temple adding pressure, feeling a throbbing headache coming on as my breathing increases.

"Omari suggested a financial settlement, but she is not interested. She wants to keep her job. I do not think it is about the money. I think it is about you and me."

Angry.

Hurt.

Shocked.

"Oh God, I feel sick." I fist my stomach, inhaling slowly and deeply, suddenly feeling nauseous. Another reaction to panic.

"Lexi, are you okay? I need to come home. Fuck my appointments. I cannot fucking stand this." He's going out of his mind with panic, sounding pained and agitated.

"No, don't come home. Finish your business trip. I'm fine. I trust you, and I know you'll do everything in your power to make this go away." Make *her* go away. I pick up several paperclips and crush them tightly in my hand until my palm hurts. Then I fire them across the desk because I'm angry she is getting to me again.

Closing my eyes, I say a silent prayer than he can make this disappear. We don't need this stress. Then I look at the red marks on my palm and clench my jaw.

"I will make sure that I do everything I can to rectify this and protect you. I do not want you to worry. I have a great legal team backing me, but I need you to stay away from her. She is up to something. I am having her monitored in and out of work, but I do not want you out on your own while I am away. Suzanne is aware and is overseeing as much as she can, but I have hired help to track every last move she makes. Lexi, you need to keep this to yourself for now."

"Of course. Lucca, I'm sorry to put you through this. She hates me so much that she is willing to jeopardise your reputation to make a point, or stab you in the back, and it's unfair."

"No, do not apologise or worry about me. I am untouchable. The girl is clearly messed up. It is you she is trying to hurt, and it is fucking killing me she is treating you like this and still interfering. I wish I was there to comfort you."

Messed up? I am messed up. She is more like an unhinged, crazy psycho.

"Will you go home with Marco? I will call you later after my meeting with the planning team here." He doesn't even need to convince me.

"Yes, I don't want to be anywhere near her when you're not with me. Lucca, I love you."

"Please be cautious and keep your phone on. I love you, dolcezza."

With these last words, my mind starts to run away from me. I just need to get out here. I grab my bag and switch on my phone, noticing dozens of texts and missed calls. I make a quick call to Mark and tell him something has come up and I need to go urgently. Then I text Jane and tell her I'll have her and Kenny over for dinner very soon.

I don't want to go back upstairs and risk bumping into Kimberley, so I quickly exit the gym and slide in the back of Marco's car. I ask Marco to stop by Mr. Carlin's so I can check in on him.

As well as Lucca, Cameron has left a series of voicemails. Ringing his number, I sing, "What's on fire?" I know why Lucca has been trying to get me, but why is he going stir frantic crazy on me?

"Where the hell have you been?" he shouts.

"Hello, Cameron. It's nice to hear from you as well." I purse my lips in a thin line and press my thumb to my temple again with the pounding ache in my head.

"Lexi, I've been trying to call. Have you spoken with Lucca yet?"

"Yes, why are you so uptight? What's your excuse?"

"What did he tell you?"

"All about that meddling little bitch Kimberley. She has some bloody nerve. Does Anna know?"

"Know what?"

It occurs to me Cameron doesn't know what I'm talking about, and maybe I need to keep that information undisclosed due to legal prerequisites.

"Never mind. What are you going on about?"

"Forget it. Is Marco with you?"

"Yes."

"Good. Tell Marco to call me when he stops the car."

"Why?"

"Oh for fuck's sake, Lexi, just fucking do it and stop asking questions." I've had enough of this. First Lucca and now him. He making me more infuriated than I already am.

"Don't you take that tone with me, and I won't until you tell me why."

"You're sucking the life out of me, and so bloody stubborn. Fine. It's a favour I need to ask him regarding Anna."

"Well, why didn't you just say so?" I mumble.

He sighs. "Just get him to call me." He hangs up.

How weird. He's a mystery sometimes and clearly has himself in another love twist dilemma. Well, I knew this would happen eventually. He can sort this mess out himself.

I spend two hours with Mr. Carlin. Marco says he has calls to catch up on so he will wait outside. I don't know why he doesn't just go then come back for me. I call Rachel and have a heart-to-heart with her and agree that we will stay friends, even if she and Cameron are not dating. I have always had a good relationship with her, and it would be a shame to lose it.

Making another cup of coffee for myself and tea for Mr. Carlin, I call Anna to enquire if she knows anything, but she's oblivious. Probably better that way, so I invite her over tomorrow night instead. She declines because she's arranged to meet Cameron.

Returning to the car, I hear Marco on the phone. "Yes, she is here ... No ... Yes ... not yet ... of course ... absolutely we are on our way ... si ... si."

"Was that Lucca?"

"Yes."

I don't bother to ask what they are talking about—probably business. "Marco, could you drive me to Glasgow before I go home? I wanted to go to my hairdresser for a trim since I have a free afternoon." I haven't had my hair cut since long before I travelled to Tuscany, and I have a terrible headache. I always think when I get my hair trimmed I feel better and lighter.

"I am sorry, Lexi, but Lucca has asked me to take you straight home." I slump in my seat, annoyed I'm being imprisoned, and call him to give him a piece of my mind.

He answers on the first ring. "Hey, baby, everything okay?" he asks with trepidation.

"Yes, but I'd like to go to the hairdresser."

"I have asked Marco to take you home."

"I'm aware of that, but you can't keep me locked up in the house. It's only the hairdresser. You're being unreasonable, and Kimberley is at the club so we won't bump into each other."

I'm so goddamn angry. Not only is Kimberley upsetting me by deliberately trying to backstab me, now she has taken away my freedom? I feel like a prisoner and that doesn't sit well. I spent far too many years as one, and I don't appreciate being locked up now.

"I will have your hairdresser come by tomorrow night, just trust me." He sighs in exasperation. I bunch the ends of my long tousled hair in my fingers, noticing how dry the ends have become recently with the sun exposure and extra growth. It definitely needs a tidy. I frown and sigh.

"Are you angry with me?" he asks.

"Yes."

"Well, then I have a lot of making up to do when I get home," he teases, using that sexy tone he uses when trying to seduce me.

"Hmmm … I like the sound of that. You're off the hook, Romeo, and only because I know you're under a lot of stress today," I say, relaxing my tense facial muscles to form a soft smile.

"Thank you. God, I love you and I meant what I said about the making up. All. Weekend. Long. I promise." Now I'm blushing and extremely excited for the making up. I think I can clear my schedule. After all, *a promise is a promise.*

"Good, I'm glad. I'll look forward it." My stomach flutters in anticipation. It's only been a day and a half and it feels like an eternity.

After I hang up, I address Marco.

"Marco, looks like you're taking me home." He smiles, nods, then drives on.

Of course, he already knew I'd fold and crumble for Lucca.

When we return to the house, I'm shocked to see two black SUVs sitting outside the front doors. Peter is talking to one of the drivers.

"Who's that?" I ask. We aren't expecting anyone.

"Wait here a moment please, Lexi." He holds his hand up to motion me to sit back down. This day is getting odder by the minute.

Marco steps outside and walks around the limo as do the two conspicuous men from their vehicles. They approach Marco and shake his hand. What on earth is going on? Peter heads off to the coach house moments later and Marco is left speaking with them.

Both men are dressed in black suits with black sunglasses and ear pieces. They are both broad and well-built and smartly tailored. The taller one is blonde and looks very smooth while the other is stocky with a shaved head and a square jaw. They nod then turn towards the limo. I'm twitching to find out what the hell is going on.

Marco opens the door for me, and when I'm out he introduces me to Lloyd and Devon.

Nervously, I stand at Marco's side and don't offer my hand, still puzzled as to why they are here and who they are. It is making me extremely uncomfortable.

"Lloyd and Devon are private security agents who have been hired to protect you, so they will be on call from now on. I will still be your main driver and point of contact, but they will be on site permanently. Should Lucca or I not be available, they will accompany you everywhere. You are not to be left alone at any point."

Men in Black keep an impassive look on their face while I stare in disbelief.

"I will see you both in the study in thirty minutes for a debriefing and a conference call with Mr. Caruso," he directs to the Men in Black. Tears prick at my eyes, ready to flood. I can't lose control, not here, but I can't handle this.

"Marco, tell me you're kidding, right?" I almost stumble back against the limo door because I'm so shocked and off balance.

"No, Lexi, I am not. You need to cooperate. It is for your own safety, and Lucca has your best interests at heart." He doesn't make eye contact, and I know he's finding this hard, giving orders when he senses my hostility.

"I don't believe this. No offense," I choke towards the stoic men.

"No offense taken, ma'am," the taller one replies.

Ma'am?

Turning my focus, I burn my blazing brown eyes right through Marco.

"Marco, did you know about this?" I choke.

"Yes. Lexi, I am sorry, but it is for the best." His left eye twitches; I sense he has no control over it, like a nerve spasm, whether it's because he's lying or that he's under pressure, I just don't know. How can he say this is for the best? It's a breach of privacy and I'm done with this ludicrousness.

"The hell it is. He's gone too far this time. Lloyd, Devon, I'm sorry to waste your time, but I don't require your services, so please excuse me." Moisture coats my eyes as I storm past them into the house and hobble into the kitchen, bearing my weight on the better ankle. I collapse in a heap on the floor, breaking down in uncontrollable sobs.

I don't even notice Rose hovering next to me.

"Oh, Lexi ... come here, petal." Rose kneels down in front of me and wraps her arms around me. I cling onto her neck, inhaling her familiar floral scent.

"Why is he doing this? He's treating me like a prisoner! I don't see why Peter can't continue to drive me places." I sob against her shoulder while she strokes my back.

"Because Peter's old and would not make a good security guard. He is better looking after the grounds for Lucca as his days of MI5 are long past." She quietly chuckles.

"I don't understand? Why do I need security? It's ridiculous. I'm suffocating. Rose, speak with him and tell him this is over the top." They are bodyguards and I don't even know them. How do I even know I can trust them?

"I won't be able to change his mind, petal. Everything he is doing is because he loves you. He must have a valid explanation. He's only trying to protect you. I know it appears extreme, but he's a wise man. A stubborn one, yes, but wise all the same. He's also the most compassionate young man I've ever known, and this is from his heart." She rubs my back and arm comforting me. "He's not trying to hurt you. He had the security firm come and fix all the cameras today. I suppose after the night that ghastly girl broke in, he's being extra cautious."

It's plausible he's worried about Kimberley breaking in, but then what can she do that needs two Men in Black to be on guard around the clock.

"Why don't you go and have a nice relaxing bath and I'll make you some tea? Are you having guests tonight?" I'm so thankful for Rose's wisdom and compassion in the absence of my mum, Granny, and Eleanor. Rose epitomises motherly love, and I feel very grateful for her love right now.

Sniffling, I tell her Lucy is coming over.

"Okay, what's her favourite dish?"

"Mexican." I whisper.

"Okay, well, beef enchiladas and chilli tacos all round. It's been a while, but I do have an authentic, spicy recipe somewhere."

"Thank you, Rose. I really appreciate it." I kiss her soft cheek once she calms me and brings me back to focus with her warm sensitivity.

As I'm walking into the hallway to head upstairs, Marco and Men in Black are standing in the hallway entrance about to head towards Lucca's study no doubt. Marco puts his hand out and lightly holds my wrist. He looks agitated, left eye twitching again.

"Lloyd, Devon, Rose will show you to the study. I will be with you shortly," Marco instructs.

They nod and follow Rose through the grand hallway towards the study at the back of the house. Seeing them up close is quite intimidating—they are strong with a steel exterior that makes them look brave, enduring, and fierce. I sense they are fearless, and they both scare the hell out of me.

"I wanted to say I am sorry." Marco frowns, and it's the first time I have seen him properly let his guard down.

"No, it's okay. It's not your fault."

"Lexi, do not be hard on him. It is for the best, and it is not forever. They will be very discreet, and it will not inconvenience you, but it is how it has to be just now. It is a difficult time for Lucca. Try and understand this is with all good intentions and just be patient with him." He undoes his top button of his shirt, as if trying to make himself more comfortable. "He mentioned that they would intimidate you, being men. There are no female operatives from the agency available just now, but these two men are the best, most reliable and trustworthy. Lucca has told me to assure you, you can trust them both, speak to him about it and he will confirm that."

Now I feel guilty, but I still think this is too far and over the top—verging on extreme. I think about the pressures Lucca has been under today and there is a chance Kimberley has made a threat regarding me. I would prefer female operatives if I need to have them at all, but I suppose at short notice Lucca is doing his best to protect me. If he says they are trustworthy, then I will need to try and learn to trust them in my own time, but I still want to hear it from him.

"Okay."

He gives me a sympathetic smile then walks to the study to address Men in Black.

In the suite, there is a massive flower arrangement sitting on the table in the living area in front of the French doors. Its decorative hues of blue, purple, and aqua are beautiful. Of course, there are blue orchids, but also blue hydrangea, which is the colour of that beautiful evening gown he gifted me, and indigo delphinium mixed in. It's the nicest arrangement of flowers I have seen.

'I love you, and will keep you safe, dolcezza, always and forever, all my love Lucca x'

Rose knocks and comes in with a tray of tea and some baked shortbread. She sits at the table and joins me. Truthfully, I think she wants to make sure I'm a little more settled, and I love her warmth and kindness—it's just what I need now.

Chapter 24: Devil's Advocate

After Rose leaves, I light the new candle Lucca gave me and place it in the bathroom before switching the lights off. I have a long soak in the tub with Lucca's tropical bath oil and only the small flicker from the candle. Feeling vulnerable, I wish his arms were wrapped around me right now. I leave my phone sitting on the marble ledge, hoping he'll feel the need to call and explain this nightmare.

I'm almost drifting off when Lucca calls. He's concerned because I'm sure Rose and Marco have both told him I'm upset with the new arrangement. I answer with the intention of giving him hell but soften a little when I hear how fragile and apologetic he sounds.

He sighs. "… Dolcezza?"

"Yes, I am listening," I croak but don't cry. I'm too tired and have exhausted myself crying in Rose's arms already.

"Are you okay, sweetheart? Tell me what you are thinking. I need to know you are okay."

I close my eyes and protectively wrap an arm around myself in the water. I don't know where to start so I blurt it out. "I'm a mess, Lucca. They just remind me of the escorts we had assigned by the police and our care team when we were leaving Australia after our escape; they even came with us on the flight back to Scotland. We had them stationed outside our hospital room and then our hotel room to keep the press away. It makes me think of the trauma and shock I went through, and how scared and intimidated I was being surrounded by strangers who were meant to protect us. To me, they were more of a threat. I associate security with being imprisoned, and that's exactly how I feel now. *Caged.*" I pick up a curl of hair clinging to my shoulder and twirl it around in my finger while my bottom lip trembles.

"Oh, sweetheart … I am so sorry … I had no idea. Christ … No wonder you were so upset. I tried to get females or at least one female, but there were none available at short notice. I know how you feel about strangers, but I did not think the security would trigger uncomfortable memories like that for you. Fuck … baby, I wish it did not have to be like this." He pauses and sighs.

"I need them there because it is a safety issue and keeping you safe is my priority, but if I thought for one minute it would trigger worries like this for you, I would have called and spoke to you about it first and asked them to come later so that they did not startle you. I need you to be brave, to believe I have your best interests at heart, and know that I love you and want what is best for you. I am sorry to cause you upset, but I need you to try, to try and be strong, for me?" His voice is so soft filled with compassion.

"I will try. Can I trust them?" I ask, now pressing my lips together trying to mask the hurt in my voice and hold tears back.

"Yes, yes of course you can. I would never put you in danger. Everything I have had to do has been for you, Lexi, with all good intentions and from my heart ... for my love for you. Always. I would not deliberately hurt you, please believe me. I have spoken with Lloyd and Devon. They know how afraid you are and to be extra sensitive and know their boundaries. It is all I can do until I am home with you." I lift my hand to my mouth and worry my fingers about in front of my mouth.

"Do you want to tell me about your fears, the memories you mentioned? Do you think it will help? Maybe if I just listen," he asks with concern.

Do I? I don't know if it will help me or not. Sometimes talking about past events makes me think like I'm reliving it. I tense up. "I'm not sure ... I think maybe I'd rather not. It might make me more edgy than I already am. I'm sorry, I know you are trying to help but thank you for asking," I mumble against the back of my hand.

"Okay, whatever you want. Dolcezza, can I ask you something?"

"Yeah," I reply, now worrying my fingers faster, along with chewing the inside of my cheek.

"Can you please take your fingers away from your mouth? I know you are nervously twisting them in front of your mouth, your voice sounds muffled, and you do that when your are deep in thought or anxious. If I were there, I would gently kiss your hand, remove them from your mouth, and then kiss your lips. I need you to breathe, listen to my voice, my words, and try to relax. I know you are tense."

God, he's good. I drop my hand and this time I admire my blue diamond and listen to him.

"I have an idea. If you do not want to talk about the memories from your past, let me tell you about the background and some personal information about both agents. It might help you understand them and give you a better sense of trusting them, if you know more about them," he suggests.

"Okay."

"Okay? As in no fiery backlash?"

"Yes, okay."

"Oh, and I was looking forward to having you so fiery that I would need to jump on a plane and rush home to claim you."

I smile. He's trying so hard to help, and I know he's trying to be light-hearted and uplifting. "I'll look forward to you claiming me. I'm sure I can find some fire for you. Now tell me about them," I say, my smile reaching my eyes as I stare towards the phone.

He does. I learn about their work experience, where they come from, their hobbies, family, ages, achievements, and skills. Lucca even reads testimonials for them both from the agency and from well-known people they have protected, and it calms me and puts my mind at ease.

"Baby, I wish I was in that bath, holding you to me."

"Hmmm … so do I," I say lazily, stretching my legs in the tepid water. "So, Men in Black … are they staying here?"

"Interesting name for them, but yes, they are staying in the guest suites around the back. Marco will put their mobile numbers into your phone so they are on call 24-7. I had an intercom installed today also which will take you straight through to the guest accommodation. Rose will show you how to work it. Do not leave that house without at least one of them. They are highly skilled and trained with the best, so you are in great hands until I come back. I am so sorry I never got the chance to explain about them. I was too busy dealing with Kimberley. I received the call from the agency to say they were on their way, just as you were leaving the club."

"Lucca, I don't think Kimberley is an expert on martial arts and she's smaller than me. It's a bit extreme, don't you think?" I want to know why she is such a threat.

"No, until I find out what she is up to, they are staying, they have to. Rose says you were extremely upset. I am so sorry I am not there, baby, to hold you and calm you down. I am glad she was there for you. I know the security must be intimidating for you. If I had time to talk to you about it first I would have, but I had to act quickly."

"I miss you, Lucca. I wish I was wrapped in your arms right now." I feel a rush of vulnerability once again now I'm gaining equilibrium.

"You are, Lexi, you are. I have you. I will be back Friday night. It is killing me, baby. I promise everything will be fine, and I will be back before you know it." He sounds damaged, as if he feels guilty or torn up again. It does reassure me he has my best interests at heart.

"As much as I would love to talk all night, Lucy will be here shortly so I need to get dressed. You can make lots of sweet love to me when you're back, and I'll try and be fiery for you, Romeo. I might even have phone sex with you another time you're away from me when I'm not so worked up," I tease in my ever developing sassy voice.

Lucca groans. "I will not be leaving you on your own again, Lexi, but I am glad you are more relaxed. Keep saying shit like that, and I will never let you off this phone. I know you need to go, so it will need to wait, but stay safe and I will call you later. Lexi, I love you."

"I love you too."

"What's with six and eight outside the house?" Lucy asks after our guests interrogated her on the way in.

"Don't ask. Come here and give me a hug," I reply, very excited to see her.

Her hair is as glossy as ever, and she has black city shorts on with a beautiful red silk blouse that matches the pillar box lipstick she wears. After the house tour, I pour her a glass of wine and we sit at the dining area in the kitchen while Rose cooks her Mexican fiesta. Marco walks through and asks for my phone, and I give it to him because I assume he's adding my two new best friends' contact information. Men in Black.

I introduce him to Lucy, and he kisses her on both cheeks and holds his gaze a little too long, and it's not lost on Lucy either. She blushes and looks away first. There is a definite attraction on both parts because I can see her shuffle in her chair and act fidgety. I excuse myself to help Rose and leave the two of them to become acquainted.

"Marco, are you joining us for dinner?" I ask, my voice hopeful.

"I am not sure, I do not want to interrupt or intrude." His left eye twitches again and I wonder if he's nervous I have put him on the spot.

Lucy sits forward in her chair and bats her long lashes subtly. She wants him to stay.

"Nonsense, there is plenty for everyone," Rose adds, and that settles it. Thankfully Rose intervenes, and I slide a chair out for Marco.

"I'm just going to find Doris. I'll be back in a minute." Lucy widens her eyes as if to say "what are you doing, get back here right now." I nod, smile, and rush off. I only plan to be a minute or two, but I think this is what she needs to break the ice and give her confidence to start up conversation.

The front doors are opened for me by Men in Black at either side. "Ma'am," the taller one says with a polite nod.

"Thank you, but please, call me Lexi." I tense because Marco is not by my side and I still don't know these strangers, so I plan to get Doris and get back into the house pronto. Until I get to know them, I can't fully trust them yet. I avert my gaze towards Doris. "There you are. What are you doing?"

She has sprawled out at the feet of the shorter one, and I am confused. Looking up with possessive eyes, she then transfixes her gaze straight ahead, ignoring me. How strange.

"She hasn't left our side. Looks as if we've gained a guard dog," the shorter one says in a thick, raspy, Southern Irish accent.

So he does talk after all. He actually has a very nice voice. He should speak more often because his voice is kind of sexy and a complete contrast to his steely, bulky exterior. He's actually not as intimidating now that I hear him speak as opposed to the stern, hostile nodding.

"She's sussing you out. I'm sorry, I'll take her inside." I put my hand under her collar to drag her but she refuses to budge.

Big bloody lump of stubbornness.

"No need, she's fine. That's a good protector you have there. We'll be rotating shifts, so you might only see one of us here at any given time. The dog can keep us company," taller one adds.

"I'm sorry ... is it Lloyd?"

"Yes, and that's Devon." Lloyd appears to be more approachable than Devon.

"I think we got off on the wrong foot, and I do apologise, but I wasn't expecting you."

"No need to apologise. We're here to help, but we'll need you to cooperate," Devon adds. Doris grumbles and does a commando crawl towards his foot placing her nose to the heel of his shoe.

"Yes, I can manage that. I suppose I don't have a choice now. Would you like dinner?" I offer. Not that they are my favourite people, but I feel sorry for them standing out here bored, cold, and hungry. I know what it feels like to be hungry, fighting sleep outside in the dark, and for that reason, I'd like to show them some hospitality and invite them inside, but I don't even know if that's correct protocol here.

"Thank you kindly, but no, we have been adequately set up in the guest accommodations and have plenty of supplies. We're here to work, ma—Lexi," Lloyd aptly corrects himself. He comes across as being the senior-superior of both guards. He seems to do most of the talking.

"Okay then, if you're sure. I suppose I'm leaving her with you." I sigh, looking down towards Doris who has pinned Devon on the spot with her curling paw over his toe cap.

Marco and Lucy appear to be hitting it off. She's giving him the lowdown on her working life, and I hear him mention his Tuscan upbringing and friendship with Lucca. I set the table while Rose finishes the meal and top Lucy's wine, giving them time to chat. I'm glad they are getting along.

"Is there enough food for me?" I hear a familiar voice behind me.

He picks his bloody timing ...

"Cameron, what are you doing here?" I place a bowl of salsa, crème fraiche, and guacamole on the table staring down deciding whether I should look at Lucy or Cameron first. I want to see who is the most agitated in this uncomfortable predicament.

"You asked me to come by and stay, remember? Plus, I wanted to make sure you're okay." He nudges me, looking for backup so he doesn't look like a complete idiot in front of Lucy for randomly stopping by when she's here.

Shit. My brain is so fuzzy and spongy recently. I forgot to get back to him.

"Oh, I asked Lucy as well because you never confirmed what night you were coming. I'm sorry, you don't need to stay if you have plans, but there's plenty of dinner." I glide my hand towards the food.

Fuck!

File A for awkward. Awkward situation, Lucy and Cameron here together.

Cameron shakes Marco's hand and gives Lucy a small, light kiss on the cheek, which she undoubtedly flusters under and worries the pendant in front of her chest. Rose goes back to the coach house when she's finished serving.

"I'm glad that the security agents are here, and I'm surprised you never kicked off about it, but it's for the best," Cameron adds casually while cutting into his enchilada. "Lloyd, he's a top guy, served with the best. Devon, he's highly skilled in combat. You can trust them both." He munches on his food nodding towards Marco.

"You knew about this?" I snap at him my fork clattering against the plate loudly. Marco exchanges a narrowed glance at Cameron—a silent warning?

"Yes, Lucca and I spoke during the night as I was on shift. They're two of the best in the industry. You're in very safe hands. Lex, he pulled a lot of strings to get the two of them." He says it as I should be eternally grateful. What I am is really pissed; he knew about this and kept it from me.

I drop my fork and stare at my plate.

"Lexi, are you okay?" Lucy asks softly, reaching for my hand.

"I'm not sure, because it seems that everyone is keeping me in the dark," I snap intentionally, for Cameron's benefit.

Silence.

Tumbleweed!

"You don't need to worry about it. You should be grateful that Lucca has the power and means to protect you like this. You're very lucky," Cameron adds.

After shaking my head, I shamble to the fridge and lift a jug of juice and fill up the empty tumblers, turning away so he doesn't recognise the heat in my eyes. Once I've poured more juice, I muster courage to retort. "Yes, Cameron, I'm well aware I'm very fortunate and extremely grateful if you must know, but I don't like people keeping secrets."

Cameron gives Marco *the look*—I've seen it before. Marco's left eye twitches; he nods and drops his gaze back to the food. Lucy doesn't know what to think, but she gives me her complete, undivided attention with warm, loving eyes. She knows I'm hurt.

I jerk my head as if to warn Lucy just to forget this. She tries to lighten the tense atmosphere and makes small chitchat.

Changing the subject, I ask Lucy if she went on another date with Harris Jones. That gets both Marco and Cameron's attention. They deserve a wake-up call for being dismissive tonight. She nudges my knee under the table, obviously mortified that I'm meddling.

"No, he's not my type. He wants to see me again and has been leaving messages, but I'm ignoring him for now. We had a lovely few dates, but I just don't know… " she whispers then takes a sip of wine.

Cameron is now very quiet and deep in thought. Marco and Lucy continue to talk about Italy, holidays, and travel. She says she would absolutely love to go travelling to Italy at some point.

"Marco, Lucca said you have your padi diving qualifications, is that right?" I ask.

"Yes, my father is an avid deep sea diver, so I have always enjoyed it. Do you dive, Lucy?" Marco asks her. I like where this interaction is going.

"I've never tried it, but I do love snorkelling and swimming. Maybe I will someday." She's being extremely modest.

"Lucy used to swim competitively," I say with my chin held high.

"Really? That is great." It's piqued Marco's attention, but Cameron stares at the table.

"Yes, front crawl. My dad and coach had high hopes I'd make the Olympics one day as I was smashing my PB, but I damaged my shoulder falling off a horse one summer up at Lexi's grandparents' place so that put the dream to rest. It still dislocates even now." Lucy runs her middle finger and thumb across her shoulder as if remembering the accident.

Cameron shuffles in his chair. He was the one who carried her across Mr. Murdock's paddock back to the house. It was our first year at university, and I had taken all the girls up for a summer holiday as we couldn't afford to go abroad on our student bursaries at the time.

"That feels like yesterday, Lucy. God, I remember it so well. It was a bad injury, and I was pissed you had to give up on swimming competitively. You were great," Cameron adds.

Lucy blushes and drops her head as Marco watches her, mystified. Reaching over, he places a gentle hand on her shoulder, and she relaxes under his touch.

Caring.

Protective.

Sensitive.

He'll be good for her. Just like Cameron and Anna have proved me wrong and seem to be good for each other.

"Well, the next diving trip, you are more than welcome to join us. My dad will love that you are a swimmer. He adores the water," Marco says.

She beams with delight, and it's lovely to see her striking movie star smile.

Cameron frowns as he watches the interaction and chemistry between them. I think she might have found her Cameron hangover cure, and he's sitting right next to her.

Tall, dark, attractive, and Italian.

Result!

I ask Cameron to help me with the plates and leave Marco and Lucy chatting away after I fill her wine glass up again.

"Are you staying?" I ask him.

"Do you think it's a good idea?" he asks, lifting his brow towards Lucy and Marco, who seem to be exchanging sweet talk and chuckling.

"I'm sure Lucy won't mind. Anyway, we're all adults and it looks as if they're hitting it off."

Devil's advocate.

"Hmmm ... I see that." He runs a shaky hand through his shaggy, waxed hair, restyling it.

"Are you jealous?"

"Nope."

He bloody well is.

Changing the subject, he tells me that he knows Jackson really likes me.

"Stop trying to divert the heat from you. Anyway, I know Jackson likes me. He told me so."

He humours me and shakes his head smiling. "No, I mean, he's hot for you. If Lucca weren't so possessive, I think he would have tried to claim you by now. I had to speak to him about not overstepping the boundaries. He's a great mate but you are out of bounds and he knows it."

Now I'm blushing.

"Oh, don't be ridiculous." I flick him with the dish cloth.

"Just saying, he's got it bad."

"So do you want to watch a movie with us tonight, then?" I like when Cameron and I joke, laugh, and confide in one another. It's much better than quarrelling, and I do adore his company.

"I suppose. I'm not seeing Anna until tomorrow, but none of that chick flick crap you watch, and definitely not fucking *Marley and Me* again." He scoffs.

I laugh because he knows I've watched that movie a million times and cry every time.

Marco leaves after coffee, but not before getting Lucy's phone number and checking with Men in Black. Lucy and I have a chat while Cameron takes Doris for a walk. She is definitely smitten with Marco because she asks why he's not in a relationship or doesn't have a girlfriend. I suggest that she go out on a proper date with him and try to get to know him since he definitely seems to like her.

I ask her if she's angry or uneasy because Cameron is here when he's outside talking to Men in Black, but she says she doesn't mind and that she's over it. I think a certain Marco da Vinci has distracted her, and I couldn't be happier.

We watch some action movie which doesn't hold my attention, so I'm relieved when Lucca calls. I excuse myself to go up to the suite to ask if there has been any development on Kimberley. Probing him, I ask why Marco doesn't have a girlfriend, and he tells me his first love died. She was terminally ill with cancer and his soul was destroyed, so he vowed never to fall in love again. Lucca's voice sounds distant.

"That's awful. I had no idea. I think Lucy really likes him. That's such a shame. Everyone deserves love."

"Yes, they do."

I press the phone to my ear as I tidy my dressing room. "Is that why you support cancer trials?" I ask innocently.

"How do you know about that?"

"I saw some documents when I was looking for a pen." I forgot all about it until he mentioned cancer. Now I feel like I've breached his personal privacy, he seems annoyed.

"Fuck. No, it is not related to that. I wish you would have told me. I would rather those documents be kept private." He's not impressed.

"I'm sorry, but they were at the top of the drawer. I didn't deliberately go snooping. It's okay, you don't need to tell me. It's your business and I love that you're passionate and generous. I just thought maybe it was the same thing." I stop sorting through my makeup because of the fallen silence. I'm worried I've overstepped the mark.

"Lucca?"

I hear him sigh then clear his throat before continuing. "No, it is not the same thing, and it is not okay, Doc. I am sorry for snapping at you. You have done nothing wrong. Are you okay?"

"Yes, of course I am." I yawn. "I'm just really tired now. It's been an eventful few days." I don't press talking about the cancer because he is sensitive about something, and I have hit a raw nerve. He will tell me when he is good and ready.

"It certainly has. Stay on the phone with me and I will talk to you until you go to sleep."

"I should get back to Lucy. Mind you, she's with Cameron and they need to clean the slate. They will be having a chat," I mutter through another huge yawn. I decide they need time alone and I am very tired, so bed wins.

I strip down to my lingerie, pull the covers back, and slide in bed. I reach my arm across his pillow and imagine he's snuggled in beside me.

"Tell me all about your property developments and how your meetings have been going. I'm still here, but if I go quiet, I've fallen asleep. So I'll tell you I love you now. I'll dream of you."

My eyes are already closed, but I'm still aware of Lucca's husky voice and breathing, as if he were right here beside me.

I'm startled in the early morning when Lucy sits on the edge of the bed and rubs my arm.

"Hey, sleepy," she says, looking refreshed, perky, and far too glamorous for this time of morning.

"Hey. Oh my gosh, Lucy, I'm sorry. I was exhausted and fell asleep. I missed our DBB. We never got a chance to cosy in bed and talk."

"Don't be. Cameron and I watched the rest of the movie then had a long chat and cleared the air, and I was really tired as well."

"You never … did you?" I gingerly ask and lift my eyebrows.

"No, we didn't sleep together, but we did fall asleep on the sofa. When he woke me up, he went into one of the spare rooms and I slipped in beside you. This house is amazing. It's absolutely beautiful. I wish I'd brought my swimsuit."

"Thank you. Bring it tonight."

"I need to go to work, darlin', but I'll be back tonight. I'll inform the girls that they need to break through the Royal Guards. Though I'm sure Hazel will find it very exciting." She winks and brushes her hand down my arm.

"Oh yeah, I forgot about them," I grumble.

"Tell Rose thank you for dinner and for the packed lunch she left in the fridge. She's so sweet."

"I will. She is very sweet. Will you be seeing the handsome Marco da Vinci in the future?" I need to ask her before she goes because I'm interested on how it went.

She smiles with those big luscious red lips. "Maybe, let's wait and see." She kisses my cheek and then she's off.

She will.

I know it.

Chapter 25: Pamper Night

Wednesday goes by very quickly. My ankle is much better today after Mark worked on it. I apply some bruise cream and notice I can already put more pressure on it. I meet Rachel for lunch in Bothwell at the usual place, Bistro & Bake, and explain everything that's happened in the last few weeks. I try to ignore Lloyd looking conspicuous sitting in the black SUV outside the restaurant, but it's difficult to do, especially since we have a table outside. He's watching my every move, and I try not to draw attention to my babysitter.

I tell her I'm sorry that she and Cameron have split up, and she says it was for the best. She's travelling again, and the long distance relationship never worked for them before. She mutters something about history and heartache then changes the subject very quickly to avert my attention, but it's not lost on me.

History.

Fucking history.

And I thought my life was complicated. Seems Cameron has his fair share of deep secrets and entangled mess.

I'm happy that Rachel and I can keep our friendship and would love to see her before she heads off to ski the French Alps. I wait until she leaves before Lloyd opens the door for me and then have him take me back home to pick Doris up.

I take her to the vet for her check-up then to Mr. Carlin's. Doris makes light work tearing through his loafers. Again.

Oh shit!

It's only ever Mr. Carlin's shoes she seems to attack. I think it's because she knows it infuriates him, either that or because she likes him. Lloyd takes us to the doctor's for Mr. Carlin's appointment but thankfully stays in the car. Then we pick up his prescriptions and stop to have tea in the coffee shop attached to the church.

I pick up some cards from the craft shop and some food shopping for Mr. Carlin then take him home and offer to make his dinner. He refuses as Julie, his home help, is due in and will take care of it. I miss doing these little things for him, although I'm thankful I did get to spend time with him today.

When we return home, I thank Lloyd for his help today. He nods, maintaining professionalism, but I see his lips form a smile. Doris growls then protectively sits next to Devon's feet. She's not wagging her tail and has the blinkers on again.

She's guarding over him, not me. She doesn't trust him ...

"Miss Robertson. Flowers, mail, and a parcel arrived for you today. I'm sorry I had to open them, it's protocol. They're on your dining room table," Devon says.

"Oh, um ... okay."

Definitely not okay. Far from it.

I walk to the kitchen grinding my teeth in anger. It could be lingerie from Lucca and he's going through my private mail and parcels. Fury twists up a storm in my stomach. They are neatly piled where he said they'd be.

The flowers are white, no blue in sight, so I know they're not from Lucca. I read the card curiously.

'Alexis,

Something to wish you well. I hope you are making a speedy recovery with your ankle sprain and taking it easy. It was lovely to see you again even under such unfortunate circumstances. J x'

Oh my God, they're from Jackson. Lucca will not be amused. The mail is all general, and the parcel is the course work I left behind at the clinic with a note from Mark.

I call Lucca but it goes to voicemail, so I leave a terse message asking why Men in Black are opening my mail.

To alleviate some frustration, I hit the gym for an hour, working on my core and doing some conditioning work, then have a hot shower and dress in clean yoga pants and a grey cotton tank top since it's pamper night.

I have six missed calls from Lucca, so I call him back. "Hey, I tried to call you."

"Sorry, I had no reception. I am in Milan now."

My heart flutters.

Agitated?

Yes.

Jealous?

Very.

I pick some dry skin from my palms. "Is Fran with you?" I know she is, so why even ask?

"Yes."

"How is she?" I ask with sincerity, as I do hope she's making a good recovery after her failed suicide attempt in Tuscany.

"She is doing very well. I am looking at properties tomorrow, some mine, some not, but they could potentially accommodate her business. And I am meeting Giorgio. He's in the city on Luminara business." He still has his business voice on, so I know his intentions are purely professional. I just hope Fran has the same idea.

Business … not pleasure.

"Where are you staying in Milan?" I chew the inside of my cheek.

I'm secretly praying he's not staying with Fran. It makes me extremely uncomfortable, considering their history, not to mention I would be envious. I do like her, and I shared an empathetic bond with her, recognising her grief and how fragile she is, but I draw the line at Lucca staying with her.

"We are having dinner tonight with Giorgio, and then I will go back to the hotel where I am staying."

"Okay, good. I don't know that I'd be okay with you staying with her." Why did I have to speak out loud? My bloody thoughts need to get filed, not voiced.

"You have nothing to worry about. I am yours and always will be. Fran has done nothing but sing your praises. She is having fashion design samples sent over to you and would like us both to visit her when we are back in Italy. I think she is being very amicable considering."

This just reiterates what a warm, kind, decent woman she actually is. Maybe it would be better if she weren't so nice. "That's very kind of her. Send her my regards."

Deadpan.

"What is wrong dolcezza?"

"Nothing," I lie.

I was handling his trip away, and I knew that ultimately he would be spending time with Fran, but suddenly I'm green with envy and regret my decision not to have gone with him.

"You are a terrible liar. I hear Jackson has sent you flowers. I am unnerved by it. I think I will be having words with our local womanising celebrity when I return."

Stop changing the subject!

"Don't overreact. It's only flowers to wish me well because I had an accident. Now we're on the subject, I'm not happy with Lloyd and Devon opening my mail. That's why I was trying to call you," I protest.

He sighs. "I am sorry, it is not forever, but it is just how it needs to be now."

I need to make my point clear because it is indeed unacceptable, and Lucca is deluding himself if he thinks otherwise. "I feel like my privacy has been violated. I don't want them going through my things."

"It is only until I come home, then I will open everything. Baby, it is only two more days."

"No one should have to open my mail, Lucca. I can do it myself."

"I know you can, it is just until this Kimberley ordeal passes. We know how malicious she can be. I would hate for you to open anything unsavoury."

"Okay ... I suppose." I lean over and smell the blue flower arrangement Lucca left for me then sigh.

"I need to go, dolcezza, we have a dinner reservation. Make sure you girls enjoy your evening. I will call you later before bed. Who is staying tonight?"

It's killing me knowing Lucca is going to dinner with his ex-fiancée, the mother of his deceased son, his childhood sweetheart. I'm struggling to be composed because I'm already imagining the worst.

"Hazel's staying." I worry my fingers against my lips.

"Are you upset because I'm having dinner with Fran?"

He's so intuitive.

Damn!

"Yes, a little," I whisper.

"It is just dinner so there is nothing for you to be worried about," he says sincerely.

"Hmmm ..."

"If you do not want me to go, I will cancel."

"No, it's fine. I don't want to be that type of person. I trust you, I'm just ..."

He loses reception and the line goes dead. I try calling him back, but it's switched off. It leaves me uneasy, but I know he'll call when he can.

And I do trust him. I hope I can trust Fran as well.

Throwing myself on the bed, I try very hard to erase all negative thoughts from my mind. I intend to close my eyes for ten minutes, which actually elapses to nearly an hour.

Downstairs, Rose introduces me to six pristine female beauty therapists who have been hired by Lucca—three from the spa at his Lanarkshire club and three from his Glasgow club. They have brought all their equipment and have set up in the indoor pool area with individual bamboo screens separating six beauty beds.

The area has been transformed into a tranquil, sweet smelling haven of exotic lotus blossom, sandalwood, and passion flower. There are candles everywhere, floating candles in the pool, the mood lighting is on with some little fairy lights, and all sorts of professional products lined up. Each bed has a white robe folded on the end, white slippers, and a gift bag filled with products and makeup for each of us.

The girls will love this. Lucca does think of everything. I'm extremely grateful.

After a commotion bypassing the Men in Black, the girls all arrive together. Samantha is really impressed with the house and décor; she's speechless even in the hallway, which reminds me of the first time I stepped foot in here. I'm used to it now, but I recall my first impressions. *Overwhelmed.*

"Bloody hell, Roo, it's easier getting into Buckingham Palace than in here. Lucca has taken your break-in very seriously, which is good, but did he really have to get the Royal Guards?" Hazel gripes, giving me a huge cuddle.

I shrug. "He doesn't do things by half."

"Um ... no he certainly doesn't," she says, tapping her middle finger on her chin.

I ask Hazel to give Sam and Carrie the tour while Devon shows Harriet, my hairdresser, in after asking for appropriate identification and searching her kit bag.

Really? As if my hairdresser carries weapons in a bag with pink rollers and plans to take me out with a hair pin. Honestly, this ludicrous behaviour is wearing thin.

The girls all squeal with delight when they see the pool deck set up for the pampering and take pleasure in their little bag of treats. I know I should be a little more enthused as Lucca has put a lot of consideration and arrangements into this evening, but I'm too preoccupied wondering how his dinner date with Fran is going.

The house is buzzing because Lloyd also brings in some catering staff and a cocktail waiter who work at Luminara—Lucca's club, bar, and restaurant—after the routine checks. Devon remains outside while Lloyd stays inside keeping watch on the extra hired staff. Hazel strops because Devon's Irish accent's growing on her.

Bloody horny flirt!

"Oh my God, we have a cocktail waiter. Girls, I wonder if he serves frozen margaritas in the buff? The Royal Guards could be the male strippers; going by the way they wear those suits." Hazel smirks. The girls laugh and I dismiss her impishness while I show the staff where to set up in the kitchen.

After introductions and completing health questionnaires, our individual beauty therapists give us the robes and a folder with a schedule and list of treatments we can have. We sit on the loungers next to the pool sipping strawberry daiquiris, gossiping, and nibbling on delicious canapés.

We've been appointed ninety minutes of treatments before dinner, then an additional ninety minutes of treatments, and maybe a dip in the pool if we have time.

We finish a second cocktail, a peach mojito, and another round of canapés before running through our choices with our therapist. I'm not comfortable with other people massaging my body, unless it's Lucca. I ask for an Indian head massage—hoping it will relieve some of my stress—an exotic moisture dew facial, and a full leg, underarm, and bikini wax too.

We're given jugs of iced lemon water in preparation and are then taken to our individual areas. The lights are dimmed as tranquil music plays. Samantha has to warn Hazel to keep quiet so that we can all relax. I chuckle, knowing it's going to be a challenge for her. All I can hear is her asking the therapist questions about cellulite, collagen, and laser treatments.

It's only a matter of minutes before everyone is drugged, deep in the heady trance of relaxation.

No sound from Hazel. Results, she's been tranquilised!

I have so many things going through my mind it's taking me a little longer to relax. I'm stiff and tense to begin with until the charming Dana triggers essential pressure points allowing my head to fall heavily until I feel light.

Inhaling the sweet tropical scent of mangos, nectarine, and papaya, I think of Lucca's exotic smelling skin mixed with the sexy masculine fusion of his aftershave, causing an unsettling pain in my stomach—worry.

Over dinner in the dining room, we are given lots more water to rehydrate us, but we do have some Kir Royals with our three course à la carte Italian-inspired meal. Everyone is thoroughly relaxed with fresh glowing skin, wrapped under their robes, feeling very soothed and pampered.

"Girls, I don't know about you, but I feel horny as hell. It's seriously turning me on. That chick has got magic hands," Hazel says discreetly with the look of mischief, the look where she raises her eyebrow and smirks impishly.

Choking, I spray my drink everywhere, holding my hand to my mouth in complete shock.

"She's a dirty bloody minx," Samantha says, chuckling.

Carrie is very quiet. It never occurred to us that she would find it pleasurably erotic, but of course, being gay she might.

"Carrie, don't you go slipping the hand," Hazel remarks, causing everyone to laugh. Carrie shakes her head, but I can tell she's amused at Hazel's sense of humour under her heated, rosy cheeks.

She says Nicole is the only girl who does it for her, and we all roll our eyes, smiling.

"I bet you two are kinky fuckers in bed," Hazel adds. Now Carrie is turning flame red. Hazel is a liability with that sassy, smart mouth. I wish she'd zip it.

Harriet adjusts a chair for me; I don't even have to give her any direction for my haircut. She does what she always does and knows best. Dana works on my fingernails, giving them a manicure, and pedicure to my toes. Once Harriet has finished my cut, Dana waxes and tints my eyebrows and eyelashes.

I can't believe the difference. My eyelashes are much more prominent now that they are darker. Not as dark and bushy as Lucca's, but still it's a great improvement.

"Are you going back in the pool?" Harriet asks.

"Yes, probably. Why, what's up?"

"Nothing, I won't dry your hair then. You can style it yourself after you wash it. Not that you need to because, you know, it's going to dry naturally in a bounce of sexy waves. You have the best hair, Lexi. You're very lucky."

I thank her profusely and offer her champagne, but she refuses as she has to drive. She does however leave me some quality hair products.

We all change into swimwear once the therapists and catering staff are packed up. They're escorted by Lloyd, and then he does another sweep of the house, switching positions with Devon, leaving only the cocktail waiter, whom we've learned is called Mack since Hazel made a point of flirting with him.

Mack makes us another two cocktails each then retires for the evening. Once he's left, Lloyd advises he will run any of the girls home while Devon stays on watch. Men in Black are not so bad after all, either that or I'm getting very tipsy and more tolerant.

The girls go into the pool and sauna while I sit in the kitchen and call Lucca to thank him for tonight. No answer, so I leave a voicemail. Smiling when I see Lucca's name light up on my phone screen, I answer quickly.

"Hey, honey."

"Lexi, it is Francesca," she says in her sexy, Italian-English. The hairs on my arms prick up as does my upper body in my chair.

"Hi, Fran, is everything alright? Where's Lucca?" I ask anxiously.

"Yes, everything is fine. Lucca has fallen asleep. He had some wine at dinner and scotch afterwards. He insisted I get home okay so he had his driver bring me back and showed me upstairs to my penthouse but then passed out, so I am letting him sleep it off. Giorgio had to leave early and attend to business so I cannot call him to come and get him." Rage burns in the deepest dark cave of my stomach.

Fuck!

File F for fiancé stealer. This is what I was afraid of.

"He's staying there, with you?" I try to mask the distaste I'm feeling for that arrangement.

"Yes, I cannot very well send him back to the hotel like this. You have nothing to worry about. I am not drinking because of my medication, and I will take good care of him."

No, please don't. I don't want you to.

That has just made me feel worse. I now feel queasy and sick.

"Why is he drinking whiskey? What's happened? Why is he getting trashed? Something's up." I feel agitated and nervous and so helpless not being there with him.

"He has had a challenging few days with the business. I am sure it was not intentional. Just fatigue and stress," she reassures.

This sounds plausible, but he knows how I feel about abusive drinking, and about him staying with Fran. It must be bad for him to lose control like this.

"Can I speak with him, Fran?" I choke.

"I can hold the phone to him, but he is slurring his words, so he will not make much sense."

"Where is he sleeping?" It is direct and rude, but I need to know. The hairs on my neck and back stand erect, and I'm stinging with needle like pricks to my skin. I'm edgy.

"In my bed. I will take the single in the spare room. Lexi, you have nothing to worry about because he loves you. He is just very drunk," she assures me.

"I'm sorry. I know, it's just ... can I try and speak to him?" I swallow a huge lump in my throat. This is tearing me to shreds. I want to look after him, to be there for him.

"Okay, hold on." I hear her muffled sounds and then Fran speaking quickly, all in Italian which I can't decipher. "I am not promising, but I will put the phone to his ear."

"Thank you."

"Lucca, Lucca, it's me. Wake up, I need to talk to you."

I hear groaning then a series of slurred words. "Le ... x ... ba ... y ... are you rea ... l? Are you ali ... ve?"

"What? Of course, I am. What are you going on about?"

"He will not ta ... ke you ever. I will not let ... it ... hap ..." A low growl emits from him.

Is he talking about Jackson? Why on earth would he get drunk because he thinks I'm being seduced by another guy? Is he trying to get me back by staying with Fran? Well, if he's trying to hurt me, he's succeeding.

"No one is taking me. Why did you get drunk, Lucca?" I soften my tone.

"I will die firs-s-st. She nearly killed me, but you will. You will kill … me because you t-t-tear-r-r me apart, I pro … tect you … uu, but he needs to kill me firs-s-s-t. Do you hear … r-r-r?"

Pain.

"Stop it! You don't know what you're talking about." He's upsetting me and scaring me with his words.

"Yes-s-s … I lov-v-vedd her, she left … you … not leavin'," he babbles incoherently.

A sharp knife is severing through my chest and tearing at my heart because the pain is acute and incisive.

Torn.

Shredded.

Lacerated.

I could bleed right here, alone and agonised. Closing my eyes, I imagine the sharp knife tip tapping slowly before it punctures right through my heart to stop it from beating.

It's not until I'm forced to breathe that I realise I've been holding my breath.

Gasping.

Air.

Gasping.

Air.

Pain.

Pain.

Air.

Disconnecting the call, I switch my phone off and put my face in my hands. Crying for the next five minutes, feeling totally crushed and wishing I had never spoken to him and glad Rose isn't privy to yet another breakdown. I freshen up, trying to maintain my composure, pour myself a large glass of water, and take a new, unopened bottle of champagne through to the pool for the girls.

I place it down for them then go into the steam room, hoping that it will help mask my teary cheeks, and it does. I manage to pass it off, although my stomach is in turmoil. Afterward, I stand under the freezing cold shower, trying to numb the burning fire scalding my heart.

It's well after midnight and we're still sitting in the Jacuzzi. Impulsively, I say something I know later I will regret. "Girls, do you want to go out tomorrow night in town? The way we used to on a Thursday, to a nice bar ... just us?"

"Yes, I'll drink to that. Chin-chin!" Sam and Carrie sing together, clinking their glasses.

Hazel's eyes light up with excitement. "What about the Royal Guards? Won't be much fun with them lurking over us."

She's right. We can't sneeze without them making a move, and it wouldn't be a girls' night with them hovering.

"I need a plan to sneak away from them for a night. I can't breathe when they're around," I reply.

"Okay, I have an idea. Let's say we're all going to Jessica's. Get them to drop you off. We'll keep the blinds closed and the music up so they think we are there. Then we'll call a taxi and sneak out the back door. They won't see from the front, and we'll use the back road." Hazel sounds like an international spy, tapping her middle finger on her chin.

Such a drama queen.

She has us huddled together and whispering, even though Lloyd and Devon are not in the pool area, and we're foolishly butting our heads together, looking over our shoulders as if we've been assigned a secret mission.

We high five on it. Then the girls towel dry and wrap their robes over their pyjamas as they gather all their items. Merrily drunk, they stagger out dressed in their sleepwear and have Lloyd drive them home.

He's getting a treat tonight. I bet he loves his job now!

Limping into the bedroom, I find Hazel standing nude next to my bed. "Eh, what you up to?"

"I'm going to bed." She shrugs her shoulders and topples over against the bed.

"Not like that. Get some underwear or pyjamas on. I don't want you slipping the hand with me after feeling all horny tonight." We both burst out laughing at her brassiness. I throw her a T-shirt, which she fumbles into, and we collapse in bed. We are too tired and past it for the DBB chat tonight. I don't tell her about my phone call with Lucca, but I'm comforted when she wraps her arms around me, and we fall fast asleep.

"Oh God, my head is pounding," Hazel says.

"Get your legs off me, blooming pest." I push her off me, freeing and stretching my hot cramped legs.

"Oh God, I feel awful," she groans, throwing her arm across her head.

"Well, you should have drank water before you went to bed." I can't hold my laughter. She looks as if she has been electrocuted when she allows her hair to dry naturally.

She pulls a pillow over her head and groans. "Lexi, go and get painkillers, or better still, ask your Royal Guards to bring them up."

Shaking my head, I shuffle to the bathroom and get painkillers and water for us both. "They're not bloody servants," I reprimand.

"Whatever, I need to sleep this off if we're back on it tonight. My body is a temple after all." She groans from under a pillow.

Oh hell, I was hoping she'd forget about tonight. "Maybe we should leave it, especially if everyone has a hangover."

Hazel tosses the pillow and stares at me. "No way. It was your idea, and you look as if you need cheering up. I know you were crying last night. Are you going to tell me what's it about?"

Like Lucca, she is so observant.

I tell her what happened, every part that I remember from the phone call. She says I'm over reacting; he was probably just drunk and rambling and then she cuddles and comforts me. Nothing a night out with the girls can't cure. We fall back asleep after she thinks she's convinced me it's nothing to worry about, but the reality is I am worried about it.

Very much so.

Rose knocks on the bedroom door a little after one in the afternoon. "Sorry to interrupt, Lexi, but Lucca has been trying to call you. He has asked you call him immediately."

"Okay, Rose. Thank you." I won't be calling him anytime soon. I'm pissed and letting him stew.

"I've made lunch. French toast BLT club sandwiches. Do you want to come down or shall I bring it up?" Hazel yawns and sits up in bed smiling at Rose.

"We were going to lounge in bed a little longer if that is all right?" I honestly do love this woman.

"Yes, of course, I'll bring it up. Did you enjoy your night?"

"It was a lovely night, thank you."

She returns with a tray of fresh orange juice and fruit, a yogurt, and stacked French toast with bacon, lettuce, tomatoes, and mayo. I kiss her on the cheek to thank her. She truly is a keeper.

"It's like being on holiday. You're so lucky. Hotel, motel, Holiday Inn," Hazel chants before she scoffs into her sandwich. "Oh God, we'll be in a carb coma with this later but it will definitely help my hangover."

I pick at my food and then fall asleep again when Hazel is in the shower. "You could sleep standing up, do you know that?"

Yawning, I have to agree I've been exceptionally tired lately. It must be all the stress. Hazel studies me and sighs and says I do look exceptionally tired and that she's worried about me. I convince her it is just all the late nights and drama this week.

Once we're up and dressed, Rose lets me know that Peter has taken Doris out on a walk for me. I decide to go with Hazel to my old house for some normalcy and check in on Mr. Carlin. Lloyd is waiting by the car, talking into a device with an earpiece in.

"Miss Robertson, Mr. Caruso would like to speak with you," Lloyd says.

I'm sure he would.

I slip my Chopard sunglasses over my tired eyes, deterring the rolling of said tired eyes.

"Please, Lloyd, call me Lexi and tell him I'll call him later. I'm riding with Hazel."

He clears his throat and clenches his jaw. "No, I'm sorry, I can't let you do that," he firmly says.

I hold my hand up directly in front of his peripheral vision. "I'm going with Hazel." I don't back down either. I'm not in the mood to be controlled right now. I've made a choice and I'm sticking with it.

His stern look tells me he objects as he mutters something into the device. Devon takes Lloyd's position as I shamble into Hazel's car. Of course, Lloyd follows us closely in his black SUV and will be infuriated, no doubt, at my lack of cooperation.

Oh please!

I'm greeted by Cameron on his way out to work, only to get a scolding for not going in the car with Lloyd. Like Lloyd, I ignore Cameron, along with his nagging me to call Lucca which gets filed in compartment – *Later!*

Fuck!

File I for ignoring. Ignoring Lucca's persistent pleas. Ignoring Cameron's brotherly bossiness.

Ignored!

Cameron actually looks very tired as if he's not had any sleep. Anna has likely been keeping him busy.

Don't care.

Can't care.

No care.

Not today anyway.

Chapter 26: Truth!

After almost overheating in Mr. Carlin's for over an hour, I return to my house and go back to my old bedroom, close the door, and slide under the covers falling asleep again. Lloyd is still outside and no doubt expecting me, but I never asked for this security, and I want time alone.

In my own bed.

In my own house.

Me ... alone.

"Lexi, wake up. You've been sleeping all bloody day. Lucca has been phoning everyone. I've had to send Lloyd away three times telling him you don't want to be disturbed, but if you don't get up and check in, he'll come up here." Hazel sits on my bed waving her hand about.

"What? Who? What are you rambling about?" I'm so disoriented being awakened so abruptly.

"Lloyd, you idiot. He's going to come up; Lucca is going batshit fucking crazy with worry."

Of course he is.

"Yeah, just like I went crazy with worry last night. What time is it?" I'm in such an ornery mood.

"It's 5:30 p.m. You need to make yourself seen so our escape plan works later." She holds her hand out for me to get moving. Sighing, I drag my ass out of bed, much against my will.

"I'll meet you at Jess's at 7:30 p.m. sharp. Bring a change of clothes so they don't get suspicious if you're dolled up. Taxi is booked for 8:00 p.m. Fine?"

"Fine. I can't believe I'm going along with this. It's outrageous." But then I can't believe Lucca stayed at Fran's last night and said some of those things and part of me wants to retaliate and make a choice, a choice to go out—let my hair down, and forget about Lucca's words and Fran being with him.

"Yes and so are we ... outrageous, now move." She smacks my ass as I hobble downstairs.

"Miss Robertson, I was just about to look for you, everything alright?" Lloyd addresses me at the bottom of the stairs. Hazel shoots the "*I told you so*" look at me.

"Yes, no need. I was sleeping. Can you take me home now, please, Lloyd?" I ask, walking out to the SUV.

"Yes, but you need to speak with Mr. Caruso. It's imperative."

"I'll call him privately from the house." He stifles his reply, an intense, strained look on his face and grinds his teeth.

Grind away. I'm not doing it.

Leaning my head against the window on the drive home, I reflect in my melancholy state. My mind is racing with confusion, anger, and apprehension. Closing my eyes, I imagine being in the Tuscan farmhouse, free of worries, just Lucca and me without complications.

"Miss Robertson, there is mail for you. It's on the console in the hall," Devon says when I reach the front door.

Although I'm warming to him, and he does have an enticing accent, I'm still peeved with my lack of privacy. It appears he's going to get the brunt of it since Lloyd took the hint and remained quiet, sensing my foul mood.

"Why don't you just tell me what it is since you've opened it anyway and save me the bother." Not waiting for a reply, I go straight upstairs into the bedroom and slump on the bed. I need to keep my eyes open before I fall asleep again, so I decide to shower and do my makeup.

I style my hair, apply my makeup and body butter cream, and add jewellery. Then I scroll through the clothes racks in my dressing room. I wear jeans and a T-shirt and my new converse, but put the sexy Alexander McQueen orange bustier dress from Firenze in a bag. I also take the black patent leather peep toes with the gold winged skull brooch and the matching clutch, some makeup, perfume, and my purse. It occurs to me that it might be a bit too adventurous wearing high heels with an ankle sprain, but they match the outfit and I'm not planning on dancing so I won't be on my feet. I'm so used to seeing bruises on my body that one to my ankle doesn't faze me.

"Are you going out?" Rose asks, placing some fresh baked goodies on the counter.

"Yes, just over to Jessica's for a movie night." I hate lying to Rose. I'm so close to calling this deceitful plan off because I hate dishonesty.

"Have you had dinner yet?" She frowns.

"Not yet. I'll just grab something quick."

"Have you spoken with Lucca?" she asks. Shamefully, I drop my head in silence. "Petal, it's none of my business, it's up to you to sort out, but he's frantic and you're obviously miserable. Lloyd mentioned something." She gently rubs my arm and says she'll make me a quick Spanish omelette.

"Thank you, Rose. I'm sorry. I'm hurt and angry now, but I will speak to him, I promise." She gives me a sympathetic smile.

While I eat she enlightens me about some of Lucca's pigheaded, stubbornness and laughs about them. I want to laugh, but I can't. Not tonight.

I finish the omelette then give her a huge kiss and appreciative hug.

Devon is my designated driver tonight, which is awkward because I was so sharp with him earlier. "I'm sorry about earlier. I've just had a stressful few days and it's draining me," I say to him from the back of the SUV.

"No need to apologise. We don't take it personally. It's imperative to remain impassive and professional at all times in our line of work, as it can be a stressful and emotional time for clients."

"Thank you."

He remains focused on the road but nods his head in acknowledgement. Who would have thought Men in Black could be so compassionate? I wonder whether they'll both be coming up north with us to visit my family. That will be interesting, turning up with bodyguards. Granny of course will love it and tell everyone in the village about our security, but my mum will be sick with worry. That's another concern entirely.

I try to convince Devon I'll just get a taxi home, but he's not flinching, so I explain it will be a late night. He nods and parks in Jess's driveway, reaching for an e-reader device from the glove compartment.

Happy reading, it's going to be a long night.

I do feel a bit bad he's going to be left for a long time outside in the vehicle. Before exiting, I thank him in barely a whisper. I'm not sure he even heard me.

The rest of the girls arrive refreshed after our cocktails last night. Oblivious to my rift with Lucca, they're exceptionally appreciative for last night's generosity and together have got him a little gift and signed a thank you card which makes my heart melt.

Smart cuff links for his suits. Jessica purchased them today, but it's from all of the girls. I need to dam the bubbling tears about to flood and clamp my quivering lip in a firm line at their gesture. They are so considerate and I love them all dearly.

The tears are there flooding my eyes, but I'm conscious not to ruin their night, so we group hug when they see me emotional. Right now, I cherish my friends, and the love I feel for Lucca is consuming, which is why I'm even sadder about last night.

They've all brought a change of clothes. Changing into our dresses, we drink two large glasses of wine while waiting on the taxi. Jess leaves the TV, music, and lights on for safe measure.

"Ready?" Carrie asks.

"Yes, let's just go before I change my mind," I reply. I'm a grown woman and am supposed to be mature and sensible, yet I feel irresponsible, selfish, and childish doing this.

"You are one sexy chick. You look better than a million dollars. Seriously stunning, Lex," Sam says, running her hand over my dress.

"She's right, you're going to stop traffic, sexy Lexi," Lucy adds, admiring my new designer look.

Blushing at their compliments has me thinking of the day Lucca nearly had an aneurism when I wore this outfit at the Four Seasons Hotel in Florence. It's very sexy and just what I need to boost my depreciating confidence today.

The taxi drops us off at BarAsta, an exclusive cocktail bar and club in Glasgow with private membership only access. One of the many perks of being the future Mrs. Caruso has proven useful. We're shown to a private booth area surrounded by silver and crystal chains hanging from the ceiling, acting as a decorative but shielding curtain, and we're surrounded by tall, exotic flowers in large shapely vases. It's very pretty.

The bar is starting to fill with many recognisable socialites; it's rather pretentious, but the girls love it, so I go along with their optimistic excitement and pretend I'm enjoying myself. Determined to stay upbeat for them, I join in on their girly fun despite my stomach churning for Lucca and the nagging ache from my throbbing ankle. I thought tonight would help me forget, but I can't seem to get him out of my mind.

I've opted to stay with Southern Comfort as opposed to cocktails tonight. It's the most sensible option having had my fill of cocktails last night. The girls squeal and bounce out of their chairs to dance when their favourite R&B club remix blasts from the speakers.

Using this opportunity to boycott the ass shaking, I make my escape to use the restrooms. Wincing as I stand in my heels, I bite the inside of my cheek, put my clutch under my arm, and signal to the girls that I'm going to the bathroom.

Shambling past the huge centre oval bar, I'm conscious of people staring at me. The hungry eyes of men linger on me, while the women on their arms are rapacious with their beady eyes like intimidating predators. Keeping my head straight, I try to ignore the sleazy glances from a group of business men at an exposed raised glass table in front of a glass and water screen.

I hobble through this futuristic maze, past the ornamental sculptures, hanging screens of silver beaded chains, and full-length glass panels with water flowing inside. These waterfall panels conceal more private booths. The screens I like; they're very swish. As I weave through, I'm camouflaged and given privacy from prying eyes. I like that even more.

It's easy to make out shapes, colours, and body outlines through the opaque panels, but they do act as a great cover-up from the painful anguish evident on my face. Right now, I regret stepping out in this sexy little dress with the attention it's drawing, and walking in these heels is proving very difficult which adds to my discomfort. I should have brought a pair of flats to change into.

Exiting the restroom, I notice the bar has become more populated and is much busier with minimal empty spaces between the suspended silver curtains and glass panels. I suppose the temporary mask between these dividers was short lived. When I get back to the table, I plan on kicking these shoes off and not moving again tonight.

I'm unnerved with an image of someone I think I see in my peripheral vision exiting a booth in the corner, but it's difficult to be sure under the hazy mask from behind these screens. Maybe I'm paranoid, but then I'm sure I'm right. Another glance.

Fuck!

File C for confirmative. Confirmative intruder. Yes I'm positive.

Shit.

Oh God. Not here, not now. Why oh why?

Taking two more unsteady steps, I'm conscious I need to discreetly fade into the crowd behind the partitions before I'm seen. My heart hammering against my chest causes me to fluster and stumble on my sore ankle. I lose balance and I'm about to topple over when a pair of muscular hands wrap around my waist pulling me back up and turning me around.

A sexy male voice says, "Falling again? It really is your specialty, Alexis."

Jackson.

Oh dear Lord.

"Thank you, Jackson, for once again helping me in my klutziness." I purse my lips and blush.

He looks sexy, smart, and handsome. His rich chocolaty eyes have doubled in size, literally staring at me, all of me, head to toe.

"You look absolutely stunning. You are simply beautiful. You always are, Alexis, but Jesus you're hot shit tonight. I like your dress it's um ... *very* ... nice." He smiles his photogenic smile, smouldering in a tailored suit, shirt, and tie.

His brown hair is styled in male model fashion. His coffee brown eyes are rich and dark and he smells divine. He's not as sexy or handsome as Lucca, not even close, but he's undoubtedly attractive, and I notice it more tonight because he's smartly dressed and well groomed.

Fuck!

File W for worst. Worst fiancée in the world having inappropriate thoughts.

"Thank you," I reply. His hands are still wrapped around my waist, and it's not lost on me that he hasn't let go.

"How's the ankle? Should you be wearing those killer heels? Sexy but not very practical."

"Truthfully, it's killing me. I can barely walk in them and they need to come off." He frowns then instantly scoops me up and walks towards one of the private booths behind a glass panel of running water. He places me down on a white leather sofa and slips my shoes off.

Again, impressing me with his chivalry. Fuckity-fuck!

It's heaven to wiggle and rotate my ankle. "Thank you, but you realise they won't go back on now?" I sigh, but he laughs.

"Well, looks as if you're in a bother then." I manage a pitiful laugh despite my humiliation and feeling sorry for myself. "Is everything okay? I mean, other than the ankle? You just seem very … distracted." Sounding more sincere, he leans back on the sofa, undoes his tie and top button of his shirt, then throws his tie on the glass oval table in front of us.

Please don't. Too friggin sexy.

"That's better. I hate those fucking things."

I smile at his honesty, and he has a way of making me feel more relaxed.

"Yes, I just saw someone whom I'd rather not have the pleasure of a confrontation with this evening, so I panicked to get away," I confess.

"Hmmm, so you're trying to hide?"

"You could say that, yes."

"I saw you come in with your friends. Where's Lucca?" he asks. I need to let the girls know where I am, they will come looking for me.

Just the mention of Lucca has me anxious. I'm pining so much for him, missing him terribly, and feel guilty for ignoring his calls. I wish he was back and I knew what the hell was going on with him. I need his arms wrapped around me. I want him close to me. I'm still infuriated, but I'm vulnerable and I want him with me even more than ever.

Sighing, I explain. "Lucca isn't back until tomorrow. The girls have brought me out to cheer me up."

"Why? What's up?"

"I've got 24-7 security, two bloody bodyguards suffocating me, so the girls helped me sneak out. Please don't tell Cameron though." I chew the inside of my cheek.

Jackson bursts into a fit of laughter with a coy cheeky smirk framing his sexy lips.

"So you're on the run?"

"Yes."

"Oh dear. I've got round the clock bodyguards too. Although, you wouldn't know it; they're very discreet. They're here with me as we had a press conference earlier, but I'm so used to it now. I just go about my business. I've no choice. I need to have them. They're not so bad."

Being a celebrity I suppose he does warrant protection, but it's ridiculous that I would need them. He watches me form a spiritless smile, unconvinced.

"Hold on, I'll be back in a minute." He moves out of the private booth to the other end of the glass panel, but now I can't see him as it acts as a complete concealed wall of water. Odd, I never noticed the water before. It just looked like opaque glass.

He's only away a moment then returns. "I've asked for a message to be sent to your friends to let them know you're here and you're good." Gratefully, I shrug and smile.

"Thank you."

"Okay, would you like a drink? And you can tell me why you need protection."

Is he serious?

I wasn't planning on staying here, but I'm not exactly walking anywhere just yet—unless I go barefoot—and I do want to keep hidden until my worst nightmare has left the vicinity. Lucca would be furious with me if he knew I was out without Men in Black, and alone with Jackson. Although, it's all completely innocent.

I hope everything with Lucca last night was completely innocent, but then the fire burns in my stomach with worry again. Meeting his hopeful eyes, I compulsively reply, "Yes, a drink would be lovely, thank you." He smiles then strolls out the booth and returns with a bottle of expensive champagne in an ice bucket and one champagne flute.

"You're not having any?" I ask. He shakes his head, disappears again, and returns with a jug of iced water and two glasses.

"I'm training tomorrow. I can't drink alcohol."

"Oh." Dear Lord.

I'll be sitting here like a drunken idiot and he'll be sober, and I'll say things that later I wish I had kept filed in the mental library.

The cold champagne is lovely and easy on the palate. I feel much more relaxed when the bubbles start going to my head and try to forget all about my worldly worries. Jackson and I talk about properties and Lucca's empire, my friends, his family, his career. I could easily be sitting talking to Cameron, Dominic, Steve, or Justin—the girls' partners.

Our conversations have been refreshing and very down to earth. Not awkward or uncomfortable. Easy, actually.

Excusing myself, I stand to go to the bathroom and with the alcohol overtaking my rationality; I intend to hobble barefoot as I have no choice. Taking a few steps, Jackson sweeps me up and carries me. "You might step on glass. I'll wait outside for you," he says.

I'm too sore and tipsy to protest. One of his bodyguards watches us from outside the booth then moves over to stand next to him. He places me down in front of the bathroom. Thanking him, I smooth out the bottom of my dress then go inside. Exiting after quickly drying my hands, he's waiting on me and sweeps me off my feet again before the door even closes.

He only manages to get two long strides towards the booth when flashing lights stop him in his track and he tilts his head downwards and turns around. Someone is taking photographs of us.

Oh shit.

Gasping, I instinctively close my eyes, turning my head away, covering my face with my hair. His body tenses at being photographed, yet he still doesn't put me down. I can't look up. I'm too ashamed but his bodyguard has intervened and confiscated the phone from the person taking the pictures. The flash is a trigger for my anxiety and sends me into a panic, my worst fears resurrected. Being photographed. Hazel must be walking towards the bathroom or coming to get me and stops in her tracks to witness the whole thing because I can hear her squawking.

"What the hell is going on?" Hazel screeches.

It's the voice objecting and whining about the phone that penetrates through me, turning my stomach and forcing me to pry my eyes wide open. I'm angry and in no way surprised.

"Does Lucca know you're whoring about with a footballer behind his back? I'm sure he'd love this. I knew you were a dishonest little slut."

Kimberley!

Stunned.

Shocked.

Soured.

"That's enough," Jackson snaps.

"Kimberley, I have nothing to say to you." I can almost taste blood because I've bitten my inside lip so hard with rage.

The bodyguard grabs her arm pulling her into the booth we were using to avoid unwanted attention. Jackson follows him in and sets me on the sofa, and Hazel also joins us, standing next to me with hand on hip.

"Please leave. I don't want to speak to you," I say to Kimberley.

"You heard the good lady, if you do not go, we will escort you off the premises." I'm now thankful for the intervention and assistance from security in moments like this.

"Not until we have a little chat." She is smarmy and devious, even her deceitful voice sickens me.

"I've nothing I want to say to you Kimberley." My tone scathing.

"You heard her, Kimberley, why don't you just piss off. No one likes you and you're like a fucking rash we can't get rid of," Hazel adds.

"You're worried because I've caught you cheating on Lucca?" She scoffs pointing at me, completely ignoring Hazel.

I'm ablaze with fury and heat and intend to lash back at her. I'm not taking any of her nonsense. I'm so enraged that I could spit venom on her and singe her with it too.

"Shut up. You don't know what you're saying. I'm not cheating on Lucca, and I never would. Jackson happens to be a friend, and he's carrying me because I have an ankle injury. Not that it's any of your business."

"I knew it all along. You're just a money grabbing slut. Now you're after his money too *and* apparently fame. Typical. Lucca doesn't deserve this." She lifts her chin and flicks her hair over her shoulder.

I practically jump up out my seat ready to launch myself at her until Hazel and Jackson both grab an arm holding me back. "You're an evil, spiteful, jealous little girl, Kimberley. I don't appreciate your fucking meddling in our lives. I've had to have twenty-four hour security protection because of you and your petulant sinister twisted fucking games. You'll never get away with it, and Lucca will make sure your resume will be so tarnished you'll never get another decent job!" I shout.

"Is that what he told you? I happen to know different." She smirks then laughs. I want to wipe that smirk right off her face.

My body temperature rises, my head pounds, and my heart thunders out of control. She's lying to provoke me. Jesus, I don't think I can hold back.

Blazing.

Hot blistering fire.

Deep inside.

"Kimberley, you've got three fucking seconds before I drag you out myself!" Hazel barks.

"Alright, you asked for it. I've done some meddling, and it turns out your past has come back to haunt you. I don't need to waste my time hating you because apparently I'm not the only one who despises you." She smiles, being very aloof.

"I don't have time for your shit," I hiss. Pulling my arms free and shaking my head, I pick my clutch up and my shoes in the other hand and turn to leave.

"Does the name Michael Parks mean anything to you?" I freeze, completely shocked, offended, and scandalised she even knows about him. I almost choke, holding my breath far too long.

No words.

No words.

No words.

"It appears he's got unfinished business and is in the UK, looking for you coincidently." She smacks her bitchy lips satisfied with her attempt to break me.

She has.

I'm broken.

"You fucking lying little bitch," Hazel spits. Losing all sense of awareness, the blood rushes from my head. I can't take it. I can't process it. I can't breathe.

Air, air, need air.

"Why do you think you need security? He's back to harm you. To take you or something. I don't fucking know why, but I know that's why you have security. I'm the least of your worries." She speaks fast, trying to get her piece in before she's thrown out. I haven't turned around but I sense her approach me, she puts her hand on my shoulder to get my attention before someone drags her sorry ass back.

Hazel.

Time seems to stand still; the quarrelling chaos behind me is nothing but a muffled echo which I've zoned out of. The shock has traumatised me. Blood thrums in my ears, jaw slack and eyes glossed over.

Staggering out of the booth in slow motion, barely breathing, I think I'm hallucinating when familiar azure blue eyes are drawing me closer amidst the bustling crowds. Seizing me. Owning me. Lucca's azure blue eyes have locked on me. He's sprinting towards me.

Is it him?

It can't be.

I want it to be him.

I need it to be him.

My head spins.

I drop my clutch and shoes, forgoing filling my lungs with oxygen. My legs give way, every muscle in my body limp, and I'm consumed by dizziness, haziness. What is happening?

"Lexi, baby, Jesus, Lexi ... Fuck!"

"LUCCA?" I cry just before collapsing on my knees. In a swift move he has me lifted in his protective arms.

I hold tight. I hold tighter than I ever have before.

My head's spinning and I don't want to open my eyes. Seconds later, I flutter my eyelashes under the reflecting bright lights of the booth, still wrapped tight in Lucca's arms on the sofa, and wonder if I'm hallucinating or if I've been drugged. I need this to be real, to feel him and nothing else.

I NEED HIM.

I inhale his masculine, sexy scent—the familiar scent that intoxicated me the first time I met him. I press into his muscular body, burying my head deeper against him, feeling his hot breath on my neck, and the realisation that it's him causes tears to flow down my cheeks.

"Fuck, Lexi. Are you okay, sweetheart? Tell me you are okay."

It's him.

My Lucca.

My love.

The love.

L'amore.

I can't speak yet because I'm so upset, but I dig my fingers into him to acknowledge I'm relieved to be in his arms. There is talking and commotion behind me but I zone out. I focus on the beating of Lucca's heart. I imagine it's him and our heartbeats still in time. I don't even know how much time has elapsed.

"Shit. Why is she not speaking? Talk to me, Doc," he begs, kissing the side of my head repeatedly.

"She's in shock. She's chalk white," Hazel says, sitting beside us on the sofa, pouring me water and holding the glass in front of me. I'm numb, frozen, and iced over, blood running cold. I stare at the glass but can't quite manoeuvre my hands to reach for it, so she sets it back down.

Without moving my head, I can hear Lucy, Sam, Carrie, and Jess chirping and asking what's going on. Hazel must have brought them in. Then I remember why I'm here in the first place.

Oh God.

I wonder what I've missed if there will be a blood bath when Lucca takes out Jackson. Lucca takes my face in both hands and drops his head, his lips marrying to mine.

Sweetly.

Tenderly.

Lovingly.

I close my eyes when his soft lips meet mine, remembering just how much I've missed this. My lips quiver and I tremble. He holds his lips on mine, breathing heavy, the hot air from his nostrils warming my upper lip and nose. I inwardly murmur, not sure whether he can hear me.

Kiss.

Kiss.

Kiss.

His soft lips have me feeling extremely helpless and needy, and for a brief moment the fright and astonishment I'm feeling subsides and it's this small touch from him that temporarily diminishes my fear.

No fear.

Just this.

Just him.

He's gasping when he slowly pulls his lips back then leans in again to repeat his touch, and this time my murmur is more of a whimper.

"Lexi, speak to me," he whispers against my top lip. I say the only word I can form.

"Kimberley?"

"Do not worry, she has been taken care of. She is gone. I'll deal with her tomorrow," he presses his forehead against mine then gently rubs the pad of his thumb under my eyes.

"I'll have my driver take you girls home when you're ready to leave." It's Jackson's voice. I don't understand. He's still here?

Alive?

Why? I thought Lucca would have asked him to leave.

"Thank you, buddy," Lucca replies. It's the familiar trauma causing me disbelief. Why is Lucca being reasonable with him?

"Lucca?" I snivel.

"I am here, I am here," he comforts me.

"Is it true?" I force a whisper with minimal emotion.

He looks directly into my eyes with pain and anguish. He's hurting for me. He doesn't need to answer because his eyes have already confirmed everything. We have a silent conversation with only our eyes.

I plead.

He apologises.

No longer bright. His insipid azures narrow into my murky brown eyes. I'm revealing to him I'm scared, and he articulates he knows but he's here and will protect me. Blinking slowly, I express my love for him.

Our love.

The love.

L'amore.

We understand each other just fine. *Silent eloquence.*

"I am taking her somewhere private. I need to speak with Lexi alone. Jackson, mate, thanks for your help tonight. On this occasion, I am appreciative that you were here with her and she was not alone. Hazel, call Cameron and explain what has happened. Get him to phone Marco and Lloyd. Girls, I will get her to call you tomorrow. She is going to be fine. No one will get near her or harm her. I have her." He rocks me gently, bundling his hands in my hair, holding me tightly.

I draw in a deep breath of air, my bottom lip quivering; unaware I'm shivering and shaking.

"Baby, I have got you," he whispers in my ear. Kissing my cheek softly, moving my hair behind my ears, he lifts my arms and places them in his suit jacket wrapping it around my body to warm me.

He stands up with me, adjusting his arms. I don't care where I am or whose company I'm in. I clutch on with all my strength. I wrap my legs around his waist and my arms around his neck and bury my face into the crook of his neck. He kisses the side of my head, holding the top of my back and my ass under the round skirt of my dress.

"Girls, can you take her shoes and bag for her?"

I feel many light hands stroke my back; it's the caring touch of my girls … my darlin's … then a warm, more masculine hand on my shoulder. "Alexis, I'm sorry. If there is anything I can do to help, I will. You're in good hands. Lucca will take excellent care of you I'm sure." Jackson doesn't sound as carefree as before. He must be shocked with tonight's revelations and drama.

I've ruined his night.

I can't worry about Jackson or what he thinks.

Lucca is my priority and he's all the matters.

I hear Jackson's voice, concerned and etched with uncertainty, but I'm too numb to respond so I move my shoulders to confirm I heard him. Lucca whispers something to one of Jackson's bodyguards. In a flash I'm on the move, exiting the booth. The loud music blares in my sensitive drumming ears.

Closing my eyes, I clutch onto Lucca as if my life depends on it. He treads through the crowds and down a flight of stairs, holding me wrapped around him. We walk through a corridor and he stops.

"No one comes through here, understand?" he orders.

"Yes, Mr. Caruso, of course."

"I mean no one," he reiterates.

"Sure," the nervous doorman responds.

Opening my eyes, I see Lucca has opened a smoky glass door to a VIP area which is empty. It's in the same style of upstairs with the screens of glass, running water, and silver chains hanging from the ceiling with modern white and fuchsia pink accessories and furniture. The mood lighting is dull and low in comparison to the pristine bright white booths upstairs.

He walks up to the empty bar, holding me with one arm under my ass while the other fixes me a drink of water.

"Drink this." He sits me on the edge of the counter, still with his arm wrapped around my lower back and his chest pressed into my body. He holds the glass to my mouth. I tilt my head back, my teeth chattering against the glass, and manage to drink almost all of it.

Attentively wiping the water from my chin, he still has given me no explanation, but right now I don't think I want one. I want him as close as I can get him. It's the only feeling that will dissipate my fear, my anguish.

"I need to explain. I am so sorry, Lexi. I did not want to worry you. I did not want you to know. I have been out of my mind all fucking day, crazy with worry. Baby, I love you, I …"

I pull myself together to collect my cognitive thoughts then make my first movement since my frozen shock and place my finger on his lips.

"Tell me later. Right now I need you like I've never needed you before, please take this feeling away and make me feel you, nothing else." Removing my finger, I lean into kiss his lips forcefully, showing him what I want, what I need.

That small gesture is all it takes for him to groan and grab behind my head, scrunching a handful of hair in both hands as he assaults my mouth with his tongue. We kiss hard, we kiss passionately, and we kiss dirty, groaning into one another's mouth until my lips feel bruised and swollen.

My fear is almost gone … almost.

I need more.

My fear is replaced by lust—heady, sparking, yearning desire—and I don't want this to end. His sexy kissing has me shifting on the bar surface, wriggling and craving his touch to my wet throbbing sex. I tilt my pelvis and push my hips forward.

We don't exchange words, only sexy moans and groans.

Desperate.

Passionate.

Understanding.

Giving.

The lust I feel igniting inside me is more intense than the lust I felt my first time with Lucca in Italy because I know how he makes me feel.

Powerful.

Confident.

Alive.

Him. All of him.

We effortlessly follow our instincts and thrash, grope, and tease. He picks me back up while pushing his hard erection up against my needy sex and clashes his tongue with mine.

Dancing.

Smacking.

Biting.

I run my hands through his wavy hair, gripping tightly to show him the intensity I desire.

Rough.

Carnal.

Raucous.

He pauses and looks in my eyes, soundlessly asking if I want to be fucked like that.

"Yes, I need it," I answer. My body is charged, infused with a surge of ignited passion.

Electrocuted, I need to feel something intense. He needs to fuck me. Fuck me hard. He walks with my back towards one of the glass panels, my legs around his waist. Every step he takes is fast, strong, and robust. He's vigorous and potent, oozing power. It's sexy, virile, and I'm melting in his arms. I'm satisfied because I know I'll definitely be getting fucked.

The cascading of rippling tremors I feel is forceful, from my heart to my abdomen to my sex. Butterfly wings are too gentle to describe this feeling; it's more like currents igniting through me, jolting me with ecstatic thrills of aches and cramps weaving down low. Vulnerable. Desperate. The pounding in my palpitating heart rhythmically beats with the dull bass blasting from the club upstairs.

He places me down against one of those glass panels with rippling water, then slides his jacket off me, pulls my dress up, and strips my tiny lace panties from me. Feeling completely aroused with my bare sex exposed, I need friction on my wet sensitive folds. I lift one leg, wrapping it around his waist, closing the space, then push myself against his hard bulge in a hard, fast thrust. Then I reach out to undo his zipper.

I'm moving fast and furious and know what I want and how to do it, but the reality is the alcohol has probably slowed me down, so he helps me out. He slides his suit trousers and boxers down, his massive, hard cock springing free. He then undoes his tie and top few buttons, leaving the tie hanging open around his neck.

I need this power, him to take control, to transport me into another world where there is no fear, only indulgent hedonism. Only Lucca can take me there. Now is the time.

I need to be taken.

Placing one hand on his firm ass cheek and the other on his thick, steely shaft, I stroke his length, massage his balls, then tighten my grip hard and work him, pleasure him until I can't take it anymore. Grabbing his throbbing cock, I pull it towards me and tease my clit with his bulbous head.

"Jesus, fuck, baby." His groaning and husky voice renders me delirious. He's real, this is real, and I'm taking him every way I can. I don't speak, I can't. I'm on a mission to get fucked senseless and have waited all week to feel this.

Lifting my leg a little higher, holding onto his girth, I circle his engorged head around my clit, grazing my sensitive nub as he tightens his grip on my hair and hisses through clenched teeth. It's a delicious sensation hitting me, but being impatient, I know what I need lies within. I slide his cock down my wet folds tempting it to my opening. Biting down on my lip and closing my eyes, I ease him into me.

Throwing my head back with the feel of him against my sex, I grab his inky, wavy hair to pull his lips to mine then bite his bottom lip. Growling, he picks me up so I'm straddling his hips as he pounds into me in one fast, forceful drive forward, banging me against the glass panel of flowing water. He thrusts again and again with strong control, shocking my nervous system with an intense electric current. He gives me what I need and fucks me good and proper.

Impaling and stretching me, I clamp around his shaft as he fervently pounds into me callously and steadfast. Tears escape my eyes once more when I thrust my body against his, accepting every penetrating, unforgiving whack, climbing the stairway to sexual heaven. Every intense slam of deep, hard incursion has me one step closer to utopia, where I won't feel fear, only gratification.

This is the best form of therapy, of distraction, and I intend to savour it. I assault his tongue as my generous, swollen cleavage spills from the bustier of my dress, squashed against his chest. Clenching around his expert intrusion, my muscles tighten; I'm quivering, shaking, but relishing every hard slam he fucks into me.

With aggressive possession in my eyes, I cry with carnal pleasure, nearly reaching my orgasm "Fuck, Lexi, I need this, baby, so bad with you." There's desperation in his needy voice causing my heartbeat to hitch in my throat I'm panting so hard knowing he needs it as much as me.

"Harder," I demand as my body cries out for more delicious abuse to my core. "I'm close ... ahhh ... shit," I bellow through the large, empty VIP area.

"Come for me, baby. Shout my name and come around my cock," he growls, losing control and panting breathlessly. It's enough to throw me into a raging, sensational climax.

"Lucca," I cry. He gutturally shouts my name as he becomes rigid and slams into me again, coming inside and pushing me up the glass.

I scream over and over, envisioning stars, my eyes rolling back into my head. He pounds into me another few times before slumping against me while the undulating ripples of erogenous waves flood my body and my senses.

He remains inside me, keeping his body pressed against mine, kissing me over and over, breathing erratically. I can't let go. I'm blissfully absorbing every nerve and flutter. He lowers me and eases out, placing me on a white leather sofa nearby. I'm not finished with him yet. I need more of that distraction and I need more of him.

Thankfully, he has the same idea. He's not finished with me either. He never is.

He slips his shoes off, then kicks away his trousers and boxers gathered at his ankles, and unbuttons his shirt all the way down leaving it open. Watching him and knowing this area is private and no one will come in, I do the same. I sit on the end of the sofa and unzip my dress. Lucca kneels in front of me and finishes the bottom part of the zipper then pulls it over my head.

"I love the dress, but you are too sexy in it. Every man up there has a hard, twitching cock for you." He unclasps my bra and flings it overhead. "I am glad it is my hard, twitching cock that is fucking you. No one else's but mine. Only mine. Always. Anytime. Anywhere. Mine."

"Only yours," I reply, feeling a pool of excitement swirl low in my abdomen with his words. His ownership.

"I love your sexy dress, but I love your sexy as fuck body even more. The body I get to fuck." He moans at the site of my naked body. "Fuck, I have missed this image."

I've missed this image also—Lucca kneeling in front of me naked, exposing his dark muscular body of male perfection. Those defined abs, deliciously ripped with his shirt hanging open exposing them, it's nothing short of a hot fantasy. My fantasy.

He spreads my legs and moves in between them, closer to my body. Taking my hard as diamonds puckered nipples, he kisses, licks, and bites, nipping the other at the same time. Arching my back, enjoying his mouth, I know I need more.

"Touch me," I beg. I'm aware he is touching me but I need him lower.

He moves his hands from my heavy breasts over my navel then lifts my feet and places my heels on the edge of the sofa, widening my legs and exposing me fully to him. Clenching his jaw, gasping at his view, he strokes my wet, slick folds.

"Uhhh." I throw my head back.

Utopia.

His thumb torments my sweet spot while he inserts two—no three—fingers deep inside me, sliding his sperm within my sheath. Arching my back and pushing my breasts forward, it's only a matter of seconds before I detonate again as I'm still very sensitive. Closing my eyes, my head involuntarily thrashes side to side as I bite the inside of my lip, curling my toes, shaking my knees and legs while tensing everywhere.

Holy shit!

"I have missed you so much. I could watch you do that all day. God, you are perfetto." He slithers his fingers out from my pulsing, hot, soaked core and trails his creamy fingers over my bare mound. He leans in to kiss me. "Hmmm, someone got waxed all over. I love it," he rasps against my lip. I love him. I love this.

I'm awfully glad he loves it, but I'd love it even more if he were back inside me.

Still trying to keep the power, I grab a handful of material from his shirt, pulling him up. Standing, I turn and push him flat down onto the sofa. His eyes are wanton for me. He watches me eagerly with that sexy dimple smile I go weak for.

Climbing up, I straddle him then run my hands all over his exposed abs, inside his open shirt that's left hanging at his sides. My Italian god.

"I've missed you so much too. I've missed this," I say in my sexy voice. Then I lean down, pressing my breasts to his chest but keeping my hips and ass lifted up and back so I'm not touching him yet. I tease him.

I kiss his lips and his neck then seductively suck on his Adam's apple, coating my tongue with a taste of his alluring aftershave. I know he loves this and I love pleasuring him like this. His virile hands firmly massage my breasts as my tongue swirls over his nipples, and without any warning I sit up, wiggle my ass, then drop my hips anchoring down onto his erect cock. I manoeuvre side to side until I have his full length inside me, making me buckle all again with that same electric current undulating through my lower abdomen.

"Fucking hell," he growls then grabs onto my hips. He feels so good. I plan to ride him fast and hard, and I do just that. I feel him ... nothing else. I bounce up and down, consuming his steel shaft and clamping tightly around it. I ride him fast and furiously.

I grind.

I thrust.

I drive.

"Christ, Lexi, you feel so good. Keep going, baby ... ahh ..." he hisses with pleasure on my next hard thrust.

Throwing my head back, rolling my eyes, I lift higher and grind lower, exerting my shameless, raw carnality, riding him senseless. I'm close, so close to explosion. The sinful greed of another mighty, mind-blowing orgasm is seconds away. I'm impatient so I move my hand and flick my clit, grasping one of my breasts with the other.

Screaming, I splinter through another euphoric, mind-shattering orgasm sparking my body into a frenzied delight. I combust.

I'm deliriously dizzy in my exultant paradise, but Lucca is still lifting me up and down on him, he's frantically ramming himself up to me in strong, impelling thrusts, grunting with fervour while taking control. My sex feels energised with sensitivity as tremors course through me. I'm crying and whimpering still, because this orgasm continues to ripple.

It's too much.

It's perfect.

I can't take it.

I'm delirious.

It's going on and on, enrapturing me while he shudders up in a hard, stiff jerk and holds my hips while he's balls deep. He's tensing and puffing out my name through clenched teeth, filling me with his release, and once more finding his own euphoric delight.

He's pumping into me so high and hard, he's lifted his own hips off the sofa, my knees coming off the leather with him. I tilt my hips forward, leaning backwards, taking him to his base in the perfect angle. Contracting my muscles, clenching my ass cheeks, and holding onto his girth, I take.

He twitches a few times in me, digging his fingers into my hips and ass. Once my shock waves have zapped through my entire body, I collapse on top of him, completely spent and temporarily clouded, sheltered from my brutal, evil reality.

Fearless.

Closing our eyes, hot, sweaty, and exhausted, we lie like this while he gently strokes my back and ass and plays with my hair, languorously kissing me. I'm not sure if minutes have elapsed when I open my eyes, but I'm still here in his arms sated and light-headed, and I don't want to move.

"Lexi, baby, I need to get you home. Are you awake?" he whispers against my cheek.

"Hmmm ..."

He sits up, still holding me, then places me on the sofa. I'm so exhausted I can't speak. I need sleep. Slumping on my side, I draw my knees up, ready for sleep, forgetting how exposed I am and where I am.

He disappears then returns with another glass of water and towels. He wipes us clean with a wet towel stroking the beads of sweat from my forehead and neck then uses another hot, wet towel for my sex. Sitting me upright, he gives me the glass of water.

I sip the water as Lucca dresses. Then he returns with my panties and slips them over my legs. He puts my bra inside his jacket pocket and slips my dress over me, zipping it up, then scoops me into his arms.

I'm safe.

Chapter 27: Picture Book

The next time I open my eyes, Lucca's loving blues are contently watching me with rapt attention. His stubble tickles my cheek as his thumb traces my lips. He's real. Smiling, I'm thrilled I'm not still dreaming and waking up with my Italian god.

"Morning, beautiful."

"Hmmm."

"I have run us a bath. I thought we could relax today, have some more make-up sex, and have that chat. I need to speak with you and clear things up. I had to bring you straight to bed last night. You were shattered, so I thought it best to wait until today." He lifts my wrist and kisses my small scar.

"Yes to the bath and relaxing, and definitely yes, to more make-up sex. I'm in. What are we chatting about?" I ask nonplussed yawning and fluttering my lashes.

A confused frown creases his brow. Searching his face, I'm momentarily clueless. Oh God, the realisation strikes me like a bolt of lightning and I gasp, panicking, and tighten my grip on him.

"Sweetheart, it is okay, I have you. You are going to be safe. I will never let anything happen to you, ever." He kisses my engagement ring then sweetly kisses my lips as I delicately hold his face in my trembling hands.

My stomach has turned over as I replay last night's brutal discovery in my mind.

I'm going to be sick.

Freeing myself from his embrace, I stumble out the bed and hobble into the bathroom, emptying the contents of my stomach into the toilet. Lucca moves my hair and rubs my back. When I think I can't vomit anymore, I hover over the toilet and vomit again. I'm not anywhere near finished. I'm sick until I'm retching and there's nothing left.

"Oh God," I groan. My stomach's cramping. I'm dizzy, feverish, and now have a throbbing headache.

"Are you okay?" he asks, rubbing my back.

"Yes, I think so."

"I will get you some painkillers and water. Do you want anything else?"

"Only you," I sigh.

"You have me forever, Doc. I hate seeing you like this."

After helping me up, he wets a cloth with cold water and holds it to my forehead. Then he pulls on his boxer shorts to go to the kitchen and returns with iced water and painkillers. I brush my teeth, swallow the tablets, then rinse with mouthwash.

He picks me up and puts me in the bath. Then he slides in behind me, pulling my back to rest against his chest, and wraps his arms around me stroking my arms and shoulders. This is the only place I want to be, the only place I feel safe.

"Lucca?"

"Yeah, baby?"

"I'm scared," I quaver softly, trailing my fingers over his forearms.

"I know you are, but he cannot touch you. I will not let it happen. You are going to be fine, Lexi." He kisses the side of my head to comfort me, and I melt into his protective embrace.

"How did you know I was at BarAsta?" I swirl my fingers over his bulky arms in another featherlike dance.

"I own the building, so the club manager called me to say you had booked in under my membership number. I flew home earlier in the day, desperate to speak to you and apologise. I was already home and going fucking stir-crazy when Devon realised you were not at Jessica's."

Inhaling deeply, he continues, "I should not have got drunk like that. I was so stressed out with your protection and the shit going on with Kimberley, but that is no excuse. I am sorry. I cannot even remember what I said, but Fran mentioned I rambled on that he would not take you, and then I panicked in case you worked it out. When you would not answer my calls, I had to come home. Shamefully, I do not even remember collapsing at Fran's. You know that nothing happened between us, and that nothing will ever happen with Fran. It is history."

I believe him.

"I'm sorry I overreacted. Between the guards, the mail, and then the thing with Fran, I didn't know what was going on, and I was consumed with jealousy and rage." I stretch my legs, moving my head, embarrassed by my confession.

"I am a fucking idiot. I hate that I lied to you, and I hate that I hurt you, baby. I was only trying to protect you."

"I understand why you never told me. I'm furious with Kimberley. The way she dug into my past unnerves me. And she had to say it in front of ..." I feel embarrassed but more than that, I'm so very angry and scared, my voice becomes shaky.

"Jackson?"

"Yes."

His body becomes rigid and he tightens his hold around me. "Do not worry your pretty little head about her. She hacked into Suzanne's emails so she has breached company data protection, which means she is fucked from a business perspective. I have reasonable grounds to dismiss her. I will ensure that little bitch gets what she deserves, do not worry."

"How long have you known? When did you find out and how?" I probe.

"Cameron found out through his contacts at CID when he was on night shift. He called me on Monday night when I was already on my trip, which is why I appointed the security." He strokes my arm then links his fingers with mine, resting them on his knees.

"How do they know about Michael?"

"He skipped parole and used a fake identity to get into the UK. They found ... err, indecent photographs of you from your childhood in his apartment. They believe he was involved with Damien Thomson, a private investigator in London, but, Lexi ... Damien was found dead."

"What? Are you serious?" I tense up and grip onto Lucca's robust arms.

"It looks like a staged suicide." He tries to soothe me by kissing my head but I'm too rigid.

"Oh my God," I blurt in a panic.

Quickly, I turn around splashing everywhere and plead into his eyes, begging for hope that he's wrong. His honest, loving eyes have confirmed he's not. They look tired and hurt, but they are honest.

"It was him. He's capable of murder," I say, shaking my head. My bottom lip quivering, the tears fall freely down my cheeks, and I can't hold back. Lucca takes my face in both hands, placing his thumbs on my cheeks and presses his forehead to mine. I'm trembling, quaking with fear. "It's me he's after." I sob.

"You do not know that. He is a psychotic sociopath, but just because your pictures were found does not confirm it is you. It is possible, but I am not taking any chances, nor is Cameron." He speaks so softly and candidly; he's trying to calm me.

Shaking my head adamantly, I raise my voice. "LISTEN TO ME. It's me he wants."

Fuck!

File C for confess. Confess everything to make him understand.

I feel sick again, and I don't think I can say it, but I need to tell him. The pain in my chest is razor sharp; it's stabbing me, trying to pull me under, and I can't breathe.

Fire.

Screaming.

Yelling.
Blood.
Tears.
Moss.
Dirt.
Dig.
Escape.
Gun.
Shoot.
Bang.
Panic.
Run.
Free.
Breathe.

"Deep breaths, deep breaths. Shhh, it is okay."

He spends a few minutes holding me, caressing me, and it has calmed me slightly, but the tears still sting my eyes and drip from my chin. I can taste them on my lips ... the tears of terror.

"I killed him," I blurt out. "I killed his father, my father. I killed him and now he wants to kill me. Don't you understand? Damn it, he wants revenge. The night I killed Simon Parks and we escaped, he said he would find me and make me suffer and now he's here." My pulse quickens, chest heaves, and heart rate accelerates.

I can't look at him; his future wife is a murderer. Pulling away, I move to stand up. "I'm sorry you had to find out like this. I haven't got around to writing it down in my journal and it's never come up. I've been protecting you from finding out the truth. You must hate me. I didn't want to tell you, in case ..." I whimper, avoiding eye contact.

He pulls me back down and engulfs me in warmth and security. "Baby, I do not hate you. I could never hate you. You saved three lives, Lexi. You are a hero, not a bloody murderer, so do not think that for a second. I am so proud of you. If you had not done what you had to do, we would not be here now, together. You are much stronger than you think. You do not need to talk about it; I know this is hard enough for you. But please know it changes nothing between us. I love you."

Looking down at him, I clench my eyes together and lift my shoulders, breathing heavily.

Relieved?

Perhaps.

Ashamed?

Yes.

His voice is breaking, and I see tears welling in his bright eyes that are losing their sparkle, the blue now changing to a cloudy grey-blue. His own tears trail down his face, and it's painful to see him torn up like this. My stomach knots and twists seeing him vulnerable.

"Please, don't cry for me." I've found some strength and have dug deep for compassion. I'm now comforting him. "One day I'll tell you about it, if you want to listen, but I'm not ready yet and I need you to be strong for me, Lucca. I need you."

He closes his eyes with a sigh then opens them again, nodding his head. "You have me, baby. I am damaged and suffering for you, with you. It kills and fucking tears me apart to see how fragile you are right now. We will get through this, I promise you. I am taking you away. Cameron suggested a safe house, but there is nowhere safer than this house, so I am taking you back to Italy until he has been found in the UK."

My cheek bonds against his like glue. My arms wrap around his neck.

Sticky.

Salty.

Raw.

I'm struggling to dam my flowing tears as they cascade down my cheeks. Burning, hot, acidic liquid trickles.

Blood.

Poison.

Red.

That's what it feels like and what I deserve.

To cry blood.

"What about up north? We need to go because I've promised them. I need to visit them, and my mum will be beside herself." I sniffle.

"We are still going tomorrow. Lloyd and Devon are coming with us. Marco and extra security are staying here, and I have also arranged security for your mother. I spoke to a CID specialist in these cases and we need to be cautious, but it is important to try and keep normalcy and continue with life. I know it is hard, but I need us to live our lives the best we can under these circumstances to prevent you from a ..."

He drops his head and strokes my hair.

Enough said.

He can't even look at me. Shit. I know what he's thinking ... *the worst.*

"Just say it. You think I'm going to have a breakdown like my mum. You think I'm emotionally unstable," I sob hysterically, knowing I'm right.

"No, I do not. I know you are much stronger than that. You are the strongest woman I know. You saved your family at such a young age, and it is admirable. It is your natural instinct to pick yourself back up and care for others. You are resilient, tough, and selfless, baby, you just do not see it. The specialist has studied your case and thinks you are exceptionally fragile, going on your past therapy. They have offered counselling, but if you think you need it, we can arrange for Casey Huddersfield to work with us again. I know you trust her."

"Let's just see how we get on. I don't think I need therapy when I have you. You are all the therapy I need." I know I do need Casey, but for now all I want is Lucca.

I tilt my head, reach for his face, and graze my fingers over his stubble then his lips. His warm smile spreading beneath my fingers shows he appreciates that I'm trying to stay focused. I don't want to give him any reason to think I'm as weak as my mum. His tears are drying up, as are mine.

"I love you," I whisper. He kisses me then frowns, noticing something. He traces his thumb over the tiny scar on the skin of my upper arm.

Oh no, we're not having the contraception discussion now.

I'm surprised he doesn't mention it. He only leans over and kisses the mark on the inside of my arm with his wet lips. Maybe he realises he'll be pushing me, not wanting to inflict any more pain or upset on me right now.

"I love your eyelashes. They are very sexy, and I notice your hair is cut. It is pretty. You are very beautiful, Lexi. You looked stunning last night."

"Thank you for pamper night. The girls absolutely died and went to heaven. They loved it. It was very generous and thoughtful."

"You are welcome. I am glad you enjoyed it, but I am sorry I ruined it by worrying you again." I remain silent. "Turn around and I will wash your hair then I had better feed you. I do not want you fainting or getting dizzy again."

Oh God. I'd forgotten about that.

Fuck!

File H for humiliated. Humiliated I passed out and in front of Jackson.

"Are you mad at me for having a drink with Jackson? He was only helping me because I couldn't walk on my ankle."

"I know, he told me. No, I am not mad at you. I am envious he spent quality time with you when I was going out of my mind with worry and wished it was me who had comforted you. But I know he would never hurt you, and I am thankful you had someone taking care of you. Cameron has told me he is trustworthy."

He slowly massages conditioner into my scalp with his expert hands, making me relax under his touch. When we've been in the bath for over an hour, he lifts me out, then dries me off, kisses my ankle, and rubs arnica cream over my bruised skin. He wraps me in my robe and kisses my wrist and the small incision on my arm then tells me he'll be back with food.

I doze off then startle when all the girls come bounding into the bedroom. They jump on the bed to hug me.

"We brought your shoes and bag, and Lucca's gift. He was over the moon," Jess explains.

"We had to make sure you were okay," Sam continues, searching my face for distress.

"Why are you all not at work today? This is Friday, right?" I ask, reaching my hands out to them. They all climb on the bed huddling in to cuddle me.

"We're going, but we wanted to see you first," Carrie replies.

"Where's Skip?"

"I'm here, I'm just finding something to wear," she shouts.

Puzzled, I look towards Lucy. "We stayed another hour or so drinking after Lucca took you away, and she's still got last night's clothes on because she locked herself out. Then she woke Mr. Carlin up and slept in his spare room because Dominic was furious with how drunk she was," Lucy says with a laugh shaking her head.

I can't help chuckling, but I'm concerned Mr. Carlin will be extremely grumpy and I'll get the brunt of this.

"Shut it, ladybug. Have you told Lexi you have a date with Marco da Vinci?" Hazel retaliates as she walks out my dressing room wearing a pair of my jeans and a T-shirt. Hazel and Lucy have been friends since they were at primary school and often tease each other without offending one another, similar to my relationship with Hazel—honest.

Lucy is blushing; she's mortified. I take her hand, smiling widely. "I'm delighted for you. That's great news. Let me know how it goes."

"I will, that's if blabber mouth doesn't broadcast it first." She chuckles and nods towards Hazel who has fallen flat across my bed.

"What are the chances of me phoning in sick tonight?" she moans with her arm resting across her forehead.

After a thirty minute visit, satisfied I'm not ready to throw myself in front of a train, they all kiss me goodbye before heading off to work.

"Roo, can I stay here and hang about today?" Hazel asks sheepishly.

"Yes, if you'd like, but I plan on keeping Lucca locked in here with me, so entertain yourself."

"Oh, check you. Where has Miss Prudish gone to? You lascivious little minx. My friend here has become a sex goddess," Hazel teases.

Sam snorts sarcastically.

If only they knew how desperate for Lucca's sex I can be.

"Next thing we know, Lucy will be shacked up barefoot and pregnant with the other Italian," Sam adds.

Lucy rolls her eyes in disgust, blushing a shade brighter than hot pink.

"Okay, ladies, I'm going for a sleep at the pool. You girls enjoy your work. Do you think the Royal Guards will fan me and bring me grapes?" Hazel asks.

After a few pillows thrown in her direction, Hazel falls off the end of the bed on her ass making us all chuckle but jumps up when Lucca walks in with my breakfast as the girls prepare to leave. I kiss them all and tell them I will call them.

Hazel steals a slice of toast off the tray and saunters back into my dressing room. Lucca shakes his head, although his lips curl up so I know he's sniggering.

"Rose will make you breakfast, Hazel. She is downstairs," Lucca offers.

"Lexi, Lucca, my friends, it has been a pleasure, but I'm off to get a three egg omelette and a cinnamon bun thing. If Dominic calls, you tell him I'm feeling poorly and sleeping. Ta-ta." After her Oscar winning performance, Hazel leaves with one of my bikinis hanging from her fingers.

Lucca closes the door after her dramatic exit. "Hangover?" he asks, referring to Hazel's mood.

"Yes, and a fight with Dominic." I shake my head, rolling my eyes.

"Oh dear. They are sweet girls and they did not need to get me a gift, but it was very thoughtful. I am so happy they thought to come by and check on you, that was kind of them." I wouldn't expect anything less. I'm very grateful.

Smiling with complete adoration, I pull the covers back and he climbs in, setting the tray in between us.

After breakfast we spend most of the day in bed sleeping and entwined as we enjoy late afternoon sleepy sex. It's what we both need—each other without disruptions and without worries.

It is almost four in the afternoon before we dress and go downstairs. Rose advises that Hazel left around an hour ago, so I send her a quick text to apologise for ignoring her. Rose prepares dinner while Lucca and I walk Doris in the park hand in hand; Lloyd walks closely behind us. We discuss the exact details the specialist gave him regarding Michael Parks. He tells me about his trip, Fran, his contracts, and a deal he secured with Giorgio for a new Luminara chain.

He confesses he was out of his mind and never slept and that's why he has Marco, Lloyd, and Devon with me constantly. He said he would have had Armando and Savio here too if they didn't need to work.

I don't eat much of Rose's beautiful meal because I can't stomach it, so I only pick at my food. Lucca watches me with trepidation.

"Lexi, you need to eat, baby."

"I'm just not hungry. I'm sorry."

"Are you okay? You are very quiet." He places his fork down, cocks his head, and pinches his forehead with his middle finger and thumb then reaches for my hand.

"Yes, I've started my period tonight, so I'm probably out of sorts with that." I am extremely light, so I assume it's because I have the contraceptive implant. My body is out of sync.

"Does that mean I will get lots of fiery Lexi this week?" he playfully jests.

"If you play your cards right, Romeo, you just might. Although my granny will have us in separate bedrooms."

"Not an option. You are not sleeping alone without me. I will book us both into a hotel together before I will allow that." He entwines our fingers tightly to reassure me he's never letting me be alone.

"Well, you better work your charm then because she's feisty and always gets her own way."

He lifts me out my chair and twirls me around in a circle, holding me against him. "Hmmm, I wondered who you took after in that regard," he teases me.

"Yeah, so they tell me. Please don't tell them about Michael Parks. Make a plausible excuse regarding the security. I don't want to worry them."

Placing me down but still pressing me against his chest, he moves an unruly wave of hair from my face. "They already know. Cameron said the CID was in touch with them, but he asked them not to call and alarm you."

God, my mum will be in meltdown—all the more challenging— but I'm filing it tonight because I want to focus on Lucca, nothing else. I'd love to run away to Italy and hibernate, but I can't. I need to be strong and face reality.

"We'd better pack. You head upstairs, and I'll sort these dishes and tidy up."

"No, your ankle is still swollen and tender and you shouldn't be standing on it too long. Rose will get them." I'm expecting a scolding about wearing the high-heeled shoes but he doesn't mention it. He's been very careful not to add to my upset today.

Before I can protest, he has scooped me up and is carrying me. On the bed there's a large silver box with a massive, pale blue satin ribbon around it. I'm intrigued.

"What's this?"

"Open it."

He places me on the bed gently then passes it over. Inside is a thick white leather book. I hope it's not what I think it is.

"What is it?"

"Look inside. I had an idea, and please, do not be angry with me, but I think it will help." I open the first page and stare in disbelief.

It's a full page black and white portrait picture of me. Wow, I've never observed myself in pictures as an adult. I've never allowed any to be taken, even on my graduation day. I run my fingers over my portrait in amazement.

"How did you get this?" I don't know how to react. I should be angry, but instead I'm shocked and intrigued so I try to keep the apprehension from my tone.

"I've been taking candid photos of you since we met, but I knew you'd object so I tried to be discreet. I had assistance in compiling them together to enhance the quality. They are all tasteful and very beautiful, and for our eyes only. No one else needs to see them, but I thought it might help you see what a vision you are and to accept that this is treasure. Something to cherish."

I'm shaking. I don't know how I feel about this. I can barely comprehend.

"Are you angry?" he asks sweetly, moving an unruly tendril of hair behind my ears.

"No, I don't think so." Actually, I don't know what to think yet.

Turning the first page of the professional photo book, there are four pictures all overlapping and all in black and white, except my lips have been coloured pink in one and red in another. I'm laughing in the bottom image, and my dress has been coloured pink. On the overlapping photo, I'm sitting on a wall in the Chianti hills with the sprawling vineyards behind me and my shoes are coloured red.

Professional. Artistic.

"I look like Dorothy." I giggle. Lucca exhales a sigh of relief; he's been holding his breath patiently.

There are continuous pages of creative, abstract, and natural detailed poses.

One of me sleeping on my stomach with a satin sheet across my back in a sepia tone, another in colour of me in a huff with my arms crossed over my chest and my designer dress is coloured in bright lime green but the background has been faded and blended.

There's one of me sitting next to the pool writing in my journal with my white bikini and kaftan on. I'm in colour but the background is grey and white, the journal coloured in deep indigo.

Suggestive.

Wow, there are so many, each as interesting and special as the next.

There are a couple of close up pictures of me sleeping, revealing certain sections of my features: my eyes and a close up of my eyelashes or my lips. Oh my goodness, the lashes have been individually coloured like a rainbow and my eyes are black and white, so intricate and detailed that its almost unreal. An explosion of colour.

Sweet.

Modern.

Intangible.

Pure adoration.

There is one of Cameron and I cuddling at the farmhouse, my head resting on his shoulder, and I stroke the photo as I recall our heart-to-heart. The journal he holds is bright blue. They are not just pretty, but very clever and expressive. It is pure art the way they've been designed and displayed. It's a story of my life so far with Lucca.

Our love.

The love.

L'amore.

I suspect he's trying to depict a theme of vibrant colour and beauty amidst the grey shadows of black and white. This is his way of bringing me into his light ... from my dark.

Turning the page, I smile realising there is one of me playing with Doris and another with Franco's dogs at the villa. Another one is of me sitting in front of the fire, hugging my knees, holding a glass of red wine with my robe on. The wine in the glass and the rug have been coloured in a deep burgundy colour. I'm speechless.

Warm.

Cosy.

Rich.

I delicately turn the next page and I'm standing in the Uffizi looking up at Botticelli's *Primavera* and *Birth of Venus*. It looks so real I can almost melt into it, touching and bringing back all the lovely memories. I can put myself back there at that precise moment; it's that clear.

Priceless.

Memorable.

There's a page of eight smaller pictures in cubes; each is a snap of a section of me making up parts of my body or subtle hints where my dress hem finishes or a strap hangs off my shoulder.

Naughty.

The next page I'm bending down slipping my feet into high-heeled shoes. Another is from behind, my hair blowing in the wind as I smell a beautiful, blue orchid flower which is the exact vivid colour of blue, purple, and turquoise that I've grown to love.

Breathtaking.

"Well?" Lucca asks impatiently

"Shhh ... I'm not done yet," I chide. He smiles and graces my shoulder with a sweet kiss.

Studying the next, I bite my lip. I have a white robe on facing a mirror, putting makeup on. There are shots of me laughing with Sofia and Franco, kissing Marissa and Antonio, cuddling Anna, having a debate with Hazel, and a close up of the blue orchid flower tucked behind my ear and my long flowing hair tumbling over my shoulder.

Fondness.

The next page shows me singing to Antonia, dancing with Roberta, and singing with Cameron with my eyes closed, perched on the sofa behind his guitar.

Natural.

I laugh at the picture of me in Rome looking at an upside-down tour map on the steps at St. Peter's Square.

Frustrated!

Then I notice there is one of me in a bikini taken from the back, my hair is tumbling down covering my scars, and has been artfully faded out. It's in colour, so my skin looks very bronzed. I'm not anxious because it's subtle and modest.

Sexy?

I stop turning the pages and frown, biting the inside of my lip.

"Do you not like it?" he asks with worry.

"No, I love it. I just don't see any pictures of us together."

"Keep turning. I had Hazel take some and Anna and even Cameron when you were unaware because I know you would trust them."

I'm desperate to see what we look like together. I smile at shot after shot of me wrapped in his arms, or sleeping in arms, or spoon feeding him gelato.

Love.

My eyes prick with tears, looking at a candid picture of us when we were out for dinner at the Jazz festival. Lucca has his shirt sleeves rolled up. His arm is around the back of my chair, and he's whispering into my ear. I'm blushing. In another he's kissing below my ear, and in yet another he's staring at me fondly. It looks like a moving picture it must have been synchronised snaps.

I hiccup, snivelling in adoration at the perfect memory right on this page.

"It's beautiful. I love this one. It's perfect, your eyes, God I love them. I loved that day."

"Me too, baby. It is a very happy memory," he adds.

Lucca and I are in the middle of his pool at the farmhouse. We're in black and white, my legs are around his waist, and I'm leaning my head back laughing as he holds me, lovingly staring down at me. He was swirling me around in circles; we had so much fun. This image catches the carefree moment and simple closeness we have.

The pool water has been coloured azure blue, as are his eyes, but everything else is black and white. The sun is setting behind us and shimmering little ripples of light across the water. His eyes are marrying on mine with the pool water equally as crystal clear and bright. I turn around smiling and see the real deal fondly gazing at me now.

Lust.

There is a side view of me sitting in the Jacuzzi at the villa with my hair bundled up in an undone bun and holding up an empty champagne glass, covered in bubbles to my shoulders. Then a photo of us kissing, dancing, me sitting on his knee while he gazes into my eyes, and one of him fastening my diamond pendant around my neck.

I'm nearing the end of the book, and sadly, I don't want this story in pictures to end. There's a double-page enlarged print of us at the Four Season's hotel the night he proposed to me. I look elegant in the cream and black lace Marchesa gown, and Lucca is devilishly handsome and attractive in his black tuxedo.

The next page is the Luminara light display: one of him behind me on the balcony overlooking the lanterns on the River Arno in Pisa, and one of me bunching up my dress to walk up the stairs to the opera.

Light.

He must have had help from the staff for these pictures because the last page is Lucca proposing to me on one knee, and the final is us dancing together in the garden of the luxurious suite. The fairy lights and bright glow from the candles have been highlighted as well as my diamond ring. I'm tilting my hand up admiring my ring as Lucca waltzes with me cheek to cheek.

Happy ending.

Throwing my arms around his neck, I jump on his lap and kiss him passionately with appreciation. When I finally let him up for air, he laughs in that masculine way.

"You like it then?"

"I love it. I love you. Lucca, you always blow me away with your thoughtfulness, but this is just amazing. I love seeing our life together in pictures. It's breathtaking. I feel so emotional, but happy emotional. I never thought I could look at myself or admire a photograph but this isn't just a picture it's a story, a beautiful story of us."

"Good, I am glad you like it. I thought it would help you see how beautiful you are, and encourage you to allow wedding pictures of us so we will have memories to show our kids one day."

"Thank you," I say it with so much appreciation I'm beginning to choke up with emotion.

"It doesn't need to finish there, Lexi. We have a lifetime to take pictures, make memories, and we can fill as many books as we like. I thought we could get your favourite ones enlarged on a huge print and frame them, or I can make a wall collage with them."

"Let's just stick to the books for now. You said someone helped you? They must be professional because these are outstanding." I flick back and forth through the pages, my eyes coming alive once more.

"Yes, when I was in Sardinia I met with Giovanni Costanzo. I explained it was a gift and asked if he would work on the images I had taken. He said you are very photogenic and would love to photograph you himself, so maybe he could do our wedding or baby pictures."

"Lucca, he's famous. His rates would be exorbitant. That's absurd."

"Don't worry about rates. Anyway, his company rents a studio and gallery in one of my Italian buildings, so I am sure I could talk business."

I lie on my side, propping my head in my hand and open the book. I spend the next hour fascinated with images, searching every expression, admiring the contrasts in colours and shapes. Lucca smiles with pride fascinated with my reactions to each photo.

"I want to take this with us to show my mum. She'll be overjoyed."

He smiles watching me turning over the same pages again and again. "Lexi, you know you just need to look at me. I am right here." I throw a pillow at him then start with my packing.

Chapter 28: The Highlands

We're not taking the BMW X5. Instead, Lucca and I will be travelling in his Aston Martin and Lloyd and Devon will both follow with their own SUVs, one getting the short straw of taking Doris.

I assumed because we're taking her we'd use my new BMW X5, seeing as that's its purpose—trips with Doris—but as Lucca rightfully points out, it's not safe to be exposed with my personalised registration plate.

Peter has locked up both my cars in the garages around the back. Doris's bed and food has been loaded into Lloyd's SUV, and they've packed boxes of groceries, which Rose purchased early this morning. Lucca makes a few early morning calls and then goes to his study to call the specialist advising her that I'm aware of the situation and asks the investigator assigned to the case for any updates.

It's a lovely day so I put on a navy sundress with thin straps. It's fitted at the bust with three white buttons and then flowing out at the bottom just above my knees.

Light, smart, and cute.

I slip into navy ballet flats and grab my white linen blazer in case I get cold. I'm finishing my makeup in front of the mirror when my handsome Italian god's image catches my eye.

"You look beautiful. I like this. It is cute and has easy access." Lucca stands behind me and runs his hand under the thin material of the dress, up my inner thighs to cup my sex, making me tingle all over with desire.

"Lucca, there is a house full of people downstairs." I draw a sharp breath when his fingers tease my clit under the sheer fabric of my panties. Oh my God, I'm pulsing for him, wet and already contracting my muscles within my sex ...

"Lucca, I'm bleeding. It's very light but still," I say, mortified.

"It does not bother me, baby. Did I not make that clear at the farmhouse?" he says, nibbling my ear as his thumb flicks over my aroused clit.

"You're shameless," I protest, but my body betrays me yet again.

"And you are sexy as fuck," he arrogantly retorts, biting down and nibbling on my earlobe.

He slides my spaghetti straps down, kissing my shoulders, then opens the bustier, popping the white buttons with his thumb. He pulls the dress down to my midriff, exposing my naked breasts to the mirror.

"No bra? You are going to kill me, but I will take full advantage of this later," he says, turning me around to face him, swirling his wet tongue over my erect nipples, which tugs on the direct link to my vibrating sex.

"Oh God, Lucca," I moan.

"Do you like this?"

I softly moan as his tongue circles around my areola, over my sensitive nipples, almost sending me over the edge, making me jerk. I'm hot, sensitive, and energised. I can't refuse; I want him to make me come.

He teases my nipples, causing a flurry of butterflies to spread their wings in my stomach. Slipping his hand under my dress, he fondles the tiny strap of my panties then rubs his fingers over my sex through the minuscule triangle of material, causing me to go weak at my knees.

Quickly, he slinks his fingers under my panties once more to tease my wet, sensitive clit as he sucks my right nipple and massages my left. He doesn't need to enter me; he has me here. Not that he would object or think twice. I discovered that in Tuscany. He's shamelessly dirty and persistent.

Leaning back against my dressing table, I weave my fingers in his sexy, shaggy, black locks.

"Oh … ahhh … Luc …" I groan when he's triggered that switch that ejects me into a spinning orbit leaving my body humming with intense desire.

I've no time to feel inhibitions. I need more of Lucca to help draw me from my dark fear, and now it's the time to make me forget. I'm drenched and pulsing for him.

I relish under his touch. I'm throbbing, shaking with a rippling shock of pleasure pulsing around me. He slides his hand up over my navel and rests on my stomach, the other on my right breast.

"Better?"

"Hmm … Yes … very." I smile.

"I wanted you leaving on a high, not worried or anxious. I am trying so fucking hard not to badger you onto the bed and slide deep inside you, but we need to go soon." He's struggling because his bulging arousal in his jeans is very prominent and pressing against my inner thighs.

"So what if I let you slide inside and we're a little late because right now I want you to take me?"

I kiss his lips, lifting myself off the dressing table, feeling very desperate to leave on said "high" he mentioned.

"You are always going to get what you want, do you know that?" He groans, thrusting against me. His hard denim-clad bulge hits my sweet spot as he grabs my ass, pulling me in closer to him. I'm glad to be demanding in this instance and get what I want.

"Yep, and I'm using it to your advantage and of course mine. Shower, Romeo," I order.

"I was hoping you would say that, baby, because my cock needs you badly."

He picks me up and carries me into the bathroom, and minutes later he's deep inside me in the shower, and I take everything I can.

Rose has prepared breakfast for everyone, with all the men tucking in for seconds and scoffing some of her chocolate brownies. I chose not to have any before travelling, plus I have an awful metallic taste in my mouth and feel sickly, so instead, I sip a cup of tea.

Peter has checked all the cameras, and Marco has welcomed two new Men in Black to our entourage. They'll remain on Lucca's property while we're gone. I call my mum from the living room to confirm were leaving shortly, only to get thirty minutes of anxiety, grief, and stress.

I hope she calms down before I get there because this could be very draining.

Cameron and Anna stop by before we leave to say goodbye. Anna saunters in and squeezes me to the point I just might break. Rose prepares to make another round of pancakes so they can dig in. She puts her hand on my forehead with concern and says I look very pale today.

"I might just need to stop by to get Rose to cook for me while you're away. Hazel's pulled the plug on feeding me," Cameron remarks, scoffing a brownie. He's actually serious too.

Leaving the kitchen, I approach the living room for my hand bag and come to a halt in the hallway hearing exchanged words. Lucca is talking to someone else. Cameron and Anna have not arrived alone. I recognise the voice.

Why would he be here again?

I wonder whether I should leave them alone, but then it could get messy so I decide to interrupt to save Jackson from Lucca's grilling. Inhaling a deep breath, I step forward. Jackson is standing in front of the fireplace with one hand on the nape of his neck while

Lucca has his back to me, rubbing his forehead with his middle finger and thumb. Jackson looks better every time I see him. He doesn't look smooth today, more rough and ready.

I stand at the doorway nervously picking at the skin on my palms, embarrassed and ashamed that Jackson is no doubt privy to my past after Kimberley's devious confession. Lucca and Jackson both silence their conversation when they glance at me, inevitably noticing I look pale and tired.

"Hey," Jackson says, settling on a sympathetic smile.

"Hey," I whisper, dropping my head.

"I just wanted to stop by and make sure you were okay. I had no idea. I'm sorry. Cameron and Lucca have enlightened me on the basics, but I wanted to reassure you that I will keep this very private and not disclose it to anyone. If there is anything I can do to help …" He's careful, decent, and appropriate around Lucca, around me.

Deep down Jackson is uneasy. He's shifting his weight from side to side with one hand in his jeans' pocket, the other still on the nape of his neck.

Lucca reaches for me, taking my hand, then gently tilts my head back up with two fingers under my chin. "You good?" He searches my face, my eyes.

"Yes, just tired I suppose." I must be strong in front of him. I know he called Casey Huddersfield this morning and that can only mean one thing. Therapy. Staring back at Lucca's eyes, we have one of our hushed conversations. He knows exactly what I'm asking of him.

"Okay, I will be in the kitchen. I will give you a minute." I nod my head and force a smile, thanking him for the understanding and privacy.

Before leaving, he graces my lips with a tender kiss in front of Jackson then lowers his eyes, silently telling me he trusts me but to keep distance. I know this wordless plea. Thanking him, I squeeze his hand before he closes the door.

The surrounding air is thick, laced with a hazy, subdued, and uncertain atmosphere. We stand and stare for what seems like forever. Finally breaking the silence, I walk over to the sofa and sit, reaching my hand out towards Jackson. Looking relieved, he takes my hand clasping it in his and sits next to me.

"Thank you for looking out for me at the club."

"You're welcome. I just wish you didn't have such an unpleasant experience with that Kimberley girl, and I'm sorry you had to experience that."

"Me too, but the reality is she's done me a favour. At least I won't be sneaking away from security from now on, and you got to witness my party piece … bonus." A gentle smile spreads across his face at my attempt to lighten the mood.

"The falling or the fainting?" he asks, which makes me blush.

"Both, I'm sorry."

"Don't be. As long as you're well."

"I hope I will be, Jackson, I do hope so." I close my eyes, filled with disquiet, exhaustion, and scepticism.

"You will. Of course you will. Lucca will take great care of you. Nothing's going to happen to you, Alexis." He smiles, stroking my hand trying to comfort me, but his look is more a sorrowful smile of pity. I lower my head because I don't think I could look into those chocolate velvet eyes right now.

"What did Cameron tell you?" I ask.

"Enough ... but please don't worry. You can trust me. This will go no further. I give you my word." He sighs.

Oh God, he knows I was abused, brutally tortured, and mentally and physically tormented. He knows how I was brought into this world, but I know Cameron wouldn't disclose how we became free leaving that world behind. Cameron will always protect my feelings and integrity, I know that for certain.

Tensing, I bite the inside of my cheek and grind my teeth.

"There are only a handful of people who know this and who I trust, Jackson, so I need you to forget about it and treat us as if you didn't know and of course keep it private. You'll understand that I find it difficult to talk about." Involuntarily, I chew the inside of my cheek.

I watch his shoulders rise and his coffee coloured eyes soften. He sympathises.

"You've really helped me this week, for that I'm grateful, and Lucca is appreciative ... even if he appears a bit alpha male. I hope you'll continue your friendship with Cameron and this won't affect that, but I know it's awkward and changes the dynamics a little because Lucca probably doesn't want you to see me, so for that I'm sorry."

I fidget, shuffle, and then continue, "I also need to ask you to keep a distance from Kimberley. She's a deceitful game player and could tarnish your reputation as well as ours and will no doubt try to meddle. She wouldn't have thought twice about releasing those photographs, I'm sure." I fidget with the hem of my dress with my free hand.

He contently listens still holding my hand but now it's his turn.

"She won't get anywhere near me. Security will make sure of that, and I have PR specialists and agents dealing with any bad press so they'll be all over it. I'd never judge so please don't worry about what I think, and it certainly doesn't change my friendship with Cameron or how I feel about you." His voice softens as his thumb brushes the skin of my hand.

Shit. Thoughts are feelings and feelings need to be filed.

End of.

Period!

"And how do you feel about me?" These are dangerous waters, but I need to know.

"I'm not going to lie. I have strong feelings for you. I like you a lot, but I'm respectful and a decent man despite what the press says about me. I would never interfere with your relationship. I accept that Lucca is one lucky guy, and you'll always be his, but that doesn't mean we can't still remain friends. You don't need to be embarrassed and hide from me because I know about your past. It changes nothing. I'm friends with Cameron, and I very much hope I can be your friend also."

Oh my.

Fuck!

File S for stunned. Stunned at his sincerity.

I didn't realise we were friends, well not really, but then we did have a down-to-earth chat at the club before the drama, one I felt rather comfortable having. He's been friends with Cameron for years and other than the occasional unavoidable meeting at events or functions, we have never had to be in each other's company. Everything is changing and he is technically our neighbour now, so I will no doubt bump into him more frequently.

"I'd like that, but I'm not so sure Lucca would." I ease my hand away and worry my fingers around in front of my mouth, the back of my hand pressed to my lips.

"Lucca and I cleared the air. He loves you, Alexis. He's a great guy, but you know that already. He's made himself crystal clear where we stand and asked what my intentions are. He seems satisfied that we could all have a friendship of sorts without this being too weird after I was honest with him. I think he appreciated my honesty and knows I'd never hurt you. I suppose he sees it as someone else to trust who'll care for you, and you need a lot of caring and people to trust at a time like this."

Optimism is in his voice if I'm not mistaken.

I'm quietly processing this. A few days ago Lucca practically threw him out of the house, and now it appears Lucca's mellowed, succumbed, and compromised.

"Okay. I'd like us to be friends, just maybe not in public so much or the media will expose us. I don't need to draw attention just now. I need to hide. I'm sure it's not good for you either." I turn around and give him an apologetic look.

"I understand. Plus, I'm not sure Shawna would appreciate pictures of me linked to someone else in the evening news. We know it's all innocent, but she gets tired of it, understandably. You and Lucca should come over for dinner when you're back. Seriously, I mean that, we're neighbours after all." He frowns at the mention of Shawna and scratches his jaw, but then finishes by smiling at me, warm-heartedly.

"Sure, I'd love to. I can meet the white fur ball." I smile.

He laughs and shakes his head.

"Don't tell Shawna I said that. She'll annihilate me," he mumbles.

"Okay deal. Since we are friends, you better have some of Rose's chocolate brownies, come on." I jump up, tugging at his hand, and he follows me out giving Lucca a reassuring nod.

I wasn't aware but he was standing at the door way and probably heard the conversation or some of it. I move to allow Jackson to walk in front. Pulling Lucca back, I put my arms around his neck and kiss him with conviction against the wall.

"I love you. Thank you for being understanding."

Moving a loose curl from my eyes he kisses my nose.

"I do not want you to have any more grief. I need people around who are willing to protect you, and I like that he is honest."

"You have changed your tune. I must be making you softer."

"Hmmm … That fucker better not think this is a friendship with benefits. I will castrate him if he does not keep to the rules. He touches you and the fucker loses his balls. He will never kick another ball again."

Lucca. Still Lucca.

I shake my head but smile. "I wondered where Lucca went. It appears you're back."

"Baby, I never left. I just want you to be happy," he says, smacking my bottom playfully.

Jackson, Anna, and Cameron scoff pancakes while Lucca and I speak with Rose, Peter, and Marco. Anna is being very chatty, even more so than normal. She'll be in Heaven having a new premier league footballer friend. Cameron's going to have his hands full with her. She'll definitely be keeping him on his toes.

"You never read the documents Omari brought over?" Lucca adds, picking up his leather briefcase.

"No, sorry I forgot." I purse my lips and shrug my shoulders.

"Take them with you and you can read them on the journey or when we get there. It's important." He slides the manila envelope into the front of my designer tote bag.

"Ready?" I have a feeling I've forgot something.

"Have you got everything?"

The concentration on my face is a dead giveaway. Running through everything I know we've packed: the photo book, the gifts, laptop and chargers. I can't put my finger on it. Then it comes to me.

"Hold on." I walk back to the study and find the rectangle parcel in the jiffy bag. The parcel is for Cathy, my granny's friend and minister. It's from Ms. Morrison, the minister of my local parish. I slip it in the front pouch of the case.

Jackson has just left, leaving us his private mobile number and an invitation for dinner. Cameron and Anna are staying longer to lounge by the pool, and when I overhear Marco telling Lucca he's taking Lucy out to dinner tonight, I could dance with glee. That's exciting I must call her and get all the details.

We stop outside my old house so I can check on Mr. Carlin. Lucca comes in with me because he won't let me out of his sight. Doris is barking like mad in the back of Lloyd's SUV.

Pinching my sundress off my chest, I shout, "Good God, turn that heating off!" I could faint in here with that blooming heat.

"Well, about time. I've waited so long this morning I'm almost another year older." He's sitting in his chair with his light jacket and flat cap on, holding his stick. His brown leather bowler bag is sitting at his feet.

"Going somewhere?" I ask, lifting my brow in confusion.

"Your grandparents are expecting us. Stop wasting time," he complains.

"You're coming?" I asked, surprised that he is.

"Oh dear Lord, please give me strength, lassie. Lucca, can you please give her a shake. You're about as bright as blondie next door." With my hand on my hip, I look towards Lucca for answers.

"Mr. Carlin is coming. I thought the fresh air would do him good and he would enjoy the company. Your grandpa is looking forward to it." He nods towards an impatient Mr. Carlin.

"Oh, that's very thoughtful," I murmur. Not that I'm disappointed, but I get enough grief from Granny. I just hope I don't get an earache from him too.

I switch off the heating, check his fridge and mail, then lock the doors and check he has his prescriptions before we leave.

"Which vehicle do you want to go in?" Lucca asks.

"Whatever one doesn't have the beast in it." He points his walking stick towards Devon. I give Devon a sympathetic smile; it's going to be a long trip for him.

Short straw.

Lloyd travels closely in front, and Devon tailgates behind us on the A9. I try to close my eyes to have a nap, but there are too many things going through my mind. I ask Lucca to make a stop near Blair Atholl in Perthshire en route to Morayshire so we can allow Doris to stretch her legs.

We don't get that far. I need to stop at Dunblane because I'm so nauseous and hot and about to be sick.

After a restroom break, some water, and letting Doris out, we're back on the road. I switch the AC up full, and Lucca watches me curiously but still keeps a skilful eye on the road. I assure him I'm fine but he's not convinced and says I look very pale.

I do feel awful.

Our next stop is Pitlochary, where Lucca and I walk for ten minutes in the park with Doris for fresh air while Devon and Mr. Carlin stretch their legs and bring back some tea and coffee. I have to confiscate a slab of Scottish tablet from Mr. Carlin as his blood sugars would be sky high, although I could be doing with a little pick me up myself.

One bite hasn't perked me up at all; it's only contributed to my sickly feeling. I drop it back in the wrapper, feeling a shade greener.

I'm exhausted and still queasy. I've not had travel sickness in a long time, and it's not even a long journey. Maybe it's nerves or stress catching up with me, potentially both. I'll be fine when I lie down. Hopefully.

I manage to doze off momentarily, despite my stomach churning. Suddenly, I jolt upright,

"Oh God." I put my hand over my mouth, barely able to hold back the threatening vomit in my throat. Lucca calls Lloyd on the hands-free signalling to pull over. We pull over at a lay-by and just manage to throw the door open in time. I lean out the car hurling at the side of the road.

Bloody hell. How embarrassing. Beam me up.

Lucca rubs my back but is agitated because I'm feeling so poorly. I lean back against the car and feel soothed when Lucca's hands wrap around my waist to pull me into him, distracting me from my sickness, but we can't stay here forever, we need to drive.

We're just outside Kingussie and I ask him to stop at Aviemore, knowing it's not too far, and I'll get something from the chemist and an energy drink. The journey has taken us much longer to arrive at this point with the added stops.

Doris and Mr. Carlin are extremely fractious, and my granny and mum have called a handful of times. All I want to do is curl up and sleep, or die, maybe both … in no particular order.

We drive through Boat-Of-Garten and into Nethybridge so I can pick up some meat from the butcher's that I know my grandpa loves to barbecue. The smell of the fresh meat turns my stomach. I step outside for air and have Lucca pay for it once I've ordered.

I can't get out the door quick enough then think it wasn't such a good idea going to the butcher's after all. Lucca exits and frowns at me as I lean against the wall taking deep breaths.

"Doc, I think you are coming down with something," he says, placing an attentive hand to my forehead. I do feel feverish and lethargic. He's possibly right. It could even be a side effect from getting the implant inserted.

We wind up the long, stony, uphill road separated by paddocks and fields and spectacular mountain views, pulling up outside Granny and Grandpa's large, white cottage.

It has five bedrooms that will accommodate everyone, and there are plenty of other rooms, some cosy, some practical. It's a beautiful house. They inherited from my great-grandfather, which they used as a holiday home and rented it out while still living in Aberdeen. It's only since they've retired that they come here to stay.

"It is wonderful. Very lovely and in a desirable location. The views are stunning," Lucca says, admiring the Cairngorms.

"Yes, they are. We had lots of lovely, long summers here during our teenage years. Scotland is truly bonnie. I love it in October when the leaves are falling. If we're fortunate enough to get an Indian summer, it's very picturesque with autumn colours, and in the winter when the snow falls it's like an image from a postcard—a winter wonderland." I tilt my head and admire the scenery.

Lucca takes my hand and leans over to kiss my lips and stroke them with the pad of his thumb. "Are you okay?" he asks. Filling my lungs with the Highland air, I'm most definitely not okay, but I need very much to prove I am.

"Yes, let's do this."

Lucca opens my door and before I step outside, he kisses my hot forehead.

"I love you. It is going to be fine ... and, baby, you are a terrible liar." A wicked smile spreads across his charming face.

Chapter 29: Mother's Intuition

The huge, aged oak tree outside the front of the house has a wooden seat built all the way around it and there sitting on the bench is Grandpa playing his beloved harmonica. *His moothie.*

My heart melts.

I lift Lucca's hand, placing a kiss on it, and walk towards his seat. Alone. His back is to us and he's looking out over the sprawling Highland landscape. He doesn't turn around because he knows I'm here.

"Come here, Apple." Hearing his words, my eyes fill with tears, pining for him. I sit on his knee and wrap my arms around him, resting my head on his shrinking shoulder.

"I've missed you," I say with a lump in my throat, feeling very vulnerable.

"And I have missed you. I think about you every day. Welcome home, kid." He kisses my cheek and temple and hugs me tightly. I nestle into him and close my eyes, forgetting the world around about me. Opening my eyes, I savour the charming natural views of the Grampians, watching the sun shimmer over the River Spey in the distance.

After what seems like hours, I whisper, "There's someone I want you to meet."

"I can't wait. Apple, do you love him?"

"Yes, more than I can even confess."

"Does he love you?"

"Yes, he does. He's my whole world. You'll love him, Grandpa, I promise." I've no doubt in my mind that Lucca loves me as much as I love him.

"Well, I love him already, Apple, if you promise. That's enough for me. Let's go and get acquainted."

I reach for his hand. "Grandpa, can you help me?"

He takes my face in his ageing hand. "Yes, of course what do you need?"

"Speak to Granny and my mum. I can't feel suffocated. They need to let me breathe and treat me like an adult. Lucca doesn't want to be separated from me. He wants to share a room with me. I'd like us to stay together, you know."

"Oh," he adds. I search his face, begging with my eyes, albeit very embarrassed.

"I'm asking for your approval."

"Apple, they love you and want what's best for you as we all do. I promise I'll speak to them so they give you space. As for the room sharing, ordinarily I wouldn't approve but under the circumstances I'm sure it can be arranged. Consider it done." He smiles, brown eyes soft and gentle.

"I love you, Grandpa."

Kissing his cheek, we turn around and realise everyone is watching us. Biting my lip, I'm drawn to Lucca's soft smile and loving blue eyes. It's all I can focus on as he watches my moment with Grandpa. I don't even notice my mum right away, who appears to have tears running down her cheeks. She drops her dish towel and runs across the grass towards me. She throws her arms around my neck, sobbing hysterically.

Love.

Pure love.

The unrest in Lucca's eyes has ripped through my heart, and seeing my mum broken like this just confirms to me that I'm going to be strong for him … for her.

"Honey, you're here, you're here. You're really okay," she chants. I close my eyes and stroke her long, brown, soft, flowing locks the way Lucca does with me, and I rock her in my arms.

"Mum, I'm okay. It's going to be fine. Shhh, please don't cry. I want you to stay strong. We have a lot of catching up to do, so don't go fretting. Let's just enjoy our time together." She hiccups, snorts, and grips me tighter.

A loving smile spreads across Lucca's face reaching his eyes, and I notice Grandpa has wrapped his arm comfortingly around Granny, who looks like she's distressed and torn watching her family so wounded and wilted.

I release my mum's grip, stretching and stepping back, holding her hands at arm's length to admire her.

She truly is a vision of beauty.

"You look well, Mum. Really great." Other than her teary, puffy eyes, she looks stunning. Her beautiful, dark hair tumbles down her back. Her olive skin glows, and she still has that amazing figure and big, sweet, hazel-brown eyes.

She has on slim fitting jeans and a simple cream blouse and wears little pearl earrings and a string of pearls around her neck. She has always been naturally beautiful, and despite her traumas she's aged extremely well.

Grandpa says such beauty comes with a price and curses that it played a part in her kidnapping. Grandpa has always worried about me, as I look very much her younger image. He always said I would melt and break hearts like my mum did.

It's unfortunate she's never found romance or love in her later years. Her emotional instability makes it difficult. She deserves some love and could make someone very happy; she just needs some light, as Lucca would say.

She's elegant and flawless, and I wonder how she manages to look so healthy despite her battling depression all these years.

I love my mum more than words can describe. Such beauty and such pain. I just wish I could take her pain away.

Hand in hand, we join the group. I hug and kiss Granny and pet the two other dogs and realise Lucca has been watching us and patiently waiting to be introduced.

"Mum, Grandpa, I'd like you to meet Lucca. Lucca, this is my mum Grace, and my grandpa." I smile lovingly at both Mum and Grandpa and deliberately allow grandpa to choose what he would like to be referred to from Lucca, giving him the same courtesy that Mr. Carlin likes. Grandpa is first to welcome Lucca while Mum cautiously eyes him up and watches his every move and expression. She's being circumspect.

"So, young man, you have stolen my Apple's heart?" Grandpa reaches for Lucca to shake his hand. Lucca clasps his hand firmly around Grandpa's then customary kisses both cheeks.

"I hope so because she has certainly stolen mine."

He glances over to me, reaching his hand out. My heart melts watching my two favourite men in the world bond. I take Lucca's hand, linking our fingers, and he kisses the side of my head.

"She is very special, which of course you know. I love your granddaughter, Mr. Robertson, and will take excellent care of her."

"I know you will, son. Please call me Alexander or Alec," he says with warmth in his eyes and softness to his voice.

I look up adoringly into Lucca's eyes as my mum looks into mine. She's paying close attention to both of us and softening her gaze, watching our intimacy, whereas moments ago she appeared scared and dubious. Hopefully she's fully tolerant and accepting my relationship with Lucca.

I leave Grandpa and Lucca talking with Mr. Carlin while I speak with my mum and Granny. They gush in awe over my engagement ring but frown noticing the other diamond jewellery I'm wearing. "Mum, I know what you are thinking. Lucca bought me these, they were a gift," I say, touching the pendant on my neck.

"Hmmm ..." She presses her lips together.

"Are you okay, you seem a little tense?" I ask, rubbing her arm and notice she's nervously twirling the pearl earrings between her fingers.

"I'm just overwhelmed. It will take me some time to get used to this. It's a shock because I've never seen you with a man before. Casey has reassured me I have nothing to worry about but, seeing you … it's just got me thinking. Until I get to know Lucca myself, I don't know how trusting I will be." She looks at Granny, who pats her gently on her back.

"Mum, I get it … I do but I would like you to try. Please try for me," I beg, staring into her eyes. She forms a smile and nods. Sighing, I pull my hair away from my neck and shake it out, feeling very hot. Then Granny feels my forehead.

"Alexis, sweetheart, you look pale and are very hot. Are you coming down with something?" She purses her lips and narrows her eyes on me.

"I'm fine. I was a little travel sick, and I think I have a bug." Lucca overhears and discreetly glances towards me with his own concerned eyes. Mum smiles watching Lucca gaze sympathetically towards me.

Lloyd and Devon have also been introduced to my family but are now doing a sweep of the house and grounds having greeted Nate, the security operative assigned to my mum. Lucca hired Nate from the same agency on the same day I got my own Men in Black. Cameron, of course, refused security. He's more than capable of defending himself being in the forces.

"Clear." Lloyd signals to Lucca.

"Shall we go in and get settled?" Granny asks. We follow her in, Lucca once again taking my hand. We congregate in the main living room to the right of the hallway. Mr. Carlin takes a seat and gets comfortable. Nate shows Lloyd and Devon where to set up and where they'll be sleeping.

Downstairs there are two living rooms: the main one and a smaller one to the left, just past the dining room. There is a huge kitchen which was extended many years ago with an attached sunroom, a downstairs toilet, study, boot room, and another room which was once my granny's sewing room but has been made up into a spare bedroom for Nate.

The smaller living room has been temporarily converted into a base for Nate, Lloyd, and Devon. Cameras have been installed all around the perimeter of the house with computer surveillance being in this room.

Extreme!

My stomach churns looking at all the equipment. It just reiterates the seriousness of our impending threat. It looks extreme but I know it's for the best and will settle my mum's fears so I try to ignore the cables, monitors, and other devices.

On the second floor, there are five double bedrooms, two with bathroom facilities, a main bathroom, and a smaller room, which is Grandpa's library containing shelves of his cherished book collection but is currently being used by my mum as a painting room.

"I'm going to give Lucca the tour. Granny, can Lucca and I take my room?"

Tumbleweed.

She is speechless and stuttering, looking at Mum and Grandpa for backup. Mum bites her lip nervously but nods. Grandpa silently confirms his approval with his soft loving eyes.

"Yes, Apple, on you go. Make yourself comfortable, give Lucca the tour, and then come down for some tea," Grandpa answers for her. My mum reluctantly nods her head towards Granny, who succumbs in defeat under the peer group pressure.

Interesting. She always tends to get the last word, yet she's speechless. Lucca has charmed her as well ... bloody Casanova. On this occasion I'm glad he's a big bloody flirt.

"Yes, Alexis, sweetheart, your room is ready for ... you both," she finally adds. It must be killing her having to falter under her own rules.

"Thank you, Mrs. Robertson. You have a very beautiful house and thank you for having us." He's persuading her with his charismatic manners.

"Why, thank you, Lucca. It's my pleasure. Please, call me Elizabeth." And it's working a treat. Result!

I show Lucca around the house, and he appears to love it—the layout, the history and character, the traditional Scottish interiors from the quality of the thick tartan carpets and sofas to the animal antlers, deer pictures, and plaques above the fireplace. Grandpa also has a wall in which all his shooting rifles, shotguns, and pistols are lined up from his hunting days.

The house has been modernised somewhat, but they have tastefully preserved some of the original features having used only local designers and craftsmen. Granny has an eye for vintage detail and quality but also loves to keep to the tradition of the Scottish Highlands.

The ceilings all boast Tudor style beams, which have been re-stained recently. I always think the house smells of pine and wood chips. There's a wood shed and barn out the back stocked with logs for the fire. My grandpa's old tractor is still there, and his old faithful pedal bike is in the newly built garages at the side. Past the wood shed and barn are their privately-owned twenty acres of pine woodland wild with fir trees and purple heather and home to deer and red squirrels.

"Come on, I'll show you upstairs." I tug Lucca along after he's admired the old tractor.

"Do we get to try out the bed?" he rasps, roguishly grinning with his sexy, dimpled smile.

"Trust you." I smile.

"Baby, you know that you, stairs, and bed in the same sentence is going to get me rock fucking hard." He runs his hand under my sundress, cupping my ass. I am blushing and looking around to make sure no one has heard or witnessed that.

My room has one of the bathrooms. It's simple and comfy. The adorning ceilings also have Tudor beams. It's actually not unlike the bedroom in Sofia and Franco's villa. There's a double bed with a white duvet cover and a purple and blue tartan throw over the bottom. A mahogany dresser with a purple cushioned stool, drawers, bedside drawers, and a double wardrobe complete the room.

The curtains are purple and navy—Pride of Scotland Hunting Tartan—with matching pelmet and thick braided tie backs. The room is simply decorated with a mirror, clock, and a vase with thistle in it.

Still feeling clammy and queasy, I open the dormer window to let fresh air in.

"Baby, come here." Lucca sits on the end of the bed reaching out pulling me onto his lap. "I am worried about you. You look rather pale. Your mother noticed too. She mentioned it to me when you were speaking with your grandpa."

Yawning, I admit I'm feeling tired and groggy. He holds me into his chest, running his hand over my hot skin, soothing me with his touch.

"So what do you think?" I ask.

"I love the house and I love your family, but I knew I would. You were not exaggerating about your mother's beauty. She is absolutely stunning, which is of no surprise having a perfect beauty of a daughter. You are her exact image, and I told her so. She is an exceptional woman, Lexi, and she loves you very much. She is caring and gentle just like you. Your grandfather is a sincere, kind man. I see why you love him so much."

"And Granny?"

"Keeping your grandfather on his toes, that is what she is." I part my dry lips to smile and giggle.

He's summed her right up.

"She's hard work sometimes so be firm with her. She likes to get what she wants."

"Hmmm … just like someone else I know." He taps my nose with his fingers.

"I do not," I protest.

"Lexi, please, those chocolate brown eyes get you anything you want and as long as you are in my arms, I will always give you what you want. I love taking care of you, just like your grandpa most likely does for your granny." He strokes his thumb over my lips.

"I'd love to go for a nap. I'm so tired. Will you hold me for a bit?" I ask before running my fingers over his stubble then his lips.

"Of course I will. See how easy that was? Anything you want, baby." He smiles.

"It's the simple things, Romeo," I say appreciatively.

Smiling, I jump up, open the bedroom door, and holler over the thick oak banister, "Mum, I'm going for a sleep. Can you wake me up for dinner please? Oh, and make sure Mr. Carlin is settled, and ask Granny to search for that herbal tea stuff to settle my stomach."

"Are you okay?" she calls up.

"Yes, I have a fever and I'm tired."

"Okay, honey, enjoy your nap. Is Lucca okay?"

"Yes, he'll be down soon. Oh, there are groceries and butcher meat, which needs to be put in the fridge. Lucca will help."

Sighing, she stares at me as I hang over the banister. "Anything else, Alexis?" Exhaustion with a trace of discontent is obvious in her tone, which could be misconstrued as sarcasm.

"Nope, I think that's it. Oh, actually, ask Grandpa to feed Doris, please." I go back into my room and Lucca is leaning against the headboard, raising his brow, looking smug with crossed arms behind his head.

"So back to our conversation ..."

"Very funny. She likes doing stuff for me because she doesn't see me very often." I smirk.

"More like lets you get away with anything." I guess she does. She has always felt a need to try and compensate for fundamental things she wasn't able to do for us when we were kids.

I smile bashfully, running my teeth along my bottom lip.

"It's lovely to see you smiling."

He kicks his shoes off then lifts me up placing me in the middle of the bed. Slipping my pumps off, he gently massages my ankle then lifts the tartan throw. Spooning around my body, he wraps us in the throw and holds me close until I drift off into a deep sleep.

Stretching my lethargic limbs, the smell of pine, woodchips, fresh lavender and potpourri fills my nostrils, and I remember I'm in a room at my grandparents, nestled in the woodlands of the Scottish Highlands.

The fresh air sure knocked me out. I search for Lucca's hand, his body, but he's not there. Lifting my cosmetic bag from a holdall next to the bed, I freshen up and brush my teeth then take some of my painkillers hoping it will lower my burning temperature.

I discover I'm not bleeding any longer. Weird! Then I remember the doctor telling me the implant reduces your period and makes it very light and short.

Excellent, I say to myself. I smile looking at Granny's coordinating purple hand towels with tartan ribbon trimming, matching bath mat, and a little vase of thistles in the bathroom.

I hope she's not too upset that Lucca will be sharing a room with me, but it's simply non-negotiable. I find a note sitting on the dresser.

'Doc, you looked so peaceful and needed a good sleep, so I did not want to disturb you. I am going to bond with your mother and tell her wonderful things about you, about us. I will be waiting downstairs for you, see you soon. Lexi, I love you, baby xxx'.

Holding the note to my chest, I smile into the mirror in silent prayer, grateful that Lucca is in my life, that I have him.

"Oh God," I groan with disgust, noticing my dark, weary eyes. I look lifeless and my face is ashen even under my olive skin tone and sun kissed glow from Italy. Pinching my cheeks doesn't bring any colour to them at all.

Sighing, I accept I look and feel like shit.

Hanging my body over the banister, I don't see or hear anyone in the hallway. Downstairs, I find Mr. Carlin, Grandpa, Lloyd, Devon, and Nate in the dining room playing cards. I wrap my arms around Grandpa's neck and kiss his head.

"I hope you're winning."

"Do I ever lose, kid?" Men in Black try to remain impartial but their facial expressions are softening, and I see a smile from under Devon's normally stern mien.

It's the first time I have seen Men in Black relax, and without those dark glasses on they look carefree and well … human. They are from the same firm as Nate so they have a lot of history together, and I'm guessing it's not going to be as uncomfortable as I initially thought for them.

"Nice sleep, Apple?" Grandpa asks.

"Yes thanks, where's Lucca?"

"Outside with your mother. Granny is in the kitchen. She might want help if you're feeling better. You have a wonderful beau there, Apple, he's a keeper. He sure is a very endearing, loving man and I'm delighted for you, kid," he says without taking his eyes off the game at hand.

I love the way he and Granny still call each other "Granny" and "Grandpa" in front of me. It's very sweet. I've only ever heard him call her Elizabeth in my presence a few times, and it's when their having a tiff.

"I know I do, Grandpa, I really do." I kiss his head and stroll outside. Leaning against the porch, I watch Lucca and my mum sitting on the bench surrounded by the tree. She has a shawl wrapped around her petite shoulders and her head rests on Lucca's shoulder. From the back I could be looking at Lucca and me.

His arm is protectively around her shoulder, and she looks tiny under his huge, toned arms. They're watching the sunset across the northern edge of the Cairngorm National Park and River Spey. The views are truly spectacular, peaceful, fresh, and unlike anywhere else on earth. It's mystical. This view fills my heart with pride every time I look at it.

Lucca also fills my heart with pride because of his natural instinct to protect, care, cherish, and love.

It breaks me seeing her so vulnerable. I'm striving to keep strength because nothing I have gone through or ever will go through will come fractionally close to my mum's own horrid misfortunes and emotional demons.

Grace Robertson has clawed and chipped away trying to shatter that glass shield, to break into her light, but she just can't make those last few punctures to splinter and crack that glass. The shield encases her, she slides back down, dragged further into the pit of Hell, deeper into the abyss of bad dreams.

On *that* side. The dark side.

Figuratively, her hands must be cut to shreds, not to mention her mind and heart. My issues seem like a mere trickle of rain on a water lily floating in a tiny pond of worry in comparison to hers.

Knowing Lucca and how he has helped me and how strong he is, he might just be what she needs to shatter that glass and find some of her own light. I hope so. I don't want to disturb the moment but little Ruby, the King Charles spaniel, is whining and clawing at my leg. I bend over to pick her up and snuggle her into my neck, kissing her head.

As if sensing I'm there, Lucca turns around and smiles tenderly at me. His eyes ask me to join them. Agreeing soundlessly, I walk across the gravel and dewy grass towards the tree bench with Ruby cuddled in my arms.

I have a desperate desire to be near him for his touch and to share his warmth. The butterflies in my abdomen flutter, anticipating his loving, gentle comfort. With Ruby in my arms, I sit at the other side of Lucca then put Little Miss Frightful down on the grass when she wriggles hearing Doris' wolf-like howl. She scurries away to hide.

Lucca kisses my cheek and moves a stray curl from my face. My mum doesn't look up; she remains peacefully relaxed into Lucca's side watching the warm amber sun lowering behind the Cairngorm National Park and distant River Spey. I reach my hand across and place it over hers, resting on Lucca's thigh. She sighs and clutches it tightly.

The golden evening sun highlights her perfect but thin body and the caramel sheen of her soft, chocolate hair. Other than the elegant small pearls, her skin is bare; there are no diamonds or expensive sparkle, only her pure, exquisite beauty which is sparkle enough for my beautiful mum. I feel a twinge of heartache sharing this moment with her.

"Alexis," she whispers.

"Uh huh." I'm waiting on something very negative, challenging, or obsessively suffocating.

"I give you both my blessing, sweetheart. Lucca is more than wonderful, and very much the man who I would love you to spend your life with. He is perfect for you, and I truly wish you both all the happiness in the world that my fragile heart can give you. I've only ever wanted the best for you and Cameron, and it makes me very happy and content to know that you have found stability, love, and security," she croaks.

I'm speechless. I don't know how Lucca managed it, but then I never doubted his charm. He's superhuman after all. Tears threaten my eyes, but I'm on my mission of strength and try desperately to contain them.

"Mum, I'm so happy you said that because Lucca *has* turned my life around, and I need your blessing, thank you ... it means so much. I love you, Mum." I squeeze Lucca's knee with my hand as my other one tightens around my mum's.

"Our relationship has progressed very fast, so I understand you have your concerns, but I can assure you I want nothing more than to be with Lucca, to have him in my life." Lucca grips me tightly, then trails his thumb across my hip. She lifts her head off Lucca's shoulder, sitting upright and turning to face me, causing the shawl to drop off her dainty shoulders.

"Alexis, I'm sorry. I'm sorry I was irrational with you. I can see now how special your relationship is, how special you are for each other. I was shocked initially, but, sweetheart, I'm so proud of you. God was watching over me when he brought you into the world, into my life. You're my breath of hope, Alexis, and you have no idea how much I love you."

The strong wall which I've tried to cement is tumbling brick by brick.

I'm demolished.

"Mum, I love you too. I'm sorry if I let you down." My lip trembles.

"Alexis, you could never let me down, ever. I've done enough of that for all of us." She's faltering, doing what I always do ... questioning herself.

"Hey, don't ever say that. You have not. You're an inspiration, Mum, look what a good job you've done raising us. We have so much respect for you. Don't ever put yourself down. Promise me," I sob with a lump forming in my throat.

Promise.

A promise is a promise.

"Oh, honey, thank you ... I promise I'll try." She smiles.

Standing up, we reach for one other and embrace tightly. In this moment I wish I could obliterate my mum's worry the same way Lucca does with mine.

We hold each other until the sun is finally down, huddled against one another. Lucca grants us our moment. I reach my hand to pull him beside me. My mum wipes my tears then smiles.

"I'll give you both a minute. I'll help your grandmother with dinner, Lucca ... thank you ..." Mum smiles, her brown eyes glisten with moisture. I see a stray tear cascade down her cheek and it looks so bright ... light ... like a sparkling diamond. I think about Lucca telling me the same thing that my tears glistened like diamonds against my skin.

Now I get it.

"You're most welcome, Grace." He rubs her shoulder sympathetically.

I watch her walk to the house, her hair swaying down her back with each light, delicate footstep.

She leaves the shawl on the bench.

"Come here," Lucca says softly, approaching my lips to kiss them, wrapping the shawl around me.

Still warm from the heat from my mum's body, it comforts me. He kisses me sweetly again and again. Ready to move, we stand. I press my body against his. Under the thin fabric of the sundress I feel his hard, toned, muscular body against mine.

One hand is behind my head softly playing with my hair while the other nestles in the small of my back. His hand travels over my ass, under the shawl. Leaping up, he instinctively catches me while I wrap my legs around his waist. Lucca places his forehead on mine and spins me around slowly in the blissful, romantic Scottish sunset.

"I love you, Mr. Caruso. You never fail to amaze me. My mum loves you, and I couldn't be happier. You've worked your magic."

"Baby, it was you. She watched the way you look at me, and that is what she noticed. That is what convinced her."

"Kiss me," I demand. A warmth of gratitude radiating from my eyes.

It's a slow, sensual kiss. The kind of sweet kiss that has me quivering helplessly with sheer loving desire, one that I don't want to end. I melt into his protective arms with vulnerability.

Closing my eyes deep in the moment, I hear Doris barking. She's jumping up and down next to me with jealously, little Tosh, the Westie, in her shadow trying to follow suit. Lucca kisses my neck tickling me, and I giggle throwing my head back while he spins me in slow motion, only causing Doris to bark with excitement and circle us even more.

Bucking and squirming, I reach my hand under his tight-fitting T-shirt to tickle him. We laugh, fondle, and giggle so much that we fall back on the grass, entangled in the shawl. The dogs are in a state of excitement bouncing around us, even Ruby the timid dog has joined us.

Lucca leans over me and moves that unruly wave of curls that falls over my face. His voice has lost its lightness, and he's now very serious. Deep. The intense heat in his eyes singes my body and makes my heart beat rapidly.

"Lexi, we will get through this. Nothing is going to happen to you. I know you are exhausted thinking about it, but I promise you …"

He leans in, holding my two hands above my head on the grass, and kisses me passionately. His tongue swirls with mine slow, soft and seductive. My grandpa's deliberate coughing shakes us from our intimate moment.

"Dinner is ready."

Oh shit. I blush.

"Okay, we're coming." I bury my head into the crook of Lucca's neck to hide my embarrassment.

"Come here," he whispers turning my head so that he can meet my eyes, silently telling me he loves me.

Amorous.

Safe.

Complete.

When Lucca picks me up and lazily hangs his arm around my shoulder walking us back to the porch, my granny and mum are both watching us from the porch, amazed with our intimacy.

"If you two lovebirds are finished, dinner is ready," Granny quibbles, ruffling her apron and her feathers. Her tone is a little sharp. I look at Mum who smiles and rolls her eyes at Granny. I never thought Mum would be so open-minded about my relationship with Lucca.

Oh God, I hope I don't get the dreaded loafer swiped across my ass from Granny.

My mum smiles in loving appreciation with eyes of respect and adoration. Understanding.

I brush the grass off the bottom of my dress and kiss Granny's cheek as I pass the front door, only to get an eye raising snigger from Mum because she knows Elizabeth Robertson does not like her feathers ruffled.

Everyone's sitting around the dining table for dinner, including our three Men in Black. Hospitality and good manners are a must in the Robertson household, so our security team has been made very welcome—like guests, not staff.

I'm sitting between Grandpa and Lucca with one hand wrapped in Grandpa's and the other around Lucca's lower back. I skim his lower back through the material of his T-shirt, tapping my fingers lightly as I hang my head on Grandpa's shoulder.

I offer to help but Granny insists I sit and relax as she thinks I look rather pale. Mum's not buying the fever excuse. She's studied every move, comment, and expression. I feel as if I'm being assessed by a triage nurse.

Mum serves the starters: Granny's homemade chicken liver pate with her own cranberry sauce, wild herbs from the garden, and Scottish oatcakes. Normally, I would love this, but my stomach is still delicate after today's travel sickness.

The smell of the pate is actually turning my stomach. It's killing me.

"Alexis, what's wrong? This is one of you favourites," Mum asks, alarmed.

"Yeah, I'm sorry, I think it's the bug, I think I'm going to …" I place my hand over my mouth and escape to the downstairs toilet and vomit into the bowl just in time, not that there's much in my stomach today.

The door opens seconds later and I know it's Lucca.

"Oh, dolcezza, you are really ill. I think you should go to the doctor's tomorrow … you must have a virus. Here, drink this."

He moves my hair and holds a glass of water in front of me. I sit back on my heels. My hand is shaking, but I reach for it and take a sip, my teeth chattering against the glass. "Oh God, I'm mortified."

"Hey, if you are ill, you are ill. It is fine. I just want you better. Are you done? Are you okay now?"

"Yes."

I know there's nothing left to physically retch out of my stomach. After washing, we exit the compact toilet to see my mum standing in the hall with her hands tucked into the pocket of her jeans looking through me.

"Alexis, Lucca, can you come here for a moment please." She's steady, serious, and level headed, so much so it's worrying me. I look at her for reasoning but nothing. I shrug, glancing at Lucca, baffled as to where this is going.

Maybe I have a mystery childhood illness that she has now decided to share with me.

Lucca takes my hand to follow Mum into the sunroom. She takes a seat on a padded wicker chair, clasping her hands on her knees, while we sit on the three seat rattan sofa across from her.

"I'm sorry about dinner, Mum. Please forgive me. I just felt so ... so sick." I place my hand to my throat and swallow slowly.

She pauses, looking down and arranging Granny's thistle coasters on the table in front. I wait for her to speak but she says nothing. I squeeze Lucca's hand, looking for help as I'm still hot and sickly, trying to keep down the lurking seediness in my stomach.

"Is everything okay?" Lucca asks.

"Lucca ..." She pauses again, taking another deep breath.

"Yes?" Uncertainty laces his voice. Mum takes a deep breathe, mindlessly twirls the pearl earrings in her ear then addresses him.

"Lucca. I know Alexis is pregnant. How far along is she? When were you going to tell me?"

Beam me up!

She's losing her mind.

"Oh God ... Mum, stop it. What are you talking about?" I retaliate with irritation.

"I know my own daughter and you, my girl, are pregnant." I can't quite process this.

"What?" I yell moving upright and turning to face Lucca.

"Lucca, I'm not. Tell her I'm not." I plead.

He's silent. *Why?*

Speak, goddamn it!

"Of course I'm not pregnant. I've just been on my goddamn flipping period and have an implant in my arm." I raise my voice towards my mum, which I'm ashamed of but she's driving me to it. I'm angry and confused.

"Calm down, Alexis. Have you taken a test?" She softens her voice. I turn to look at Lucca for backup, but he's frozen on the spot, shocked with this conversation, staring at the stupid bloody coasters possibly with a paler complexion than me.

"Lucca?" I yell, shaking his arm.

He blinks from his momentary trance, then stares at my midsection. "Lexi, are you? Are you pregnant with our baby?" It sounds more like a hopeful wish than an inquisition.

"What are you two going on about? You both sound ridiculous."

Flustered.

Irate.

Hot and bothered.

"No, I'm not pregnant. I had to take a test at the clinic with the doctor before I got the implant and it was negative. I was bleeding yesterday and early this morning so I can't be." I begin to shake nervously.

"Alexis, sweetie, that doesn't mean you're not. I bled all through with Cameron, and halfway through my pregnancy with you. It can be very common," she adds.

Lucca is white, like a frozen snow statue. He hasn't moved, and I've never seen him like this before.

"Mum, please stop. You're freaking him out and getting his hopes up." I don't know what I'm saying, I don't know what she's saying but I do know that I feel like disappearing into the ground below me.

She quizzically looks at him, and me, then him again. "Oh, goodness gracious ... I'm sorry, Lucca, you poor thing. I thought you both were aware. I thought maybe that was the reason you fell head over heels so early and got engaged. Of course, I might be wrong but, Alexis, you need to do another test. Your Aunt Eva had to take four tests before it showed positive with the twins."

"Oh, I think I'm going to be sick ..."

I lean over the rattan chair and vomit up the glass of water.

Splash. All over the floor.

The room is spinning. I need fresh air. I can't hear this, not from my mum anyway. Once I sit up, Lucca takes my hand, sweetly stroking it but I feel him trembling. It's the first time I have ever truly felt him shake like this.

"Jesus, Lexi, baby, you *are* pregnant. You must be." His glistening eyes meet mine, hungry and eager for answers. Answers that I can't give him because now Mum has put ideas in my head and I'm wondering about the effectiveness of the test I took.

"Lucca, I'm not. I must have a virus, please don't make an issue of this. I have enough going on. I promise you I'm not and I had a negative test. Sickness is a side effect of the implant." I choke and break.

I'm not. I'm not. I'm not.

Denial. File. Compartmentalise. Ignore.

Mum nods towards Lucca, giving him the look. The "mother knows best" look and confirms to him that I very much am pregnant.

"I'll clean that up for you. Lucca, take her for fresh air. I'll make something else to eat if she wants it." Then she wraps her arms around my shoulders and kisses my head now covered in sweat.

"Alexis, I'm sorry to alarm you. I just know my own daughter. I'd like you to take another test tomorrow. I'll go to the chemist for you. Please don't worry, sweetie. We will work this out, and after seeing you both, I know this can't be a bad thing. You love each other. Everything will be fine, I promise you."

Promise.

A promise is a promise.

These are her words. She would always promise to make things better and protect us when we were kids. If she promises, then she means it and does everything in her power to make sure it happens. She's soft and caring, speaking the way she would when I was a young, vulnerable girl. She is serious but she's compassionate. These words end me. I cry.

"No," I retort. "I'm not pregnant. I can assure you. Mum, please don't … just accept I'm not. I want to marry Lucca first before thinking about children, and with everything else going on I'm not equipped, I can't be a mummy. I can't do it, I can't because I'm too …"

I fall onto my knees, breaking down in sobs, holding my stomach as if in denial, searching for another sign. *Confirmation.*

"Grace, I am taking her out for fresh air. I will come back with her if she is hungry." Suddenly Lucca has snapped out of his trance and is taking control while I just need to evaporate into space. Forever.

Fuck!

File F for fate. Fate interrupting my already complicated life.

Lucca lifts a heavy shawl that's folded and sitting on top of a wooden trunk and scoops me up in a swift move. Then he opens the sunroom door and walks with me around the back of the house to the wood shed. It's pitch black.

"There's a switch to the right," I sob.

He flips the switch and a strip light above flickers then shines brightly.

"It's full of logs. I was hoping to sit with you. To talk."

"There's another section to the back. It's a barn. There are hay bales but no lights, only lanterns," I inform him, snivelling through my broken sobs.

He walks past the rows of logs and finds the door into the barn. I signal towards the lanterns, and he balances me on his thigh while he fidgets with the lantern. He has two lit, so he leaves one at the entrance and carries the other, finding a corner by the hay.

He stands me on my feet then spreads the thick shawl out over the hay. Setting the lantern on a nearby ledge, he lifts me up and places me on the shawl, then kneels in front of me, leaning protectively over me.

I stare at the pine timber roof, nervous about how this discussion is going to go. He straddles my legs, lifting my sundress, then leans over and runs his thumb along the edge of my panties.

Softly, he kisses my navel, covering every piece of skin. He kisses, strokes, and tenderly rubs the pad of his thumb across my stomach.

I ripple in a delightful flutter under his touch. I've never felt such soft, gentle butterfly wings flickering so tender, desperate, and profound. Involuntarily, I lace my fingers in his hair.

"Lucca, I don't think I'm pregnant," I whisper, not wanting to spoil the moment or burst his bubble, but I need to be honest.

He doesn't say anything. He brushes feathery strokes, kisses, and softly licks along tummy. Then he rests the side of his head there, his stubbly chin and cheeks tickling my abdomen as his fingers skim my lace panties' edge.

I'm breathing heavily. He's breathing heavily.

My chest rises and falls with such sweet attention. Closing my eyes, I actually don't want him to move. I want to stay here forever with his cheek pressed against my fluttering tummy. Safe.

"Lucca, I took a test, and it was negative."

"I want you to do another one tomorrow. I think Grace is right. It makes sense."

The dizziness, sickness, headaches, tiredness, and loss of appetite.

More tears break the dam and cascade down my cheeks. I'm shaking and sniffling with the realisation.

Metallic taste to my mouth. Shit.

I *am* pregnant. I must be.

He lifts himself up, looking into my wet eyes and quickly wipes my tears away.

"No, baby, do not cry. Do you know how happy you would make me if you are carrying our baby? I love you more than anything in the world. I thought I could not love you any more, Lexi, and I do every day. I would love us to have a baby. I know this is a little quick for you, but we agreed to have a family at some point. It is just unexpected, but not unwelcome."

"Hmmm ..." I sigh. This is not what I expected, perhaps in a few years' time, not now.

"We are lucky and blessed to have one another, but a family ... God, Lexi, I cannot tell you how much that excites me, how much I want you to be the mother of my kids, now or in the future. There is probably never a perfect time. It is a miracle and will happen when God sees fit to bless us with this gift."

His warm hand splayed across my stomach causes light tremors of internal desire deep in my core. The other hand is on my cheek. He leans into me, kissing my cheeks, my eyes, my nose, and then my lips. I'm trying to block out the fact I've just been sick.

Yuck.

"And what if I'm not? I don't want you to be disappointed. You seem pretty convinced and *hopeful,*" I say cautiously.

"If you are not, we live our lives. I protect you. We get married and think about it when you are ready. I feel awful about putting pressure on you before when you have all this other stuff going on. You need to know either way I have you and you are the most important person to me, the most important person in the world and always will be. If I can keep you safe, I will be a happy man. Then we will concentrate on our future when this all passes."

He always says the nicest, most sincere words when I'm in despair.

"And what if I am pregnant, what then?" It changes everything."

In the dim flickering light of the lantern, I see a glimmer of excitement cross his eyes.

"I will take great care of you, both of you. I will spoil you and we will have a baby, a very lucky baby I might add to have parents like us to care for it, and we will cherish and love our baby and live our lives, and we will be the happiest parents in the goddamn world."

"And what about getting married?" I ask a little more rationally now that my tears are subsiding.

"We can marry as soon as possible if you want. You know I want to. I can make it happen or if you want to wait we will until after the baby has arrived then that is fine too. Lexi, I need you and want you to be my wife, baby or not, we are going to get married and have a future together."

Could I love this man anymore?

I close my eyes.

"You sound like you already know I am."

He's so near my mouth, his nose pressed against mine and his warm hand splayed across my abdomen. With one finger hitched under the lace edge of my panties, the other rests on top. He pulls me closer to him. His hot breath gusts over my lips and neck, and it's deliciously exhilarating. He's raspy, sexy, and attentive.

"I just know you are. Your mother is right."

He graces my lips with a chaste kiss. Then he slides back down and kisses my stomach causing little reverberating ripples of pleasure. Sweetly circling and kissing my skin, his tender caress has my sex so electrified with a pulsing desire that I need him. It's a feeling like nothing else.

For a nanosecond, I'm thinking I may be able to handle pregnancy if this is the pleasure I get from the man I love smothering me in protective blissful caress. I like it, I feel secure, safe, and special. Lucca's hot air from his nostrils travels across my abdomen, only to turn me on because he's so near my hot, damp sex.

His attentive fondling is pacifying and pleasing, and I've forgotten all about my day of sickness beneath his considerate and thoughtful touch. Rationally, I feel as if I need to pull him away from caressing my tummy in the event I'm not pregnant, but it feels so perfect and I just can't. My head is full of mixed emotions, but the one thing that pulls me back from fear, doubt, and anxiety is Lucca's love.

Always, Lucca's love.

"Lucca?"

"Hmmm?" He sighs, moving his jaw so his bristly stubble grazes across my soft skin again.

"I love you ... but I'm scared. I mean I was scared about Michael Parks but this just ... well, I don't know if ..." My voice trails off, sounding broken. It scares me on a whole new level. I don't know that I'm ready right now to be a mum. Lucca is supportive but it's me, I question my coping mechanisms. What if I screw this up? He's already talking about having extra therapy sessions with Casey. How am I supposed to be strong and supportive, set a good example to a child, when I can barely do it for myself?

He kneels in front of me on a lower haystack and slides his hands behind my back, pulling my upper body up so he's between my legs: his chest to mine, my sundress scrunched up in between us. He looks into my eyes, closing the space between us, claiming me, owning me and wordlessly calming me.

I know he's telling me everything will be okay, and I want to believe in us, our light and our future.

"Tell me what you are thinking." He searches my eyes, so close and sincere.

Here goes.

"I'm ..." Breathlessly, I carry on through my nerves. "I'm worried I won't be a good mummy, or be fit to look after a child. You said yourself that the specialists suspect I'm on the verge of a breakdown similar to my mum's."

Pain and upset lace his voice, but his eyes are so warm and compassionate that they are filled with honest love. He's hurting that I would even question myself. "Christ, Lexi, they do not know you, but I do. You are strong, loving, caring, and selfless. You put everyone before yourself the way your mother has done with you and Cameron. You have endless support, and I will always love and protect you. We can do this together. I give you my word, I promise. I will be a hands on papa and be there every step of the way, at every aspect of our child's life. And for you, dolcezza, I will be here for you, always. If you are rotten at changing the nappies, I will tell you so."

I giggle because he's alluding to my insecurities and trying to be light-hearted.

"Lexi, your mother may have had issues to face, but she has done a pretty damn fine job of raising you both, especially under the circumstances. She is stronger than you give her credit for, and so are you, Doc. Believe me. Do you feel better?"

"I don't feel as sick as I did."

"That is good. I am pleased. Do you feel better now that we have spoken?" His thumb trails down my stretched neck, my chest, my breasts, and to my stomach again.

"Yes, you have a way with me, Mr. Caruso, and I'm thankful you can always centre me. I need your reassurance, and you've helped me see a little clearer tonight, so thank you."

I imagine everyone has doubts and this is normal. I had an amazing weekend with Lucca's nieces and nephews and I could see myself care for our child someday, but now the reality is overwhelming. I've not even had time to file and revisit these thoughts.

His hand travels under my dress, over my thighs, and up to my tummy again. These palms of his are going to be splayed over my tummy for the next nine months if I am pregnant.

"You know, Lucca, it's the same tummy you felt seconds ago."

"Baby, get used to it. If you are pregnant, which I am sure you are, I will be stuck to your tummy like glue."

"Hmmm, and what if I'm not? Does that mean I won't get any of this TLC?" I challenge, wrinkling my nose.

"I will still be giving you plenty of TLC because I told you I am stuck on you, but that is *if*, baby. I know you are."

We talk and cuddle for so long my stomach rumbles, which stifles a laugh from both of us.

"Time we fed you. Are you ready to go?" He places a final kiss on my abdomen, then my lips.

"Yes, I hope my mum didn't tell Granny. Oh God, can you imagine? I might be dragged into church tonight after she wallops me with her loafer." He laughs, fixing my dress. "Then she'll wallop you," I add.

We lift the blankets, blow out the lanterns, and walk back to the sunroom.

Chapter 30: Church

Everyone has finished their meal when we return to the dining room. Mr. Carlin and Grandpa have a dram of whiskey in hand as they share familiar stories, playing chess.

"Alexis, Lucca, I'm glad you joined us. Would you like some dinner?" Mum asks.

"Yes, thank you, but it's okay. I'll fix something," I say, squeezing Lucca's hand.

"Okay, I'll help you." She picks up the rest of the empty plates and carries them into the kitchen.

"I'll bring you something. Please, sit down and relax," I tell Lucca. He picks up my hand, kissing the front of it, and nods for me to go with my mum.

I follow her into the kitchen. My fingers feel tight, my heart rate is quickening, and my head is dizzy. I'm nervous about what she might say.

"Is peppercorn fillet of beef, Diane sauce, potatoes, sautéed vegetables, and soda bread okay for Lucca?" she asks, fetching the ingredients from the fridge.

"Yes, perfect. He'll love that."

"And you?" she adds.

"It sounds lovely, but I don't think I'll manage tonight. It would be a waste."

"Did you two talk?" she asks as she seasons Lucca's beef fillet. I watch her sear it in the hot pan then put the potatoes back onto the cast iron stove to crisp.

"Yes, but I'm so confused." I lean against the counter and worry my fingers in front of my lips.

Stopping, she turns around to face me. "When did you get this implant thing?"

"Monday, but I've been on the pill." I rub my finger over my arm where it was inserted.

"The pill can be unreliable. Did you take it correctly?"

"Yes, I've been very cautious." *Or have I?*

"Have you been sick or taken any prescription drugs that could interfere with the effectiveness of your pill?"

Then like a jolt of lighting shocking me into reality, I place my hand over my mouth. "That's it. I had antibiotics in Tuscany, but I still took my pill and never realised."

Shit, how could I be so careless?

"And did you use other precautions?"

Shamefully, I drop my head, embarrassed to be having this conversation with her. "No."

"There you go. That's why you're pregnant." Noticing the disbelief on my face, she smiles. "Alexis, please don't worry. It will be fine, I promise you. Regardless of the outcome, you have Lucca and you have us."

"I don't think I'm strong like you."

She walks over and wraps her arm around me, stroking my hair. "Nonsense. You're stronger and you know it. You're loved and in love, so it's completely different. If you had called me and told me you were pregnant, I would have passed out from shock, but this is different and I'm honestly happy for you. Ideally, I would love you to be married first, but it doesn't matter. Watching you both, I've no doubt in my mind that you'll be great parents together and have a happy life. I don't want to miss a minute of my grandchildren growing up, and I hope it will bring us closer together again. Second chances, right?"

"I hope so. Second chances," I whisper.

We hug in the middle of the kitchen, and a few tears escape her eyes. She assures me they're happy tears, and in this moment I feel love for my mum. I watch her flipping the steak, and the smell of it cooking is making me queasy again so I hold my breath, spreading my toast with cheese and Branston pickle. I fill the whistling kettle and place it on the stove.

"Have you told Granny?" I ask, standing back from the sizzling, bloody beef.

Taking a nibble of my toast, she moves me to get to the clean plates. "No, let's just wait and see first, but she suspects something. Then I'll be in the bad books for not telling her."

"Mum, either way, I just need to know ... are you proud of me?"

She drops her utensil and walks towards me, wrapping her arm around my waist. "Every blooming day, more than yesterday and less than tomorrow, so don't ever doubt that, ever." I wonder what she would make of this predicament if she was in one of her fragile episodes.

"I'm worried about what Granny and Grandpa will think of me." Chewing the inside of my cheek, I fidget with an envelope with their name on it that is sitting on the counter.

"Don't worry about that. If we're right, it will be lovely news and good for this family to have something positive to focus on for a change."

My goodness, someone has virtually reprogrammed Mum's mind. I think she has stared long enough into Lucca's azure blue crystals and she's under a trance.

I take his meal through to the dining room, stretching it as far away from my line of scent as I possibly can, turning my head. I pass Granny as she walks to the kitchen to help Mum clear up. She'll likely ask what we've been talking about. Interrogate.

"Thank you, but are you not eating? You need to eat," Lucca says.

"I've had toast. It's all I can ..."

"Okay."

"Would you like some wine with your dinner?" I ask.

"Absolutely not. You cannot have wine, Doc."

"Keep your voice down." I signal towards Grandpa and Mr. Carlin, who are too lost in their world of Kings and Queens to have even noticed.

"Sorry." He frowns.

"I offered it to you. Obviously, I'm going to have tea." Crossing my arms across my chest, I take umbrage to his insult.

"Come here." He holds his hand out and I stand by his side. "I am sorry, I know you would not. I will have what you are having. I am not going to drink wine on my own when you cannot have any," he whispers in my ear.

"You don't need to do that."

"I want to." He moves a stray tendril from my face.

"Oh God, oh no ..."

"Doc, what is wrong?"

"I've been drinking all this time. If I'm ... shit, I've been abusing my body, and this can't be good." I mentally count the weeks back.

"You must be early on so do not worry about that. We can speak to the doctor, but I am sure it is fine this early. Most women do not know right away." He's right of course. It would probably be the size of a seed right now, but it doesn't help my concern any or make me feel better about it.

"Eat your dinner before it gets cold, and I'll bring some drinks." Mum shows up in front of us and shoves two glasses of chilled cranberry juice in my hands and says she will bring the tea. Granny and Mum both join us for tea to chat with Lucca, and Granny finally gets her teeth into him by interrogating with a million questions.

They engage in chat about Lucca's businesses and Tuscany. Granny asks me all about our holiday, but I'm too drained to talk, Lucca kisses the front of my hand and tells her all about it.

Lucca and I wrap up and go for a short walk outside with the dogs, hand in hand. Now that we have privacy again, I feel I owe him an explanation.

"The antibiotics I took for the infection for my foot in Tuscany must have counteracted against my pill. Mum helped me work it out because I thought I was very careful."

"Well, then it is fate and meant to be. God, I love you," he says, pulling me in close to him. "Let's get in. You are chilly."

The space next to Grandpa is free on the sofa. I look at Lucca, silently asking if he minds.

"Go ahead, I will sit here."

I curl into Grandpa's side, resting my head on his shoulder. Everyone is in the main living room, sitting comfortably in front of the fire. Mum and Granny are looking at my photo book with tears in their eyes.

Lucca and Mum talk about Tuscany and our holiday while Granny smiles at Grandpa with sweet, loving eyes. Her eyes are tired, but I'm sure I notice a glimmer of pride as she passes him the book.

Opening the front cover, he inwardly catches his breath. "Well, would you look at that? This is really something. Apple, I never thought we would see this day. I couldn't be prouder of you right now, kid." He's referring to my fear of being photographed.

"I will have copies of this book ordered for both, for you to keep if you would like." Lucca gestures towards Mum and Granny.

"Oh, thank you, yes, that would be very kind. We shall cherish it. You're so photogenic, sweetheart, and you remind me so much of your mother before ... well, before ..." Granny says trying to mask hide her sobs. Grandpa comforts me, patting my back, but at the same time he's smiling fondly at Mum. He adores his girl. He's hurt.

"Yes, she is very beautiful, Elizabeth." Lucca adoringly smiles at me, causing me to blush.

I place my hand on my lower stomach, and Lucca tilts his head, watching me with warmth in his eyes. It sends little waves of serenity through my body. Mum looks at Lucca watching me with a sense of mirth.

"Are you ready to go to bed?"

I thought he'd never ask. We kiss everyone good night and hold hands as we walk upstairs. This walk to bed feels different.

Young.

Serene.

Naive.

He strips me of my clothes as I'm too weak to move. Then we shower together under the hot water, which is invigorating and refreshing against my weak body. Keeping my eyes closed, Lucca stands behind me, holding me against his rock solid body, his arms wrapped around me and his hands protectively splayed across my abdomen. My sleepy eyes open with the feel of his erection pressing behind me.

"Are you too tired?" he asks.

I smile.

"For you, never." And now I'm wide awake. His touch is all I need.

"Good, I was hoping you would say that. Tell me what you want," he rasps, then nibbles my neck, moving one hand to cup my sex and the other to tweak one of my budded nipples peaking under his touch.

Shaking with desire, I've never been so aware of my body. I lean my head back against his shoulder, holding my hands on the back of his neck and gripping his shaggy hair.

"Touch me, kiss me, then take me to bed. Slowly bury yourself deep inside me then make long, passionate, sleepy love to me."

And that's what I get, over and over until I'm so spent and cocooned with love that I sleep all night engulfed in Lucca's embrace.

The noise of rustling paper stirs me from my sleep. Prying my eyes open, I witness Lucca fully dressed and propped up against the headboard with a mint green paper bag, reading instructions on a thin piece of paper.

Far too early for this behaviour.

"What are you doing?" I lift the paper from his hand and try to focus, still bleary eyed. It is instructions to a home pregnancy test. Good Morning. I've woken up to reality.

"Where did you get this?" I scowl at his impatience.

"I asked Grace to go to the chemist this morning. I bought you six."

I nearly choke

"Six?"

"Yes, I left you sleeping as long as I could, but I am getting restless. Can we do this now?" He holds out a glass of water for me.

"You need a full bladder," he informs me.

Bossy.

Persistent.

Bloody pest.

"I'm well aware of how they work, and what do you mean *we*?"

"I'll help you."

I nearly drop the glass from laughter. "You realise I need to pee on a stick, right? How on earth will you help with that, Romeo? We can't use your urine."

"I will hold, you pee. Simple." He shrugs.

He has an answer for everything.

"No ... Ewww. I'm not peeing onto your hands. I can hold the stick myself." He is losing his mind.

"They will wash. Just aim straight for the stick, come on." He pulls the duvet off me.

Is he for fucking real?

Yes he is.

I throw the duvet over my head only for him to pull it back again and lift me up. I drink the water and argue that I'm not having him hold the sticks. We compromise when I finally convince him to stay outside the bathroom when I take the tests. Then I say he can come in while we wait on them.

"We are doing this together, baby. I do not want to miss a single thing." He's so persistent on the verge of obsessed, but I realise he's referring to his regret the day he missed the scan of his and Fran's baby, the day the baby was stillborn.

He follows me into the bathroom with a massive smile and lifts all the tests from the boxes and lines them up. I step into the shower.

"What are you doing? I don't think you need to be clean first." He pinches his forehead with his middle finger and thumb because he's antsy.

"I'm just having a quick wash." I'm conscious that I'm scented with sex from last night's lovemaking.

Drying off, I wrap myself in my robe.

"Ready?" he asks impatiently.

"Yes, here goes. Stick one, Mr. Caruso," I instruct. He hands me it then kisses me before I order him out the bathroom.

Six test strips later and he actually did wait patiently in the bedroom without chapping the door every two seconds to check if I was finished.

I wash up, ask him to come in, then we both stare at the sticks lined up on the vanity for what seems like hours, although only seconds have passed.

"How much longer?" he asks, shifting side to side and running his hand through his hair.

"Lucca, can you just ..." I sigh, picking some skin on my hands.

"I am sorry, I am just excited."

"And I'm nervous."

I turn him away from the sticks so his back is to the vanity and distract him by wrapping my arms around his neck and kissing him. After running my tongue along his bottom lip, I slide my tongue into his mouth and kiss him, knowing he'll relax under my touch. It works.

We've been kissing so long that I know my sticks are ready. I open my eyes and sneak a peek over his shoulder to see two blue lines, two p's, and two smiley faces. When we pull away from each other's lips, I search his eyes, a soft smile lighting my face.

"Wow. That was sexy, Miss Robertson." He smiles with his sexy dimple.

I move his hand from my breast to my stomach and smile. I don't say anything, I wordless tell him with my eyes. A simple evocative confession so deep and honest it means more than any words. His eyes are so wide with delirious excitement that he drowns me in his clear blue pools.

Turning around, he picks the sticks up and studies every one of them. We pass them back and forth, checking and double checking with the instructions. They are definitely positive.

Pregnant.

Positive.

Life changing.

"Lucca, say something."

He drops to his knees and unties the sash around my robe, exposing my naked body. His lips lightly kiss my abdomen. I hold onto his shoulders, trembling, and close my eyes enjoying the sweet sensation. He presses his cheek against my tummy.

I'm carrying his baby. I never thought in a million years I would have a child, and here I am experiencing this tender moment with the man I have fallen in love with, and the love I feel right now is all consuming.

"We are going to make great parents, I know it. You have just made me the happiest man in the world, Doc." His voice breaks with a shaky quiver. He's exposing his helplessness.

I can feel his tears on my navel. Sweet, happy tears. "I hope these are tears of joy," I softly say, raking my hands through his hair.

Standing back up, he holds my face in both hands with wet eyes. God, he looks so sexy like this.

Raw.

Emotional.

Vulnerable.

"Lexi, we are having a baby. This is real. I am going to take great care of you, both of you," he says in his rapturous bliss.

He picks me up, taking me back to the bed, and leans over me, moving unruly waves of hair from my eyes. His profound loving attention elicits more flutters low in my stomach.

"I love you with all my heart, but you're going to need to keep me strong because I'm a little scared," I confess.

"Do not be, dolcezza. You have me. We will get through this together."

I think about what people might think, how my girlfriends will react? And I feel torn because I want desperately to share this with them. I want to tell Hazel and have our friendly DBB chat. We tell each other everything and I would hate to keep this from her and Cameron, but if I tell them I would need to tell the rest of the girls. I feel it's too early and I need time to myself to process this and be content that I'm fully accepting the life fate intended for me. I know it's ludicrous to file this because it's real and I need to deal with it and address it gradually every day.

"Lucca, I'd rather not tell anyone about the baby. I know you want to, but I'd rather wait until after I have a scan. Please, promise me. It's just overwhelming and I want to make sure everything is okay first and I need time." Just saying the word baby has my skin hot and prickly and my stomach twisting in knots. It's so surreal.

"Dolcezza, anything for you. How do you feel?"

"Weird."

Emotional.

Nervous.

Stunned.

Apprehensive.

Anxious.

Scared.

Excited.

Content.

Blessed.

"Are you happy?" he asks with hope.

I have my reservations, lots of them in fact, but knowing this is making him so elated makes me feel unexpectedly happy—blissful.

"Yes, now that I'm over the shock."

He kisses me, showing me just how much he appreciates me and just how much he wants this. "Do you feel sick? Are you hungry? Do you need anything?"

Bloody hell, this needs to stop.

"Lucca, I only need you. You need to stop treating me like a china doll because I won't break. I love that you care for me, but can you stop being overprotective with me?" I ask.

"Never. What do you want for breakfast?" He smiles.

"Hmmm, this is going to be a very long pregnancy," I say with snark because he's ignoring my request.

"I hope so because it is turning me on thinking about your growing bump and body changing," he replies.

"So you have a fetish for pregnant women?" I raise my eyebrows in disbelief.

"No, only you because you will be sexy as fuck." He runs his fingers over the slender curve of my hips.

"Lucca, you'll need to stop swearing. She might hear you." I try to keep my swearing to a minimal and mostly I mentally swear but Lucca has an awful habit of swearing out loud.

He chuckles. "She?"

"Yes, definitely a girl. I have a feeling."

"I would love a little girl." He smiles. "Or a boy." He raises his eyebrows and curls his lip at one end then casually shrugs.

"Lucca, you want a baby, period, so I'm guessing it doesn't matter."

His excitable smile is so sweet and endearing that it melts me. "You are right, it does not, but the idea of having a papa's girl is growing on me, and she will be every bit as beautiful as her mamma."

After Lucca brings me breakfast in bed, I dispose of the pregnancy kits so Granny won't find them. While Lucca makes some business calls and checks if there have been any updates from the CID on Michael Parks' whereabouts, I venture to the window to check out today's weather before picking my clothes.

"Are we expecting visitors?"

Lucca puts his phone on hold.

"Why?" he asks with scepticism.

"There was a car driving down the road, but it stopped for a while then turned and drove away."

"What colour? Did you check the model or the person driving it?" He walks over to the window and pulls the curtain aside.

"No, it was too far away." I shrug.

"Marco, I will call you back." He disconnects the call.

"Lexi, this is important, what colour was the car?" he stresses.

"I don't know. Burgundy or plum, I think. It's probably someone getting lost. They've realised this is a private road and drove away, happens all the time," I reassure him.

"Maybe. I am going to speak with Lloyd. See if he can pull up the video surveillance for a search on the registration plate. Do not worry about this. What do you want to do today?" he asks, tapping his fingers on the windowsill staring outside.

I shrug feeling a little deflated now.

"What time is it? Granny will want us all to go to church. I need to give Cathy that parcel anyway, do you mind?"

"No that is fine. You better get dressed though." He smacks my ass as I walk by.

I dress in one of the lingerie sets he gave me—the sexy blue satin under black mesh with lace flowers on the straps. I'll need to make lots of use of all my sexy lingerie before I'm too fat and unable to wear them. I pick the new blue dress to wear in the hope it lifts my spirits from this lethargic feeling.

Throwing my hair up in a shaggy, messy bun, I apply some light makeup hoping it will conceal the darkness under my eyes and my pale complexion today. Standing in front of the mirror, I observe my body and place my hand on my flat tummy thinking in a few weeks' time none of my lovely clothes will fit me.

"Jesus, Lexi, if you are going to look so goddamn fucking fabulous, we are never getting out of here today." He grabs my ass pulling me closer.

I swipe his hand off my butt. "You're just saying that because I look like death, and just so you know, I feel like it as well," I grumble.

"You look beautiful. I love your dress. Your tits and ass are hot in this, Doc. Very sexy." He can't restrain himself, his hands are back on me, roaming over my curves.

"I still feel awful but, thank you, and I have something hot for you underneath it," I reply seductively.

"How long is this service so I can get you back here and unwrap you?" He grins.

Lucca speaks to the security team about the mystery car while I take Mum by the hand and sit on the porch with her to confirm her suspicion. Lucca has been very supportive and always says the right things but I'm glad I have my mum here supporting me as well.

"You're pregnant, aren't you?" She smiles warmly, staring at my flat abdomen.

"Yes, you were right. All the tests were positive this time." I shrug.

"I thought so. Well, congratulations, sweetie, and please don't worry. Everything will work out fine. I promise you. You have a special man there. He really loves you. You're very fortunate, Alexis. I've no doubt in my mind Lucca will be an amazing father and husband." She hugs me in a warm, loving embrace.

"Thank you, I know he will too. Mum, please don't mention this until I've had a scan at least." I pick at a splinter of wood on the edge of the deck.

"Sure, sweetheart, but please look after yourself, and if it's okay with you I'd like to see more of you. Lucca offered for me to come and stay for a while. Would that be okay?" She takes my hand.

"Yes, I'd love that." I actually haven't felt as close to her as I do now for a long time. Perhaps the baby will help keep Mum focused and give us both a new perspective. Something special we can bond over and experiences we can share together. It pleases me that she is being so level headed and accepting; it makes this easier for me to cope with.

Nate stays at the house while the rest of us go to the church in the village for Sunday service. After the service we stay behind and Cathy welcomes us into the manse next door for some tea. She's heard a lot about Lucca from Ms. Morrison with his continual support for charity and is thrilled to hear all about his plans for this year's projects.

Men in Black are parked outside the church in their SUVs on security watch, most likely bored from waiting.

"The grounds look super, Cathy. Those flowers are coming along nicely," Granny compliments.

"Thank you, Elizabeth. Mr. Carmichael retired, as you know, so I have temporary help, a South African gentleman. He's very quiet, keeps himself private, but is a tremendous landscaper and handyman. Anyway, tell me how everyone is getting on."

After thirty minutes of catch up, Mum, Granny, and Grandpa leave with Devon to pick some fruit and vegetables up from the farmers' market before it closes while Lloyd waits for Lucca and me outside.

I give Cathy her parcel. Thanking me, she then disappears into another room. I shrug my shoulders to Lucca, nonplussed, as I have no idea what she's doing. She returns, dusting her hands across a box and muttering to herself.

"Hmmm, it's in here somewhere." She's searching through a box of books scanning the names on the inside pages.

"Ah ha, here it is. Alexis, this is your Bible from Sunday school. I had them all sent over from Aberdeen. I thought you would like to keep it if you have your own family one day."

Oh my goodness, does she suspect I'm pregnant or am I being paranoid?

She hands me the white leather Bible engraved in gold then walks over to a drawer. Searching through a binder, she pulls out a folded piece of paper and slips it inside the Bible.

"I hear congratulations are in order." She chirps very upbeat.

I cough, almost choking in amazement, and Lucca has to pat my back. Seriously? How does she know?

"Your recent engagement is wonderful news. That's a copy of Corinthians 13:1-13. Something for you to consider for your marriage readings." She nods towards the Bible.

And I can breathe.

"Oh, thank you." I don't bother to tell her Lucca is Catholic.

"May joy and peace surround you both, contentment latch your door. May happiness be with you now. God bless you ever more," she chimes.

Lucca takes my hand and grasps it tightly. We thank her profusely for her kindness and agree to come back and say goodbye before we leave Grantown-On-Spey.

When we exit the manse, the sky is grey with ominous clouds. The heavens have opened to a torrential downpour. Lucca holds his blazer over the top of my head as we make our way to the car across the path back to the front of the church, dodging soggy puddles. The rain is so heavy it splashes off the ground and up my bare legs. Heralding thunder roars from afar causing me to startle.

Frightful.

I turn to wave goodbye to Cathy and catch a glimpse of a man in the distance between two trees. He's well-built, wears a long, black rain mac, and holds a golf umbrella above his head. He watches us from the distance. He must be the new groundsman Cathy was referring to, or perhaps someone visiting a graveside, but why stare at us?

Weird.

It's creepy. Shivering when the cold breeze bites across my bare, wet legs, I feel a chill to my skin. The hairs on my arms stand still with an icy wariness.

Lucca opens the Aston Martin car door for me, but instinct tells me to stop. I have a shudder of nerves and a twisting in my stomach.

"Lexi, get in. What are you doing? You're soaked, get in the car," Lucca says.

I pause to look back across the graveyard, but the mystery silhouette has vanished. Once in the car, I watch out the windows at the spot where the mysterious man was standing. Lucca wraps his blazer around my shoulders and signals to Lloyd, then we drive off leaving Lloyd to follow us all the way back.

I shiver all the way home, sitting in the wet dress. We stop at the gas station for Lloyd to refuel. Lucca asks Lloyd to buy some newspapers while he's at the kiosk. I watch a long haul truck driver bend over to kiss his little girl and lift her up onto the passenger seat of his delivery vehicle. As he pulls away, I can't help but notice a burgundy estate car in the side mirror despite the lashing rain. It had been concealed behind the large truck, but now it manoeuvres to a pump behind us. It's driven by a hatted and cloaked man, but he's not refuelling. Odd ... Why sit at a pump?

I'm about to mention it to Lucca but hear some text messages coming through on my phone which startles me and holds my attention. Hazel's name on my screen makes me feel melancholy that I'm keeping a secret from her. I would love to be able to tell her about the baby but it's too soon. I read the texts, then my thoughts are back to my pregnancy and I forget everything else around me.

Lloyd is back, so we pull out of the station to drive the few minutes to Granny's house. Lucca gives me a hand towel from his glove compartment to dry my legs. I lean over and dab them dry, and when I sit up the burgundy vehicle is gone. I choose to forget it and concentrate on curing this pregnancy sickness instead.

When we return home, Grandpa has the fire lit and Granny is in the kitchen making a pot of butternut squash and chorizo soup with baked bread for lunch—my favourite. Maybe this is what I need to cure my queasiness.

Mr. Carlin is having a nap and Mum is painting in the sunroom.

"We're just going to dry off and change, then we'll be down shortly," I shout through to the kitchen. I close and lock our door and shiver as I realise I've left the window open and the wind is gusting through. I secure the window closed and rub my arms to create some heat.

Kicking off his shoes, Lucca takes his wet jeans and T-shirt off. Moistening my lips, I admire his glorious body. Every time he's exposed, I marvel at his sprawling, bulky shoulders. There is something very attractive and sexy about his masculinity.

"It is freezing in here. I am so cold," he says, checking the thermostat on the radiator.

"It is, but you're very, very hot, Mr. Caruso, and you're core teasing me looking like that," I seductively say, watching his cock harden and expand in his tight fitting briefs.

"Am I now? I might just have to do something about that," he rasps, striding towards me.

I lift my dress over my head, my teeth chattering together with the cool air, and undo my messy bun so my hair tumbles down my back.

His breath hitches. "Wow, I love your new lingerie. You look very sexy. I would say you were a cock tease. Fuck the towels, I am heating you up in bed."

Suddenly, I've lost my chill and my temperature is on the up and boiling away as he presses his erection against my lower tummy with his hands on my ass, pulling me further into him and dirty kisses me.

Lacing my fingers in his wet hair, I thrust my heavy breasts against his chest. A drop of water falls from his hair onto my cleavage, and I watch as he leans down and licks it away.

Sweet Jesus.

Erotic as hell.

Oh my.

I move my hands to his ass, my grip firm as I bite his bottom lip. "Pregnancy is making me extra horny. I need you desperately," I moan into his mouth as his tongue assaults mine. I'm always horny, but my body seems to be extra sensitive and responsive to his touch.

My panties are drenched with my arousal. Moving the tiny piece of wet satin, he slips two fingers inside me, tormenting the contracting muscles in my sex. Then he slides the moisture over my folds until he flicks my clit.

"That's so good," I groan, spreading my legs for him.

He slides his fingers out of my hot core and brushes my bottom lip. "Open," he instructs.

Taking his fingers, I seductively lick my arousal from his fingers.

"Jesus, you are going to undo me right here. Now that is hot. See how good you taste?"

I turn him around so that he's near the bed then push him down so his back hits the mattress. Propping himself up, he leans on his elbows to stare at me, and I can't help myself. I step back and give him a view. I suddenly feel like a siren and want to seduce him. Then I want to ride him senseless.

His blue eyes greedily lust for me, trying to draw me closer. I wave my finger at him cheekily.

"Quit tormenting me and get that sexy ass over here," he guffaws. He reaches his hands out to grab me but I move back.

"No touching yet, Romeo."

I wave my finger at him again, looking very devilish, raising my brow and spreading my lips with a sultry grin. I take my hands down to my tummy then trail them further so that my fingers are hooked just under the edge of my panties. I ping them and leave one hand there and the other travels up to massage my sensitive breasts.

"Fucking hell, are you trying to kill me?" His erection strains and twitches against the fabric of his tight boxers, and he's ready to launch himself on me. I'm torturing him.

I seductively trail my fingers over the blue flower motifs on my bra strap then over the swell of my breasts. My thumbs flick over my erect nipples and I softly moan. Gripping the mesh of my bra, I pull the cups down so my breasts spring free. The heat in Lucca's eyes scorches right through me, burning every inch of my skin.

This flame is still rising. I'm not done yet. I sensuously move both my hands over my breasts then pinch my nipples. Lucca chokes watching me, and his cheeks inflame. Then I slowly unfasten the bra freeing my breasts completely.

"Lexi ..." He warns me. The last time I touched myself for him, he was in control and still had contact, his hands were still on my body and he was pressed against me. This is killing him, he has no control.

The sound of my name on his tongue in the sexy, husky rasp arouses me even more. Yearning for this, I move one hand back down to my panties and slip it inside to feel my hot, wet sex. I smile seductively at my handsome Italian god then run my teeth across my bottom lip.

"Fuck me," he hisses, and because I'm feeling confident, I give him a little tease.

"Are you asking or telling?" I reply.

"Both," he grinds out, clenching his jaw.

"Good, because that's exactly what I want."

Pregnancy is screwing with my hormones. I kind of like this new me.

Screwing?

Appropriate!

I'm not going to make myself come. I want him to do that, but I do want to tease him. Hooking the fingers of my other hand under the elastic, I wiggle and slither them off my legs, planning to touch myself again, but I don't get that far.

In a flash, Lucca pounces and grabs me around the waist.

"That was hot as fuck, but now I need to touch you. That was cruel, baby, and I cannot wait." He devours my mouth with kisses so hard that my lips will surely bruise. Then he leans back pulling me down so my knees straddle him.

He slides up the bed then pulls me further up so my sex is spread above his face. His tongue slides into me again and again. Then he teases my clit. I arch my back, circling my hips and pushing my folds against the incursions of his delicious tongue.

He slides three fingers inside me, rubbing the wall of my throbbing sex while his tongue penetrates my sweet spot. Coming undone, I bite down on my lip to stifle my cries as a rip-roaring orgasm shreds through me, stiffening my body with pleasure. Every vibrating nerve ending orbits me into a euphoric fantasy where all I can see are stars behind my eyelids.

He kisses my sex and flicks the tip of his tongue over my clit another few times after sliding his fingers out. Then he kisses my tummy in several places, spreading my arousal.

Still shaking, I slide down his body, but he already has his boxers off. He grabs my hips and my eyes jolt open from the intense force of his cock thrusting into me. I drive further down onto his shaft with every plunge as my body trembles.

"You are driving me crazy," he whispers, conscious we're being too loud, then hisses through clenched teeth.

"I cannot take this slow right now, baby. I am going to fuck you fast." He flips me over just before I reach climax, and I'm on all fours as I moan at the loss of his cock.

"Do not scream." He bangs into me with such force that he slides me up the bed.

Bloody hell.

Slamming.

Shoving.

Pounding.

He grips my hips. Then, with might and determination, he fucks me over and over, breathing frantically and muttering as he tries to muffle his own cries. I have to bite down on a pillow to mask my cries.

"I know, baby, let it go. Come for me now." He yanks me upward so he can grasp my breast while his other hand teases my clit again.

I whimper, biting my lip when an earth shattering orgasm tears through me sparking my fuse and setting me on fire. My knuckles are white from gripping the pillow so hard.

"Jesus fuck, Lexi."

He stiffens, gently smacking my lower back and digging his fingers into my skin. Reaching his own climax, he buries himself deep inside me filling me with his sperm. He doesn't stop. After another few quick thrusts to my hot, already sensitive sex, he collapses on top of me.

Intoxicated.

Satiated.

Relaxed.

We are wet all over again but from perspiration.

Holy shit that was amazing.

"Warmer?"

"Hmmm, roasting hot," I reply lazily.

After soft, sweet kissing and lazy strokes across each other's skin, Lucca eventually pulls the covers back. He gets some tissues from the bathroom to clean us up and comes in beside me pulling the covers over us.

"Doc, did I hurt you? Is the baby safe?" He realises he couldn't refrain and take things slow and gentle. There's panic in his voice.

"Yes, it's perfectly safe to have sex, Lucca." I turn around to lie on my side to face him.

"I know that, I mean, is it safe for me to fuck you so hard and deep?"

"Yes, I believe so."

"Good. The thought of not being able to fuck you would kill me." He bites his bottom lip and brushes his thumb over my own lip.

"Fran ... and I, we ... um," he doesn't elaborate.

He notices the look of hurt on my face. I don't want to think of him and Fran experiencing this.

"Do not worry. I know what you are thinking, and Fran was not ... well, she never let me touch her when she was pregnant, so I did not have to consider if sex is safe during pregnancy. We were not romantically close during that period. Our relationship was different and in no way like what we have." Instantly he regrets mentioning Fran because his face tenses up.

"Oh." He's said it diplomatically and without elaborating on their sex life, it's enough to pacify me.

"But, Doc, forget that. I plan to satisfy you all through your pregnancy. I am glad it is safe and you still want sex. It would seriously kill me not being inside you," he says cupping one of my breasts then settles on my hip.

"Well, Romeo, just as well because I'm very horny and plan on having you in me as much as I can, like anywhere and anytime," I reply, yawning.

"Thank the Lord for that. Lexi?"

"Hmmm?"

"I love you, dolcezza, and I love our baby. You have no idea." He kisses my temple and moves a tendril of hair away from my face.

"We love you too. So much it hurts."

I snuggle into his chest, fighting against my heavy eyes until I drift off. When I wake, he's not here but the bed is warm. I hear the shower so I sit up and hold my stomach. I run into the bathroom and curl over the toilet to vomit. Groaning, I hug the bowl before flushing.

He moves to the end of the shower curtain and frowns watching me.

"Doc, I wish I could take this feeling away." He sighs.

"I hate being pregnant, it sucks," I moan.

He chuckles. "You were not saying that earlier on when you were frisky."

"Well, that's the only perk. This is torture. Why on earth do women put themselves through this?"

I brush my teeth then hop in the shower and wash him all over. He then reciprocates, cleansing my body and washing my hair. Because I know we're not going anywhere and it's turned into a rainy, miserable day, I put on tartan pyjama bottoms, a grey yoga top, and thick sleep socks.

I manage to eat some soup and keep it down. When we finish our late lunch, Lucca offers to make dinner tonight. Granny, Grandpa, and Mr. Carlin go to the senior citizens club in the village community centre, accompanied by Nate, so Mum and I cuddle up on the sofa and watch *Marley and Me*.

It gets me every time. I have a hormonal sob at the end of the movie and feel guilty for neglecting the dogs. I slip into my hunter Wellingtons and put Mum's wax jacket on to take the dogs out. Lloyd lurks closely behind, but I don't mind so much now. I'm grateful for their protection.

I offer to help Lucca but he says he has it under control. I'm desperate for the family to enjoy his wonderful culinary skills since I've been bragging on about them.

Mum shows me the paintings she's been working on as part of her therapy, and I'm amazed at how good she is. She has a natural talent, and she's very creative. Mostly, they are landscape portraits of various Scottish sceneries, but there are also a few still life drawings.

"Wow, these are amazing. You're very gifted. You could sell these. They're that good."

She blushes. "It's just a hobby, but I do enjoy it. I've been taking lessons. I go to a class in Inverness, hence the still life drawings." I remember Grandpa telling me that Mum applied to art school before she went travelling to Australia with her friend. *Before she was taken*. It was always her aspiration to paint and I'm glad she's now pursuing her dreams. I'm so proud of her.

"Mum, you could sketch or paint a portrait of the baby when it arrives. You know how I've always hated photographs, but Lucca has truly helped me with that photo book. I'm thinking I might like paintings or portraits of our baby, you know canvas memories."

"I would be thrilled. I think it's a wonderful idea. One of my biggest regrets is that I don't have any baby pictures of you and Cameron ..." Her voice trails off. "I've photographed it up here." She taps her head and smiles. "I remember everything. Every little look, expression, giggle, frown, cry, and laugh. Cameron hated being cuddled, but you would lie in my arms all day, every day, and I would just watch your face for hours."

"Oh, that reminds me ... I have something extra for you." I've already given them their gifts, but I haven't given her the journal. I take her hand and lead her into my room and find it in my case.

"Here."

"What's this?"

"It's just a journal, but this is how Lucca helped me communicate with him. If I was struggling to talk and needed to relieve my anxiety, I'd write it all down. I have a few now, and I still try to write in them because it really helps me. Sometimes I can't because I find it hard, then other times I can't stop. I thought maybe you'd like to try it."

She strokes her fingers over it. "It's precious, thank you. I'm very blessed to have you."

"Don't thank me. It was Lucca's idea. Mum, I love him so much. He's so good for me." I sigh with contentment, feeling a warm and blissful flutter settle in my stomach.

She draws me in close for an affectionate embrace, stroking my hair and kissing the side of my head. "I know, honey. I know you do."

Lucca's food is delectable and pleases everyone. Granny sings his praises. He incorporates butternut squash—my favourite vegetable—with the main meal, hoping I will eat something, and I do manage some of the risotto and chicken.

Lucca skips red wine to drink water with me. I'm confident we've convinced Granny I have a virus, so Lucca is refusing alcohol in the event he needs to drive.

I clear and tidy the plates, filling the dishwasher, then we sit around the coffee table in the lounge—Men in Black included—to play scrabble, cards, and dominoes while Grandpa and Mr. Carlin carry on with their chess game.

My eyes are closing so Lucca scoops me up to carry me to bed. Grandpa leans over and kisses my head and pats Lucca on the shoulder at the bottom of the stair.

"You know I'm envious of you, son. It wasn't so long ago that she was wrapped up in my arms. Hold her tight, young man, and cherish her."

"I intend to. She will always be yours to hold, Alexander. That will never change."

I'm too exhausted to shower, so he strips me of my pyjama bottoms and top to nestle against my bare body. I sleep sprawled across his chest with one leg wrapped over him and my face nuzzled into his neck as he holds me.

Chapter 31: Angel

The next day is spent relaxing indoors because the weather has been horrendous. My mind has been far too preoccupied with my pregnancy. I've been sick regularly and have slept almost around the clock, but I have comfort knowing Lucca is attentive and ensuring I'm well-cared for.

We have a surprise visit from our therapist and her husband, Terrance. They were on their way to their holiday cottage, so they stop by for the day. Terrance and Lucca go way back and catch up while Mum and Casey spend most of the morning together. I sleep.

Mum asks if I want to talk with Casey in light of what's been happening with Michael Parks. At first I don't want to, but Lucca convinces me. He's worried about the dreams I'm having and my doubts about impending motherhood.

Lucca confesses that he's deliberately asked them to come by. He's been encouraging me to speak with Casey regularly again, and he thinks that I might feel more comfortable talking to her outside of the clinic. I agree, but I ask him to join me in my talks with Casey.

Casey listens with compassion; gives advice and a new theory based on the concept of my journal writing that she thinks will help me. She suggests I write a list of everything I'm feeling now, then beside it write how I want to feel. She's convinced that I will feel most of these good things already. It's all about painting the bigger picture, acknowledging the negativity and past in order to accept positivity for my future. After a long session of talking, crying and more talking, Casey and Terence join us for dinner before leaving.

Mum later tells me that she had a very positive session of her own with Casey, despite being very tired afterwards and that she has started writing in her journal.

I don't sleep as well tonight, talking with Casey has stirred and provoked memories and highlighted my current situation. The pregnancy has been taking my mind away from Michael Parks, but now it's all I can think about because Casey spoke about it and I slept way too much this morning so I'm wide awake.

Turning on the lamp, I open my journal and sigh. I can't bring myself to write anything down. Next I pick up my e-reader and try to read but I drop it as I'm too agitated and can't concentrate. I've now disturbed Lucca.

He asks me what's wrong. I tell him and we talk. After comforting me, he asks me to tell him about my summers spent here at the cottage. I think he's trying to distract me. It does relax me and makes me smile. I tell him about the summer I brought the girls here and Lucy fell off a horse and it gets me thinking.

Lucca picks up my e-reader. "Do you want me to read to you?" he asks switching it on.

"Yes, okay." I snuggle against his chest and draw lazy shapes on his body. He plays with my hair and reads a chapter from the book I'm re reading, *Sense and Sensibility* by Jane Austen until I drift back off to sleep and dream of horses and picnics.

The thunder and rain finally pass, and it's now Tuesday. I'm wearing denim shorts and a tight fitting chequered lumberjack shirt on this bright, sunny day, and I've found my old riding boots. Yesterday's therapy session with Casey and our discussion last night inspired me to share something else with Lucca. I take Lucca to the Murdock's stables, as there is someone I want him to meet. Angel.

We spend hours with the horses. He watches me feed, groom, and walk them around the ring. I explain my history with them and he contently listens, watching me.

I've always found solace here. After our years of incarceration in Australia, part of our therapy was AAT—assisted animal therapy. In order for us to learn how to trust, we were encouraged by our care team to work with the horses. Every time I'm home I come back here. I normally ride the horses through the woods for hours on end, but not today.

Angel is a strong, black Friesian and my favourite. Our souls joined together years ago. I'm delighted she's still here, but she's certainly not as youthful or spritely as she was back then. I remember at first I was petrified of her because of her colour, intimidating size, and powerful muscles but soon I discovered she was sensitive and very intelligent and moved with such elegance and agility.

She made a great companion during the summer months up here. Cameron would ride Jambo, a Dutch Warmblood. We would follow the River Spey, trot, sprint, and jump for hours through the woodland, and it would be after dusk before we went back home.

Grandpa would ride out on Hamish, an English Thoroughbred. He'd accompany us with his rifles but encourage us to ride on in front; he was teaching us valuable lessons, to break free and move forward, and how to be independent and courageous. We just never realised it at the time. Hamish was known for his agility, speed, and spirit but was sold to a family in Germany when his hunting days were over.

Our first block of sessions with the horses, Mum also had to participate. It wasn't only Grandpa that joined us, but the whole care team, who were there to help and assess us. Cameron and I never left Mum's side; the whole process was a daunting experience, not to mention we were not used to being around groups of people, never mind huge animals. Mum was experienced at riding because she had learned when she was younger, so when she got up on Hamish for the first time to show us what to do, I cried.

I cried, because he was so big and I was so little. When Mum first pulled his reins and Hamish began walking, I squealed in hysterics. I thought she was leaving us and I begged her to come back, although she was only circling the ring. Grandpa tried to console me but at that stage I was still nervous around him and would run towards Cameron and cling onto him. We weren't used to having grandparents, it was a foreign concept, and so it was difficult understanding the importance or their role. To me, I was angry because Mum was our parent, no one else, and I only ever wanted her help ... *on everything.*

We didn't have interaction with any adults other than the Parks during our imprisonment, so the transition going from the isolation and confines of our life to having so many adults being involved in our new lives was an extremely terrifying experience.

I knew Grandpa was trustworthy because Mum told us lots of sweet stories about him and she loved him dearly, but for us he was just another stranger in the early days, someone to be wary of. Cameron came around quicker than I did; Grandpa played football with him and so built on their relationship through the aide of sport. Cameron showed lots of promise, Grandpa recognised his skill, and eventually once he had Cameron's trust he got him training in a local under-fifteen football team where Cameron truly came into himself.

I was harder to crack. Granny tried teaching me to sew and knit, but that petrified me because I didn't like the knitting needles. Then when she cooked, she would ask me to watch so I could learn new skills and understand all about healthy food and local produce. I was still too withdrawn to try and cook myself as everything was overwhelming, but I did silently watch taking everything in. I think that's where my passion for cooking comes from, her cooking lessons, our previous lack of food in our childhood years, and Granny's perseverance with trying to encourage us to try different foods.

Granny then suggested I try dancing because all the other little girls did it. Truthfully, I think she just wanted to give us the experiences which we missed out on and to do something with me that she could be involved in. She had taken me to Ms. Saunders I.S.T.D Ballet School in Aberdeen, but I panicked and ran away when I saw all the other girls because they were following commands and instructions. The structure and concept of being ordered around scared me, and I found it intimidating that they all looked the same in their uniforms. Pink seamed tights, plum leotards and hair in tight neat buns.

Ms. Saunders agreed to give me private lessons at home until my confidence was built, then gradually we went to local dance shows so I could see the other girls perform what they'd been taught on the stage. Within two years, I was attending classes with everyone else my age but still having private lessons too so I could catch up on the grading work.

By that time the twins were turning three, so Aunt Eva enrolled Hayley in the little baby ballet class. I liked that because Ms. Saunders allowed me to be a helper with the little ones. I found them exceptionally cute and it gave me responsibility. Hayley fell, skinning her knees, screaming, but it was me she ran to and cried into my neck. The same way I would do with my mum. My natural instinct to care and protect kicked in, and I swayed her around the floor, shushing her and kissing her knees until she stopped sobbing. From then on, I knew that I wanted to help others.

The turning point for me was the day after Mum got on the horse Hamish for the first time, Grandpa was determined to win my trust. It broke his heart that I was petrified and withdrawn. He asked Mum to stay off the horse for the time being and he would go on Hamish in her place. Instead of trotting, he galloped fast around the paddock but always came back. This went on for days, until he ventured outside the paddock towards the River Spey for a short time at first and then gradually increased his time away.

I panicked because I couldn't see him. The care team thought this was a breakthrough. Although I hadn't fully trusted him at that point, I was showing new emotions. I wanted him back because he made me feel safe and I didn't want Mum to be upset or lonely.

Each time he would return, Mum would give him a huge cuddle. This was his way of showing me that he would always return and he would always be there for all of us, always. This went on for a few weeks. At the time I had no idea it was intentional. He didn't return for a full day and our routine was all messed up. I hated that. Mum said, "Keep looking out for your grandpa. Tell me when he returns."

I looked out into the empty paddock for hours and silently sobbed because I thought he was never coming back. When he trotted back, instead of telling Mum, I ran towards him. Once he reined the horse to a halt and got off, he crouched down and opened his arms and I threw myself in them and latched on so tightly while Grandpa whispered in my ear that he would always take care of me and never let me be hurt ever again.

Grandpa cried when I was responsive and voluntarily cuddled him for the first time. He barely let me go after that day; I was always by his side. Our relationship then gradually progressed. Every day we built more trust and he taught me new things. He knew we never had any choices in our previous life, so he always asked what I'd like to take from Granny's store cupboard to feed the horses; he would let me choose. The first time I suggested the yummy butternut squash soup Granny made, he smiled and explained what the horses were allowed to have and why. Normally, we would take carrots, sweet potatoes, or turnips.

Granny had tried getting me to eat apples as part of our new diet. I hated them. She used to buy green Granny Smith apples but they were awfully sour and I always thought they were better used in cooking than eating raw. I tried telling her, but she thought I was being fussy. I soon discovered the horses loved them, so I would sneak them out of my packed lunch on my AAT days and give mine to Angel on the sly.

Mum's one-on-one therapy sessions were normally at lunchtime, so Grandpa used to take us on walks with a packed lunch, weather permitting.

Sitting at a bench on a sunny June day in 1997, the summer after we escaped, I noticed a red apple in my purple *Spice Girls* lunch box. Granny thought I'd appreciate having something modern that was fashionable at the time. I had the T-shirts, sweatshirts, posters and pencil case.

The red apple was big and juicy; Grandpa told me it was a Red Mackintosh. I held it in my hands and turned it around, admiring its pretty colour.

"Go ahead, try it. I bet you like this one better than those green ones Granny gives you," he said. Cameron scoffed his and I desperately wanted to try it as he seemed to enjoy it.

My teeth sank into it and juice trickled down my chin. He was right, I loved it. It was delicious. I ate it so quickly I don't think I stopped for a breath. Afterwards I was very silent. I stared at my empty lunch box, then over at Angel in the paddock and I looked down at my hands. I felt guilty for eating my apple because I always liked to give her an extra treat, Grandpa watched me inquisitively.

The next day, Cameron opened his lunch box, fisted in the air shouting, "Yes!" pleased with whatever he got. I opened my lunch box, excited to see if I had another red apple. I smiled when I saw the red apple but wrinkled my nose when I saw a tuna mayo sub wrapped in cellophane. This was another food I was encouraged to try. I sighed because I thought I'd be left hungry. I wanted to give Angel my apple, but I didn't like the smell of my sub and I wouldn't be allowed the treat until I ate my lunch.

The treat was always a surprise. Grandpa kept it in his backpack, sometimes he even brought extra that Granny didn't know about because he liked to spoil us, but the condition was that we ate lunch first. That was never an issue for Cameron; he would have eaten his hand given a chance. I was a little fussier. I think this is why I liked to give Angel an extra treat. I cared for her the same way Grandpa cared for us. Or I thought it was the same at the time.

Pouring some freshly squeezed lemonade for us, Grandpa sat back and looked in his Tupperwear tub. He asked why I wasn't eating. I dropped my head and told him I wasn't sure about the tuna. Cameron was already half way through his by this point, like a typical ravenous thirteen year old boy, making grunting noises and wiping his mouth across his T-shirt.

Grandpa gave me his cheese wrap, and he ate my tuna sub and said it was our secret. He then said if I ate my red apple, I would get my treat. I wanted the treat but I also wanted to give Angel my apple so I chewed the inside of my cheek and worried about it.

"Lex, if you don't eat that apple I'm going to eat it," Cameron teased.

"No way, you've had yours," I retaliated. I didn't know what to do because Grandpa was already rummaging in his backpack and I knew Cameron would be getting his treat.

It was clotted cream fudge. *Yummy*. Grandpa laid the box on the wooden table; I stared at it, thinking how much I liked fudge the last time he had given it to us. It was soft and creamy and tasted like heaven. Grandpa wouldn't tease us, so I wondered why he was laying it out in front of me. Cameron then moaned and told me to hurry up and eat my apple so we could open the fudge.

I did.

I took massive bites of the juicy apple, practically swallowing it whole. Satisfied, Grandpa allowed us to rip the confectionary box open and devour the fudge while he smiled and poured tea from his flask. Once the fudge was finished, I shifted restlessly on the bench. All I could think about was poor Angel missing out on her apple for two days running.

Cameron grabbed his ball and started kicking it around the field; I sat quietly with a full stomach but worried about Angel. I knew what it was like to feel hungry. What if Mr. Murdock forgot to feed her and she felt hungry? The thought made me restless.

"Alexis, I have something for you, an extra treat," Grandpa said, clearing up the bench. When my big chocolate eyes flicked up, he held another red apple in front of me. "This one is for Angel, let's go and give it to her." I jumped up and wrapped my arms around his neck and told him thank you about a million times. "Hey, come on now, kid, it's only an apple and from now on, you and Angel will have your own at lunchtime. Alexis you are a very special little girl, so thoughtful and considerate, and your Granny and I couldn't be prouder. I knew you were feeling guilty about the apple. I love you, kid, in fact you are the apple of my eye." He sobbed because I was so appreciative and held him so tightly. It's a memory I will always cherish.

I smiled all afternoon that day and couldn't wait to tell Mum all about it. Of course a plain old green apple would still be sufficient for Angel, but I wanted her to have the same as me. It tasted better and she was my friend, after all, and Grandpa knew that. From that day forward Grandpa has called me Apple … *his Apple*.

Lucca is adamant I'm not getting up on a horse today. He's fearful I'll harm the baby or injure myself. I comply only because I'm happy enough just to spend time with Angel and have no desire to be running off with her when I have Lucca right here. I even brought a few red apples for her from Granny's fruit bowl.

"If we have a daughter, I'd love her to take lessons and ride," I say, following the contour of Angel's glossy muscles with my palms.

He kisses my head and runs his fingers down my braid.

"I'd like that too. Maybe we need to upsize and invest in stables."

Rolling my eyes, I shake my head, but I'm thinking he might actually be serious.

Lloyd and Devon are not too far behind and waiting patiently in the SUV at the end of the road. Lucca is leaning against a gate inside the indoor stables, watching me bend over to brush Angel's legs.

"I know you're looking at my ass," I say, looking over my shoulder and catching his sexy dimple, his lips curling up at one end.

"Hmmm, your ass is pretty amazing in those cock-teasing, denim shorts. What do you expect when you bend over wearing hot fucking shit like that?"

Smiling, I ignore him until I feel him pull me back into his denim-clad erection, pressing against said denim shorts, causing me to drop the paddle brush. He turns me around and picks me up in a swift move so I'm straddling his waist. Angel neighs, nodding her head but doesn't flinch her body.

Gripping my ass and slipping his tongue into my mouth with fervent desire, he strides backwards, carrying me to the very back of the stables where there is a dark empty stall. He shoves my back up against the timber wall and assaults my mouth then pops the buttons on my chequered shirt to free my red lace bra.

"Jesus, I have not seen this one before," he rasps.

I thrust my hips forward to meet his hard cock, hoping the friction from the denim presses onto my throbbing sweet spot and gives me some relief.

"Looks as if you are getting that ride after all," he groans into my mouth then places me on my feet. He unbuttons my shorts and slides them down over my boots and off my legs in one fluid motion, leaving me breathless in only riding boots, red bra, and a matching thong, my long braid hanging over my shoulder.

"Lexi, Christ ... you are every man's fucking fantasy standing there like that. You are my fantasy, and I want to fuck you senseless right here, right now."

I grab his shirt to pull him back towards me. "Take me," I beg.

Fast.

Hard.

Now.

He pauses for a moment, admiring me, his lustful eyes burning my body.

"You have no idea how sexy you look right now. God, you are beautiful." He slides his belt off, unbuttons his jeans, then lowers them with his boxers, freeing his impeccable cock. I grab his T-shirt, pulling him to my chest, and he picks me back up to straddle his waist.

I squeeze tightly around him with one arm around his neck and the other on his ass. He holds me firmly against the wall then uses one hand to move the tiny red lace material from my wet folds. He slams into me, riding me zealously until my eyes water and I bite down on his shoulder, crying his name in pleasure.

Fast.

Hard.

Furious.

He grips my braid and pushes me further up the wall as he comes deep inside me, wildly shouting my name and spilling his release until I come hard and desperate around him.

After showering and changing back at the house, we go to the Boat Hotel for some late lunch. I'm surprised to find Aunt Eva, my mum's younger sister by two years and her husband, Uncle Jim. My eighteen-year-old twin cousins, Hayley and Hayden, are also waiting for us in the private dining area.

"Oh my goodness," I scream excitedly and greet them.

It's been so long since I've last seen them. Mum must have planned this surprise. Lucca is introduced and we spend forty minutes hugging and catching up before actually sitting down to look at the menu. Mum and Aunt Eva look alike, but Aunt Eva's hair is auburn—wavy, and stylishly short.

Hayden is Cameron's younger image; he looks very much like him, and he too has the boy band persona. I suspect he's going to have females flocking around him everywhere he goes if he doesn't have a girlfriend already.

Hayden's twin Hayley is gorgeous. She's slim but curvy, has massive blue eyes, and her light brown, highlighted hair is piled on top of her head in a messy bun, similar to how I like to wear mine. She wears a slinky, green maxi dress which hugs her curvy figure. Her eyes blaze when she admires how handsome and attractive Lucca is, and of course, he has charmed both her and Aunt Eva.

Bloody flirt.

Lunch has been lovely and it has been nice catching up with the family and hearing all about Hayley's escapades at Dundee University. She's such a free spirit, and I admire her confidence and footloose qualities. She's very intelligent and studying to be an optometrist.

Hayden's apprenticeship is going well. Lucca has offered him permanent work with the contractors for Osurac Industries, which blows him away. Hayden's so much more laid-back than Hayley, to the point he's horizontal. It's endearing to witness them mature into young adults. They are both so grown up now.

They are coming back to the cottage with us to stay the evening. The boys are away in the fields clay pigeon shooting with Doris. Mum, Aunt Eva, Granny, Hayley, and I go to the Hilton Coylumbridge in Aviemore for facials and some wine and drinks in the bar—mine being a decaf coffee—with Lloyd and Devon.

They choose to sit at a table next to us. Aunt Eva is aware that Michael Parks is in the UK. Mum called and told her, but they've kept that information from Hayley and Hayden for now. I suppose they don't need their minds warped with this. Although they are adults now and should be made aware, they will find out soon enough when they discover the room that's being used by the security team. It's only a matter of time before they ask about our Men in Black.

It sometimes feels as if we're walking on eggshells as we very rarely bring it up or talk about it—forbidden discussion. I don't think it's just me in denial. It's a family trait. I guess they're trying to protect our feelings. Distraction works but my thoughts always go back to the matter at hand, as does Mum's. It never truly goes away.

Lucca calls no less than four times to check on me, and I tell him that I'm fine every time. Granny, Mum, and Aunt Eva go with Lloyd an hour or so before Hayley and I are ready to travel back with Devon. It gives Hayley and me a chance to have a girl talk, alone.

"Oh no, I've left my purse, shit. I'll just be a minute." Hayley panics once we are seated in the back of the SUV. I think she's a little tipsy with the four glasses of wine she consumed and the two blue concoctions. God knows what was in that. Conveniently, she waited until Aunt Eva left before she ordered them. She throws the door open and quickly runs back inside to the bar before I get the chance to say I'll come with her.

While I'm waiting I check my emails and text messages, sending a quick one off to Lucy asking how her hot date went with Marco. Getting impatient, I think it's been at least ten minutes since Hayley's left. Surely it can't take that long, unless she's waiting on management to check if anything has been handed in. I do hope she finds it. I mention to Devon we need to go in and check on her if she's not back in ten minutes. He agrees and says we both need to go as I'm not to be left alone.

I call her phone but it rings out.

After ten minutes, she still isn't back and I have an awful feeling in my stomach.

"I'm worried about her. I'm going to get her." I open the car door.

Devon calls Lloyd but disconnects when a tipsy Hayley tripping towards us, giggling from the front door of the hotel, holding her wedge shoes in her hands. Dear Lord, she's properly drunk now. Pissed, no less.

She comes to a halt, staggering backwards, when a burgundy car nearly runs her over. I jump out and storm over to her and help her into the back of the car.

"What were you thinking? You nearly got yourself killed there. What took you so long?" I snap.

"Chill out. My purse wasn't there, so I asked management to check while I waited at the bar and a guy bought me a drink. In fact, he bought me a couple of shots which, of course, I threw back." She giggles.

"Are you insane? Taking drinks from a stranger? Hayley, Jesus, you should be more careful."

"Oh relax! I saw the bartender pour them in front of me. It's all good. Please, don't tell my mum. She's been yapping on about my party lifestyle, but I'm an adult. I can do what I like." She slouches across the backseat of the car.

I fasten her seat belt. "Well, start acting like one and don't you do that again. And stop talking to strangers you have no idea how risky that is," I yell. I'm so angry with her because I love her and I'm only looking out for her. How could she be so irresponsible? Then again, she doesn't know why I'm on edge but it doesn't excuse her carelessness.

"Stop shouting at me, Lexi, you sound worse than Mum, just cover for me and I'll owe you. Anyway, he had the sexiest accent." I sigh and start to tell her the reason I'm being extra cautious but she falls sound asleep. I protectively cuddle her into my side until we reach home. I call Lucca and tell him about it because Devon will tell him anyway.

Devon lifts Hayley up and puts her in my mum's bed. I'm so embarrassed by her antics today. I thank Devon profusely but ask him to keep it to himself. She mumbles and thanks me. I kiss her head and leave her some water.

Mum and Granny start preparing dinner, my stomach taking a turn for the worse after lunch with pregnancy sickness and nerves over Hayley's drama. I sip a camomile tea, leaning against the counter talking to Aunt Eva.

"Where's Hayley?" Aunt Eva asks.

"In bed. She's feeling poorly. We need to talk."

"Oh, I hope she's okay," Aunt Eva replies.

"She's sleeping it off," I say.

Mum looks at me curiously, hoping Hayley doesn't have the pregnancy bug as well. I lift my hand to my mouth, tilting an imaginary glass of wine when Aunt Eva turns to roll out the pastry for Granny. Mum understands nodding her head discreetly.

I tell them about her carelessness today, because while we're all walking on eggshells, she's being idiotic and it's not safe to behave in that way, especially given the circumstances we are in. She needs a good talking too, but it's Aunt Eva's place to do it. I asked her to wait until Hayley's sobered up to speak with her. I don't want Hayley thinking I'm going behind her back, but it's for her own good. I have her best interests at heart.

The boys return and we have a cosy night with a homemade steak pie dinner, sharing lots of old stories, minus an intoxicated Hayley, and Hayden who has gone away to Kingussie to meet an old friend. Lucca tells me he's really gone to meet an old flame from the ski school and had Nate drive him. At least someone will be with him.

Avoiding the steak pie, I have parmesan chicken and some salad and say I'm trying to build my appetite back up. It's hard as Granny makes an amazing homemade steak pie, but the smell of the meat curls my toes.

Mr. Carlin has retired to bed, feeling exhausted after his outdoor walk today. Lucca informs me that he never actually walked that far, but it's still good exercise and the fresh air is great for him.

After dinner Lucca makes some calls to the specialist and CID for updates and other business calls. Then we decide to have an early night. It's been a long day.

Checking on Hayley, I place some water and painkillers down next to her and a bowl in the event she's is sick. Aunt Eva and mum have both checked on her, but she has been sleeping soundly. Hayley will be getting a good telling to in the morning.

In the shower, I update Lucca on her antics this afternoon. He knows I care deeply for her and is concerned with her careless behaviour as well in our current situation, but he doesn't challenge the conversation any further. His mind is elsewhere. Distant.

I shampoo his hair, massaging his scalp to try and relieve his tension. It seems to relax him until his phone vibrates on the vanity shelf. He leaves me in the shower so he can check his messages. I switch the shower off, towel dry, and apply my body butter cream.

Lucca is sitting at the dressing table with his towel around his waist, using his laptop and phone at the same time.

I walk around him and lightly skim my fingers across his upper back as I place a soft kiss on his shoulder to let him know I'm here. He drops his shoulders under my touch then lifts my hand and kisses it. He needs five minutes so I use the time to read a magazine in bed.

He seems very irate and anxious as he runs his hands through his hair while checking emails. He pinches his forehead after a phone conversation with Omari. The defined muscles in his back flex, showing just how brawny his body actually is, not that I'm complaining about that view, but I know he's tense. I ask if it's regarding Kimberley, to which he comes over to the bed kisses my nose and tells me it's nothing to worry about, just business that he needs to address.

I hate seeing him stressed. His face reveals a thousand worries, but he's still magnificently beautiful. I need to relax and distract his mind because this tension is not good for either of us right now. We have enough to deal with, like a crazed lunatic on the run likely trying to track me down.

"You still have not read those documents Omari gave you," he says.

"No, sorry. I've been distracted, but I'll do it tomorrow. I promise. Is that why you're so tense?"

"No, of course not. I just remembered when I spoke to him tonight. I am sorry, I do not want you to be uptight because I am tense. It is nothing I cannot take care of, so please do not worry." His voice softens when he notices me picking the skin on my palms and biting my inside cheek.

I'm sitting propped up against the headboard naked, allowing the cream to absorb into my skin, as I look through a pregnancy magazine that Mum secretly bought me at the store. We change the subject and talk about the baby and our future. I'm hoping this will distract and relax him.

It does.

Lucca's cheek rests on my tummy. His fingers lightly tickle the skin of my abdomen with gentle strokes, which elicit that deep fluttering sensation inside.

Comfortable.

Tranquil.

Blissful.

"I want you to see a doctor as soon as possible, and we will get you all checked out. I have arranged full private health care coverage for you, here and in Tuscany in case we are there."

I don't argue because he'll be persistent, and I do want to know everything is how it should be with my pregnancy.

"I need to get this implant in my arm removed also." That was a pointless exercise which caused a huge fight with Lucca afterwards. I never even knew I was pregnant at the time too.

He runs his thumb over the skin where it was inserted, sighing.

I read some facts and recommendations to him from the pregnancy magazine until I feel his body relax and his cheek sink heavier against my stomach. His slowing deep breaths billow across my skin. Knowing he's fallen asleep, I turn off the lamp but don't move just yet.

I close my eyes and reflect on the past few months, these crazy few weeks. Gently, I stroke his muscular shoulders and weave my fingers in his hair with the other hand, twirling my fingers.

"Lucca Caruso, thank you for giving me your light. I love you, and you are going to make the best daddy in the world," I whisper. He stirs and splays his hand across my tummy. I'm not sure if he heard me, but it doesn't matter. I'm only thinking out loud. A few moments later, I need to move to get comfortable until we are positioned in a warm embrace.

Sleep.

Lucca wakes me up the next morning by showering me in kisses and caressing my body all over, apologising for being stressed and falling asleep last night. He gives me three early morning orgasms no less, which my body is more than grateful for.

"I love these *gifts of the days*," I mumble, completely sated and relaxed.

"Hmmm, you have no idea how much I do too. That was amazing, baby. You need to keep your energy levels up because I am planning to give you these gifts of the day, every day, forever and always."

"That I can manage. It would be a shame to deny my horny, pregnant body such gratification. It makes me feel so much better," I say with bashfulness, wetting my lips and smiling. Playful.

"Well, in that case, I will need to do this throughout the day for my own physical wellbeing, as well as yours, you understand. I cannot have you unwell," he says, picking me up to place me in the shower.

"Of course. Then we'll both be grateful and feel so much better." I lean over to kiss him with my bruised lips.

"Did you mean it when you said I would be the best daddy in the world?" he asks while we get dressed.

"Oh, I thought you were sleeping." I blush.

"I thought I was dreaming," he replies with so much hope in his eyes.

"I don't just think that, Lucca, I know it. You will be an incredible father, and I feel very blessed right now, even if I do feel si—" I run into the bathroom to vomit again.

Chapter 32: Ghosts

The family is taking a trip to Inverness for some shopping today. Hayden and Hayley choose to stay at home with Nate because Hayden slumped on the sofa at four this morning after Nate brought him back from a house party and Hayley has a horrendous hangover, although she's pretending to study. Nate will be pissed about babysitting all night.

Hayley and Hayden have been briefed about Michael Parks, and she now feels guilty about yesterday and apologises for her carelessness. I suspect she's avoiding everyone because she received a family intervention this morning. I wouldn't be surprised if Granny swiped her ass with her loafer and gave her a very rude awakening.

I ask Hayley to take the dogs out for me as the fresh air will do her good. I'm not particularly in a shopping mood, especially after being sick again this morning, but it pleases Granny, Mum, and Aunt Eva when we spend quality time together.

While they try outfits and accessories on, I have coffee in a little tearoom next door with the men. Grandpa and Mr. Carlin browse the newspapers, Uncle Jim checks the share price on his tablet, and I catch up on my texts sending a quick one to Cameron telling him about Hayden and Hayley's drunken behaviour, to which he replied with a thumbs up, smiley face, and the word "legends."

I refuse to let Lucca buy me any more clothes, especially since I won't be fitting into any of them soon. While we're having coffee, he sneaks off leaving me with Lloyd and Devon. He won't tell me what he's bought, but I'm sure I'll find out soon enough.

We have an early dinner at La Tavola Italiana—the Italian Table—Rafaello's restaurant chain. Everyone appears to be in high spirits after shopping, and even Uncle Jim is delighted with his new leather briefcase for work.

I sit between Grandpa and Lucca after we meet more of his extended Scottish-Italian aunts, uncles, cousins, and second cousins who work here. I'll never remember them all as there are so many names to memorise.

"Alexis, you've barely touched your pasta, and you look washed out. Are you not hungry?" Aunt Eva asks.

"My appetite is still not back to normal. I'm good, just tired," I reply. She nods and gives me a sympathetic smile then gives Mum "the look".

Shit, it's "the look". She knows I'm pregnant.

Fuck!

File W for what. What happened to complete disclosure?

Mum and I will need to have words about this. I can't believe she told her. Lucca protectively places his arm around the back of my chair and fidgets with a loose curl, comforting me. Surprisingly there is nothing else said. Maybe I'm just paranoid and she doesn't actually know.

We ask for a few main dishes and sides for Hayden, Hayley, and our Men in Black team to take home with us. While we're waiting for our lunch to arrive, Lucca's phone rings. He excuses himself then returns with Lloyd and Devon, and I can tell by the look in his eyes that something is wrong.

"Who was that?" I ask.

He sits down on edge and whispers into my ear. "It was Nate," he whispers.

"Oh, is everything okay?"

"I'm not sure. Hayley was out walking the dogs earlier and noticed something." He pinches his brow and temple with his middle finger and thumb.

He tries to shrug it off, but something isn't right. I feel myself aware of the surroundings and consciously glance over my shoulder with a slight shiver, as if we're being watched. Paranoia creeps in.

"What did Hayley notice?" Aunt Eva asks, having overheard. Now, the full table is listening.

Lucca searches my eyes and sighs, contemplating whether to mention it in front of the table.

"Please, Lucca?" I beg for his honesty.

"Evangeline, she is fine. She was out walking the dogs and saw a strange vehicle parked on the private road. Probably nothing. Perhaps someone was looking for the Murdock's stables. We should go back soon. I would like to speak with Nate."

That silences the table like rolling tumbleweeds, until Grandpa addresses me. "Apple, don't you worry. You're as safe as can be at the house with Lucca and all of us. It's probably nothing at all. Hell, it might even be the photography club stopping to shoot landscape pictures of the sunset. They do that frequently."

"Maybe," I say, twiddling my fingers with worry in front of my mouth. I'm worried that by telling Hayley about Michael Parks, it's scared her and she's being extra paranoid

When we arrive home, the air is thick, grey and dusty and smells smoky, like burnt wood. Aunt Eva reheats the meals we brought back while Hayley whines about being starving and asks what took us so long. She says she heard fire engines and we missed all the drama. That would explain the smokiness. I hope it isn't serious.

"Lexi, I hope you don't mind, but I borrowed your toiletries and makeup," she adds.

"No, honey, that's fine. Are you feeling better?"

"Yes, I feel much better, and I'm starving."

Lucca disappears with Men in Black to pull up the video surveillance from today. It's not lost on me that he clenched his jaw all the way home.

I knock lightly on the door to the small lounge to take in a tray of the hot meals for Nate, Lloyd, and Devon. Lucca opens it then signals to Lloyd to switch off the monitors and close the laptops.

"Is everything okay? What's going on?" I ask. "Did you find out about the suspicious vehicle?"

Lucca takes the tray from me and sits it down on the corner of the table. "It was that photography group your grandpa mentioned. We can see from our cameras that they were taking photos." He narrows his eyes towards Men in Black.

"Oh … well, I'll be back with drinks. Just a minute," I whisper. I can't help but feel Lucca is keeping me in the dark, and that doesn't sit well as he's done nothing but promise to bring me into his light.

"Thank you for dinner, Lexi. This looks great," Lloyd interrupts.

Lucca stretches for my hand before I leave the room. "I promise you, everything is fine, so stop worrying."

Closing the space between us, I whisper in his ear as tears fill my eyes, "You're a terrible liar."

He runs his fingers through his hair, shifting his weight. "I will get the drinks. Boys, you should start your meal. Lexi, can I speak to you upstairs in a few minutes?"

I knew it.

Dishonesty.

Without saying a word, I shake my head, drop his hand, and storm into the dining room, grabbing Hayley's arm.

"Ouch," she squeals.

"A word … in private," I demand, pulling her into the boot room and shutting the door behind us.

"What's eating you? And why are you yanking me into a bloody cupboard?" she asks, dumbfounded.

"What colour was that car you saw today? I need to know."

"It was maroon or burgundy, why? What's the drama?" She absently plays with her hair.

I don't explain. I turn on my heels and go upstairs into my room. With every footstep, the murky storm building in the deepest, darkest cave of my core rises to my throat.

For a girl who's supposedly very bright, Hayley can be such a dumb-ass sometimes. The stabbing in my chest is sharp and imminent. My throat is constricting. I'm hot, I'm breathless, and I'm having an anxiety attack.

I search in my bag for an anti-anxiety pill and pop it on my tongue. I don't even consider if it's safe to use during pregnancy. Right now my heart has skipped so many beats that I might just have a heart attack. I pace the floor, angry at Hayley, angry at Lucca, angry at myself, and angry at the whole goddamn world for screwing with my karma.

Angry.

The door opens. "Jesus, Lexi, come here, baby." He grabs my waist and pulls me into his chest. Involuntarily, I throw my arms around his neck, needing his contact.

My own chest rises and falls as I try to control my erratic breathing. Beads of sweat form on my forehead, and my skin feels clammy. I'm so dizzy from lack of food and this pounding headache and stabbing heartache.

"Lexi, please calm down and breathe. It is not good for you or our baby."

"I feel so dizzy," I manage to gasp.

"Christ!" He panics, picking me up and taking me over to the bed. He places me down on my back then lies on his side, still not breaking the embrace. He kisses, soothes, and caresses me until I've slowly regulated my breathing, reducing the tightness in my hands and fingers by allowing oxygen and blood to flow properly. My heart and lungs are working more efficiently.

"You scared the shit out of me. Are you all right?" He wipes the trail of sweat running down the side of my face.

"Yes, I think so." His hand rests on the top of my thigh. He runs his thumb over the skin of my thigh and slips it under my dress to rest his hand on my tummy.

"Doc, I know it is hard, but you need to avoid getting worked up like this. It cannot be good for either of you."

Slumping into the mattress and slamming my hand on the cover, I cry, "I can't do this anymore. I can't act like everything is normal when it's not. There's a fucking lunatic after my blood, and you're keeping things from me. I don't like it. Stop treating me like glass. Just be honest with me." He moves a stray curl from my face and stares into my frightful eyes.

"I am not keeping things from you. I am protecting you from the truth. I was afraid you would end up like this, and this is exactly what I wanted to avoid. God, the last thing I want to do is hurt you, you know that." The pain in his eyes is honest.

I reach my hand up and cup his face. "I know. I'm sorry. I'm just tired and sick, both mentally and physically. I want to lead a normal life, Lucca. This is killing me slowly," I sob.

He kisses me with such force that his teeth bite at my bottom lip. "You are very much alive and I would like to keep it that way. Nothing is going to happen to you, I promise you. I love you so much. Please, just trust me to look after you so you can concentrate on looking after our baby."

He moves his hand to slide my dress further up to my waist, then moves down the bed and softly kisses my abdomen until his mouth meets the trim of my purple lace thong, his tongue slipping along the edge of the delicate fabric.

"I did say that I would be giving you this whenever required," he says with that velvet tone deep in his throat as he slides his fingers inside my already wet sex.

Oh God!

Folded, crumbled, and melted.

It's exactly what I need to take my thoughts somewhere else, somewhere much better. Sated and more relaxed, my mood has shifted thanks to Lucca's Love.

Our love.

The love.

L'amore.

He passes me some gift bags. "What's this?" I ask.

"You would not let me buy you an outfit, so I had an idea. It is something practical for you ... well, for us."

I open the bags to find various baby books explaining all things pregnancy, childbirth, and babies.

"Thank you. This is great."

I flick through the pages then wrinkle my nose in disgust when I come across a page showing a woman giving birth vaginally. I shut the book closed, faking a smile and filing that awful thought to the back of my mind. He laughs and I smack his chest. "Yes, laugh all you like. You don't need to deliver a baby from somewhere so—"

"Perfect and tight? If I could do it, I would, but I will make sure you have the best medical care, and I will be there every step of the way."

I purse my lips as I put the books back in the bag. "What's in this one?"

"Look inside."

I pull out a professional camera. Puzzled, I look at him.

"It is to take photos of our baby. It is a Leica M9 Titanium compact digital camera. I wanted something professional so we can take great family photos. Then we can email photos to my parents

416

and your family when we do not see them." I stare at it for a long time, focusing on the lens. Memories of the dark room in the house on stilts ring through my mind. Michael Parks taking photos of me, Mum being forced to help develop Simon's photos for his business.

Shit.

I never envisaged being in front of a camera, never mind holding one and actually shooting pictures. I don't know what to make of it. My face must be pale. So many emotions run through my mind. Is it a good thing that I'm holding a camera? Or is it going to send me into a panic attack? Will it help me be more tolerant and move me forward? Or will it trigger nightmares?

I'm confused. Lucca notices the conflict written across my face, he walks over to the dressing table, lifts the photo album he gave me and holds it out towards me.

"Baby, I understand ... I do. I know this is challenging for you, but I want you to remember how you felt when you opened that photo book and looked at all the beautiful memories in those pictures. We have an opportunity to take pictures of our baby, our happy times together as a family. Would you not like to cherish and look back on them in the future?

Immediately, I think about what my mum said about not having happy photographic images of Cameron and I and it makes me realise, that yes, I would like this for our family. I don't want to miss out on anything or have any regrets.

I want our baby to have a normal life. Whatever normal is.

"Wow, it's wonderful, thank you. I never thought I would see the day I'd have a camera in my hands. I would love to be able to photograph our baby," I say, upbeat.

After my initial reservations I warm to the idea, witnessing the proud smile on his beautiful face and the thoughtfulness behind his gesture. I kiss him, worshipping his lips because if there's one thing Lucca Caruso is ... it's thoughtful.

He growls into my mouth. "So am I in your good graces again?"

"You were never out of them. I was just in a bad mood. You had me right there with your gift of touch, but thank you for the camera. It's great."

"I owe Hayley an apology," I say as we walk downstairs. I lashed out at her because I was angry Lucca was keeping things from me.

"Oh, that reminds me. I got gift cards for Hayden and Hayley today."

"You're amazing, do you know that?" I plant a kiss on his cheek.

"So you keep telling me. If you kiss me on the lips, I cannot be held responsible for what will happen on these stairs, baby. I know how you like that exercise."

"Shhh," I gasp and blush.

Hayley and Hayden are absolutely delighted with their gift cards. I don't ask how much is on them, but Hayley says she'll be set with new clothes for a full year at university. Lucca sits at the dining room table to email and make more calls while the rest of the family gathers in the main living room to watch a movie.

Mr. Carlin complains about Doris chewing his slippers, and Hayden tosses popcorn across the room towards Hayley, so of course Doris jumps across everyone's legs trying to catch it and knocks Mr. Carlin's spectacles off the arm of the chair.

"Right, I'm taking her out. Toshums, Rubster, walkies," I chirp, calling on Tosh and Ruby.

Just as I'm about to take the dogs out, someone knocks. I look through the panelled glass. Devon asks me to move into the living room before I get a chance to open the door for the well-dressed couple. He shows the two visitors into the small living room then asks for Lucca.

From the door of the dining room, I watch Lucca nod his head and follow Devon out the room with Nate and Lloyd. Shuffling around, I'm agitated and have the front of my hand against my mouth worrying my fingers.

"I'm going to the bathroom. Be back in a bit, then I'll take the dogs out," I tell my mum, who's too engrossed watching *The Notebook* to notice. I deliberately close the door and venture through towards the other side of the house where the small living room is being used as a security room.

The door is slightly ajar and the light is shining through the crack underneath. There are lots of heated discussions going on with Lucca's voice being the most significant. I tiptoe outside the door. Pressing my ear against the pine, I can hear Lucca swearing and cursing, raising his voice and probing the couple.

Oh shit, this can't be good news. I'd love to file this and pretend it's not happening, but this chapter needs to be addressed.

I think they may be investigators or specialists or something because he's going on about developments and updates, questioning them. I hold my chest, tapping my fingers against my skin when the conversations turn to the burgundy vehicle I saw outside.

"So you are telling me it was a hired car?" Lucca asks.

"Yes, it was hired under the name of Kyle Saunders, which of course we've traced. He died four years ago in a house fire in London. Someone has used a fake identity, passport, and cards."

"Is it him, goddamn it? Is it him using different aliases?" Lucca is furious as he rants at the couple.

"I'm afraid we're not sure yet. The burned vehicle was found tonight near the Ospreys nature reserve. The team is working for prints, but the person was very clever and clean. We can't rule out the possibility that your man has help ... professional help."

My stomach churns at the thought.

I can sense his heated tension radiating through the door and feel every stomp of his feet as he paces.

"Bodies?" Lucca asks.

I need to slap my hand over my mouth to muffle my gasps.

"No, empty."

"I do not fucking believe this. Surely you have video footage or can trace the handwriting or credit card used when the car hire was made," he protests.

"We haven't found any links, but you'll be informed as soon as we do, Mr. Caruso. There is something else. The church minister reported a raid tonight. She came back from the senior citizen club and her manse has been turned over. Nothing was stolen. They are dusting it just now, but again, another clean job."

"Are you fucking kidding me? We were there on Sunday. Maybe it is linked!" he shouts.

"It may be coincidental, but we're treating it as suspicious. Also, there was a deliberate fire this afternoon over at the Murdock's stables. The family is okay, and so is the house, but the stables burned down. They managed to get all but one horse out and into the paddock, and they've been transported to the riding school in the village."

"Jesus, Lexi and I were there on Tuesday," Lucca snaps.

Oh my God, no ... please no ... Angel.

I feel a deep-seated pit in my stomach, the horses, the Murdock's, and Cathy. This is catastrophic.

He must be watching me. He's trying to break me and get to me by destroying everything important to me. My hand moves from my gaping mouth to my stomach. It isn't just me we're protecting now.

Our world is crashing down.

I must protect our baby ...

I push the door open, protectively holding my stomach, and feel my legs go weak beneath me. Shaking and startled, I stare at Lucca.

"Christ. Lexi, did you hear any of that?" He's beside me in two fast strides, his eyes still fierce with rage and a trace of uncertainty.

"It's him," I stutter.

"What? You do not know that." He narrows his eyes towards the female detective.

"Yes, I do. There was a man standing in the graveyard on Sunday watching us," I say towards the female detective. Everything is coming back to me, I've been so focused on the pregnancy, but I recall the event trying to visualise what I remember seeing.

He grabs my shoulders tightly. "Jesus, Doc, why did you not say anything?" His voice is broken with panic. My grandparents and mum enter the room, having heard the commotion.

I'm numb.

I can't speak.

I only stare with an iced glaze over my startled eyes. "Miss Robertson, this is very serious. We need a description."

I refrain from turning around to look at the probing detective this time. "Black coat, well-built, golf umbrella," I splutter, utterly dazzled.

"Jesus ..." Lucca sucks in a sharp breath of air.

"What's going on?" My mum demands.

The female detective relays the information to someone on her phone while her partner flips through the notes in his hand. Lloyd opens up his laptop, frantically searching for something as Devon makes a phone call.

"Alexis, elaborate ... please," Mum begs.

Chewing the inside of my cheek, I force myself to speak.

"Car ..." I stammer.

"What about the fucking car? Jesus Christ, tell me!" Lucca shouts, shaking my shoulders.

"Lucca, please calm down. You're scaring her," Mum scolds.

"Sorry ... Lexi, please tell me. You need to help us because we cannot help you if you do not tell us." He softens his tone, letting go of his grip and running his thumb over my cheek.

"Lexi, stop havering, kid, and tell us." Grandpa follows Lucca's begging with a softer more rational tone. Peacemaker.

"The burgundy car ... it was here today. Hayley told me. And yesterday it nearly ran her over outside the Hilton. I saw the same car on Sunday morning, remember? Then there was a stranger, a creepy guy in the graveyard watching us. It unnerved me but I assumed it was the groundsman. At the gas station on the way home I saw a similar car, but he never refuelled. I'm sorry; I was too distracted to mention it." My voice breaks.

I struggle to take air in.

"Shit," Lucca hisses.

"There's something else. Hayley said someone with an accent was chatting to her in the bar, but she was drinking and doesn't remember anything." I sob and tremble.

The detectives both look at Lucca, nodding, and move with great speed around the desk making more calls, pulling files from their briefcases, and firing up their tablets. The man has an earpiece in calling the CID followed by the local police station and notifying the specialist.

"The team will be here shortly," the male detective says. Lucca paces towards the table to pick his phone up, punching the wall another few times on the way.

Everything from that point happens in slow motion. Granny's squawking and my grandpa is beside himself with worry. Mr. Carlin is grumpier than normal, pinching his suspenders, unsure what to do. Hayley and Hayden think they are on a movie set, totally stunned, and Lucca and my mum have just freaked out under the pressure of stress.

She calls Cameron in a frenzied fit, and I'm still standing in the same spot, my arms dangling by my sides. I can't focus on anything in particular because of the humming noise in my ears.

There's a moving picture all around me, only now it's a jumbled image with lots of distortion which I've zoned out of. I don't hear them, I only see what looks very much to be a nightmarish dream and my blood runs cold.

Stumbling backwards, I try to ignore my impending fate. My head can't quite process this—discovering I'm pregnant one minute, then realising I'm destined for abuse or death in the next or worse ...

My friends and family.

This is all so extreme, but it's the reality of my screwed-up life that I need to accept. But I'm angry and don't want to accept it. I want a normal life without complications.

The whimpers and worries from within the room over spill into the dining room and push me further back into a quiet shelter within the hallway.

I'm merely a fading flicker among all the fire. I slip out the hallway and stagger out the front door, hobbling around the perimeter, holding onto the white pebbled walls outside, until I've found the quiet corner inside the barn where I can sit on the hay and pull my knees up to my chest.

Doris has followed me. She whines at my despair then jumps up beside me, burying her velvety head into my neck. I hold onto her tightly like my life depends on it and cry uncontrollably against her mink-like coat. My heart breaks like nothing else because I simply can't comprehend this ... fucking mind cluster.

Doris has now wrapped her two lanky front legs around my neck. That's the thing about Weimeraners, they have human like tendencies. I clutch onto her and close my eyes.

Chapter 33: Queens and Kings

I don't know how much time has passed, but I open my raw eyes and startle when I see a torch blaring in front of me. I'm swiftly lifted into Lucca's arms and he carries me through the wood shed, into the house, past the chaos, and into our room.

He sits me on the bed and grabs our suitcases from under the bed, throwing them on top of the mattress. I'm frozen, blinking nervously, just watching. He grabs everything from the wardrobe and throws it in the case then empties the drawers and does the same.

I stare dumbfounded at the dressing table when he runs his arm across it in one swift sweep depositing my cosmetics in a bag. My brain is all out of appropriate motor skills to make me manoeuvre, the signals temporarily malfunctioning as I simply can't move.

Lucca stuffs my toiletries, gifts, shoes, chargers, and anything lying around into the holdalls then places his laptop in his briefcase.

"Wait here. Do not move," he orders, giving me a tight reassuring squeeze to my knees.

He calls Lloyd and Uncle Jim to come upstairs and help him with the luggage while Devon keeps an eye on me. I yank my Wellingtons off then pull my knees up to my chest and hug them, feeling very vulnerable and small in this fucking mind puzzle.

Devon sits on the dressing table stool watching me but remaining silent.

Lucca returns and hands Devon a piece of paper then asks him to go downstairs. He gives him an appreciative pat on the shoulder in a silent exchange.

"Lexi, you're perfectly safe. We will make sure you and your family are well protected, gal. It will be grand. Your guy is an amateur," Devon says in his sexy Irish accent.

I give him a lacklustre smile but appreciate his sentiment. There's nothing amateur about Michael Parks. Evil is ingrained in him.

Lucca runs his hands through his hair, and on that cue Devon leaves and closes the door. He drops to his knees on the floor in front of me, pressing his forehead against mine.

He's shaking.

I'm shaking.

"We are going away," he says, gripping my thighs, breathing heavily against my face, his blue eyes stormy.

No reassurance, no spark. Shit, it's bad.

"Where are we going?"

"I am taking you back to Tuscany tonight."

"No! What about my family?" Suddenly alert, I clench onto his biceps in fear, begging him to be rational.

"Your Aunt Eva, Uncle Jim, Hayley, and Hayden are being transported to a safe house under police protection because they feel Hayley is too exposed and a target. Your grandparents and Mr. Carlin are going back to our house in Bothwell and will be monitored and looked after with lots of security, and your mum is coming with us; she is already packed. I need to take you out of the country. I cannot have you at risk here until he's found."

"Oh my God, I'm going to ..." I scramble off the bed, hunch over the toilet, and vomit again and again until my stomach's empty. Lucca is right by my side holding my hair and wetting a cloth.

"Doc ... we need to go."

Certain.

Sharp.

Focused.

"Hayley?" My voice falters, quivering and breaking. My lips tremble with dread for her.

"They are pulling video links from the bar, but it looks as if Hayley was used as bait. She will be protected around the clock." He runs his hand over my back. "Are you okay, baby? We need to move quickly."

"No, not my little cousin. She's too innocent to be part of this. She doesn't deserve this." I stand on shaky legs, rinse my mouth, then look down at my stomach and pause.

"Lucca?" I cry.

"No, do not. You do not dare. I have you. You are both going to be safe." Without another word, he picks me up and carries me downstairs.

It all happens so fast—the policemen, detectives, and Men in Black sprinting back and forth, my mum sobbing into Aunt Eva's neck saying goodbye, my granny heartbroken on the chair being consoled by a specialist, Hayley wrapped in Uncle Jim's arms, and Hayden chalk white. I'm motionless.

When Lucca carries me towards the door something sparks inside me.

"Wait!" I shout and wiggle from Lucca's embrace. I walk barefoot through the frantic crowd and find Hayley. I walk past the chaos and stop right in front of her.

"I'm sorry," I say, cupping her face. "I wouldn't wish this on my enemy. I'm so sorry. Everything will be okay, and you will be fine. I promise you. We won't let anything happen to you." She looks terrified. My heart is breaking and I just want to take her with me. Why does it need to be like this?

She's in shock with terror in her eyes and doesn't respond. She's confused. Anguish strains Uncle Jim's face as he rubs my arm.

"It's not your fault," she eventually says. I kiss her, cuddle her, and tell her I love her.

"Apple," a broken voice says.

Oh God ... Grandpa.

He stands helpless—a wounded soldier—with his hand on his heart like a broken man. I wrap my arms around him believing it's the last time I'm ever going to see him, breaking my heart. My hair at the side is soaked with tears and my grandpa is shaking. I've never seen him so afraid.

"Apple, I love you. I love you as much as life itself, you know that. You're my breath of fresh air, kid, but I need you to go with Lucca. He will keep you safe. We can't protect you here. Call us as soon as you get to Tuscany. We're going to join you there shortly."

"You are?"

Hope ... I now have hope. I thank my lucky stars.

"Yes of course we are," he stutters.

"Oh, Grandpa, I love you so much. I'd love for you to come. I hate the thought of ..." He places his fingers to my lips to shush me. I hold him for what seems like only seconds, but Lucca puts his hand on my shoulder gently prying me away. It's time. I don't want to go.

"Lexi, we need to go."

"No, wait ..." I cry, noticing Mr. Carlin pacing in the hallway.

"For fuck sake, Alexis, we need to go!" Lucca shouts over the commotion while banging the wall with his fist. I yank my hand away and wrap my arms around Mr. Carlin's neck while I have the chance.

"Please tell me this is going to be okay?" I beg for his promises because he's a wise man with wise words and always centres me.

"I don't know that, lassie, but I will pray for everyone," he says in a stern, gruff voice.

Lucca is cursing and swearing behind us, which causes me to sigh. I close my eyes and shake my head. Mr. Carlin does something he's never done before—he takes my face in both hands.

"Don't be angry at him. He's hurting too and falling apart because he wants to protect you, lassie. You know, in a game of chess the queen always protects the king. You remember that because I know in the end, Lexi, you'll always be the strong one under pressure. You keep it buried deep, girl. Hell, you always do, but when the time's right, you dig and fight and protect your king. He's a strong man, but sometimes men can be so blinded by love that they become weak and falter. He's stressed but trying very hard to mask it. Lexi, be strong, have faith and courage. Eleanor will guide you, lass."

"No, I can't, I'm not!" I yell, dropping to my knees. Lucca lifts me off the floor in his protective, masculine arms and storms to the front door with me.

I don't get the chance to say goodbye to anyone else in the house or comprehend what's happening before Lucca carries me out and places me in one of the SUVs. He fastens my seat belt and gets in beside me. I hear Doris barking from the porch, which tugs right at my heartstrings.

"Wait!" I yell.

"No, you can't take her, Alexis." Mum sobs from the front of the vehicle, rummaging in her handbag; I hear the familiar pop of pills from a packet. Mum's obviously had to take her medication because of tonight's discovery.

I focus on Mr. Carlin standing at the front door next to the detective, rubbing his head in confusion and pinching his suspenders. I lower the window. "Mr. Carlin, can you take care of her until I'm home? Please make sure she's looked aft ..." I'm barely able to finish, my throat raw.

"Lassie, don't worry about the beast. You get yourself to safety. We'll all be fine, but I give you my word, I'll look after her." He coughs then blows me a kiss. I catch it and return the gesture as Lloyd slams his foot on the accelerator and drives off with us into the fearful unknown dark of night.

Mr. Carlin's shrinking eyes are the last image I have because my eyes are squeezed shut so tightly that I'm seeing white distorted shapes flickering through the darkness within the car.

Lucca pulls me into his chest protectively, but all I can think about is the family we have left behind.

"Alexis, are you okay?" Mum asks, but she sounds broken.

Like me.

How can I be so mindless wallowing in my own anguish when she must be absolutely ready to shatter and break? When she doesn't have anyone holding her or protecting her?

"I will be fine. Mum, are you ...?"

"Yes, don't you worry about me. I'll be all right. We will all be fine. Just focus on you and your baby."

I don't care that she's said it in front of Lloyd because her heart is in the right place.

I wish I could pull her over into my lap and caress her the same way Lucca is doing for me, to give her some comfort.

The ringing of Lucca's phone startles me, and he answers it almost immediately.

"Yes, is it ready? ... Good ... Yes, the ladies may want to sleep ... Good ... Negative ... Yes, four ... Passports are with me ... No fucking about, Claude, ensure she is ready to go, ETA thirty minutes ... yes, it is fucking imperative ... I understand ... refreshments yes, food, blankets, and one cabin crew member only ... Yes, off radar and no manifest ... CID, security, and the case specialists are more than aware, all above board ... Claude ... Thanks."

He disconnects as another call comes through.

It's Marco who he gives further instructions regarding the enhanced security and details of our flight. Then he speaks with Cameron to ensure that he, Hazel, Dominic, and Anna leave my house in Uddingston and move into Lucca's temporarily where there is adequate security.

Shivering from fright and because my feet are bare, I lift them up on the seat and place them under my ass. Lucca takes his suit jacket off and slips it over me, realising I'm shaking and cold.

He continues making his calls to Peter, Antonio, and Giorgio—his business partner at his Luminara chain—and finally another to Suzanne.

"Are we going to Inverness airport?" I whisper when his calls have finished.

"No, we are going to a private airfield nearby. We should be arriving shortly." He kisses my forehead.

"How did you get my passport?" I ask.

"I brought them with me out of habit. I always carry mine in case I need to fly for business at short notice."

"We're not going on a standard flight are we?" I ask, parting my dry lips.

"No, we are not."

"Then how?"

"My private jet. I have chartered it before for business use, but decided to buy it for us and it will be utilised as a company jet as well. When we returned from Tuscany and we were on the flight, it got me thinking that I would like you to be more comfortable and have privacy, and with my business we will need to do a lot of travel." He sighs, running his fingers through my hair, peeling the salty wet strands away from my cheeks.

I'm not surprised he has bought a jet. I'm only thankful Lucca has the means to protect me like he can and get us out the country quickly.

"I have no shoes on," I whisper, ashamed. Through all the turmoil and drama, I think of my feet. I think of running barefoot, I think of the bush and trying to escape. I cry.

I'm trying to escape. I'm running through the bush.

He's chasing me ... he's shouting at me ... my bare feet are hurting and bleeding.

It's dark ... it's hot.
I'm scared.
I can't get away.
I need to get away.

I panic, crying uncontrollably against Lucca's chest. He hushes me and calms me and tells me to keep focus and be brave.

"Do not fret about your feet, baby, that is the least of our worries. You can shower and change on the flight. We are here," he says, holding my hand while looking out the window scanning the area.

Shower? Like shower, as in running hot water in a cubicle shower? Oh my goodness this night is just getting crazier by the second. I wipe my tear stained face and try to gain some composure.

I've been too busy fretting about my bare feet to notice we're in a secluded airfield. We drive across the tarmac approaching a sleek, private jet with Osurac in bold capital letters on the side, and the engine noise intensifies as we edge nearer to it. Mum glances back towards me and gives me a reassuring nod, but I see in her eyes, she's just as petrified as me.

It's the look, the "be a big brave girl and you'll get a gold star" look.

Lucca unclasps my belt, rushes outside, and shakes hands with two smart men and a beautiful female.

Oh, just great. I look like I've been in a car crash or bushfire and have no footwear on, and she's like an air flight angel standing like a model from the frequent flyer magazine.

Lloyd passes his car keys over to another man waiting nearby in a smart suit speaking into a mouth piece. Lloyd lifts the luggage from the boot of the car.

"Can you bring the suitcases on board please, Lloyd?" Lucca shouts over the revving engine. Lloyd nods and proceeds to lift the cases up the ramp into the aircraft as opposed to the hold.

Lucca opens my door and I have to grab onto the bottom of my chiffon dress to prevent it from riding up thanks to the forceful gust of wind from the engines. He scoops me up in his arms, and I wrap my arms around his neck as my wild, wavy hair flies everywhere. Then he climbs the stairs with me into the jet.

Walking past the cockpit and crew kitchen and another private room, we settle in the main cabin. He sits me on a leather reclining bucket seat, and he takes the seat in front. Mum and Lloyd take seats on the other side.

Looking around, I find there are empty seats behind us and a huge lounge at the back with a modern corner sofa, plasma television, bar, dining table, and study area. There's a closed door in front of us and also towards the back further down the cabin.

The interiors are ultra-modern and not what I would expect to find on an aircraft, but then this is not any ordinary aircraft. There are comfortable lime green pillows, blankets and cushions, modern accessories, and lots of state-of-the-art equipment. It looks more like an exquisite suite at an upper class hotel than a plane.

Claude is the captain, Eric is the co-pilot, and Bethany is the flight attendant. Lucca passes over all four passports for inspection, and Claude casually pats him on his shoulder in a friendly gesture. He turns to address us all, giving the mandatory "welcome aboard" speech, then Claude shakes everyone's hand and walks off to the cockpit followed by Eric.

Bethany performs her safety demonstration, then disappears for take-off. She returns shortly after with bottles of water and some savoury snacks. She offers Mum and Lloyd some champagne. Lloyd refuses while on duty, but Mum takes one and throws it back then takes another.

I frown towards Mum. She says she called Casey and she's told her to take sleeping tablets with her other prescription drugs to avoid any episodes or anxiety on the flight. Mum's eyes are rolling in her head already, and I know she'll be out cold soon. Lloyd sips his water then places earphones in his ears.

Lucca pinches his forehead, contemplating what he wants. "Bethany, I will have a Peroni and a chaser of double Macallan Scotch, no ice please."

Fuck!

File - W for whiskey. Whiskey is the devil.

He's struggling, I know, but I don't want him to get sloshed, not when I need him.

He needs me.

I need him to be strong. I need to be strong for him.

I have him.

Bethany returns with our drinks, and Lucca asks for another double scotch. I turn away so he doesn't catch my distaste. He hasn't spoken to me since we got on board, and there's an oppressive silence between us. I've seen this behaviour before, and it scares me, but I love him and I'm willing to forgive his stressed-induced alcohol intake if this helps him deal with what's happening.

"Bethany, can you show me where I can use the bathroom please?" I follow her into a private bedroom when I'm satisfied Mum is sleeping.

Wow.

Under normal circumstances, I would be starstruck by this amazing bedroom with a full size bed and all the expensive hi-tech, modern conveniences, but I'm too dispirited to appreciate it.

She shows me the shower room and lets me know where my luggage has been stored then instructs me how to use the stereo system and plasma TV.

"I'll give you some privacy. If there is anything you need, press the call button over here."

"Thank you."

I drag my suitcase onto the bed with a heavy thump and pull out some clean clothes. I struggle with the weight, but I manage to lift the case onto the marble topped dressing table and strip out my dress.

As I lean over the bed to find some toiletries, I hear the door open and the lock close. Before I get the chance to stand up, Lucca presses his body against mine, ramming his hard manhood against my ass and cupping both my heavy breasts.

It's very sudden but not unwelcome. My breath hitches in my throat, and I realise just how badly he needs and wants me. I'm giving myself to him and plan to rip my anxiety to shreds.

To be numb .... to forget.

No whiskey ... just him.

Just us ... together.

He pulls me back towards him with a fierce, strong prowess, and his hands skate over my body as he bites down on my shoulder, groaning with burning desire. He pulls my hair to the side and kisses and bites my neck while his hands rip my panties off my body.

I'm lusting for him.

Desperate.

I want to make his pain subside. I want to make my pain subside.

"Lucca, I want you to fuck me. Fuck me hard, fuck me so deep that your pain becomes pleasure. Don't hold back," I beg. This helped me in BarAsta after the Kimberley ordeal and I think it will help him tonight. To feel. To feel something other than fear and heartache.

He spins me around and stares at me with dark, foreboding eyes full of anguish. "If you ask, you will get it, and I do not want to hurt you."

Desperation ...

I circle my hips and push my sex against his massive erection. He growls with deep carnal desire and unhooks my bra, freeing my tender breasts, then he picks me up and places me onto the bed. I watch as he strips his belt off and lowers his jeans and boxer briefs. His hard cock throbs with angry veins.

And I'm angry to have it.

Fuck!

File A for angry. Angry is good. It numbs the pain.

He kneels on the bed and I expect his shaft to plunge straight into me, but he waits, tormented by mixed emotions. He leans over me and his tongue dives into my mouth, fighting with my own tongue in a battle of indecency as he finger fucks me with three fingers.

Relentless.

"So wet, baby," he slurs into my mouth. I push my hips to meet his hand cupping my sex. His breath is laced with single malt sherry oak, and I almost feel drunk as I taste his tongue.

When his thumb touches my nub and flicks my clit, I explode and scream into his mouth. He swallows my screams by continuing the onslaught of his tongue. I am drunk, in scotch, sensitivity, and surging sensations that spark through my veins.

When I've jerked and twitched through the last of my orgasm, he slides his fingers out of me and rubs them across my bottom lip.

"Lick," he demands. His eyes have once again lost their bright blue hue and are now cloudy grey. I want him to fuck me so badly so that I paint colour back into those eyes.

I slip my tongue out and seductively trail it across my moist lips then reach up and grab his fingers with my teeth and suck hard on them.

"Good."

I stifle a sharp yell, his fingers still in my mouth, as he bites down on my hardened nipples, assaulting each nipple in turn. It throws me into another eye rolling orgasm when the fingers of his other hand torment my clit and slides back into my sex.

"Lucca, please I want you."

His gaze twists up a storm in those cloudy eyes. "I am sorry, baby." He clenches his teeth with possession in his turbulent eyes.

"Sorry for what?" I pant for air.

"For this."

He growls, flipping me over onto all fours. Then he slams into me with such force I cry and bite down on my lip being shunted further up the bed with every hard blow and ram. He pumps me hard and strong, each time assaulting my core as he impales his angry shaft inside me.

Violently.

He grabs my hips, yanking me back and slamming deeper into my womb with his abusive intrusion.

His hand moves back to my nipple, he pinches it hard and I groan with the intense pleasure rippling through me which builds me up towards another peak of ecstasy. With his next deep shudder, his hand meets my ass with a hard fast slap as he throatily groans my name. I bite on my arm to muffle my cry as my eyes ears fill with water; the stinging sensation takes me off guard at first until an intense jolt of pleasure courses through me. He doesn't stop until he stills inside me rubbing my ass cheek then leans over to kiss my back.

Once we have come down slightly from our climax, I reach around and grope his balls, massaging them, and feel his still erect cock twitch and expand inside me.

"Again?" he rasps sexily.

"Yes," I moan. I want it. I want more of it.

Pleasure.

Pain.

I don't want him to stop. I need it.

More.

Lots more.

I wiggle and circle my hips, encouraging him to move with me even though my legs are shaking still from our first round. He makes a low groaning noise then slowly picks up rhythm.

Oh God. It feels so good.

"Harder, deeper!" I demand then scream when his fingers dig into my skin with another intense, penetrative stroke inside me. I do want the carnality; I do want him to have me this way. If this helps him feel and gives me what I want then yes. I want it.

He's rasping, besieged with wild breath. He forces every painful emotion into every thrust. He's pushing me to an explosive orgasm. Clenching my tight walls around him, the pressure builds inside me.

His fingers flick over my swollen clit, then using the arousal from my damp sex he spreads it to lubricate my rear entrance and pushes his finger in. Trembling with the intense feeling, my eyes roll in my head as I grip all around him. He orders me to touch my clit and squeeze a nipple. I do. With his next slam inside me, his hand meets my other ass cheek with a hard slap at the same time his finger presses into my back entrance, my fingers flicks my clit and squeezes my nipple.

I erupt in an explosive orgasm.

I scream his name through a reckless climax. I continue to buck and quiver with wave after wave of stimulated pleasure from my orgasm. "Fuck, Lucca, mmm!" I cry, feeling a violent rush rippling through me.

"Shhh, relax. I have you. Breathe baby."

"Yes." I pant breathlessly, coasting through this sensational feeling.

Groaning.

Cursing.

Mumbling.

He picks up rhythm. I'm a slave for him.

He controls each thrust with more power as I push my hips back to accept more of his girth and length. He drives me forward but I'm not sure how much more my shaky muscles can take.

"Jesus, fuck, so fucking unbelievable. You are driving me wild. You feel sensational." He plunges deep inside me again with force.

"That bastard will never hurt you again," he moans, letting his rage and distress tear through him.

I asked for it, and he keeps true to his word—he fucks my core like his life depends on it.

"Touch your clit," he orders, pounding into me again. My muscles contract around him.

I can't. I'm still exhilarated from my last orgasms.

"I am close … goddamn it, Lexi, touch your clit. I need you to come!"

I barely need to touch I'm still so sensitive.

Oh my holy God … intense, sensational pleasure.

Seconds later, I come undone, screaming and erupting into a mind-blowing shattering orgasm like nothing else I've ever felt before. Lucca shouts my name, followed by a string of curses as he fills me with his second release.

I've never climaxed so violently.

Numb.

Weak.

Sated.

Euphoria.

We collapse face down on the aircraft bed, panting, breathless, drenched in sweat, slick with body juices, and utterly spent. We lie for some time, silent other than the sound of our breath. I'm on my stomach facing the dressing table, away from Lucca, with my cheek resting on the mattress.

Dazed.

My legs are spread wide on the mattress because I'm simply too weak to move them. My ass cheeks feel tingly and inside my legs are soaked with the cream of our passion.

Lucca has vigorously abused me with his sexual prowess, and I devoured it. I enjoyed being subjected to such rough sex, and it helped me ignore my fear this evening. I only hope it's done the same for Lucca because I hate seeing him in pain.

I've had no less than eight orgasms today—worthy of eight days of sleep as my body has been on a climaxathon. Tiredness prevails. I may just need medical attention, perhaps an intravenous drip of pure glucose to help me recover from today.

Lucca's arms are draped over my back. "Lexi?" he asks once he's caught his own breath.

I can't respond. I'm so sleepy.

Scotch.

Sensitivity.

Sedative solace.

"Lexi?" he asks again. When I don't answer, he turns around to snuggle his head against my neck and hooks a leg over my ass and back rubbing my ass cheek tenderly.

"Lexi, baby, answer me," he pleads.

Silence.

"Jesus fuck, Lexi, shit."

He shakes my shoulder gently, then flips me over and straddles my waist in a swift moment. Cupping my face in both hands, he hovers over me.

"Fuck, no. Baby, did I hurt you? I never meant to hurt you. I am sorry, Lexi. Jesus, I am sorry," he cries. "Please, talk to me. I am sorry."

Closing my eyes, I fall deeper into the skies below—weightless.

"Oh shit. Did I hurt you? Did I hurt our baby?" He's alarmed and I need him calm.

With my eyes hooded, I mutter, "No, you didn't hurt me. I asked for it. I wanted to help you fight against your pain."

"Jesus, that does not excuse what I did to you. Causing you pain only hurts me more. Open your eyes, please. I am so sorry."

I'm wounded to see his azure blue eyes have not returned, but they are no longer grey. They've changed to a pale, white-blue colour, just like the clouds we fly through. It's not enough. I want azure.

"I wanted it and I loved it. I'm not angry at you. I … enjoyed it. You help me feel. I wanted to do the same for you. I just wanted to help you to forget. I'm damaged, Lucca, but not because of this. I'm damaged because I've broken you and I thought this would fix you, not make you worse." I nervously bite my lip.

"Dolcezza, do not ever think that. You have not broken me. You have made me. You are right, I did need that, and it helped because the thought of losing you is slowly destroying me. The feel of you and knowing you are aroused drives me insane. That was amazing for me. I love to own every inch of your glorious body and be that intimate with you. It did help me forget, but now I am angry with myself for putting you at risk and in that situation."

He presses his nose against my cheek, holding my face with one palm, then skates the other down to my tummy, showing our baby love from the heat of his palm.

"You didn't put me at risk. We had rough sex, yes, but amazing sex. It's not as if you were beating me up. The baby is completely safe. I trust you and I needed it too. Hell, I asked for it. Those orgasms nearly ripped me apart, and you gave me that. It was incredible. I love you."

His facial muscles relax and he flutters those beautiful, dark lashes at me. The colour of his eyes brightens along with his loving smile. "I love you, dolcezza, so goddamn much that it fucking tears me up."

Deep-rooted fear.

I kiss him softly, a contrast to our recent roughness. It's light, sensual, and sexy, our lips barely touching. Pausing, I take his face in both my hands and share my thoughts.

"Lucca, I need you to promise me that you won't deliberately get drunk when things get tough and you stress. If you need to exert that anguish, I want you to love me, lust for me, and use my body if it helps, but don't get yourself wasted."

"I am not going to use you, Lexi. The love and lust I will always have for you, but I am not using you. Fuck, I could never do that." He looks offended I even suggested it.

I don't reply because it's exactly what I asked him to do a short while ago, and boy, did he do it. I don't object because when I need to take advantage of him, I know he'll willingly allow me to do so. He already did in BarAsta that night.

He lowers himself to kiss my tummy and whisper sweet promises to our baby as he tickles my lower abdomen with his stubble. I carefully play with his hair with one hand as the fingers of my other hand lazily waltzes along his shoulders. My body hums, still sated from our rampant fucking.

I feel myself drifting off to sleep.

"Lexi?"

"Hmmm?" I mumble.

He scoops me up in his strong arms with my toiletry bag in his hand and takes me to the shower. My head is so heavy I struggle to keep it up. Lucca washes my hair, my sex, and up and down my legs with my soapy sponge. Then he runs his hands over my ass and kisses my skin. He lifts me out the shower to dry me off then combs my hair, running my leave-in conditioner from my scalp to my ends. He rubs body butter all over me and wraps me in a towel, placing me on the bed while he shaves and brushes his teeth.

I don't remember him dressing me, but when I wake up I'm fully dressed and sitting on Lucca's lap in the main cabin. He holds me close to his chest and lifts my hand up to his mouth, placing soft kisses on it.

"Hey, I need to put you back in your seat for landing. You feeling okay?" He brushes my hair behind my ear. I don't want to move. I don't want him to let go of me. Ever.

"I'm tired and still feel a little sick. Where's Mum?"

"She just woke up. She is getting washed and dressed. I think her sleeping pills have made her quite groggy."

I'm about to go and get her to check she is okay when I see her return looking a little fresher than before. I reach my hand out for her. She stops by our seat and leans over, takes my hand and places a tender kiss on my head. I pull her into me and wrap my arm around her waist, kissing her hand and telling her everything is going to be okay while Lucca plays with my hair and rests his chin on my other shoulder.

I've been leaning over to cuddle her for so long that I have uncomfortable muscle cramp. I stand up and stretch, which feels good, then hold her in a warm embrace, rocking her in my arms while she sobs quietly against my cheek. I swallow down my fear and anguish but don't cry. I want to be strong for her. If there is ever a time she needs me, it's now.

Once I'm back in my own seat, I lift my journal out of my handbag. Lucca smiles at me and reaches for his engraved pen from inside his blazer pocket and passes it to me. I place a hand over my abdomen and think of our baby—our next chapter.

Taking Casey's advice, I begin writing on the empty page with a new approach. *With colour.*

I focus on my aspirations as opposed to writing about my fears, the past, and harrowing memories. It's time to write new, happy memories. I begin with how I feel now, today at this very minute, so that I can reflect and hopefully accept that these emotions are a fragment of my past.

Dark Black
Today, again I run ... I run to safety.
I am petrified.
I am confused.
I am empty.
I am vulnerable.
I am angry.
I am shocked.
I am exhausted.
I am hurt.
I am sick.
I am anxious.
And I am nervous.
Nervous of the unknown. Nervous of what tomorrow brings. Nervous my new found happiness will be taken from me. Nervous to become a mother. Nervous I might get hurt. Nervous Lucca might get hurt. Nervous of losing Lucca. Nervous of losing the baby. Nervous I get dragged back to Hell and becoming black.
Nervous of losing my light. Forever.

With that being said, I turn a page and write how I want to feel, how I imagine my happily ever after will be and will myself to believe I'm deserving of everything Lucca promises me.

I write about the lust, love, and light I feel for Lucca. I scribble meaningful words from deep within my heart and know this is how I want to feel. Always.

L'amore.

The love is Lucca's Love.

It's Lucca's love that's going to see me through the next chapter of my life and keep me in his light. His Luminoso.

I don't know what my future holds, but I know this—I don't intend to live my life in the dark. I need light. Our baby needs light. We need light.

I am loved.
I am in love.
I am loving.
I am confident.
I am carefree.
I am happy.
I am blessed.
I am positive.
I am bright.
I am grateful.
I am desirable.
I am secure.
I am strong.
I am safe.
I am protected.
I am complete.

When I read over the words I've scrawled, I realise Casey's intentions by asking me to do this.

I am all these things with Lucca.

He has me.

He makes me feel.

Closing my journal, I turn around to see Mum back in her seat and writing in her own journal.

I place the pen down and watch her. No ... I admire her. I'm so proud of her in this moment that she's utilising the journal I bought her and hope it brings her the same comfort as it has done for me.

She's an inspiration, and I'm glad to have her here with me. I don't want her to suffer anymore. Alone.

We will get through this together with love.

Our love.
The love.
L'amore.

The End...
For Now

Epilogue: Michael Parks
Inferno Burning

After Michael arrived in Glasgow last week, he drove to the safety deposit box in the town centre to pick up his supplies left for him by his reliable source. He drove up north towards the Scottish Highlands on the warm Monday afternoon then swapped his hire car in Perth for a burgundy coloured estate car.

His reservation for the small room in Newtonmore was under the name of Uuka Benadi, the false South African Immigrant and whose name he would be using. *It's far enough away from the church but still close enough for driving,* Michael thought, pleased with his location.

Michael unpacked his trolley case and holdall, stripping out of his stuffy, smart tailored clothes. He dressed in jeans and a casual tee. The owner of the guest house had offered him hot food, but he declined. Instead, he chose to eat sandwiches which he bought from the same shop where he picked up the hired vehicle. He did not want to get close to anyone while here. After all, this was a mission and he would do well to maintain privacy. Discretion was essential.

Michael brought up the blueprints of the church on his smart phone. The desolate forgotten crypt underneath the ancient church would be the perfect dungeon for torturing Alexis Roberston. He wanted to be prepared for meeting Cathy and desperately needed this position, so he studied the church's undercroft and grounds. Michael knew it was a clever decision to use the church as a base, and it would be the making of his devious plan.

"Uprising," he muttered, hissing through his teeth focusing on the diagrams.

It was not by coincidence that this church would be his target. The contacts that Damien Thomson assigned to scout out the area researched the inconspicuous location and discovered the crypt under the chancel.

Somewhere out of prying eyes, somewhere underground, and somewhere sacred.

Symbolic.

The next morning Cathy offered him the position of groundsman and caretaker until the Church of Scotland sent a replacement. She gave him the tour, rambling on about the history of the church, the local area, and even about his retired predecessor. Michael remained impassive and quiet. He kept to himself and went about landscaping the lawns and gravesides. Cathy gave him a key to the church, and he spent the next week staying until late into the night.

He set up an area in one of the cavern like rooms within the crypt with all his tools, and sourced an old mattress and other supplies. He would eat and occasionally sleep in the dungeon undercroft.

Cathy's manse was off limits for now—she had cleaners and church elders frequenting and various visits from members of her congregation. He didn't want to raise suspicion, so he deliberately stayed out of Cathy's way. She was of no use in this mission.

Until his first Sunday ...

Michael's source had discovered Grace Robertson's address on some private acres uphill just outside the village. He drove to the property to assess. He watched patiently. He was looking for patterns and routines. His plan was to enter the property when everyone had left then he would search out information on the evil little bastard whore Alexis.

He was forced to leave when he noticed security of some sort standing on the front porch behind two black SUVs. He realised then that the family must have protection, which would mean that they were aware he was in the country. This complicated matters and made things more challenging. He would need to stay underground in the crypt and perhaps seek assistance from his contact.

While Cathy performed her Sunday service, Michael exited the vestibule and sat on a bench around the back of the church. After smoking three Marlboro cigarettes, contemplating what his next step would be, he closed his eyes, until the heavens opened up and unleashed an almighty torrential downpour.

He entered the vestibule and lifted his long black coat and golf umbrella. Exiting the church to cross the graveyard, something caught his eye. Through the lashing, wet rain he stared in disbelief, gritting his teeth together and clenching his fists until his knuckles were white. He bite so damn hard on his lip that he drew blood.

Blood ... sweet blood!

He couldn't be positive but instinct told him the vision of beauty staring at him could be Alexis, the whore from his past. He never thought of her as his half-sister; the thought made him sick. She wasn't worthy of that title because she had taken his father's life, her own father's life. He thought of her as a piece of fucking scum who should never have been born and who deserved to pay and suffer for her sins.

The brunette beauty turned around and stared at Michael. Those timid chocolate eyes made her look like deer caught in the headlights, as if she instinctively sensed his presence. There was no mistaking those eyes. Fear.

It was her. *It had to be*, Michael thought.

This was his only chance, so he had to follow her to confirm his suspicions. The tall, bulky, dark haired man holding his blazer jacket above her head was not the brother because he kissed her on the lips. He had to be her partner.

Well shit!

"Inter-fuckin-fering son of a bitch," Michael cursed, then he noticed the same black SUV that was outside Grace's house this morning. "Fuckin' entourage." He hissed.

He would need to follow the vehicle to be sure. Not wanting to lose his chance, he turned on his heels and headed for his own hidden car parked on the side of the church out of view. He followed the ridiculous fucking sports car and black SUV into a gas station.

"Rich bastard," he spat, watching the motherfucker driving an Aston Martin. He was sure the girl caught a glimpse of him, so he used the opportunity to drive off before she realised it was him.

He spent the next two days following the girl. He couldn't get too close because of the rich bastard and the arsehole pricks protecting her. Each time he thought of her at the stables, his cock was instantly hard. The image of the whore with those little denim shorts on hugging her tight little ass and those long dark legs and her hair in a braid imprinted into his mind. He visualised yanking coarsely at that very braid while he brutally took her from behind and tore her apart.

He reached the climax of his masturbation, spitting her name as rage fuelled his whole body imagining her incoherent screams. He slumped on the mattress in the inhospitable crypt and devised a new approach.

It was time for a new tactic. Michael took advantage when the minister disappeared. He trashed the manse, ensuring it looked like a breaking and entering, searching for information about the rich bastard. He would need to study this fucker in order to get to the girl. Find his strengths and weaknesses and every detail right down to his national insurance number.

Nothing ...

He couldn't find anything of importance and assumed the rich bastard wasn't from here. He was about to give up when something piqued his interest, finding crumpled wrapping paper in the trash can. He studied the brown paper and found an address on the back, a church in Uddingston, South Lanarkshire.

He copied the address then placed the paper back in the bin. He called his contact and gave him the registration number of the flashy fucking sports car the bastard had been driving around in to see what came up. He waited patiently back at the room in the guesthouse.

He opened a bottle of vodka and slugged it down just as his phone alerted him of mail. Scrolling through, he found all the details he needed.

The empire—Osurac Industries flagged.

Property ... Health ... Fitness ... Club di Energia ... Construction ... Property ... Italian ... Hospitality ... Entertainment ... Restaurants ... Events ...

The next paragraph detailed a chain of clubs linked to Lucca Caruso.

Luminara ...

Bingo!

He finished the rest of the vodka, allowing the poison to burn through his veins while he formed his plan with vengeance. Michael knew he wouldn't get close to Alexis here with her protectors around her, so he needed to lure her to him, all in good time, and the rich bastard's empire was somewhere to start. He would find something or someone to use as leverage. In the meantime, he would taunt, intimidate, and emotionally scar her. If she were vulnerable and pathetically weak, she would be easier to break before he shattered her.

Deleting the information, he threw his belongings into a bag and looked for another fake identity and credit card. Before heading to Glasgow for his new mission, he had some business he would take care of first.

He cast his mind back to the stables, his cock straining against his jeans.

The inferno burning.

Heat flaring.

Flames scorching.

Fire blazing.

The stables.

He would leave her a message that she would not forget.

"Fucking Bitch. Fucking rich, useless bastard and her meddling, godforsaken family," he spat after he wiped his release from his lower abdomen then fisted the wall in rage.

Patience. He would wait.

He'd hurt the ones closest to her and lure her to him. He'd torture her and keep her in misery until her time was up and she begged for life to be taken from her. Dark black was the colour of her life ... and is the colour of her *afterlife.*

Alexis Evangeline Robertson is going straight to Hell.

To be continued ...

Glossary of Characters

Primary Characters

Alexis Evangeline Robertson (Lexi): Sweet, caring physiotherapist with a private clinic within Club di Energia; a young beautiful woman with deep dark secrets and insecurities. Scarred by her past, she's learning to trust and break her rules in order to discover lust and fall helplessly in love with Lucca Caruso.

Lucca Caruso: Italian/Scottish wealthy business entrepreneur. CEO of Osurac Industries – Property Development & Management, Hospitality & Entertainment, and Health & Wellbeing Clubs. Handsome, virile, insatiable, romantic, charming, and possessive. Falling quickly and deeply in love with Lexi, sweeps her off her feet, protects, loves and cherishes her with endless promises.

Secondary Characters

Grace Robertson: Lexi's mother. Abuse survivor. Beautiful, fragile, emotionally vulnerable, loving, caring and protective.

Cameron Robertson: Lexi's older brother, fire arms agent in the special forces. Roguish, handsome, and talented.

Hazel Scott: Lexi's best friend, fitness instructor, extravert with a quirky sense of humour.

Dominic: Hazel's Fiancé.

Ted Carlin: Lexi's next door neighbour, retired pensioner, wise and grumpy.

Franco: Lucca's nonno (grandfather), owner of Villa di Tartufi (Villa of truffles) Tuscan cook school and hotel.

Sofia: Lucca's nonna (grandmother), co-owner of Villa di Tartufi (Villa of truffles) Tuscan cook school and hotel.

Marco: Lucca's friend and right hand man.

Antonio Caruso: Lucca's papa (father), owner of Casa sulla Collina (House on the hill) Tuscan cook school and hotel. Sister property to Villa di tartufi.

Marissa Caruso: Lucca's mamma (mother), co-owner of Casa sulla Collina (House on the hill) Tuscan cook school and hotel. Sister property to Villa di tartufi (Villa of truffles.)

Orianna Caruso (Anna): Lucca's younger sister, marketing director for Osurac Industries.

Francesca (Fran): Lucca's ex-fiancée, fashion designer.

Tertiary Characters

Casey Huddersfield: Lucca and Lexi's therapist at the private M. Martha Clinic.

Terence: Casey's husband. Friend of Lucca's.

Doris: Lexi's German gun dog.

Rose: Lucca's house keeper.

Peter: Lucca's groundsman and landscaper. Takes Care of his Scottish home.

Eleanor Carlin: Mr. Carlin's deceased wife. Neighbour and dear friend to Lexi.

Michael Parks: Lexi's Australian half-brother. Evil, sinister, sadistic, and corrupt. A disturbing memory from Lexi's past. He was her abuser, recently released from prison and tracking her down.

Simon Parks: Deceased Australian father to Lexi, Cameron, and Michael. Unstable, psychotic, sociopath that abducted Grace, Lexi's mum. Held them captive for fourteen years in a tragic case of Stockholm syndrome. Tortured and abused Grace mentally and physically.

Mary (Scary Mary): Simon's Australian wife, Michael's mother. Worked at the local hospital. Drug user, bi-polar, evil, and vindictive.

Kyle Saunders: Fake identity used by Michael Parks for car hire and flights.

Uuka Benadi: Fake identity used by Michael Parks disguising himself as a South African immigrant working as a groundsman at Cathy's church in Grantown-on-Spey.

Damien Thomson: Private Investigator helping Michael Parks obtain details on Grace Robertson and her family and providing him with resources.

Vladimir: – Russian drug dealer and assassin who killed Damien Thomson for Michael Parks.

Mark: Physiotherapist, Lexi's business partner at their private clinic within Club di Energia.

Jane: Physiotherapist, Lexi's work colleague.

Kenny: Jane's partner.

Rena: Chef within Club di Energia.

Lucy: Lexi's friend. Beautiful single, and besotted with Cameron, Lexi's brother.

Jessica: Lexi's friend. Caring, sincere, and optimistic.

Steve: Jessica's partner.

Samantha: Lexi's friend. Smart, sharp, and intelligent. Marketing manager.

Justin: Samantha's partner.

Carrie: Lexi's friend. Pragmatic, sensible, and mature. A & E nurse in Glasgow hospital.

Nicole: Carrie's partner.

Rachel: Cameron's on/off girlfriend. Young, sweet, and loves to travel.

Maurizio: Head chef at Villa di tartufi.

Rafaello: Franco's twin brother, owner of a chain of Italian restaurants in the UK.

Savio: Lucca's brother, owner of his parents' former restaurant in Carluke, Scotland.

Kate: Savio's wife, co-owner of his parents' former restaurant in Carluke, Scotland.

Armando: Lucca's brother, manager at Rafaello's Glasgow restaurant branch.

Sarah: Armando's wife, stay-at-home mum.

Roberta: Lucca's niece. Savio and Kate's daughter.

Emilio: Lucca's nephew. Savio and Kate's son.

A-Jay: Lucca's nephew. Armando and Sarah's son.

Antonia: Lucca's niece. Armando and Sarah's daughter.

Suzanne Myers: Lucca's personal assistant, sister of Casey Huddersfield.

Jonathon Myers: Suzanne's husband.

Kimberley Franks: Suzanne's assistant. Troublemaker, blackmailer, and ex-conquest of Lucca's.

Jackson: Cameron's friend. Footballer/local celebrity and is attracted to Lexi.

Shawna: Jackson's girlfriend.

Adam: Footballer, Cameron's friend.

Jordan: Footballer, Cameron's friend.

Ben: Footballer, Cameron's friend.

Ethan: Footballer, Cameron's friend.

Tyler: Footballer, Cameron's friend.

Lloyd: Lexi's security guard. Men in Black.

Devon: Lexi's security guard. Men in Black. Irish.

Nate: Grace's security guard. Men in Black.

Julie: Mr. Carlin's new home help aide.

Terry: Mr. Carlin's previous home help aide.

Fiona: Mr. Carlin's previous home help aide.

Dr. Harvey: Lexi's doctor.

The young Doctor: Inserts Lexi's implant at the family planning clinic.

Omari Farid: Lucca's best friend and solicitor.

Chris McCarron: Lucca's best friend and accountant.

Lyle Graham: Lucca's head contractor.

Andy Johnson: Lucca's Project Manager.

Giorgio: Lucca's business partner at The Luminara nightclub chain.

Leila: Blonde, scantily clad female who broke into Lucca's house. Ex-conquest of Lucca's.

Cathy: Local minister in Grantown-on-Spey. Friend of Lexi's grandparents.

Aunt Eva (Evangeline): Grace's sister. Lexi's aunt.

Uncle Jim: Eva's husband. Lexi's uncle.

Hayden: Eva and Jim's son. Lexi's eighteen-year-old cousin.

Hayley: Eva and Jim's daughter. Twin sister to Hayden. Lexi's eighteen-year-old cousin.

Ruby: Lexi's grandparents' King Charles Spaniel dog.

Tosh: Lexi's grandparents' West Highland Terrier dog.

Angel: Black Friesian horse, Lexi used to ride.

Jambo: Dutch Warmblood horse, Cameron used to ride.

Hamish: English Thoroughbred horse, Lexi's grandpa used to ride.

Ms. Morrison: Local minister at Lexi's local church. Cathy's friend.

Mr. Carmichael: Retired groundsman at the church in Grantown-On-Spey

Ms. Saunders: Lexi's childhood Ballet teacher.

David: American, Mystery Man, owner of Tasa, upmarket bar and nightclub in Firenze city. Rival and a threat to Lucca, attracted to Lexi.

Adorna: Art history tour guide within the Uffizi gallery, Firenze. Previous conquest of Lucca's.

Gina: Tour guide and representative at Castello di Brolio (Brolio Castle), winery of the Ricasoli family Chianti classic wines. Previous conquest of Lucca.

Giovanni Costanzo: Famous Italian photographer, wealthy, smooth, and sophisticated. Infatuated with Lexi's beauty, offers to photograph her.

Melissa: Roberta's four year old friend.

Millie: Roberta's four year old friend.

Dana: The beauty therapist hired by Lucca for Lexi's pamper night.

Mack: Cocktail waiter, works at the Luminara nightclub. Hired by Lucca for Lexi's pamper night.

Harriett: Lexi's hairdresser in Scotland.

The Murdocks: Neighbours of Alexander and Elizabeth Robertson and owners of the stables.

Detective one: Female detective working for the CID. Visits Lexi's grandparents' house.

Detective two: Male detective working for the CID. Visits Lexi's grandparents' house.

Claude: Pilot of Lucca's private jet.
Eric: Co-pilot of Lucca's private jet.
Bethany: Flight attendant on Lucca's private jet.

Acknowledgements

I truly am eternally grateful for all the love support and encouragement I have received. I have so many gratefuls I'd like to share with you, and every day I feel blessed and am thankful for these gifts of the day. I'm going to keep it quite short as I said most of my gratefuls in Lussuria.

T, A & A – My wonderful husband and two daughters.

Thank you to the moon and back for being patient, supportive, and encouraging me to get through another crazy hectic few months. I know it's not been easy on any of you because of the time I have had to commit to my writing and all the changes I've had to make.

I didn't think it could possibly get any more time consuming than it already was. I was wrong. When I decided to go back and work on the developmental edits for *Lussuria* and re-publish, I was juggling between three books at one point and things were a little hectic and intense to say the least and it affected us all. Thank you for taking my worries, stress, and mixed emotions in your stride and still loving me through it all.

I'm sorry if I ignored you on many occasions, but you knew I had to see it through by re-writing some of *Lussuria* and lots of *L'amore*. Just when you thought you were getting your mum and wife back even for a little bit, I crossed over into the world of developmental editing and sold my soul for a crazy few weeks, and boy, it was challenging getting there.

You come in from work and school with a smile on your face when dinner often isn't ready, the washing isn't done, and the chores are piling up, and you never judge or complain. You accept that that's how we are rolling just now, our own little chapter of chaos. You stay upbeat and positive, and on the days when I am thoroughly exhausted but refuse to stop, you leave me to it. Then when I do stop to breathe, you pull me back into normal family life, your light. This has always given me focus and a sense of warmth because it reminds me why I do this and it touches my heart. I might be spending a lot of my time in world of *The Luminara*, but you always bring me home to you and will have my heart first and foremost.

I promise things will get easier, and a promise is a promise.
I love you all. Xxx

Joanne Carlin Sinadinovic – Design Divaz.

Again, thank you to Joanne from Design Divaz, for providing an impressive professional design package for me. I am absolutely thrilled with the amazing graphics, personalised designs, logos, and images you have created for my cover art, website, Facebook page, and of course marketing and all the swag for my branding.

You never fail to impress me and know exactly what I'm envisaging, even when I go off on a tangent, and your results are always amazing.

Thank you for the new re-branding and the covers for *Lussuria* and *L'amore*. We got there in the end and the results are amazing. I absolutely love the iconic symbolism, vibrancy, sharpness, and prettiness of your design. I have even had readers ask for the image of the blue orchid as they would like it as a tattoo x.

Vera.

You know I don't need to elaborate. I said it all in *Lussuria*. Thank you always for being a great support and always being there and being the best 'go to' anyone could ask for. Thank you for loving, protecting, and encouraging me. Thank you for knowing me so well. You have an uncanny sense of knowing when and how to rein me in, motivate me, know what's best for me, and ultimately steer me in the right direction. Always.

You never complain when I'm Skyping, messaging, and emailing you at all hours looking for advice and for that I am always entirely grateful x.

Evelyn. *My Assistant Eve.*

Eve, my little book gem. Thank you for being my organiser, my diary, my consultant, my assistant, and advisor. Thank you for helping with my admin, giveaways, and for looking after my social media when I'm out of action or not around. You are a little gem and I'm very grateful to have your help. Thank you Eve, a million times over x.

Maxann – The Polished Pen.

Max, I don't know where to start. It's been an absolute pleasure working with you again. Your professionalism, efficiency, productiveness, and excellent guidance have been outstanding once again. You aren't just teaching me valuable lessons and skills throughout this editorial process, but you've set me up with the best footing possible for the rest of the series. You've shaped *Lussuria* and *L'amore* into an overall flawless, consistent, and sharper read. I love that I'm learning so much from you throughout this process.

Without your expertise and insight, these books wouldn't be what they are. I'm extremely grateful for everything you've helped with and that you noticed something in this series and wanted to make it the best it can be. Thank you for offering me solutions, alternatives, and accommodating date changes, answering my questions, and teaching me valuable skills. I can't thank you enough and I look forward to working with you on the rest of this series.

Also thank you for polishing *L'amore* off and making it so much better x.

James Ramsey.

James, thank you once again for helping me shape this novel into what it is. It wouldn't be *L'amore* without all your honest critique, advice, and help, and I have you to thank for that. You have a skilful knack for planting the seed to let my ideas grow into so much more, and to expand and develop on your own ideas.

I think now you are getting me and my made up words that drive you crazy, and I am getting you and your bazillion comments. Which of course, makes me want to scream, cry, and hibernate in my tartan pj's with a large glass of merlot until I pull myself together. Eventually when I get over the shock and get focused, it's these comments that make me smile and keep me sane. When I come to the sections that make you want to throw your laptop, I know we are getting somewhere, and these are the sections of the novels that do particularly need more depth and reasoning.

It goes without saying, that often I want to mentally kick your ass sometimes, actually a lot of the time, because you give me so much work. With that said, everything you suggest is for the best, and I know you want to help me do these novels justice so it's with all your good intentions.

We finally got there, after the blood, sweat and tears and I'm so thankful to have you on-board keeping me on my toes. Thank you James for everything, I look forward to more torture while working on the developmental edits of *Luminoso*, I say rolling my eyes and dreading it already x.

K Bromberg.

Kristy, I have you to thank for setting me up with Max and James and it has been a breath of fresh air having them both work on this series. It's truly made these books by having such professional help and direction, so thank you for being insightful, kind, and understanding x.

My wonderful Readers.

I wrote this acknowledgment in *Lussuria*, but I want to share it with you again because you are so important and keep me going. You remain supportive and you have been exceptionally patient during all my dates changes and delays while I went back to re-write. And after finally publishing *L'amore*, you are still as loyal as ever and continue to follow and read my work. Thank you everyone.

It goes without saying that this book is for you and would not be anyway near as successful as it has been without the continual support, appraisal, interest, and passion for *The Luminara Series* I have received from you all. I can't tell you how happy I am that you are falling in love with Lexi and Lucca as much as I am on their romantic anecdote of Lust, Love, and Light.

I'm absolutely astounded and overwhelmed, albeit delighted, with the positive response you have shown me and my debut Adult Romance Suspense series. I started writing with the mind-set that it was something that I always wanted to do, and I was doing this for my family. With that said, I never anticipated I'd be launching them publicly. It would have been be way too selfish for me not to publish. I decided to bring this series to light by sharing it with you all and I am ecstatic I did and hope you are too.

Obviously I was nervous sharing this, and to be honest I still am. It's a very nerve-racking experience, and I never know how my writing will be received and reviewed. I try to stay positive and have faith in my characters and my unravelling storyline. I prayed that you all fall in love with it as much as I have to give me a solid foundation to work on.

When you were receptive and showing positive enthusiasm with good feedback, I began to relax and enjoy the writing experience even more and found I couldn't stop even if I tried. I then knew I was making the right choice sharing it with all my readers.

The love and support you show makes this experience completely fulfilling and worthwhile. It's because of the readers' enthusiasm and support that I'm able to write with complete passion and conviction to give you the best emotional and romantic story I can.

From the bottom of my heart, it's a privilege to be able to share this with you and I hope you all continue your support by following Lexi and Lucca through their intense, impassioned, and complicated relationship which will unravel throughout the coming series. Readers, you're the reason I've made so many compromises in my life to do this because like you, I'm also an avid, self-confessed book junkie and lover of romantic fiction novels. I have been blessed to read so many wonderful creations from magnificent, talented authors out there and I wanted to give something back—to you—and hope it's every piece as wonderful. For you readers, I am eternally grateful x.

Dolcezza's – My Street Team.

Ladies, thank you to the moon and back for all your ongoing pimping, support, advice, comments, and sharing. I'm very lucky to have backup and support from such a lovely, wonderful group of women who share my passion for all things lust, love, and light. For you all, I'm very grateful x.

My Darlin's.

Girls, thank you once again for being my shoulder to cry on, my biggest cheerleaders, and for listening to several months of my book chat. Thank you for putting me to bed when I'm tipsy, for the DBB'S, for making me laugh, showering me in your infectious positivity and affection, cuddling me and distracting me in the best possible way. You are a wonderful group of friends and I want you know I love you all dearly x.

For my beta readers.

Thank you to my Beta readers who took the time to read *L'amore* in the early stages before I worked on the developmental edit and who gave me honest feedback.

Athina.

Thank you so much for proofreading *L'amore* and being so helpful and professional. You're such a lovely person as well as efficient and I have truly enjoyed working with you. Thank you Athina x.

Lucinda – Design.lkcampbell.com

Thank you Lucinda, for your exceptional e-book formatting, correspondence, and understanding. You have accommodated my crazy schedule again and are always happy to oblige. You've provided such a great professional service and worked in a timely manner to meet my deadlines. It's been a pleasure working with you, and you have the patience of a saint. For you I am grateful, Lucinda x.

Kassi.

Thank you for another exceptional professional service and for formatting my MS for POD so quickly and accommodating my changes. It's been a pleasure working with you also, and I love your work. Kassi, for you I am grateful x.

Debra – The Book Enthusiast.

Thank you, Debra, for organising and arranging my cover reveals, release day events, blog tours and providing such a great service and reaching out to so many bloggers. You have been beyond patient and accommodating especially with the date changes. That you for putting up with me, Debra. I am very grateful x.

Book Bloggers.

A massive gift of the day – every day is to the entire book blogger social network community who have liked, shared, pimped, and supported, followed, participated, and reviewed. I'm stunned and totally blown away by the interest you have all shown. There are far too many of you to name but you know who you all are x.

About The Author: Bio

SJ Molloy, first time British Author of The Luminara Series, was born in Edinburgh, Scotland. As a young child, her family moved and raised her in Lanarkshire, Scotland where she currently resides with her husband, two daughters, and her energetic, hyperactive loving gun dog who is utterly spoiled.

SJ is a qualified Fitness Instructor and Health & Fitness Motivator of various fitness styles and disciplines. Music and dance aerobics have always been a pleasure and passion for her. SJ will sporadically make up dance style routines at any hour of the day when a move comes to her or piece of music moves or inspires her. Currently not teaching classes, she is focusing her time into nurturing her yearning passion for creative writing, exchanging one visualisation for another.

As a child, SJ loved to write in journals and make up short stories and has a flare for all things creative. With an overactive imagination at times, SJ adores to make notes and visualise scenes and settings to create characterisations.

While on holiday with her family one summer reading book after book, she had a flash of inspiration and has had various ideas whirling around in her mind ever since. It was not until she pulled back on teaching classes that she found the courage, time, and insight into actually bringing these ideas to life.

In February 2013 she decided to bring that imagination to light by beginning her writing journey with *Lussuria* the first instalment in The Luminara Series.

Being a self-confessed book junkie, she loves nothing better than to get lost in an emotional and moving book. A true romantic at heart, her guilty pleasure is reading heart-warming, passionate stories and falling in love with her favourite fictional characters.

With seven books already mapped out in The Luminara Series, SJ's busy, creative mind has already planned two more fictitious novels, both stand-alone romance books and very different in their own right.

When she is not writing or reading, spending time with family and friends, or exercising and walking her dog, SJ loves all things practical and creative. Dancing, music, cooking, travelling, good food and wine, and painting are her favourite past times along with laughter, lots and lots of laughter.

Share and review

I encourage you all to, like, share, tweet, and follow my social media links for updates, news and teasers for the rest of the series. I will be eternally grateful if you would kindly leave a review for *Lussuria* and *L'amore* on Goodreads and Amazon and any book groups and blogs. It's really important and crucial for the rest of the series. I will be eternally grateful if you would kindly leave a review as it gives us great foundation to work on and helps develop our writing to make it the best it possibly can be. It also assists with publicising our work so that the future books of the series can reach a bigger audience.

I'm currently working on Club Luminara, a facebook group dedicated to discussing anything about the Luminara Series for readers and fans. This will be advertised on my Facebook page and website, and will contain exclusive advance excerpts, giveaways, and information on Luminoso Book 3 in the Luminara series. www.facebook.com/Authorsjmolloy. www.sjmolloy.com

If you would like to join the official Dolcezza Street team for the Luminara Series and put your name on the wall, apply via link below. Street team member receive Luminara privileges.

http://www.sjmolloy.com/dolcezzas/

Author Links

Website - www.sjmolloy.com

Facebook -
http://www.facebook.com/pages/Authorsjmolloy/1419001364992793

Twitter - https://twitter.com/AUTHORSJMOLLOY

Pinterest - www.pinterest.com/authorsjmolloy

LinkedIn - www.linkedin.com/pub/sj-molloy/80/280/536

Stumble Upon - http://www.stumbleupon.com/stumbler/sjmolloy

Tumblr - http://sjmolloy.tumblr.com/

Goodreads - https://www.goodreads.com/user/show/23883969-sj-molloy

Wattpad http://www.wattpad.com/user/sjmolloy

Booklikes - www.sjmolloy.booklikes.com

Independent Author Network -
http://www.independentauthornetwork.com/s-j-molloy.html

Email – author@sjmolloy.com

Email – info@sjmolloy.com

Email – authorsjmolloy@gmail.com

Coming soon by SJ Molloy

Luminoso.
Book 3 in the Luminara Series is scheduled late summer – early fall 2014.
Luminoso is Italian for light.
The continuation of Lucca and Lexi's life. As they plan for their future together, many secrets and plots are conspiring which will re-write their destiny, perhaps forever. Fate works in mysterious ways. After the sweetness of love and the closeness it brings, unimaginable events rouse emotions in them both that they fight hard to control. Will she fight, surrender, or run this time? Intense and gripping, this book is filled with angst and suspense leaving you gasping for breath.

Book 4
Yet to be named. This is the conclusion to Lucca and Lexi's turbulent journey. In order to find the light, you must first see the darkness. Will Lexi and Lucca find their light again after their story reveals dishonesty, hurt, grief, and guilt? In the most emotional, sensitive, and painstakingly disconcerting tear-jerking conclusion, our hearts will weep. Can they bury the past, forgive, accept, and move on to have their happily ever after?

Book 5
Wildcard and a mystery book in the Luminara Series. I will announce later this year the name and title of the book, as it will be worth the wait, but I'm keeping it a little mystery for now.

Lacerato.
Book 6 in the Luminara Series from Camerons POV. Scheduled for 2015.
Lacerato is Italian for torn.
Lexi's brother shares his own anguish and title of the book as it will stop pulses with his roguish insatiable desire to lure and seduce woman, but can he stay faithful and love only one?

Levare

**Book 7 in the Luminara Series from Grace Robertson's POV
scheduled for 2015.**
The prequel.
Levare is Italian for taken.
A story of courage, strength and hope.
Lexi and Cameron's mother shares her trauma, fear, and devastation.
Life was taken from her, yet she had to breathe and keep faith in
order to protect her children and keep them all alive. A dark,
harrowing, suspense-filled physiological thriller of one woman's
miracle—saving grace.

More future projects

Indestructible – Late 2015 - early 2016

After her father's death, a contemporary ballet dancer struggles to
accept the debt, crime, and debauchery left behind. Inheriting her
father's share of a pretentious exotic strip club, she is determined to
sell because she's is disgusted with the seediness and cliché attached
and does not care for it. Her mysterious, handsome, powerful, and
sexy business partner has other ideas. Falling for the womanising
business partner, she loses all her composure, self-control, and
respect. Feeling bereft and used, she verges into the darker side of a
different person after continual protest and seeks solace from the
exotic dancers whom she once despised and belittled. She learns how
to strip and lap dance provocatively to distract her from her grief,
hurt, and emptiness in return for her ballet tuition and gets caught up
in the dark side of crime, drugs, and betrayal.
A woman so very fragile but strong, determined and ruthless.
She is indestructible…

Almost Is Never Enough – Available spring 2016.

A heart-wrenching love triangle between a woman and her two
childhood sweethearts. One man provides, protects, and makes love
to her. He's safe, reliable, and he's typical. The other ignites,
electrocutes, and burns her in a way she always dreamed of and
makes her feel very much excitable and alive. She always imagines
what life with the other would be like. It takes a natural disaster for
the woman to experience these fantasies, another life of amazing sex
and passion. Ultimately is it what she wants?

Tragedy has an ironic way of manifesting your dreams into an earth
moving shattering reality.
Guilt can almost strip it away.

www.sjmolloy.com will contain all updates on these future projects.

Thank you and happy reading x
Lust, love, light.

43705936R10270

Made in the USA
Charleston, SC
06 July 2015